Download

To order additional copies, please contact us.
BookSurge, LLC
www.booksurge.com
1-866-308-6235
orders@booksurge.com

HOWARD J. PETERS

DOWNLOAD

—A trilogy—
An Alternative Story of Noah and his Ark

2006

Download

'Download'

A sensational story of Humankind . . .
. . . Man's inhumanity to man and his environment

CONTENTS

"Religion is a gift from G-d.
Cherish it,
Do not abuse it, and never fight over it.
Why cannot people forget their differences by remembering their same's?"

I dedicate this book to humanity,
that it should have the intelligence
to use its knowledge in a responsible manner
for the sake of its survival.

With apologies to 'Adam & Eve' (Old Testament)

Rusty,

Enjoy a good read.

Thank you for your great services on Manuela's car. I hope that this novel helps you to open your horizons that you will be better able to remember your future!

Kindest regards y'all,

3/13/09

FORWARD . . .

The bible was originally written by human beings, for human beings of that time, to understand in the way only they could understand at that moment in the span of development of human life. This book does not pretend to have any inside knowledge, and does not question the authority or inspiration for the original or popular version of this story, but no apology is made for the interpretation of the events that could well have happened.

Likewise this story has to be read in context of the time in which it was started. Today was 1987. It would have been beyond the comprehension of a man in Oliver Cromwell's army, and more so by Moses or Ishmael. Perhaps Winston Churchill or Dwight D. Eisenhower would have understood some of it, and Queen Victoria or Benjamin Franklin would have frowned upon it but it will still be soon rather than early, that this story may unfold to full comprehension. Don't forget...they all ridiculed Christopher Columbus, and everybody laughed at Noah!

CONCLUSION . . .

This could have been what really happened. If this had been written even twenty-five years ago it would have been considered a folly of imagination, but surely, the original story, as we know it today is far less credible?

***

—BOOK ONE—

'Castle in the Sky'

"Ba'reshit"

Itruly am amazed that as I lie here naked on my back, I am not afraid. That which is to come is of my own design with the loving help from Lika, my wife, without whose energies I would never have achieved this great event. I am the last to undergo this experience and I am contented that all downloads before mine, with one exception, have been perfect. Loukash, a few days previously was a problem, I believe that in truth he really did not want to go and eventually we managed to upload his entire memory back to its place of origin. He then tested positive and was scanned containing no errors. He has elected to stay on board and will travel with the others.

At last it is my turn and I am ready, I am awaiting the experience without trepidation. I am so looking forward to rejoining Lika. I use the word 'experience' so lightly, but in no more than a few long moments I will have no experience on which I can any longer dwell my thoughts. I am about to be downloaded onto a disc for posterity. No longer will my thoughts be available to me, I will just be basic instinct and life essential brain memory. The only luxury that will be retained is the love recognition emotion of family and close relatives. I will know Lika and she will know me.

"Svi? You OK?" The soft voice of a young male nursing attendant enquires as he brings the headset to my side. "I am ready to complete my task, you are positively the last one to be done. You have done enough yourself to know how easy it will be. The last transport is waiting and your place is secure next to Lika and company. The shuttle is pre-programmed to return here empty and as planned there will be no crew. Your disembarkation from the shuttle is to be completely automatic and aided only by robotic androids. They cannot stay with you and if one does in error it will self-destruct, dissolving into the atmosphere. That is what was arranged is it not?"

"Yes! Exactly!" I know that I smiled as I ask him once again his name.

"My name is 'Porgelet' but surely that is of no consequence as within moments from now you will no longer have need of it and your memory will be gone?"

"Not quite Porgelet." I answer, wishing that I hadn't for I knew that my brain is to be downloaded and with all the others secretly directed to a multiple backup disc elsewhere for data record in the possible event that humanity will catch up with itself in many thousands of years yet to come.

I feel warm all over very suddenly; the headset is now in place and has a very high-pitched whine. I know what that is. The first thing that the headset will do will be to make my brain cool my body down by about ten percent which is why I feel so pleasantly warm and sleepy.

My thoughts are beginning to race, a strange feeling indeed. It is so real as if it is really happening just here at this very moment. My memories are in their most infinite detail; so immediate and yet so short lived.

***

CHAPTER 1

Another time, another place and approximately half a lifetime previously . . .

Svi was getting tired now, he had been walking in a circle for nearly four hours, and had had very little to drink. It was hot and sticky, and beads of perspiration were pouring like rain down his bare body. He was wearing his old sandals, and they were somewhat only an excuse for a foot cover. The pole he was carrying was still cold against his naked chest. It was made out of one of those new lightweight metals that kept cold for days without change in whatever temperature it was placed. The banner he carried was self-explanatory, and needed very little reading. There were many other people parading around in this marching circle, not one man or woman wore a stitch of clothing with the exception of ragged shoes. They seemed to be competing with each other for the least likely looking footwear and managed somehow to look scruffy even in their nakedness.

"Crisis for Nuclear Danger" had been around since the bomb itself, and this was just another of its organized displays of protest. Each banner or notice gave a similar message. What they actually said was never of any consequence, but the fact that it *was* said meant a great deal. "CRISIS" had been the catalyst to the endeavors of those innocent moralists in their attempts to stop man's own destruction of man.

"They're coming!" A shout rang out from somewhere down the street. "Get out of here quick!" The same voice was frantic now, "They've got paresifiers, and they look very very mean. They're coming this way fast. *Good God*" they're over the ridge, they..." The voice stopped in mid-sentence, just as abruptly as it had started.

Svi dropped his pole and threw himself over the low wall that was only three paces from where he was. The shallow wall offered very little cover for him, even in the crawling position. He had to be quick or they would surely get him. He inched along on hands and knees at a speed he never thought was possible. All the time he could hear the noises of his friends trying hard to scatter and the gargled yells as they were overcome with terror, then silence. He was now just a few body lengths from an opening in the wall of the building. They were coming nearer; he could sense it. He moved faster, on all fours. Throwing himself a second time, into the darkness of the opening that he knew was his only chance.

The ground came up, and hit him hard, as if he had fallen on an onion grater. He had landed on a bristled mat, used for wiping the mud off shoes. He was so hot and sweating. Perhaps it was the greasy effect on his body that saved him from further pain. He still could not afford the luxury of languishing there; he had to move fast. He was in a small lobby with a staircase going up, and one going down. Which one should he choose? He gently closed the door behind him while still on all fours. Only then did he allow himself to stand up. He bolted the door and decided to ascend the stairs. He thought he would be safer if he was higher, rather than lower, and perhaps he could escape across the rooftops. He had been lucky so far; they obviously weren't following him. Had any of the others got away? What was happening to his girlfriend? What was going on below? These were all thoughts that were racing through his mind as he climbed the spiral staircase, ignoring all exits until he reached the top. The door was closed but not locked, only bolted. He carefully loosened both bolts, and the noise seemed to echo as if he had shot both barrels of an old fashioned shotgun. He froze for a moment, feeling his heart pounding in his naked chest. It was his imagination. Opening the door slowly a thin pencil of bright light widened until the full glory of the hazy sunshine presented itself to reveal the flat roof outside. Through the salty tears of perspiration he could see a narrow parapet wall only feet away. He turned around the tower wall, trying not to make himself visible as the doorway had opened pointing inwards to the roof. He could not have been seen. Now at the parapet wall he looked over very carefully. He just couldn't believe the carnage. About thirty of his friends had been caught directly beneath him and they were burning their bodies with flamethrowers. Wait! One of the women was not paralyzed; she was now running for cover. Had they seen her? Her naked body looked truly beautiful, as, like a sprite, it seemed to take off straight towards the base of his tower. Svi couldn't make out where the shot came from but she went limp and her body carried on, with the same momentum as it fell to rest at the low wall he had jumped only minutes before. He would never forget her strangled shriek as at full speed, her living running body, so full of physical beauty and yet so full of obvious terror transformed into a limp lifeless mess, like a rag doll being thrown against the low wall.

Two of the guards moved over to investigate. They turned her over. She was certainly dead. The taller of the two uniformed men gave a signal as they took a very careful look at her lifeless form. Their examination was very much more detailed than necessary. They were enjoying it. Their lusty pleasure obviously satisfied, they moved away. Then the "crack" as the flamethrower changed the lifeless form into a puff of smoke and carbon deposit.

Svi froze as the shock of the event began to dawn on him. He watched as the dozen or so guards collected the remaining proof of their demonstration that afternoon and threw it into a truck. The bodies were already only dust. The black and silver uniformed men began to move large vacuum cleaners to clear the remains. Within a few minutes there was no trace apart from the thirty-two burned marks on the pale gray concrete.

Svi was exhausted and soaking with sweat. In the last hour whilst he had been lying there on the parapet motionless it had become a little more windy. Feeling very naked and cold, he decided to make a move and head for the college. It was then that he realized the worst. He was bleeding from the shoulder blade. It must have been when he grazed it as he went over the low wall. Bleeding in public was against the law and meant instant incineration, for the public fear of incurable disease being carried. Even unprotected bleeding in private was illegal. No one, not even his nearest and dearest could help him now.

***

The black and silver uniforms of the security forces looked very smart as the truck drove into the yard. They belied the character of the event that only a while before had taken place in the square in front of the municipal buildings several miles away. The men were jolly, and eager to praise their own efforts in suppressing a rioting mob of uncontrolled hooligans. No trace had been left, apart from a few burned stains on the concrete, which would wash away in time.

"Lets get rid of the evidence," shouted one of the men as they emptied their vacuum cleaners into the garbage cans at the side of the building. They decided to keep the poles for ball games, but burned the banners and notices on a bonfire in the middle of the yard. Two of the men detached themselves from the activity and went into the building in order to make their report.

***

Not very many miles away from all this, a happy couple was contemplating each other, seated by a running stream. It was a beautiful summer's day, and the river was flowing free as they sat there looking at the steamy water passing by. The river was only young, as it had a long way to travel in order to reach the sea, and yet they couldn't even touch the water for the fear of the danger from poisonous pollutants that were now quite common. An industrial egestion a short distance upstream only added more to a rapidly worsening situation. Nothing seemed to matter to this young couple as they sat there under the spreading leaves of the large tree that somehow seemed to be surviving man's inhumanity to its environment. It was a beautiful place, away from the hubbub of the city. 'Quiet' these days was very difficult to find, and 'Peace' was at a premium.

"Shall we ever marry and if we do, what future for our children?" Naamah said wistfully. The depression seemed to be there all the time, a feeling of melancholy and anger. "Even my very own brother, Tubal Cain, is active in creation of this destruction!"

"I won't have that!" said Noah. "It is his arms and munitions factory that has contributed to many years of peace on this planet. The severity of the destruction that would follow if those armaments were used would be of holocaust proportions and nobody wants that, do they? It's with thanks to him and his like that our enemies have been kept at bay for so long. Anyway, his factories don't only produce weapons, they do a lot of other things."

"I know." Naamah was getting upset that the day was being spoilt by the turn of the conversation; it was so often like this. "Perhaps my brother's contribution with his large worldwide conglomerate 'Science and Welfare' mitigates the warlike functions of some of his factories, but the 'Nuke' will destroy everything, like that flick of a switch, or touch of a button. What then?"

"It's been around now for over a millennium and nothing has happened," said Noah becoming bored.

"It only has to happen once!" Naamah stood up. She was annoyed, picked up a broken twig, and broke it again "That's how easy it would be if things went wrong."

Noah was upset now that such a beautiful day was being spoilt by a silly argument. "Let's go for a walk, we haven't been to the hills for over a year. Perhaps there is still some greenery there and the blossom should be out by now". He said, trying to change the subject.

They reached the top of the hill and could feel the warm wind coming up from the other side. There were birds singing to each other. As they walked arm in arm they could see the ground was becoming very slightly brown in appearance where once it was so very green. The atmosphere was much thicker than it used to be and at that altitude it should have been easier and cleaner to breathe, but the humidity was still quite unpleasant, and the black dust, it was everywhere.

Away in the distance, in the valley between the three larger hills there was an occasional flash of light, as something moved and gave reflection to the hazy sun. It was the large turning radar and ventilation beacon that announced intruders and took samples of the external atmosphere. This was an entrance to a 'secret' underground bunker, which could act as home locally to at least 20,000 people in time of war. Safe and secure it was, secret it was not. Everyone knew about it. It was one of the national and international networks of inter-connected underground bunkers, which were meant to support the population when 'Nuke' happened. They all knew, they all knew what to do, and where to go. It had been tested many times. After all, the bomb has been around for the past eleven hundred and thirty five years.

"There must be some other way." Noah lay down on his stomach. He pulled at a piece of dry rye grass and put it in the side of his mouth like a cigarette. These had been made illegal sixty years previously. "There must be some other way...," he repeated, "...to avoid this depravation, there *must* be another way!"

***

Naamah's brother, Tubal Cain, was in a board meeting, when it happened. The power station in the north was flashing emergency on all channels throughout the building. All hell was breaking loose.

Tubal Cain's consortium of businesses under the flag of "Science and Welfare" boasted many assets throughout the entire globe. Many power stations, arms factories, scientific laboratories, space labs and most civil-engineering plants that were still functional were under his control. 'Science and Welfare Consortium' could claim to be capable of doing and creating anything that was involved with fashioning of metal or metallic substances. It was wholly responsible for all the worldwide engineering industry. A tragedy in the north would not help the image, and could really damage public relations if many people were hurt.

The messenger burst into the meeting unannounced. "It's happened! It's happened! It's happened! "He was near to crying now, and finding it almost impossible to speak.

"Sit down! Calm down!" commanded Tubal Cain, in a manner of panic only likely to make matters worse. There in the chair, slumped the messenger; a well built, mature handsome blonde haired man, who had obviously experienced the rigors of life. He was crying.

"A grown man crying!" shouted Tubal Cain, not helping the situation at all. "For God's sake what's happened?"

"Mel...Mel...Melt down! The whole place has cracked apart. People...people...people...

just thrown away like matches out of a box. Smoke, fire, steam and tar everywhere, and then the video receivers went blank! We've sent an emergency force out to look at it. They're all geared up and properly prepared, but the real horror! Oh dear! Oh dear! Oh dear!" He buried his face in his hands, as if in prayer.

"Meeting adjourned" called Tubal Cain "I'm going out to see what's going on. You come with." He suggested to Erash, now a little calmer, but still slumped cringing in the chair. "After all, security is your responsibility."

The whole area of headquarters was now galvanized into activity, but what could they do? A thing like this had never happened on such a large scale before. Everyone was running around trying to do something but not knowing what to do, a form of panic inertia was taking place. As long as the person had a telephone to the ear, or was tapping at a keyboard, he felt justified in being there.

Tubal Cain and Erash had been airborne for about twenty-five minutes, when the steam appeared on the horizon and the radiation counters started to rattle.

"We had better stop here and put on protective field belts" called the pilot, as he pulled to a stop at vigorous but unnoticed deceleration. They were now stationery at five hundred feet above the ground. The hemisphere they were traveling in was new, and could cope with rapid changes of speed. Passengers no longer had to wear seat restraints to hold them in place due to deceleration or acceleration, as the cabin was internally compensated. The field belts emitted a powerful "vibral" field, a form of three-dimensional magnetism, which not only repelled and attracted but also penetrated. It did no harm to the human body, but protected it completely from any radiation in the electromagnetic spectrum to which it was tuned in.

"Are we all tuned in?"

They all affirmed.

"Let's go in." The pilot suggested, as he pulled the craft out of its stationary position to circle the disaster area. The smell was the first thing that hit them. It was acrid, but also smelled of something akin to vomit mixed with ammonia. In spite of the craft's ventilation ducts being almost closed the strong smell was horrible and so unusual. "Perhaps we'd better go back" called Erash, his face going white with fear. "On the other hand, we owe it to them down there" he muttered when he realized what he'd said.

The telefax was turning over and over with newsworthy events at the reception hall in "Science and Welfare".

—Explosions in the north, as power station collapses—
—Many injured—
—Tubal Cain flies out—
—Unrest in the South East – Small town riots quashed –
—Hooligans arrested—
—Coupe d'etat in Bylia—

The trouble in the North seemed to completely diminish the importance of a minor event that killed thirty-two friendly souls in the south.

***

Nightfall was a friend to Svi, as he found his way into the hills not far away from the town, which had left him with such vivid memories, so real, so horrific and so recent. The congealed bloody wound on his left shoulder blade constantly reminded him of that afternoon. He was very grateful that at least it was a warm evening, as he hadn't thought it prudent to collect his clothes. He was making towards the wooded hills, where there was a reasonable amount of cover, and running water that might be fresh to drink. He had forgotten how thirsty he was. It was surprising how far he had gone and how much had taken place since he last had a drink. He didn't seem very hungry at all, and hadn't eaten all day. Crawling through the undergrowth, and sometimes running through a clearing he had found his way in the half-light of evening to a small pool fed by a lightly flowing waterfall. Exhausted, and semi-comatose, his body collapsed on the grassy bank. He carelessly drank from the cool fresh fall of nature's wine. The tranquility of the scene seemed to offer him the security he needed. He turned over; it was dark, very dark. The occasional crack of a branch, or the hoot of a night owl, the distant scuffle of a night creature, the "cheek, cheek" of a cricket—this was the scene that he left behind, as he committed himself to a welcome sleep . . .

 . . . An arm reached out, and two staring eyes looked down at the naked sleeping body. The hand gently moved curiously through Svi's hair, and then casually down his torso until it reached his thighs. It stopped and stroked the area with gentle movements. Still Svi slept, but his organ didn't. It rose like a snake to a charmer's flute. The hand stopped again and moved underneath the body upwards to the lumber region as if curious rather than deliberate. Eventually the other arm came to its aid, and softly took the buttock from underneath, while the other took the shoulder, carefully trying to turn him over. Still Svi slept, oblivious to all around him, as the stranger moved him onto his side. One hand stopped with sudden apparent surprise. It had found the wound. The fingers rubbed at the congealed mess, and then moved quickly to the stranger's mouth. A lick gave all the information that was needed...BLOOD! The night visitor thought for a moment, and got up and left abruptly. Svi was still asleep when the visitor returned with three others and a stretcher. They quietly put the stretcher down on the flat ground alongside his body. Again he was rolled onto his side. They slipped the stretcher under his back and rolled him carefully onto it. They proceeded to carry him with one of the group at each end, and another pulling back the low branches for them to pass, the fourth covered their tracks, so that no one should follow, using mustard to confuse the dogs.

The original member of the group that found him sat with him all night, gently washing the wound that had become infected. They had covered him with a blanket and put him to bed in one of their mud huts, in a small clearing deep in the forest.

It was midday when Svi began to show signs of consciousness. He murmured satisfaction, when with eyes still closed he smiled as hands again gently caressed his vital parts. Even in his slumbers, the sexual arousement was becoming uncontrolled. The hands were now working hard, he was waking up, and he was coming through the most sensational experience he had ever known. He opened his eyes. He screamed with satisfaction and shock as there staring at his penis was a female gorilla in full ecstasy. . "Where am I? What are you doing?" Svi was wide-awake now. "We help you." said the gorilla, very happy that her treatment had had the right effect. "I find you at stream. You have wound. Lots of blood. If they find you, burn you. You die. We all help you here; you not die. You stay with us until you better. Baldape must heal before leave." Svi was confused; he knew that to go back to town would mean certain death whilst he had a wounded shoulder. On the other hand, gorilla people were known to be schizophrenic and he could fall victim to their pleasures just as easily as benefit from their help. He had no choice but to stay.

"Thank you very much for saving my life." He murmured.

"My name 'Zarby'" Thumped the lady gorilla on her hairy chest. "You name?"

"My name is Svi"

"Nice to meet you 'See'!" The gorilla offered her open right hand, and Svi took it in his. "We must bannage your wound. Make better!"

After five days on a diet of nuts, tree fruit, and water from the local stream, Svi was beginning to feel his old self again. The gorillas' hospitality was excessive. They were treating him like royalty as if preparing him for his coronation. It worried him a little. His fears were well founded. He was being prepared for his celebration of getting back to health again, after being saved from the 'fire dragon' and certain death as a pile of soot. The day of celebration was soon to arrive.

"Tomorrow we have big party" said Zarby. "We celebrate, you back to health".

"That's nice?" Svi was worried.

Zarby had tear filled eyes as she spoke. "I bring you yellow Laurel to wear on head for party. You also wear zis shirt and open fronted shorts. We give you a gown tomorrow to wear on top.

She gave Svi a yellow colored shirt with blue and white strips hanging from the mid-chest region, back and front. The shorts had the same strips of cloth hanging from the legs where they finished, just above the knees. The color scheme was the same throughout. "Gown we give you tomorrow". Certainly Svi was pleased about something. At last he had got some clothes, no matter how silly they look. He was fed up with the lusty looks from his nurse. Zarby was a nice girl, but the wrong species.

As morning dawned he heard the laughter and giggles of the whole village.

"Today, the day". A passing native was heard to say. Svi was sure it was mockingly said for his benefit.

Zarby appeared at the door. "I stay wiz you until they come".

Svi was bewildered. Why was she so distraught and yet obviously trying to conceal it? They sat together in silence for about half an hour Zarby quietly whimpering occasionally with Svi pretending not to notice.

A drumbeat started. It was in time with his heart, or was it that his heart was in time with the drum? Anyway the rhythm was the same. It got perceptively a little faster and the reeded door was pushed apart. Three very large male gorillas entered. They were much taller than him and more stoutly built.

"You come wiz us". The smallest one handed Svi his gown. It was yellow with the same blue and white strips around it at about waist height. It also was open fronted.

"You put zis on" he repeated, "You come wiz us". The other two gorillas knelt down and the leader, who had already spoken, gestured for Svi to mount their shoulders. He sat with one buttock on each shoulder. They held his feet to stop him from falling.

He had to bend down as they left the hut. There in a large circle must have been every gorilla in the village. The audience was probably five deep all the way round. In the middle there was what looked like an old fashioned two-noose scaffold, with a large pot underneath. There was a well-established fire under the pot, and something in it was boiling. He couldn't see what was cooking but there was a great deal of steam.

"You climb zees steps," the smallest gorilla said to Svi, "You get best view from here" he said, as he pointed at the scaffold-like construction. Svi's hands were now tied, one in each of the two nooses. He stood on the wooden platform over the pot of boiling fluid. It smelled of menthol and eucalyptus, and certainly would have cured his cold if he had had one. The mist was getting thick, and very hot. The nooses were tightening as the steam got to them.

"We offer our sacrifice, to zee" They began to chant.

"We zank you for saving friend's life . . . we offer his life as zanks"

Svi didn't know whether to laugh or cry. Surely they don't mean to kill me, he thought. They were all so serious.

The speed with which they removed the supporting floor meant that it almost passed unnoticed. He felt jarred as he fell, but he had the foresight to hold onto the nooses higher up, so that he could reduce some of the momentum from the weight of his body when dropped. He was now hanging free, but held by both hands in the nooses.

They were all laughing, and scratching themselves. It was all so unreal. He must hold on. Surely they can't mean to harm him. It's all so stupid. Through the steam he could see Zarby sitting there crying.

"Huh, huh, huh, huh" They were all laughing and scratching.

He now knew that he had outstayed his welcome. "We all zank god for help in saving his life" They all laughed. Svi was getting anxious now. This wasn't a joke. He was surely going to die. Panic was beginning to set in. He was not going to get free. His brain was going into shock; he began to urinate into the cooking pot. As the sizzling steam rose, cheers rang out, the gorillas went mad and into a frenzy....

"Cut him down. We have had our answer. He shall live." Zarby was first to the front. "You passed zee test, you go free!"

***

CHAPTER 2

Noah was at his desk, the hologram of Naamah was looking at his every move, and he was comforted that he could have such a wonderful partner in life. They must surely marry very soon; he would love to start a family in the conventional way. How wonderful it would be, he thought, to father Naamah's children.

A noise of sudden movement from the corridor outside his office caused Noah abruptly to return to reality. He had much work to prepare for his coming meeting with Tubal Cain. A government office was a continual 'in and out' tray, a conveyor belt for paper, a production line of edicts, statutes and orders of law, plans, propositions, and procrastinations. Most of all, it always had the appearance of a grand central station of computer terminals, a mass of stroboscopes causing havoc and damnation to all who gazed upon them. Noah was on the threshold of becoming anxious. He had been given a government report to prepare on "National Civil Protection in time of 'Nuke' war". He had delegated a great deal of the work, but he knew that to do the job properly he should get directly involved as well.

Tubal Cain was ill at ease; the neatness of his dress in no way indicated the tension and anger that was on his face. "Accountability!" he muttered to Noah. "Accountability is something I just can't prove. I am very worried Noah, we've often had problems at 'Science and Welfare', but now they are getting serious. For sometime we've had 'shrinkage' in our stores in Subterranean Sector 26 in the South East, but now it's come to my ears that its not just petty pilfering.

This source tells me that above ground, the same unit organized destructive disposal of an entire 'Crisis for Nuke Danger' protest rally at which the only violence was from our guards"

"Can't you prosecute?" enquired Noah with interest "You must have plenty of witnesses".

"They won't testify! They're terrified of recrimination on them or their families, the organization has got it all tied up." Tubal answered.

"Why don't you discipline them?" enquired Noah. "We can't let them have the slightest suspicion that we know what they're up to, or they will cover their tracks even more".

Tubal Cain hesitated for a moment as if deciding whether to break a confidence. It was obviously hurting him very much. "Listen Noah, what I'm about to tell you is very strictly for your ears only. You will not report it, write it, or act upon it in any way…other than through me?"

He relented slightly

"Is that agreed?"

"Yes!" Noah answered immediately, "Except if it's against the national interest." he added as an afterthought.

"It probably will be!" Tubal Cain was a worried man, and it showed. He appeared to Noah like the little boy who was trying to tell his father that he has just been expelled from school. He hesitated again, and then swallowed..."I'll tell you, but will you help me deal with the problem?"

"I will consider it" Noah was now beginning to realize that this was no ordinary problem. "Tell me, and we will work at it as one, so long as we keep it in the national interest as we see it". He compromised.

"Well", said Tubal Cain, almost inaudibly, "As you know we have had trouble up north, where we had a melt down at our nuclear power station there. After extensive surveys and tests during the last few weeks we have discovered a systematic regular theft of 'Radiact' from the station's plant supplies!"

"Radiact!" exclaimed Noah in full volume "That's the material used in making nuclear bombs!"

"We've got to find out where it's gone!" They said together, both of them in a chorus of severe shock. They decided that an investigation had to be completed at all costs, but in complete secrecy. If the news were leaked then there would be serious recriminations. The public only accepted atomic power under sufferance, and this would give antagonists all the ammunition they needed.

The two men decided to follow the trail before it went cold on them. It would seem easy to follow a main clue such as pilfering in Section 26. There *must* be a connection, they thought, because of the engineering equipment that was stolen. Specialized 'vibral magnetic induction tools' which would be needed to handle radioactive materials. Protective belts and headgear were also missing. It was all happening at the same time.

"Sinister things are going on!" Noah made each word count "I believe that there could be troubled times ahead if we don't act fast."

"Let's go visiting!" agreed Tubal Cain.

They had decided to take public transport, and go unannounced as Revenue Inspectors; they both looked the part, sitting on the bench at the transportation center. This way they could get into all security areas without much trouble, and not arouse any suspicion. Noah had arranged fingerprint passes at a moment's notice through his ministry department. It was useful sometimes having bureaucratic connections.

Going by public transport down to Section 26 was sensible, but they had forgotten how uncomfortable it was. Why did it always have to be so utilitarian? The hemisphere arrived on time, and was really very clean, but the seats were so hard, and the safety restraints were outdated. It would be a rough ride, stopping often to exchange old passengers for new ones. They traveled at an average height of 500 ft., sometimes going between tall buildings. It was amazing how some of them stood up to the strong winds. It was usual to see them wrapped in long strings of twisted lattice work, which acted as a variable "sprung" support tying the buildings to the ground around a central pivot. They would take a severe blast, and would withstand the worst groundquake. Sometimes the craft would "land" on the roof of one of the taller buildings to exchange passengers but more often than not, it would drop to 1 ft. above the ground and throw out the ramp that people may enter or leave. These older machines became less efficient on ground contact, so while the gyros were running the sphere never completely landed.

Eventually they were over the wooded forests where the gorilla people lived, in another few seconds they were vertically above a hemisphere entrance port. It was not clearly marked, but the craft dropped very gently to the center of the valley into what seemed like a muddy pool. The area of sludge opened out allowing the circular vehicle to drop into the ground out of sight as the terrain replaced itself to its original state above it.

The vehicle came to a stop in what appeared to be a vertical empty lift shaft. Security Check 1 must have just taken place, as the apparent flashes of photographic light seemed to penetrate the cabin from all angles. Noah could see Tubal Cain's pass glowing through his shirt. He allowed himself the luxury of a single smile. "We are in." he mouthed to his friend.

The craft again began to drop, and in seconds they were in a large very grand entrance hall, in which many modes of transport had their terminal, or interchange point. The main subterranean monorail, which was driven at the speed of sound by silent electro-magnetic engines, was the latest addition. Eventually it would be possible not just to travel the entire country on this, but to most other countries in the subterranean network, but at the moment it was still having teething problems. Security Check 2 was at the immigration control desk that all newcomers had to pass through no matter from where they had come. "You are entering Subterranean Section 26" The stern computer voice said, "Please insert your pass into the slot and press your personal code." This they both did. "Processed and verified. Enter freely" came, the polite welcoming reply. "Have a nice day". This computer obviously had been programmed with a sense of humor. "I wonder what it would say if we failed the check." Tubal Cain remarked to Noah, who was now looking at the illuminated three-dimensional hologram map, which greeted them as they turned the corner. Location of the section's stores was not difficult, they were clearly marked in the "Private No Entry" section which was off limits to all except high security personnel, and of course Revenue Men!

The Subterranean world was really very beautiful, considering where it was, and for what purpose it was being built. Two and three miles below the surface of the planet, this network of living, leisure and industry facilities were being created to be self sufficient in perpetuity. All who entered should be able to support themselves and their children and their children's children, from generation unto generation for ever and ever. In the event of "Nuke", 20,000 people could occupy Section 26 in comfort without problem, and as long as they didn't increase the adult population at any time beyond 10 per cent of the original entry, they would never run short of supplies, and the supportive industry would cope with ease. It was hoped that this scheme would never be needed and would be a permanent museum for peace. Its' underground lakes and artificial sunlight made an atmosphere of tranquility that would have been much better if placed on the surface. Real sunlight hadn't been seen on the surface for decades. The hazy sky was always bright but never the bright blue it used to be. It was now a muted silver or yellowish gray, due to the changes in the environment created by man during the last two or three generations. It was known as the "greenhouse" effect. The atmosphere could only take so much of industry's effluent, but nobody believed it. Efforts to clear it only seemed to make it worse. The first thing that hit you when entering the under surface world, is the definite lack of humidity.

As the pair of them entered the Extra Security Zone they were stopped by a very realistic robotic computer. It looked like a human but was obviously all metal, and very black with silver trimmings. The head had no face but was shaped like a triangle with apex to the top. It was shrouded in a black metal hood. The effect was meant to be frightening. The two men were standing in a narrow beam of light, and could barely see the image of the robotic, but as it stood in its own half light it still looked very impressive, which of course was what it was designed to be. "Whom have we there?" came the question, in a very matter of fact manner. "Show me your passes, the two of you. Place them on my hand." The robotic held out its left hand. Noah placed his first in the metal hand. The machine then placed its other hand on top. There was a rapid whine, and then the black figure offered back the pass. "You are welcome to enter. Pass in friendship". The whole episode was repeated for the benefit of Tubal Cain. Both having been admitted to the high security area, they felt relieved and could fully understand why the checkpoint was manned in such a manner. No stranger could go through this check without some form of misgivings. Within another few minutes they reached 'Stores Center', using special mini-bicycles that were available for local travel within the special area. They made straight for the office.

There was a hive of activity at the top of a few short steps. Noah felt at home. The office obviously offered all the facilities for moving paper around, just like his own. "We are from the Revenue, and we need a full schedule all goods and materials belonging to the management of this Complex 26. Here is our warrant. We want the list *now* and *on demand*. There is not to be any delay!" Tubal Cain was in his element and enjoying every moment of it, grudgingly. "This could be a long job," he hinted to Noah.

***

Jabal was delighted to see the smiling face of his half sister. Naamah had decided to pay him a surprise visit on his farm estate in the South West. She was very fond of her older brother, and had a strong admiration for the manner in which he conducted his business. Jabal was full of enthusiasm, he had just purchased a new all purpose gyrosphere which he could use for aerial crop spraying, additive dropping, and spreading soil nutrients. It would also double up using an undercarriage attachment, as a massive combine harvester which could process ripe crops into sorted grades, and pack products ready for distribution. He held his sister's hand with brotherly warmth as he spoke. "We are going to have a bumper crop yield this year. These chemical fertilizers mean that we can grow more and more of the same crop every year. It's fantastic! We don't have to leave the fields fallow any more, and crop rotation is no longer necessary."

Jabal was so happy, it was a long time since his sister had been in his home, he suggested a casual tour of his estate. After a drink and an exchange of family pleasantries they both mounted the steps to the gyrosphere.

"You will get a much better view from above" shouted Jabal, from the other side of the sphere as he bent down to enter. He had to stoop to get through the entrance in spite of the door's high opening. He was very tall; Naamah only just came up to his chest. He must have been the tallest man she knew. Had he not been her half brother she could possibly have liked him in a different way, in fact she was certain she could. He was dark in appearance and his firmness of attitude and temperament was enough to excite any girl's admiration. He was a complete gentleman. Naamah could understand what all the girls saw in him.

They were airborne going south, and she was very impressed with the acres and acres of fields all the same color, all identical, and all equally becoming ready for the harvest. It was a soft silken carpet of green, maintained by artificial means, on soils that should have died a natural death many years before.

"How do you avoid the acid rain?" queried Naamah. "We don't" snapped back Jabal. "We spray everyday with dilutent that renders it harmless, but it is very expensive, so we can only spray profitable productive areas. Our forests and lakes suffer very badly."

"Industry has a lot to answer for!" Naamah sighed, "The fumes and exudates into the atmosphere all come back to the land somewhere. Our rivers are polluted, our air is impure, and our soil is being suffocated. Don't you realize that nature's fine ecological balance is being destroyed by us, the human race, like maggots eating at a rotting apple!"?

"I'm a farmer!" Jabal was becoming impatient. "I don't have to worry about these things; after all, I'm growing good things from the land and creating food and raw materials for fiber production. That can't be bad."

"But look what you are doing to the land in order to produce it. Look over there, at the very edge of your growing area, just over the other side of that low perimeter wall". Naamah was leaning over as far as she could for a better view. "Sand, rocks and gravel where the polluted river has eroded the ground during earlier years. We are desecrating this planet and total destruction can only be a few generations away. Machinery and science have changed the natural habitat that our great grandparents may have known. The balance of nature is almost on the point of complete collapse. Many species that we read about in books or see on old videos, don't survive any more, *even in the zoos*. The human animal has a great deal to answer for, doesn't he?"

"Survival! That's what it's all about!" replied Jabal "The human has evolved in just the same way as all creatures, the best go on to greater achievement, re-generating themselves and retaining the stronger qualities whilst the weak go under. All creatures go on that way; it's just that we are better at it than others."

"Do you call *that* being better at it, when we are destroying everything we come in contact with? If there were to be a nuclear war, there would be nothing left to destroy. The rain forests are nearly cut down, the rivers are being bled, and the soils are becoming chemistry sets. Is this the right way?"

Jabal was a little perturbed by such a lecture from his young sister, but he tried to keep his feelings to himself. As they approached some small hills after many miles of travel he decided to set the machine down on the ground. They were just outside the cultivation zone, the green silky carpet only a few paces away.

As they walked away from the fields into the hills the ground became hard, dry and rocky.

"Do you remember this place Naamah?"

"I can't believe it!" exclaimed Naamah "This was the spring that we used to play in as children. It was green and cool here. There were birds, and the trees all had leaves…an oasis in the middle of flat farmlands. We used to come here on our hoverbikes to picnic in the long grass over there by the….. dead tree trunk!" She hesitated, the dead tree trunk was still lying there, complete with the carvings that she and her two half brothers Jabal and Jubal had made, next to an earlier more carefully cut treasure engineered by her full brother Tubal Cain. She was shocked "The dead tree trunk! It used to be the only one, now they are all dead tree trunks, except that the others are still upright, leafless and fixed to the ground." The stream was nothing more than a dried out gully carefully lined with Mercury salts. Nothing lived there any more, not even vultures bothered to fly. "I feel sick" cried Naamah "Lets go back home! There is nothing here for us but memories. The trouble is this is just a small example of what is happening everywhere. They laughed about it in our grandparents' time. They nearly stopped it happening, then. It's too late now. Oh, I only wish that those people had listened! They always laugh or pass it over, and then when things happen they always blame *something*, or *someone* else."

The return journey to Jabal's residence did not seem to take very long, and it was mutually decided that Naamah would stay overnight. They could relax, gossiping over a hot meal, and enjoy each other's company as semi-siblings who hadn't seen each other for a long time…so much had happened!

It was not long after they finished eating that Naamah saw the dark figures in the half-light, through the early evening window. Jabal stopped in mid conversation as shock appeared very noticeably on his sister's face. "What's wrong Naamah? You look like you've seen a ghost!"

"Those people at the window, they are looking straight at me.

Who are they? What are they?" She looked terrified.

"These are my 'hybrids'. They work my land, and are just coming in from their daily toil in the fields." Jabal tried to re-assure her.

Naamah was very concerned; she had never seen a hybrid man before. They looked very fierce with their thick black curly hair, wide noses, and such very dark skin. She had heard about them, and how they were misused and ill treated, but she had never seen them so close before. She couldn't understand why there were so many of them. It was illegal to have more than fifteen together in any one place, unless under certain protective supervision. They were very dangerous, especially in a herd. They were a genetic result of human relationship with a species of ape found in the far central eastern continent two oceans away. This sexual relationship was now also illegal but it still seemed to go on in a clandestine manner.

A hybrid had his face so hard against the window that his nose was squashed to nearly three times its rightful width, and his breath was rapidly misting up the glass on the outside. His eyes were so staring and curious. They were so large, so dark, so round. His thick lips flattened against the glass, and showed white teeth so strongly contrasted in the black leathery face. His curiosity seemed to be fixating on Naamah's shapely legs. He seemed to be getting pleasure and surprise at the same time, from the sight of a well-formed human female. He was getting some perverted satisfaction out of his apparent lust for Naamah…Crack…Naamah was sure she heard a whip!

"That will teach you to play with yourself!" The voice came clearly from outside the window, and the face dropped from view just as fast as it had appeared.

"What's going on?" squeaked Naamah as she tried to clear her throat. The astonishment at what she thought was happening was confirmed when Jabal told her.

"Oh, some hybrid masturbating at the window. It happens quite often when they see a woman. They are very highly sexually motivated, both the male and female. Keep away from them unless with one of us. They can be very friendly and have a very keen sense of humor, but can easily turn dangerous without warning. We have a carefully vetted herd on this estate; they work well and play hard. We understand each other and never have we had an escape. We reward them well, feed them and treat them like humans but still have to watch our backs. Four years ago, when one of the females had lost her baby, she stole a child from the local nursery. When we found her we had to make an example of her. They knew it was wrong to steal a human. It's bad enough that we let them steal from each other. It's their way. Anyway we put her on the gallows. She hung there for two days before she died. We had a riot and we had to destroy half the herd. Since that time we keep them locked up at night, and they are constantly under guard."

"We have increased the size of the herd up to full strength again, and allow them a form of self government, as long as they fit in with our rules on the estate. It's taken them four years to get back to this very high level of efficiency and mutual understanding. On many other farms they use worse forms of discipline than the whip, but then are they creating their own problems? Be very wary of all hybrids. They don't really trust us, so we can't really trust them. It's not their fault, but that's the way it is!" Jabal continued, "There is going to be a hybrid wedding tomorrow, Naamah. Would you like to see it before you return home? I'll take you."

Naamah was full of cautious enthusiasm, "What a wonderful idea!"

***

Svi returned to college with very mixed emotion. He couldn't believe all that had happened during the last few weeks. Worst of all was the conspicuous absence of some of the colleagues and friends whom he had known so well. It was with shock and relief that his friends greeted him as he returned through the common room doors. "We thought you had been incinerated!" Came a girl's exhilarated voice from the corner of the room.

"You are alive! You are all right!" Svi shouted and took rapid breath. He was almost airborne as he jumped a small sofa and landed at the young woman's knees. "Lika! I thought that they had got you too!" Svi was filled with emotion. He had tears in his eyes, not having dared to think of his loved one since that horrible day which seemed to him almost a century ago. He didn't want to face life without her, but he did not dare think that she had escaped. "How did you get away Lika?"

They embraced each other oblivious of the understanding onlookers who were just as pleased to see the happy couple, as they were to be one.

"I hid in the hollow trunk of a dead tree, and prayed". Lika whispered into Svi's ear. "It was horrible, the noises, the screams and that awful smell of burning flesh! I was sure that they had got you and that I would never see you again. I just prayed that you wouldn't suffer any pain. They say that you don't you know. Paresifiers make you go stone cold. There's no feeling at all, they say." Lika went on, "I waited in the tree until everything was quiet, then when I was sure that all the guards had gone, I crawled out of the tree and down the ditch on the side of the road until I reached the field where we had left our clothes. I knew as I waited, huddled with cold, under the old burnt out hedge, that I wouldn't see you again. Your clothes were still neatly piled in the little corner where we had put them. We thought we were going to have a good fun day. Oh! We lost so many of us, it was horrible. I stayed with your clothes until midday the next day. I felt that I was still with you, just being with the clothes so recently worn by you. Eventually when no one else came, those of us who had stayed back, picked up all the remaining belongings and took them to the 'Crisis' office. I took yours home with me!" She smiled in that familiar cheeky manner that always warmed Svi's heart.

When eventually it was Svi's turn to tell his story, he narrated it to all the people gathered there. They all showed keen interest, having all had miraculous escapes. One other of the people present had made it to a roof and then seen all below just as Svi had done. Svi and Lika decided to cut out the morning lectures and go back to her home for a long 'talk' as they had not now seen each other for over three weeks.

Lika's apartment was very much that of a student. Although there had been an attempt to keep it feminine, tidiness was obviously at a premium. She was noticeably very much involved in her studies. Books, tapes, video discs and holographic recording sheets filled the many shelves that made up three walls of her small study. Work that was immediately at hand was laid on the center pad of her desk. She had interrupted her work for some reason and not returned to it. Lika walked over to the desk and shut her books.

"No work this morning!" She said with a cheerful and extravagant smile, as she pushed the little button by the desk. The wall started to move, and the lower half of it began to drop forward towards them and form a sofa bed. Svi sat down. Lika disappeared into the small kitchen area out of sight.

"I couldn't believe it when you appeared at the common room door this morning" Lika's voice came from the kitchen. "I had given up all hope of ever seeing you again!"

Svi stared at the floor, in a dream, feeling very happy. A private sensation of glowing warmth and gratitude that he was re-united with Lika after such a horrific chapter in their lives. He was thanking God for their deliverance. "I didn't realize that I still believed in the Almighty" Svi said to Lika as she came in through the door and saw him in his state of apparent daze.

"In truth, I understand" came Like's reply. "We all turn to him at some time in our lives. Our forefathers used to give him a lot more time than we do."

She sat down at Svi's side, as he continued to stare at the base of the wall opposite him in a blank dream-like manner. Putting her arm around his neck, and softly across his other shoulder, she pulled him close to her. She pushed her fingers through his curly blonde hair, and could feel the movement coming back into his thoughts. His comatose withdrawal from his immediate surroundings was beginning to wane; he was regaining his old alertness and keenness of interest.

"I'm very sorry darling" Svi began softly "I didn't realize how much the last few weeks had played on my mind. It was quite traumatic, and finding you alive, well, and still so very loving and beautiful as ever, when I had given you up without even daring to hope. I feel so….. so guilty, so ashamed? It is so hard to explain. I love you so much, that I could not bear to think of your destruction, so I completely deleted you from my mind. Today I found you alive and wonderfully well, and feel so guilty and sorry that I neglected you in my thoughts."

"I understand, perhaps more than you could believe." Lika offered warmth in her manner, as she stroked his head more purposefully and pulled it toward her bosom. She cuddled it like a mother nursing a baby. She kissed his forehead as he turned to face her. He was now on his back, with his feet up on the bed. She moved her fingers slowly across his chest and he let out a sigh as he looked up at her face. He could see the very faint suggestion of a tear starting in the corner of one eye.

"Why are you sad?" Svi asked.

"No! I'm so very happy! I seemed to have waited what seems like a decade for this very moment. I was never completely certain that you were destroyed and forced myself to push the affair to the back of my mind, but you were everywhere. I could not study; I was like a robotic machine. I performed my daily tasks, but I cannot remember doing so. When you walked through the common room door, it took a good few moments for my brain to register. I just thought I was dreaming. There you were, alive and well, my Svi!" She caressed his hairy chest, with one hand and ran the fingers of her other hand across his lips, as he kissed them one at a time. They looked at each other, their eyes were drawn together, and they understood what was happening to them. Svi's hand reached for Lika's ankle and began to gently feel the mould of its design, while Lika's hand moved secretively from Svi's chest to his naval where it made a house call, only to move on to its next destination in a place so full of opportunity. She had just arrived in this very warm and sensual hairy region in the loins of love when likewise she felt Svi's other hand gently encircling the nipple of one of her breasts. She must have moved, her nipple became enlarged at the same moment as Svi's masculinity became very obvious to her. She was sure she hadn't grabbed at it; it just went straight into her hand. Solid, vibrant and warm. She was very aware of her sexual desire. Her loins had become very warm and needed something. She took Svi's hand and put it there, she was losing control of the situation. Svi moved her onto her back and very carefully moved onto her, within a space of a single heart beat Lika had opened herself and admitted Svi. He entered with serenity. Their pleasure, their singularity, they together were one. No other human could ever know what these two souls had experienced at that moment.

Midday had passed and given birth to early afternoon, when the dozing duo awoke from their well deserved slumber. Svi woke up first; he was holding his Lika's head all tucked up in his hairy chest. She was still asleep in the pre-natal position snuggled up to her partner in a manner of complete trust and devotion. She was so very much at pleasure, secure and peaceful. Svi reached down to her forehead and gently kissed her. He took his right hand and kissed his index finger, then carefully placed it on her lips. Almost imperceptibly, Lika kissed the finger in return. She was surely awake now.

"I can hear the thumping of your heart" murmured Lika, "It sounds very happy."

They must have lain there on the bed for quite a while when finally Svi decided they should make an attempt to go back to college. After all, they were meant to be responsible students.

Getting out of bed they freshened themselves up and prepared for an afternoon's study. They had missed the first afternoon lecture, but arrived in good time for the second. They took their places next to each other in the Lecture Theatre, putting on their audio-phones so that they could understand as the knowledge pulsated and programmed into their brains. Lika always had problems tuning herself in to her unit, and Svi was always there to help. She was so pleased to have him returned to her side. Having the information data-fed into their brains was very pleasant, and often very interesting, but it was what they did with that information that was important. The tutorial sessions where they had open discussion with their tutor in small groups was the occasion when the newly acquired knowledge was put to the test. It was to be in one of those groups that Svi and Lika were going to find an interest that was to be the test of their abilities. This was an interest that was to destine them for achievement that would be beyond the aspiration and comprehension of any human mind.

***

Noah and Tubal Cain had become very much involved in their adopted characters as Revenue Men. They had almost forgotten who they really were. The two friends had been working for more than ten days, with little time for sleep, and certainly no leisure. They were listing stocks, checking invoices, cross-checking files with computer entries and with the help of three more government clerks of the 'Revenue Department' who had come down from the surface, they had finally matched everything possible with computer data and ledger-tape entries and the real thing that they could see in front of them. Every aspect of checking had been completed...*There was a great big hole...Enormous quantities of valuable and not so valuable goods had been lost...disappeared...acquired by foreign powers???*

Tubal Cain was very worried, Noah was not very happy either.

Why would so much equipment disappear, and where had it gone? Why did two countries keep buying the old used empty storage cases? He was sure that Bylia and Cabu were not innocent countries in an international intrigue which smelled very much of danger on a very large scale. Where had the 'Radiact' gone, and why had so much heavy equipment and high technological hard and software been purloined in such massive quantities? Why had there been so much effort in concealing the theft, and where had it all gone?

They finally made a decision to return to the surface in order to correlate their findings and of course make the necessary reports to the authorities. Noah could also add some of his personal findings to the government report on national security that he was in the middle of preparing. Had they known what was going on only a short distance away they might have wanted to be a little more careful with their own personal safety?

Two hands were squeezing plastic explosive into the doorframe of the only exit from the section in which Noah and Tubal were working. As the door was to slide open the whole area would be torn apart in a major local explosion, certainly killing anyone within ten paces of its center.

Noah and Tubal decided to pack their pooled information from the days of research together. Their colleagues were organizing a warrant for the removal of all the material that was needed for the investigation. Noah was at the far end of the room talking to Tubal Cain when it happened . . .

A strong blue flash of light, followed by a loud bang, which almost rendered the two men deaf on the spot. The force of the explosion threw them to the ground hard against the wall. There were blooded bits of bodies and lumps of what looked like sugar all down the wall against which they had found themselves lying. The carnage, the smell, and the revolting mess that was all around them was enough to make anybody vomit. Noah had blood all down his left side and he hadn't even been hurt. It was not even his own blood. He went to his pocket for a cloth to mop himself. That did it; he nearly threw up as he pulled out a single human finger, which was recently detached from its owner. It was warm and bloody.

Tubal Cain looked at Noah and did not know how to react. The fear and revulsion in his brain became very close to mirth as he tried to imagine how Noah could get into such a mess. An entirely illogical reaction at that time.

Noah felt filthy. He was amazed that at a time when he should be worried for his life and sickened by the obvious carnage, all he could think about was how filthy he was. An explosion had ripped open the exit wall and thrown two of his colleagues in shreds, perhaps seventy paces across the room. They could never have known what happened, and would not even have seen the flash, having been dead even before that instance in time. The three men stood there looking at the wall that was not there any more, bewildered.

"There is certainly a lot of damage!" Noah made the inane remark, "We can't clear this up." He was stunned.

Tubal Cain decided at last, that it was a very dangerous place to stay in, and perhaps they should make a rapid departure with whatever they could salvage from the ruins. They seemed to be very lucky that all the important paper work was already in a bomb and fireproof metal cabinet, which had been blown across the room in the blast. The two men asked their colleague to take it to the surface, and return it to their office. He reacted very well considering that he had just 'lost' two of his closest workmates.

Tubal Cain walked over to the subterranean guard who had just arrived on the scene, along with a small crowd of very curious people. He showed his Government Pass, as a Revenue Inspector, and using its authority, demanded that an investigation into the source and cause of the blast should be immediately carried out.

The guard's hand barely indicated that he was about to answer when there was another sharp blue flash of light. They never consciously heard the explosion . . .

***

CHAPTER 3

Naamah's face showed a pleasurable curiosity as she sat with Jabal in the chair as the guest of honor at the wedding of the two hybrids, Rastus and Glenshee. Each one stood naked in a large bath separated by a screen so that they could not see each other. They could only be seen by friends or relatives of their own sex, who each took their turn to help wash the body of the bride or the groom while drums gently beat in the background. They were using sweet smelling herbal dressings, which gave forth the most beautiful smell of lavender. As guests of honor, both Jabal and Naamah were allowed to sit in a privileged position only permitted to non-hybrids. They were able to see both sexes at work at the same time. The only hybrid who was allowed the same privilege was the celibate priest who was to perform the ceremony of "Walking Through The Trees". After the washing, (which was accompanied by joyous wailing from both sides), the rhythm of the beating drums became slower and heavier. The marrying couple stepped out of their baths at exactly the same time as the drums changed tempo. It was as if each knew what the other was doing and had pre-rehearsed the event. Part of the beauty, Jabal told Naamah, was that neither the bride nor the groom had ever attended a wedding before. It was customary for only married hybrids or celibates to attend.

This was as new an experience for Rastus and Glenshee as it was for Naamah.

The guests began to dress the couple in colored ribbons and silks, still out of view to the other partner, and guests of the opposite sex. Each ribbon was tied in a very special way to the next until the whole body was covered. They looked very impressive, like the large black children's dolls in multi-colored clothing often seen decorating toy displays in many city department stores.

"The tying of the ribbon represents the tying of the marriage knot, and it forms a simple chain around the body. The way the ribbons hang together gives the illusion of a solid sheet of clothing. A single break in the chain, a single knot coming loose and the costume will break up and fall to the ground. This is meant to show how fragile a marriage can be." Jabal explained.

The singing and the drum tempo went slower again, as the preparations of the couple reached near completion. Crowns of twigs and valuable fresh green leaves were finally placed on the heads of Rastus and Glenshee.

The screen came to an end almost in front of Jabal and Naamah and they could see full length of both sides. The celibate hybrid preacher stood in front of them, facing the couple that still could not see each other. All the guests now came forward in front of the couple and at the side of the preacher as he gestured for them to do so, the males and females still in their separate gatherings. They all cheered as the drums began to "roll" in a rapid beating rhythm. The preacher raised his arms forward and lifted his hands upward, palms forward, to show friendship to the couple and that nothing was concealed. A male guest and a female guest then took a length of thin brightly colored twine and tied it between the two trees that were one either side of the front of the screen.

"You will now see why the screen was erected in this position" Jabal leaned over to Naamah. "Sometimes they bring trees in pots, but they have to be real trees with leaves. They represent life to these people, and you know how scarce trees are."

The singing changed to a warlike cry "Ajah! Ajah! Ajah!" They all cried together, and as the third call came the couple reached out to the screen with their nearest hand. They moved until they touched whilst still looking ahead at the preacher's hand, from which they never removed their gaze. When they made touch contact they then moved forward until the moment they could leave the screen and hold hands, this they finally did. The roar went out "Jaha! Jaha! Jaha!" On the third call, the couple stepped forward to the twine. The preacher opened his arms wider and the assembled crowd again roared "Mawa! Mawa! Mawal! The preacher dropped his hands to his side and the couple jumped forward between the trees and broke the twine.

"They are now married" Jubal stated the obvious. "The marriage takes place as they jump their first step together between the two trees. The twine is only a modern extra so that all the guests can be sure of the moment that it actually happens".

The place went into uproar, singing and dancing. The music started. The drums softened and other instruments began to play and music became rhythmic and joyful. A large circle was formed around the bride and groom and all guests mixed and danced.

Jabal was very contented, seeing his hybrids so happy, and he felt good, knowing that not many herds would invite their owner to one of their weddings. But then, he was a good and generous man.

Naamah's face went white, her jaw dropped, as her mouth went dry with shock. Jubal her half brother, and brother to Jabal had just arrived with the news of Noah and Tubal Cain.

"There has been a terrible incident in Subterranean Section 26. Two explosions, but both Noah and Tubal Cain have been brought to safety. They are in the intensive care department of the local hospital on the surface of Lublia the nearest town to Section 26. We have a very rapid hemisphere at our disposal to get us there now".

Naamah mouthed as if to answer but could not. With Jabal on one side and Jubal on the other, she ran to the hemisphere.

Erash, Chief Security Officer of Science and Welfare greeted them with a somber face when their hemisphere landed at the Lublia hospital only a short time later. They must have traveled at four or five times the speed of sound in order to get there so quickly.

"Their condition is critical." said Erash. "They are very very lucky to have got out of that inferno. They have all their legs and arms. Noah may have lost some sight in one eye and Tubal Cain has been bleeding a great deal into one lung, but both have a possible chance of recovery. The guard and the surviving government clerk were badly buried and died. Thirty onlookers also died. Their ghoulish curiosity in the results of the first explosion caused their death in the second one. Casualty Officers say that seventy-two other injured people have been brought in, but they could not treat everybody at once and a few more of the injured died on arrival. The wounds are horrific. The second explosion had metal bolts and shrapnel in it. They caused devastation and horrible wounds.....!

"Enough" shouted Naamah, regaining her composure. "I want to see Noah and my brother now!" she shouted, "Let me see them!"

"This way, follow me." he said.

There behind a glass screen were three beds, all with monitors and video screens at their foot. Noah was on the left easily recognizable but an awful color. Unconscious, next to Noah was Tubal Cain. His face and upper body all swathed in bandages. The only way Naamah recognized her brother was by the old scars across both shins where he burned them with a red-hot poker as a boy.

Who's that man in the other bed?" enquired Naamah. "That's not a man, that a young woman" answered Erash. "She has lost all her hair and a hand. She is also very lucky; we think that she was one of the crowd who came to 'see', when the second explosion happened. They had nowhere else to put her. All the other wards and rooms are full. This is only a small hospital. You should see the injuries that these bastards have caused to other innocent people! They are evil blighters and have got to be caught. We don't yet know who did it, and nobody claims credit for this cowardly deed".

Naamah, Jabal and Jubal decided to stay at the bedsides taking it in turns to sleep only one at a time, so that there were always two of them there, changing every third day.

It was early evening three and a half days later, when Noah realized that something had happened. His head was ringing and there was pain in his ears. His right eye felt bruised. He opened his eyes. Oh the pain! The light! What had happened? Where was he? Why could he not see properly? His legs felt numb. That's not logical, he thought again. How could they 'feel' numb? No, he thought, they must feel cold with very little sensation. He must be rambling, he thought. 'I must say something.' He just could not work his mouth. He *must* say something, even if it was just '*Help*'. Perhaps if he lifted his hand. Yes he could feel his hands, so that was alright. He tried to move his eyeballs. They were frozen looking at the ceiling. That would not work either. Could he hear a voice? He knew that voice. It was soft and very familiar.

"Na...Na...Marn...Naarm...Naamah!" He managed to shout, he managed it, he managed it. He was very pleased with himself. He was sure he must have been smiling.

Naamah leaned over his bed and looked straight into his face. "I'm sure he spoke very faintly," she said to Jabal "Look I'm sure his lips quivered very slightly and his eyes seem slightly open."

"Your imagination", Jabal consoled Naamah as he also leaned over Noah's face to investigate. "No, not a sign of life" Jabal tried to believe Naamah. "He must be in a very deep coma, look at the monitors, not a single flicker. Just a vegetable! All we can do is hope."

Naamah did not believe Jabal. She was certain Noah was conscious. She *knew* he was, there was no question about it. How could she prove it? She could feel Noah's thoughts in her head. This had never happened so profoundly before. She knew that Noah was thinking. What is more, she knew *what* Noah was thinking!! She had never believed in mental telepathy. She had heard of thought transference, but now she did not just believe, she 'knew' that it was possible.

She looked at Noah's slightly burned and bruised right hand, so tense and tightly clenched. Perhaps he was worried that he could not communicate. She looked at his hand and 'thought' at Noah, but that did not seem to work. Naamah knew that Noah was trying to tell her something. Then suddenly she felt an incredible knowing feeling in her head. He had got through to her. He was alive and conscious. He was talking; he was calling her name again. This was unbelievable. No one would accept this. She knew he was aware of his consciousness. Think with him she thought…she encouraged him to relax and concentrate on his right hand.

"Look!" shouted Jabal, the enthusiasm registering in his voice. "Look at his hand, he's relaxed his right fist!"

Naamah spoke to Noah "I know you can hear me" she said "Don't try to strain. Just relax. I'm with you. Together our strength will get you through this. I know you are hearing me, and I will stay here by your side". Naamah could see in her mind the first explosion in Section 26. Noah was obviously thinking about it. He was muddled. He didn't know about the second explosion at all. He could not understand. Where was he? Why was he here? Why was he so helpless, and why could not anyone hear him whilst he was shouting so loudly?

Naamah tried to tell Jabal, but gave up before she even spoke her first word. She would never be believed. They would say that she must have been suffering from delusions. Pure coincidence, but she did not doubt that her knowledge was as certain and beyond question as the ground she was standing on. Why did she have to prove it? She knew, and Noah knew. They were one in thought together. She moved her hand under his head and gently lifted it, so that his eyes could see more of the room. She put his hand to her mouth and kissed it. A love so pure that Noah understood. Naamah could see his lips soften as if to smile. She leaned over to kiss them. His tongue met hers, as contact was made. He had managed to give her the sign she was waiting for.

"Why are you crying? What's happened? Jabal was asking. "He has just kissed me!" came the answer. "He is going to be alright!"

Naamah was so involved with the welfare of Noah that she had almost forgotten her brother Tubal Cain laying there. She tenderly laid Noah's hands to rest and gently stroked his brow. She could feel the love between them. She knew all was well. Knowing that Noah understood made it so much easier for her to go over to Tubal Cain's bed and spend more time with him. He was a real mess, covered with corrective bandages, which in their time would help to create fresh skin on the body and facial areas, which had been so badly burned. He was lucky, by normal reasoning he should have died. Naamah believed that it was divine intervention that had placed the "Medical Defense Unit" on maneuvers in Section 26 that day. If medical treatment hadn't been there, on the spot, it was certain that Noah and Tubal Cain would have died within minutes of the second explosion. Treatment bandage was also very scarce as some natural products were still needed in its' manufacture, and this meant that it was rationed, but the Medical Defense Unit always carried it. Tubal Cain would otherwise have been scarred for life.

Tubal Cain had had several occasions of consciousness in the last three days, but at no time had he been completely coherent for long enough to estimate his mental welfare.

The nearly bald excuse for a woman in the next bed was crying and moaning incessantly. She kept talking in vague repetitive sentences. She seemed very much the aggressive type, and yet she was sad and pitiful as if all alone and bewildered. Something about her made compulsive observation, and Naamah was very much attracted to her. It was as impossible to estimate her age, as it was her sex. She had got flat breasts, as far as one could see, the reason being her left handless arm was strapped across her chest in order to help it heal.

Again she started to writhe in agony or frustration but this time she kicked off the bedcovers only to expose her completely naked unspoiled femininity for all to see. If she knew what she was doing she did not care. Her legs were flaying out in both directions at once. Naamah came to the conclusion that this must be a young dark haired woman about the same age as she was. She had been strapped to the bed around her waist and her right hand kept trying in vain to loosen the buckle, but it was locked and no way could she escape. Naamah felt very sorry for her. The treatment she was getting was really the best available. Why was she so frustrated?

Naamah stood by her bed, and reached out to stroke her right shoulder. That did it. The woman turned her face to look at Naamah straight in the eyes. A balding head with fierce staring eyes the pupils vaso-dilated. Then it happened…she bit hard at Naamah's right hand, she missed but caught the forearm just behind the wrist. Naamah let forth a scream that would waken the dead. The woman's teeth had drawn blood. Naamah was badly bruised and slightly bleeding. A nursing attendant appeared on the scene immediately and administered a clean dressing to the wound from an aerosol can. Plastic skin took only a morning or an afternoon in which to heal. Naamah was bemused that so many things came in aerosol cans. So many hospital treatments used them, as they were always sterile. Yet these very articles used to save life were potentially destroying the environment.

The woman was now shouting very loudly, very coherently, but made no real sense. Naamah did not know whether she was ranting or trying to tell them something. "Glarka forg wungle Fadfagi!" The woman cried.

That was clear enough thought Naamah, but what did it mean? The woman repeated it several times and the nursing attendant returned. A quick short spray across her nose and the poor demented soul was fast asleep. Naamah offered to cover her up and make her comfortable. The body was soaking with perspiration and she was very hot. Very nearly a fever Naamah thought.

***

Svi arrived at Lika's door. It was very early in the morning. Lika was not looking her best. She was semi-dazed from being aroused from her sleep. Her curly blonde hair fell carelessly brushing her shoulders. With half closed eyes she gestured to Svi to come in, and despite her obvious displeasure at being woken so early, she closed the door behind them and threw her arms tight around Svi's neck almost strangling him. She loved him so very much. She had not really understood the excitement that Svi had brought with him to her front door. He was bursting to tell her something, and all she wanted to do in her half awake condition was make love. His enthusiasm to tell her about it overpowered all desire for lovemaking. She pulled at his collar; she wanted him to kiss her. Finally, without much fight, he gave in and within a very short moment, they were laid out together on Lika's bed. Svi could not contain himself any longer...

"I have got to tell you the wonderful news." He whispered in Lika's ear. She was still trying to kiss every hair on Svi's chest. "I must tell you, please listen," he begged. She carried on as if everything depended on the result of her efforts. "Oh alright" he went on "I'll tell you anyway". She was still not taking any notice. "I've been offered the project and I can take another student with me. *Will you come?* "

Lika thought she heard Svi say something. She was still half asleep; her eyes were still not properly open. She looked beautiful to someone who really loved her. Svi melted when she looked up at his face and her almost closed eyes met his.

"Of course I'll come." She answered soporifically, "Where am *coming* to?" She asked, as an afterthought.

Svi could not resist any longer, he looked at those cute sleepy eyes with sleep still encrusted in the corners. He leaned over and with his wet tongue kissed both eyes until they were clean and wide open.

"That was lovely" Lika said as she purred and cuddled up to Svi. "Where are we going? What project and when?" For the first time she appeared to be awake.

"Our final year project." Said Svi as he regained his enthusiasm "The examining board have recommended me for one of the plumb jobs for next term and I am allowed to choose a colleague from a list of approved students. You were on the list. We must have done well in our studies to be recognized for such an exciting venture."

"You mean, *you* must have done well in our studies," replied Lika "If it hadn't been for you I would never have reached the approved list of candidates, and anyway you must have been of extremely high standard to be nominated as a project leader. By the way..." asked Lika as an afterthought, "What project is it?"

"We are going to study the effects of the extra-terrestrial environment on Social Welfare, with particular interest in the prospect of long term involvement on the human mind! In other words, how to survive in orbit."

Lika's mouth dropped open, "But that's the blue-ribbon experiment! That's the one you always wanted. You will be the envy of everyone. I can't believe it! And you want *me* to join you! I'm surely not up to it. I could never have done what I did, without your help, so how could I do such advanced work? I would only hinder you!"

"No! No!" shouted Svi. He was angry. "I would never have even finished my first year of studies without you to inspire me." He was getting quite angry. "If you won't come with me, then I won't go. There are only two things in my life that matter to me. One is my love of my work; the other is the love between us. Every night when I am with you, or without you, I pray to God and thank him for bestowing this love upon the both of us. We are very lucky. I pray to him that he will let us keep it."

"That's the nicest thing you've ever said to me!" Lika was almost crying. "Please, I would love to come with you, and we will make a success that will do full credit to the sponsors whoever they are. They are giving us such a chance in life; we must repay them the only way we know how, with the pursuit of excellence, and to the best of our ability."

Svi was sitting up. "That was quite a speech." He kissed her on the forehead. "Let's get dressed and go to the board to enroll. I've got all the forms. Oh, and while we are about it, lets get married at the same time".

***

The monitor screen was beginning to register a brain pulse. The high pitched whining that had been a characteristic of Noah's care unit for the last week, gently started to lower in key. Jabal and Jubal both noticed the casual change of note at the same moment. The change in the audiometric scan, which announced an improvement in the brain impulses, caused the two brothers an immediate joyous reaction. Noah was past his critical stage now; they decided to call Naamah who had not long before retired for her rest period. They were still deciding who was to inform her, when she walked in the door, smiling and happy.

"Isn't it wonderful?" she cried.

"What are you so pleased about?" called Jubal, not quite understanding the situation. "How did you know?" Jabal enquired when he realized why Naamah was there. She brushed passed and stood at the side of Noah's bed with very happy tears in her eyes. Leaning over she kissed his lips with such force that their teeth touched.

"My darling, of course I'll marry you when this is all over. We have been through so much together." Naamah took his hand, but this time the hand reciprocated and would not let go.

"I love you darling." Noah mouthed very carefully. "You have been such a comfort to me, you don't have to.....". He fell asleep. Jabal took his half sister's hand and Jubal wrapped his arm around the back of her shoulders. Together the trio knew that now it was only a question of when, rather than whether, recovery would be achieved.

That evening it was decided to move Tubal Cain. The doctors who had been treating his wounds were very pleased with him, and his breathing was now normal. They instructed the staff to move him to a separate side room that had recently become vacant. Tubal Cain's periods of coherence were becoming almost continuous now, but he had lost all memory of the explosions and was still very dazed.

The woman had been moved to a woman's ward the day before, and the police pathologists had been to examine her. They were suspicious about some explosive gel found under the finger nails of her left hand which they had found in the debris and the hospital laboratory were preparing it, with care, for suspended animation. Surgery at a later date to re-attach it to the woman's wrist was possible, and they were very pleased with themselves for finding it. Suddenly all that changed when they found the gel.

If she had been found guilty of taking part in the conspiracy to cause the explosions, she would be treated as a terrorist and would never have her hand returned to her. In fact it would be the only thing left of her that would survive, and it would be kept in the museum of 'Punishment and Crime'.

She would be garroted and incinerated for such an evil crime. 'How could anyone do that to innocent people?' would be the prosecution's call when sentence was being considered. The garrote was thought to be the cruelest form of legal execution and was only used in cases of proven terrorism. The executioner's prowess was in his ability to keep the prisoner conscious for as long as possible, so that their punishment was complete. A wide metal band was secured around the neck of the prisoner, who was seated in a chair with both arms secured at the elbow and both legs secured slightly apart at the knee. The handle was turned, causing the wire to tighten, and the prisoner began to feel the tension. A gentle executioner could keep a prisoner in agony and pain for a long time. This form of execution was very much feared and its' often televised public performance only added to its deterrent effect. Criminals would rather kill than be caught, but they would rather not kill in the first place. Villains seldom carried weapons of murder any more. Televised executions had a great deal to do with that.—This woman may have been a terrorist and they would soon know.

Naamah was with Noah when Tubal Cain walked into the room as if nothing has changed and the explosions had never occurred. During the last couple of days his recovery had been rapid. He still had lapses of memory, but on the whole he was generally fit, and his physical wounds were almost invisible. Fibrous compounds were very efficient in their curative qualities. Noah's recovery had been a great deal more difficult because his trauma was not entirely physical. He had to fight his problems by himself, and this he had attempted to do. With great effort and Naamah's continual involvement somewhat relieving the strain, Noah was pulling through and Naamah was never going to leave his side.

"We have some wonderful news for you" Noah was smiling as he spoke to Tubal Cain "I'm going to be your brother-in-law. Naamah and I are getting married!"

"When?" Tubal Cain tried to show surprise in his voice, but he was never a very good actor.

"Very soon, when we are clear of the hospital...." Noah was replying.

"We are going to take a special license and get married as soon as possible". Naamah interjected. "Jubal and Jabal are full of it and they want to throw a big party, hundreds of people, music, dancing and lots to eat. What do you think?" Her enthusiasm was flowing forth as she ran over to her brother and threw her arms around his neck, not letting him answer.

Lights above the door began to flash vigorously, and a hospital alarm could be heard from some distance away. Tubal Cain looked over to Noah, as Naamah turned round with concern. The door swung open and a hospital guard looked in, and rapidly disappeared again. A few moments later two police arrived and looked into the room where the woman 'terrorist' was meant to be recovering. They re-appeared and mounted guard outside.

"What's going on?" Naamah asked one of them. "There has been a theft from the path-lab. This lady's hand has vanished. It has probably been stolen".

***

The Palace of Memories always created a sensation of awe and curiosity in Lika. Her imagination would run riot, as she would walk between the exhibits of civilization as it used to be. How did people really think, behave, and feel amongst themselves when they lived so many years ago, in times much less damaged by technology and scientific interference? Many of the people of earlier times did horrible things to nature. They used to catch whales and drag them up the sheer cliff faces at the sea's edge, but if they caught three or four in a year that was an achievement. Today they go out with large factory ships and catch and kill hundreds in a year. Soon there will be none left. The environment was so much cleaner then. The people did not have to wash their clothes every time they returned indoors for fear of contamination, or black dust, which would get into everything including their hair.

Lika let her imagination run wild. The rainbow demonstration always caught her interest. That was something that never happened any more. The sky was permanently silver gray in haze, the sun never breaking through. When the rain came there was never a chance of a natural rainbow. Two generations ago her grandparents would have been the last people to see one of those beautiful creations. The green covered hills, which sometimes boasted a proud tree line, or a forest. Could they really have looked like that? How did they smell in the early morning? What did the fresh cool air feel like on one's face as the light of early day began to create long shadows which would shorten as day reached for its maturity, only to die again with the lengthening shadows of evening? Shadows were no longer sharp, but vague and hazy. Their meaning had been digested into the stomach of progress. The colorful world of yesteryear was disappearing very fast into the drab monotone of tomorrow.

A hand laid itself to rest on Lika's shoulder, and a soft whisper entered into her ear. It was Svi, raising her from her deep meandering thoughts of life in other times. "I've got the certificate." He said in muffled tones. "We have to go for our blood tests today if we want to get married tomorrow".

"Must we wait that long?" Lika mused with concentrated enthusiasm.

"We don't want to register for the project until we are married, or we won't be allocated to married quarters." Svi retorted.

"That's true, but we have three more days to accept the offer, and we can do that tomorrow after the wedding. We shall get married here in the Palace of Memories" Lika decided. "It is the nearest we can get to what G-d had originally intended for us!"

Later that afternoon, Lika and Svi's happiness and anticipation was to be badly shattered. They were seated together in the health center's interview room secretly holding hands below the level of the desktop and staring at each other. They did not even notice the gowned man entering the room carrying their file.

"Eh, hem" he grunted for their attention. "I have some news for you. The blood tests did not prove a result and will have to be done again, perhaps the day after tomorrow"

"What do you mean?" shouted Svi as he stood up in a fury. "We *have* to get married tomorrow!" He was becoming aggressive now, and Lika pulled him back down.

"I'm sorry, but you can't!" said the Welfare Officer. "What is the urgency? We shall have the results in a few days or so. You need some extra special tests, because your blood groups do not match. These are not simple checks and need advanced equipment, which we don't have here. We shall have to send your blood samples to another center in the North, and they are still not completely back in working order up there since the power station melt down".

"That will take ages" Svi was beginning to become angry again. "That's not good enough. We have to enroll for our project within the next three days and we want to be married first or we will be domestically segregated for a year."

"Oh, I understand" Came the reply. "Perhaps there's something that we could do" The official was trying to be kind when the situation had become clear to him. "You must travel to Lyboncher yourselves and have the tests done there. That would be quicker. If you left now, they could do the tests immediately on your arrival, and then you could possibly be back here with your certificate tomorrow evening. You could marry the next day and even register for your project with a day in hand. How's that?"

Svi and Lika stood up in unison and threw her arms around the neck of the unsuspecting official.

"Thank you, thank you, thank you" she kept saying.

They were very lucky to reach the local transportation center in time to catch the fast hemisphere going direct to Lyboncher in the north. The queue was long and the conductor was calling for everyone to hurry along. It was their turn next; Lika was in front of Svi.

"You are the last" called the conductor to Lika. "You must wait another 2 hours for the next hemisphere he said to Svi. "It may not be direct, but you will get there by midnight". Svi could not believe his bad luck, and Lika began to cry when she realized what was happening. "We've got to get there in a hurry. Everything depends on it" Lika pleaded, "We want to get married, and we must go to Lyboncher first, this evening. Please Please Please!" she was earnest in her manner.

The conductor was sympathetic "I would love to help, but someone else would have to get off, and we are already a few minutes late".

An ape-like creature appeared from behind the conductor, and tapped him on the shoulder. The Conductor turned around.

"Plees, I weel wait for the next hemisphere. Let this man have place!" The gorilla made a move to get off.

"That's alright with me!" said the conductor with some relief. "Come on, get aboard" he gestured to Svi, who mouthed a thank you to the gorilla. Svi looked very hard at the ape. He couldn't work it out. Where had he seen her before? Then he realized, but it was too late to acknowledge to the ape, as they were already airborne.

"Did you know that gorilla?" Lika was curious. "You seemed to recognize her, and I know that she knew you. Who is she?" asked Lika as they sat down and strapped themselves in.

"Zarby!" Svi mumbled "Zarby!" he confirmed.

***

Tubal Cain was looking at Erash across his desk. One of the agents of 'Science and Welfare' had reported in that some contraband Radiact had turned up in a city in the country of 'Bernia' a neighboring state in the South East. Tubal Cain wanted Erash to go there himself to make the investigation directly produce immediate results. They had to locate and find that stolen deadly material, Radiact. Tubal Cain was very serious; Erash had never seen him so sincere.

"The future safety of mankind depends on your successful mission" Tubal Cain was obviously nervous as he spoke "If this material finds its way to Bylia or Cabu, the power crazed governments there could hold the rest of the world to ransom.

Erash did not believe that such a serious mission could be entrusted to him. Tubal Cain continued to speak. "You will report to our agent in Semir, that ancient, old walled city, where the best Bernian sparkling wine is made. We believe that the external organization of Bylia is working through there to secure all their needs for fabrication of dangerous and offensive weaponry. That would almost be acceptable, but we know they are obtaining stolen 'Radiact' and also other important components needed to make their first nuclear device. This would add one more member to the 'Nuke' Club, but what is even more dangerous, these people who have no sense of responsibility, and no stable government, are quite capable of using a nuclear device just for kicks, or worse, just to prove a point politically!!" Tubal Cain was becoming immersed in his political argument and continued. "The major nuclear powers mutually respect each other's possession of these destructive weapons but would be quite defenseless against a suicidal maniac country, such as Cabu or Bylia. This organization must be stopped and smashed into oblivion" He thumped his hand hard down on the desk, and the whole room seemed to vibrate. "It took many years for the major world powers to agree on defensive intervention from orbital space, but the defenses are not complete yet. A typical example of what happens when involved in a joint effort. The Stellar Defense System was created in the peoples' minds many years ago, but was misunderstood in its motivations. Anyway it will take another ten years to complete and use it in absolute safety. There will be the capacity and capability to neutralize any nuclear weapon when primed, even in full flight on land, in the air, or under water, but at the moment against Fadfagi of Bylia it would be impotent."

Erash was very conscious of the importance of his mission, but he was only a company security agent, not a glamorous international detective that you read about in books.

"I shall leave tonight" he replied.

He did not want to admit it to himself that he was scared. He packed his belongings for the trip to Semir, feeling very worried. He had never had to work on his own like this before, and was certain he would not be coming back.

Sitting down, Erash did something that he had also never done before; he recorded his will on a holographic recording sheet then identified and sealed it, using his personal identification number and finger print. This having been validated, he posted it to Central Registration Department for Security.

He decided to travel to Semir as an ordinary tourist, a short holiday being his cover. He had already arranged for this to be noted at his office in Science and Welfare. If he was to be on his own, then he had decided to make it official. He was going on a wine tasting holiday to Bernia and where better to start it than in Semir for the wine festival?

Anybody arriving at Semir for the first time could not fail to be impressed by the size and splendor of the ancient walls of the city, built on an island hill with a natural moat surrounding it. The walls had turrets and ramparts, an old portcullis in excellent working order, and a drawbridge still in use, for pedestrians only. The city was still as it was many generations ago when built to protect the main valley entrance into the high mountains behind. The river that supplied the moat was born in that mountain range, and supplied water and irrigation from its ever-flowing currents, as it traveled down and on to the sea. In ancient times this city was a hive of civilization as a center and a market for all surrounding areas. Through the centuries it had maintained a very similar function no matter what technology was thrown at it. Wine grapes were grown in abundance in the local countryside and every landowner in the region boasted a better vineyard than his neighbor. Once or twice a year the market place would be the center for an auction in the open air, when the great wine cellars would offer large casks of the local wine from their vaults. The wine cellars dominated this city, and they honeycombed underneath the buildings, and made good use of all the old caves in the hill on which they stood. There was an abundance of secret passageways and hidden hallways that accommodated many a suspicious activity.

Erash made his way on foot through the main gate, by going across the drawbridge into the large market square beyond. There were no motorized vehicles allowed in Semir, only horse driven carriages. Carts or wagons were permitted, and in the winter season when the snow came, the wheels would be substituted for sledge runners, which added a graceful quiet to the neighborhood as they slid silently through the snow. This small geographical area had been one of the very few that had hardly been affected by the changes in climate over the years, although snow did not come every year now, and then did not stay very long when it did. The sky there and in the mountains was still a gray haze, but seemed to be so much higher than elsewhere, except when low cloud came with rain, snow or mist.

Standing in the market square Erash turned full circle, he was very impressed. The scene could have been out of any theatre set, and it completely surrounded him. Being inside the old walled town was more striking than being outside. The first thing Erash has to do, was find a place to sleep, he needed an Inn, a Tavern, or a hotel. He decided not to go too cheaply as he did hold quite a well paid position in Science and Welfare, but he wanted to play it low profile, so possibly an average choice of hotel or tavern would be most suitable. He also thought that perhaps the main square would not be the best place, as he did not particularly want to draw attention to himself.

Eventually he finally checked into a small hotel in the wall of the city itself. He was given a room on the first floor with a small window overlooking a courtyard. It was almost a taverna, but its accommodation was very much better. He had a room with a toilet, a bath and sauna shower. 'The House of Four Eyes' promised to be a useful center from which he would be able to work. He decided to go bed early and read the copy of the report that was given to him of the irregularities in Subterranean Section 26. . . . Good bedtime reading.

***

Lyboncher would not have merited a place in any illustrated tourist guide. It was a drab town, heavily lacking in personality. Geographically it was inland, of completely flat terrain and even before the incident at the nuclear power station it was very gray and always covered in fine dust. The only redeeming feature was the canal, which was wide in parts as it carefully wove its way through the center of the city from east to west and on to the sea. The people of the northern half of the town were very different from those of the south. Affluence and social position was more the character of the southern half, whereas the north was deprived of development. In earlier days it was thought that the nuclear power station in the outer northern suburbs would bring about a change in the fortunes of the local population, but now tragedy had very much left its mark. More than two thirds of the people in the northern neighborhood of the 'melt down' had migrated to other parts, but those who had stayed were facing disease and poverty. It was mostly the old who did not want to leave when they had been given the chance. The southern neighborhood were comparatively unaffected by the incident although the people were very nervous to talk about it.

It was beginning to get dark as Svi and Lika's craft came in to land at Lyboncher, but the stark difference between the well-lit and lively south, and the darker sparsely lit north was very noticeable from the air. Lika leaned over to Svi and took his hand; she tucked her head into his shoulder. She felt very sad. The damage done to countryside and urban areas beneath them affected her very personally, just as one would be upset if they saw someone's pet dog being tortured. It was a strange feeling but Lika did not realize how much she loved her country, and to see so much destruction offended her very emotionally. She gave a deep sigh; Svi tightened his grip on her hand. She had not said anything but he knew that she was sad.

"Don't worry." He said, "We are nearly there, we should land in a few moments. This is a very old hemisphere and it will be quite 'hairy' you will feel the reverse forces as we drop, and the change of speed will be quite sudden, but as we land and make ground contact the whole floor of this craft will carry on downwards as it buckles to take the impact and then return to its original shape, like a large elasticized trampoline".

"Just like it did on take off". Lika replied indignantly. She was not happy at being told the obvious, but they had had a long stressful day, and she was getting very tired and irritable.

As if to rub salt in her wounds Svi carried on. "We have a great deal to do when we land," he said. "We must rush to the Municipal Pathological Laboratory Center immediately if we are to have our blood tested overnight".

"That should be fun". Lika had substituted sarcasm for indignation in an attempt to suggest to Svi that she wanted to slow down a bit, reduce the hurry. In her heart of hearts she was as desperate to complete the job as Svi, and she knew that they were working to a deadline; they could even lose the project. They could always marry, but the project, which was the chance of a lifetime, never to be repeated.

The landing, although 'hairy' was uneventful, they were urgently making their way from the transportation center when they decided to take a fast taxi, rather than trying their luck on the monorail, which they knew by reputation, was very unreliable as to time. Svi successfully managed to hail a green rota-cab, which would land them directly on the roof of their destination. It was not the cheapest way to travel, but it was very reliable in spite of its noise. Lika commented to Svi that she was surprised that even in these days of modern technology, rota-copters were still so very noisy, but Svi could hardly hear her, as they traveled across the roof tops, their goal now clearly in sight; a large neon-lit building, which in normal daylight would probably be creamy yellow. Now in the artificial evening light of the neon, it was more a bright orange.

Rooftop reception was deserted, only one young boy sitting behind a desk reading a girlie book, busily biting his nails. He was so consumed with interest that he barely looked up as they entered through the automatic doors into his warm nighttime domain.

"Hello" called out Lika. "We have an appointment for premarital blood tests".

The young lad did not even lift his gaze when spoken to. He was quite absorbed in his fantasies. "Go down to the 3rd floor along the red corridor until you reach the crossover with the blue one, then turn right, down the blue one, and you want room 3216 for "Blood Group Reception".

Lika flunked down onto the friendly settee the moment they arrived at the reception center. She was completely exhausted. Svi went over to the desk to check in. He was not very wide-awake himself, but he had to go on, he pushed the service request buzzer, and stood there waiting. Eventually two youngish girls appeared giggling from a room behind the desk.

"What do you want?" called one of them in a most vulgar manner, and then started giggling and laughing with the other girl. Lika looked up; with one eye open and the other half open, she could sense that Svi was becoming very frustrated and angry.

"I've come a long way to get here, and I'm utterly exhausted, we both are." He suddenly remembered Lika. "We have an appointment this evening for a pre-marital blood test. Would you please oblige and inform your colleague that we are here." Svi's patience was wearing very thin; he would soon explode. "We are in a hurry!" He managed to restrain himself.

The two girls looked at each other and one of them decided to pick up the telephone. "Two more for the condemned cell". She mouthed down the hand set, and then started to giggle all over again. Within minutes, the door opened at the other end of the room and a senior looking couple, wearing clean starched white coats, walked in. The woman looked eager to help, and the man seemed to be very much someone whom you could trust.

"You must be Svi and Lika?" The woman clinician enquired. "I'm sorry about the reception but it is very difficult to get staff these days. Most people have moved away if they lived in the northern parts of the town, and the people who live in the south don't need to work."

"What did she mean by the condemned cell?" asked Lika. "Oh that is just one of their jokes; they see marriage as a means of condemning themselves and prefer their own sex. I'm sure you understand. We employ them, because although frivolous, at least in this line of work, they are safe!!"

***

A long throaty scream rang out loudly; it was the middle of the night. Erash awoke with a start, and sat up in bed. He was sure that he heard a woman's scream for help. Someone was being attacked. He was already out of the door grappling to do up his dressing-gown, running down the corridor in the direction of the scream which came again, although not so loud this time and slightly muffled. The third room down the corridor, that's the one, thought Erash as he reached for and opened the unlocked door. There, in the dimness of the bedside light he could see a male figure standing at the side of the bed holding a cushion over the head of a half naked female who was struggling to get free. She seemed to be fighting for her life. Her nightwear was all torn and naked flesh was exposed. She was punching and kicking wildly into the air with no effect. She was lunging out and must have scratched her assailant's face as Erash was entering the room. The man stepped back with shock straight into Erash's arms, and an arm-lock on the rogue enabled him to stop the man in his tracks. Erash grabbed a water jug that was just within his reach from the washstand and broke it over the man's head. He fell to the floor, out like a light, of no use to anyone. The woman was now sitting up in bed, her head in her hands, elbows on the offending cushion and crying. Erash went over to her; she looked up at him, stopped crying and leaned against Erash's chest, and started again.

"He would have killed me!" She sobbed. "He was trying very hard. Oh thank you for coming so quickly. You must have saved my life!" She was still crying, but not so much now. Erash could not take his eyes off her. Her breasts were hanging loose through a torn nightgown and yet he felt so natural holding her head against his body. He ran his fingers gently through her long curly hair. She had the most beautiful deep blue eyes.

"Don't worry, you will be all right" Erash consoled her. She turned her face upwards. She pursed her lips as if to ask Erash to kiss her on the mouth. He was feeling aroused. He was unbelieving, but he leaned forward and their mouths met in an ecstatic first kiss. He put his arm tighter around her shoulders and she pulled at his dressing gown collar as if to ask him to come closer. He was becoming very interested. It did not seem right but he felt something for this young woman and did not want to take advantage. She must be in a state of shock, and he was sure that he must have been sticking out of his trousers. How could he look? He did not even need a downward glance; he felt her searching hand as it gently fondled his protrusion. They kissed even more firmly, and Erash got on to the bed. Their love became very physical and would have gone on through the night, had there not been a groan from the floor, which brought them back to stark reality.

They decided to tie him and bind his arms so that he could not move freely. Then they would call the police for help.

The night patrol must have been close by, as they came very quickly to collect the stranger whom they handcuffed and threw vigorously into their wagon. When they had gone, Erash bade the young woman goodnight in a more polite manner, they kissed gently and Erash said he would see her in the morning. She saw him to the door and her eyes followed him down the corridor as he made his way back to his room. Suddenly he turned round and ran back.

"Pardon me," Erash said "but I don't know your name!"

"That's true" she replied with surprise. "Neither do I know yours!"

"My name is Erash"

"My name is Rula"

They again kissed goodnight, and Erash returned on his own to his room. It was just beginning to get light outside, and he knew he was in love.

Erash must have awoken with a smile on his face, he was so happy he could not believe that it was such a short time before that his sleep was disturbed. Was it a dream, or did it really happen? She was so beautiful and soft. He could not stop thinking about her. Had he really saved her life? Why did that man want to kill her, and was she alright now, all on her own?

For Erash getting dressed that morning was a necessary chore. He was in a real hurry; he nearly didn't apply his facial hair removing cream. He had not forgotten that since the adolescent days of his youth. He felt like that again, he could not wait to see her. Was she alright, or was it a dream? It was too real to be fiction. At last, checking himself in the mirror, he looked neat and presentable. He could go visiting.

The door to Rula's room was unlocked. He gently pushed it open. Daylight was coming in from the window; the room was neat and tidy. The bed not slept in, the curtains wide open, and the windows slightly ajar. (It was never prudent to open the windows too much as it allowed in the dust.) Erash could not believe it. The bed was made, the room was empty. No soap in the shower dish. No toothbrush in the clip. No shoes by the bed,—nothing. He went over to the chest of drawers. He felt very mean, but he opened one. He knew it was empty by the way it pulled out. Where had she gone? Had he been dreaming? Was it the right room? He went to the door again, and looked back down the corridor. Yes, he counted the doors and it was the right room! He sat on the bed and looked at the washstand. The jug was not broken. He must have been dreaming. As he sat there feeling very depressed he realized that he had not done up his right cuff link. He reached to do it up, and it fell to the floor rolling under the bed. Erash got down on his knees to pick it up, but could not find it. He ran his flat hand uneasily under the bed, and as he retrieved the cuff link, a sharp stab cut into his finger. He pulled out his hand. He had cut himself on something. It was only slight but what was it? He got down low and looked. There it was, a small piece of the broken water jug. He looked at his finger again and smiled to himself, he was right. He picked up the few tiny pieces of jug that were left and put them in his pocket wrapped in tissue paper. At least he knew it was not a dream, but where was she? Had she been kidnapped, is she safe? He should have stayed with her all night he told himself. Why had he been such a gentleman?

He had a very long day in front of him and a lot to do. He had not forgotten about the job he had been sent to do, but he was worried about Rula. He decided to pursue her later, but not having eaten since traveling down the day before he wandered into the Hotel's own restaurant for breakfast. As he walked in the door he was sure he could smell a familiar scent. It was Rula's! He would never forget that perfume from the middle of the night. Why had he become so worked up about nothing? He looked around the restaurant. She was nowhere to be seen. Then out of a door marked 'private' the back of a woman appeared. She was carrying a large ledger with both hands, so she had to push open the door with her behind. It was Rula. Erash would know that hair anywhere. He went up to her, and took her by the elbow and turning her round just to make sure he asked...

"Can I help you carry that, it must be heavy?"

The woman turned round and Erash smiled at her warmly, he was right. Those beautiful eyes looked so much more vivid in daylight. She was very attractive. She smiled a thank you to him and handed him the book.

"Where do you want me to put it?" he asked "It's very heavy".

She gestured to the desk near the entrance door. They walked that way together. When Erash put it down, Rula thanked him for being so kind, and she smiled. Erash was so happy to see her; he put a hand on each of her shoulders, and pulled her towards him as if to kiss her. The kiss enjoined, he felt some hostility, and stepping slightly back he felt a powerful pain across the side of his face as he saw the bitter anger and genuine surprise of Rula's face. She had slapped him very hard!

"How dare you!" she was red in the face now, with rage. "I won't tolerate such attentions from guests in my hotel. If you wish to continue your stay in this establishment, keep your hands to yourself!"

She disappeared through the door marked 'private', and Erash sat down to breakfast. He was astonished. He could not believe the change in the woman. She was genuine in her surprise. No one could act like that. He looked around the restaurant and made a mental note of all those present, just in case Rula knew she was being watched.

***

CHAPTER 4

At that same moment in the City of Lyboncher a young couple were awaiting with great trepidation for the results of their pre-marital blood tests. Svi and Lika had not slept at all. They knew that it was very unusual to need a second blood test, and they had traveled a long way to have it done in such a hurry. The tension and stress were beginning to show between them and they were hardly on the best of terms. Lika thought that Svi could have been a little more attentive, she was obviously worried about the results and also the deadline that they had set themselves to get back to register for the project. Everything had happened at once. If they failed in the tests, she knew that they would be banned from getting married, and would never be able to co-habit under any legal circumstances.

Failure of the medical tests was almost unheard of, and she knew that she would take it personally, but in truth if they failed, it would just be bad luck. These blood tests were just a precaution, to make sure that they were not related by blood. Not everybody knew who his or her true parents were any more these days. Also these facts would detect if there were any chance of genetic malfunction in their possible procreation, that they would have deformed offspring. Finally, whether there was any disease that could be transmitted between them. It was fair that the other partner should know. With the exception of transmittable disease, the law stood, and was accepted globally, that if any of these conditions existed, and one of the partners accepted sterilization the marriage could take place.

Lika knew that she would be to blame if the tests proved damaging. She did not know her parentage. She knew that she was a pure Caucasian, but she could only boast that she was pure of race, not of mind. She wished so much that she could know who her parents had been. What if she was a close relative of Svi! Her father she knew was a semen donor to the local ovary bank in her old village, but her mother was surrogate to an embryo implant so she would never know her Mum and Dad, just as they would never even know of her existence. Lika was becoming very morbid and depressed. She felt that she would soon explode. "Why could not Svi understand?" she thought. She realized that she must be about to start her period. Everything was going wrong. They hoped to get married tomorrow, and it was too late to change her menstrual cycle now, it must be imminent.

Svi gripped Lika's hand tightly, the door slid open, and a woman clinician came in carrying a white and brown folder with their names on it. She had a sullen look on her face. Lika's heart was thumping. She could feel the pulse in her neck; she turned to look at Svi, who had a glazed expression on his face as he turned to look at her. She knew the result before it was announced. She was sure that it would start with 'I regret to inform you...'

"I regret that I have to inform both of you that the tests have proved conclusively that there is an impediment to your forthcoming marriage on the grounds of incompatible blood grouping". The woman turned away. Lika believed that she saw her starting to cry as she ran out of the room after handing the notes to a male colleague. Lika became hysterical. She could not control herself. Svi slapped her face. This had an immediate result; he pulled her hard against his chest and said down through her skull. "Do not worry darling Lika, my beloved, I love you and I always will. We shall never be parted. We will marry. We will have a sterilized marriage, and adopt children, or perhaps you could be a surrogate, or have a donated sperm. There are lots of ways round it. I will be sterilized". Svi said firmly "this afternoon, so that we can still get our license for a marriage tomorrow ".

Lika screamed. "No, it must be me. You must not destroy yourself like that for me. No. No. No."

Svi felt terrible, it was his entire fault for taking such a risk in rushing things. He knew that he was not thinking logically, but he must make what appeared to Lika to be firm decisions or she would cave in completely.

They decided to depart immediately for home, and would discuss their mutual problem on the journey back. Lika was white with rage. She kept blaming herself for the problem, when in fact it was just a bad stroke of luck.

Aboard the hemisphere high above the ground, life seemed to assume a different meaning. Lika became more rational and a great deal calmer.

"Never mind" she said, "I'll be sterilized and you could be a donor to another ovary. Maybe, I could be surrogate to your baby." Lika said wistfully.

"I don't think that would be possible," Svi answered, "because our blood groups are incompatible. We'll have to find out!"

Back at the Institute of Common Welfare in their hometown they decided to take advice that afternoon, and act upon it there and then.

Medical opinion stated that the quickest way to confirm sterility would be a radio-vasectomy on the male. That was painless and quick. It was guaranteed to work and a license to marry would follow immediately on the spot.

Lika begged for a stay of execution, she loved Svi so very much, and wanted to have his children, even if they were not hers. "Please!" she begged. "Please! Let's wait a year until the project is finished. We'll live separately on the project". She was begging now. Svi stayed firm, with great difficulty.

They were taken into a large square room with a flat metal bed in the middle. There was a track in the floor, which was marked out in angles, and the wall also had a track going up the sides of the room. There was a silver gray machine with a gun and video camera attached to it, which pointed at the bed. The bed could be watched through a small window from a tiny anteroom next door. This second room contained a control desk, which would operate the machine by remote control, moving it around the bed to the position required. The bed could also be moved to any angle from the same control-room.

Svi was taken into the main room and strapped to the bed so that he could not move inadvertently. The doors were closed and Lika and the staff went into the control room. All the lights were put out, and Lika could watch in the half-light through the window. She began to feel faint, as she heard the engine start inside the machine, as it built up to power.

Svi felt like a condemned man about to be gassed, executed or magnetized. He was helpless, lying there waiting. He could hear the high-pitched whine as the machine hovered over him. This machine was used for many kinds of treatment not just vasectomy. He was waiting. The light went out, and at any moment, no longer would he ever be able to father a child. The lights went back on as he heard Lika scream and scream and scream. He could not move because he was strapped down. What was going wrong, why was Lika screaming? What's wrong? The next thing he could see was Lika's face as it came down hard on his with a kiss like never before.

"Everything is going to be alright." she said. "They have arrested the bitches. We can get married".

Svi was still strapped down.

"Please tell me what you are talking about" He demanded. "Why have we stopped? Have I been done and why did you scream? What's happened?"

"No, you are safe; you can still father my children. We are clean. Our blood tests are normal. Those lesbian bitches that you had an argument with in Lyboncher, switched our test results so that we would fail, but they had a petty argument with each other and one snitched on the other to get her into trouble. The bitches!"

"The doctor there thought that they were safe. That they certainly weren't!" Svi could not believe it. All they had been through together. He had nearly lost his virility, and possible children, at the whim of a pair of lesbians. "If I ever saw them again," Svi said "I would kill them, for what they have put you through." He sat up on the bed and gave Lika a magnificent kiss that seemed to the watching staff to go on forever.

***

It had not rained in Semir for months, and the sudden downpour seemed to be going on all morning. Erash was delighted; he was not used to the hot and sticky atmosphere that had prevailed the day before. He had decided not to pursue his problem with Rula immediately. Things like that were best left for a more appropriate time and place, there were more important fish to fry. The need to get involved into the local subterfuge and secret trading was his most pressing requirement. He had to trace the path of the trade in "Radiact" and locate its' final destination. So much depended on him. Thinking to himself that he couldn't go up to the reception desk at the hotel to ask where the center for illicit dealing in arms was located, he decided to stay put and let them come to him.

He waited for some while in the entrance lobby of the hotel looking and watching out of the front doors into the roadway and beyond. The rain was pouring down and the little rivers in the street were washing away the dust and any memories of hoof prints in the muddy and cobbled roadways, which still existed as they were a few centuries before, now uneven and in many places cobbles were missing, only to be replaced with mud and dirt that had collected over the years.

There were many people now gathered in the entrance lobby, like Erash, waiting for the rain to stop. This was his big chance to make an impression. He would do his busking now, while they could all hear clearly without trying. He walked casually over to the telephone booth, which was hardly very private. He had been listening for the last ten minutes to a man telling his son how to set their burglar alarm at home. Everyone in the hotel lobby now knew his secret combination code, and what to do if it goes off by accident. That gave Erash the idea. It was brilliant, he thought.

Erash placed his card into the slot and dialed a number. It rang three times at the other end then it was answered.

"This is Erash, Chief Security at Science and Welfare. You have come through on my private line, and I am not available at the moment" it said. "Your call is obviously important so please when you hear the tone, speak and leave your message. I will get back to you as soon as possible. Peep...peep...peep."

Erash then started to speak into the phone very loudly for all to hear.

"This is Erash from H.Q. Please put me on to my contact known as 'Pollo'...Pollo? Good. The long journey was worth all the work...Good...my case is full of equipment. All available at the right price. I have some very good wines, and one of them is very volatile...You are interested?...Very expensive...No...yes. If not, others might be...my superiors are not aware of any...you will meet me? Good. I will be at the "Flagon and Bottle" in the market place of Semir, at the point of Noon. How will I know you? A red button on the lapel of your jacket, and a red briefcase in your left hand. I will carry a red umbrella, and a newspaper. If you can't make today, then I will be there again at the same time, tomorrow and again on the two days following. Same conditions."

He put the phone-set back in its place, and then lifted it again dialed another number, so as to cancel previous memory e-dial. He obtained an engaged signal as he had dialed the same number as the call set he was using at that moment. He again replaced the handset removed his card and left the booth hoping that the job had been well done. He did not stay in the entrance lobby long enough to see the next person who used the phone booth, trying over and over again to obtain a ringing tone from a seemingly permanently 'busy' line using the memory recall button with the third finger, as the index finger was missing!

The Flagon and Bottle was a small wine-tasting bar that he had noticed on his arrival at Semir. It was well appointed on the market square and all people would know it, who enter the town. It was a lovely place to sit. There were tables and chairs on the pavement outside. A friendly and very busy atmosphere. Also there were only three approach routes to reach the Wine-bar, and if the opposition were interested in him, they would be able to stop any contact getting to him before they did, had there been one. Erash was well satisfied as he sat there on the street with a cup of wine and cold ice. He was a little early, but he had his red umbrella and newspaper.

After a few moments of sitting down, Erash had a strange visitor, who asked if the other chair at his table was free. Erash recognized him as one of the people at breakfast, when he had been in the argument with Rula. Erash sent him away; he was not wearing a red button, and certainly no brief case. Was that a con-incidence or not, thought Erash, as the man moved over to another table that had just become vacant. He was a strange looking man, wearing a pale-gray hemi-spherical hat with a brim, which came down to his ears, pushing them outwards like wings. He also wore a pale gray suit of the same material. Very drably dressed, he would certainly get lost in a crowd. It was his walking stick that caught Erash's eye. It was obviously a length of natural knotted wood, cut from a living tree. It was well polished and a brass handle and tip had been attached. It looked far too good to be just a walking stick.

Erash took out his snuffbox, the man had now sat down behind him, and unless Erash turned right round, he could not see this stranger at all. In his snuffbox, Erash carried a small wide-angle mirror under the lid; he could use it as a rear view mirror, which was what he was doing. He noticed that the man had walked with a slight limp on his right leg and he had a very slight stoop, but the stoop was very much more noticeable when he was sitting down.

Erash must have been sitting in that seat for over an hour, he was thinking of giving up his vigil for the day. People had come, and people had gone. There were still three people that had been there since he had arrived, and one of them was the hunchback in the gray hat, then there was a very attractive young woman who was deeply immersed in her stereo headphones, and writing a great deal, and finally a peasant type, long haired youth who looked like he needed a square meal and a wash. He was probably on drugs as he had very constricted pupils, and he seemed to be in a daze. Any one of these people could have been interested in him but Erash was sure that they were not whom he was waiting for.

Erash decided to leave. There was no point in sitting there all day, and if the connection was to be made they certainly weren't coming today. He thought that it would be an opportune moment to go looking at the wine vaults, in order to miss some of the mid-afternoon heat. At this latitude with the heavy silver gray skies, the humidity built up in the afternoon even after heavy rain. It was always best to try and avoid being outside at that time. He got up from his seat feeling quite damp around his rear quarters. The humidity was already uncomfortable. He paid his bill and then walked across the square, and up one of the narrow cobbled streets that climbed above the city center. The narrow street was bending and weaving between the very old buildings. Although on opposite sides of the road, the people upstairs could almost hold hands with each other across the street. The roadway under these circumstances was well shaded and the cool stone work of the building somewhat reduced the humidity. A pair of mules was pulling a cart up the steep incline, and Erash had to step aside as a peasant with a very long whip was driving the passing vehicle. The whip was tightly in his hand and the sight of which was enough to persuade the donkeys to move. Erash had his back hard against the wall of one of the buildings as the cart came by. If it had been any wider it could have ruined his sex-life. The man smiled as he passed and Erash smiled acknowledgement. They had obviously both agreed that it had been a tight squeeze and yet not a word passed from either of their lips.

It was getting quite busy, another cart was coming up the hill and Erash was getting tired, he was not used to the heat. It was the same distance yet again to the top of the hill and one set of wine vaults. He decided to rest, and sitting on a low window ledge, he watched the cart struggling up the hill, being pulled like the other by two gray donkeys with the whipping boy or in this case, man, behind. Looking into the cart as it went by Erash was surprised to find it empty. Not for long. He never knew what hit him, but unknown to Erash he was now the load that was to be carried to the top of the hill.

It was colder and felt slightly damp in the wine-vaults, and as Erash regained consciousness the pain from the blow on the back of his head began to reverberate through his cranium. He thought he was surely going to die. Was that someone speaking to him and where was the beautiful smell coming from? He recognized it, but he couldn't place it.

***

The green piece of paper that granted license to marry was burning a hole in Svi's pocket. The earliest possible moment for their wedding ceremony was to be the following morning at the "Palace of Memories". The venue was the choice of Lika. The time was the choice of circumstances. The two happy people had been for preliminary enrolment at the project registration department and had applied for married quarters on the basis of their license and forthcoming marriage.

The wedding morning was slightly cooler than it had been for some while, as if the day was meant to be perfect in every way for the two of them. Svi was amazed that so many people had turned up, and at such short notice. When he saw so many of his old friends together he had a momentary twinge of sadness, when his mind wandered back to those whom he had lost in the 'Crisis' massacre. That incident in his life and that of Lika's would leave an everlasting scar in their memory.

Svi was standing in the middle of the aisle usually used for weddings in the "Palace". The 'Palace of Memories' in its original state was built as an Abbey, and the original central aisle and old alter was preserved and used for solemn functions such as weddings whenever a member of the public requested. Svi was facing the old alter, that used to be used for animal sacrifice to god when it was legal. The society for prevention of cruelty to animals soon stopped that about a century before. The recent conversion of the old Abbey into a museum was done in a very careful and tasteful manner, maintaining a considerable degree of the old original meaning. Occasionally marriages were held there, as the ambience was particularly conducive to decorum of prayer and respect of the marriage vows. It always gave the full feeling of cleanliness and sanctification with god, for those who truly believed. In these days religion and the belief of a supreme being was generally neglected. Most people would say that they believed if asked, but in truth, they only thought about it if asked. Births, marriages and deaths were still always accompanied by a suitable token of worship of the almighty creator, but in most circumstances in these "enlightened" days, the last thing people thought about was religion. People would pray only when they wanted something, and seldom when they wanted to give thanks. It was under these strictures of religious belief that the preacher was willingly going to conduct the wedding of Svi and Lika that morning. He knew that they loved each other very much. He knew that their belief in the creator was only roused at this type of occasion in their lives, but he was still prepared to marry them spiritually.

Svi stood there looking up the aisle at the altar, on which a large single candle burned. He had his back to the entrance door and his eyes were fixed on the burning flame of the candle. The old organ was being played and the music was filling the hall. Svi watched the candle intently as it seemed to dance in time with the music. All of a sudden, the musical rhythm changed. Svi could feel Lika's presence as she entered the hall behind him. He knew she would have a little tear in her eyes as he was very conscious of her, and could feel her gaze directed at the back of his neck as he still stared at the flickering candle.

Lika was dressed in "grass-green" the color used to represent natural life and purity. In these polluted days green meant "life". A green wedding meant a hope of luck in health, and purity of life being long.

Svi put out his right hand as Lika came to stand beside him. She was very nervous and seemed overcome by the event, which was very out of character for Lika. She took his hand with her left, and they remained enjoined as they then walked together to stand in front of the altar under the canopy prepared for them.

Lika turned her face to look at Svi. He smiled re-assuringly. Lika felt warm inside. She was so very happy. No one else had ever experienced this feeling. She felt so rich; she was praying selfishly that it would last forever.

After the words of prayer, the questions of honor to each of them and the promises of commitment to each other, the couple exchanged tokens of their love and devotion. Svi placed a narrow metallic ring onto the forefinger of Lika's left hand; in return, Lika did the same for Svi.

A glass cup of red wine was held, that both of them might drink from the same glass, as a gesture of friendship and the joining together in marriage. They each drank three times from the cup, alternately, and then they handed the cup back to their preacher who placed it on the floor. Svi stamped on it hard, breaking it into pieces. This meant that no one else could ever drink from their marriage cup, and the actual impact of the glass underfoot was the time recognized as their moment of marriage. Everyone together, even the visiting public shouted together in unison, "Hallelujah! Hallelujah! Hallelujah!"

Unknown to the newly married couple there was another wedding party waiting outside. There were to be two weddings in the "Palace of Memories" that day and in the very near future events were going to bring all their lives very closely together.

As Svi and Lika departed for their wedding breakfast another groom took his position in the aisle. Noah was feeling well pleased with himself, he had managed to take up his position completely unaided, although he knew that there would always be help close to hand if he became unsteady. He knew that Naamah would not keep him waiting long as he watched that candle on the altar, mesmerized.

For Svi and Lika their wedding party had seemed to go on all day and all night, but they had to be up early the next morning, as they had important business to do.

"You certainly left your project registration to the last minute!" The official smiled to Svi and Lika, as they reached the front of the queue for applicants.

***

The pain in his head seemed to be subsiding very slightly, thought Erash, as during his first moments of consciousness, a cold damp cloth was placed on his forehead. Yes he was sure that someone was trying to talk to him. The conscious world was suddenly very strange. He had opened his eyes and tried to look about him. There was a lot of marble, and many large 'old' wooden casks stacked in various places in this very dimly lit semi-basement type establishment. Of course, he realized where he was...a wine vault, and he was on a marble slab. There were three or four people with him, but they were above his head and behind him, so without arching his back, there was no improved method of being able to see them, although he could certainly hear them. He knew that smell, it was very important to him, he would try and look around again, but the water from the damp cloth was getting into his eyes, it was difficult to see. A soft familiar voice was speaking to him, but he could not see the face. It was a woman. That smell, yes, he recognized it. The perfume that Rula uses. Why did he not think of that before? He was bewildered.

"Erash! We wish to ask you some questions" the soft voice was speaking "For what purpose have you come to Semir?" Erash had made contact, he was delighted, but how it hurt.

Was all that necessary, he thought to himself.

"I'm a tourist, who wants to buy wine," he answered, "That's not illegal, is it?"

"No, but you have also come to sell. You were overheard offering to sell wine. We wine growers, don't like interlopers with inferior goods."

"My goods are not inferior, they are the genuine article." Erash was getting impatient, but he had to be careful. "I have come to meet 'Pollo' my business is with him, and no-one else." Erash hoped that he had not shot his bolt. He was also beginning to feel very uncomfortable lying on the hard marble. The back of his head was on something soft, but it still throbbed with a dull pain. He must have taken quite a nasty blow with something hard.

"Pollo? What do you know of Pollo? What are you willing to sell him?" This time it was another deeper, and more mature male voice, which was showing concerned interest in his tones. "You will tell us, or we will make you tell us" he went on...

"Is Pollo not a friend of yours?" Erash asked, in a surprised manner. The reports from subterranean section 26, showed orders for requisition of packing cases to Bylia signed by Pollo. Surely he must be one of them. They must have dealings with him. Erash could not understand. Something seemed wrong, and facts were not matching up to circumstances.

"He deals in treachery!" The man interrupted again "Pollo is an agent of the Bylean leader Fadfagi, and not to be trusted. What dealings do you have with him?" came back the question.

Erash was beginning to realize that this sort of conversation would go on forever, and neither side would give much away.

"If you don't have dealings with him" Erash continued, "What do you want with me?"

"We want to know what you are selling to him." The woman was now speaking again.

Erash tried to sit up but he could not. He was partly strapped down to the slab. He thought it strange that he had not noticed that before. He desperately wanted to see if that was Rula speaking. This was like a nightmare; there was nothing that seemed to make sense. He decided to keep quiet until he found out more about his inquisitors. He again tried to lift his head, and again the water from the damp cloth poured into his eyes. He couldn't see, the water made sure of that. How very clever, he thought, his head was tied gently down with a soft pouch underneath and whenever he moved up to try to lift his head, more water ran into his eyes. This method stopped him seeing his surroundings except by keeping reasonably still, and would have rendered him very susceptible to questioning had his motives not been so strong.

"Please will you tell us?" The question came again in a pleading of apparent desperation from the woman who sounded more and more like Rula, and even through all that water, he was sure he could smell her perfume. She carried on with her plea. "It is vital that you tell us. Please! We must know!"

"Don't demean yourself, young woman!" The man interjected "We will manage on our own" he muttered quietly "Like we always do. Tie him up properly and put him in green section for the night. He'll possibly be ready to talk in the morning."

***

Svi and Lika could not believe the size of the place. Ground control for the extra-terrestrial orbiting network known as 'G.C. Eton' was massive. It was almost a small country in its own right. The whole complex nearly completely covered a large island just off the coast not far from Lublia. The entire island was devoted to maintenance and support for the major business of space research, and unknown to many it was one of the many subsidiaries of Science and Welfare. Tubal Cain's business interests were indeed global. This island was security itself, the happy couple had gone there directly on the day following their wedding, which was now a happy memory left behind them. Entering the complex was not easy for them; their marriage documents were not yet completed, and were following them on from behind.

They arrived on the island on a hovercraft and then traveled down the main avenue to central research institute number one. It was a very tall building typical of the design that had gone into all the buildings on 'G.C. Eton' as the island as a whole had become called. There were two hundred and thirty floors, and the building was built around a central tubular core that went deep into the ground. The hollow core, which contained eighteen elevators, acted as a central support pivot around which the rest of the building was 'woven' with supportive high-tension cables. This gave the building tensile strength in all weathers, and in case of groundquake, which was still quite possible in that region. Subterranean network had a service monorail to this island, which linked up with the central elevator systems of most buildings on G.C. Eton. In a case of severe groundquake, if the tunnel system were to 'snap' then each section would automatically seal itself off, so pressuring the main system underground. Svi and Lika had not been near the island before, although they had seen pictures and movies, or holographic studies, but never had the vastness of its size made its strong impression on them, as the actual impact of reality. It was like twenty or thirty of the largest old-fashioned airports that catered for horizontal take-off craft that used only wings for their levitation. It was like twenty of those airports, spread out altogether as one. One needed a geography lesson just to find one's way around. Modern flying vehicles were all vertical take-off, although, once losing contact with the ground they could move off at great speed in any direction. The size of ground base was not due to the type of take-off required, but to the much needed scientific support on the ground, as most orbital work was controlled and supplied by G.C. Eton.

Lika's mouth dropped wide open with astonishment as they entered the main reception area of the Institute building where they had to register for their accommodation. The entrance hall must have been capable of housing about thirty five thousand people still with room to move. The internal roof of the hall, which was at least eight floors high, had a gallery, which allowed visitors to walk around with an excellent view of the business going on below. Each of the eight floors of the building, which abutted the reception hall, had its own gallery balcony running the full perimeter of the hall. The main entrance and the full width of the building was solid transparent glass-like material that she had never seen before. It was very cool to touch, and yet outside where it was very warm, the same material was warm. Novel, she thought. She tightened her grip on Svi's hand as she felt the excitement of the dawn of a new era in her life. It was something that she could share with the one that she loved. Together they were doing something new, a joint venture, she felt so happy.

"I love you" Lika said, as she looked up to Svi, she was overflowing with excited happiness "I love you" she repeated for no apparent reason. She just wanted to hear her voice say it, at a time when she was so exhilarated by events, and environment.

Svi turned to Lika, gripping her hand even tighter; he pecked her on the cheek with a gentle kiss. "I love you too," he whispered, as they walked slowly over to the long reception desk across the hall, just drinking in the busy atmosphere of an important venture that was laying itself out before them. They were both beginning to understand the gigantic scale of the task that lay in front of them. Svi was chomping at the bit, anxious to get started.

All the reception officials were dressed in pale blue; the men looked so smart and efficient in their peaked caps with dark blue braiding. The woman behind the long counter also wore a cap but its peak was smaller and the hat had more shape. It was silly little touches like that, which made Lika feel that there was strong meaning in what they were about to do. If the feminine touch was so important even at this stage, then perhaps her involvement in the project will be just as important as Svi's.

"You will be staying overnight in this hotel" said the reception official talking to Svi. "Then tomorrow, a courier will come, who will show you around ground base before your departure for central orbital command where you will be stationed. Married quarters are allocated for you. Here are your keys. "The official handed Svi his keys for the night, and another set to take with them to their billet in Orbital command "and here is an envelope for you. Your sealed orders, I believe." The man in blue smiled, and shook Svi's hand. "Good luck. It can be good fun."

Svi felt good. All that work during the previous years had not been in vain. This would appear to be a climax in his career, and so early on. He couldn't believe his luck. He turned to Lika and smiled. She understood he did not have to say a single word. Lika smiled an even broader smile back to Svi. They threw themselves together and for the second time in recent weeks, they embraced each other carelessly in public.

"I love you" Lika said again. "I feel butterflies inside me every time I'm with you."

Svi covered her mouth with his as she was talking and gave her the longest public kiss she had ever known. Passers-by were politely amused at the public, but harmless demonstration of passion; only a honeymoon couple could perform with such dignity.

Their accommodation for the night was executive style. Never had they been able to share a double bed together before, and in such luxury. Their room was high up in the towering building. They had to take the elevator to get there. The view was truly magnificent. They could stand on the balcony and if they looked across the buildings they could see the sea some distance away. Along the coast-line could be seen the Museum of Original Space Flight where the old empty gantries still stood, that used to support the early departures of the simple rocket propelled re-usables. One of the re-usables still stood in gantry as a memorial to all those pioneers that lived and died trying to improve the lot of humankind. How progress had changed all that, Lika was thinking. No longer did you have to be specially trained to go into orbit. No longer did the human body have to suffer the contortions and pressures of anti-gravitational take-off. Today they could sit in a restaurant on the craft and drink a light beverage while taking off into the vacuum of space. Opposing rotation of spinning bodies had created the most incredible ability to move in an upward direction without much force and no noticeable rotation. Lika could see a 'globe' just taking off at that moment. She pointed out to Svi.

"How serene it looks as it spins and moves so fast out and upward. It looks almost weightless!" Lika remarked.

"That orange ball has rooms and people inside it, but they are not spinning or they would all be quite ill, with the centrifugal force of gravity acting against them. No! Inside the exterior body that you see rotating at high speed there is another main body that rotates at exactly the same speed as its exterior shell, but in the opposite direction. This means that in relation to the ground from which it departed, the inside is not rotating at all. Those radial stripes around the circumference are transparent, and act as a permanent window for the internal contents. The engines are powered by solar magnetism, one of the most important forces ever discovered by mankind." Most gyrospheres and hemispheres are powered in the same manner. Tomorrow we will ride in one to the stars. An experience I am told that will never be forgotten". Svi took Lika by the shoulder and turned her round, closing the balcony door behind them. Brushing off the black dust he suggested to Lika, as the night was young perhaps a last walk through an urban metropolis on solid ground would be a pleasant way to spend the evening.

"Why are there so many toy manufacturers represented here?"
Lika asked Svi.

"Many inventions can often be tried out on childish toys before being put to use in a big way full size." Lika wished she had never asked, as now she had given license to Svi to talk unending.

Svi continued. "Look here for instance," as they passed one of exhibits in the hotel entrance hall. "This children's construction kit. Invented a few years ago with pre-programmed magnetic joints, like the padlocks with multi-magnetic keys. Each time a length of the material is made, the ends have small moveable joints, which locked together in three dimensions. The other strip that it is meant to join onto is also programmed magnetically to click locked together when the two pieces meet at the correct angle. These joints are highly secret, and if taken apart, they become useless, so no-one could copy them without knowing how."

"What's that got to do with space research?" asked Lika.

Svi continued…"They send many flat packs of this kind of structure out into space all the time. They are hundreds of times the size of the children's toy, and made of very strong and tensile materials. When in the non-gravitational 'weightless' state, each pre-programmed magnetic joint will find its mate. Each joint is programmed only to have one possible mate. Eventually, without any external physical help the entire flat pack constructs itself into one very large unit of solid volume. In this way very large constructions are being made in orbit at a very cheap and speedy rate. Cities are being built as we talk. That's what we are going to research. How the human mind, and way of life is affected by the orbital environment."

Lika was tired, she had found the day so full of excitement, and she pulled gently at Svi's arm.

"Tomorrow will be another day" she said, "Let's not talk shop now. I'm hungry!"

***

Green Section was very dry and extremely dusty. Erash had been tied up very securely with leather straps usually used as a martingale with the bridle for the donkey. He had one hand tied to his ankle and his feet were also strapped together with the bindings passing through a metal loop that was cemented in the wall. The loop may have been used in earlier days, for a fixing when the workmen were stacking the wine casks, now it was substituting as a jailer for the night. They had left Erash with one hand free in order that he could eat and drink or scratch his nose. Nevertheless he was very uncomfortable, he managed to shuffle along the dusty floor on his bottom, and he just managed to reach the corner of the room with his feet still secured to the wall. His left arm was secured between his ankles and he could save his back from breaking by just squeezing up against the return wall of the corner. He could still just reach the food and drink that had so thoughtfully been left for him. He took some of the bread and put it in his mouth. It was fresh, and quite tasty; he had not eaten since, he didn't know when. They had even left him cold water, which he also found very welcome, but he was so uncomfortable, and knew that if he was to last out the night he had to get free. His left leg was beginning to suffer from 'pins and needles' and lack of circulation. It was so cramped and he was suffering already. He had to get free, but how? The straps were padlocked and like manacles, the leather was very thick. There was no way he could undo the buckles, he would have to….. he remembered. He put his hand in his pocket to see if was still there. It was wrapped in tissue paper from Rula's bedroom, the broken water jug. It was sharp enough to cut his fingers on, with persistence he should be able to cut through the leather. He was already fired with enthusiasm as he set to it. He took the largest piece with the sharp edge and started to cut away at the leather bindings.

All Erash could see was the back of her as the next morning the door opened, and in she walked, carrying his breakfast tray. Hiding behind the door was a game he used to play as a child, but on this occasion it seemed his only chance as he grabbed her from behind and pulled her to his chest. She was still holding the tray, and still smelled just as she had that other morning in the restaurant-bar of the "House of Four Eyes".

"Why do you ignore me, why don't you acknowledge me?" Erash whispered in her ear.

"What are you talking about?" she answered in a cold fury, desperately trying to get free from his grasp. Erash could not understand. Why was she resisting so much after all that they had been through together. This change in attitude was so unnatural, there was no one else about to see them but still she was estranged from him. She carried on talking, still with her back to him.

"May I put this tray down? The water is very hot and might scald you if I move suddenly. You would not like that, would you?" Erash released Rula, and she turned around putting the tray on the little table in the middle of the room. "How did you get free?" She asked in a matter of fact way, as if she was expecting it of him. Erash showed Rula the broken jug piece, which was easily recognized. Rula went white. "How did you get that?" She exclaimed with a shocked reaction. Erash was now completely mixed up. Nothing was making sense.

"Don't you recognize me…?" Erash was caught by his own trick. He had his back to the open door, and someone else had managed to surprise him from behind with a cloth, which was jammed into his mouth.

"He was about to talk", called Rula, "Let him speak."

Erash was allowed to turn round, and the gag was released to fall free to the ground. He could see the owner of the aging male voice for the first time. It was the old man with the hemi-spherical hat and the walking stick. He was now certain that it must have been the brass handle that struck him across the back of the head the previous day, dropping him into the cart as it was climbing the hill. This man had been following him since the incident with Rula in the restaurant of the hotel. Who are these people, Erash was wondering.

"Well!" The old man grunted. "What have you got to say for yourself? We don't intend to wait forever for you to talk. We have ways of making people talk."

"No!" shouted Rula. "Let him speak! Where did you get the broken jug from, and who are you? Why did you telephone about selling wine when we know that you have no intention of selling wine? What are you selling to Pollo? What do the Bylians want from you?" Rula was almost crying now.

Erash replied, feeling now more at ease. They were obviously on the same side, as far as Bylia was concerned, but who are 'they' he wondered.

"You know where the jug was broken, and yes, I am not selling wine, I am in the technology business. I sell expensive hi-tech components to whoever will buy them. They are usually used in power stations, and energy plants, but sometimes they get into the wrong hands. We have to be careful." Erash was in full flow, he was beginning to believe he had found unsuspecting allies in his cause. He continued. "Who are you, if you are not working for the Bylian Government? Why are you so interested in the dealings with Pollo?"

The elderly man stepped forward, for the first time showing a possible gentle hint of a smile on his face. He offered Erash his hand.

"I have also come to that conclusion," he smiled in return.

But there is still a great deal which does not make sense". Erash mused, quite audibly, as he watched Rula still fondling the broken jug piece in her hands.

The older man continued. "We are terrorists," he exclaimed "or freedom fighters!" That is depending on which side you happen to be on. We are actually fighting to destroy the present puppet dictatorship of Bylia. Since that autocratic, self-centered, monster of a creature, Fadfagi took over the reins of power in Bylia, life there has become almost intolerable unless you subscribe openly to the regime. He has turned a once fully democratic independent country into a despot of tyranny. We are a group of people who want very much to restore genuine government to our homeland and rid ourselves of that foul smelling, power thirsty tyrant who is destroying our country with such ease. He calls us terrorists. We call ourselves freedom fighters. He is the terrorist!" Erash was quite impressed by the enthusiasm of the gray curly haired man. He was so full of purpose and resolve, perhaps he and his group would be willing recruits to his own cause exposing Fadfagi for what he really was. "Perhaps it would be a good idea to return to the Hotel, as somewhere more conducive to private discussion." Rula interrupted. "I am sure that we have a great deal to discuss now that we all understand each other."

***

It was still dark outside when Svi woke Lika with an early morning kiss. Their big day had at last arrived. This day was the culmination of all their efforts during the last years of study. Most people would never get the chance in their whole lifetime ever to show their noses for a few minutes outside the environment of their planet, but Svi was going to be a year out there, with his Lika as the icing on the cake. He was so happy; he had to keep on pinching himself to 'prove' he was not dreaming. He was still sure that soon he would wake up and it would all be gone. How could he be so fortunate? He thanked god in his thoughts. He was always grateful, and never took good fortune for granted.

Lika was purring in his arms.

"Surely it's too early to get up" Lika was only semi-conscious. "It is still dark outside, and haven't we only just gone to bed?"

Svi moved over and pushed a button in the bed's headboard. A bright well-spoken woman appeared at the foot of the bed. The hologram was giving details of the day's events, and the global news.

"That always un-nerves me," Lika announced to Svi "Breakfast, and early morning hologram broadcasts always seem to so real. I feel quite embarrassed. It is just like having a public visitor when one is most vulnerable. First thing in the morning!"

"Come on, get up!" Called Svi as he climbed out of bed, and disappeared through the speaking hologram into the bathroom. "I very much prefer fixed screen television, its more impersonal Lika shouted after Svi.

Most of that morning Svi and Lika were taken on a guided tour of what was later to be commonly known to them as 'ground-base one', another name for G.C. Eton. The couple were going to be in constant touch with home, and it would all have to be through this ground base. It was important that they should have a comprehensive knowledge of the functions and capabilities of the base.

Svi was amazed at the size of everything and the amount of area devoted to experimentation. Many of the complexes already in orbit were re-produced accurately on the ground. Lika was amazed at the explicit detail given to the simplest of things like automatic food preparation, which in certain conditions of weightlessness or very low gravity needed special treatment, or methods of use. It was a whole new education. They were going to have to pick it up as they went along. Although their course-work had covered some of the problems they would meet, the real training for the engineer-astronaut could take up to two years, even with stereo-auto-thought methods of pre-programming the human brain.

It was mid-afternoon when the happy couple entered the embarkation center, full of excited anticipation, like two young children going to a friend's birthday party on their own, for the very first time.

The formalities for leaving their world were very much less involved than the formalities required for traveling from one part of it to another. All that was required was the demonstration of their new identity discs at the checkout as they entered the loading capsule. They inserted the disc into the slot at the gate and put their hand on the disengaging lever. If their fingerprints matched their personal disc, and the identity was on the permitted list, which was checked electronically, direct with registration, then the lever would lift allowing them to pass through into the capsule.

They felt an acute state of satisfaction when the gate lifted for Lika, as this single act in itself verified that their newly married status had been formally recognized for the first time in the use of their new discs. Lika smiled her cheeky smile to Svi, and he clenched her hand tightly to indicate his understanding of her. He put his arm tightly around her waist, as they entered the capsule, taking a seat right at the front sitting in the oval panoramic window, which gave them complete all round vision. It was only to be a short journey to the gyro-globe but it might as well be in visual comfort, and there did not seem to be any other fellow travelers. This last observation was soon to be proven quite untrue, as only a few moments later, the capsule doors re-opened and five people entered carrying all kinds of gear.

They had many tubes; brushes and what appeared to be a vacuum cleaner. Svi remembered the horror of the massacre only those weeks before, when they swept the ground with just such objects. Under the thick padded protective gear these men were wearing, he could just see the flash of the same black and silver uniform those men wore that fateful day. His grip on Lika's hand tightened from caring comfort to shocked horror.

Lika was not sure that she understood Svi's reaction to these strangers although she certainly knew that he was very tense. Svi tried very hard to act as if nothing happened, and ignore the newcomers as if they were not there. This was very difficult, as with all their gear, and protective clothing each one of them took up the space of two people.

***

CHAPTER 5

Erash never wore his uniform, but on this occasion, back at the "House of Four Eyes" he was pleased that he had at least brought his identity badge with him. There could be no question of whom he was, with the personal hologram of his face and profile, set in the black panel with silver flashing down the side. The five silver stars on the top indicated his most senior rank as the chief of security of the whole firm of Science and Welfare. This he needed as proof of his true identity for his new found 'colleagues' in the attempt to uncover the chain of supply of his firm's goods to the tyrannical government of Bylia. His new friends would need him as much as he needed them, but it had to be founded in trust, and they wanted proof of whom he claimed to be.

They would be waiting for him downstairs in the private lounge bar. It was lucky that he had packed his disc in the secret compartment in the handle of his suitcase. He hurried downstairs; they were all busy talking when he entered the room.

He wasted no time; he walked over to the small group, and gently placed his 'badge' on the table in front of them and still covering it with the palm of his hand announced.

"This is who I am, I know that we can trust each other, we have to, as there is no other choice if we are to beat this Fadfagi at his own game" Erash watched their faces as he carefully removed his hand, revealing the beauty of his gleaming, well polished black and silver badge of office.

"You are Erash" The old man choked. "Chief of Security, Science and Welfare, a five star general. Do you believe our cause serious enough to come here yourself?"

"Your cause is only of secondary importance. We support you only as far as we want Fadfagi out of the way as much as you do, for the sake of stability and peace, but we are very worried. There have been very serious thefts from our workings in Lyboncher and also in Subterranean areas only known to us. We keep finding discrepancies in our stocks and equipment all the time. These are often very skillfully covered up."

"What kinds of things are being taken?" A young man in the group enquired.

"Precision, high-tech tools and some heavy equipment, but worst of all…'Radiact' in quite large quantities!"

"We suspected that!" shouted the old man as he stood up and marched away across the room, only to turn around and return to his place waving his stick at Erash, as if to accuse him personally for the trouble. "Pure negligence!" The man shouted.

"Sheer brilliance" Erash replied. "The people behind this are very clever and know in great detail what to do and how to cover their tracks. This Pollo character has an organization, which has to be respected although it must be defeated. Have any of you ever met Pollo? Tell me about him".

"Her!" came the answer in chorus. "Yes" continued the old man "We have had dealings with her, but only as a cover for monitoring their movements and possible sabotage to their operations. One of our best agents is on to her at this moment; we are trying to trace their center for operations. We have tried everything. We have put bleeping transmitters in their goods, but somehow whenever they get near Bylia they become 'neutralized' and disappear. We have paid them in marked money, which re-appears all over the place in tiny amounts. We cannot locate the central H.Q. or where they keep their ill-gotten gains. We have access to a friendly country's satellite information data of Bylia, and also close-up infrared photography, and nothing. Our agent has been over there now for two days. She reports back later tonight. Perhaps she has had a meeting with Pollo.

Erash looked around the room; there were nine people in the room excluding him. They were a motley group of characters. Each person obviously had his or her own individual identity, but together the appearance was one of a rugged bunch of conspirators. The only person who looked even remotely lacking in austerity was the elderly man with the brass-handled stick who spoke with a strange accent. He was very obviously their leader, if only by virtue of his general air of authority. Erash was thinking that this was the gentleman he would have to deal with, and he addressed him directly.

"I am sure that we could give you any facility within our power. We will ensure that your group never needs to go without equipment or supplies..."

At that moment the door opened behind him. He could smell that perfume again, very much stronger this time. He turned round to face the door and gasped, he now knew something that explained everything. Four eyes were looking at him; two identical pairs of beautiful blue eyes. One pair showed astonished surprise as they started to move towards him with a little tear in each corner. The other pair showed surprise at the reaction of her identical twin and then she too began to understand the situation. This must be the stranger in the night that had saved her sister's life.

Rula threw her arms around Erash and smothered him with open-mouthed kisses. Erash pulled back after a moment of sheer ecstatic pleasure at the sudden reunion. He looked at Rula's smiling dusty face.

"Now I understand, it all fits into place. I thought you were your sister and no wonder she thought me forward." Erash was grinning all over his face.

Rula pulled Erash down next to her on the two-seater between her sister and herself. "You have obviously met my sister 'Marla'. We often get confused; in fact, we sometimes even get confused ourselves in circumstances similar to this. Anyway, what we are you doing here?"

"Don't you think you ought to give us your report? Did you meet with Pollo?" The old man interrupted. Erash couldn't believe his ears, but now everything was beginning to make sense.

"No, I didn't." Rula turned to face her inquisitor, and continued to give forth a de-briefing. "There was a problem somewhere along the supply-line. One of their agents was hospitalized for a few weeks. She was seriously injured in an incident and lost her hand. There was quite a commotion, because she was one of Pollo's best agents, she may even have been Pollo herself. They have managed to steal the hand back, but it's still some way back down the line."

Erash interrupted "I know what woman. If we find that hand, we have a strong bargaining counter. This might be the chance we've been waiting for!" Erash was positively delighted with his progress. He put his arm tightly round Rula they smiled at each other.

***

Jabal was very pleased with himself, as he rested after a hard day in the fields. Dusk was just beginning to show the earliest sign of approaching and he was allowing himself the luxury of sitting back in his basketwork chair, rocking gently, enjoying the early evening air. From the verandah of his home he could see a very long way to the foothills that formed the northern perimeter of his vast estate. He was smiling to himself as he sipped at his refreshing iced drink of cable-juice. He had just completed his full harvest. The crop was completely prepared, and the distributors would be there for the morning collection. He had not had time to unwind for nearly two weeks now, and he was savoring every moment. He allowed his chair to gently rock backward and forwards in a pendulum fashion to the soft beating drum of the distant festivities of his hybrid herd as they celebrated the completion of the work on the harvest. Where else would hybrids find a master who would allow an early finish to the day, and also donate food and cable-juice for a celebration party? The best a hybrid could usually hope for on any nearby farm would be a day off from being whipped or punished severely. Jabal treated his hybrids almost like people. He was respected and obeyed in return. If any one of them stepped out of line it was often their own kind that performed the punishment. Jabal found it the best way to run a good business, and he was very much admired, and equally very much envied by those who didn't understand.

He was almost asleep when he noticed in the early dusk, a long line of lights moving across his gaze against the darkening mistiness of the lower foothills at the perimeter in the northwest. He had never seen anything so strange before. A moving line of lights was snaking itself down onto the plain beneath. His plain. He was sure it was coming nearer, and perhaps lights were afire or torches. 'That's right', he thought to himself a torchlight procession would match the identity quite surely.

He wondered who and why such a beautiful thing should be coming to him, as it certainly was moving in his direction. He could now make out that there were many lights each with small figures carrying them. 'Torches' he thought, 'that was definitely what they were, moving slowly in a zigzagging line nearer and nearer'. There were many different colors, green, blue, magenta, crimson and many more. How thoughtful, was this a surprise for him, and who was responsible? He watched its movement with keen interest, as it approached nearer and nearer.

He didn't notice the change in rhythm of the hybrid drumbeat that had been gently patting away in the background. He didn't notice the fine 'hum' in the air, a melodious high pitched chanting noise, that was beginning to make itself heard. He didn't notice the smell like burning rubber, which was beginning to fill the dusty air. He sat there, content, sipping cable-juice, contemplating the following morning's collections and the end of his harvest responsibilities for at least another half year. All his stocks were locked away in the barns ready for the morning.

With distinct awareness, Jabal began to digest the sound of the approaching column. The softened hum in the air began to make itself known, and Jabal was beginning to make out the figures of the people carrying the torches. They were hybrids, and they were chanting. That was not a good sign, as hybrids only chanted when they were very happy or extremely angry, and as his own hybrid herd had gone very quiet on him, he was beginning to worry!

Then it happened, a very loud scream or was it a shriek and one of the crimson torches was racing through the air in a very threatening manner, towards one of the largest hay-barns!!

He could see one of his hybrids up on the roof of the barn in a crouching position as if waiting to catch it, which he immediately did. He very wisely threw it down into the water trough for the pigs or similar beasts.

Jabal controlled himself; he must not be seen to panic. The fact was that he had no other choice than to be brave. His farm estate was under attack by hybrids. From where they had come he just did not know, but what they were about he had a very shrewd guess!

He couldn't believe his eyes, there must have been swarms of them they were coming in droves. He couldn't remember ever seeing so many hybrids at one time. Some of them, he could see the whites of their eyes. The occasional one was apparently foaming at the mouth. They would do that to work up angry enthusiasm; it seemed to help their adrenalin in preparation for a fight. The next thing he saw was the darkening hazy sky, and the occasional streak of light as another flaming torch flew across his view he was being carried fast, in his chair by his very own hybrids.

"Quick, to the water tower" he heard one of them say, a hybrid voice he recognized. "He will be safe there!"

The screaming and yelling was now at increased volume, as apparently the attacking strangers were over-running the domestic area of the farm. His own herd seemed well prepared, they must have known about his attack well in advance. He was now in a position high above the ground in his well-structured water tower with a parapet surround. The entire specter of warfare was laid out beneath him. He was amazed that with all the burning torches and malicious intent of the aggressors, there was only one barn that was afire. Against the background and under the brightly lit sky he could see terrible things. Two male intruders had taken a young female into a darkened corner and were holding her down on the ground, while a third and fourth were attempting to rape each end of her body at the same time. One of them was entering her mouth, muffling her screams, while the other was doing the same at her other end. Jabal nearly laughed if it hadn't been so sad, the one with his penis inserted in her mouth, screamed so loudly, he must have been in sheer agony, as obviously to defend herself she had managed to bite so hard, they hybrid-man went mad. He was running around in circles half naked from his waist down, holding himself, screaming and yelling. He found the nearby pig's drinking trough and jumped in. He was exhausted. The other three men started to beat the young woman with bits of dead wood that were lying around. She screamed. It was pitiful. Her screaming became frantic; she was cowering and curling up in the corner now. Her screams were becoming hoarse. The noise was never ending. Why didn't somebody come, he almost wanted to help her himself, then suddenly nothing. He saw the three men running away. No movement from the girl whose body was like a broken doll, limbs all splayed out in the corner. She didn't move and her eyes were open. She must have been dead; her head was at an impossible angle. The neck must be broken. Jabal couldn't believe the carnage and destruction, there were now four barns on fire.

At last, he could sense a change in movement as some human faces began to appear; three of his men, with paresifiers drove into the yard. The hybrids started to run in all directions like scolded cats. One was climbing the steps to the water tower. Jabal looked for his knife, which he always kept down by his ankle. Their eyes met. The hybrid was a stranger and the shock on his face Jabal will never forget as his knife entered the hybrid's chest within seconds of it being drawn from Jabal's sock, he was very accurate when it came to throwing the knife.

The fighting went on for a long time, and his own hybrids fought very well. They were out numbered by three or four to one and they still seemed to be coming out on top. They knew the lay of the land in the dark, and also had a great deal to lose if their farm was destroyed.

He had seen so many terrible things. There was the old man who was running around with his hair on fire, the young very pregnant woman with a stake through her vagina hanging dead upside down from a post. A little baby crying in her dead mother's bosoms and worst of all, the little girl with half a face, the other half burnt away by the vicious use of a hybrid torch. Jabal prayed for it all to end. He wanted to help but it would be non-productive, and if he were to be hurt there would be no one to run the farm.

Peace and calm took a long time coming to Jabal's home. Sunrise greeted him before the last stray scream or crashing timber. An eerie silence eventually seemed to fall across the yard. The occasional fire was still burning and many farm vehicles were damaged but as Jabal climbed carefully down from his tower he thanked god that things were not worse. He believed that under the circumstances he had probably got off quite lightly. He started to get his men together to survey the damage.

Two fair-haired men stood on a small hillock across the valley not far from the scene of devastation, smiling and joking with each other. Their pale but pink complexions becoming slightly reddened as their delight became evident, that their hand in the carnage had been far from innocent.

"That should set the cat among the pigeons!" Malek said to Jodl. "We sure will see some results from this mess". They began to curl up with laughter. Jodl could hardly contain himself; he was doubled up, almost tearful with wicked glee. "Come on" he whispered to Malek, we must not be seen anywhere near here. The sold gold signet rings on two of his fingers flashed in the early morning dawn, and the red snake emblem could be clearly seen on both of them. The two men turned away and made a silent but hasty retreat.

***

The black and silver uniforms, hidden under the over clothes of the newcomers to the loading capsule, created an acute anxiety in Svi's mind, bordering on a neuro-phobia. Why, he thought, did they need those heavy vacuum materials, what evil doing were they concocting now?

He moved up closer to Lika, who of course not many weeks before had had no visual contact of the carnage and destruction from her concealment, as she hid from the guards as they unleashed their punishment and murder on that peaceful gathering of "Crisis for Nuke Danger". Svi contented himself with her ignorance; at least she would not be upset so badly by the sight of those uniforms, as they would have little meaning for her.

"Move over," came the arrogant command, "Make room, there are going to be another ten of us for this capsule. You may well have to get out and wait for the next one." One of the guards was gesturing with his baton, as the entrance door again broke open, to allow more than ten of these heavily dressed 'thugs' to enter the capsule. The tallest one of the newcomers signaled with his little finger to two others, and with an obvious wave of the finger gestured that Svi and Lika should be removed.

The two men obeyed the command and moved over to Svi, one of them brought his baton hard down across his back in a punishing blow almost sweeping Svi into the floor, and certainly temporarily driving all the breath out of his body.

"Get out now, we need the room. Go on both of you leave while you still have breath to do so. You can take the next capsule. We don't mind that." The man said with a calculated smile half appearing across his face.

"We were here before you!" Lika interrupted. "We have more right than you to be here. We shall stay!" She stooped to help Svi regain his seat.

"You woman may stay. That would be fun!" The same guard replied with a lecherous smile on his face. Svi grabbed all their belongings and taking Lika's hand, they made an abrupt exit to await the next capsule. They could hear the corrupt and vicious laughter, and looking back through the large windows into the craft the mocking gestures and filthy suggestions of the small army of thugs was enough to make Svi console Lika that at least they had got away in one piece more or less unscathed apart from their pride.

"Don't worry darling" Lika took Svi's hand and wrapped her arm into his "One day Svi, we will get our reward at their expense, I am sure, indeed, I am certain, I see it in the stars."

There was another capsule in the neighboring docking station which had the next departure time indicated above the entrance module. The couple went through the same performance as the previous time as they sought entrance into the capsule through security. They finally took up their positions in the loading capsule in exactly the identical position as before. The only things different were the color schemes of the capsule and possible departure time.

The waiting seemed to go on forever, although it could not have been more than a few short moments before their original capsule loaded with the thugs secretly dressed in the black and silver uniform slowly left its loading bay on its short journey to the gyrosphere, the large orange ball towering high above the metropolis.

"I wonder what type of stranger we shall see on this capsule." Svi whispered to Lika, as suddenly the entrance door broke open again. 'Medical and baby care supplies' was neatly imprinted on the metal casing of the delivery crate that a very attractive female medical orderly had carefully wheeled into the capsule. She sat down next to the box, as if to guard it from all-comers.

"Why would they want 'baby products' on a gyrosphere and especially abroad the orbital crafts. Life out there would never support a family. What would they want all that for?" Lika was very curious.

After what seemed an interminable wait, only two more people entered the capsule, and then the announcement came.

"We welcome you aboard staff flight 008 to the gyrosphere.

Please secure all loose belongings, as rapid entry is required into the sphere, and this can sometimes result in rapid deceleration being felt in the capsule. Have a good day. You depart on the count of forty, thirty-nine, thirty-eight......"

Svi could see the surprise in Lika's face, as she mouthed a question to him.

"Why is this so primitive? The latest hemispheres used for local transport don't even have seat restraints any more, but on these short journey machines everything has to be strapped down, including us?" They were beginning to move, very slowly, almost imperceptibly, as the count had reached zero. Their speed was increasing at a very high rate of acceleration and before Svi could answer Lika, they were already half way to the gyrosphere.

"We have to enter the gyrosphere at great speed, and then come to an almost sudden halt once inside. This is due to the planet's gravitational pull on the gyrosphere being counteracted by constant magnetic spin. This with the opposing inner wall spinning in the other direction means that as long as we approach the sphere in harmony with its revolution, then at the correct speed we will enter without any problem if the outer and inner doors are open. If they were not then we would be repelled like simple same pole magnets...! Svi was not concentrating, he was bent over double, as his chin nearly went down to his knees they had slowed down violently to no more than a snail's pace, and then gently glided to a stop. "They still haven't perfected this system, and I feel quite sick!" Svi finished. Lika had almost passed out; she appeared to be completely drained. She looked up at Svi who was quite green. "What did you say?" she enquired. "I'm sorry; I didn't hear any of that." She managed a smile, and gently kissed her new husband on the cheek. "We are on our way at last, and they say that part of the journey is always the worst. I am sure one day it will improve."

The couple retrieved their belongings and followed the medical orderly and her trolley down the narrow moving corridor into the heart of the very large gyrosphere.

"You could easily get lost in here". Lika was very impressed with the size. "It looks large enough from the outside, but when you realize what this place can accommodate, the proportions of size become astonishing."

Svi decided that as it was late afternoon, and they would still be stationery above the metropolis for at least a couple more hours, they should spend their time at leisure. They were amazed at the reality of the gyrosphere. A small plastic ball of little weight could be placed in the center of a polished tabletop, and it would not move or roll at all. Such was the stability of the 'stationery' craft. At different places scattered throughout the sphere they noticed spirit levels at many different angles. These also remained immobile, as the ship remained wholly fixed in its position of no movement. They later learned that these spirit levels helped passengers and crew judge the plumb line, or direction of artificial gravity when the ship is in extra terrestrial flight.

Svi and Lika were now very nervous, full of cautious anxiety and childish anticipation of their very first flight outside the natural atmosphere of their own planet.

"Not very long now," Svi put his arm tight around Lika's waist and he guided her to a table near the window "Come on lets eat here, and we can watch the events of terrestrial departure from this very useful vantage point."

Lika put her head on Svi's shoulder as they sat looking out of the window. She fell asleep.

***

Noah was very anxious about Tubal Cain's possible involvement in covert arms dealing with certain foreign powers, without the full knowledge of the Board of 'Science and Welfare' and certainly without the official backing of the government defense ministry. Noah had finally completed his report on "National civil protection in time of Nuke-war", and he knew that if it were ever published, the evident controversial nature of its contents would cause a public outcry. He had not spent much time at his office desk that morning; the file was already compiled in triplicate and had been recorded in the proper manner on electro-magnetic tape. Noah packed his dispatch case as neatly as space would allow and departed from his office to cross the central square on his way to the central government building. He was climbing the eight steps up to the entrance module when he resisted that sudden urge to look round, he was sure that a stranger was fixating a stare on the back of his neck. He casually walked up to the darkened window glass that formed the majority of the front wall of the entrance hall of the very large building and carefully tried to appear as if he was looking through the window, when in fact, he was using it like a mirror. As he moved his gaze from left to right and then the other way, he could see the sharp reflection of a thin flash of light from what would normally be called a pair of binoculars. He knew he was being followed. Noah tightened his grip on his valise and entered the building with some strong feeling of relief at having that wall of glass behind him. The fact that it was there seemed to give Noah the feeling of greater security from the intruding inspecting glances into his privacy. At the double he made it across the foyer into a lift that was already just closing its doors. He didn't care where it was going; it was his speedy escape route. Getting out on the seventeenth floor he ran down one set of stairs to the half landing and then entered another lift, which took him down to the fourth floor. There he felt safe, surely no one could have followed him that closely so as to know where he was now? He walked carefully up to the door of room 4010, and pressed the bleeper with strong purpose.

"All right! All right!" came the answer from the other side of the door, "keep your shirt on, I'm coming!" Noah felt re-assured that he could hear Tubal Cain's voice so clearly, he was certainly very enthusiastic about meeting with him before the coming government meeting. Noah had to talk with Tubal, he had to brief him in advance, they had gone a long way together, and had to produce a unified argument for changes in development to the committee. The door opened and Tubal Cain showed surprise on recognition of his friendly visitor.

"What are you doing here?" Have you been followed? It could spoil everything, you are mad! Come in quick!" Tubal Cain grabbed Noah by the elbow and pulled him into the room closing the door behind him as if with the speed of light itself.

"What's wrong?" Noah enquired, astonished at Tubal's reaction on seeing his brother-in-law. "Why are you so worried? You look dreadful, and we have that meeting in one hour."

"That does not worry me, we are well prepared for that, and it's the security forces I'm worried about!" Tubal Cain had gestured to Noah to come over to be near him at the sideboard, and indicated that silence was the policy of that instant by putting his finger to his lips. Tubal had already turned the hot drink machine to boiling, and it was hissing and blowing at full volume sound.

"I don't know who is listening!" Tubal whispered into Noah's ear, "We have got real problems at Science and Welfare. Our security forces have been compromised and infiltrated. There are groups of anarchists that have formed 'cells' within our forces, they have done a lot of damage and are highly ruthless and dangerous. What is more they are doing their dastardly deeds in our name. They have formed small 'Action groups' all over the place, and are doing terrible things, committing horrific atrocities. They are turning our uniform into something, which is always to be obeyed and even worse feared beyond belief. The black and silver uniform is being tarnished even as I speak."

Tubal Cain had a tear in his eye as he continued to speak in a whisper to Noah.

"Everything I've worked for, all the purity of ideal, the endeavor, and successes in achievement, everything is being washed away, as brutes, thugs and criminals use our organization to further their own ways and means."

Noah was beginning to see Tubal Cain in a different light. Perhaps he had misjudged his brother-in-law. These dealings on the secret arms supply markets that he had uncovered; perhaps they were nothing to do with Tubal Cain after all. Noah was listening intently to the exhortations, it was obviously not the simple problem he had originally expected, this was much worse, and very serious. They had to act.

"Don't you think it would be a good idea to mention all this in our report?" Noah asked. "It would give more credence to the belief that you are not implicated."

"No!" Tubal interrupted, almost so loudly that he must have forgotten the importance of discretion, he then started to whisper again "No," he repeated. "Let it ride with me as the bad guy, we don't want to warn our enemies, and with me as a rogue, it may help the true cause, the destruction of these infiltrators." Tubal was satisfied now that he had got his worries off his chest, to be shared with Noah. Shared problems he believed were much easier to solve. "We will stay with our original arrangement, you Noah, must present the unexpurgated version of the report. No holds barred and with full conviction. Do not miss-treat the truth, or it will become very sick and possibly throw up all over you. Let the panel hear what you have to say and then stand back, they will become very interested. Watch each member's reaction to each point raised; it should then pay dividends."

Not much later, the two men walked the short distance down the corridor to the elevator; they had found a new bond of friendship and mutual trust often uncommon between brothers-in-law. Their arrival at the meeting was unannounced. There on the slightly raised platform sat the panel of government representatives. They were all sitting there feeling very important, trying very hard to look important and being given confidence in that fact by the other people present who actually believed them to be important. Such was the working structure of a government committee. Noah and Tubal were about to be interviewed and their report would be dissected by all assembled on that podium. There was a small degree of nervousness on both their parts, because the report that Noah and Tubal had put together was going to open quite a few eyes. Noah was to speak first and he had decided to go for it. The truth needed no deep preparation; it was only lies that needed rehearsal.

***

Erash could not easily remember going to bed, but he awoke with a smile on his face, and an unbelievable feeling of deep pleasure. He felt very warm, as he lay there cocooned between his two sleeping bedmates Marla and Rula. He lay there looking at the ceiling, with the thoughts of the previous night's experience replaying through his mind. The two beautiful women had kept him carnally amused to the very early hours of the morning. He gently turned to the right and to the left; two smiling contented sleepy faces cuddled up to him. Such joyous pleasure was feeding his emotions. How could he love two women so much? He gently moved both hands down under the covers and found both pairs of buttocks. The twin sisters were both lying naked on their stomachs, but they were mirror images of each other in the manner in which they had put their arms across his naked hairy chest as if to hold him down, that he shouldn't escape their embraces. He carefully and almost imperceptibly stroked their behinds with loving satisfaction. Two beautiful women. One of them would have been more than he could have deserved but two identical adorable lovers were more than any good man could ever wish for.

Now that he had been with the pair for so many hours, nearly an entire night through he was surprised how easy it was to distinguish the two girls apart. Marla was on his left as he lay on his back, and Rula, his first love, was on his right. He felt somewhat guilty that perhaps he had let Rula down, by showing such bold affection in Marla's direction, but he would happily have married either one of them. In fact, he had already made up his mind; he would marry both of them, if they would have him. With his senior position in Science and Welfare he could certainly afford it.

DOWNLOAD

It was several hours after morning daylight had broken when the sleepy threesome lifted their warm sweaty bodies from their love nest and took a steamy shower before meeting what was to be for them a very important day. Erash had made it clear to both girls his honorable intentions and they had cried together. The three of them were deeply in love, a perfect trio.

"Yes" they had said together, they would both be Erash's wives. Rula and Marla were so very happy, but certainly Erash's joy must have been equal if not greater.

Their joyous planning was carefully trimmed with caution, as yet they still had a major task to perform and reality had to be faced. They still had the problematic Bylian question, and their route had to be found to Pollo's organizational nerve center. Erash had agreed to go with Rula; while she retraced her steps back down the line of connections until she could find the lost hand. That being found would then give them a wonderful introduction to the Pollo's organization, which they desperately had to crack.

Saying goodbye was very painful for the three of them, as Marla had to stay behind but Rula and Erash took a pair of homing pigeons with them, they agreed to keep in touch with Marla. There was an emergency safety hospital at Larden on the Bylian border with Orcamo, which by nature of its recognized international status gave it diplomatic immunity. It would be at a place such as this that the possibility of tracing the "wandering hand" could come to fruition. A strange arrival of a singular detached hand in deep freeze without any identity would not even raise an eyebrow in such a refuge. There would be no questions asked. The administration would assume that sometime soon a qualified claimant would turn up on their doorstep. If no one appeared within half a year then it would be destroyed. These hospitals were meant only to serve as safe medical havens between two aggressive parties. This desert oasis was the destination for Rula and Erash as they left Marla at the "House of four eyes". All three of them had tears in their eyes, and they had each taken it in turns to cuddle a goodbye with one another. Erash held Marla in such a tight embrace, that if she had been any closer to him, she would have been standing behind him. Rula and Marla also kissed each other, but much more meaningfully than ever before, as now they were not only twin sisters, but also they were going to be joint wives of Erash. The emotions of the moment left their spirits in limbo; it was not easy for any one of them. Marla remained in the doorway waving to them until they eventually disappeared, walking through the large city gateway carrying what little luggage they had needed to take with them. She wondered how long it would be before she would see either one of them again.

**

The back of the man's head was vibrating and his shoulders were bouncing indicating most definitely that he was having a great fit of laughter as he joked with the two men who stood before him. Malek and Jodl were reporting their deeds of the previous night. The stranger in front of whom they were standing was obviously very pleased with them. It was very difficult for Rastus to identify the man, who continued to have his back to the view of the binoculars through which he was viewing the scene. Under Jabal's orders he had been surveying the comings and goings of all strangers to his farm during the last few weeks, and he had noticed Malek and Jodl getting friendly with some of his hybrid friends. Why were they asking all these questions and poking their noses into everything? Then they appeared under his nose that fateful night while he was doing a border patrol. He latched onto them and followed discreetly.

The interview seemed to be going on for some time and Rastus was finding it very boring watching three figures talking and laughing from such a distance. He could not make out what they were saying and could not perceive even a profile of man whose frontal image was eluding him. The interview came to an end very abruptly and the two men gave a very strange military-style salute as they stood to attention, then clicking their heels together, both men in unison, lifted their outstretched right arms forward, unbent and just above the level of their heads, they had their palms flat facing down with hand, thumb and fingers all in a perfect straight line. They seemed to mouth a greeting or salutation and then purposefully dropped their arms standing to attention once again. The other man repeated the exercise in reply. Malek and Jodl moved backward slightly bowing to an obviously higher rank. The man that Rastus could not see properly was seemingly very important. How he wished that he had brought his boom radio-microphone with him that fitted into his binoculars. With that, he could have picked up the talking voices of the trio without much effort at all. One thing was certain though; they were very pleased with themselves.

Rastus was now in a dilemma. Who should he now keep under his observation, the two rogues, Malek and Jodl, or their senior 'Officer'? He decided that the higher rank should be more fruitful, but he had yet to identify him. Rastus decided to get as close as possible to his quarry in the attempt. It was essential that recognition should be achieved.

On all fours, Rastus moved carefully through the dry decaying undergrowth taking great care where to place his hands and feet. He was well trained in this form of tracking and could travel unheard through the driest of dead forest without a sound of cracking twigs. He bared his feet and carried his shoes around his neck. Hybrids were highly skilled in stealth. It seemed to be a racial characteristic, an instinct. They could appear from nowhere, completely unannounced, and were extremely accurate with the knife or bow and arrow. Their attacking prowess was always their silence. He knew that the night before, they were so noisy, that was done for a purpose to create an effect. They must have been under someone's direction. Not an arrow was fired; their attack was not the usual kind expected from the hybrid species.

The door of the building was around the other side and Rastus was fortunate that there was a great deal of cover for him to get around to that direction. Finally, he managed to hide himself behind an old dead tree that had cracked open on falling to the ground. The drying heat had opened out the trunk to allow him more cover than he could need. He now could lie on his stomach and see down the gentle slope into the window of the room. The stranger was still there talking to four other men, also in their black and silver uniforms, but obviously of lower rank. The stranger was getting annoyed and took his officer's baton and thwacked it hard across the unsuspecting subaltern's face. He reeled backwards in pain and went to wipe his hand across the bruise; the baton came in hard again from the other direction. "You will do as you are told. You will obey orders always. Do you understand?" The angry officer was now in a rage, venting his fury out on his junior. "Do you understand?"

Rastus could hear them clearly,

"Yes!" came the one word reply.

"Then take your paresifier and point it at your colleague."

He then addressed the other man who was now terrified. "You will face him and stand to attention." This he obediently did. "Now", the man continued, "Set the paresifier to kill." The soldier did this, and the other man was rigid with fear and anticipation of immediate death. "Fire!" The order came, and the soldier pulled the little trigger. The other man collapsed to the floor. "Get up!" shouted the enraged general; Rastus could now see his rank. "That paresifier was not armed. I took out the fuse; you are only suffering from shock!" With that, the other soldier collapsed to the floor in shocked relief that he had not killed his friend and he had retrieved his dignity by obeying the order in full. "In future you will understand that orders are issued to be obeyed under all circumstances at all times. Do not ever question an order. You may not survive if you do!" Without a sign or gesture, he threw his head back replaced his black cap with the silver trimmings and marched with great speed out of the door into his waiting hoversphere. The other two men followed sheepishly behind. Rastus was not prepared for a rapid get-away. He could not follow a fast moving hoversphere. He took a magnetic device out of his pocket and with his small hand-bow; he aimed at the underside surface of the sphere. The small device hit the target attaching itself to the metal curtain on which the machine was supporting itself. Rastus set the activator by remote control, only just in time, as the hoversphere moved off throwing dust and debris in all directions. The signal being transmitted from that device would last for days, but so long as the machine sees some daylight then the solar cells will re-charge and the device will transmit forever. Rastus will be able to find that vehicle without any difficulty whenever he wanted to. The signal being sent out was in stereo, and this made its direction and distance easy to collate within less than one second. Rastus returned to the farm to report to Jabal.

***

"We are beginning to move" Svi gently nudged Lika. She was fast asleep on his shoulder, and he knew that she would have been upset to miss any of the excitement. Lika looked up at Svi's face and smiled a thank-you. Movement of the craft was imperceptible and the only way that they knew that the sphere was moving free was by watching the parallax change as the two radio masts started to move in different directions and the reflections in the large office windows down below started to move across the frontage of the building. Svi could just make out an almost unnoticed change of direction, as the vehicle was beginning to ascend. The ground had disappeared below them as if the whole event was taking place on an artificial screen. There was no "feeling" of movement but the dull hazy sky outside was becoming very bright only to go paler again as they rose above the misty cloud. Suddenly the deep blue of clear space dissolved into black with shining spotted lights curtaining itself around the craft.

They could look back at the globe from where they had come with great-unnoticed speed and they could see a misty white surface over the entire globe with the startling exception of the ice caps at the two poles. These were two areas that were completely cloudless, and the whole landmass underneath was covered with white ice and snow. The surrounding coastline at both poles was quite vividly colored blue, but this was so narrow it was almost hardly visible. Svi knew it was there, and he managed to point it out to Lika.

"In our great grandfather's time, two thirds of our planet was that fine shimmering blue color, the rest was a green and brown. The cloud would be visibly changing its pattern of cover in gentle rotating swirls and drifts, which appeared to move very slowly from this distance out in space. The further we go out into space, the bluer the planet would have become. That is all different now as you will see; the globe will become a silver gray and will look cold and lifeless to a visiting stranger, as we move further away." Lika shrugged at Svi's remarks.

"Look, the globe has stopped shrinking. We must have stopped and we didn't feel a thing. Lika mouthed to Svi.

"There are 'momentum compensators' fitted to this craft, and we experience no movement of any nature when the engines are running". Svi answered. "Until the compensator was invented, everyone and everything had to be strapped down or locked-up before take-off. Today things are so different, but that's progress for you." Svi sighed as if sadly. "You know Lika," he continued. "Perhaps we would have been better off if we humans weren't so inventive!"

In the peripheral edge of his vision, out of the corner of his eye, Svi could see the construction approaching. In fact, the sphere on which they were traveling was approaching the construction at a very slow speed. The construction was in a stationery orbit around the planet, and mirrors from the loading or disembarkation center in the middle of the construction were steering them in.

The construction looked the size of a small building, but it kept growing. Perspective meant nothing when out in space unless there was more than one object to compare distance with. Their spherical vehicle was quite large but the construction that they were approaching was growing larger and larger, it was impossible to ascertain how far away they were from the arrival point. The little dots down the side of the vessel that they were moving towards were thought to be windows but as they were getting nearer the construction was still growing, and the 'dots' turned out to be too big, and becoming bigger. This was amazing. How huge was this building going to be. Those windows turned out to be large solar cells, which must each have been the relative size of the very vessel in which they were traveling.

The approach seemed to go on forever, the construction was now completely obliterating any view of their planet behind it, and as they were arriving on the sunny side of the building the reflected light off the surface lit up the interior of their restaurant so brightly, that Lika remarked jokingly to Svi that she could get a sun tan from it. The illuminating power of the reflected sun paled even the strongest interior lighting in the sphere that had brought them there.

Lika lifted her hand to reach for Svi's, but she missed completely misjudging the weight of her hand as she lifted it from the table.

I forgot that we were on half gravity!" She laughed to Svi, as a sign came on above them warning against sudden movement. The gravity reduction had been very gradual since leaving their planet's gravitational field, because the artificial gravity system only took over very gently, and the standard mode for temporary transit work was only half gravity as too much cyclonic power was needed to create a full artificial gravity condition.

Through the large restaurant window Svi and Lika could see the surface of their destination but it was still growing and becoming much more detailed. The detail was beginning to show a slight roughness with shadows. At last the true dimension of the construction was coming into perspective as the small shadows began to move in relation to the movement of their own craft. Suddenly, a great big gaping hole appeared right in front of them. The great building began to turn through an anti-clockwise movement by about a quarter of a circle and stopped.

"That was our craft, that rotated" Svi remarked "We are obviously now lined up for entry". Everything seemed to go dark, and then as they re-adapted their vision to the lower illumination they could see that their hemisphere was traveling at moderate speed down a well internally lit tunnel. A pre-recorded voice broke into the silence; they seemed to be coming to a stop.

"Pick up your belongings, take young children by the hand and make your way to the nearest exit point. Do not make rapid movement; your sensation of gravity will be new to you. In this section of the transit station you will still be on half your usual gravity, so take care, and watch the children."

A child pulled away from his mother and decided to jump, just to try out the situation. 'Thwack' his head hit the ceiling with quite a thud, and back down he came again with tears rolling down his cheeks. The young mother tried to console her naughty young mischief. Lika smiled to herself with a tongue in cheek. That's just the kind of thing I would like to do, she thought to herself, as they moved with the crowd towards the exit.

Svi and Lika continued to be amazed at the size of everything. So far from home, and yet so many familiar home comforts, and such a vast expanse of area. Real estate acreage was infinite and so cheap in an extra-terrestrial environment. With radio-magnetic construction techniques size and difficulty was no problem. Everything was made on the ground back at home and brought up in flat packs. A whole new shell could be erected in hours from just one short shuttle trip. Svi took Lika's bags and threw them over his shoulder, he put his arm around her waist and as they stepped down onto the floor of the station, he whispered to Lika. "We have to report to the 'Bureau' over there and then we will be able to register for our accommodation. Only then can we open our sealed orders."

He gave Lika a hug, and they walked through without effort towards the Bureau. They were so tired, but so very happy.

"They say that making love in a state of weightlessness is the most incredible experience!" Lika smiled cheekily.

***

CHAPTER 6

Noah was becoming very angry and frustrated, his face was going redder and he was showing beads of perspiration on his forehead. The inane stupidity and lack of ability to grasp at the nettle of the problem was always typical of self-appointed government bodies, but this was the limit, thought Noah. Tubal Cain could see how Noah would explode if they continued with the sort of cross questioning that they were putting to him after he had delivered a very informative and detailed report. It was obvious that each member of the committee was only interested in furthering his or her own position of importance. Each member was using the period of questions to Noah, solely to get one up on his colleague by trying to score points, trying to be clever. Not one of the people present seemed genuinely concerned about the incipient dangers of neglect and treachery in the security system, and in very sensitive government departments in the Ministries of Defense and Safety. Noah had spent weeks preparing his report for the government, and the committee was only interested in how they could each use it for their own ends, he felt sick.

"Do you not realize that while we talk here, *bicker* and *argue*, serious breaches are taking place under our very noses? The Lyboncher explosion was not a result of neglect or bad management, but due to insufficient material thickness to the protective wall of the main core of the nuclear reactor. This was a result of deliberate pilfering and purloining of substantive building material that was needed when the reactor was re-furbished only a year before. These thefts were meticulously carried out and the final loss was very carefully covered up. Security forces have proved that only an insider would have been capable of doing what was done. We know that valuable raw material in very large quantities, not to mention the missing 'Radiact' has been finding its way to the state of Bylia. This is very serious because as you are aware, these materials need not only be used for peaceful purposes, but are the basic ingredients for the construction of a nuclear weapon. I would like to suggest to the committee that we give Tubal Cain's Science and Welfare Security Department full government backing to use the full force of the law to dig out the roots of this problem. Global peace itself could be at stake. The security forces should have full power to go unhindered in the pursuit of these villains.

Tubal Cain was watching the committee's faces very carefully as Noah asked for the absurd. He was sure that at least one member of the group would take the bait, but no one was so foolish. They all looked at each other and the main spokes person suggested that they put his suggestion before their committee in private. Noah then carried on.

"More of the defense budget should be allocated to the orbital extra-terrestrial program, as this means of global defense within the next ten years, could yield much more effective use of deterrent weaponry and also more global control of existing weapons. Also the resulting scientific developments in orbital space would benefit the human race as a whole. All major conflicting powers could be invited to take part and pool their ideas; true world peace with great depth of meaning would evolve as a result. Mutual trust and understanding between different cultures and social-economic groups could be a reality. We must expand the orbital defense system."

Tubal Cain was just about to interrupt Noah, with a suggestion to close, when Noah thanked all present, finished his summing up, and sat down to a mixed applause.

"You did go on a bit" Tubal mouthed to Noah "I am sure that some of them were bored to tears, and the platitudes at the end were somewhat obvious."

"We have to give them some excuse to make a decision. We all know that real decisions are made behind closed doors." Noah replied with a smile.

Tubal Cain stood up and walked over to the rostrum. The next ten minutes were taken up with a very carefully prepared supportive speech for Noah's report and suggestions. It was well presented without notes and Noah was very pleased, because it gave the very good impression that it had been impromptu.

It was a full working day before an indication of an answer came from the committee. They had agreed to recommend to the government a new policy to increase some expenditure on the defensive use of orbital space, but they were reluctant to offer any encouragement to the increasing of the powers of the security services. It was agreed that these services should be able to work well within the existing constraints. Nevertheless serious encouragement would be forthcoming from government resources if this were required.

Noah was delighted that the orbital development was to expand and he intended to get involved in that but he was a little bit concerned that no mole had shown up on the committee, because there was obviously one around.

***

The desert border between Orcamo and Bylia was very fierce under the midday sun. The permanently clouded sky still allowed the strength of the noonday sun to beat through. Small pale shadows could almost be perceived beneath their bodies on the ground as they walked across the sandy dunes in the direction of the wire fence of the International Emergency Safety Hospital at Larden. It was very hot, and the two people looked nothing like the Erash and Rula who only the day before had left the "House of Four Eyes" in Semir. To some extent, the couple had tried to look as if they had been in the desert for over a week, broken down in their hoversphere many miles away and had trudged overland to arrive with luck at Larden. In fact they had spent only the last hour and a half trudging through sand dunes in thick dry dust in the arid heat of the midday sun. They did not have to try; they already really looked the part, as refugees in time of war.

Erash had carefully burnt the back of his left hand and left leg before being dropped to the desert surface. The condition of his wounds looked suitably realistic to need attention in the hospital, and Rula's moral support was certainly needed. Erash was in acute pain, and the agonized expression on his face was definitely genuine, he would need treatment clearly very soon for his wounds or infection would follow.

The moment he entered the door, there was no need for rehearsal, Erash felt terrible, the heat, the pain and the thirst, he was quite giddy and the ground was moving like water. He couldn't remain upright, he just keeled over. It was a fortunate piece of luck that the male nurse just happened to catch him or his head would have hit the step as he fell. Rula did not have to look suitably worried; her concern was real. Another nurse appeared with a stretcher, and Erash was carefully taken into a small room where his wounds were dressed and he was made comfortable. Rula remained at his side all the time.

"Keep your eyes and ears open" Erash whispered to Rula "We may not be able to stay here very long. When my wounds are clear they will throw us out."

"Don't worry," Rula kissed him on the cheek "They will look after you, we will be out of here very soon" she tried to show Erash that she had heard and understood, by answering in that manner and in a loud voice for all to hear.

A nurse or young doctor came into the room carrying a large clipboard.

"Where is your identity disc?" he was asking Erash "We need to know who you both are."

"We are both refugees and have disposed of our discs on our way here. We didn't want to be picked up by the wrong side" interrupted Rula, "My colleague needed medical help urgently."

"And which is the wrong side asked the man with the clip board?"

"The other side" Erash interrupted this time.

"Very well answered," the man retorted.

"You know that you are not allowed to ask these questions" Rula interjected "This is an international haven for all wounded. Your duty is only to help the visitor, then send him on his way. The motto is clearly printed in stone above the main entrance of this establishment; you should go out and read it." Rula was becoming quite argumentative.

The man made a few notes on his clipboard excused himself to them, and then left. Erash and Rula were very tired. Although it was only early afternoon, they were not used to the strong humidity and the hot hazy sun. They had traveled a long way from Semir, and it had not been over comfortable, but they had at least arrived in one piece...at least almost. Rula sat next to Erash holding his right hand. She sat back in the chair that she was sitting in, and almost immediately fell fast asleep. Erash felt her hand go limp as she drifted off. How he envied her. She could fall asleep anywhere. He lay there just looking at Rula, a perfect specimen of woman kind, he would let her sleep, she obviously needed it.

He didn't know whether he had dozed off himself but he was brought to full consciousness by the noise outside of heavy running footsteps going past his door. There must have been at least six pairs of feet, like a small group of soldiers on fixed forced march, on the double. He thought that odd, because soldiers were not allowed to operate within the area of the hospital without express detailed permission.

There was a commotion some short distance away, perhaps down the corridor in one of the adjoining offices. Erash could hear shouting and someone was fighting, there was a loud noise, as if something had fallen from a great height. All hell seemed to be let loose, and suddenly they were plunged into darkness, all the lights had gone out. It was pitch black; Erash realized he must have slept through, past nightfall. There were no windows to his room, but there was not even a chink of light coming from under the door. He tried to awaken Rula, but she was out cold, as if in a drugged stupor. He carefully climbed out of bed, and managed to stand in the corner behind the door. At least in that position he would have the advantage over any stranger entering the room. He tried to leave his bed in a mess with one of the pair of cushions tucked up under the bedclothes in order to give the appearance that he was still in it. There were great difficulties for Erash trying to do all this on strange territory, without any light. His eyes had dark adapted, but it was still very difficult to see in his 'cell'.

Suddenly the door opened without warning and a beam of bright white light entered the room and went straight to the bed. The brightness of the beam showed the image of a sleeping mound, but a side cabinet near the door seemed to protect Rula from the searching beam of light. Her experience on active duty and her built in instincts save her from the devastation of the paresifier gun that was to follow. She dived to the floor out of sight, completely unnoticed. The paresifier's attack on the bed was short lived and left positively no damage. The intruder could be heard moving on farther down the corridor. Erash gently putting his little toe on the bottom of the still open door, he nudged it back into the closed position as if it had done so under its own weight. He was trying very carefully to give the impression that there was no one in the room. He could still hear his pigeons in the corridor but apart from that the noise seemed to have abated. There was the occasional vehicle and now and again the sound of a person running but otherwise not a sound. The quiet periods seemed to get longer and longer, eventually Erash crawled over to Rula, which was a very difficult exercise in total darkness.

"Are you alright?" He whispered across to Rula who offered an affirmative reply. They knew to keep the conversation down to the barest minimum.

The announcement on the tannoy came from nowhere.

"We of the Bylian liberated army are assuming complete command of this hospital and its enclosure. The Orcamo government have many of our people as political prisoners, and until they are released you will remain here as our guests. We apologize for any inconvenience. The light will be restored immediately, or even sooner, but those of you on dialysis and life support machines will be safe. You are on automatic emergency power supply running off the generator. We appeal to any hospital worker who cannot see his or her way to continue working in this hospital under our command to please come forward to the reception office where a free passage out of this establishment will be guaranteed into whichever country you choose, Bylia or Orcamo. Please be quick, this guarantee will only last one hour."

Erash took Rula's hand and they made for the door, crawling on all fours. The first thing Erash saw was a pair of feet on the other side, under the door, as the lights all came back on. Rula had seen them as well, and indicated this to Erash. "He must be on guard" he stated the obvious. The two of them stood up and brushed themselves down. There was dust everywhere, and black atmospheric dust mixed in as well. They felt very dirty, but they decided to take a calculated risk. Erash stood behind the door, as Rula opened it and beckoned the stranger to come in. He was only a young lad and Rula felt guilty setting the trap for him. Erash was now behind him, as he took the cover off an anesthetic aerosol and squirted it at the back of the stranger's head. The noise of the rush of the spray made him turn around, and he received full frontal force of the anesthetic in his face. He felt to the ground, they left him where he lay, as they disappeared down the corridor. That sleep had given Erash newfound energy, he was feeling much better. They climbed the staircase at the end of the corridor and found themselves on the galleried landing of the reception hall. Looking down they could see about nine members of the hospital staff in an orderly queue for the reception desk. There were two young lads, three young not unattractive women, and four older members equally divided between both sexes. They were all showing their identity discs and signing a piece of paper that was put in front of them, they were asked to move along to the front door and be prepared to leave. They were well kitted out for this event. The three young women were called back to reception, some error in their papers the guard announced to them very clearly. Erash watched the three women with great intent. They were certainly very attractive and had lovely bodies. He felt Rula's hand freeze hard with shock as she showed Erash what she had perceived. The six departing work people marched to the long high perimeter wire near the exit gate. The column of six was queuing up against the wire awaiting their allowed exit to the outside world. It happened so quickly; it was as much as Erash could do to stop Rula screaming. The line of six people were just mown down where they stood, and seconds later, the guards came along with flame throwers to burn out the evidence. The three surviving girls were quite oblivious to the goings on outside, in fact it was quite possible that nobody would have seen what had happened outside in the forecourt area, as the flood lights were all directed at the building and it was very difficult to see through the glare, unless on the first floor landing, which was above the glare level. It happened that only Erash and Rula were at first floor level at that moment on that side of the building and therefore were the sole witnesses to the mass murder of the hospital staff. Rula as a very hardened agent had seen plenty of action, but she was shocked to bewilderment on the sudden surge of violence which was wholly unnecessary, totally unprovoked and without any apparent real purpose. Erash was not timid by nature, but since his arrival in Semir and his meeting with Rula he had found more confidence and certainly more courage. This happening only showed Erash in a better light as he tried to offer solace and direction to Rula's broken pride.

"Where have they taken the three girls?" He asked Rula trying to distract her from the immediate memory of the massacre. "They seem to have disappeared!" Erash whispered quietly to Rula.

"They will have numbers tattooed permanently on their backside like cattle, and then they will be sent for 'usage' by the troops in the Bylian command. Those poor girls will be diseased and dead by the end of the year, if they are lucky. They will suffer such humiliation, and punishment they will pray for death to release them. They would have been better off with their colleagues out in the yard.

They heard approaching footsteps, coming their way. Erash grabbed Rula's forearm and pulled.

"Quick!" he mouthed as loudly as he dared "Let's move or we will be found here and that could be our lot. Back to the room, before we forget what we are meant to be."

The intrepid couple eventually made it back to their room and closed the door.

"He's gone!" Rula showed surprise "That anesthetic should have knocked him out for two or three hours!"

"Look at the bed sheets, they have been pulled at the bottom, he must have been dragged out, while still unconscious. That means he might think they did it to him, as he never saw me" said Erash, feeling quite pleased with himself. Rula did not know how to take that, as she knew that she would easily be identified. Then Erash continued "Come on, we had better bed down or they might get suspicious….."

The door flew open and three men stood there in yellow Bylian uniforms. The one in the middle spoke; he had a wide toothy grin. "Mr. Erash, you and your friend will be our guests in this hotel for some while, so please help us to help you make your stay as comfortable as possible."

***

The Orbital station had no symmetry; it was not designed to look beautiful from the outside. It had no need to be built in a formal manner, as natural gravity was so minimal from the mother planet. It was almost immeasurable. Each section was added whenever needed, and whenever most convenient. The orbital station was growing with nearly every shuttle visit. Flat packs were arriving all the time and were being added with great vigor. In the year that Svi and Lika would be on board the station, it should increase in size multifold. It was with this pioneering spirit that Svi and Lika had accepted the allocation of their new apartment in the new sector on the outer edge of main section "6". This area was still under partial construction and had not had any artificial gravity installed as yet. Total weightlessness was a novelty to the happy couple, but they would soon get tired of it.

They entered Section 6 through an old air lock, which now acted only as a safety valve in case of trouble. The section in which they were to be resident was very new and only recently connected to the main shell of the orbital station, a natural atmosphere had only just been infused, and Lika remarked to Svi how much it smelled like 'rust'. After passing through the 'air lock valve' into new section 6 they felt a weakening of the gravity and they were beginning to feel somewhat lighter in their walk. They began to take hold of the guide-rail at the side of the corridor, which helped them along their way.

"Look!" said Svi, "You don't have to walk we can just glide along now floating free" Svi was beginning to look silly, he had apparently lost his balance and was moving away from her quite fast along the corridor with his feet straight out in front of him and his whole body tilted backwards. He had their entire luggage moving along next to him but quite unattached. Lika put her hand to her mouth she could not believe her eyes. Her husband looked so funny. She was finding it very difficult to suppress her mirth.

"That's our door, the pink one, on the left. Number 167. Lika was thrilled that they had arrived. Svi grabbed the handle as he went passed and he managed to stop. The luggage carried on down the corridor. Lika shouted to Svi to watch out for it, but he had had foresight to tie the belongings to his waist on a long tow for just such an occasion as this. He gave a very gentle pull and the cases started back on their return journey up the corridor. Svi managed to stop them at the apartment door.

Svi took Lika's arm and put his own arm under her thighs so that she was cradled in his arms in the seated position, and she, holding the key, which they had been issued in G.C.Eton, put it against the door handle and magnetically it opened the door. They entered the apartment in that manner in tight embrace. Their luggage obediently followed behind.

They closed the door, and were together at last, in their new home for the first time, they were totally exhausted. It was a whole new world of strange experiences, and so very different. The reality of the situation was impossible to take in all at once. They took their cases and attached them to the luggage clamps so that they could un-pack. This was like a holiday. The apartment had three areas made up as a kitchen and eating area, a bathing, washing and toilet area, and a sleeping and leisure area. Its size was that of a large hotel apartment, not too big but definitely not small. There were all facilities that they could need. They knew that they were going to be happy there. Too tired for anything else, they slid into bed among many pillows and zipped themselves in. Svi and Lika were asleep, they had postponed their pleasures until they were awake enough to enjoy them, their energies were zapped, and the journey had taken its toll. They would open their sealed orders in the 'morning'. They just lay tied together in each other's arms oblivious to anything other than themselves, in total darkness.

Lika's eyes opened to the sight of color images moving across the opposite wall, like running water but changing through all colors of the spectrum. She had seen that reproduced in the Palace of Memories, and also in Laboratory experiments using prisms, but where was this coming from. It was most unusual, she didn't want to waken Svi, but that would prove difficult the way they were laying. She watched the colors; they were getting brighter and stronger. There appeared to be no windows to their rooms, so where was the light coming from? Lika tried to look around without disturbing her husband's slumber, and she noticed that the wall was not completely opaque in places. There were in fact, several areas of size that seemed very slightly translucent, and it was light from outside that was passing through that surface which was breaking up into the various spectral colors so easily. Then she realized that it was dawn. The sun was beginning to appear on the horizon of the mother planet, and the brilliant illumination was starting to break its way into the apartment. The walls obviously had window material built into it that was photochromic, variable light protective to the inhabitants. Also she could see its surface was double layered made of very fine grooved stripes which helped to regulate the blur, as two surfaces were in opposition to one another. The inner surface could be magnetically moved sideways thus allowing a perfect match of surfaces and a full picture of the outside would be freely available. She had learned all about this at college. She decided to leave well alone, the sun should be fully exposed to the Orbital Station within a very short time, and she would let its blurred image awaken Svi.

Svi's face was going red with rage; he had just opened their sealed orders.

"We've been duped! This is outrageous and totally immoral! I can't believe it Lika; they surely can't mean all this! It is terrible. Here, take a look." Svi threw the notes across the room at Lika in disgust. He had completely forgotten the weightlessness situation and they just kept on going straight into Lika's face.

"Thank you!" smirked Lika as she took the full force of movement in her face "That hurt."

She took them in her hand and opened the file. She became equally startled at the message that was unfolding.

"How could they do that and why? What are these people out to prove? They can't be serious, and it is immoral if ethical at all. "Lika was very indignant, they had come all this way in good faith and were given a task such as this. It was against all morality to go forward. How could they use humans for experimentation, especially young babies? Lika began to read the sealed orders all over again out loud to Svi, she thought maybe that way it would sound more realistic, and less incredible.

Lika read:

"A study of the effects of environment on the human mind. There is a deep and full examination to be conducted in the strict ethos of the extra-terrestrial community.

The aim of this experiment is to discover how the human character can develop from its primitive and natural state without any interference or help from the outside world environment.

Subjects for these experiments will be newly born infants who have been taken directly from their umbilical cord. They should neither see or be seen by their natural or surrogate mother. Children are to be monitored at all stages in their development, in an unobtrusive manner, and in complete secrecy. This research has already been in progress many years, and will now continue on a permanent basis. The facilities are given top priority from Science and Welfare benefit-research funding, but complete secrecy is positively essential. ANY BREACH OF CONFIDENCE WILL RESULT IN SEVERE DISTRESS FOR THE CULPRITS' FAMILY. The mere fact that this knowledge is in the reader's possession commits him/her to its confidence and the consequences. This work is of major importance in man's understanding of man."

As Lika looked at Svi, the astonishment was expressed clearly in her face.

"What do *you* think we should do?" Lika questioned. Svi sat there in silence, meticulously tapping his fingers on the arm of his chair. He was deep in thought. "I look at it this way," he started to reply after a seemingly never ending period of careful consideration "this research is on-going, and other fellow human beings are involved as subjects. We cannot stop the experiment and if we drop out someone else will step in our place and they may not be as conscientious as the two of us. I believe that we should stick it out for the year and do what we can to guide the research project in the right direction."

"I couldn't have stated a better case myself." Lika answered very delighted, she nearly hit the ceiling as she stood up from her seat; again forgetting the non-gravity effect and gripping at the arm of the seat protected her from further embarrassment.

"It says that we have to report to the central core of 'B Section' this morning in order to pick up our briefing, and we are to be given a short instructive lecture on progress so far." Svi was showing some enthusiasm in his voice.

"You know" Lika remarked, "I am getting quite keen on this myself" she smiled, and flew over into Svi's arms. He didn't argue. Making love without gravity, was more than remarkable, it was highly skilled. They would obviously both have to learn, but that should be fun.

***

Naamah's face could hold no secret from Noah, he knew what she was going to tell him, and before she could even open her mouth he was already holding her tight in his arms, and kissed her passionately. "I know," he said "I am so happy, you are with child, you are pregnant," he whispered in her ear.

"How did you know?" Naamah asked in astonishment. "I knew, I just knew. The moment I left the meeting this afternoon, something came into my mind..."

"That's when I knew!" Naamah interrupted "I was at the doctor this afternoon for my test reports. He showed me the scan. It was positive. We are going to have a boy. I'm a quarter of the way through already. Can we call him 'Shem' after the little oasis in the dry dusty desert where we met? It was a place full of life and promise. It is where we fell in love, and I gave you my virginity." Naamah tucked her head deep into Noah's chest; she had a single tear in her eye. She was so very happy.

"That's the most wonderful news 'Shem' a son please god our first-born will thrive and that Oasis will never be forgotten." He took Naamah's face in both hands and looked straight at her. She was looking so beautiful. Her eyes were looking directly up into his. This was a moment in both of their lives that they would never forget. Noah took her face and kissed it very hard on the lips. The response was immediate and within a moment, Noah and Naamah were on their rug in front of the open fire. It was an otherwise cold evening, what a wonderful way to keep warm.

Naamah cuddled up tight into Noah's arms, she could feel the strength from his chest, as she tried so hard to bury herself into her husband's grasp. She so desperately wanted to be every part an extension of his mind and body.

"I do so want to have your child" she murmured "I am so happy." She was smiling very softly to herself. "I find it so wonderful that I am walking around with a part of you permanently inside me. Everywhere I go, I can't stop thinking about it. I walk down the street and smile for no obvious reason. I foolishly believe that people can see my baby inside me even now, but I can still get into my bikini without any problem, and I know that in truth I still look the same." Naamah was rambling on, but for once, Noah was listening.

"You make me feel so proud my darling. I will watch you grow, and please be careful; we want Shem to be born a fine and healthy specimen of man. You must help me to help you. When you need me, you must tell me, after all I am only a man." Noah was rambling now, he realized it, and changed the subject, very slightly.

"What kind of world are we bringing a poor unsuspecting child into? We owe it to him to give him a chance for his future, but instead of creating an environmental dream, we are creating an environmental nightmare. Our world could explode around us, I have said it before, and I'll say it again we are eating the fruits and drinking the wines that were planted and laid down by our forefathers, but we aren't replenishing our stocks, and soon if not already, in some places, there will be nothing left but desert. I am determined to do something about it, people are fickle, but perhaps one day they will listen to me. It should be remembered that as we shall sew, so should we reap."

"That's very profound" Naamah sighed into Noah's right ear.

They were obviously so very much in love with each other. "By the way," Naamah whispered as if she was keeping a secret from anyone else in the room "Did you know that 'Thopia' just south east of Bylia has suffered a third year of total drought. That country is really suffering from the effects of man's destruction of the environment. It has been proved that the lack of rainfall is due to the 'Jastics' cutting down their forests a whole western ocean away. Will this tragedy ever end?"

"Or is it just beginning?" Noah answered glumly. The two people cuddled up together in front of their fire and fell asleep wrapped in each other's embraces. Little could they have then known that which was to be their destiny?

***

Glenshee was crying hysterically, she was kneeling on all fours in front of Jabal, begging him, that now she was with Rastus's first child inside her, could he please save her husband from going away again. She knew that it was very dangerous and that she may never see the father of her future child again.

"If he is discovered, he will be tortured . . . and killed if he is lucky. If he is unlucky he will be allowed to live a little longer. They do terrible things to the hybrid." Glenshee was nearly exhausted from her pleading.

"I understand" Jabal answered "but Rastus is very familiar with the problem so far, and I can't trust many of my hybrids more than I can trust your husband. He would be like my own son, had I had one." There were very few herdsmen as kind as Jabal. It was certainly unusual for a master, to listen to the unsolicited pleas of one of his hybrids, but then Jabal *was* different.

"We have to follow up the only good lead that we have" Jabal continued "These people are organized and they have tried to let me know by their visit here the other night that they disapprove of my friendly attitude towards the hybrid. Take great heed Glenshee; these people could destroy us if we are not careful. Your husband is a very brave member of your race. He must go, and will. In fact he would be very upset if I didn't let him."

It was at that moment, the door behind Jabal opened, and the eyes of Rastus and Glenshee met in surprise.

"What are you doing here?" Rastus asked his wife. "No don't bother to answer, I know. I thank you anyway but I can handle it. I am not intending to be a martyr to the cause, but I am determined to inflict a great deal of damage on the aggressor....."

"You will do no such thing" interrupted Jabal "You will seek the roots of this movement, and report back to me. Until we know who and what we are up against, we cannot afford to strike back. I am sending a human companion with you." Jabal pushed a small button on his intercom unit. "Send up Lex. Tell him that Rastus is here."

'Lex' was a very well built curly haired blond man who was a good head and shoulders above Rastus. When he arrived on the scene Glenshee's face changed from frustration to hope. This man, she knew would protect her Rastus from almost certain death if he went alone.

"Lex" Jabal spoke "You will be Rastus's master and prefect. He belongs to you for the purposes of this mission." Jabal was speaking with authority "You will be able to go almost anywhere as a partnership. Seek out that vermin and you shall find it. Please report back here, we need to know whom we are up against. Oh, by the way, you are both charged with the order to guarantee the safe return of your partner."

Rastus could not stop thinking of Glenshee's woeful face as he had left her two days previously. Her concealed worries had been somewhat placated by the arrival of Lex, but he wondered whether he would ever see his child. Terrible things were going on, hybrids were easy prey to these thugs and bullies and no law seemed strong enough to protect them.

Waiting was something that Rastus found very unnerving. All these thoughts just kept passing through his mind as he lay there in the thicket at the edge of the old railway sidings. Lex had been gone for more than an hour and should be back very shortly with some news. They had followed the stereophonic signal to this location but all they found was the empty hoversphere. What in the world would anybody want in these old railway sidings? This form of transport was archaic. It was known to be the most uncomfortable form of transport in modern times. It moved along the ground and maintained permanent contact physically with metal rails underneath. It was so primitive that the only vehicles seen in use nowadays were cattle trucks with large sliding doors and no windows except for an old barred hole for air. They were used for transporting livestock from one part of the country to another.

The silence seemed to be death itself. Rastus could not see very far because a mist had fallen overnight and the early morning dew did not seem to improve the situation. The dampening fog gave him a mixed feeling of fear and security, while simple sounds seemed to be at full volume as even the tiniest noise seemed to echo through the low cloudy haze. The fact that the silence was so clean seemed to suggest to Rastus a serious impending danger of which he should be acutely aware. He didn't know why, but he felt that something he was not going to like was about to happen. The atmosphere was electrifying in Rastus's mind. The complete non-existence of aural stimulation was an impossibility in Rastus's understanding; he was beginning to pray for something to happen.

There was a broken twig cracking not far behind him. He made to turn around, and then he felt the grip on his left arm.

"Lex! Am I pleased to see you" Rastus exclaimed in a loud whisper. "Where have you been? You must have been away about half the night."

"I can't make it out." Lex went into detail as he lay down next to his colleague. "The tracks are well polished and have been used recently. One of them leads into an old barn where it stops. There is enough room in that barn to house a whole train length. There are old stable areas, which have obviously been recently renewed for some form of private use, as they have been re-fenced and partitioned with the correct materials. Through the wide door at the end of the barn there is a walkway, which at a small turnstile type gate divides into two, and goes on in different directions. One of them leads to a shower room and then through another door into a gym. The other side seems to go nowhere, except toward another shower room with a door in the side that could never open. Its just decoration, but it looks real enough, from the other shower room. There is a terrible feeling of...I can't describe it...in the air. I knew that I shouldn't be there. It's very frightening. If I were not sane, I would say it was a haunted place. I then walked another short distance down another railway track, which is also well polished. It runs out from the shower room with the artificial door, down through a gully that can't be seen from the road into another yard of a large gray concrete building with three tall wide chimneys. This may have been a large metal forge many years ago, but today the smell was sweet and strange. I have smelled it before, and can't place it but I do know that there is a feeling of the presence of danger...great danger!"

Rastus was hypnotized by Lex's description of the nearby buildings and out houses. He was busy trying to work out the true meaning for these places but unfortunately very soon these questions were to be answered.

Perhaps they had slept, and perhaps they had not, but the time while they were together seemed to be a lot easier to face, at the side of those tracks. They must have been there a long time. They saw the mist rise and day became quite bright by modern standards. The whole geography of the place did not seem too spoilt by environmental changes. There was still some green grass, and a beautiful rose hedge that led from the railway track up to the shower room, on the outside. The roses were in bloom and Rastus could smell the scent from where he was lying. He just could not take his eyes off them. He so much wanted to break cover to go and smell them. The pink colors with a tinge of red, so very beautiful, a piece of godliness in this seemingly completely unholy place. He was very tempted to run for it. He looked at Lex he was deep in thought, as if many miles away. Yes he thought, he will go for it, a short dash, it was only ten or fifteen paces, and he could be back with his bloom. Oh what a prize. He had not seen the like before except in picture books. He certainly had never experienced that perfumed fragrance he could smell from afar.

He was already running, it was not very far; he pulled the knife out of his sock and took two blooms, why not he thought. The smell nearly overpowered him it was a touch of ecstasy. Then he saw not much further along the path, an orchid, he could not believe his luck. Nobody will miss that; the colors were a vivid blue. He had to have it he turned to move on, he must have it, and he would be quick. He might be seen, and he was a hybrid, he was running again, and without warning he was falling on his face. He had been felled by someone jumping for his legs. As he fell he was more concerned about his flowers than his person. He gathered the two blooms with his grazed hands and looked behind at his feet. It was Lex who had brought him down. Lex was standing up again he brushed himself down and picked up a long piece of cane from the side of the road. 'Thwack", hard right across Rastus's back. He did it again 'Thwack' with real venom in his voice. Rastus yowled!

"You are nothing but vermin, trying to escape from me like that. Your master would have you castrated for less. 'Thwack' again across his face this time, but not enough to draw blood. It was just enough, Lex hoped, to satisfy the curiosity of the two guards in their black and silver uniforms who were approaching rather hurriedly.

***

CHAPTER 7

The lecture continued . . .

"This is a farm, essentially a farm for breeding and observing the habits of the human being, unadulterated by a developed environment, but totally enclosed in the confines of this space capsule in Central Core of B. Section. We only observe. Under no circumstances must any non-recognized experimental involvement ever take place. This would invalidate the project and result in prosecutions. The sentence is death by garrote or electrocution for any instigating offender. Just remember you walk the tight rope of knowledge, a very tricky one, and it cannot be treated lightly, it is a privilege to be here."

Svi and Lika were completely absorbed in the lecture. The idea of watching the human in his primitive state seemed immoral to both of them, but they could not help agreeing with each other, that it was both exciting and extremely exhilarating. Farming human beings in their natural environment was a concept that had been discussed for many years back at home. The reality of doing it seemed an impossibility, as well as an absurdity, but today, anything seems to be accepted as normal. Svi nudged Lika with encouragement, he gave her a soft smile, which she acknowledged and returned. She put her finger to her mouth for quiet, as the lecture continued…..

"Several versions of this project are taking place within laboratories in many stations throughout orbital space. We are all collaborating with each other, and you will be able to visit the other areas of study. It is important to maintain complete all round observation, and never should any of the subjects be allowed to suspect or have even the slightest rudiment of suspicion that he is not his own creature and in his own world. At no time should you feel remorse or pity for these beings. Just remember, they have either been bred in the laboratory specifically for this purpose and would otherwise never have existed, or they are unwanted children for one reason or another, who would by law have had to be destroyed at eight days old if no parent was available and ready for them. All these children would otherwise not be alive if it was not for the experiment. The children in this section are all white and fair skinned, but other sections have got hybrids, green human giants, a very rare species indeed, and there are several versions of clones in other areas of orbital space."

"Clones?" Lika queried in a whisper to Svi, "I thought that they were illegal?"

Svi turned to Lika "They are illegal at home, but out here the laws are set by orbital Government, and cloning is legal by virtue of not being illegal."

The tall blonde man in a lecturer's black gown with its striking silver edging, which was swathed down to his ankles, continued with his oration. His voice was full of authority. A confidence of manner, which Svi was sure, was generated from that gown.

"You will be required to take notes and make summary comments and reports on your observations. As you will soon see, you will be able to watch these people from many positions and vantage points throughout the thousands of acres of experimental area. They cannot see you at all because the surface through which you are viewing them only allows light to pass through in one direction towards the observer. Any light outside the observation cubicle will stay there. You will be pleased to know that this will make your observation of them completely invisible. Indeed, they could be looking straight into your face, and they will not see you. You will find this very disconcerting I am sure. The observation bubbles that you will be inside will appear to these people as large rocks, or boulders and they will be completely solid in appearance to them. There are also holographic telescopic cameras in the natural habitat and some video two-dimension cameras as well. This will allow you freedom to refer to the screens or holograms in your own apartment. You will be able to record and replay any situation that you think important to your work. This on going experiment should benefit mankind in the long term as our knowledge of human psychology and interdependence will be viewed in a very unusual manner. This work is vital and is one of the subjects at the top of the project list for our research work out here in orbital space. There will be possibilities to visit one of the observation areas at the end of this lecture. It is important that you can assimilate the problems and recognize changes in behavior, you will be given some time to settle in, and I am sure that when we ask you for your first reports they will be very interesting and original."

After a few finer points of information the hologram had dissolved and the blonde gowned figure had disappeared. The lecture was terminated.

Svi and Lika made their way to a nearby observation post at just above ground level in the side of a small cliff about three miles into the experimental area. This position as with all others was reached by silent magnetic 'underground' monorail. 'Underground' is only a descriptive term as meaning undersurface, as this part of the station had full half gravity, and therefore direction did have some meaning. "What a magnificent view" Lika couldn't believe her eyes. There seemed to be a whole geography laid out in front of them. There were hills, woods and plenty of greenery as no longer seen on the mother planet. It was so clean and pure in appearance. Running water, the odd waterfall, the fruit trees, and sunlight, 'real' sunlight! Svi and Lika knew that the entire area was enclosed, and cocooned away from public view. There was no way that the 'real' sunlight effect could be other than artificial, but it was so ingeniously reproduced as if real. The use of prisms and a small moving single light source produced the overall effect of a moving sun on its' daily journey across the sky. This was certainly something that had not been properly seen back home for many decades. Lika pulled gently on Svi's arm; she had seen something and pointed it out. "Look! That is a young child over there, at the edge of the stream. It's taking a drink with cupped hands. "The naked little girl, sat there on crouched knees with her feet in the stream as if playing with the water as it ran through her open legs. "How old would you say she was?" Lika turned again to Svi, who had not said anything since they had arrived. He was completely overcome in awe of the occasion.

"She is very young." Svi easily assessed the obvious. She is a very pretty little thing, her chubby little face with a wide grin, and little dimples in her cheeks. She is really enjoying herself isn't she? She loves the water. She sounds like she is cooing or singing. The noise is very beautiful, but nothing I recognize. It's like an overgrown baby singing in her cradle. That is a baby! That child has never heard real language she has been there fending for herself since the day she was born, and with the exception of artificial teat feeding by remote control as a baby, she has never had conscious contact with the outside world ever in her short life. How could she have learned to speak?" Svi turned to Lika; the new enthusiasm in his voice was showing in his face as with a loving smile, he gave Lika a warm, passionate kiss on the side of her neck. Lika could not take her eyes off the little child. She was obviously becoming a broody hen.

***

Tubal Cain appeared at Noah's door early that morning. His face was angry and full of urgency.

"I must talk to you Noah, it's very important; I couldn't even use the scrambler on the televideo in case the news leaked out. I had to come and tell you in person.

Noah invited Tubal to enter his abode, and they went together to the toilet where Tubal turned on the running water, in case there were secret listening devices about.

"Security is perfect here" Noah's pride was obviously hurt. Tubal Cain interrupted Noah before he had the chance of becoming quite verbal.

"It's Erash! He's in trouble. He is being held as a hostage. They have sent us some of his hair and his security disc. They threaten to kill his young woman if we don't reply to their demands. We don't know who has him captive, and we don't know of any woman. The last message we had from him, he was in Semir and had made contact with a friendly organization of freedom fighters, perhaps from Bylia. We certainly don't know where he is now. They have given us one day to reply."

Tubal Cain seemed embarrassed and perhaps Noah was unwittingly rubbing it in. "They are sending a courier to my office of Science and Welfare tomorrow morning. They want to know if we will trade arms and supplies for Erash and his woman's release, but we don't talk to kidnappers or terrorists, how can we make an exception? They might kill that poor woman, and we don't even know who or what she is."

Noah started to think aloud, he started tapping his fingers on the window sill. He was getting very impatient with himself there must be a counter measure that would protect the situation. "The most urgent matter to attend to, is to keep them thinking that we are interested in a deal, but we must not be seen to take part in negotiation. That young woman's life must be taken out of danger." Noah was wandering on "We either defend against these people or we attack. We cannot ignore them. They won't go away." He turned to Tubal and showed signs of an inspiration…"What about the hand? That would be a gamble, but it might work. Do we know where it went?"

"It is just possible that a transmitting device may have been implanted in it at the police pathology lab, when it was in custody. It is standard practice in some places for purposes of identity at a later date." Tubal went out to the televideo phone in the hall. "I'll ring the office, let's find out right now." Noah went over to the small low table and sat in one of his easy chairs; he took out a pencil and started to doodle on the note pad. In fact Noah was quite an artist, often he would sit and sketch out diagrams, drawings or patterns on any spare piece of paper. It was a mild form of escapism, or relaxation when his mind was in tension. He found it worked well for him.

"What's that?" Tubal said, looking over Noah's shoulder. "You have drawn a pattern of that children's game we used to play so many years ago. What was it called?" Tubal scratched his head "'Clargy, beat your neighbor out of doors!' That's it. That is the game where one used to try to commit a misdemeanor and get someone else to take the blame. It is also where one tried very hard to get the credit for someone else's good deeds. Do you remember? We used to play it for hours. Jabal hated losing but he always took it in good fun."

"What happened about the hand?" Noah asked in a veiled whisper coming back to the point.

"They are going to check and ring us back" Tubal was still amused at his recollections of his childhood. "That's it! You have given me the answer in that game. "Tubal was full of himself. The germination of an idea was beginning to explode in his mind and he was becoming quite excited. He sat down next to Noah and in a whisper gestured him back to the toilet room and the running water.

"We shall deal through a third party, and even they won't know what the real situation is. There will be no dealing with terrorists, at least not directly. Someone else can take the blame. We shall keep our noses clean, and still rescue Erash and his 'friend'!" Tubal Cain was thinking aloud, and the ideas seemed to be forming a plan in his mind as he spoke.

Noah was listening with an interested patience. "One thing that the Postations have a great deal of are nuts." Noah mused quite audibly to Tubal Cain.

"What on your life, are you talking about? Queried Tubal Cain. "What have nuts go to do with Erash, and why Postia?" Noah was now fully aware of his own new idea.

"Postia is a friendly country to us, and to Bylia. It is quite neutral in its politics with Orcamo and Cabu. In fact it is a state of few enemies and poses no threat to peace. We could easily buy large quantities of their 'Postation nuts', in exchange for arms and supplies of munitions. "Noah had a wicked grin on his face, completely out of character for him. "What Postia did with their 'loot' would be their business. If they chose to sell them on to….. Bylia for example, then that is up to them. That's how we get out of this one!" Noah was very pleased with himself.

"A wonderful idea!" Tubal Cain exclaimed. The relief that a possible solution had been found had given him a new hope. "In negotiation Postia can seek the return of Erash and his friend as part of their deal, which of course would be our deal, as Postia would only be in it, acting as agents for profit." Tubal Cain had relief in his voice. "But we are still not sure where Erash is. We had better work fast."

***

The two guards bodily lifted Rastus from the graveled path, and held him securely between them. The heavier guard then thumped his knee brutally into Rastus's lower spine from behind while the other held him very professionally. They turned him to face Lex who now had a nervous sweat pouring down his face.

The shorter of the two guards the one who had given Rastus his knee in the back addressed his attention to Lex whilst still maintaining his grip on Rastus. They almost had the hybrid bent back double in the standing position, looking directly up at the sky.

"Is this one of yours?" The guard asked Lex "He's mine on loan for a few days. You can check his markings and identification number. You will find that he is one of Jabal's herd and he is helping me collect rocks for a geological study we are doing." Lex was thinking quickly. Keeping as near to the truth as possible, was always the best policy. That way it was easier to prove one's cover story.

The guard gave a visual command to his taller colleague who immediately took both of Rastus's arms and bending them behind his back pushed him forward head first bent over a metal barred gate. The other guard pulled at Rastus's clothes exposing his bare backside. There, neatly tattooed across the right cheek just above the thigh was a string of numbers, and a badge-mark 'seven sheaths of corn by a river'. The guard made a copy of what he saw and then without warning the two guards took Rastus and threw him into the shed at the side of the track.

"We will investigate his credentials. Let him have some solitary confinement for the rest of the day. The heat will do him good, a suitable punishment for his running away." The shorter guard smiled to Lex. "You may come with us for some breakfast if you wish while we check him out." The guard was bolting the small shed, which was no larger than a dog kennel.

Lex accepted their invitation to a late breakfast graciously, but feeling a certain degree of sadness at leaving his friend and colleague behind in a 'dog's kennel' no matter how temporary it may be. The heat of the sun although hazy could wreak havoc on a poor encapsulated body locked up with no water for a day. A hybrid his size could barely move cooped up in such a small space. He could not even unfold his arms to full length, and his legs would be in a permanent crouching position. He would surely be in pain before long.

The two guards took Lex to a small mobile cabin not far from the sidings but quite high up on the side of the hill, which gave a good panoramic view of the whole area. Lex could see everything that was possible from this vantage point. If the guards had been watching earlier they would certainly have seen Rastus and Lex arrive. They may even have had their suspicions aroused when Lex went investigating the buildings. He was worried but covered it up very well, as he tucked in to a cooked breakfast.

"Don't you think you ought to check-out my hybrid's credentials" Lex asked casually "So that we can get on our way?"

"Not a chance" The shorter more authoritative guard replied. "We have to let him stew for a while. He did try to make a run for it, didn't he?"

"I suppose so" Lex replied "Perhaps I'm rather soft, but he is usually a very good worker. They are difficult to find these days."

"How right you are. We have to use the whip more than ever now, but they are becoming a little more resilient all the time. Only last week I had to break one of their ankles with an old rifle-butt before I could get one to move. Hybrids are beginning to get too forward and somewhat independent. We have to stop them before it gets out of hand, and they overrun us. Don't you agree?" The guard stood up, as an old railway bell rang in a nearby signal box. The bleeper started in the other guard's breast pocket.

"It must be due very soon sir." The second guard spoke, a very rare occurrence indeed!!

"I'm afraid you can't leave now, until tomorrow at least" The short guard turned to Lex. "You certainly have turned up on our patch at an inconvenient time." The guard was embarrassed. "We will have to lock you both up for a short while. Until our job is done!"

The two guards were already holding Lex and tying his arms to the chair he was sitting in. They lifted him bodily, chair and all and took the struggling Lex into a small room at the back of their 'office'.

What could possibly be about to happen that they should be locked away? Lex was wondering to himself. Surely they must be up to something. He must break free, but both his hands were tied rigidly to the back of the chair in which he was sitting.

Lex was worried. He knew that the very essence of this mission was to find out what these people were doing, and he was sure that something was about to happen that was to be very important. He had to break free while he had the chance. He was on his own, and could easily escape if he could dislodge his arms from the back of the chair.

He sat there. The most important thing he must not do is panic. He made himself relax. First the left foot then the leg, his right foot then the leg. He kept his eyes fixed on the handle of the door. It meant a slightly downward gaze, but the whole combination of movements helped him to become completely relaxed. He calmed his body, his arms, and then his hands. He just became like a jelly. He then realized that there was a small degree of vertical mobility in his lower arms where they were tied to the chair. He could move them at least three inches upwards and downwards. This must have been because he was severely tensed up when the bonds were tied. What else could he do? He thought. Both of his feet were on the floor, perhaps he could lean forward and holding on to the back of the chair lift it. This he did, and leaning forward bent double he could shuffle forward. This would take him ages to get anywhere and was extremely painful on the arms. He tried lifting the chair and moving backwards in short jerking movements. Thank god for the soft floor surface. The movement made very little noise.

He made his way backwards towards the door. It took a great deal of effort but he made it. When he was almost up to the door he stopped for a rest. He just prayed that the door would not be opened while he was in action. Taking a deep breath, Lex made the supreme effort and with three or four shuffles, he turned completely around and was facing that door handle, sitting there still fixed to his chair. His luck would surely not hold out, he thought, he had better work much faster. Carefully measuring the distance from the door handle he sat back as far as he could in the chair and lifted his right leg upward and forward. The curved handle of the knife concealed in his sock protruded just enough to hook onto the door handle. He made several attempts at the connection and eventually with the pain now very severe from his hands he made contact and with a very careful downward movement of his leg he released his knife onto the door handle, hanging freely. He moved forward and then taking it in his mouth, he almost dropped it. A few more shuffles and he had backed up to the small low table. Turning the chair as he had done before eventually he was able to carefully drop the knife a very short distance onto the table. He wanted to relax and take a break, but this was a luxury Lex could not afford. Very smartly, he turned his back on the table with the chair and edged carefully towards it so that his hand was within close reach of it. He lifted the chair over the table and in one quick movement, he was very lucky, he retrieved the knife by its' handle into his hand. The rest was relatively easy, although seemed to take an age. Eventually he had cut right through the cord binding his right arm and replaced his small knife into his sock.

To his amazement the door was unlocked and the office was empty. He was soon outside and in the heat of the mid-afternoon haze. He had to release Rastus. The climb down the hill was difficult through dead dry bracken. He was attempting to remain under cover until he was within reach of the kennel that was Rastus's prison. He reached the ditch at the side of the road very close to the kennel. It was well covered in foliage and the ditch seemed slightly damp and muddy. The land was in a valley, and was obviously almost still self sufficient in its water supply. Perhaps that was why plants still seemed to grow so well and grass was still evident around the lower section of the valley and around these railway sidings. Plant life just did not survive at any higher altitude in that valley. It was all dried out and dying, a complete contrast of green on the floor and the gray brown on the surrounding hills. It was strange valley indeed. Lex lay there in the damp ditch. He was exhausted, and the heat was powerfully oppressive. He fell asleep.

It must have been the noise of the arrival of the train that woke him. He could see the steam from its engine as it climbed the last few track lengths to a stop just outside the sidings, not far from where Lex was lying. He had to act fast. He sensed that something very eventful was about to happen, and there was danger in the air. Lex was worried about Rastus. Edging along on his stomach he reached the road. He took a good careful look, and could see both the guards walking up to the train. In a moment they would disappear from view behind the engine. He chose the moment, and was across the road at the kennel door. It was a simple sliding bolt and the door was open. The stench and the steam were incredible. The only visible evidence of there being anyone in there was the curly black hair on the back of Rastus's head. He must be asleep, or unconscious. He was curled up on all fours with his head bowed to breathe the cooler air from under the door.

"Rastus" Lex whispered into the kennel. There was no reply. "Quick! I've just got to get you out of there" he had urgency in his voice.

Lex was a well-built man. He decided that physical action was going to be the only way he would be able to get Rastus clear and into his protection. With both hands, he pushed one under each shoulder and felt the limpness in Rastus's body. As gently as Lex could, he pulled his friend out of the kennel into his arms and then throwing him sack-like over his shoulders Lex quickly made it back to the ditch. He lay Rastus down in the soft earth to rest. They were well covered by overgrowth in that position and would certainly be safe from discovery from any superficial search.

Lex could not believe the reality of what he saw next. The two guards had come back round the front of the engine and were again quite visible. They had at least six similarly dressed guards with them. The group paced out into a symmetrically spaced line of 'honor' for the newly arrived train. One of the guards went up to the sliding doors of the carriage-truck, and one at a time he released each catch, allowing the doors to open freely. They slid open quite easily. Lex was filled disbelief. The sudden realization of what was going on made him pinch himself for sanity.

***

Larden was a hot sticky place. Erash had been kept in a very small room with a skylight only big enough to allow him the knowledge of whether it was night or day. It was only at about mid-day when there was enough light for him to be able to see well around the tiny empty hospital storeroom that was his prison. He must have been there a long time. He was unshaven, hot, unwashed and sticky. They had allowed him a bucket for his toilet which they kindly removed and replaced once a day. Food was scarce and very simple, and he was not sure about the water. It may not have been safe. It tasted of chalk he thought, but he drank it anyway, he had no choice. Where was Rula, what had they done with her? He could not stop thinking of her. He was blaming himself. They had seemed to treat her as if she was one of Erash's chattels and had taken her away as if to punish him. What had they done with her? He was very worried. They didn't seem to have any interest in her other than she seemed to belong to Erash, and for that she was to be punished. They obviously didn't know her true identity, and would have left her alone if it hadn't been for Erash who they had certainly identified.

They had left him to stew in his own juice quite literally and he was not enjoying it. He was in solitary confinement; the only companions were the two caged birds that he had brought with him. They had allowed Erash to have them in his room for company after he had pleaded for something just to maintain his sanity. Time was passing so slowly. He knew that it was only into his second day of capture but it seemed like weeks. On several occasions he had been brought to a nervous state of 'fear' exhaustion whenever anything stirred outside. When it was peaceful and quiet, he was too, but then it was the other extreme of lethargic worry and boredom. Earlier he was sure he had heard a woman's screams from down the corridor. It didn't sound like Rula, but what if it was. She was obviously experiencing extreme horror and excruciating pain, and he heard men laughing and joking. What kind of world is this? All that he had left was his profound believe in god. He prayed. With tears swelling in his eyes, Erash got down on his knees in half light, with head bowed over the small mat that was his bed, he pleaded with god that he should help his friend in her time of need.

Rula had been taken into a nearby room and had been kept prisoner in the company of the other three girls who had been 'taken' from the exit line only that previous day. 'At least they were alive,' Rula kept saying to herself, 'and so far untouched and unharmed'. 'How long for?' She pondered. She could not understand why they would not talk to her or each other. They were terrified and each one kept very much to herself. Rula knew that the three other girls were friends, and therefore it was a sensible deduction that they must be very wary of her. Perhaps they thought she was a 'plant', a spy of some fashion to watch over them. Rula was very much on her guard. If she fell asleep, they could quite easily do her a damage or worse. She could not tell any of them who or what she was, as they could break under torture, and that she knew could be very severe. She had seen previous results on her colleagues before. One of her friends no longer had her tongue and could not properly scream when she was raped by four men at once, while she was held down with her hands tied to her feet. They forced her knees apart and she could not get them back together. The more she screamed the more the men seemed to enjoy it. She was splayed out on her back like a piece of meat. A once beautiful young woman, she was sent back by these people to her friends in Semir. It was a warning not to interfere in internal Bylean politics.

Rula decided that the best way to get some sleep would be set for herself a booby trap that would arouse her if something happened. She pulled some thread from her already torn shirt and carefully tied it around her ear lobe unnoticed. The other end she tied to her shoe, which she placed across her gangway between her excuse for a bed and the other nearest excuse for a bed. The only way that they could get to her would be if they walked through the thread.

The night passed without event, and Rula felt that she was a little safer, by the morning. They obviously were not going to attack her, but she knew they didn't trust her.

That morning Rula and one of the other girls were taken out of the 'cell' much to the horror of all the girls. There was shocked disbelief on the faces of the two remaining girls as Rula and her new nervous companion were led away down the corridor into another much larger room. There was a strange smell in the room of disinfectant and something else. Rula could not place the other smell but she had known it before. She was beginning to become very worried. The room was dimly lit, but in the center under a strong spotlight there appeared to be what looked like a religious altar of a type sometimes seen for kneeling at, with a candle alight at each side. The first girl was held firmly in a standing position at the door and another man gestured to Rula to face the altar. Am I to be a human sacrifice in some religious ritual? Rula was thinking. The man pushed down on her shoulders for her to sit down. She moved backwards and sat down. At that moment another door opened and many smiling men came in as if to enjoy some entertainment. They looked at the girl standing petrified at the door, and then at Rula, as each one took a seat as if to take part in this forthcoming event. When all the seats were taken, several more men stood behind and by the nature of their actions they were competing with each other for the best view of whatever was to happen on that altar. Rula was almost wetting herself with anxiety, what was going to happen to them. Was this a sacrificial ritual, were they the sacrifice and was she to be the first. She could smell her own body odor as she began to sweat. Under her arms, between her legs and the back of her neck she was soaking. She had never been this scared. She had heard of torture, she had seen evil doings and had been out in the field on active service. She had seen limbless men on the battle field, headless bodies and bodiless heads but never had her imagination run so wild with the tension of not knowing what was going to happen next. She could feel her heart beat resounding throughout her body. She had goose pimples. She was sure that her head of hair must have been standing on end. She felt a cold metal baton under her chin, pushing upwards. A Soldier was standing there trying to attract her gaze by lifting her head with some force; it was almost breaking her jaw. "You will note all that happens. It is very much in your interests to be well behaved" he seemed to be threatening her. He had an evil wry smile. She bit his hand hard. He yelled in shocked surprise.

"You may live to regret that" The soldier replied. "That is if we allow you to!" He stepped backwards and moved away. There was some commotion from the left, where Rula had entered the room. Rula could not help looking, but did not want to. The other girl had been manhandled by two guards who were 'frog marching' her towards Rula. She was now looking Rula straight in the face and was furious and very scared. She summoned up all her strength and with a venomous movement, spat straight into Rula's face with full velocity.

"Be brave" Rula offered a conciliatory gesture "I'm your friend please believe me" The girl shrugged as best she could and spat again as if to confirm her disbelief.

The two guards turned her round. She now had her back to Rula who was seated at the front in the middle of an audience of men. Rula was praying for the girl's deliverance in safety from whatever was about to befall her. She wanted to get up and give this poor victim some help but what could she do? Nothing!

The girl was now standing rigid in front of the altar. One of the guards took a long staff and placed it between her ankles indicating that she should part her legs slightly. This she did without objection. The other guard then with both hands took her by the waist from behind and pulled her clothes downward from her stomach until she was half naked down to her feet, with her lower clothing around her ankles. She was forcibly made to lean over the altar and Rula could not look any more. She turned away. There was a yell of approval from the audience. She could see all their elated faces. The men were becoming very sexually aroused. She felt sick; she was prisoner in a sadistic den of iniquity. Suddenly Rula felt her hair being torn out by the roots. Her face was being forced upwards. A guard the same guard as before spat into her open mouth.

"You will watch this or you will have a face scarred for life. However short a time that may be." Rula was feeling near to throwing up. She had to control herself. The captive girl screamed and screamed. Her screams were so penetrating. She seemed in such pain. A guard was drawing a picture on one of her buttocks. She was bent double. Her whole modesty was displayed for all to see. She must have been going through hell. He was drawing a picture with an electric needle. Rula could see the smoke coming from the burning flesh. That was the other smell. Now she recognized it. The girl was now alternating between crying and screaming. She was trying to shake off the instrument but that only delayed the pain and indignity for longer as the guards held her rigid. All the men seemed to be enjoying the spectacle with a perverted glee. Rula's heart was bleeding for the girl. The punishment was for both of them.

With one buttock completed, she had a beautiful badge burnt into the skin. If it wasn't so sick Rula could have admired the finished work. It was truly very beautiful, well formed and a nice decoration. She had only seen it before on a hybrid but never on a human, and never had she actually seen it done.

The rest period was short lived. The girl started screaming again and was trying very hard to wriggle free. The guard now appeared with a slightly larger electric needle, which was glowing, red in the darkened part of the shadows. He moved into the spotlight and started his work on the other buttock just above the thigh and after much more screaming and intermittent crying, the girl had a six digit number burnt into her rump. The guard stepped back. The all male audience showed their appreciation by rapturous applause. It was all Rula could do to stop herself from being sick.

The girl was still being held, as two more men appeared this time accompanied by a woman in uniform. She had a long tampon in her gloved hand. She dipped the tampon into a steaming sticky solution, which it seemed to digest like a sponge. The woman than inserted the object completely into the girl's vagina in full view of everybody. She screamed with sustained shock, and her body seemed to writhe with the impalement thrust upon her. The audience roared with gasps of approval. She started to cry with relief as she realized it was almost all over. The 'nurse' sprayed her buttocks and genital areas with an aerosol with obvious healing properties. She was allowed to stand up and reassemble her modesty by putting back her clothes, as they should be. She stood there bewildered not knowing what had been done to her. The woman who had administered the tampon stood in front and addressed the crying victim.

"You are now the property of the Bylean State and as such will always obey the orders of its servants. You have no rights and will only survive if you do your work well. You have been disinfected and after further internal examination you will be removed from this place and sent to a suitable place of lodging where you will be able to fulfill your duties to the best of your ability. You will be properly trained and if you survive you may be released when your use to us is over. That of course is up to you. You will be privileged to offer service to our troops in the field. If you are good you may be able to work in civilian life. You will meet some very interesting people."

The girl was nearly dressed. She hadn't taken it all in, but as the young girl was marched off into another room; the nurse took off her gloves. Rula missed a breath she couldn't believe her 'luck'. The woman had an artificial hand on her left arm.

Within what seemed no more than a moment, Rula was back in her prison with the other two girls. The guard threw her into the room and slammed the door behind her. She looked up at the startled faces of the other two girls as she lay there on the floor. "Where is Rebecca" One of the girls spoke accusingly to Rula. "They have taken her away," she answered. The two women jumped onto Rula and threatened to gouge out her eyes if she didn't tell. "She is safe" Rula struggled. "Please...." Then Rula threw up. For the first time the girls might believe her. She looked so pale.

***

The incident did not take very long but was going to have severe implications for the future of the gorilla people. Life was back to normal; it had been a long time since Svi had been their guest. He had made a strong impression on Zarby. She had fallen in love with him and could not get him out of her mind especially since that chance meeting on the hemisphere on its way to Lyboncher. She had become jealous, he obviously had a girl friend of his own, but her memories were rekindled. She kept remembering the feelings she had perceived at that time. Perhaps they were about to be married.

Zarby was busy at her home doing her usual menial chores of domestic necessity, deep in thought about the short few days she had had with Svi, when the commotion and screams from the other side of her village woke her from her day dreaming.

A strong smoky smell of burning reached Zarby's nostrils, causing her to drop everything and run out of her hut into a moving river of panicking gorillas. In her own language she asked the nearest terrified male what had happened.

"Three K's people have attacked us," he answered, "there are many of them on horseback and hoverbikes. They are all hooded. They have captured many of us and taken prisoners. Fire is everywhere. Thank god our mud huts don't burn very easily. They just turn into ovens, if you try to hide inside. We are all heading for the hills! You know that if any one of us were to be captured the 'Three K's' have been known to cook and eat our kind or serve us to their domestic animals." He ran off into the moving crowd.

Zarby was worried; she had to find out what was taking place and whether anything could be done for their protection. They shouldn't run away like cowards but should stand and fight. She knew that it was pointless trying to edge back through the moving crowd. She joined the crowd on the periphery and continued in its movement until she could see a break between the huts and made her way round one of them until, by repeating the same movement on at least three occasions she managed to transverse the entire village crossing the moving torrent of scared gorillas. She could now see some wounded members of the community as the crowds coming past were from the part of the village that had been attacked. She saw one terrified screaming female gorilla running with one child crying, sitting on her shoulders, and another cradled in the gorilla woman's arm. It was very dead. The front of its' face was all burned away. The center of the head was just one great big gasping hole. What are these people doing to us? Poor Zarby was crying inwardly and she was even more determined to reach the center of this horrific attack. The nearer she was getting there were fewer people and the crowd was becoming increasingly more depleted. She knew she was in danger herself. Zarby made for the peripheral cover of the forest where at least she could remain safe. She ran as fast as her legs would carry her into the bushes. Down on her hands and knees she moved very fast jumping and running like her ancestors quietly but with much speed. Soon she was up a tree. She had not jumped like that for years. She had to be careful only to use heavy well formed branches when she jumped from tree to tree as otherwise the noise would attract attention to her. Within only a few minutes she was above and behind the areas of attack on her village. There were other like-minded members of her species up in the surrounding growth of trees. Climbing trees was something only children would do these days. The gorilla people had become much more ground loving than their ancestors. They now used tools and could defend themselves against normal dangers so the Three K's would never think of looking up into the trees.

There down below her in the clearing she could see everything. She had managed to get around to the back of the attack and could see what had happened. Some brave gorillas had managed to make a large barricade across the main gap between the central huts in that part of the village. They had created for themselves a protected stockade, using wagons and old water barrels. They had obviously managed to obtain two paresifiers, which they were using very effectively every time someone attacked. Unfortunately the equipment was either very old, or not well enough charged with power as the effect of the paralysis on the enemy was only short lived and the attacker revived after a few moments. This attack would overpower them very soon and there was nothing she could do. She just hugged the trunk of the tall tree that had offered sanctuary to her.

Zarby was looking down on a dreadful spectacle. Virtually the whole village was now afire. These horrible hooded monsters were everywhere. They spoke with human voices, and had human hands. It was rumored that they belonged to a sect, a clan that depended very much on secrecy of identity for its existence. Even their own members did not always know each other because they wore hoods when in their groups. They were a clan with secret signs and secret language that only their own members could understand. Once admitted, the only way out was death. They would prey on the weaker communities. They hated the hybrids as deformed and sub-human. It was only recently that they had started on the gorilla people. She couldn't believe what was happening and things were getting much worse down below.

Four members of the Three K's had managed to crawl unseen to underneath the upturned wagon nearest to Zarby's tree. From that position they could pull down the wagon and gain entrance. Zarby so much wanted to shout warning to them. She could see her old friend Borza on the other side of the wagon completely ignorant to what was about to happen. He was busy helping to renew the support of another part of their stockade wall. Apart from the two underpowered paresifiers, and their own personal knifes, they had nothing else with which to defend themselves. They had spent all their arrows very much earlier, and their bows lay idle in the center of their defensive compound.

Clan members were continually bringing captured screaming gorillas back from the center of the village and throwing them into caged vehicles. They had taken many prisoners. A very large percentage was adult female or children. They were easier to catch, and it was said that they tasted better. More flavor.

It happened suddenly, the four members of the Three K's turned over the wagon with extreme effort on a single signal. Borza turned around only to receive a steel shaft straight through his neck. He could not breathe, his eyes rolled; the breath came pouring out of his body followed by blood and muck. Zarby threw up, as she saw her friend dive to the ground as his brain previously had directed it to do before he suffered the fatal blow. He was certainly almost dead, but it took a long time for him to go completely. The physical movements of his body took a while to subside. Zarby was going to remember this event for the rest of her life. So clear, so vivid, so horrid. Her friend skewered like an animal.

Zarby had been sitting in that tree position for some long time. Her feelings had been routed; she was numb with shock and grief. The only thing passing through her mind now was the fiercely strong feeling for retribution. She was determined to fulfill her motive for revenge. She was going to fulfill her feelings for vengeance on those people who had come to destroy her village. These people were cowards; they did not even have the courage to show their identity but hid in their hoods with tiny slits for eyes and mouth. They seemed to have all gone now, taking their prisoners and their spoils with them. Perhaps now was the time to do something she had not done since she was a child. She stood at full height, with her feet wrapped around the branch on which she was standing. At full voice she called for all to hear, pounding fiercely on her chest to initiate a drum beat which was picked up by several of her kind who were also sheltering in the nearby trees. Her warlike call was echoing throughout the local forest, enough to put the fear of death into any human. Within moments her tree was beginning to wilt under the strain of all those gorillas that had come to join her. There were at least twenty in her tree and many times more in the surrounding trees nearby.

"We shall seek revenge!" she shouted. "They shall not go unpunished. They will rue the day; will KKK, when they came our way. We live to fight, we'll make them pay!"

Her 'poetic' warlike cries went down very well with her new friends. Zarby was sure that she had found a new role in life, their leader.

***

CHAPTER 8

Noah burst into Tubal Cain's office unannounced followed very furiously by Tubal's reception secretary who immediately tried to apologize to her boss for the intrusion. Tubal waved his hand in a friendly gesture to her, that she should not worry.

"I've done it" Noah announced to Tubal Cain. "I've been in contact with Postia . . . through diplomatic channels, using our embassy over there. We had to go to the top as quickly as possible. They will be delighted to be of help, and they are grateful for the 'business'. Perhaps we can get things moving now." Noah was very pleased with himself.

"We have to act fast" Tubal replied. "The agents of the kidnappers will be approaching us in the morning." Tubal continued.

"We have still no news about the hand, but we have received a cryptic message from one of our agencies in Semir. It seems that Erash had made contact with a group of the Popular Front for the liberation of Bylia. Essentially they claim to be a fully democratic organization, which would like to see Bylia 'redeemed' into a country free of autocratic government and tyranny. They are mainly a group of well meaning Bylians living in enforced exile. They could well give us a chance to break into the Bylian problem. If we help them, perhaps they will help us. Erash has obviously worked this one out for himself, and he has gone off on a mission with one of their best agents."

"Is she a woman?" Noah showed inspiration. "That's a point. You are probably right. That woman he was taken prisoner with. Perhaps she is with them. We must get them both out and quick!" Tubal was thinking faster than he could talk, and it was showing in his stilted sentences. He sat down on his desk, sidesaddle. He wanted to make the discussion informal. "Perhaps one of us should go to Semir."

"No we must finalize this Postian deal with their Postation nuts. They must have the money to deal with the 'Bylians'. That is assuming it is they who are the kidnappers. We don't know that for certain. "Noah was always very logical in his manner.

"They have already had their first payment and have promised to send a small group of representatives over here to buy arms from us. While they are here tomorrow morning, they are coming to my office to meet these couriers from the kidnappers. The plan is beginning to fall into place." Tubal was full of enthusiasm.

"By tomorrow evening we should have some news of Erash and his friend." Noah was hopeful.

The thumping of the muscular walls of the heart was pounding away at the inner linings of Tubal Cain's rib cage. The blood was flowing fiercely in fits and starts, as it seemed to pulsate through his fully conscious brain. Tubal believed that the noise of his heart beat and the vibrant throbbing in his head must be wholly audible to anyone in his close vicinity of his office that morning. He was sitting at his desk, nervously playing with his televideo wishing to negotiate' the release of his employee Erash. Tubal was not generally one to become over anxious, but on this occasion he was worried. He was the person who had put Erash in this position, it was his fault, and he was almost powerless to help. Tubal was determined to bluff this through.

The red light above the door, when would it start flashing. Tubal could not take his eyes off it. Who would arrive first, the Postians, or the kidnappers' agents? How would he deal with it? He would have to ad-lib. He had to be seen to deal only with the Postians. He could not be seen to deal directly with the 'terrorists'. He just sat there watching that light. He thought he was going to burst. Something must happen soon. His mouth was dry and his eyes were almost glazed. His fingers were playing a recognizable tune by beating on the lid of his personal televideo index. He stood up, walked around the office, picking out the squares of the pattern in the soft floor covering with his feet on each step he made. He was working himself up to a crescendo of nervous anticipation. This was all wrong he thought in this state of mind they could be at the advantage. He must calm down. He must make himself settle his mind before they arrive. He took a drink from the Cable-Juice machine and sat down to enjoy it. The red light seemed to flash at the same moment as the buzzer sounded on the intercom.

Tubal reached for the hand piece, and the buzzer stopped, but the red light was still oscillating on and off above the door. He could hear Noah's voice as he held the hand set to his ear. "The Postians have arrived, they are here in my office, will you see them now?" Noah asked.

"The terrorist agents are also here" Tubal replied. "I believe that they are in the foyer now. I will see them first. I will hear what they have to say. Keep the Postians happy for a short while. I'll call you back soon." Tubal pushed the entrance button and bid the visitors to come in.

There were four of them. They smiled, but still looked very stern. The three men looked like they could kill, but were being friendly. The other could be a woman, but only just. She was very 'butch'. She was to be the spokes person. She stepped forward, flanked by two of her colleagues and the third stood behind her. She must have been in her middle years, and was certainly no beauty. She held out a hand to Tubal. There was an envelope between her fingers. "This is for you" she said "A proof of identity." She handed it to Tubal, who took it, and opened it. He took a deep breath..."Erash! What have you done to him? He is so badly scarred, and bald. What are those marks on his chest? Have you used electricity on him?"

"What about the woman who was with him?" Tubal dared to enquire." What have you done with her?"

"Woman? She is no concern of yours. We only offer Erash in return for arms supplies to help us in fight against counter-revolutionists. The woman will not die, we can promise you that. Let us call it an offer in return for you having met with us today. She will remain our prisoner."

Tubal Cain was angry, but he had to be careful. He guarded his tongue and walked across his room in temper. He did not like to be spoken to like that, and in his own office. Turning around, he pointed his index finger at their Lesbian leader.

"Now listen to this," he said, with an attempt to control the fury in his voice. "We do not deal with terrorists, and never yield when under threat. We cannot deal with you and we despise your cause. "He was wishing he had not said that, as the words were pouring out. "What I mean to say," he continued "we will deal with you through intermediaries, the 'Postians'."

The three men turned to the woman; Tubal sensed that he could see a faint smile on the woman's face, which was immediately imitated by the men.

"I am pleased that we are in business. This is our first list of requirements..."

"No!" shouted Tubal, we will not deal with you, but wait here in my office, and you will meet the people who will." He picked up the intercom-hand set and called Noah "Please send them in" he spoke into it.

Not many moments later, the door opened and Noah walked in, in the company of five people, who were representing the country of Postia. Tubal was surprised at the clean and smart appearance of these people. He could not take his eyes off the woman. She was slightly plump, but had the most captivating smile. Her fresh pale pink skin was just begging to be kissed, while thick curly blonde hair just finished her off like the icing on the cake. He knew he could fall for this woman, and what a damn fool time to do it. She had her own individual type of beauty, as he had never seen before. He particularly noticed the dimples when she smiled, and her little chin, which seemed to pout. He could not wait to hear her speak. He wanted to hear the sound of her voice. He walked casually over to Noah.

"Shall we all introduce ourselves?" Tubal said as if trying to give the appearance of an attempt at breaking the ice.

"Then let me begin." The business like answer was coming from the Lesbian terrorist. "My name is Vilia, and these gentlemen are my aides. Now who are you? She turned to the Postians.

Tubal Cain could not believe his luck the woman was going to answer.

"My name is Tsionne, and these are my friends." she pointed to each one in turn saying their names. Vilia shook each one's hand, but Tubal was not listening to what they were saying. He was overcome by the magic of meeting Tsionne.

***

Rastus was beginning to regain his consciousness while lying there in the muddy ditch under the luxurious green overgrowth. Lex was almost regretting that he had his hybrid friend with him; it will be a trauma for him when he sees what was about to take place. Somehow Lex had guessed correctly that they were about to witness terrible crimes of humanity. The sliding doors of the railway wagons were now fully open. Sad, worried faces, full of anxiety and shock, were greeted by the outside world. There were hybrids of all ages and of both sexes, jammed together in those trucks so tightly that they had barely room to move. There were old men, young pregnant women, and young mothers with their infant in their arms suckling against a bare bosom. They were all bewildered, and some were crying. There was one man in the second truck kneeling down at the edge of the open door. He seemed to be up to something. Lex did not see him move, he was so quick. The stray young hybrid had somersaulted under the train onto the lines. He was trying to escape on the other side. It was a brave attempt but doomed to failure. It was only a few moments before he was back at the original side of the stationery train to answer for his deed. He was being held between two security guards who were forcing him to stand with his back fully arched with the chest pushed forward. Another senior officer called the newly arrived 'guests' to attention that they should listen to his announcement.

"This is what will happen to anyone who tries to escape." He ordered another guard to pull two hybrids from the wagon. They were made to stand next to the captive prisoner. The guard had chosen a man and young, not unattractive woman. The officer was relishing the situation. He was going to teach these newcomers a lesson that they would never forget. He gave the male newcomer a knife with a long shining blade, then he put his hand under the woman prisoner's chin and grabbing hold of her collar, ripped her clothes completely off her, revealing her brown naked body.

"Now take the blade down the woman's front from below her neck to her pubic mound. Split her open!" He screamed at the man.

The hybrid man could not contain himself, and took a wild swipe with the knife at the officer, catching him off guard across the shoulder.

"Now you've done it!" The officer shouted "Hold him he must see this. Bring down two more prisoners!"

This time it was another woman and a baby in arms. "Excellent." The sadistic officer was enjoying himself in spite of his shoulder wound. "For each offence you commit, you will take two others to die with you." He shouted in the direction of the wagons. He took the knife and with one single, but gentle downward movement split open the body of the poor horror-struck woman. "That is what you have done to her!" he spoke to the original escapee, as the writhing, bleeding body of the woman was allowed to fall free to the ground, where it seemed to take an age to die.

The officer then wrenched the baby from the other woman, and held it aloft upside-down by its legs. Then as if splitting a chicken he pulled both legs apart until he had torn the little infant in half. Lex threw up. He vomited up the whole contents of this stomach. He couldn't look any more, but he owed it to those poor people. He had to watch. The poor woman had feinted in traumatic shock. She lay next to her broken offspring. She would never have seen the knife coming down across her throat releasing the life from her tormented body.

All that was left of the hostages were the two men. The one who had struck the officer and the original who attempted to escape.

"Now." The officer held the knife high in the air and threw it to the ground. "Whichever one of you kills the other will go free. The knife is there, take it!"

Neither man moved. The knife was the same distance from both of them. "If you don't make a start on the count of five I will kill two more hybrids from the wagons. One, two, three." The two men looked respectfully at each other. "Four" Neither wanted to make the first move. "Five". They both hesitated but only an instant, and were then lying together on the ground fighting a duel for possession of the knife. They were rolling in the dirt. Then one got up and started to run fast towards the spot where Lex and Rastus were lying. The knife came flying after him just missing and landing at the edge of the ditch within arm's length of Lex. The stranger fell to the ground and looked Lex straight in the eyes. It was the original escapee. He grabbed the knife, picked it up, and turned. He ran at full speed at the other stranger, stabbing him hard into his rib cage in the region of the heart. The poor man fell dead without a murmur. Blood was everywhere. The officer asked the *'winner'* for his knife back and told him to kneel in front of him. The officer took the knife and placed the long blade on the right shoulder of the hybrid. "You have done well, but arise," He then moved the blade across to the other shoulder "and take your place in our ranks. So long as you work with us, you will be fed and you will survive. If you disobey an order, two of your compatriots will be killed. You must not die. If you do you will take two of your friends with you. Now go to that officer over there and he will give you an armband with which you will always be recognized. Now go!!" he shouted. "I have seen something that will interest you, over there in the….." The hybrid mumbled.

"Shut up! Only speak when you are spoken to. Now go!" The officer was mad with rage. He certainly had not heard what the hybrid was trying to say.

Lex decided it would be too dangerous to stay where they were now that they had been spotted. They must move when it gets dark. Rastus was beginning to get his strength back, but he was very thirsty. Lex discovered that underneath them was very muddy, and by digging down he came to a damp area, which was becoming damper the further down he went. Scooping out the soil with his hands the hole seemed to fill up even more quickly with water. It was cool mountain water. Perhaps this ditch was filled by a fresh running mountain stream. Lex scooped some more. The water was no longer just oozing but pouring. The hole in the ground between Lex's legs was becoming filled with muddy water. Lex took a cloth from his pocket and dipped it into the well. The relief on Rastus's face became very evident when the cool damp cloth was placed on his forehead.

"I must have a drink," he mouthed to Lex "I am parched dry".

Please can I drink?" He pleaded.

"Your stomach is certainly stronger than mine, but this water has to clear before you dare to take any to drink."

The two men sat there watching their puddle, when suddenly bubbles appeared to surface as if the water was draining away. The well quickly began to empty of its contents as quickly as it had filled. The two men looked down in disbelief. An empty wet hole.

"Listen" Rastus whispered to Lex as he put his head to the ground. "Running water. Fast running water." Rastus could not believe his luck. He put his hand down into the hole and came out with a palm full of clear clean mountain water. He lay there drinking until he had fully quenched his thirst. "We must have broken into the original mountain underground stream that follows this ditch underneath us."

Pandemonium had broken out. There was screaming, crying and shouting. The hybrids were being unloaded from the trucks. Lex was of two minds whether he wanted Rastus to see the happening. The new arrivals were being lined up along the side of the railway train three ranks deep, a motley crowd of people.

The guards started walking up and down the columns of gathered hybrids. There were some very old with gray hair; some very young, crying in their mothers' arms. There were children wanting to play, and complete families fraught with uncertainty as to their future. Each of them was pitifully carrying a small bundle of belongings that they had managed to collect and bring with them blatantly at short notice.

A guard appeared from the end truck. He was immaculately dressed in his black and silver uniform, with high black boots on his feet, and two large strips on the epaulets of his jacket. He was obviously more senior ranking than the other guards who gave him the salute by lifting their right arms towards him with flat hands and thumbs pointing forward, they mouthed a greeting, retracted their arms and stood to attention clicking their heels together.

Lex looked at Rastus whose eyes were transfixed on the spectacle, which was laid out before them. Lex could not even try to imagine what was going through Rastus's mind at that moment. He was just praying that he would not lose his temper, and give their position away.

"Selection! Stand in line. You will all be allocated to sections for your stay at this camp. Get in line! Now!" The senior officer was carrying a megaphone. He seemed to be enjoying his enforceable authority. The reality of the danger these people were in was permanently demonstrated by the four bodies lying in their own blood; there on the ground untouched where they fell. As the columns of people filed past the dead lying there, they became very sober. Some of the prisoners had not seen what had happened before, as they were too far down the track at the time.

The moving column was being made to march in single file passed guards seated at a desk that had been erected unnoticed by Lex. They were making each prisoner expose his or her naked buttock so that the officer at the desk could make note of the registration mark that labeled the identity of each hybrid. Any defect error or omission and the person was pulled to the side and given a new mark; intended to be a truly public degradation. Surprisingly there was very little reaction from the crowds of prisoners. The early murders had made their effect, and they were moving passed quite obediently.

The guards started to separate them into groups, which consisted of able men, and some women into one group. Children were taken from their screaming mothers and placed into another group. Some sick, old and nursing mothers were also put into the same group as the children. There were scenes of husbands and wives kissing their children and elderly parents, as they were pulled apart. Whole families were fragmented. The situation was becoming too much for Rastus to watch any more, but he had the sense to know that there was no point in him declaring his presence. "Please. Can we go from here?" He called under his breath to Lex.

"We must wait until dark. We must make sure we see what happens to these people. We owe it to them not to get caught. When it gets dark we will go around the other side of those buildings. I have a theory that I must fulfill before we leave, but we must be very careful."

***

Several days must have passed since Rebecca had been taken from the cell. Rula had now spent her time with the two other girls very usefully breaking down the barriers of mistrust that had existed between them. She had discovered that the three girls including Rebecca, were immigrant Nurses who had readily been offered work when the hospital was run on neutral political lines. When the 'terrorists' took over they just did not want to stay. It was that simple. They had now got themselves into a real messy situation. What would their poor folks at home think? Rula was growing to like them a great deal. The three girls were becoming good friends in their close confinement. There was certainly no privacy for any one of them. They even had to perform their excretions and ablutions in front of each other. They politely turned their backs, but it was still very embarrassing.

Lara was almost devastated when Rula related to them the punishing deaths that their friends had suffered at the exit gates of the hospital encampment. Lara's blue eyes swelled with tears as she heard about the premature death of her friends, one of whom was a young lad barely out of adolescence. He had been something very special to her. This young girl with long blonde hair, blue eyes and pedigree figure had confided in the other two girls that she had given everything to this boy. He had died taking her virginity with him. She felt that part of her had gone forever. It was an experience that she could not relate. It was private to her. She sat in the corner, took her long hair in her mouth and cried for nearly a whole day. Rula and the other girl, Mela was her name, who was also blue eyed but more a brunette in hair color, tried to console her, but the poor girl had to cry it out. . Rula found she had a great deal in common with Mela; they seemed to be very 'sympathetic' with each other. It was as if they could read each other's most secret thoughts without even trying.

The door of their cell opened without warning. There were always people walking past. It was only when the footsteps stopped outside, and the handle moved, that the in-mates Rula, Lara and Mela realized that the door was about to open.

The guard was stern but friendly. He was carrying a small paresifier.

"Come on the three of you. You are going to take a warm bath; there is no doubt that you all need one." The Guard gestured to them, "Pick up your belongings; you won't be coming back here again".

The warm fluffy towels were wrapped around their steaming wet bodies. The three girls sat on the bench in the changing area lapping up the luxury of warm exuberance. No one would believe that only a short while earlier those three ladies had been suffering the horrific privations of abject captivity.

Rula was inwardly concerned about the sudden change of atmosphere with regard to their captivity. She was a veteran soldier, and knew in her heart, that this could only be the calm before the storm, but she didn't want to spoil this moment for the other two girls. It was to be that that moment was only to last a short time longer.

Rula was still considering the situation when the woman appeared. A cold shiver went through her body as she tried to conceal her horror from the others, but the loud involuntary gasp of breath from Rula's mouth indicated to them that danger was present. This intruding woman who had appeared without warning was carrying three large parcels. She gave one to each of the girls. They were fresh clean clothes and boots.

"Get into these. I will be back very soon." She said, and left.

Lara was amazed. "Did you see her left hand?" she asked innocently. "It was artificial, poor woman!"

"We don't have much time" Rula interrupted. "I believe that we are now in grave danger. Horrible things usually happen when that woman is around. Just take care to stay on the right side of her. Try to keep calm."

They finished dressing and each put the final adjustment on the other's clothes. The three girls looked a picture of health and cleanliness. They each put their wet heads into the rapid drier and styler. Having pre-set the drum to a design of their choice within a moment all three had neat, tidy and dry hair, each in a slightly different fashion.

Again the door opened. This time the woman was accompanied by four guards, who each had an expression of sweet anticipation on their faces. Rula did not like the situation at all. She was sure that she recognized one of them. "You are coming with us. Bring all your things with you please." The one-handed woman was asking politely.

The three women were marched along the narrow corridors in single file so they did not even have the security of seeing the face of one of their friends. The uncertainty was affecting all of them. Rula was already perspiring and she had just had a bath. They came to large unmarked doors. Through the small porthole windows Rula could see that it seemed quite dark inside.

As they entered through the opening doors, Rula realized what was about to happen. There was a stage in front of them. There was an altar on the stage with two candles. The auditorium was crowded with men. It was a lecture theatre of the hospital being used for 'other things'. The three girls were being made to walk down the steps into the auditorium where Rula could see that the front row had three central seats reserved for them. She had been here before, but had come in from a different entrance. She was first in the line, and she carefully stepped down the gangway to the front. Then it happened. She felt a clammy hand up through her clothes. It was groping away at her soft behind. She felt it try to get between her legs as she was slowly walked passed. She swung her right arm as hard as she could and caught the man fairly and squarely in the face. She went mad, as with his other hand he grabbed her whole body and pulled her down into the seat on top of him. His hand now had very busy fingers. She had to do something. She bit his nose so hard that the man let go and screamed out loud. He was bleeding. Time must have stood still for Rula at that moment as he was physically pulled and dragged out of the theatre by two guards.

Rula regained her composure as best she could. She was determined not to give in to her emotions and did not dare to think of the things that were possibly to come. Her friends would have no idea what they were probably about to experience. She was made to sit in the right hand seat in the front row, and Mela was shown to the left. The center seat was left empty. Rula looked around for Lara. Then she heard the scream. Lara had been blindfolded from behind and was being held between two guards. The woman with the artificial hand was taking her place in the center front seat between Mela and Rula.

One of the many guards came over to Rula and Mela's seats and took away their belongings with the remark…"You won't be needing these for a little while." He then went over to Lara and said the same thing.

Lara's blindfold had slipped a little since it had been put in place. A guard went over to her and tightened it even more. 'Poor Lara' thought the other two girls, as they sat there watching.

The pretty young thing was frog-marched onto the raised stage where she was made to stand with her hands tied together in front of her. She was turned with her back to the audience.

"Now bend over!" Shouted a senior guard officer. "We are going to remove your clothing from below the waist."

Rula could not stand the thought of having to sit through another branding ceremony, but she knew that it would be impossible for her to miss it.

The young Lara was beginning to sob. The uncertainty of what was happening, and the painful humiliation in front of all these people was making its indelible effect on this innocent soul. She had only known one man in her life on intimate terms, and he was only a young lad. Now she was blindfolded and half naked reversed up in full demonstration to a large lusty all male crowd.

She was beautifully formed thought Rula as her naked backside was presented and specially illuminated for all to see. Her dark pink slightly hairy private parts seemed incidental in the neatness of her body form. Rula suffered a cold shiver. Surely they weren't going to spoil the beauty by desecrating it?

An officer appeared with needles and solvents. Within a short space of time he was well into his work. Rula was amazed at the strength of character of the young lady. Hardly a sound came from her mouth once the work was started but she desperately strained at the item of equipment keeping her knees slightly apart. The tension was evident and very visible as her naked thighs took the strain. Finally the job was finished. Both buttocks bore the label. The woman seated next to Rula got out of her chair and mounted the stage. She was to deliver the coup de grace. She took the large tampon and dipped it in that sticky disinfectant liquid, then with a purposeful thrust, penetrated her genitals in full view of everyone. Rula was not sure which was louder, the horrific scream from Lara's mouth, or the gratified cheers from the gathered crowd. Rula's stomach was turning over. She so much prayed for it to finish. Eventually Lara was allowed to re-adjust her clothes, and restore the neatness of her body form.

"You may sit down if you wish. Take this rubber ring and use it as a 'comfort' to sit on while your wounds heel." The one handed woman said in an almost friendly and motherly manner to Lara.

"Come take this Lady's seat." They were moving in the direction of Rula. "She won't be needing it for a while!"

Rula could not believe this was happening. Surely it was not going to be her turn next. It never even dawned on her that they would do it to her.

The blindfold was not comfortable, but the cold around her bottom was very unnerving. She had seen this twice now, and knew what was coming, so she was trying to convince herself that in a way it would be easier for her. The block between her knees gave her something to press upon as the first contact of human fingers on her groin began to press. She felt the needle but it didn't seem to hurt. It just felt uncomfortable. She felt wet and very draughty. She managed to contain her emotions not to cry or scream, although she had to fight with herself, not to give in. The workmanship on her behind seemed to go on forever. She wondered how many men's eyes were fixated on her genitals and would carry that image to their beds with them that night. Strange unrelated thoughts were passing through her mind when suddenly without any warning she was impaled with the internal thrust of the tampon that she had clearly forgotten was due. Rula let out an involuntary scream with shock. It seemed so hot and fiery. It was an experience she had not suffered since she lost her virginity. She felt she was afire from within. No wonder the other girls screamed so.

Rula was allowed to tidy herself, given a rubber ring cushion and ushered gently to the seat in which Mela was seated.

Rula and Lara were numbed with disbelief as they watched their companion squirm and yell as she prolonged her agonies until her job was done. The one handed woman then made the three girls stand together in a line on the stage, while she gave her word perfect speech about them being the property of the Bylian state and what was to be expected of them. They had no rights and would only survive if they did their work well.

They were removed to an anteroom for an internal examination. At least for the present they were still together, thought Rula.

***

The dark damp evening mist clung tightly around the crouching bodies of a small group of carefully conspiring gorillas. The attack on their village two days previously was very much the subject of their conversations, as they sat there in a circle among the trees. A small glowing fire dying in its embers only enough to keep them warm and give them the smallest amount of illumination. The secrecy of their meeting was of prime importance; they did not want to attract any attention from the world outside. This was a committee of war.

"The best form of defense is attack," Zarby was whispering to her friends in her own tongue. "We must prepare ourselves to go to their meeting place and create a rout. They must be taught a lesson with fire and explosion. That kind of argument they understand.

"What about the prisoners they have taken from us?" A young male gorilla was asking.

Zarby quickly interjected. "They are probably slaughtered by now. We will no doubt find their carcasses hanging neatly in their abattoir. See you have little hope of finding any survivors. Just be careful not to add one more corpse to the pile yourself. These people have no respect for gorilla people. We are fair game to a member of the KKK. Three K people are filled with their self-indulgence and see us as trespassers on their culture. They hate us and despise us!"

Zarby was scraping away at the ground as she spoke. She was becoming very worked up within herself with the hunger for retribution. She continued . . .

"We must attack them in their own home on their own ground with surprise and full vigor. They must be taught to leave us alone."

There was a general undercurrent of verbal approval, as they all indicated with their soft approving grunts.

"We go when we are ready, and not before" Zarby continued, "Tomorrow, three of our group will go and scout out their positions. Soon we have full operational plans to prepare for attack. If three others go to our friends in Science and Welfare, we could 'borrow' and 'buy' necessary weaponry to help us in our deeds. Some of us have very good contacts. Soon, perhaps in three or four days we will have gathered together enough information and ammunition to launch a successful assault with little risk. This plan of war must not fail. We must teach them a lesson from which it will take them a long time to recover." Zarby was showing her anger. Her blood pressure must have surely been raised as the adrenalin was pumping around her body.

Six days had passed since that meeting of gorillas within the trees. They had achieved a great deal in such a short time. The scouting party had returned, and their friends in Science and Welfare had 'found' some ex-surplus war materials. The small band of gorillas under Zarby's strong leadership had created the wherewithal for a calculated and probable low risk attack on the legion of the KKK. They had old fashioned but fully workable mortars with at least two dozen shells. They had three modern paresifiers with re-charging units, several laser-led short-range rocket launchers complete with range finder and instruction manual. The last item along with several others were to prove too difficult to use without proper training, so they decided to put them into storage. The simpler equipment, Zarby decided, the more efficient they would be as a fighting force. Paresifiers, mortar common, small arms, even bow and arrows they could use with good effect. Hand grenades and flame throwers were also very useful, but low tracking heat seeking, laser led, pulsating vibrant, force-field exploders were too much for any gorilla to understand. Anyway they would wipe out their enemy with one blow. They would never know what had happened to them and would certainly never tell the tale. The whole point was to teach the survivors a lesson that they would never forget. That they should remember the expression of shock, pain and anguish on their dying friends faces as the attack makes its way forward. The three K's must be taught to never again meddle with the gorilla people, who are a force to be reckoned with.

The following evening not many miles away from the wooded hills of the gorilla enclave, and not far from the small town where Svi's friends met their doom at the hands of the renegade guards during that peaceful demonstration, a group of men were donning their hoods and habits in preparation for that night's assembly.

These were the officers for the meeting that evening. They were lighting the fire, which would burn in a high column behind the altar, which stood at the far side of the large room. It was called a room, but in truth, there were no walls and there was no roof. The structure was made up of columns of dark gray stone standing on end in a circle around a center point. The columns acted as support for large lintels that went all the way round to complete the circle. When a meeting of the three K's was in progress this eternal pathway was important and put to good use. In the center of the room at the 'pivot' or 'axle' as it was sometimes called there was a circular stool on which the second senior officer would be placed before the master called the meeting to order. The master would sit diametrically opposite the altar in a large stone chair with a small column at each side of the backrest. On each of these columns a large stone saucer supported a small fire, which these officers were also now lighting in preparation of the impending meeting.

Eventually the stage was set and the whole area of the 'room' was aglow with the beautiful pale yellow light that was radiated from the peculiar fibers that were used to fuel the flames. The magic of the way the flames of pale yellow flickered in the darkness and reflected off the dark gray speckled stones, created an aura of extravagant mystery which would overpower even the most strong minded observer to the ritual of the oncoming feast.

There was deliberate tapping on a piece of hollow dead tree wood with a small but hard stick. It was beating out a tempting slow rhythm, which seemed to be very much in tune with the flickering stroboscopic effect of the flames, even as a gentle wind sometimes drew across the flames to create an exaggeration to the movement of the occasional dark shadows on the stones.

There must have been nearly three hundred hooded people marching in single file as they appeared from nowhere. They were marching slowly but with purpose to the rhythm of the stick that was now beating on that hollow piece of wood. Eventually as the rhythm lifted they found their way still in single file to the eternal pathway that went around the top of the columns.

Every so often in unison and without warning but possibly linked to the rhythmic beat of the stick, the masked and habited bodies turn and face inwards to the circle's center, and murmur a chant, and lifting out their robed arms to nearly horizontal and shake their hands before returning them back to their sides. The bodies then returned to single file and continued to march in rhythm until the whole function would be repeated at some time later on. The evening had set a thin yellow haze, low, on the stones. The magic of the visual effect with the robed Klansmen walking around the elevated perimeter would have struck mystery and curiosity into any stranger's mind.

The senior Klansman, the master himself, moved forward to the center of the circle from which he was then carried by two other members of the group to the main chair between the two burning saucers. When he was seated by the two men, the rhythm of the sticks became faster, and another slightly deeper noted hollow stick was introduced into the rhythm. The mood became somber all of a sudden as the man in the master's chair raised his arms forward and almost vertical. It was as if to announce the arrival of outside visitors. The smoke seemed to increase, and then newcomers were carried in on very large trays shoulder high. There were two scared young female gorillas and one large male who was very angry.

The trays were put down on the large alter table and the tempo of the beating sticks changed again as one more stick was added. Now there were three sticks beating the rhythm. The three gorillas had been dressed in white cloth, and their hands and feet had been tied together very much in the appearance of being trussed up as for a sacrifice.

The three gorillas were laid on their backs and a long metal rope was passed through the loops made by their bindings. The three trussed bodies were then lifted above the gathered crowd for all to see.

The master was about to speak when it happened.... a grenade landed at his feet. Every one fell flat on the ground, except the Master Klansman. He bent down and picked it up and threw it back in the direction from where it came, but first he removed the pin. An explosion was seen and heard in the darkness not too far away.

"Who ever is attacking us has a sense of humor. They did not remove the pin!" The master called to his astonished audience now back on their feet.

"Zen I have removed Zis pin Ziz time! Eeeah!" A small angry gorilla had run into the circle of stones and had made it into the area. He was holding an open grenade close to his chest, and was running fast to the Master's chair. He threw himself to the ground at his feet. There was a terrible explosion, and fragments of gorilla mixed with stone and Master Klansman went everywhere. The suicide run, a courageous act of revenge by this small gorilla got its mark clearly with the first blow. The rest of the KKK meeting went completely into disarray. They were completely surrounded and searchlights once used for searching the skies were turned onto the circle of stones. Within moments the place was a blaze of fire and flames as inflammable liquid was sprayed over the stones, only to be set afire at the same moment. Klansmen were burned and dying everywhere, but Zarby wanted a few, a very few, to escape to tell the tale. The three trussed up gorillas were released without a problem and no sooner had the attack begun, then it was over, and Zarby and her 'army' were in full withdrawal.

"We teach KKK, We live to fight anuzzer day!" She shouted in the tongue of the Klansmen so that perhaps, maybe they would understand!

Zarby stood there thumping her chest. She was very proud of their day's work. She had turned a peace loving species into a strong organized army of defense. She felt good. They had become a determined group of people, the gorilla people. Zarby smiled to herself, although tinged with a little sadness. They had lost one gorilla this night. Biza was her nephew, and he was out to avenge the murder of his parents by the Three K's. His mother was Zarby's sister.

***

Noah was certain that Tubal was not listening to him. It was already three days since their 'meeting' with the Postians and the 'others'. Since that moment Tubal's attitude had completely changed. Noah was sure that he heard him singing before entering his office at Science and Welfare, there was certainly an embarrassed look on his face as Noah marched in through Tubal's door. Tubal Cain was a very happy man, and tucked away in a world of his own. Noah did not very much want to disturb his brother-in-law's dream world, but there was business to be done.

"Sorry to interrupt your contemplations, but we really must discuss developments." Noah had his voice slightly raised. "I don't know what has got into you but would you kindly come back to the world of the living, and wipe that stupid smile off your face." Noah was not usually sarcastic, but this was becoming a problem. A fully-grown man of high intelligence, and enormous responsibility acting like a young adolescent. That sickly expression on his face could only mean one thing. Noah did not know how right he was.

Tubal Cain adjusted his composure as if waking from deep thought.

"Er. Yes. What was that you said? The Postations? They are certainly doing a good job of it, are they not? They have already bought a great deal of thermo-metal, and heavy-duty tracking. I wonder what they want with so much magnetic wire, and lead."

Noah broke in saying "I thought that they would be buying arms and weaponry, not items of light and heavy engineering like six heavy-duty construction vehicles, and six high-rise cranes of half-tracks for desert work. None of these items make a great deal of sense when grouped together."

"Don't you notice something strange? Tubal interrupted. "The goods being ordered all come in large sizes, or bulk of such quantities that would easily be missed if acquired any other way. This way they are able to rob us openly, and with the purloining of other materials that 'firm' are definitely up to no good. I think I ought to go to Postia and meet again with our intermediaries. Perhaps they could find out more information for us."

"You mean ask a neutral country to spy for us? There is no way that they would agree to anything like that." Noah commented.

"I do believe there may be another reason that you want to go to Postia. A rational thinking man like you, going off on a wild goose chase when you could send a junior to do it for you."

"No I don't want that!" Tubal was worried. "I will go. I need to be close to the action. It is necessary that I get the facts first hand."

"You mean you want to see Tsionne again?" Noah guessed correctly.

"Who?" Tubal asked trying very hard to stifle a smile.

"Go on then and good luck to you" Noah was pleased for Tubal. Why shouldn't he have some happiness in his life?

"We need to know what is going on in Bylia and that is as good an opening as we will get at the moment. Perhaps we will have more news of Erash shortly." Noah knew that Tubal was off in a dream again. He knew that Tubal was not listening to him. He must be besotted with this woman with whom he never spoke more than just 'hello'. He has to quench his thirst and quell his hunger for this woman, or it will drive him mad. If things went wrong for the both of them it could prove very awkward.

"Perish the thought" Noah was thinking.

Tubal Cain's arrival in Postia was meant to be quiet and unannounced, but things never quite work out that way. A small delegation of industrialists met him at the transportation center in the central city. The news media had heard of his impending arrival and had swarmed around him like bees at the honey pot. Tubal's visit was on the Televideo and Holographic screens within moments of his rumored arrival. It was almost as if someone had put them up to it. The Bylians would be delighted to see Tubal Cain's face in every home in the country of Postia. He could certainly not remain anonymous under those circumstances.

Fortunately the arrival crowds were left behind as quickly as they had appeared, when Tubal and the entourage were quickly ushered into a small hoversphere which left with great haste for its local destination, but for Tubal Cain the damage may well have already been done.

Tubal's fears were put to the back of his mind as he entered the strangers' office. There silhouetted against the hazy daylight from the large picture window was the back of a woman that had been indelibly imprinted on his heart during the last few days. He had suddenly become very nervous. He had built this meeting up in his mind to such an extent it was dwarfing the real reasons for the business at hand. She was turning around. Her smile met Tubal's. Their chemistry was joined. They both knew the other one's mind. Not a word needed to be said. They knew that they had been blessed. Tsionne and Tubal's eyes were united. Perhaps business could wait for a short while. Tsionne and Tubal were transfixed.

Only but a moment later one of their colleagues suggested they all sit down around a table with some light refreshment to discuss developments. It seemed to Tubal and Tsionne that they had been standing there for an eternity as each with a very warm satisfying feeling sat down at opposite ends of the table.

***

CHAPTER

The loud wailing of hybrid women who had been
seemed very much to dominate the quiet of the eve.
cover of darkness had crawled through the undergrow.
the complex of buildings, which were situated at the edge of the

It was the sweet smelling but acrid smell, which seemed to
Lex. He knew that smell. It was familiar to him but he could not q
cooking, no, he thought, not just cooking. It was a smell of roasting
believe that these thugs would be feeding all these people with portic
What, he wondered could they be cooking at this time of night. The thic
smoke that was climbing out of the tall chimneys, collecting with it fragm
burnt ash that was depositing itself almost everywhere within range. Lex put
that had landed on his sleeve, to his mouth. He touched it with the tip of his tc
a slightly salty and fat-like taste. Lex could not work this one out. It was definitely
they were cooking. But so much of it! Why? This completely destroyed his logic.
previously thought that these people were to be used as the worst type of slave, and
be taken to the depth of depravity until they had been worked to death. He never dre
that they would be so well fed with cooked meat of such quantity. He was beginning to
quite hungry himself.

They carefully moved closed to the large building that looked like a warehouse. It was
the one next to the shower room, which was fitted out like a gymnasium.

"The best thing we could do" whispered Lex "is climb up on to the roof. They are all
joined. The buildings either touch one another, or there are gantries that we could climb
across. Look over there. A ladder built into the side of that building."

With great care, the two men started to climb the rungs in complete silence. They
removed their shoes and tied them around their necks, daring not make the tiniest sound.
They knew that their lives depended on it. Without shoes they would be silent, but they
would also be very sure footed; it was an old trick that Rastus had learned in the army.
Moving slowly but skillfully they edged their way across the roof of the main building to the
center. There was an internally illuminated skylight not far from where they were. Perhaps
they could look down into the building underneath.

Rastus was the first to the skylight; he could not believe what he was seeing. The
expression on his face was of acute horror and panic. In an almost audible shout, that Rastus
managed to contain to a muffled whisper at the last moment, he called to Lex, with tears and
emotion in his voice. "That's my Mother down there, and I know that she has seen me. She
waved to me to go away. My Mother, my Mother!" The full-grown hybrid man of impeccable
qualities was crying. Lex could not believe what was happening.

a moment or two in the darkness, away from that skylight." Whispered
yourself a moment or more to calm down. Don't forget, you are an agent of
ob, which has to be done. If you give yourself away you betray everyone below
the farm. Possibly your entire race!"

e a lot to do." Came the reply from Rastus. "We have to be away from here by
d we must see all that is going on. Look over there. There were other people on
black uniforms. They have gone now; it was the silver braid that caught my eye.
something into that building down those vents. We ought to go and look, follow
us certainly had become very positive in his action. Lex hoped that he was not gong
e careless. Still with their shoes around their necks, they crawled on. Over a gantry
o the next building they climbed, with stealth. Great care was needed. The darkness
very little illumination with which to see by. There was the glow of the flame from
imney and the illumination coming up through the various skylights in the roofs of
uildings. Rastus and Lex did very well to reach the section of roof without making a
d or a slip. Rastus was determined to see what those uniformed officers were doing with
e vents.

Lex and Rastus lay flat on the slightly inclined roof, they could see directly into the area
low.

"It's the shower house," Lex whispered very quietly to Rastus who was so close to him
that their faces almost touched. "Look, there are several officers down there in the changing
area. They are making those women undress. Look that woman has hidden her baby in the
pile of clothes." Lex was astonished. Why should she do that? He thought to himself.

It was not long before he saw the woman in an orderly manner take their naked bodies
in double file through the heavy open doors marked 'De-lousing'. They were about to be
slammed shut when the sound of a baby's crying came from under the pile of clothes. In an
instant, a female guard found it, and with a strange grimace on her face, she threw the child
onto the shower room floor. The child's mother went hysterical and pulled the child to her
naked bosoms. They were both crying now. That was the last Lex and Rastus could see of the
women from that position. They crawled a little further across the room to the next skylight.
Now that the doors had been slammed closed on the shower room, they could see directly in,
from this new position.

One of the women tried to turn on the water. Nothing happened. She banged the tap
with her hand almost to the point of pain. Still nothing happened.

Lex could hear the screams of horror. All hell was let loose as out of the ceiling vents
poured a yellow-orange vapor which dropped rapidly to the floor. Within moments the
women were dying choking on the floor, and others were climbing on top of the dead and
dying to reach a higher level to escape the heavy fumes. Possibly only a short moment later
they were banging with glazed sore and red eyes at the very skylight through which Lex and
Rastus were viewing. Rastus's instinct was to break the glass to help those possible survivors
to escape. He lifted his shoe, as if it were a hammer, about to use the heel to break the glass.
Lex grabbed his arm.

"No!" he almost shouted into Rastus's ear "That gas will kill us on contact, just as it is
killing them. Don't be mad, you can't help them, they are as good as dead already, look!"

Rastus looked very sick, but he was trying very hard to control his emotions. "I know, I knew" he corrected himself, "some of those poor souls down there. One was a cousin, another an ex girl friend and an old aunt. What are those thugs doing to us, and what rights have they to our lives."

Lex was very upset for Rastus. He was very much a part of what was gong on, and there was nothing immediate that could be done for them.

The two men lay there for what seemed an eternity. The pile of bodies seemed to fall away slightly. There was no sign of life. There were dead women and children in all different positions. So tangled up it was difficult to see whose limbs belonged to which body. Modesty was completely forgotten.

Then came the water. The showers really did work after all. The water came out in floods, washing the bodies and the area free of all the contaminating gas or gas powder that may have still lingered awhile.

The doors opened, and a guard entered with that hybrid he had seen in the duel earlier in the day. He was wearing an armband with the markings 'Kapo' on the ribbon. This must be his new rank, as an aide to the guards working there.

The 'Kapo' was being made to turn over all the bodies and untangle those that needed it. Every body was examined for concealed valuables, valuable metal teeth, some things secreted in the most personal places. Lex could not believe where the man was putting his hands. Was nothing sacred any more? He turned to see how Rastus was taking the trauma…he had passed out!

"Wake up! Wake up!" Lex was carefully and gently slapping Rastus's face, on each side. "You must wake up" Lex whispered.

"Erhh! Erhh!" Rastus started to grunt an acknowledgement he was beginning to regain his consciousness.

"We must leave here now Rastus! We cannot stay any longer or we might be caught. I think that we have done very well until now. Let us not outstay our 'welcome'."

"No." Rastus was indignant. "I want to see what they do with the bodies."

"You will have your answer almost immediately" Lex replied, getting hold of Rastus's arm to indicate the direction to look. "Do you see the small railway truck on that narrow gauge track? Look it goes directly into the shower room."

The intrepid couple lay on the roof watching them loading the bodies of the poor wretches, who not long before had been so full of life. They were being thrown carelessly into the trucks until not one body was left. The remaining valuables were left by the Kapo, in the middle of the room in a neat pile. He then pushed the trucks off down the gentle incline in the direction of the building with the chimneys.

"That's it!" Lex gasped at the realization. "The smell of roasting meat. They were burning the bodies. They are removing all proof of their existence!!" Lex then used vocabulary that was very rare for him to mouth. What an idiot he felt he had been.

"Let's go!" he called sharply but quietly to Rastus.

Erash was getting desperate. He had been in solitary confinement for many days. His main objective was to keep his mind and body fit, alert and well. The walls of his room were not thick, and he was easily able to hear the comings and goings of people as they passed by along the corridor outside. On the rare occasion when somebody came into his room with an excuse for food, a change of his ablutions, he tried very hard to engage them in some form of conversation, but he never received more than a polite reply. Instead he would speak at length to the small birds that shared his prison. Sometimes he would run on the spot, counting until he became tired, other times he would sit down in the corner nearest to the door, and listen very hard to what he could hear of the outside world. He was sure, that once, quite recently he heard Rula walking past with at least two other women, but he was not sure. He would sit there in the corner and think of Rula, and Marla very often. It was their images in his mind that kept him motivated to survive.

He was completely surprised with himself, the most obvious gesture that he could perform in the pursuance of his release. The idea came to him and he felt such a fool. Why had he not thought of it before? He needed pen and paper. How could he get that? It was forbidden to him except…Erash remembered the old 'International Code for the Conduct of War Prisoners and Wounded'. One of its clauses read 'at no time, and under no circumstances should any prisoner of war, or wounded of war, ever be prevented from making his Will. Also complete personal confidentiality should permanently prevail'. Erash decided to make a Will. That way he would be able to obtain pen and paper.

There was no problem in obtaining the materials with which to write his 'Will'. He re-wrote it in much the same way as he had when he left for Semir, but this time he tried to mention Rula and Marla without actually writing their names. The will had to look somewhat authentic, or they may have wondered what he was up to, and caused him many inconveniences. He certainly did not want to arouse his captors' suspicions.

With the very fine blade he had kept concealed in the sole of his shoe, he managed to cut off, very neatly the lower quarter of the sheet of paper on which he was writing.

"I am a captive, in the International Emergency Safety Hospital in Larden. My companion has been taken away. Erash. S & W."

He took the message, and rolled it up very small, and inserted it in a clip that was attached to the leg of one of the small birds. He pulled the little stool over to the middle of the room. He found that if he stood perilously on the stool which he perched on top of the bucket of his 'slops' it gave him just enough height, using his shoe he could force open the skylight sufficiently to allow his pigeon to escape through. As the bird flew away, Erash felt a tremendous sense of achievement.

Rula, Mela and Lara sat naked, but wrapped in towels, together, in the recovery room. They were bewildered, at the polite manner, and the treatment that was being meted out to them, since their horrific ordeal at their 'branding'. The three girls had spent the last few days together under very traumatic circumstances. They had become very close to one another. The fact that there were consecutive numbers engraved on their posteriors was only part of their fond relationship. Rula had become very much one of the girls; they had evolved into a real team, a family. There was a newfound wealth of fellowship between them. The absence of their fourth, Rebecca only added to their endeavors to remain together. They found mutual strength in their unity; they had been through so much together.

A friendly male guard burst in through the door. He had a polite smile upon his face, as he threw three large bundles onto the floor in front of them.

"Here you are, put these clothes on, then report to the duty nursing supervisor in the office where you will be issued with your orders." The guard was very pleasant, and as an afterthought he added, "By the way, I wish the three of you well, and the best of luck." He smiled a warm smile and departed.

"Why are they all so polite and pleasant to us now?" Mela was thinking aloud, as she began to get the clothes together.

"They are certainly doing us proud" Lara interrupted "I have never seen such beautiful underwear. These clothes are beautiful. Look at the quality. They are all well known designer names." Lara started to parade around the room in her new underwear teasing her two friends with her beautiful see through blouse, a clear looking black net fabric which seems to dance through the air as she moved so gracefully as if dancing in the wind.

"Set to music, that would look truly professional" Rula remarked "but be very careful, don't run away with yourselves. We have not been dressed up in wonderful clothes for nothing. What are we going to do? What is going to be expected of us? Take care, and be careful." Rula's comments at that moment seemed to tame Lara who stopped in mid-flow. She collapsed back on to the chair and started to cry. Rula went over to comfort her. Perhaps this once, she felt guilty, perhaps she had gone too far. On the few occasions that one arises, after what they had been through, they should enjoy the happier moments to their full.

The trio looked dressed to kill as they entered the duty nurse's office. They even felt quite pleased with themselves, as they had helped each other with their make-up. The three of them looked a dream, and the nursing officer said so. "You are to be taken from here within the next few moments, so please collect your belongings from that desk over there, and you will be settling into your new base which will be your home for as long as is necessary. You may enjoy your new position or you may not, but it is very much suggested that you try to. Your base will be in the romantic city of Politir, at the house of the Dolls.

The building was very beautiful. It was just getting dark as they arrived at its' old fashioned and over decorative main entrance. The atmosphere of grandeur, and times past became very evident as the three girls entered the 'palace'. The ornate chandeliers and the beautifully hand-carved furniture made out of wood. *That* was a material that had disappeared from use in furnishings, a whole generation ago. Only antique furniture was legally wooden. Even in Bylia. It was a result of the World Convention of preservation of Wildlife, and the environment.

The trio, were standing in the foyer of this superb magnificent hotel, bewildered and curious, when all of a sudden Lara let out a yell, as she threw her arms around the neck of a stranger. "Oh am I pleased to see you. What have you been doing? Have they been kind to you? Lara would have gone on and on, but Rebecca turned away as her eyes caught Rula's.

"What is that bitch doing here" she spat in the direction of Rula.

***

Well over thirty days in orbit had passed by so quickly. Lika could not believe that she had completed one whole female cycle in space. She was a little concerned; she was usually *so* regular that one could tell the time by her. She was now very late, but she consoled herself with the knowledge that some women had been known to go very irregular when affected by reduced, or zero gravity.

Perhaps she was one of them. Nevertheless she was consumed with her concern. It was not that she did not want a child, but the truth was, she did not want one just then, this project was so very important to her. She decided to give it another few days and then perhaps go for medical advice at the orbital unit health center. If she was pregnant, there was a strong possibility that she would be sent back home below. She could not anticipate such a calamity. That would represent a complete failure and defeat in her mission, if she was forced to put her feet back on the ground. They just did not allow pregnancy in space. It was a forbidden sin due to an earlier dated suspicion as to the possibility of the embryo being affected by cosmic radiation in space. Recent tests disproved that theory, but old rules were very difficult to change. She had decided not to tell Svi until she had to.

"I've marked off sixteen different children in experimental section eight. Each one is easily identified by their color sex and build. I have already listed some of their individual strange habits".

Svi was waking Lika out of her daze. She was deep in thought in some other world. He continued . . .

"I'm growing quit fond of one little so and so, who keeps making strange noises at the girls. He's a real character you know." Svi was trying to involve Lika in casual conversation, but he was having communication problems. He did not understand it, Lika was not herself, and was not saying a word in reply. Not at all like her.

"Lika, wake up! Snap out of it!"

Svi walked up behind her, and put his arms lightly around her waist. She turned around to face him with a feint childish smile. They kissed. There was a slight tear in Lika's eye. Svi knew that on this occasion, he should not press the subject, so he tried to change the mood. He continued.....

"Do you notice the one prime problem that these young people have is difficulty in communication? They have advanced brain ability just like us. They are human offspring, and yet being completely cut off, and devoid of any knowledge of speech or language, they have to create their own. Do you see how they came together in small groups, and how one often tries to become a leader as they endeavor to combine their wills together to perform a task too big for one to handle. At the moment they seem to understand one another using whines and grunts. They even have some form of simple use of one 'word' language. Listen hard and occasionally you will hear a word that is often repeated. 'Lok'. That seems to mean 'come' but it sometimes is used in a completely different context. These people are growing up very fast; soon we will find it very difficult to keep up with their progress. I do find this study very rewarding. The strange instincts that these humans have and the way they adapt to their community certainly show many of the qualities, errors and characteristics of the human race. A study of this nature would never have been possible back on our Mother Planet. It is an honor and a privilege to be here on this project with you Lika, and I couldn't do it without you!" Svi pulled tightly at Lika's waist trying to cheer her up.

"I wish, I wish . . ." Lika was very dismayed, she was being slightly wistful.

"There is something very wrong isn't there." Svi began to try and break the ice. "What is troubling you? I know you are now happy. There is something worrying you. What?" He stepped back and went round to the front of Lika; he wanted to see her face as she answered. The truth was very important to him.

"I might be pregnant!" The words came out from Lika's mouth in a quite involuntary manner, as if they were not hers to keep and had to be returned to their rightful owner.

"WHAT!" Svi shouted so loudly he frightened Lika who cowered back for a brief moment. "I can't believe it, when did you know? How absolutely marvelous! When is it due? I'm going to be a daddy. I love you so much, you are the best thing that ever happened to me, and now you put more sugar on it. Let's celebrate!"

Lika was amazed at Svi's response; she couldn't get a word in edgeways. She never expected this response.

"I'm not certain yet" she began to reply "and anyway, if you think about it, I could be in real bad trouble, I could be sent back home without you until the baby is born, and if I or we want to keep it, I would have to stay below until the child was of school age. There are no 'long stay' children allowed in space, and certainly no pregnancies.

"That is not strictly true" Svi replied. "Certainly pregnancy in space is frowned upon, but you have been out here already for more than five weeks, and I know that you can't be more than two months into your time, so if any serious damage was to be done it has happened already. You can have a scan, which will show the genetic health of the embryo."

Svi continued without interruption, Lika was enthralled lapping up his every word.

"Secondly, there are young 'long stay' children up here in orbit."

"Where?" Queried Lika, with a cautious tone in her voice.

"Here!" Svi delivered his coup de grace. "Here at the project. We can give our first born to the project, which will ensure that we can stay up here and work together at least for this next year as planned.

"You mean I should give our baby away before it is born! That's a typical unfeeling reaction of a male chauvinist!" Lika hesitated in thought for a moment and then continued in her reply. "I'll do it if you want. It may be the only way that I would get to stay here with you and the project, and we can always have more children later" Lika knew her logic made sense, but it was not at all feminine, and if she followed it, she would surely regret it.

"I'll go for tests immediately…. next week." She corrected, with a cheeky smile.

***

Noah felt very much on his own at the government sub-committee meeting on orbital defense. Tubal Cain was always there to support him with notes and background material. He did not like being inadequately prepared for such a crucial discussion, he was determined to pull out all stops and speak his mind. He had a wealth of knowledge to draw from; he just had to be sure that he could find the correct facts when he needed them.

There were twenty-two people present plus the Chairman who seemed to be very little aware of the importance of coming to any decisions. He was just content to contain the discussions on an informal basis, hoping that a policy document could be prepared to put forward to the correct government ministry. Noah was determined to cut the bureaucracy and get a strong policy recommendation put forward to update the orbital defense system. He wanted to increase the experimental manufacture of interplanetary travel vehicles.

"We must maintain our vigilance in defense of our territories, from above" Noah was at last able to speak, he had been sitting in his seat for a long time, listening to a great deal of garbled uninformed drivel being put forward by members who very much liked the sound of their own voices, and had a self interest in making themselves heard.

Noah continued…..

Following on from previous decisions made in government committee some weeks ago, inroads have been made in to the expansion and enlargement of several orbital space stations, from this our ability to increase our ground defense system has very much improved, but I would like to seek permission for a variation in policy to update vehicle development to enable us to improve our ability to travel outside orbital space. At present we only visit dead planets and make use of their raw materials. We have no local living planet in our system. The only living planet in orbit around our sun is our own and we are killing that off fast. In three more generations if we are lucky and less if we are realists, the very planet that mothered us will be no more than our cemetery. We must strive to improve our environment, and we must strive to reach farther into deeper space. There are areas where we are sure human life can be supported unaided. If this committee would grant permission for the planning of a proto-type vessel that will be able to travel at many times the speed of light, we have the engineers and scientific know-how available to start it."

The committee seemed completely hypnotized by Noah. He had a way of speaking that would carry his audience along with him. It was not always what he said, but the manner in which he made his points that seemed so professional.

"My second point, as I have said many times before, is the environment. We are killing this planet very quickly. In time there will be nothing left. This planet will die, and will join the other dead or weakened planets in the graveyard of space."

"They say that it is impossible to travel faster than the speed of light!" A voice came from the far end of the room.

"That is not true, and we will prove it very soon. For example, if you have two objects traveling at just less than the speed of light, towards each other, after they have passed one another their joint speed of separation will be nearly twice the speed of light."

"They won't be able to see each other then?" Came a question from the floor.

"That is not exactly true," Was Noah's answer "But this is neither the time nor the place for a science lesson."

"Why not?" The voice was very persistent almost bordering onto being that of a heckle. Noah was getting annoyed, and felt that he was being pushed into giving an answer.

"The answer is really simple." Noah condescended to enlarge on the subject. "As the two bodies move farther apart the light leaving them will travel more slowly than the bodies moving away from each other, as in relation to each other they are traveling faster than the speed of light. If you can imagine light having its time at the moment of transmission or reflection, then as it moves away from its source at great speed, the light will still retain the characteristic images of the moment it left its origin. Eventually, if the objects slow down in relationship to each other, either by one, the other or both reducing speed eventually the light from the original meeting will 'catch up' and the passing object will become visible. The only problem will be that it would be too small to see. Certainly with the correct apparatus the distant image will become visible as it was at that moment in the past, if the magnification were to be available to find it."

Noah could see that his theorizing was going way over the heads of the people gathered there, and decided to follow his original instincts and continue his first line of argument. "The Ostrich bird buries his head in the sand when he senses danger. It is suspected that he does this for two reasons. *Either* to hide from the danger, if he cannot see it, perhaps it will go away, *or* to camouflage himself to appear as a 'bush' amongst the surrounding dead dry bracken in which he lives. Are we trying to emulate the achievements of this poor species? Do we not see the dangers around us? Are we oblivious to the self-destructive nature of human attitude to the very planet that is our own home? Our rivers are overflowing with pollution and poison. Our fields are being sprayed into deadly wastes. The rain forests are being reduced to the timber yards for the sake of progress. The atmosphere carries vengeful chemicals that drop out of the sky on a daily basis. When did you last enter your homes without having to brush yourselves down, possibly take a shower to get dust out of your hair? Do we have to live like this, and what hope is there for our children and our children's children."

Noah felt that he was going over old ground and no way would these ignorant people understand his argument. He just wanted their agreement, he didn't care whether they understood or not.

"Thank you Mr. Noah, if you would kindly leave." The Chairman almost interrupted Noah in full flow. He had not yet made the full force of his plea. "I think that we have heard enough now to form an opinion, so if you would kindly leave, and we will advise you of our decision in a few moments.

Noah picked up his papers and backed away from the lectern, he was most surprised by the Chairman's outburst. It was very unusual for that man to take any action in the proceedings. Noah left with great trepidation. He had a troubled look about him.

Noah threw his arms around Naamah. He had tears in his eyes. "I've won!" He pulled his pregnant wife tight against his body. "The committee has agreed to increase our funding. They have given us everything we wanted. I can't believe it."

"There must have been divine intervention!" Naamah replied looking at Noah straight into his eyes.

***

The soft shadows of the frail flickering flame of candlelight were very complimentary to the distinctive friendly features of Tsionne's face. Tubal Cain had not been so happy in his recent memory. He could not recall how he had arranged that he and Tsionne got away from the gathering crowd of VIP's, in order that they could go off together for a quiet romantic meal. He just knew that he had done it, and he was elated. Tubal could not take his eyes off Tsionne's face. He adored her beauty, as the dimples appeared in her rounded cheeks as she smiled. He was completely absorbed in her presence with him. They sat facing each other across the candle lit table completely enwrapped in each other's company. The restaurant was well known for its anonymity. There were small alcoves and hidden seating sections where anyone wishing to be discreet could conceal themselves.

Tubal found himself talking with Tsionne in a trivial manner that he had never understood before. Previously the only person he ever felt so close to and could speak so freely with was his sister Naamah, but that was slightly different. He could not believe that people, who only a few days before, were perfect strangers, could now be such close friends. He felt that they had known each other for years.

Tsionne happily allowed Tubal to order her meal; somehow she was completely captivated by the air of Tubal's authority. He seemed to carry it so very well. There was not even a hint of arrogance in Tubal Cain's manner, and yet his strength of character outshone anyone she had known before. Being entirely at ease in his company, she felt complete trust and admiration for this man whom she had only just met. There was no question in her mind, no doubt, not even a whisper of caution; she knew that she had met a person who could be a man to her. She knew that she could easily fall in love with him. That is if it were still to be in the future tense. Perhaps she had done so already.

Tubal had ordered the sliced meat that was to be cooked at the table. While they were waiting Tubal organized some drinks. Tsionne was delighted at his choice of fruit dip. An alcoholic beverage in a large communal bowl which was placed in the center of their table into which they would dip the soft sponge-like quinoa-fruit, in order that it would soak up the liquid. Tsionne was always amazed at the power of these fruits, and their capacity to hold the juices without spilling a single drop. The skill was being able to handle the soft substance without squeezing it thus expelling the fluids too early. The quinoa-fruit in its natural state is a small edible round sponge, which is naturally very absorbent and yet has its own very distinctive flavor. Tsionne was amazed at the miraculous blend of tastes so carefully chosen by Tubal Cain.

Tsionne reached across the table for another fruit. Tubal had the same thought and intention at that identical movement. They both reached for the same fruit and their fingers touched almost apologetically at first, but neither hand retracted even a fraction. Tubal made the first move as he carefully took the tips of Tsionne's fingers between his thumb and forefinger. There must have been bells ringing somewhere, as the electricity seemed to conjoin the couple into a warm happiness. They were completely oblivious to anything around them as their eyes met, not a word needed to leave their mouths. They both knew that heaven was theirs and they had been blessed.

Tubal Cain could remember little of the meal as he escorted Tsionne back to her home. He knew that they had enjoyed it, and he had a very warm feeling inside him as he walked along the covered mall with Tsionne's hand tucked into his. They had indulged in nothing more than small talk, which Tubal did not even know was in his vocabulary. He never usually had the time for such things. He could not believe that he had achieved such pleasure from trivial conversation. Not a word of politics or foreign policy. They were just a happy courting couple that had found themselves very much in love.

Tubal Cain thought that she would never ask, but it seemed to come out so naturally.

"Come in" she said "Let us have a night cap together. You can always get a hover-cab or rota-bus back to your hotel" Tsionne was smiling as she spoke.

They disappeared into Tsionne's apartment. Tubal was very impressed. A lot of thought had gone into the decor. A woman's touch made all the difference. He thought of his own apartment and the utility approach he had, to the manner in which he had decorated his home. The feminine touch seemed to make things gentle, more comfortable. She had done things no self-respecting man could do, but to what wonderful effect. He could grow to like this kind of life.

An hour later, Tubal and Tsionne were asleep in their own beds, having had a superb evening together. Each would dearly have liked to kiss the other one goodnight, but as usual Tubal acted the perfect gentleman and took his leave of her after only a short while. They were both determined to keep the kindled flame of their love burning. They never admitted it to each other, but they did not want to destroy this relationship by rushing it.

***

Marla was unsure about the noise coming from the pigeon loft. She was certain that she heard a familiar sound. Surely one of the birds could not have returned. She must be imagining things. Rula and Erash had been away now for well over a week, in fact nearly two. Marla was sure it must be another false alarm. She had been up there every day, sure that she had heard an arrival of one of the birds taken by Erash. Each time she had opened the attic door, there had been nothing, just the polite wind making itself heard against the beaded curtain on the window pane. Again she climbed the steep metal stairs that led to the trap door into the roof-space of the "House of Four Eyes." Each time she pushed it upwards above her head, a shower of fresh black dust would fall down into her hair. She kept re-proaching herself. By now she should have come prepared, possibly wearing a plastic shower cap that she could keep at the bottom of the stairs. She promised herself every time, and then inconveniently forgot when she returned to the lower levels. Taking a careful breath to avoid the dust, she clambered through the opening on all fours, then standing up at full height she walked over to the corner window which led out into the pigeon loft where the little flap would allow entrance for the returning feathered friends.

Pulling very carefully at the beaded drape, Marla carefully peeked through a small gap between the curtains. Sudden surprise and incredible relief simultaneously registered dramatically through her tense body.

Perched on the side of a small water trough, the little body of a friendly pigeon. Marla was sure that his little face was smiling, proudly announcing his arrival from a successful mission. She walked over to pick him up, and there on his foot she found what she wanted. She could not wait to undo the protective wrapping. Marla was desperate to read that message.

Noah was in the bath when Tubal Cain's secretary called. There was a televideo in the bathroom and Noah was dripping wet as he reached across for the videophone. The sweet smile on the face of Tubal's secretary announced the good news. Noah was delighted to hear about Erash, he jumped straight out of the bath with surprise. He had to go and tell Naamah, he forgot all about taking a towel and his wet footprints found their way very quickly to Naamah's dressing room. Had Noah realized it he may have been quite embarrassed, as he had displayed his full but wet masculinity to Meryl, Tubal's attractive personal secretary. She will probably always carry that strange memory with her; he had forgotten to turn off his screen transmission.

Naamah and Noah could not stop talking about the arrival of the message in Semir. Now many things were falling into place. It seemed that Marla had explained in great detail the happenings in Semir and how Erash and Rula had teamed up together. Marla was now very concerned about the safety of her sister and was trying to arrange to trace her. It was hoped that when Tubal returned to Science and Welfare, he would organize a rescue effort to release Erash from the Bylian's grip in Larden. Meryl was sending a message to Tubal Cain in Postia. It was now urgent that he should return. Noah was already constructing and planning a rescue. Noah, although now only half dressed had already arranged a meeting for later that evening, and had cancelled all other arrangements for the next few days. Naamah had agreed to act as hostess and was already preparing their home for the visitors. She was hoping that Tubal would make it back in time. His authority was very desperately needed.

Meanwhile in Larden, Erash could little have known how much change he was making to so many lives at that moment, solely due to that scribbled note he had attached to a little pigeon's leg.

Naamah never got flustered when out to entertain, and in spite of having staff to help, she always took a personal pride in making any guests to her home feel comfortable and welcome. She put a great deal of personal effort into the preparation even at such short notice. She knew that this was to be very much a business meeting, but they would get through it more easily in a relaxed comfortable atmosphere. She had the large dining-room table laid out like a boardroom, for a very well attended meeting. She also had a running buffet laid in the same room, so that they need never go hungry or thirsty during the long night's discussions. She sincerely hoped that Tubal Cain would return in time.

His attendance was possibly crucial.

As people started to arrive Naamah found it difficult to put names to faces, so she issued each delegate with an external nametag for them to wear in their lapel. There were people from the security forces directly under Erash in Science and Welfare, there were two people from the special commando unit, and one well established officer from the scientific special effects department. Most interesting of all was the attractive woman who appeared a little late with Tubal Cain's secretary. They walked into the reception just as Noah was about to call the meeting to order. Naamah walked over to Meryl who she knew very well.

"Won't you introduce me to your friend, and I'll make up a badge for her." Naamah enquired.

"This is Marla. Her sister went off with Erash to Larden and now she is missing." Meryl continued "Marla and her sister Rula are Bylians by birth, but they had to give up their country and fight for its integrity while in exile. They are members of what they commonly call 'The Popular Front for the Liberation of Bylia.' They are working with us; they have the same mutual interest, to unseat Fadfagi from power."

"Aren't they terrorist's?" Naamah enquired innocently. "No! They are on our side." Meryl was shocked that such an apparent insult could come from the lips of her friend and Noah's wife Naamah.

"Don't worry" interjected Marla, "we are used to it, but we don't care what we are called so long as we win in the end. A name is only a name, the deed is more important than the breed."

They took their places at the 'board room' table. The meeting was being called to order. Noah was in full force....

"We have a problem, Erash, the security chief of Science and Welfare has been taken prisoner, and is being held hostage in Larden on the border between Bylia and Orcamo. The purpose of this meeting is to decide how and whether to affect his rescue. He had teamed up with a member of the Popular Front for the Liberation of Bylia but they have been separated.

I cannot give you the identity of the other person, because we do not want to break their cover in case there is still a chance of security. Let it just be noted that our two organizations are working together for a common cause. One of us here today is a member of that group, and I am sure that we all wish that person heartfelt support at this time. I am sorry to be so vague but, although we will display our first name tags as a form of identity, you will notice that none of us are identified by interest or department. If you happen to know each other anyway, so be it, but please do not volunteer information about yourselves or your position in your organization to anyone here. Security is of prime importance, as was explained to you all when you arrived. Every person here is representative of a department of government or commerce directly affected by this situation, and as such, has been empowered, through me to make the necessary decisions and act upon them. Breaches of security have become very common, and all attention must be made to the secrecy of this meeting, as it may affect the outcome."

At that moment there was a commotion outside in the lobby, and the door to the room burst open. A guard entered looking somewhat flustered.

"Excuse me sir!" the young man saluted and addressed Noah in a formal manner. "Tubal Cain seeks admission, but he is accompanied by a woman from another country. Her name is Tsionne."

"Inform Tubal Cain that he is most welcome, but it would be imprudent at this stage to embarrass his companion with knowledge of the discussions that are about to take place. Perhaps she would be entertained elsewhere" Noah replied.

"Please ask Tubal to come straight in, he is needed."

The meeting went on late into the night. Naamah kept everybody well supplied with food and drink. She even found time to go into the anteroom where Tsionne was resting and had a long conversation with her. Naamah liked Tsionne; she was a seemingly honest natural and kind woman. They seemed to strike up a fond friendship even in only that short space of time.

It was the early hours of the morning when the meeting broke up. Naamah and Tsionne could hear the delegates leaving and the hustle and bustle of casual conversation eventually dwindled to a mere murmur. The voices of Noah and Tubal Cain began to become more distinguishable from the thinning crowd until all that was left were Meryl, Noah and Tubal. The door to the ante-room opened, and the trio walked in with a friendly greeting for Naamah and Tsionne. Noah had a smile of satisfaction on his face.

"I did not expect to find you both still awake at this time in the morning." Noah spoke to Naamah. "It's very late, but let us all have a drink together. We achieved decisions last evening that will have far reaching consequences."

***

CHAPTER 10

Marla entered the front door of the 'House of Four Eyes' most carefully as it was very early in the morning and she did not want to break her own house-rule of peace and quiet whilst her guests were asleep. The early staff were already in the kitchen, she could hear their every move, but she was more concerned that she should not be seen arriving back at such an early morning hour. She pushed the entry-key pad of her private living quarters and as the doors slid silently apart she was taken aback by the brightness of what should have been a darkened room. Through the glare of the full illumination she could see familiar faces. Her 'gang' had been waiting there to meet her.

"We are in business!" she smiled "We have got a job to do, and we have the full backing of Science and Welfare and all that involves. There is a big 'but'…this project has to be kept 'Top Secret', for our eyes only, and of course those in our organization that need to know. I am afraid that excludes three of you here this morning, the most recent arrivals to this group, so I must ask you to leave. If the others disagree when I have briefed them, then you will be notified and called back. If after the initial briefing the secrecy cannot be agreed, then the project is off! Marla was almost out of breath as she spoke. With that the three discarded figures smiled an embarrassed acknowledgement, and left the room together. Marla closed the door behind them and turned to the others.

"I am very tired, I have had a very long day, but I owe it to my loyal friends to give you an initial de-briefing before I get some well earned sleep."

They all took chairs and sat down in a semi circle around Marla who took a small sample of cable-juice to dampen her mouth as she spoke…..

"I said that we have the full backing of Science and Welfare but that is only part of it. We have the full support of their government, but they cannot and will not admit to it. This is the major reason for complete secrecy. As you know, we have located Erash but not my sister Rula. Science and Welfare, with their government's backing will help us to capture Erash back from Larden, and then we are to hold him for ransom to the Bylians, who cannot afford to lose him. He is their meal ticket for supplies. We will have Erash back with us and Bylia will pay us for the privilege. In the meanwhile Erash can help us to find Rula."

Her audience was stunned and open mouthed at such subterfuge, but there were those amongst them who could not resist a smile.

"If you accept in principle, the plan that I have put before you so far, then I will have to ask you to show signs of fidelity to the government of Science and Welfare and sign their official secrets act by which you will be bound, by agreement. I have already done so. I am now going to bed; give me your answer later in the morning. I put the word answer deliberately in the singular, as it must be entirely unanimous. I must ask you to leave now as I am very tired, and you will have a lot to discuss."

If it weren't for the bright hazy cloud, Marla would have been able to see the brilliance of the hot sun almost vertically above them. It was midday, as she awoke from her well-deserved slumbers ready to face the 'new' day. Would her colleagues agree to take part in helping a foreign country? Would they agree to help to release Erash whom she was missing wildly? These thoughts had lain with her as she slept, and now they were turning over and over in her mind. She had to find out. She had arranged the recall of the meeting for mid-afternoon and was hoping that all would be sorted out then.

Marla's friends were all smiling, as they arrived back at her rooms, somewhat like a returning jury, waiting to give their verdict. Marla looked at each one's face to see if she could trace even the smallest gesture of revelation. None whatsoever, she would have to wait for them to deliver in their own way.

The group finally resumed their positions of the previous meeting early that morning. Marla was becoming impatient, but she dared not show it. To her the passage of time seemed so slow, but she knew that in reality it was her impatience that was slowing everything down in her mind. How long now, she thought, before she would know Erash's fate.

The old gentleman spoke first. He was full of authority in his voice, and the others were looking on with respect in their faces, enough to convince Marla, that the answer she was about to hear had their full unanimous support.

Marla could feel her heart beating in her chest as her friend mouthed his words of agreement to her proposals. She became elated and her whole demeanor was lifted to new heights of happiness. Involuntary words came out of her mouth, she was almost crying..... "Does that mean that we will be on our way? We are really going to get Erash back, at risk of our own lives?" She was crying now, and her friend, the old man came over to her to give comfort. They were all so happy, and very resolute.

The following day a small group of the P.F.L.B. all hand picked and carefully chosen for the job met with a similar group from Science and Welfare to begin training in special arts.

***

Daylight was just beginning to present itself. The faint haze of low cloud was beginning to turn a deep magenta as the darkness of the night was turning into early day. Lex and Rastus had made some distance from the horrors of that previous night. Traveling in the dark, down the valley and through the thick dry bracken had not been easy. They had finally made it to the low hill that would lead them back on their homeward journey to Jabal's farm.

Rastus heard the noise at exactly the same moment as he felt Lex's hand on his arm.

"Did you hear that?" Lex whispered in Rastus's ear. "I am sure that was a woman's muffled scream! "It came from over there amongst that clump of bushes just near the top of the hill. Do we dare to investigate?" Rastus was unsure and they had to be cautious. Their report had to reach Jabal at any cost. It was imperative that nothing should stop them. It could be a trap.

"I will go in very carefully, and you watch my rear." Lex mouthed to Rastus. "If a poor woman is in pain we must help her. Listen those cries are of agony. Somebody must be torturing her.

It went quiet once more as they approached the clump of bushes very slowly. They did not want to make a sound. No sooner than they had reached the point where Lex was going to go on alone, when the muffled screaming started again in real earnest. That poor woman must be in real pain thought Rastus.

"Be careful, and be cautious" he called quietly to Lex who began to move off, as it had gone quiet once more.

"Ahhrgh!" The noise came again, and Lex disappeared into the bushes, out of sight of Rastus, who immediately followed behind taking care to watch for others, or the possibility of a trap being sprung. The noise started yet again, just as Rastus arrived at the scene only seconds after Lex.

Rastus could not believe what he was seeing. It was unreal and completely incongruous. Daylight was almost full by now and the sight that had presented itself to both men was one that neither of them would ever forget. Lex very obviously did not have any idea what do to. Rastus made the first decision.

"Water! You must get some water. There is a fresh mountain stream over there, take our nearly empty water-cans and re-fill them. Be quick, we will need plenty of water."

The hybrid woman was naked from the waist down, her mouth had been gagged with a thick handkerchief tied behind her head, and sweat was pouring down her face. She was sitting in a crouching position with her legs well apart. She was holding her very pregnant stomach and was in the process of giving birth. The head of the yet unborn child was clearly visible, well blooded and messy as the woman even as Rastus watched, helplessly pushed in a desperate attempt to dislodge the infant. The head was now fully exposed as Lex returned. Then all hell seemed to let loose as the entire infant just dropped clearly out into its mother's waiting arms.

"She had done that all by herself" Lex said the obvious "What courage!"

"What else could she do" Rastus replied as he took off his shirt and tore it to help wash the baby. The woman shook the child and gave it a thwack across its back. It let out a yell. The woman looked shocked even though she was still gagged. Rastus had seen this all before many times on Jabal's farm. It was not so new to him and he knew what to do. He had cut the baby free, and they washed it with the water from the nearby stream. "Who did this to you?" Rastus asked as he removed the gag from around her mouth.

"My husband, so that I could scream, and bite into something without making too much noise. He has gone for water, but that was a long time ago and he has not returned. "The woman was becoming distressed, as she began to realize her worries since the birth was now over.

"My husband, what has happened to him? Have you escaped, like us, and who is your friend. Did he help you?" She was nursing her baby's face to her chest, and stroking its head. At least the newcomer to the world was happy. He was wrapped in what was left of Rastus's shirt.

"What do you mean escape?" Rastus was asking. "Where have you come from? Were you on the train?"

The woman did not know what to say. She seemed scared to answer. "Well yes. When they made every body get off the train we crawled underneath and hid on the bogie wheels of the engine. We couldn't be seen as we were well above the ground. When a terrible duel was taking place we ran for it into the bushes and waited for darkness. No one saw us. They were all intent in watching the fight. Were you there, did you see it?"

"Yes we saw it!" Lex interrupted. "It was horrible. You are very lucky to have got away. Where could your husband be and why had he been so long. Its broad daylight now and we have to move if we are not to be discovered soon. I will go and look for him."

"He was bleeding badly" The woman called "He was badly cut when he fell last night in the heavy bracken. You can follow his trail. It was bad wound under his right shoulder blade. There was a lot of blood. Please find him, he may need help." She began to sob with relief at having someone to be there, and shock at the realization of the culmination of events. Lex disappeared, but he found a trail, and Rastus sat with the woman. He helped to clear her up and then return her to her modesty. She was a very attractive woman. Rastus nearly forgot his Glenshee for a few tantalizing moments as he helped to replace her personal clothing.

The trail of blood became easier to follow as Lex pursued its course. The poor man must have been bleeding very badly.… Lex came to a sudden drop, and there in a trench, lay a male hybrid, very bloody. Lex climbed down, taking great care not to drop soil onto the poor man lying there. He lifted his head. There was life in the body but only just. It lay in a pool of blood.

"Can you hear me?" Lex enquired in a calm, warm manner of voice.

The hybrid nodded in the affirmative, trying very hard to speak, but without success, as a full mouthful of blood poured out into Lex's lap. The man was choking; Lex turned him on his side to help clear his channels for breath.

"Better?" He enquired. The man was still conscious. Again he nodded in the same manner, but this time not attempting to talk. "You are now a proud father of a delightful baby boy, and you have all successfully escaped the clutches of the people of the train. Well done. You can come home with us to our farm in safety." Lex felt the man's grip on his arm as the pleasure of what he was saying was striking home. Lex was just about to go on, when the man suddenly exhaled and became just a blood soaked body, lying in a soggy red trench. A life form was no more. There was no pulse, and the wound stopped bleeding.

"Did he know that he had become a father before he died? Tell me the truth, it is very important." Were the first words that the woman said when Lex returned to give them the sad news.

They buried him where he lay and Lex, Rastus, the woman and the baby all made off together in the direction of Jabal's farm.

They did not realize it at the time, but they now had a 'live' witness of those past events leading up to the destruction of many hybrid people. Unfortunately, it had been a very successful mission.

*****

Erash was certain that it was becoming warmer in his cell. Usually at night the heat was not so severe, but the humidity seemed to be increasing. His shirt was soaking and his underwear was clinging to his vital parts. He wanted to strip off completely and lie on the cold stone floor. Perhaps that would help to cool him down. The condensation was everywhere; it was even dripping from the ceiling. The occasional drop would land on his forehead or his now naked shoulder. He had removed his shirt and had even tried to wring it out. It was soaking wet. He was so hot and clammy, he could not believe it. It was so debilitating, He was feeling very tired. The sweat was pouring through his hair and running salty into his eyes. He had never known anything like it before. He curled up into the corner, naked, on the cold, wet, stone floor. He wrapped himself between the two abutting cold walls. He knew that stone nearly always remained cool in these conditions. He was sure that he was shivering a little. Perhaps he was going to lose consciousness. His head was beginning to swim. He was sure he saw Rula standing in the other corner, but she was gone no sooner than she had appeared. He must be delirious. It all seemed so real. He was sure it was she. He was certain that he recognized that smell, her perfume.

The three men and a woman were wearing breathing apparatus when they entered the cell. Their dark thin airtight suits made them resemble ballet dancers as their clothes clung tightly to every intimate part of their bodies.

They found Erash in a deep sleep, curled up naked in the corner of his cell. With the greatest care they very carefully lifted the naked sleeper onto a simple stretcher and quickly carried him through the corridors of the sleeping hospital to their waiting hoversphere. The entire hospital was asleep in a deep anesthesia, an ingenious result of secret work over the past year in Science and Welfare. Within moments, the four protected people with their captive sleeper were on board their rescue vehicle and away from Larden, on the way to Semir. In about another half hour, the hospital complex will begin to cool down as the air conditioning system returns to normal and the substitute gases begin to fade. Nothing dreadful would have happened, and there would have been no major tragedy, as the people concerned would have been fully aware of the heat and humidity and would not have undertaken any risky or dangerous work as they began to lose their efficiency, and became increasingly more uncomfortable.

Erash collected his thoughts as his sub-conscious mind began to give way to his consciousness. He felt warm, but comfortably so. He was surrounded by soft material. His head was on a cushion filled with goose-down. Where was he? That familiar smell of perfume. Yes, he thought, that was what he recognized. It was still there as he awoke from his slumbers. He opened his eyes very carefully. It was daylight, and he was in a room, darkened by nearly drawn curtains. He could smell that perfume. He knew it well.

"Rula, is that you? Where are we? What has happened? Where have you been? Erash sounded as if he was rambling on, but he wasn't. He did not yet know that he was no longer in Larden.

A voice came from across the room in reply.

"I'm not Rula, I'm Marla" she walked over to Erash and kissed his forehead with great tenderness. She had at times never thought she would see him alive again. "We have brought you back to Semir. You are back with our 'gang of thieves'. I hope you don't mind."

"Mind!" Erash sat bolt upright in the bed. "Mind! Of course I don't mind. It's wonderful to see you again. He grabbed hold of Marla's hand and pulled her to him. I have missed you so much, you would never know." He hesitated. "Have you brought Rula back as well? Where is she?

"No" Marla replied with regret in her voice. "We don't know where she is. We think that they have taken her away to service the Bylian army. We are trying very hard to trace her, but at least we have you back!"

"Even if it is only for a short while," Erash replied. "I will have to go as soon as I am fit. I have a job to do, and I would also like to find Rula." Erash was adamant.

"No!" Marla was being very firm. "You are to stay here at present. You are under our command, by directive from HQ at Science and Welfare. Nothing is written down for security reasons, but Science and Welfare's Tubal Cain needs you to work with us. He said you would agree if we show you this."

Marla held out a photograph of Tubal and Erash together after coming back from the explosion at Lyboncher. There were only two copies and they each had one. Erash kept his in his identity disc. He had cut his face out because it was just the right size to fit in the hole. Tubal knew about that. They had joked about it. Tubal would know that his photograph was the only intact copy. It was a trivial piece of information but excellent for security. It worked. It convinced Erash of the honesty of the order.

"Alright" Erash smiled. "I agree, and await your next command." He liked the glint in Marla's eyes. He was sure that he was going to enjoy the next mission. She had a very cheeky smile as she locked the door. It was just the two of them in the room. He smiled likewise. For the next little while he was going to be a very happy man.

***

Rula had mixed feelings about her new situation in Politir. The lush surroundings, the friendly treatment, and the satisfaction of every whim, was not the kind of life to which Rula was accustomed. She was resting on her bed, admiring herself in the mirror that took up best part of the ceiling. Her room was truly beautiful, and very lavishly fitted with heavy drapes and very deep long woolly carpet. If she had ever dropped a pin or a needle into it, there would only be one way of finding it, and in bare feet that could be very painful. The toilet facilities for internal cleanliness, the Jacuzzi with soap foam. The rubber suction system for removal of all unwanted body hairs. She had been recommended not to use this, having been told that the Bylians liked their woman with body hair. It was nevertheless advisable to keep the legs well stripped. She had a complete stock of all the best fragrances and perfumes. Nothing had been forgotten. She was allowed complete freedom of movement, but had been warned that she had been security tagged, and if she was caught outside the gate of the "hotel" unless escorting a registered client, she would be made use of in a public place, and then executed in public shortly afterwards. Strangely enough it was the thought of carnal mutilation in public, the shame of it that frightened her more than any death penalty. Death was terminal, but shame was something one had to live with for however short a period. People had been known to choose death, rather than face shame; she could understand that feeling considerably more now. She had not yet had a client since she had arrived, but the four girls had met together in one another's room, and they had had three briefing sessions in the manager's private lounge. Rebecca had been there although she had already started work. They obviously liked to train their new girls in groups.

Rula could not understand why Rebecca seemed to hate her so much. She knew that Rebecca did not trust her, and Rula was very concerned, even slightly hurt, that she should be the object of the poor girl's frustration. She seemed to blame Rula for their being there. The other girls were quite the opposite, they seemed to adore Rula, and though not much younger than her, they looked to her as someone they could trust, someone that to some extent, they could lean on. Rula wondered how things might change when they started work. That she was sure would be very soon.

It was at one of their social gatherings in Mela's room, that the full realization of what they were there for first hit Rula. Lara had her first assignment directed to her for that forthcoming evening. She was very nervous and didn't look forward to it at all. She knew that she was getting a top executive in the 'Secret Police' and she had been told that she had been chosen because of her almost innocence, and purity of appearance. This upset Lara very much. It made her come back to reality and remember the boy she had left behind never ever to see again. She had given him her everything, and he had known and loved her for it. How, she kept saying could she ever desecrate her body and give it freely to someone else whom she didn't even know. She was crying bitterly. The other three girls could do nothing to console her, or calm her down. Even Rebecca who had already had two different clients on separate occasions could not help her.

It was finally Rula who managed to take the young girl in hand and suggested that she took her back to her room. Rula would help her to dress and prepare for her forth-coming meeting. Rula had decided in her own mind that she would try to talk young Lara out of her innocence and give her some confidence. In truth, she had not a small clue how she would do it, but do it, she would. Rula never gave up a challenge, and she could see a lot of her own younger self in that girl, who needed some rescuing or cushioning from the rigors of this type of life.

They reached Lara's room, with Rula having to mop away floods of her friend's tears. Lara had sat on the bed and with Rula's arms around her; she had placed her head to Rula's breasts like a baby and sobbed as if in her mother's arms. Rula could not believe the situation she had got herself into, but she had to see it through.

"I am not very much older than you," Rula started "and I've seen some of the seedier side of life. My origin is true Bylian, and I was born there. My mother was raped in front of my sister and me, when we were very young, and we have a half brother to prove it. We only know his father as being in Bylian soldier's uniform. Our father was away at the time. He was so enraged when he found out that we ran away from the Bylian state and settled near Semir. Ever since we have fought these people. We want our country back. I was a young girl in the fields helping to bring in the cable crop, when an old man grabbed me from behind and dragged me into the bushes. With the help of two other equally horrible men I was stripped and my virginity was torn from within me as each one in turn took his frustrations out on my bleeding body. How I never became pregnant god only knows. I cried for weeks afterwards. On one occasion I was close to committing suicide. I had already dissolved the tablets in my drink, when I then remembered my own mother and the grief she had suffered and would suffer again at my hand. My twin sister in whom I had confided my troubles managed to talk me round. After a month or so I could again face the world. The feeling I had for men was stilted. I was ashamed of my own body. I felt that those 'footprints' were all over me. Those men had left scars that were only in my mind but I perceived them as being visible and dirty and ever present. I became less feminine and fought off any man in shame of something that was no longer visible, and long past. I couldn't look at the opposite sex and certainly became very shy of any friendship with any man. I had doubts about my own sexuality, and was worried whether I was sexually normal. I almost began to find solace in friendship with other woman, but there I stopped and drew the line in my life as that was almost abhorrent to me. There was one man who finally released me from this soul-destroying perversion and we are now very much in love. He has given me back my identity as a woman and perhaps when all this is over we will get married."

Lara had been quiet for some while; she had been very intent in listening to Rula.

"I did not realize how you had suffered. You make me feel so mean; I have had a wonderful introduction to sex. I gave my virginity with pleasure in love. I gave it. It was not taken from me. We were in love. I will always have that memory whatever else happens in my life." She could see a feint glimmer of a tear in Rula's eye. Perhaps she was about to cry, something she never thought would be possible. "I'm sorry," she continued, "I've been a fool, I must just think of this as being a job I have to do. It is a duty that I have to perform to secure a possible future for me in this life. If I were religious I would say that god would forgive me for what I am about to do if only to save myself for the future."

She smiled, and so did Rula. They took each other in their arms and cuddled. Both of them whimpered a little but it was in comfort, not sadness.

***

Svi didn't know if he was more concerned about the results of the test than Lika was. He was waiting patiently with her outside the main examination room. The slides, smears and holographic plates took a short while to process and the consultant physicians would have to analyze the results. This usually took no longer than it would have taken Svi and Lika to have a short snack in the nearby cafeteria. The problem was, neither of them felt hungry. Svi had taken two cable-juices from the drink dispensing machine and they had both sat there silent holding hands and sucking at their juice. It seemed like an age since the slurping noise had announced the approaching end of any liquid left in their drink containers. Svi and Lika sat looking at each other becoming increasingly more impatient. Svi was contemplating biting his nails, something he had not done since he was a child when he looked at Lika's face as he felt her hand tighten on his. Her face showed it all. Someone was coming, and she had seen that person first. Svi looked round, a young orderly, possibly male or female was walking towards them. He or she beckoned the couple to follow, down a corridor into another room. This room was pleasantly and warmly decorated, and it resembled a sitting room in an average home in the area from where Svi and Lika had originally come.

"Please be seated and make yourselves comfortable." The orderly said. "We will be reporting to you in a moment."

Svi and Lika still could not be sure if he was a man with a high pitched voice, or a woman, with a deep one. They only had to wait another moment when another door broke open and a very pleasant matronly woman appeared in the room. She walked over and sat with them saying......

"I have good news for you both." Svi's heart missed a beat, and Lika's must have missed two. They knew what was coming and didn't need to listen. "You are two months with child. The child is perfectly normal, and is a girl. You will have to make immediate plans for your return home." She was addressing her remarks to Lika.

"No!" Interrupted Svi "She will not return home if she doesn't want to." He was exhibiting annoyance; he had not even anticipated himself. The two women were quite taken aback at his sudden outburst.

"Why ever not?" The doctor enquired. "It is much safer down there for the unborn child."

"That is an old wives tale!" Svi was argumentative. "Today's thinking is that we can handle any radiation that we are born into if we have the special pre-natal treatment."

"That's true," said the doctor "but it isn't well proven!"

"Somebody has to prove it" Svi again interrupted.

"Is that what you really want to do?" She turned again to Lika. "Yes" Lika replied unenthusiastically.

"Is there any law that prohibits pregnancy in orbital space?"

"No, only recommendations and codes of conduct. There is no law, exactly. It just is not done. Pregnant woman never risk their offspring in this situation. They always return home."

"Once my wife has gone home she would not be allowed to return, would she?" Svi was making his point.

"No she would not" The doctor was beginning to understand.

"It is illegal to send a pregnant woman into space knowingly. Your wife would have to remain with her child until it could be schooled, and you know how long that can be."

"I will stay here, and have my baby here. Let us look at this episode as part of the project we are on. *A donation to science.*" Lika was unsure, but she was trying not to show it.

The doctor smiled, and indicated acceptance of the situation. She told Lika that she would have to sign the forms acknowledging the problems, and her willingness to undertake continual monitoring of the embryo's progress. Lika was overjoyed that she could stay and felt that she had taken part in a simple trade off. Her baby for the project. Svi was not so sure; he was beginning to think differently already. Would she want the trade off when it came to the crunch? He wondered. Would they want their newly born daughter put into the unnatural environment in which they were working? Would they be happy never handling or even touching their child once born? A terrible, terrible thought that Svi knew had not yet reached Lika. There would be no other way for mother and child to stay in orbit. He felt sick, but he dared not show it.

***

Rula was feeling very unsure. Her first assignment had been presented to her, in a sealed envelope at lunch. This was the identical manner in which Lara had been presented with hers. Rula could not take her mind off Lara's reaction to her first assignment. She came back in the early hours of the morning crying at Rula's door. She described in vivid terms, the way this middle-aged 'gentleman' had laid her down naked on her back and nearly suffocated her as he tried to make what would have been an excuse for love. She could not even look away, or behind his head, as he had insisted that all the time she should look straight into his eyes and that horrible face with hairs growing out of it. Even his ear lobes had hair. He was horrible, he had an unkempt beard which she was sure had the smell of his entire day's menu, and he insisted in putting his horrible greasy, dirty fingers all over her body. Lara wanted to throw away all the clothes she was wearing; he had had his horrible hands all over them. She wanted to have a hot bath, and she begged Rula to help her to scrub herself clean. Rula had agreed and let her use her bathroom. The psychological effect on Lara of having someone else scrub her clean was immense. She began to return quite quickly to herself and her own sweet personality the more Rula helped her in her ablutions. Lara had two more guests to her room since, and she had become less tarnished by them, than she was by her 'first'. Possibly her attitude was becoming harder or maybe she was just getting used to it.

Rula was concerned, she was very unsure. She just did not know how she herself would react and what lasting effect her 'first' guest would have on her. She thought of Erash, and what he would feel if he knew what was happening to her. Was he still alive, and was he still in Larden?

Her thoughts were wondering all over the place as she sat there in the hotel lobby-lounge, her lunch having been completely spoiled. She looked around for one of her friends but there were none to be seen. There was just the usual changing mélange of people coming and going about their business. At one point she was not sure but she thought she saw that woman with the artificial hand, but it would only have been momentarily, as someone walking past blocked her view. Then the woman was gone. This nevertheless jolted her mind back to her real reasons for being where she was, and the thought suddenly struck her that she was in one of the best places to find the information she needed. She began to realize what a strong position she was in, if she played her cards close to her chest. She began to feel better. She had a new motivation to do her job 'well'. She knew Erash would approve, in fact she would make him proud.

Her attitude changed dramatically in that short space of time. The kind of person she and her friends were meeting was high, very high in the administrative structure in Bylia. She would put this to good use, and play one up against the other. These people often talk too much for their own good. The right question here, an innuendo there, and if her friends would co-operate they would have quite an espionage organization without even going out the door. If they became really expert they could play one up against the other and create real problems for the Bylia administration. Her forthcoming guest that evening was the Chairman of the Public Accounts Department.

It was with a strong sense of purpose that Rula walked back to her room that afternoon, but unbeknown to her, someone had been there before her. Rebecca, had covertly been through Rula's personal things in an attempt to discover more about her identity, but Rula being an old hand at the espionage game, naturally didn't have anything to incriminate her. Rebecca, not wishing to be disappointed in a completely wasted journey decided to doctor Rula's contraceptive powders. She substituted into the same sachets a similar colored but inert powder which was identical in appearance. Her instant contraception would now be nothing more than a reasonable cure for a headache.

***

'Transition'

Noah and Tubal Cain could not control their merriment; they had together consumed a little too much alcoholic wine. The happy duo sat together on the high stone wall, while laughing and joking with one another, like a couple of lads who had been cheating a day out of school.

"Shem is such a beautiful baby." Tubal giggled, "You can be a very proud father. Such clear blue eyes, and he is the image of Naamah" Tubal Cain was in full flow with a little added help from the alcohol.

Noah interrupted.

"Baby girls are beautiful, or pretty. Boys should show strength and leadership. He may be a 'handsome' little baby, but no, he is not beautiful!" Noah was a very slurred firm in his manner. He knew what he meant, or meant what he had said. Nevertheless he managed to continue...

"I am a very very happy man today. I have always wanted to be a Daddy, and especially to a son. Shem, I hope will be the first and eldest son of many brothers. Naamah is not so keen, but I would love a very large family. Hey! Noah changed the subject "What about you? Isn't it about time that you, Tubal, settled down with a woman. Do you still see Tsionne, that young woman from Postia?"

"Yes, we are still in contact with each other, but she spends most of her time in Postia, liaising with the Bylians about their payments. We miss each other but at present we have to tolerate the situation until we can see each other again."

"When will that be?" Noah enquired showing genuine interest in spite of his inebriation.

Tubal was trying very hard to concentrate on his answer to Noah, but his face was beginning to go a pale shade of green. "Not until Erash can come out of the wood work." Tubal began to reply, trying to remain coherent and purposefully pronouncing every word very carefully.

"We are having to keep him out of sight in spite of the fact that he is out on a mission searching for Pollo. If I were to be seen with Tsionne, it could compromise her in front of the Bylians. They might smell a rat. Bylia is still paying the Popular Front for the Liberation of Bylia ransom money for their silence on Erash, while Erash unknown to the Bylians is wandering around searching for Pollo. Nearly seven menstrual cycles have gone by and they still haven't found out. Erash has been very lucky, and so have we. We are still feeding the Bylians through Postia with heavy goods in return for...." Tubal was running out of steam very quickly, he turned away from Noah and went to put his hand to his mouth, but he was too late. He threw up vomit which flew like a jet propelled lump followed by its trail of muck and strong smelling rubbish, to the ground beneath them. Noah made movement to grab at Tubal, as he started to lose his balance on the top of the wall. Tubal could hold on no longer and he fell clumsily to the ground beneath them. Noah jumped down to follow him. He had to see if his friend was all right.

The two men stood up, looked at each other, and putting their arms across the other's shoulders marched off in the direction of the dying sunlight, that is in the direction where the setting sun would be, if it were to be visible behind the darkening cloud.

Noah was a happy man despite the forthcoming hangover, and Tubal would have been happier if only he could be re-united with Tsionne. How long he wondered to himself, quietly and privately, would it be?

***

There were men in black and silver uniforms everywhere. The entire area of the section of the Orbital Space station was in mild panic. There were sirens, bleepers, buzzers and chimes all repeating the alarm warning with consistent panic. Automatic doors were opening and closing in a seemingly uncontrollable manner. People were standing still and some were wondering around aimlessly.

"What is going on?" Lika looked up to Svi. "Why the sudden panic and why are the amber lights flashing on and off everywhere?"

"Stay sitting there" Svi stood up and went behind Lika, placing his hands gently on her shoulders. "It is only an amber warning, so there is no danger involved, don't worry. In your state of pregnancy I don't want you running around like a lost sheep in the wilderness. Wait until another guard goes by and we shall solve this mystery." Svi reassured Lika. "We don't want you giving birth just now. Do we? He half smiled. A guard in the familiar Black and Silver was carefully moving past their project observation position underneath them.

"What's going on out there?" Svi called down to the guard.

"Why is the alarm going, can I be of any help?"

"Show me your papers. At once!" The guard took no notice of the polite questions put by Svi. He reached up to the observation platform and tried to take a grip of Svi's left ankle. Svi turned around and knelt down looking the guard straight in the face.

"Don't you know how to be polite, you people?" Svi was taking a chance in being rude to a guard. They could turn really nasty. They were always flouting their authority on anyone whom they chose. Often they would treat themselves to the sport of inciting others to create an offence in order to obtain an excuse for their authoritative actions, although they did not often need an excuse.

The guard took out his paresifier and cracked it hard down across Svi's face, then pointing it at Svi...

Both of you get down from there. At once! I want to see your papers. You could both be in very deep trouble."

The expectant parents climbed carefully down to the level of the guard. Low gravity meant that their movement was quite clumsy. Although they had been in orbit for more than eight months, they still had not got used to the gravity changes, and often over reacted in movement.

Svi did not like the leering eyes and the facial expression of the guard, who seemed to be taking a distinct interest in Lika's body form. The guard had complete power over both of them. Even if he had an accident and 'fell' on his paresifier, Svi and Lika would be held up to blame regardless. These guards were a complete law unto themselves. Anyone who attempted to discredit them would come to an 'unfortunate' end.

"Stand over there. I wish to see your papers. Show me!" Svi reached to his chest pocket for his identity disc, the guard stepped forward and took Svi's hand out of his clothing. "I will do that." He opened Svi's shirt, and with warm, sweating, fumbling fingers he found Svi's disc. He pulled it out and inspected it. "So you are one of 'them' I should have expected that." he turned to Lika. "Your papers or your disc please." The fact that he said please was either an accident, or as an excuse for his aggressive manner. He moved very much closer to a very startled Lika who was now pressing her backside hard against the smooth wall of the corridor. The rear of her body was becoming flattened as she was leaning back as far as she could go. The wall seemed to be pushing her helplessly forward as the guard approached, hands outstretched. His face was almost directly in front of her. His eyes were looking straight into hers. She could smell the foul stale breath coming from the steamy damp mouth that was getting very close to hers. She had to resist, but that could be fatal. She tried to convince herself to hold her ground and think of her unborn child. Guards on the mother planet had been known to severely disfigure the stomachs of pregnant woman to the point of killing the child and sometimes the mother as well. They had been known; rumor has it, to jump with pleasure on naked hybrids stomachs in their later stages of pregnancy, often killing both mother and child. These men are worse than beasts and often act without reason purely for self-satisfaction, in the name of 'duty'.

Lika was beginning to feel very wet under her armpits, and she was very scared. She prayed that Svi would not interfere. Had he done so, she knew that he would be killed on the spot, and while he was there watching it gave the guard even more sadistic pleasure. This was Svi's guarantee for survival.

The salivating, sex crazed guard was now face to face with Lika, but she felt his hands on her stomach. He was feeling her stomach with curious carefulness. He didn't seem to want to miss anything. He was savoring every moment as he felt her stomach with moving fingers.

"I can feel your child. Is this his bottom or his head?" The guard inadvertently spat small droplets of saliva onto Lika's mouth as he spoke. His hands were moving slowly and inquisitively all over her lower abdomen. He was poking her with his fingers, and kneading her with his palms. Lika stood rigid as she felt his hands reach through her clothes onto her naked flesh. She let out a little gasp as his hot sticky hands made contact with her skin. His eyes were becoming glazed as he continued to look Lika directly in the face, as if in self-punishment not wanting to allow himself the pleasure of looking at what he was doing, or perhaps enjoying the sadistic viewing of Lika's horrified face.

Lika fought back the shrieks and nearly choked her scream as she took a deep, deep breath. His hand was now between her legs, pushing well into her naked crutch. She was trying not to scream. Her self-control was absolute. She managed to remain silent and she gritted her teeth in trying to ignore this heinous invasion into her personal privacy. She knew where his fingers were. She was even finding the feeling quite sensuous. She was disgusted with herself, and pushed her face to the side of his neck and bit him as tightly as she could. She achieved such pleasure from the salty taste of revenge. The adrenalin was again flowing through her veins. She completely forgot the moment of disgust at the fact that she may have enjoyed the intrusion into her genital regions.

The guard reeled back with his hand tightly held at the side of his neck. He dropped it and pointed his finger at Lika, exposing a magnificent 'love-bite' at the side of his neck.

"You bitch!" The guard was angry at being embarrassed. His pride was hurt and it showed. He had been quite gentle to Lika compared with the treatment often meted out by his colleagues. "You shouldn't have done that," he yelled.

"Have you never had a love-bite before?" Lika demanded of him. "You should take it as a compliment." Lika nearly choked on her words, but for Svi and her own sake she had to be convincing.

"A small child has escaped from the project area and has to be found and destroyed." The guard announced in answer to Svi's earlier question.

***

Naamah's brother Jubal was nervously winding his way through the moving crowds in the center of the city. The poisonous exhaust fumes of the moving hover-traffic and various assorted forms of mobile vehicle were extruding themselves into the atmosphere. Jubal was very much the playboy of the family, but he often envied the peace and tranquility that his brother Jabal enjoyed on his farm away out in the countryside. The metropolis was very much Jubal's home. He enjoyed the nightlife and slept through most of the days. His waking hours were generally spent under artificial illumination. His skin stood as witness to this fact, as it was always so pale and colorless. Jubal's nocturnal habits were the bane of his family life. His only saving grace was the wonderful music that he and his group of skilled musicians would orchestrate when they were working. Jubal's work was internationally admired and his orchestra had made many recordings, holographs, and videos. Fame and fortune had been kind to Jubal, but his way of life had been tainted by its benefits. Jubal was on his way to see his sister and her new baby. He was late as would surely be expected of him. It was part of his character to run close to the wind.

"What do you look like?" Naamah shouted across the room at her breathless brother, who had run up the stairs because he could not wait for the elevator, he was so late. "I haven't seen you for nearly a year. Not since Noah was in hospital with Tubal after that terrible accident, and look how you come to see me. You look terrible. Have you been out all night?"

"Well yes, actually I have." Jubal answered casually as he walked over to the seated Naamah and gave her a peck of a kiss on her cheek. "Here these are for you." He handed her a beautiful bouquet of foliage and flowers, which was a very rare gift indeed, these days.

"I managed to bribe somebody to get more than my ration. I am completely out of environment coupons, and I had to give you something for your new maternal status." He then put his hand to his pouch. "This is a little gift for Shem. Where is he? "Jubal looked hopefully around the room. Naamah stood up and took her brother's hand; she threw her arms around his waist and gave him a hug.

"It's so good so see you again. Come we shall put these plants in water, and I'll show you your nephew. He is lovely, and I think he looks like you. He's got your pale pink color, especially after he's broken wind!"

Jubal put his arm tight around Naamah's waist and hugged her close to him. Together they walked into the other room.

It was the first time so many of Naamah's family has been together in one place for a very long time. Even at her wedding to Noah, the speed in arrangement caused many of their relatives not to be there at such short notice. But then, at that time Noah had been so ill that the quiet celebration was what had been needed.

Great grandpa Methuselah was holding Shem who was in full volume. Old man Methuselah was obviously very proud, he felt like a young man again, and certainly did not look his age. Naamah's mother, Zillah was full of smiles as she greeted her step son Jubal on his sudden arrival, but she indicated to Naamah that she go back to the other room for her rest, as Jubal knew everybody anyway. They were such a happy gathering. Grandpa Lamech, who was now completely blind, held the hand of Shem, and Noah who had recently returned was quietly smiling content and satisfaction in his face. Jubal wondered why he had stayed away for so long, and was pleased to see all his family together again.

He was surprised to see his brother Jabal looking such a mess, with a broken arm in a sling, and a very badly cut and bruised face. Jubal had heard that his brother's farm had been raided yet again and that he had lost half of his herd of hybrids, but the true facts were obviously concealed behind that blooded mask of Jabal's face.

***

CHAPTER 11

Tubal Cain was missing the fun and merriment at his sister's home. He was feeling a little sad that at this time he should be deprived of the very person who meant so much to him. He had seen Tsionne only three times since their initial meetings, but they had gelled together and both had undying love for each other. They communicated often on the televideo, but there were often fears of being listened to, and their friendship had to be kept secret. An unscrupulous computer hacker somewhere between his terminal and Tsionne's in Postia could unscramble even their own personal telefax machines. They would almost be incommunicado with each other until Erash had located Pollo and the Bylean connection had been broken. Meanwhile the trade between Science and Welfare' and Postia was increasing as the demands of the Bylians were becoming more and more complicated. Tubal Cain sat in his office with his head on his hand thumbing through sheets and sheets of data. He was sure that he would find a good reason to visit Postia.

Suddenly his fax machine stirred into action. Tubal was shaken out of his lethargic slumber. The machine was clattering and buzzing with some urgency. Tubal Cain stood above the rolling feed-out as it printed its message. The blood ran fast through Tubal's breast. He could not believe his eyes; he had to read those words again. His life could be about to change…..

———*'Tubal Cain. Science and Welfare. Urgent for his*
notice. Pollo uncovered. Proceeding to follow
with a view to capture.
Will contact again very soon.
I have to watch my back. Eh!'———

'Eh' Tubal recognized Erash's call sign. Tubal could not help feeling quite elated; a long chapter in his life may soon be coming to its climax. Never since he had set up the development of his business Science and Welfare, had he concentrated his mind and actions on a single event. Tubal sat down in his seat and tried very hard to unwind but he could not come to terms with reality.

Erash knew that he had taken a great risk in using the telefax machine, especially sitting there in the open reception hall of the largest International Hotel in Postia. He had managed to get behind the counter for just those few moments to attack the keys of communication, and hope to get his message to Tubal Cain. Erash reached over the machine and tore off his copies and then quietly went round the corner to the toilets where he managed to dispose of the torn shreds of evidence into the sewage! He had to be careful not to lose sight of his quarry.

Erash and Pollo had never knowingly met, and the likelihood of him being recognized was not very great, nevertheless Erash had taken the rude precautions of taking on a disguise. Even his best friends would not easily have recognized him. He had grown a heavy beard, and given himself contact lenses to change the color of his eyes. He wore a tooth cover giving a different shape to his mouth, and slightly altering his voice and manner of speech. He had tried built up shoes, which gave him extra height, but they were too cumbersome so he discarded them very soon afterwards. His main change of appearance was the dye he had used on his curly hair, which in the end completely changed his appearance. He looked at least fifteen years older than his age.

Being ready to leave at a moment's notice was an attribute that all 'spies' needed to have in their repertoire. Erash had learnt a whole new way of life in his role as an agent on active duty. He traveled very light, and only carried a small hand-case, which could give him a change of clothing and help with his personal hygiene. He had carefully taken possession of his luggage from behind the reception desk, and had kept it with his person as he sat down in the reception seating area, waiting for something to develop.

He did not have to wait long. Two young children came out of the elevator, followed by a well-dressed woman with only one natural hand, her right one.

Erash tried very hard to look nonchalantly at the Hotel's local magazine, with great interest, while out of the corner of his vision he was watching the woman with her two children at the reception desk. He was finding it very difficult to hear and understand her conversation, there was so much other noise going on, and people kept coming across his view. He then realized he could get a clear picture of her by looking in a mirror not far from his seated position.

A small brown leatherette satchel was being passed across the reception counter. The woman seemed very pleased with herself as she placed it into a larger handsome valise, then taking the children who were holding hands; she walked towards the front entrance of the Hotel, pushing the valise with in built wheels before her. Erash had to move fast if he was not going to lose her. Picking up his small case he meandered across the foyer to the same exit door, slightly behind the departing trio, just in time to see them climbing into a chauffeur driven hovercab. Erash ran to the cab-rank only around the corner, hailing the first vehicle as he ran. Within moments he was in his cab in hot, but subtle pursuit. Fortunately for Erash, his quarry was traveling at a moderate speed that would befit a lady of substantial means, with two small children in tow. Erash was very impressed with her cover. An urban terrorist would not be expected to walk around, dressed in the highest fashions accompanied by two sweet little over-spoilt and well-turned out children. Whoever created her disguise deserved a medal for brilliance. She would be waved through any security check. Designer labels could often work wonders.

They were making for the transportation center for international travel. Erash had made this journey in Postia so many times he knew the way with his eyes closed. In no time at all, he was following the woman into the booking hall. She went up to a pay-window and showed her disc, in return the woman behind the glass handed her three boarding cards. Erash walked up to the window as he saw the two children with their companion disappear into the departure lounge.

"I have just missed my wife, and children, may I also have a ticket please?" Erash felt rather tame, but that was the first idea that entered his head.

"Which one was your wife?" The woman replied.

"She only has one hand" Erash was inspired.

"First class for Bylia, Politir," The woman answered. "No!" Erash interfered. "That would be just like her traveling expensive. Give me one ticket, second, tourist class please. I'll suffer, I don't mind," he said sarcastically!

The journey was uneventful, except that after traveling about two thirds of the distance, the one handed woman left her first class seat with both children and disappeared into the toilet with them, only to re-emerge a short time later, all dressed in peasants garb and looking a real mess. They were certainly very obviously out of place in a first class compartment. She had even taken the smart cover off her valise. It looked so simple and plain now, just like any other. Why Erash was wondering.

The arrival in Politir was very undignified. The very smell of rotting fish greeted Erash's nose as he alighted onto the hot sticky tarmac. Politir was an unfortunate town that had seen better times a generation before the revolution. It was still somewhat romantic in its reputation, but the horrible smell was with you everywhere. Erash was always amazed at the complete paradox that the city exhibited. Romance and abject poverty seemed to go hand in hand.

Following a sophisticated woman, with two well dressed children through the streets of Politir would have been easy, but staying in pursuit of a drab peasant woman with two ragamuffin children was a very different proposition.

Now he understood the change of identity. Erash turned his jacket inside out and pulled his shirt out at the waist. He no longer stood out in the moving crowd. He managed to cover his case with a muddy dust as he passed a small building site. He had managed to camouflage himself very satisfactorily in a very quick time.

Erash was determined to follow his trio to their ultimate destination. He kept at a suitable distance, but through the busy winding back streets it was not too difficult to keep in visual contact with a woman, a valise, and two young children.

It was not long before they turned into a narrow dark street, which was a cul-de-sac. The street just came to an end. He saw the children helping the woman as she struggled to lift the valise up a very high step into the doorway of a tradesman's entrance of an establishment whose name was proudly announced in a small illuminated sign above the door. *'The House of the Dolls, kitchen entrance'*!

***

Jubal had been delighted to accept his brother Jabal's invitation to return with him after the celebrations. Jabal's farm offered a tranquility and peace that Jubal was very seldom able to enjoy with his busy urban habits, and the demands placed on him by his orchestra.

They had traveled most of the way out to the farm from the city center, by underground monorail, which was connected into the subterranean defense system and had only recently been extended to an input station not far from Jabal's home. They completed the final distance in Jabal's new rota-cropper.

Jabal was very proud of his new acquisition. He was delighted to be able to show it to his brother. One of Jabal's weaknesses was new equipment. He loved to acquire anything that was new, that would reduce his heavy workload. He showed Jubal that with his new rota-cropper, he could hover in any single place in a stationery position at a fixed distance from the ground, and perform most agricultural functions. He could dig a hole, drill a well or in longitudinal motion, he could plough a trench. It was a genuine multi-purpose machine; it even substituted as the reasonably fast and comfortable mode of general transport, which was taking them both back to Jabal's home.

Jubal's anger was very visible in his face as they approached the once very beautiful home of his brother.

"What happened? Who did all this? Why?" Jubal was almost hysterical with wild fury. "What the devil is going on here?" he shouted at Jabal, who seemed quite resigned to the situation.

Jabal was obviously inwardly shocked as he placed the feet of his new Rota-cropper on the hard ground.

"When I left here yesterday there had been considerable damage from a raid we sustained the other day, but it was nothing like this." Jabal said trying very hard to control his feelings. "This is horrific!" The grown man was holding back the tears, as he looked around the garden area of his lavish home. The front door had been daubed with graffiti; the guttering had been pulled from the roof and thrown to the ground. There was a pool of dried blood outside the front porch, which was the feeding ground of a multitude of flying insects. Across the yard the tower was pouring out water, which was falling wastefully to the ground from three different fractures. There were vehicle tracks across his beautiful lawn, which he had spent months on getting to a green velvet finish. Jubal's gaze wandered up to Jabal's roof…he grabbed Jabal by the arm…

"Don't look up!" he said. "There is a half naked hybrid woman hanging by her neck into a hole in the eaves. These people must be of the worst evil. How could they do that to anybody even a hybrid?"

Jabal was furious and he turned on his brother. "What do you mean, 'even a hybrid'? They have as much right to their place in this world as we have. They are also people. How could you say something like that? My brother. Our family. We were brought up to be decent people, not to sink to the gutter like the perpetrators of this crime."

"Some of my best friends are hybrids!" Jubal replied in sincere innocence. This made Jabal even more riled.

"Don't be so patronizing, that means that you still differentiate between 'them' and us."

The two men began to bicker and were becoming more and more angry with each other. A sudden sad crying noise interrupted the flow of their argument. The two men began to realize the reality of their situation as they turned around and walked over to a pile of rubble from where the noise seemed to be coming.

"Can you see that foot? It seems to be moving!" Jubal was pointing to a darkened shaded area immediately below the center of the pile of rubbish and debris. There was a trial of trickling blood running along the ground into a drain. The foot was wearing a loosely fitting torn sandal, and was sticking out, toes upwards, the bruised heel to the ground.

"Quick!" Jabal continued, "You help me lift that heavy stuff and be very careful."

The two men knuckled down and worked with fury to remove the excess of the rubbish, which seemed to be trapping the body beneath. The pale sound of crying continued, but seemed to be getting weaker, and more of an effort. Eventually the identity of the body was becoming clearer. The owner of the body was a young semi-conscious female hybrid who was forcing a great deal of effort into an attempt at speech. Jubal bent down on both knees and placed his ear to the youngster's mouth.

"I'm listening," he whispered into the young girl's ear.

"More...! More...! There are more of us...under...there!" She tried to point, and then lost consciousness.

Jabal and Jubal acted in unison. They gently placed the unconscious hybrid in the safety of the corner near a solid standing wall, and then moved with relentless speed into the task of removing the heavy debris from the pile in front of them.

Moments later, to their sudden surprise two more hybrids appeared on the scene from nowhere, to add manpower to their rescue efforts. Jabal knew them both by name, but they never spoke a word. The four men were determined to clear the way for possible survivors. It would have meant too much effort to exchange words at that moment.

Not much later, an arm appeared from the wreckage, followed by another one. One was human female and the other was hybrid male. It was not long before two more semi-conscious bodies were released from their trauma.

"How many more? I wonder how many more!" Jabal was inwardly crying to himself as he spoke out to whoever chose to listen.

Jabal and Jubal placed these two people next to their first discovery, and then Jubal took a large bucket over to the leaking water tower and filled it from the pouring flow of water that was casually falling to the ground.

"There are at least two more in there!" One of the helping hybrids spoke across to Jubal. "I can hear two voices very faint from below ground." He continued.

"I believe that there is a cellar underneath. "Jabal had sudden inspiration. "There could be many more under there. We need help." He ran to his rota-cropper and to his telephone. Why had he not thought of this before?

"Help is on its way." Jabal returned to find a large gaping hole had been opened into what could be a tomb or a sanctuary for several sad souls.

Jabal looked into the dark yawning chasm, which had been so successfully exposed by hard working hands. A blackened dusty face appeared to the light of day. It was the whites of the eyes that Jabal saw first, and then the white teeth as the mouth opened to give a yell of positive delight at the prospect of obtaining rescue from above.

The hybrid helpers had found a length of rope. Tying one end to a secure bollard in the ground they dropped the long length into the hole. They had rescued eight fully conscious hybrids and two human women by the time the rescue services arrived. Sadly only two more survivors were brought to the surface. Ten dead bodies, including two babies were discovered buried, crushed under fallen debris.

Frustrated anger was all over Jabal's face. His initial reaction was of revenge.

"Who did this? He asked one of the shocked survivors. "Tell me what happened." He pleaded, with tears in his eyes. "They will be punished. A punishment that they will never forget!" A Hybrid's hand was placed gently onto Jabal's shoulder. It was one of the two helpers who had appeared on the scene not long after they had arrived. He softly whispered a few words into Jabal's ear.

"Come with me, and bring your brother Mr. Jabal I have something I must show you, but don't make it too obvious what you are doing, or where you are both going." He indicated that they should move away, across the yard.

The two men found it very difficult to look casual as they 'nonchalantly' followed their hybrid friend past some partly destroyed out buildings, to the perimeter dwellings of the village. The hybrid brought them to a narrow alleyway, down which they had to walk in single file. In fact as they walked their shoulders could touch both walls at the same time in some places.

Eventually, half way down this street they came to a place where a hole in the wall had been blocked up with bits of plastic waste, and also some straw. Initially it appeared as if it has blown there on its' own, it was so casually placed. The hybrid suggested that one of them should pull away at the rubbish until the entrance gap was large enough for the three of them to pass through one by one without much problem.

Together they went down a short flight of stairs into a semi-darkened basement. There was a very dim light burning in the far corner. Jabal and Jubal's eyes began to adapt to the darkness after having left the brilliance of a 'bright' although hazy warm day.

"Look over there!" Jabal took a grip of Jubal's left arm, as the horror and surprise simultaneously registered on both of their faces. There were two men sitting on the floor back to back, tied up hands and feet. They were both wearing black uniforms with silver braiding, and high black leather boots.

***

Ground-base one was alive with expectancy. The chief government minister was due to attend that morning for the launch of the new reflecting probe. It was one of the first of its type. The previous two attempts to launch it had resulted in disaster. For this reason, Noah, as minister of state was to be present in order to show how important was this new development.

They all liked Noah at ground-base one. They knew that so long as he was around there would always be a forward-looking space program.

The two previous failures were not necessarily accidents or technical error. It was generally considered amongst those who knew, to be arson or sabotage. The first probe fell-off its mount position at take-off, breaking into pieces on the ground. The second blew up when it was not more than just outside the planet's atmosphere. Everyone was 'rooting' for the success of this new effort. This project was the first step to plotting a passage through deep space. It was to be the first of many more that would follow.

The probe was to be launched at just enough speed to get it out of the mother planet's gravitational pull, and when in extra-orbital space, booster power packs were to be fitted manually out in space while the satellite was in its full exit trajection. These power 'lobes' would generate sufficient acceleration when activated from ground-base, to throw the probe-unit complete with the lobes out into hyperspace at many times the speed of light. For many generations of scientific discovery it had always been claimed that nothing could travel faster then the speed of light. This experiment would certainly quash the cynics.

The method of obtaining maximum power was still secret, that was the reason for direct ground launch and orbital workshop enhancement to its function to get it on its way. Within days the vehicle would be at least that many light weeks out into space if all went according to the schedule. The astro-probe will be greatly accelerated many times on its journey away from its mother planet. It will be monitored by reflecting electromagnetic waves off its specially constructed reflecting mirrors back to ground base control. These electro impulses will be transmitted at the speed of light from ground-base one, and will be measured on their return. This will therefore mean that a 'beacon' will have been placed moving out into deep distant space. It had been decided to slow down the first probe when it was far enough away, or near a planetary system of interest. It had a built-in sensing device to locate natural water, oxygen, nitrogen and carbon. The device would slow down the probe to stand at a fixed point in relation to its original launch. This would be done automatically within the probe itself. The probe would then be stationery in space relative to its mother planet, but it may well be moving in relation to its local geography.

The red carpet had been put down in front of the large podium. Noah was careful as he helped Naamah up to her seat. This was the first time that she had been seen in public since the birth of their baby Shem. She was looking very pleased to be there and had a broad smile across her face as she waved to the gathered crowd.

The circular probe was in free anti-gravity suspension under its own magnetic power. It has the appearance of an upside-down saucer, suspended in the air above them, very much like an ancient, historic air balloon, or dirigible, attached to its anchor mast. Everybody was looking up at it. The majesty of such a large object sitting in the cloudy sky so high above them was enough to impress any doubter in the crowd. The other thing that was very noticeable was the silence. The new magnetic-anti gravity engines were so smooth, that the entire scene seemed like something out of a science-fiction book.

The entire island of ground-base-one had been sealed off from the mainland. Security was as high and acute as it had ever been, but there was still a great deal of concern that he launch should be a success and the probe should depart unscathed.

Three men were now climbing aboard the small leading capsule that was attached to the underside of the 'saucer'. These men would help take the probe into orbit and help guide the power-lobes into position before it moved off into deep pace. The three men would travel back via the orbital space station where they would rest for a night before traveling back to ground base.

Noah rose to his feet. The nation's media were all waiting with anticipation. He was about to make a major speech. He gave a little cough into the microphone and the crowd fell silent.

"This planet is filled with violence, we, the human race are like maggots eating at the core of a rotten apple. We are greedy, selfish and disrespectful of the wonderful home that was once our heritage. Our children, and if we survive that long, our children's children will have nothing left here to destroy. We must change our ways before it is too late..."

There were some soft ripples of applause in agreement, but there seemed to be a startled reaction of disapproval from the main body of the crowd. The applause was eventually 'stifled by jeers and catcalls but Noah tried to continue, Naamah sitting resolute at his side.

"…. I pray that one day these things we are doing in the advance of experimental astro-science will enable our future generations of man and womankind to save this planet from its folly, and perhaps give our future a probability, rather than a small possibility. Let us prepare for the future in order that we may still be around to remember our past."

Soft broken egg yolk was pouring down Noah's face. Naamah immediately jumped out of her seat to be at Noah's side, she leaned over to him to try to wipe his astonished face. The yellow sticky matter was running down his neck. Naamah let out a short yell as another egg caught her across the side of her shoulder. The mess seemed to go everywhere.

"Why are they doing this?" Naamah asked Noah as they both knelt down behind the podium for protection.

"The majority of people think we are scaremongers, worrying about the future. They cannot see farther than their noses" Noah whispered, forgetting that he was wearing a chest microphone that was still switched on to broadcast to the outside world, although it could not be heard in the immediate auditorium. Naamah smiled into Noah's wet sticky ear, as she said.

"They may not be able to see farther than their noses, but they can certainly see far enough to throw an egg in the direction they want."

Their whole private conversation was being broadcast on the airwaves. Possibly it was the good-humored way in which they had accepted their plight that prevented Noah's authority from being undermined by the incident. Unbeknown to them, Naamah's remarks may well have saved the day.

There was a short commotion in the center of the crowd, and as disheveled Noah and Naamah arose to their feet, they could see two young people being dragged to the exit by security guards. A polite applause greeted them as Noah resumed his position at the podium's microphone, and for all to hear he continued....

"At this point I greet you all well, and wish the team in charge of this launch good luck. If you all care to turn your eyes upward we shall hopefully see the accurate departure of

'Reflection probe three'. These mirror probes will serve to one day open our windows into a wider world. An infinite universe available to all who care to take account of it."

There was mild applause this time, which seemed to grow slowly to an ovation, as the anchor straps were released from the mast and dropped away from the main body of the probe.

Reflection Probe One stood perfectly still in its own right for what seemed to be many moments, giving the strong impression that perhaps the anchor was not really a necessity to the launch at all. There was a downward gust of cold air as if a refrigerator door has been opened above them. The machine started to rise quite quickly within less than a minute it had disappeared through the hazy cloud.

They all stood there looking at nothing at all.

***

Lika was back in their room, 167, in section 6. She lay there exhausted in her bed of soft cushions. She was completely zipped in. Svi was curled up beside her, gently caressing and soothing her through her stressed state of minor after-shock. There was still no artificial gravity in section 6, although it had been scheduled a long time before. There had been some technical problems with its function and the re-designed system was a long time coming. Svi and Lika didn't mind in the slightest. They found weightlessness quite good fun, and certainly easy to relax in. They had completely padded the small cubicle they used as a bedroom with many small soft colored cushions and often played wonderful sensuous love games in their little room. Fifty percent of the volume of the room was filled with loose cushions.

Svi was worried about Lika. She was shivering and her teeth were chattering as if she were bitterly cold. He knew that she was suffering from nervous exhaustion. Her general shocked condition could bring on an early birth of their child. He decided to call the medical department on the intercom. The doctor arrived very quickly.

"Your wife is about to give birth." He announced to Svi with a worried look on his face.

"I think that we should transfer her immediately to the surgical department. That is the only place I know that will have the necessary facilities for a difficult birth of this type. The baby is in breach position, and will come out feet first unless we open your wife up. This happens frequently among the few births that take place where the mother has spent the last months of her pregnancy in a non-gravitational environment. It seems that maybe the baby does not have the motive or instinct to turn around in the womb, and it is very difficult in these conditions to do it artificially. We must move Lika now."

"No wait" shouted Svi "That's not possible. We have agreed to offer the child to the 'Extra-terrestrial environment project' and the child must be born directly into the reception cubicle. It must not be touched by human hand."

"The natural birth technique is the only way a child can be born into that environment" The doctor interrupted. "Any birth of that nature would be very dangerous for your wife but much more so for the child. I'm not sure that I could sanction it."

"If my wife cannot donate our child to the project, she will have to return home on the mother planet. We must follow the original plan." Svi was getting very agitated.

The doctor turned to Lika, and purposefully stroking her forehead began to question her.

"I would love to have my child. Of course I would." Lika answered him with tears tucking themselves into the corners of her eyes. "I would love to have my own child, but this one was an accident of fate and will be lucky it exists at all. So it is a bonus life that would not otherwise have happened. In those circumstances I must hope that the environmental experiment will offer my child a life that by rights should never have been created anyway."

"That is very logical thinking" The doctor continued. "But do you really believe it?"

"No!" Lika replied "But I'm going to anyway!" Lika was beginning to become worked up once more, and Svi was most concerned about her.

"Look doctor, please leave her alone. The tension is coming back again. That cannot be healthy."

The doctor smiled some encouragement, for the first time. "All right, let us see what we can do. There is a birth room in the 'environmental section' not far from here. As long as you both are aware of the possible problems that can surely arise, I will come with you and help."

It was not difficult to move Lika to the nearby birth-room. It was a very strange place, dark, with low gravity. There was a bed in the middle, which appeared to be half the length of a normal bed, but it's end butted up against the widest wall of the room. The wall was mirrored which gave the impression that the bed was full length, but the illusion did not fool Svi. He certainly could see what was really going on. The mirrored wall at the end of the bed was soft and made of woven material. Svi helped the doctor to put Lika on the bed and her now naked lower body was allowed to pass through the mirrored wall. Lika was instructed to lie there with her legs splayed apart. She was lying on her back with her knees up. "You will lie there like that until we have taken some measurements," The doctor said to Lika. "That should not be very long. "If you go into labor, so much the better, otherwise we will have to induce it for you within the hour. Don't worry we have some special tools for helping you which we can work by radio control through the 'wall'.

Svi stayed at Lika's side holding her hand. The poor girl was becoming very nervous now that the reality of the time had caught up with her. She was no longer suffering from the 'cold' of chattering teeth, but the tension of the anticipation of the unknown was pushing its way into Lika's mind.

"I have a dreadful feeling, lying here like this with my legs apart." Lika was saying quietly into Svi's ear. "I believe that I am about to betray our unborn daughter, by passing her directly from my womb and out of our lives, through that mirrored window into an uncertain world where she will always have to fend for herself." Lika was beginning to cry. Svi felt her hand suddenly take a firm tight grip on his, and then release itself slowly.

"What happened?" He queried as he gave Lika a loving kiss on her cheek.

"A dragging pain!" I've felt that sort of pain before, but it has gone now."

The two expectant parents held hands and looked at each other bewildered at the event they had become involved in. Suddenly all their ideologies and plans for the future seemed dwarfed by their immediate thoughts and consideration. Svi was feeling guilty that he had allowed his Lika to end up in this situation. Lika was feeling guilty that she was letting her family down. She was depriving Svi of his child, and their daughter of two loving parents. She did something she had not done for a long time. She prayed to god for forgiveness and guidance. A sign she needed a sign. She squeezed Svi's hand again.

"That pain was deep I felt it again, a little longer this time. I think our daughter is on the way. She wants to get out. Oh Svi! What are we doing, giving our baby away?"

"No we are not!" Svi decided to be resolute. His strength was needed now or Lika's state of mind could collapse. "No we are not giving our baby away. She will be entering into a new world, a privileged pioneer in a strange new environment. We will be with her and will see her in her development years if we are lucky. Do not worry just think of NOW! You have worked for years to reach this level of academic achievement. We must carry on with the good work. You wouldn't like some stranger to come along in our place would you. Who knows whom those poor children will end up with?" Svi tightened his grip on Lika's hand, and affectionately sponged her forehead with a slightly moistened cloth.

The doctor returned just as Lika was having another pain.

"Don't worry. You have obviously started on your own. Everything is prepared. The suckling apparatus and the respiratory initiation equipment are all in place. The only problem is getting the baby out without any difficulties, because it is feet first. We have a special suction machine, but it has only been used successfully up until now on gorilla people and hybrids. If you insist on going through with this we will have to use it to stop the baby drowning at birth. Are you sure? You still have time to go to surgery. The operation theatre is already prepared."

"No!" Lika shouted, and pushed her legs as far apart as she could manage.

The lights in the room were turned down low and both Svi and Lika would be able to see the birth through the two way mirrored wall. The bed had been slightly elevated and Lika was more in a sitting position. For her it was the strangest experience. The lower half of her body was completely isolated from the rest of their world. Special equipment was wrapping itself around her lower body. The spasmodic pain was becoming more frequent now. The pain was more severe and dragging like waves in her lower abdomen. They kept coming and coming again. Lika thought she might pass out. Her waist seemed too constricted in the rubber waist-belt, and yet she was amazed at her instincts telling her what to do. She screamed. The pain was so great this time she lost control. She started to push. Svi felt her grip tighten. Her nails were digging in to his flesh.

They were both physically and mentally exhausted when Lika gave out the most threatening scream of her life. Her eyes began to roll and then settle. Svi showed Lika the machine through the glass. It was there, doing its job, bringing their daughter, the new baby to life in its new world.

Lika began to cry uncontrollably.....

***

Erash had a problem. Registration as a guest in the 'House of Dolls' was not difficult for him under his guise as a tourist. In fact his room was very comfortable and of exquisite taste. The prospect of 'room-service' was also quite promising, but none of this was a reason for Erash's visit. His problem was how he could maintain his careful watch over Pollo. He was determined not to lose her, having achieved so much and gone so far. Somewhere he must get into the staff quarters, he thought. Perhaps if he used the 'service' offered by the establishment, in the name of duty, of course. Then he may be able to befriend somebody on the staff who in their innocence could help by keeping him informed. After not too much careful thought, Erash convinced himself, and in the name of duty he made a decision. He pressed the button above the bed-head.

It was not long before the lady of the house appeared at his door.

"You would like some friendly entertainment this evening." Erash nodded in the affirmative in reply. "Then," she continued "would you like to help me with your choice?"

"Of course!" Erash was somewhat surprised. He had never done this before. He had always obtained his 'fun' free of charge, so to speak. It seldom cost him more than a meal, or an evening out.

"Do you like blondes or brunettes? Young or experienced? We even have one very nice young lady who is several months pregnant if you like that sort of thing. She is very popular and can be a little unwilling. Some men find that very stimulating. Would you like it straight or kinky? We suit every taste." The enthusiasm on the woman's face made Erash quite excited. He had very mixed feelings, and had come to Politir with a specific job to do; he had two wonderful sisters promised to him in love and marriage. They were not only his fiancées, but also his friends. How could he betray them especially when Rula was missing and probably in serious trouble? Who knows what problems she may be suffering at that moment? Erash was feeling very guilty. He tried to chastise himself out of the thoughts of exciting anticipation.

"Would you like to choose from holographic video, or would you like to be pleasantly surprised and take a chance unseen?" Erash did not need time to think. He would look at the holographic video he decided.

"Good." The woman turned to the internal videophone and dialed a number.

"Please connect me to the holographic video circuit." She announced down the mouthpiece. She turned to Erash. "Now look on the bed!"

At that moment, the woman pushed her control buttons and dialed in another number. A beautiful full size scantily clothed woman appeared in hologram on the bed next to him. Erash could not believe the reality of the situation. Some men pay a fortune just for this experience, and he is being offered the real thing.

"This young woman came to us a few months ago, innocent and a child at heart. Her name is Lara, and she is very gentle and caring. If you choose her she must be treated well. She is quite fragile, but works very well. She is extremely highly recommended. Some very important people regularly service her. She is very expensive, but worth every cent."

Erash was becoming amused, and indicated that he would like to see more. The woman pushed another set of numbers on her control set. The young girl disappeared and another appeared lying on the bed right next to him. Erash felt that he could almost touch her. He reached out his hand to touch her flesh and it went right through it. Erash knew that would happen but she looked so real. Again the woman gave a commentary about the sample of the female sex on display. She comes from a poor family and has very strange ideas about giving pleasure to men. If it was the 'unusual' that Erash wanted, then she was for him. Erash waved her on to the next choice. Erash's face changed. His mouth dropped open. He was certain, but his better instincts told him to keep any outward appearance of surprise to himself. The woman evidently did not notice.

"Move on" he said, while inwardly thinking, perhaps he had seen that woman before, but he did not know where. He definitely knew her from somewhere, but where?

Several women appeared on the bed next to Erash, one after another. Erash was becoming numbed by the variety. It was almost becoming boring for him. He liked the aggressive type like Rebecca, and the friendly appearance of another, but before he became over exposed by too many female images, he decided he had chosen, and asked her to stop. "I have made up my mind." Erash said to the woman with the remote control panel. "I'll take the first one. Lara."

Erash made good use of the hotel's wardrobe and managed to find an outfit of clothes that fitted him well. Any smartly dressed man would have been proud to be seen in them. He found perfumes, soaps and most pre-requisites for a comfortable and 'friendly' evening with a young woman. Erash kept thinking of Rula and feeling guilty. He would reproach himself and then condescend to make what he believed to be an excuse. After all, he was on an important and certainly dangerous mission and this was to be an essential part of it. He just hoped that Rula would one day forgive him.

There was a polite knock at the door, which was almost timid. Erash felt that he could understand a great deal of the character of the person to whom that knock belonged. He felt a warm sadness. He was sorry for her and he had not even opened the door to her yet. The embarrassed knock came again, although a little more urgently this time. Erash moved a little faster towards the door. "I am so sorry." She walked in the door before Erash could open it completely. She looked young, virginal and beautiful. Her lovely long locks of golden hair dropping to her shoulders. She was wearing a silken kimono, and one leg was peeking out at the knee.

"I am so sorry" she repeated. "I hate standing out there in the corridor when I go visiting. I feel that everybody suspects, and that they are laughing at me."

"Come on." Erash decided to change his plans. "I will take you down to the restaurant. Let me feed you well. That way people will see you with me and they may not think these things. Perhaps that will help you to feel better?"

"You are very sweet. Thank you. That would be very nice."

The restaurant was crowded. It was the busiest time of the evening. Erash and Lara had to wait at the headwaiter's desk before they could be given a table Erash had a good look around. He wanted to see if he could see his quarry. Pollo must still be there, he hoped. He looked hard at each face and recognized none of them.

"Come this way please." They were to be given a table near the window looking out onto the front.

Lara was quite impressed with the beautiful beard so proudly sported by Erash. She could not take her eyes off it. Every time Erash spoke his beard seemed to roll under his chin. There was so much of it, but he looked rather distinguished nevertheless with the dark brown with the occasional touch of gray. She wondered how old he could be. It had a reddish complexion, which seemed to indicate a younger man, but his appearance was much older. He seemed very fit and probably quite macho. She was thinking as she sat there looking through the menu, she could quite like this client. He was not the usual type. He seemed to be a real person with some depth to his personality.

"Do you come from far?" Lara spoke. "I can tell that you are not from around this way."

"How?" Erash replied.

"You have an accent that I can't place, but it's definitely not from around here." Lara smiled.

"You don't have an accent from these parts either. Do you?"

He enquired, trying not to answer the question. Lara turned red and looked unhappy. She took a quick look around the restaurant and leaned over to Erash. "No I don't come from around here. I am….!"

She stopped in mid-conversation and buried her face in the menu. Erash realized that it would not be time to pursue the subject of conversation. For reasons best know to her she had terminated the discussion abruptly. He was sensitive enough to realize his position. There may be a chance to continue later, he considered.

Erash decided to turn the conversation in a slightly different direction.

"Have you worked here long?" He enquired.

"About half a year, I think. One loses track of time." Lara was obviously not used to talking with her clients, as she was strangely uneasy with Erash's questioning, yet she continued in a somewhat friendly manner that encouraged Erash to talk to her. He continued.

"Have you made many friends while you have been here? Do you like the people you are working with?"

"Oh yes! I came here with friends and we have remained friends all the time, but we will not talk to anyone else about our personal friendship. That is the only private thing we have left. My job. Well that is a different matter. I will not talk to one client about another so there is little I could talk to you about my job. I certainly won't give you a cheap thrill at someone else's expense." Lara finished in a higher volume, almost a little angry.

Erash looked around. He wondered whether anyone might have heard that previous remark. He put his hand on the table to take Lara's. She smiled, and their grip was enjoined.

"No. I didn't mean that at all. I completely respect your 'professional' confidences as I hope you will respect mine when I am gone from here." Erash continued, slightly tightening his grip on Lara's hand.

"What I really meant was do you like your employers."

Lara went red and embarrassed just as she had done before, and pulled her hand away from Erash's.

"I don't get treated badly!" she was becoming abrupt again. "There are two women that run this place. They may be sisters, or just very good friends. One of them I believe only has one hand, but she is hardly ever here."

"Is she here now?" Erash's blood was pounding through his veins. What luck he thought this may be the break that he had been waiting for.

"Yes, I believe that she came back last night or today sometime. Why do you ask...?"

Erash noticed her gaze was moving to a distinct direction behind him, and she stopped speaking and nodded recognition.

"What's the matter?" Erash questioned. "Who did you see?"

Oh nobody really. Just one of my friends that I work with. She's pregnant now, but she is like a mother or a big sister to me. I would have failed miserably at my work by now if it were not for her moral support. I don't know how she can go on working the way she does. I know she hates it really." Lara put her hand to her mouth. "I should not have said that should I. We are all meant to show love in our work!"

"Do no worry, your secret is secure with me." Erash tried to look behind him to see if he could see this woman. His curiosity was getting the better of him.

"No. Don't bother." Lara said to Erash across the table. "She has gone now. She had a very young client with her. We both made a secret sign to each other to acknowledge it. You know, I have never spoken so openly with anyone like this except my friends, since I've been here!" Lara was gazing straight into Erash's eyes. "I think that I like you." She mouthed quietly to Erash. "What is your name?"

"You should know better than that. We do not give our natural names, but in this case I'll give you mine, but you must not tell anyone. Promise?"

Lara smiled sweetly.

"I promise." she said.

"Then call me Alram." Erash gave his alias name, given to him by the P.F.L.B.

***

161

CHAPTER 12

Girk was crawling through the undergrowth, he was sure that he had seen a small group of pandas chewing at the bamboo not far from there, that very morning. It could possibly have been a whole family of them. Girk had come back, and this time, was not alone. Those skins would make a valuable profit on the fur exchange in the distant metropolis of Varg. The most beautiful black and white fur with those big sad looking fur blackened eyes. He was determined to get a large kill to take home. Those pelts would be worth a small fortune.

The three men eventually arrived at a small clearing near a group of caves that buried themselves into the bamboo and wooded mountainside. There was very little left of the wooded countryside, as more generations of humans that had come before had taken their choice of large wooded areas destroying them for their own uses. Girk was very fortunate to find any of these beasts left in the wild. The few that were left in captivity would not procreate for some strange reason, and they would often miscarry when artificially inseminated. It was thought that there was a strong lack of motive in captivity. For this reason Panda-skins were very valuable. The trio of stalkers lay in a small sunken ditch at the edge of the clearing with their paresifiers fully charged. They waited. In fact they waited until practically nightfall. One of Girk's companions was becoming restless, but they dared not make a sound. The least little noise or sudden movement would frighten off their prey.

It was Ludo, Girk's youngest companion who saw it first. A large hairy male panda crawling on all fours out of a very small cave only a spitting distance from where he was lying. Girk had trained Ludo and Velmitz to act only on his command and they had to lie perfectly still until the whole group had appeared. Then they would be able to kill them all in one go.

Velmitz was getting cramp in his elbows and the ground was beginning to feel rougher and rougher underneath, but he had to lie there, still and waiting. Eventually two more pandas crawled out of their holes and more or less walked on hind legs over to the other one. Now there were three pandas on show. They wondered how many more? Girk has said at least five must show before they attack. Still longer Velmitz had to lean on his sore elbows, and Ludo had to stop himself becoming trigger happy.

The three men lay there almost in suspended animation as they waited for two more pelts to appear from the tunnel. Ludo could see his breath condensing on the dried leaves that surrounded his perspiring face. He could feel the salty tears running down into his mouth. He was sure that he could feel something long, and thin crawling up his right leg. It felt strangely smooth next to his skin. The hairs of his leg seemed to stick to its movement as it meandered up his thigh.

Ludo forced himself to exercise extreme self-control. It would not be long before that snake would reach his crotch.

He knew that to move would wreak poison into his flesh and if he lay permanently still nothing would happen and the intruder may remove itself from unwelcome territory. Ludo lay transfixed to the spot with his eyes glued on the cave entrance straight in front of him. An age seemed to pass. He felt the movement rising into his private parts. Was it going to stop and curl up around his penis? Ludo's eyes were watering now for a differing reason surely this was unreal, it couldn't be happening to him. He allowed himself to take a shallow breath, as the creature seemed to move into even higher regions. It was moving past his stomach. He felt its tail slightly flapping in his groin as its entire length now stretched from his lower abdomen its head was under Ludo's armpit. Now where would it go? Ludo's hand was tight on the trigger button of the Paresifier as the snake decided which way to go. Neckwards was the path it chose. Its head broke through for air.

Ludo's left hand was around its neck so fast that a lightening flash would have missed it. He grabbed its head between his thumb and forefinger pulling its full body-length out of his hiding place. With one almighty swing, he threw it through the air in the direction of the cave. He collapsed face down in earthy ground exhausted. His arms outstretched before him and his legs straight out behind him.

He didn't see the three more pandas exit from the cave. He heard the cracks as the paresifiers of Velmitz and Girk downed all six in the full blink of an eye. They did not wait for him.

"What's wrong with you? Fall asleep or something?" Velmitz called to Ludo.

"Come on we've got work to do" Girk called out to both of them. He was obviously unaware of Ludo's failure to fire a single shot. "Let's get the animals skinned before the darkness collapses around us completely. I want us to be out of these woods before nightfall. Taking out his large knife he started cutting out the torsos from their valuable protective wrappers.

"I hoped for five, but we take home six. Not bad for a day's work is it?" called Girk.

"No! Not really!" Ludo smiled to himself.

***

Tubal Cain's arrival in Postia was silent, and certainly unannounced. He was determined this time to keep his visit low-key. He had even been to the trouble to organize a well-publicized trip to Lyboncher. He viewed the work being done to decontaminate the area destroyed by the explosion at the power station years previously. Tubal Cain made a big media event of it. He wanted the world to see that Science and Welfare really cared and was doing its' best to recover the situation. It was a real public relations effort, at which Tubal Cain was a real expert. The delegation from Science and Welfare left Lyboncher in a great fan-fare, with a parade of guards to see them off. Their gyrosphere lifted off the pad and moved south towards

Lublia. When out of view from any media presence the sphere came to a stationary situation not too far from its destination home base. Another smaller gyrosphere pulled alongside and while hovering in close proximity Tubal Cain made the transfer with a hover-jet pack on his back. Within moments Tubal Cain was secretly on his way to Postia in his own personal vehicle.

Tsionne was nervous. She had tided her apartment at least a dozen times. She had re-positioned six ornaments so many times that she had almost forgotten where they went originally. She could not believe that in only a few more moments Tubal Cain's smiling face would appear at her door. She had changed her clothes twice and thought about re-doing her hair. She knew that he was not due to arrive just yet but he might be early. On the other hand he had said that he would videophone first as he arrived in Postia. On the other hand he might not. He may come early and surprise her. Tsionne was certainly not relaxed, but she was full of pleasant anticipation. Twice she had painted her nails only to decide that she should have a manicure. Oh dear why had she not done that. Tubal Cain is bound to notice. She sat down in her lounger, and then she got up, she felt that would make her untidy. Again she brushed herself down, then sat upright with her legs strategically placed knees together in a very lady like manner. She had decided to sit at the dining table and read a book. Having looked at each word on the page without taking any notice of one of them, she turned the page like an automaton. This is very silly she thought. He might even be late. She went over to the holographic-video cabinet and took out a pre-recorded disk. Placing it into the play back machine, she sat down in an easy chair and watched an excellent recording made some years before by Jubal in his early professional years. The music was excellent, the quadraphonic sound. There was an entire working orchestra in three dimensions in her room. She began to calm down until she realized she might not hear the doorbell. No! She decided. She turned on the video-door alarm that would flash red in the middle of her video holographic recording. Tsionne sat still and tried so hard to relax. The flashing alarm would not have been needed Tsionne knew that Tubal Cain was about to push the door button a good moment or two just before he did so. She sensed his presence she knew that he was there. The door alarm was almost redundant. It only served to confirm her happy anticipation. She tried to walk nonchalantly to the door.

The door opened. They stood facing one another, static and unbelieving. It had been such a long time. They each looked at the other taking everything in. The smile on both their faces said everything. Not a word was said, and after what seemed an eternity, they fell into each other's arms. It would have taken a nuclear explosion to tear them apart. The door automatically closed behind Tubal Cain, as Tsionne pulled and guided him over to the low settee at the far side of the room.

"That is lovely music," Tubal Cain said as he walked straight through the hologram of his brother's orchestra. "That's not one of Jubal's early hits is it?" Tubal sat down.

"If you don't recognize your own half brother, then you ought to be ashamed of yourself." Tsionne sat down next to him. They just held hands, and sat for a time looking at each other, smiling. True warmth of friendship was running through their veins. It is said that love can come in many forms, but Tsionne and Tubal Cain knew that theirs was purity personified.

"I pray to god often, and thank him for finding you for me!"

Tubal Cain whispered into Tsionne's ear, as she cuddled up close placing her head on his shoulder.

"You know it." she replied, a phrase she often used. "I love you, and never want to lose you. I also pray that our feelings will never change. Such a wonderful experience, I hope will never die." She turned away from Tubal Cain, and allowed a tear or two to spill. This was a whole new world for her, and she guessed correctly for Tubal Cain as well.

"How long are you staying?" Tsionne turned to Tubal Cain.

"I have the spare room ready for you."

"Three days is all I have time for, and I could do a little work while I'm here. Perhaps on my last day, we don't want the media to plague us with their intrusions do we?" Tubal Cain took Tsionne's face into his hand, and examined her features in great detail. Their eyes met in a hazy concentrated gaze. The two faces approached each other, and gently, very gently, Tubal Cain pursed his lips and gave Tsionne the most passionately felt kiss of all time. Their tongues met in curious friendship, and teeth touched as if to confirm their unity in a singleness of one. It was an experience that seemed to go on forever.

***

The two captive security guards were showing signs of nervous exhaustion. Their captivity on Jabal's farm was certainly no holiday for them. They had been taken back to Jabal's house under cover of darkness. Had they been removed in daylight, they would most certainly have been lynched by the mob. Feelings were bitter now among the families of the hybrid herd on Jabal's farm.

It was essential that these men be questioned in depth. Jabal and Jubal decided that in the absence of Erash, it would be a good idea to bring these men before Tubal Cain. After all, security was responsible to the authority of Science and Welfare. The two men were stripped of their uniforms and again bound and gagged. They were removed to an attic room in Jabal's own home, where they were very secure. The only way out would have been across the roof from the eaves window, or internally they would have had to break open a well secured magnetic door and climb down a narrow staircase through an alarmed "ultrasonic-ray" which would sense any movement on that staircase. The windowsill and frame were also alarmed. No way could either of the two captives escape their fate. They were to be kept there in joint confinement until Tubal Cain could be reached.

A day and a half later sending the telex to Science and Welfare, a returned message was received on Jubal's own telex receiver. It had come from Science and Welfare's office in Lyboncher.

"Tubal Cain left here yesterday. No certain knowledge of next destination. Trying to contact him on his portable telephone, but so far, no success. Head office suggests they could send someone else, as Erash is still not available. What is the problem? Shall we send one of his assistants or a senior security officer?"

Jabal decided that a quick reply was essential. They certainly didn't want any more security guards on the premises however clean they might be. Jabal was not alone in his doubts about internal security in Science and Welfare. He sent out two messages. One on his telex to Science and Welfare at Lyboncher.....

————*"No need to worry, everything under control"*————-

He also sent another message to Tubal Cain's own office on his private number at Science and Welfare headquarters. He scrambled the message onto Tubal's answer-machine. Only Tubal's own key-code could unscramble the message back to him. Security was now obviously of prime importance.

————*"Take heed! We have two of your security guards prisoner after a horrific raid on Jabal's Farm. We need you here, very quick. Urgent response essential. Top secret, for your eyes only.....*
Ja"————-

Jabal used his call sign and Tubal would understand the urgency. They now had to sit and wait. Jabal at last had a little time to sort out his home, the damage, and his wounds.

Not many hours later a coded message appeared on Jabal's Telex, which finished with the words...

"...arrive Jabal's farm tomorrow, mid-afternoon. Please oblige...TC."

Jubal and Jabal now knew exactly what was required of them, and it had to be done.

Later that night, all hell broke loose, as alarm bells rang, the two brother's and a hybrid member of the household staff ran up the stairs to the attic, they threw open the attic room door. The security window was still locked closed; there in the middle of the room was one of the near naked security guards. The other one was missing. He had gone.

***

Svi was concerned about Lika's reaction after the birth of their child, but he was delighted to sit beside her while she slept so soundly, very much like a baby herself. He was at her bedside in the recovery area for several hours while Lika's mind and body had the chance to sleep off her traumatic experiences of the last two days. Svi hoped that the passage of time would heal the scars of attempted rape and unrewarded childbirth. Lika cried forever, that she would never hold her baby. She did not realize what a punishment that would be. Especially after seeing her daughter so clearly through the mirrored screen.

Words of encouragement were all that Svi could present to her as she awoke from her slumbers in their private sleeping quarters in section 6, apartment 167. The nursing staff had removed her back to their apartment.

Svi kissed Lika's wet thumb. She had been sleeping very deeply with it poked firmly in her mouth, something that Lika would certainly never do under normal conditions. Svi sat there carefully caressing Lika's forehead and running his fingers through her short curly pale brown hair. Lika was waking up, she was becoming quite conscious.

Uncurling herself from the sleeping embryo position, with a small degree of effort, she eventually sat up and cradled herself in Svi's open arms. She was purring like a domestic cat. "I must certainly look after you now" Svi whispered to himself in thought, as he looked down into Lika's friendly sad smiling face.

"I must treat you with kid gloves. You are likely to be very brittle at this time after what you have been through." Svi continued to think quietly to himself while closely examining every contour and pattern on Lika's face.

"I am so lucky," Lika spoke "to have someone like you." She gave Svi a kiss on his cheek. "You haven't shaved! Your face is rough with stubble."

Svi smiled. "Complaining already. When did I get the chance to shave during the last 'day'?" Perhaps we could both do with a rest, a break from routine."

"Yes, that's a good idea. Let's go out to the new recreation area for a walk." Lika took Svi's hand and started to tidy herself up, indicating that he could well be advised to do the same. "There could be a three dimensional ball game in the 'globe' that could take our minds off things for a while". Lika disappeared into the bathroom leaving Svi to tidy himself up.

Svi was positively astonished at the immediate change in Lika. Not very many hours previously she had given birth after a physical struggle that must have exhausted her. The trauma of 'losing' her child should have left a mental stain on her conscious thought, but she was carrying on as if nothing had happened. Svi was suspicious it was not possible. She must be covering up. Perhaps she didn't even realize it herself, she was doing so well.

It had been a very good idea of Lika's to go to a ball game. There were crowds of people walking from the direction of the enclosed globe. These games were always incredible to watch. The skill of the players in zero gravity as they moved the ball around the internal volume of the enclosing globe was ingenious and deserving of high admiration. Secretly Svi would have liked to have been an active participant, rather than a seated spectator on the outside looking in. Each team had its own home patch, which it had to prevent the ball from entering. The ball was almost the same size as an average human head and was reasonably solid to touch. There was just enough 'give' in it to prevent body injury, and allow a bounce off the side of the globe. A point was achieved when the ball was 'allowed' to enter the base of the opposing team. The players had small propelling fins, which helped them to move unaided through the air at atmospheric pressure in zero gravity. There was a similar game played on the ground in full gravity at home, or in half gravity in the main core area of the Orbital Space station, but that game had to be played in two dimensions and was much slower. Three-dimensional ball games were far more exciting.

Svi and Lika walked hand in hand away from the game that had been played to a very exciting and closely matched conclusion. The couple were exhilarated by the rapid changes in fortunes of the opposing two teams. The complete change of environmental influences was genuinely what they both needed to relieve their tensions.

They returned to their apartment in a much happier frame of mind. Svi remarked to Lika as they approached their door, that they appeared to have left it ajar. Svi saw the look of startled shock on her face as Lika pushed the door of their sleeping quarters open much wider. There, curled up in a little ball, was small naked female child asleep, in amongst their cushions.

***

Erash would have been quite content to spend the entire evening sitting in the hotel restaurant talking with his newfound friend, Lara, but the conversation started to take a different turn a short time after they had finished their meal.

"Whose room would you like us to go to Alram?" Lara threw at him like a bolt out of the blue. A rapid change in a friendly conversation that Erash was certainly not prepared for. He certainly fancied her physically very much indeed, but he also liked her and found her to be a very good friend.

How could he lower the level of his friendship to that of prostitute and client? He had almost forgotten her purpose for being there. She continued, "You seem surprised at my question. Don't you realize that I am working here and I have a job to do? I must be seen to be doing it, and doing it well. If I fail to achieve excellent results of a very high standing, I am forced to leave these plush surroundings and go out and service the troops in the field. Life there is very hard, and few women survive. The exiled woman sometimes has to allow groups to make love to her all at one time. Horrible stories come back to us from the front lines. I shouldn't really be telling you all this, but I feel different with you Alram, and I trust you. If I am not seen to be making an attempt at making love with you I could be under suspicion and it would go against my record."

"What do you mean?" Erash was showing an amazed expression. He could not hide his astonishment at the frankness of this sweet little Lara, who came to him so timidly." How would anybody know what goes on between us? I certainly won't tell them!" He said sarcastically.

"You won't have to. They will know all they need to without you telling." Lara was starting to show the anxious state that had appeared sometime earlier, and Erash understood not to pursue his questioning.

"Please," Lara continued, "Which room shall we go to? Yours or mine?" Please Alram, please decide." She took his hand across the table and lay her face on the inside of her elbow exposing the back of her head to Erash who started to run his free hand through her long golden hair. He thought for a few moments, and then Lara heard the words she wanted.

"That's fine" he said, "We shall go to your room" Erash smiled inwardly. He felt so guilty; he loved his Marla and his Rula, yet there was definitely something very interesting and sexually seductive about this young wench. He kept trying to tell himself it was all in the line of duty, but it was becoming much more difficult for him to believe it.

Lara's room was exquisite. There were long high and extravagant silken drapes. The view was beautiful from her balcony. The entire coastline of Politir was spread out beneath her with the sharp sea edge eating away at the rocks below her window. The sun was setting on the ocean and was almost visible through a thick red mist, as it slowly would have been disappearing below the distant horizon. The onset of darkness seemed to give Erash a little more confidence, and possibly a natural excuse to continue with this charade they had set themselves. He looked around Lara's room as they re-entered from the balcony. It was lavish to an extreme. He had seen this type of setting before in an old estate house that dated back many generations. There were several in Semir, and two large estate homes in Lublia near Science and Welfare H.Q., but this room was very different. It didn't smell musty and the bed linen smelled fresh. In fact it was perfumed. There was also something else apart from the glistening chandeliers and the old hand carved and marquetried furniture. Erash was quite bemused; it was so strange that the ceiling and a large area of the four walls were mirrored. The room seemed so very large and everywhere he looked, there was an Erash and a Lara.

Lara sat down on the bed and indicated for Erash to join her. "Can't we just sit and talk?" Erash enquired. "I do like talking to you so very much."

Lara's face whitened with embarrassment.

"Am I not good enough for your pleasures?" She retorted, with a sad embarrassment in her tone of voice.

"Please come and sit here." She touched the bed next to where she was sitting on its edge, indicating that Erash should sit there next to her. "Come on Alram, come and sit down." She produced a truly seductive well-rehearsed smile.

Erash found himself involuntarily sitting himself next to Lara. He was completely taken by the change in her since they had entered her bedroom, and what is more he was enjoying it. He could not believe how good she seemed to be. She sat there with her kimono slightly falling forward at the neckline as she leaned forward carefully taking off her shoe. Erash could see her beautiful rounded breasts completely unprotected, bouncing around inside her clothing. She had done that beautifully and certainly intentionally. He couldn't wait for the other shoe. He watched with the keenest interest as she repeated the movement on the other foot, but this time she slightly lifted her knee, causing her thighs to show in the mirror. She opened them slightly. She was not wearing anything underneath. Erash was becoming very aroused. He could feel fullness in his groin. She was certainly very good. She returned to her seated position and smiled at Erash. "Come here Alram. I have a present for you." She leaned over and gave him an open mouth kiss, forcing his mouth to open with hers. Erash felt something highly perfumed and very pleasantly sweet entering his mouth from hers. It seemed to dissolve slowly in his mouth, and he felt that Lara was indicating that he should pass it back to her. With his tongue he pushed it back into her mouth. They continued to share the tablet until complete dissolution was achieved.

"What was that?" Erash asked, taking a deep breath.

"A sexual stimulant" Lara replied. "Although I am sure you won't need it." She continued with sarcasm, as she rubbed her hand gently across Erash's now exposed red-haired chest.

She kissed him carefully on each nipple, and then looking up at his face smiled a message of encouragement. "Now you do that to me." Erash's mind was completely taken over by the sexual stimulation of this innocent looking charmer. He obeyed her instruction, and gently pulled at her kimono. It just fell away from her chest. She sat there naked from the waist upwards. He obliged her request.

It was not many moments later when Erash had his shock. Lara was lying completely naked on her stomach on the bed; Erash was progressively stroking her back and moving lower down her body when he saw it. The tattooed figures of seven sheaths of corn by running water on her left buttock, and a six digit number on her right buttock. He followed his instinct and kissed each one as if in sympathy with the unfortunate owner.

"Who did this to you?" Erash enquired with trepidation and subdued anger.

"Please don't remind me of it" Lara was about to cry. The evening would suddenly have been spoilt if Erash hadn't taken Lara with sudden affectionate clinch. It was not long before pleasure was reciprocated with further pleasure. Eventually the couple moved from gentle to physical passion. Erash could feel a whole orchestra playing in his body and Lara let out an ecstatic scream as they exploded together in unison. They fell asleep in a pleasure of heavenly peace.

Daytime was beginning to show its first signs of light. Lara lay awake alongside Erash. He had a baby like appearance of happiness across his sleeping face. Lara turned onto her stomach and lay there naked next to him. She placed her chin on her hands as she bent her arms at her elbows, and looked closely at Erash's blissful state. She wanted very much to kiss him on his forehead, which was no more than three fingers width from her mouth. She didn't. The last thing she wanted to do was wake him from his peaceful slumbers. Lara examined every detail of his naked sleeping body. She was beginning to realize that she could be falling in love with him. This was so strange. She couldn't believe what was happening to her. Alram was only her client, and yet she knew that she loved him. She desperately wanted to shout it from the rooftops, but that was not practical. No she decided she would definitely see him again somehow. She had to tell someone. She decided.... she must tell Rula.

***

Rastus had not wanted to go on another mission, he was soon to be a father, and he felt it was unkind to leave his wife Glenshee at such a time. The only consolation was that he was still with his old friend and colleague Lex; they worked very well together. It was a tremendous responsibility following the escaped security guard they had taken great pains to release. They had been under strict security instructions from Jabal that Tubal Cain wanted to trace the root of their security problem. The intrepid duo had given their captives their hot soup that previous evening when they were held prisoner in the attic in Jabal's home. One of the bowls contained a large quantity of stimulant, whereas the other bowl contained sedative as an ingredient. It had not mattered which guard had which bowl as long as one slept while the other broke loose setting off the alarms. The escapee had to believe that he had escaped or he would not necessarily return carelessly to his base. So far the plan had seemed to work. The short moment when they hybrid guarding the prisoners turned his back after removing their 'slops' from within their cell, the stimulated prisoner broke loose through the door leaving his sleeping pal behind not knowing what had happened. The door was closed later and as the captive awoke from his slumbers he was greeted by a 'surprised and astonished' Jabal and company ready to question him under pressure. It was in this way that Tubal Cain hoped to discover the depths of the organization of the rogue organization in security of Science and Welfare.

Lex and Rastus could not believe the speed with which the half naked security guard had left the confines of the village. He had found an old-fashioned air-bike that was self-powered with compressed air when pedaled. He obtained extraordinary power from his legs under the effects of the stimulant. Lex and Rastus had difficulty in keeping in sight of his image in the darkness of the night as they followed on their silenced hover-bikes. They had had the foresight to put mini-bleepers in their soup, which they had swallowed along with the vegetables, but being so small its range was not very far. Lex and Rastus each had a stereo mini-receiver to track and locate, but this man was moving away at a great speed. By the time daylight had come the pursued and the pursuers were well into the local mountains and gaining altitude.

"That stimulant certainly worked". Rastus remarked to Lex, "He should slow down soon and possibly break off for a rest as the stimulant wears off."

No sooner had Lex agreed, than they noticed the bleeping signal had gone to a single monotone. It had stopped moving and therefore stationery.

"We know where he is so let's circle around him and watch him from above". Lex suggested.

The day was becoming brighter and certainly more humid. The black dust also seemed thicker than usual. The two men had reached a ledge over-looking a gully in which the escaped guard had secreted himself to sleep. Lex and Rastus fixed their bleeper receivers to aural alarm and placed them in their ears. This way they could also sleep without worrying that they would lose their quarry.

Lex was not sure what it was that first awoke him. It was either the loud bleeping in his ear, or Rastus striking him softly across his face. Whatever it was, they both knew that they had to move fast or they would lose him. The mountain trail was very dusty. The warm humid atmosphere still seemed to allow the black dust to collect and mix with the sandy surface of the mountain path. The bicycle they were following was leaving clear tracks for them to follow.

It was very late that afternoon when the bleeping once more turned to a monotonic single unbroken sound. They had stopped several times that day but never for more than a few moments but this time seemed to be for ages. Lex and Rastus were physically becoming exhausted. The heat was taking its toll of them. This guy that they were following must have certainly been very fit. It was a known fact that men in black and silver uniforms and wearing the badge of Science and Welfare had the most strict and rigorous tests for fitness twice a year.

"He has been stationery for a long time. Perhaps we ought to take a look at him. I wonder if he is alright." Lex showed concern in his voice as he spoke to Rastus.

"Shall we circle around him like before?" Rastus questioned Lex, who immediately agreed, but emphasized caution. Moving very slowly along a ridge above the level of the dusty path, the two men came alongside the bike that the escapee had stolen the night before.

"He's gone!" Rastus mouthed the obvious.

"No. Of course he hasn't" Lex retorted. "His bleeper is still on monotone. It seems to be coming from over there in the bushes. Perhaps he is asleep in there."

They decided to get much closer. They put their hoverbikes on lock and set them down next to his. Very carefully they clambered slowly trying very hard not to make a crack or crunch of breaking dead wood as they both trod trepidly forward. The monotone sound on their receiver was becoming much louder and clearer.

"He must be within spitting distance." Rastus whispered very quietly to Lex. They slowed down to a mere snail's space. They just could not understand. They made enough noise to warn an army, and still the bleeper was not moving.

"I wonder if he is hurt, and fallen into a gully." Lex pondered as he climbed a small mound into a small copse of bushes.

"There is your answer!" shouted Lex, as he pointed to the ground in front of him...a little pile of excreta!"

***

Velmitz, Girk and Ludo appeared at the edge of the forest. They each carried a pair of Panda pelts hanging down their back. The three men seemingly looked very tired after their difficult journey through the mountain woods of Varg. Large areas of the forest had been cut down, destroying the habitat of many creatures, but the government had stepped in and tried to control the desolation before it became too late.

The effect in this part of the world at least meant that there were still very large areas of heavily wooded and overgrown forestry under government protection. The government of Clarb for several years had been attempting to stem the flow of timber from its once rich jungles in the north and east. The president of Clarb was an elderly man of failing faculties, but he was still very much in control. Or at least he thought he was. He was reported to be an ignorant man but he had a strange and deep understanding of human progress. He was very much an environmentalist.

The three trappers were physically and mentally exhausted as they reached the edge of the thick overgrown forest, which had acted in the dual role of protector and enemy during that day's events. Ludo was showing his anxiety in his manner, and also in his voice.

"Do you think we've been followed? Are we safe?" Ludo asked the others. "There will be terrible trouble if we get caught with these pelts. The Panda is a protected species. We could be shot or paresified for less!" Ludo was almost crying with worry now. He was very tempted to run away, but he just about managed to remain calm.

They retrieved their air bikes from the hiding place in the bushes near the roadway, and within moments were off down the road at a reasonable pace of movement. They were so intent, in contemplating their future profits that they did not notice right above, on a ridge overlooking the roadway a uniformed man looking down on them through binoculars. He spoke a few words to his colleague with keen enthusiasm in his voice.

"Three of the bastards! There's three of them down there and we'll catch them, red handed if we are careful."

Velmitz and Girk had started to race each other down the hill leaving Ludo on a much slower bike trailing behind trying very hard to keep in contact. The two leaders disappeared around a bend in the road, Ludo began to get worried. He was quite a long way behind and all alone. He had two very valuable pelts very openly displayed on his back. He stopped his bike and dismounted. If he had to make the homeward journey on his own, he had better protect himself. He removed his jacket, and then very carefully hung the pelts as they were before, down his back and then placing his jacket over them he just looked like a very fat man riding an air-bike on his way home from a day's work. He found it very strange how warm they were across his shoulder blades. How heavy they were becoming. He thought. In spite of the fact that Ludo was much younger than his two friends he was finding the return journey very hard going.

He kept expecting to see them around each bend, but they had disappeared already from view. Ludo was very impressed with their apparent speed, but what he did not know was that not long after he first lost sight of them, they were captured and taken into custody by the government police.

Ludo approached the gates of his village, a suburb of Varg, it was already very dark, but he was positively delighted to have made it back with everything in one piece. He ran up the pathway to his home, with sweat pouring from all parts of him. He could not wait to tell his wife, he rushed in through the door with his valuable pickings across his shoulders. He didn't see the man in uniform standing behind the door. His wife's face told him all, as he turned around. "You are under arrest. You could get life in prison for that." The Policeman said as he pointed to the pelts on Ludo's back.

***

The fury and controlled anger in Tubal Cain's mind when he arrived at Jabal's farm was very much concealed as he walked through the ruins and debris of the living quarters of Jabal's herd. He was accompanied by his two half brothers Jabal and Jubal. Finally after much deliberation and consideration Tubal Cain spoke.

"We must root out the thugs and scum who would do such a thing as this. The fact that they are a shameful example of the human race is bad enough, but they purport to be members of my security guard of Science and Welfare, that is unforgivable. We must seek them out and destroy them before they become established as a positive force which will then have to be reckoned with on much more dangerous terms." Tubal Cain did not know why he did it, but he had to let off steam. He took a short run and then lifting back his right leg he kicked hard at a small loose round stone sitting harmlessly on the ground. It traveled fast and relatively far into the ditch at the far edge of the perimeter field. He felt a lot better for doing it.

Jubal suggested that Tubal Cain should see their prisoner and possibly watch while he was being interrogated. They made their way up to Jabal's attic-room.

"As your message ordered," Jubal began, "We have let the other prisoner think his colleague has been re-captured and taken away for questioning. He does not know that we planned his pal's escape and that we have been following him all day. We may even have to stoop to their tactics of torture and deceit to trace their nerve center and origin of command. It has to be irretrievably destroyed."

They arrived in the attic-room only to find their prisoner asleep, and the radio terminal on the lower landing was bleeping. Jabal walked over to it in order to take the message. It was Lex's voice that came across the airwaves.

"We've lost the prisoner on a temporary basis, but will re-establish contact as soon as possible. We know which direction he has moved in. He could not have gone far."

Tubal Cain instructed his stepbrother that an interrogation should begin on the remaining prisoner, forthwith. "Wake him up! Put him in that chair and tie his hands behind his back. "Jabal gave his orders to the two accompanying hybrids. The prisoner was still slightly drowsy as he was manhandled into the chair.

"What is your name?" Jabal continued as he addressed the semi-conscious prisoner.

"Joyahhh……." He drifted back to sleep.

"I am so sorry to disturb you," Jabal's sarcasm was becoming obvious, "But we do have some questions that have to be answered."

Grahyyy….." He was still semi-conscious.

"How much sedation has he had?" Tubal Cain addressed to any who would answer. He walked over to the prisoner and stood in front of him. Lifting the back of his right hand up to the left of himself, he pulled down hard smiting the prisoner a severe blow across his face.

"What the devil were you doing here?" Tubal was becoming very frustrated. He had drawn some blood from the prisoner's nose. It started to bleed. "Quick mop it up, and dress it quickly. Let's stay legal!" Tubal Cain could also be sarcastic.

"He's not fit for questioning as he is at present. Sober him up and call us back". He addressed to the hybrids, and suggested that his half brothers joined him downstairs for a drink and a rest.

Tubal Cain found the contrast between his brother's war-torn farm, and the wonderful few days he had just spent with his adorable loving Tsionne, too much to understand. How could so many beautiful things have existed elsewhere, at the same time as these violent horrible scenes were manifesting themselves under the same skies? A cold shiver went through his body. He felt so ashamed, but how he wished he could be back within the loving arms of his Tsionne. No, he thought, for a moment, he was there on Jabal's farm. He came back to reality. He had a very necessary and important job to do, nevertheless, Tsionne was constantly on his mind. He saw her smiling face continually in his thoughts. He knew something then, for the first time in his life, and he wanted to tell her to her face.

He was determined and had made up his mind. He loved her and could not survive without her.

***

Lara felt wonderful as she walked along the lengthy corridor to Rula's room. Her heart was warm, she felt so clean, and yet she had hardly washed her body since her lovemaking with Erash the night just past. She had said her fond farewells to him not many minutes before, insisting that they should 'liaise' once more, as soon as possible. Lara could still feel the touch of his hands and the warmth of his body close to her as if their lovemaking had left its indelible mark on her person. She did not want to wash away the images that may still remain where he had caressed and kissed her so carefully and well. Lara had adjusted her hair and put on a small degree of face cover, just for appearances, and thrown on a robe. She was anxious and she had to tell her friend about the new joy in her life.

Rula was wearing a very thin paper-like Kimono when she opened the door to Lara. Its pale blue color and thin white fringes complimented the slight touches of silver-gray make-up Rula had used as face cover that morning. Rula's state of pregnancy was becoming much more obvious; she no longer had her slim egg-timer shape. Her tummy was clearly visible through the paper-thin clothing, which was almost completely transparent as the light passed through it from the large window behind her. Rula's entire anatomy was on show for Lara to see, and yet Rula was completely dressed. Light can play some very strange things thought Lara as she unashamedly launched herself into Rula's arms pushing both of them into the privacy of Rula's bedroom.

"What has got into you? Why are you so happy?" Rula questioned into Lara's ear. "I've never seen you like this.

What a tonic so see, especially after the night I've just finished."

That young chap?" Lara queried "Was it the one I saw you with at dinner? He looked nice, but very young."

"He was a virgin. Not only in body, but also in mind."

Rula continued, "He was the son of a former client, a man of great importance in the government treasury department. He insisted that I 'break-in' his son to the pleasures of life. The fact that I was pregnant and becoming very obvious, he said would only make his son's pleasure even greater. It was horrible. The poor lad had never seen a naked woman before.

I had to show him everything, and he was so shy. I had to be careful not to scar his urges for life. To begin with he was very timid, and then when he became more confident he began to man handle me. He drove himself into a brutal frenzy. I felt that he had put his whole arm into me. I feel like a have ridden the whole night through, astride a galloping horse with me hanging underneath. I will be amazed if my baby survives." Rula finished, and then continued.

"Anyway, enough about me, what about you? You obviously had a wonderful night. You have a happy smug look about you that always means only one thing. You have fallen in love. Was it that man you were with at dinner in the restaurant last evening? He looked nice, although I couldn't see much of him. I could only see him from behind. He reminded me of someone….. that's another reason my evening was spoiled. I couldn't stop thinking of my love, lost and away somewhere. I don't even know if he is still alive. It's more than half a year now since I heard any news. He was being held prisoner at Larden, and rumor now has it that he has disappeared, although the Bylians won't admit to it. It is said that they are still collecting the ransom for him. Oh I do miss him; I pray every night for news of his safety. He was on my mind all through last night's mockery of lovemaking. I felt I was letting him down." Rula sighed wistfully. "I really felt close to him last night, as if he was very close by, he is always in my thoughts."

"This Erash guy must be quite something to affect you so deeply." Lara remarked, "You are usually so level headed about these things. I am certain that one-day you will both again be together. I will pray with you, for you tonight as I meditate my evening hours before supper. I do want you to be back together again. Wouldn't it be wonderful" Lara had an inspiration and a smile broke right across her face, she repeated. "Wouldn't it be wonderful, if Erash and you together with Alram and I could go out and celebrate our freedom from this place!"

"Shh!" Rula put her finger to her mouth "Be careful, as you know walls have eyes and ears in this place. Anyway who is Alram? Is he the one who has changed your demeanor over night? If so, he has made a new woman of you. He must be some hunk of a man."

"Oh he is! Lara's smile was becoming slightly sickly as she began to drawl out loud, the qualities of the man with whom she had spent the previous night. Eventually with the two girls sitting together drinking cable juice on the bed Lara continued her oration of happiness.

"He has promised to see me again, soon. I can't wait. I know, I will ask the housemother for a copy of the room video. That way you could see what a lovely man he is, and how well he makes love."

"That would be nice" Rula replied with a small degree of disgust in her voice. "Don't let these people completely destroy us into the depths of depravity!" She whispered deeply into Lara's left ear, and then gave her a gentle sweet kiss, as if for her forgiveness. "I would like to see your video, anyway." Rula smiled. "And I would love to meet Alram, he sounds so nice!"

***

CHAPTER 13

Lex and Rastus must have wasted a great deal of valuable time searching the surrounding undergrowth for a clue to the whereabouts of their lost quarry, the escaped security guard. Lex was already on his fifth encirclement of his half of the search area when he found it. A small broken dry twig, which had been snapped, very recently as something had passed it by. The direction of the break gave very good indication as to which way the movement was proceeding. Lex and Rastus were overjoyed at their find. It was not long before they found an unending trail of small clues, which led them for over a mile through heavy dead dry undergrowth. The rocky face, and changing gradients of a mountainous trail which left little choice of direction to go, became a great aid in their pursuit ability. Eventually they arrived at what seemed to be an ancient observation post that was well secreted high above the valley below, tucked carefully into the mountainside.

On their hands and knees, the duo crawled and edged diligently along the narrowing pathway that many years of time had savagely corroded into a dangerous ledge, just wide enough to perilously support the weight of one man. A sudden movement or a misjudgment of balance and the crawling adventurer could fall without warning into the deep yawning chasm waiting below. Lex had decided to attempt the last few paces on his stomach in an attempt to reach the old wooden door without doing too much damage to the crumbling pathway. As Lex's hand reached up to the old circular ring, which was the handle to the ancient wooden door, the ledge started to crumble beneath him. His heart must have missed several beats as it accelerated into action and the adrenalin in his veins raced around his body. He could feel his left leg go over the edge as his hand finally made firm contact and took grip of the door handle immediately above his head. He managed to regain his composure and then carefully and slowly achieved an upright position outside the door.

"It's not locked." He whispered to Rastus with caution in his voice. "I'll open it, and then perhaps I can help you across the cracking pathway." Lex continued. They were certain that the creaking noise of the opening door must have echoed across the whole valley. They would definitely not surprise anybody with their arrival after that aural announcement. With Lex standing in the open doorway he could throw out a helping hand, and some verbal guidance as Rastus carefully sidestepped along the final few paces of distance on the ever rapidly crumbling wall which was supporting the mountain ledge pathway. Rastus managed to reach the touch, then the grip of Lex's hand as he moved in an upright position along the ledge with his stomach firmly against the face of the mountain.

The two men were inside the ancient watchtower. Their relief was mixed with astonishment as they looked around its contents. It was fitted out with very old-fashioned radio and telegraphy of at least two or three previous human generations, but it was in almost immaculate condition. It had the very old standard faced visual display units with the regular keyboard. Rastus and Lex were amazed.

"This kind of gear went out decades and decades ago." Rastus exclaimed. "It must be over a hundred years old, and it looks like new!"

"This tower has a wonderful view over the entire geographical area, and if there were to be any antennae above us on the peak of this mountain then the total circular range that this tower could observe would almost be as far as Jabal's farm. This equipment looks as if it could be in use currently. Let's look for a waste-bin, which would soon tell us." Lex was inspired with enthusiasm, which abruptly changed as they both heard the whirring noise, which seemed to be coming from within the mountain wall of the watchtower itself.

"Quick" Lex whispered to Rastus "Close the door and hide in a cupboard or somewhere, I think someone is coming." They both managed to hide like children playing a childhood game of hide and seek. Rastus in a tall cupboard and Lex stretched out in the eaves of the roof space. He only just made it as he saw the wall in the mountain side of the watch tower open and two men in black and silver uniforms appear immediately beneath him.

"I was sure I heard something." One of them said to the other. Lex could see right down his neck. He prayed that they wouldn't look up. He was rigid and didn't even want to breathe. He could see that they both carried paresifiers in their belts.

"Over there! In the cupboard, I heard a noise!"

Lex knew that was his cue, he had to act or they would discover Rastus. One of the guards now had his back to his colleague and was moving towards the cupboard. Lex took hold of one of the rafters with one hand and threw himself onto the guard beneath him grabbing his paresifier from his belt on impact. Not a moment too soon. The other guard was just about to open the metal cupboard to reveal Rastus. Lex watched the guard fall helplessly to the floor a limp fleshy mess of lifeless body, as the man had taken the full short-range blast of his colleagues captured weapon. Lex managed to use the element of surprise to maintain his hold on the startled guard who lay flat out on the floor beneath him, and threatening him with his own paresifier he had a new captive.

"Come out Rastus" Lex was pleased "We have a new prisoner, and two paresifiers, on full charge."

Rastus emerged from the cupboard and retrieved the other weapon from the distorted body of the man lying awkwardly across the floor.

"Come on, you will be our guide." Lex pushed the paresifier into the prisoner's neck. "If you value your life."

It was not very long before they were in the downward motion of a rapid moving elevator, going deep into the mountainside. Lex knew that there was something familiar about the machine that they were traveling in but he felt it seemed to be out of context. It was the same form of transport that took people to subterranean protective areas. Their decent although rapid came slowly to a stop. The doors yielded to an open space of a bright subterranean monorail station. Lex finally understood the entire situation.

***

Rula was standing just inside Lara's bedroom door; there were just the two of them in the room that sleepy warm Politir afternoon. Lara was sitting unashamedly with her feet apart, and her knees drawn up to her chin at the very center of her bed. All she was wearing was a pale peach 'see through' negligee.

"I have been thinking" Rula said to Lara as if she were to make an announcement of momentous proportions. "I have changed my mind about watching your Room Video. I feel that your lovemaking is your private affair, and certainly no concern of mine. You can introduce me to Alram when you get a free opportunity. I would really love to meet him!" Rula smiled. "Perhaps you will let me know when you are next seeing him, and we could have a chance meeting or something, but remember don't become too attached, you know that it is against house rules!"

"Now that Pollo is back, the regime is becoming much stricter" Rula tried to tell Lara something that she would obviously have known already.

"But I can't help my feelings and there is no house rule against that is there?"

"No, but as long as the client doesn't find out." Rula smiled and turned to leave. Lara lifted herself from the bed and with almost nothing on, followed her to the door. Holding her door ajar, she tried to whisper to Rula in the outside corridor where security was less formal.

"Will we ever escape from this horrible prison? I believe that Alram can help. He seems so knowing, and so strong!"

"Don't talk of such things. If we are heard it will be the end for both of us. Please be very careful, one day our time will come, I am an optimist. I don't intend to have my baby here." Rula kissed Lara on the cheek as a passing waiter coughed and politely smiled at the state of Lara's undress. With acute reddening of her face and a deeply felt blush, she backed gently through her door, throwing a friendly, understanding kiss back to Rula.

Erash was certain he saw Pollo enter the building those few days ago, and he was determined to capture her if possible. He had never knowingly killed anyone before, and certainly, he had never killed a woman.

He didn't want to start now, but his brief was to capture her, or kill her as a last resort, and not to break his cover under any circumstances.

He decided to meet up with Lara again. Perhaps he could use her to get through to the service quarters. He had to find Pollo while she was on the premises. He rang for service in his room. He would like the same young woman that he had had previously, he repeated into the house phone.

"You look wonderful" Erash felt very guilty again, on seeing Lara enter through his bedroom door with her passkey. He was beginning to hate himself for using such a sweet young thing. He had forgotten how lovely she was. A 'spritely' nymph in a sea of evil. How he wished he could take her with him. "You are beautiful" he smiled, and gave her a friendly peck on the side of her neck. She returned the compliment by putting her arms around his neck and giving him a full frontal kiss almost digesting him in passion. Erash was quite taken aback. He knew that she was genuine, and he was feeling even more guilt, at her sudden exhibition. Had he led her on unintentionally, he wondered.

"Let us go and get some fresh air." Erash suggested. "We could go for a walk along the front and watch the evening arrive."

"We have to check-out and we cannot go beyond the limits of the hotel security, without permission or we will lose everything, and possibly be subject to public rape. I would love to go with you, but we must get proper permission."

"Alright!" Erash replied, "I'll come with you."

"You will have to," Lara replied. "They need your guarantee of my return. You would be in critical trouble if I escaped Alram. They could castrate you and even blind you, if you let me go. If they caught me, their vengeance is fierce and prolonged, and you would be forced to watch as a Eunuch. This part of the world is very brutal, but they have very little crime, and a great respect for discipline." Lara had a feint tear in her eye as she spoke. "Alram. Please be careful, I would hate anything to happen to you because of me. Come, let's check for permission. I promise to be good." She smiled re-assuringly.

Erash was becoming guilty again. These feelings of guilt worried him. He was an agent out in the field. He could not afford soft sentiment. That could be a killer.

"We have to go to the office." Lara beckoned Erash to follow her.....

"After dark" the official behind the desk spoke to them both "After dark, you cannot re-enter the hotel by the main entrance this evening. We are expecting an important visitor. You will have to come in through the staff quarters. We apologize to you sir. As our guest you deserve better, so you may have the use of this lady free of charge tonight, but I am duty bound to warn you that you are under all other circumstances obligated to the 'rules of return' as stated to you, for which you have just signed acknowledgement."

"Who's coming tonight?" Erash leaned over the desk as if for a quiet off the cuff hint from the man in the office. "I'm not aloud to say..... but..... ahem..... there is no higher office held in this country." He took the payment from Erash unseen by anyone. Erash's discretion was so superb, that even Lara who was standing next to him, holding his other hand did not notice Erash pass over the bribe.

Their walk along the promenade in other conditions would have been full of warmth and romance as they looked at the rocks below the promenade where the sea lapped gently around them. The tidal lift was very slight as the sun's effect on the tidal movement was very low at that time of year. The sea was almost at a constant depth.

Erash picked up a small black stone, and threw it hard across the surface of the calm sea. It bounced three times before it sank.

"I can't get it to bounce more than once," Lara whispered to Erash as she tried to emulate his prowess at stone throwing onto the sea.

Erash smiled. He felt even guiltier now. She seemed to trust him, and he could well be about to destroy her. How could he do it? He felt terrible.

It was already quite dark when the happy couple arrived back at the staff entrance of the House of Dolls. There was quite a commotion going on along the promenade at the main porch way entrance. There were people with protest banners waving into the center of a crowded street area just in front of the main entrance of the House of Dolls.

"They have got courage!" Erash spoke quietly into Lara's ear. "People in Bylia have been executed for less. If the visitor is who we think it could be he will be furious. He could have them all shot, there, where they stand!"

"He probably will too!" Lara replied with a sad smile.

"They are so cruel in this country. I do hate it here....! Lara realized that she had said too much, she had broken a cardinal rule. Rula had warned her, never to speak ill of their hosts of the country. "What is that you say?" Erash enquired "You hate it here. Where do you really come from, and how and why did you get here?"

Fortunately for Lara, they had just reached the staff entrance on the front of the hotel. It didn't look quite so sleazy as the kitchen entrance at the back, where Erash had last been two nights before. As they entered, Erash took Lara's hand and they moved towards the staff's reception desk.

"You can't go into the main hotel at the movement, our VIP visitor is in the entrance hall with his guests." The woman at the reception desk spoke to Erash. "You can check your woman in here if you wish, and take the back stairs to your room."

Lara and Erash made their way back to his room then decided to go down to the restaurant for a meal. Erash was aware that this could well be an ideal opportunity to search out Pollo while all of the staff were so very busy with the major distraction of the visiting VIP's. He had overheard a casual remark that the guest was taking the bridal suite for his nocturnal pleasures and would be staying at least for the night.

Lara and Erash were given the same table in the restaurant as they had the night before. Their meal was uneventful, but Erash had the distinct feeling that Lara wanted to tell him something. Erash desperately wanted Lara to speak out her words but she seemed to lack the confidence and clammed up always at the last moment. He sincerely wanted to know what Lara was trying to say. Erash was also trying to work out a plan of action to locate Pollo; he had to complete his mission. Perhaps he could get some help from Lara. Could he trust her? They had been as close to each other as any humans could physically get, but they still could not communicate. Erash was becoming unknowingly as frustrated in their communication problem as Lara was. Lara desperately wanted to ask Erash to help her to escape, but it could mean catastrophe for both of them if they were caught. How could she ask that of such a man? A complete stranger? The poor souls sat opposite each other during their meal completely ignorant of what was going on in the other one's mind. Then it happened! The catalyst they needed to set them on their way.

Lara looked over Erash's shoulder; she could see her friend coming into the dining room. She was not alone; she had a client with her. The headwaiter was directing the couple to a table on the left and just across Erash's right shoulder. Lara wanted very much for Rula to meet her Alram, this could be the chance that she had been waiting for. Lara's pulse was accelerating; she wasn't sure whether Rula had seen her. How could she attract her without making it too obvious? It would be very difficult for Rula as she has a client with her, a real greasy dark haired character with a spotted and pimpled face. He was well dressed and clean-shaven, obviously was a man of position or wealth, but he didn't look like a person that she would like to have taken into her bed. Lara was thinking to herself in deep nervous contemplation.

"What's the problem?" Erash asked, bringing Lara back to reality with a bump. "Why are you so engrossed in thought? You look like you have seen a ghost. What's the problem?"

He repeated.

"Oh, nothing. I have just seen my best friend come in for dinner with one of her clients. He looks horrible. I feel so sorry for her."

"Where?" Erash made to look around behind him.

"No please don't make an obvious move." Lara put her hand out to Erash! "Please Alram, I don't want them to think that we are talking about them."

Erash tried to change the subject of conversation and acquiesced to Lara's request, but he was finding it tough going. He so desperately wanted to seek her help with Pollo. Would she agree? He was so uncertain of her.

"Can we go to your room" Erash suggested. "I want to speak to you privately."

"Oh no! Not there". Lara was quite put out. "We get no privacy there…..!" She realized what she had said and went bright red with embarrassment. "Take me into the bar, where it is noisy and there is music. We can talk there without being heard."

They got up from the table Erash turned taking Lara's hand….. he became transfixed to the spot where he was standing. He could not believe his eyes. He wanted to run towards her.

They must have both seen each other at the same time. Rula's eyes met his. She knew who he was. No disguise could fool her, but how why and when? She kept her cool. She was unbelievably calm. Rula knew. Erash knew, but neither Lara nor Rula's client could have known the sudden change in their partner's fortunes. Both Rula and Erash were experts in the field and this was a case for composure for both their sakes.

"I would like you to meet my good friend Rula" Lara introduced Erash to her. "This is Alram a passing friend." She used the term commonly understood amongst the sisterhood as describing a client when in their presence.

"I am so pleased to meet you Mr. Alram." Rula stood up slightly and shook his hand, smiling nervously.

"Delighted to meet you also," Erash smiled in return. He turned to Lara. "Perhaps we could ask your friends to join us in the bar afterwards for drinks." He turned to Rula's client, a real greasy mess. "Would you like that?"

"Ah…. yes. That would be pleasant. For drinks you say? Yes, would you like to do that?" He turned to Rula, who immediately agreed.

Erash and Lara took their leave of the dining couple and went off to the bar to wait for them. They found a secluded noisy isolated spot very near to one of the loudspeakers. They could almost 'feel' the music bellowing forth.

"We can talk here." Lara whispered at the top of her voice to Erash.

***

The display digits on the 'Estimated Time of Arrival' board in the subterranean monorail station had stated six minutes for the last two hours or more. It was obviously malfunctioning. Lex and Rastus were becoming slightly nervous and certainly very impatient. They had to keep a constant eye on their captive. Not that he had anywhere to go. They had sent the lift back up. He could only risk his life by running along the tunnel. He was unarmed, and they each had a fully charged paresifier.

Time is only a luxury when you need it. It becomes a liability when you have plenty of it. They were beginning to become very anxious and a little irritable.

"How often do these trains run?" Rastus prodded the captive with his paresifier under his shoulder blade. The prisoner was sitting cross-legged facing the track with his back to his captors.

"Do you expect another train soon?" He prodded him again.

"If you kill me, you'll find out nothing. So stop jabbing me with that."

"The prisoner spoke!" Lex turned to Rastus with interest in his voice. "Perhaps he's alive after all," he continued with sarcasm. He walked in front of the prisoner and faced him "What are you doing here and who are you?"

The prisoner spat in the direction of Lex and put his head between his knees as if to reject Lex completely. Rastus was just about to club him across the back of his head in anger, with the butt of his paresifier.

"Cool it! Lex interfered. "We will have our time. Let's keep him alive; we might need him. It would be a terrible shame to waste him."

Conversation ceased again for at least a quarter of an hour and tedium was almost beginning to take its toll.

"What if we are stuck here for days? There is no water, no food we could starve to death." Rastus suddenly shouted to his friend.

"Precisely!" came the reply from Lex "That is why I am convinced that a train will come soon. There was only enough water upstairs for a small refreshment and no more food than a man would eat for his morning break. This is their only way down so there must be a way to go from here. Believe me Rastus; we are on the right track. Something will happen soon."

The prisoner's face exhibited a feint smile.

"What if there are more of these villains on the next train. We should have dressed in those uniforms upstairs." Rastus showed some initiative.

"No! Have you ever seen a hybrid in one of those uniforms? That would be madness, but you have given me an idea." He turned to the prisoner. Take off your clothes. They are about my size."

Rastus smiled. "What a good idea. If you put him in your clothes we both become your prisoner."

They completed the dressing of the prisoner just in time. A train was approaching the opposite platform. They could feel the change of air pressure in their ears as the silent vehicle came into sight. Its lights shouting from down the dark tunnel.

"It's going the other way" Rastus interjected.

"You tell me which is the right way?" Lex remarked in jest, as they bundled the prisoner and tied his hands. Holding him close to their paresifiers they moved towards the arriving train.

"You say anything out of place and you're dead." Lex murmured into the prisoner's ear. "You had better come around onto this side of me and give me the other weapon. You are also meant to be a prisoner do not forget." He called to Rastus.

The well-lit empty train arrived at the platform. Not a living soul was on board. The doors automatically slid open, so quietly that even a blind man wouldn't have heard, or felt the vibration. The three men stumbled on board and took facing double seats. They sat their prisoner on the inside of them so that he could not even contemplate escape.

"Where are we going" Rastus was thinking aloud. "These trains can travel faster than sound, and cover very long distances. It could be going anywhere."

"No this one" Lex replied. "This is one of the early prototypes. It cannot travel very fast. We are probably on an old branch line, which should now be out of use. I would guess that these hooligans have converted this system into their own use and if we are not careful we will find that we are in fact still their prisoners."

Their captive's face broke out into a knowing grin as the train began to turn through a gradual bend slowing down, and then cruising carefully to a stop. Within a moment they were on the move against slowly gliding into a brightly illuminated station. There were several guards in black and silver uniforms on the platform but they didn't look as though they were especially expecting anybody. The three travelers alighted from the train and made for the exit steps—Lex was fully expecting to be called back. He must have looked an odd sight with his two prisoners. He was amazed that he was not even challenged. They reached the elevator and pushed the control. When they reached the highest stop and the elevator had come slowly to a halt, they emerged into an open area that was still very obviously underground, although quite near the surface, they had traveled upwards a long way, and there was that sweet surface smell in the air. There were also small deposits of black dust here and there. These were only evident near the surface as it generally came down the surface ventilators.

"Quick, sit down on that bench and look as if you are waiting for someone." Lex whispered to Rastus. "There are several people coming and they are wearing very high ranking uniforms." He pushed the captive onto the bench. "One out of place gesture or word and you and your officers will be dead!"

The three men sat still trying hard to look part of the scenery. Lex made the necessary salute as they passed. He was quite perked when they returned his recognition. He was obviously well disguised and was very pleased with himself. Rastus almost gave the game away but he managed to control his smile.

"Did you see who they were?" Lex asked Rastus "They are generals, in high command. Look at our prisoner. His face tells us all. This must be their H.Q. We have to leave fast! They seem to be very highly organized. We've found out what we came for let's get back to base….. fast!"

Lex and Rastus waited for the strangers to get out of sight. They grabbed their prisoner and ran for a hoversphere that they seen parked near a ventilation shaft. Lex had it working and with the help of Rastus they were soon moving. There was a vertical exit shaft immediately behind the machine. It became clear that within moments they would be away. Lex and Rastus held their breath as the globe started to rise very slowly.

"I hope you know how to drive this thing." Rastus called to Lex. They were amazed to see daylight as they broke from the vertical shaft into 'fresh' air. They were even more amazed that they had done it without incident.

***

Erash was not really listening to Lara as she continued to try talking in fierce competition with the music belching forth from the stereo system. He so much wanted to ask Lara more about Rula, but he didn't want to seem too interested in her. He could not properly clear his thoughts from the shock meeting he had just had. Thank god they were so well trained. No one could know that they knew each other. What had happened to Rula? Was she really pregnant or had she just become a little overweight? No. He had to admit to himself, she was definitely the woman who was advertised as pregnant. He tried so earnestly to search his thoughts for all those things he had recently heard about her from various sources. 'She was unwilling, but she put herself into the job with skill.' That would be just like Rula, though Erash, she knew that as an agent in the field she had to survive best way she could. How did she get herself pregnant? He just could not come to terms with that.

"You are miles away. Your thoughts are very far from here, what is your problem? It's all over your face!" Lara had noticed. Erash became slightly startled by the question. He did not know why, but he felt that this time he had to give a fair answer. Things had changed; he had to work very fast. "Are you sure that we cannot be heard?"

Lara nodded the affirmative.

"I need your help" Erash continued. "We have to leave here tonight" He saw the shocked expression on Lara's face. He could have kissed her. She looked beautiful. He knew that she was on his side.

"I will take you, and your friend Rula, but I must also take a prisoner as a hostage. "Please will you help?"

"Oh yes! Alram!" Came the spontaneous answer. No thought was required it was a reflex action. "My darling I love you, and thanks for including Rula. You don't even know her, and you will risk your life for a friend of mine. You must like me a lot?"

Erash could not bring himself to spoil her illusion. He just hoped he could play along with it. He had to be sure of Lara's help and he did have quite a soft spot for her.

"Who can we take as hostage?" Lara continued. "What about Rula's client. I believe that he is related to the President somewhere along the line."

"No!" Erash was firm. "He may not be one of Fadfagi's favorite cousins. No. We want Pollo. There is no doubt that with her we will secure safe passage out of here."

Lara was numbed by Erash's resolution. He was certainly positive in his thoughts. Oh what a man she thought. She is so lucky to find such a man. She was completely confident that he would succeed in the impossible. Capture Pollo and use her as a hostage. Lara could not take it all in. She was shattered with admiration for this man. Disbelief did not enter her mind.

"That's easy." Lara found herself answering positively but completely involuntarily. "She does her accounts on her own, every night in the staff office, but how will you capture her. She is always armed when she counts her money, and the place is heavily alarmed."

"Don't worry about that just tell me her routine, and her times of normal habits. I'll do the rest." Erash stood up to greet his guests as Rula and her 'client' arrived on the scene. "What would you like to drink?" He played the perfect host and ordered drinks from the bar for the four of them. Unseen when he arrived at the table he placed Rula's drink in her hand, and made it impossible for the greasy gentleman to refuse the one he was offered. Lara always drank pure cable-juice with ice, which was very boring. So Erash had no problem making sure of his endeavors. Rula knew what Erash was doing. It was part of their training.

"Your friend has gone to sleep" Lara pointed out to Rula.

"I do believe he has" Rula smiled "What a terrible disappointment!" She continued with some sarcasm.

"For him!" Erash interrupted with a smile from cheek to cheek. Lara grabbed hold of Rula's arm as if she had not a moment to lose. "Alram has a wonderful plan. We are leaving tonight, and he wants us to take you with us." She was effervescing with enthusiasm. Erash was praying that no one would notice. It could cause problems. "There is only one sure way to do it..." Erash put his hand on Lara's knee to indicate she should shut up. She did.

"Rula. I am gong to help Lara out of here tonight and I will take you with her as her friend, but we must act very fast while all this commotion is going on with the President's visit."

"How are you going to do it?" Erash's heart melted. Her voice. "This place is like a fortress. No one has ever 'escaped' successfully. You must be crazy!"

Erash wanted to kiss her there and then. Oh how he would have liked to embrace her. She was so special to him.

"No! We will take a hostage. Pollo!" Erash murmured almost inaudibly under the dramatic tones of bellowing music. He then outlined his plan to both the girls, as they leaned over the sleeping body of the greasy gentleman.

Pollo was busy with her eyes becoming very heavy as she poured over the many figures of her accounts. She was having a bad time. The book would not balance. The Visual Display Unit was blurring then clearing. Why was she so tired? It was so unusual for her. She never needed her sleep. She took another swig from her coffee. The only noise was the percolator bubbling away on the sideboard. It was beginning to annoy her. Why was her screen beckoning her in that way? The figures were dancing in time with the percolator. Her head dropped onto the keyboard. She tried to lift it. She had work to finish. She was so much better now. She had had her hand returned and re-affixed. She could work the keys so much more effectively now. Why could she not control her thoughts? She was becoming delirious.

Rula, Erash and Lara entered the office very carefully. They turned down the light to very low, and then carefully lifting the sleeping drugged body of Pollo from its position at her desk. They carried her to the couch. Erash helped the girls to strip her, and Lara put on her clothes. There was a feint likeness in the dark. They dressed Pollo up in Lara's clothes, and then wrapped her in a blanket and Erash threw her over his shoulder. It was so simple a scheme it had to work.

They walked straight through the staff exit out onto the street. It was a very dark and warm humid evening.

"Who are you, and where do you think you are going?" Two men appeared from nowhere.

"My name is Alram. You should know Pollo. We are taking this young woman to the doctor. She has taken very ill, and with the Eh…. Hm…. VIP staying with us we don't want any embarrassment. She is very contagious and has been bleeding!"

The two men would have been seen to go white with shock had it been daylight. They moved three steps backward and allowed them to pass.

"Where are we going?" Lara asked discreetly.

"The port." Erash replied. I have a boat there at my disposal. Soon we shall be sea borne.

The four people fitted very neatly into the tiny cabin of the small cruiser as it guided itself out of the harbor. Rula and Lara were asleep as Erash set the automatic pilot on a course for the nearest friendly port. Pollo began to stir, as Erash returned to his bunk.

"You! I know you! She screamed like a tiger awoken, with venom. "I have seen your photographs. I know you! What am I doing here? Where am I?" She succeeded in waking everybody up. Erash would have answered, but a searchlight caught them in its beam.

"Who are you? Identify yourselves."

Came over a loudhailer. Erash was not exactly prepared for this eventuality, not two problems at once.

The loudhailer continued. It was obviously a local Bylean patrol boat.

"We believe you have a valuable passenger on board. We will blow you out of the water if you don't release her. Pollo is too valuable. Our orders are to sink and destroy all of you rather than allow you to capture Pollo. Decide. You have two minutes for her to appear on the life raft. Then we will let you go. You have a choice."

"Erash!" That's who you are! You bastard!" Pollo spat full face into Erash. No one saw the shock on Lara's face. She was devastated. She had been used, and yet she loved him and she loved Rula. He would always be Alram to her. She had to act fast. Carefully and completely unnoticed, she crawled in the half shadows of the searchlight into the life raft. She launched it out into the sea.

"It's alright, I'm safe" She stood up and shouted into the searchlight. "Let them go! That's an order."

Rula pulled Pollo back from the door and struck her a searing blow across the back of her head. She was out cold. Erash was bewildered.

"That's Lara out there. She's almost at their boat." Erash seemed defeated. "What have I done?"

"You couldn't avoid it. She is so young a sweet girl. You meant a great deal to her. She was falling in love with you, but she loved me too, and she knew how much I loved you. She put together her sums very quickly and made a run for it. I really believe she has done it for us. We must not let her down!" Rula whispered into Erash's ear.

"I feel so guilty!" Erash suddenly changed his mood. "There is nothing we could do for her now, she is too far away. While we have the chance and they are busy with Lara, let us get a move on. We must get out of range of their laser cannons. This boat is a racer and built for speed."

As Erash spoke he had moved over to the bridge and pushed hard on the supercharged throttle. The boat almost took off out of the water just as the other boat was helping Lara out of her life raft. Within moments Rula and Erash were together gliding across the sea with their prisoner now well secured in the locked cabin. They would be at sea for a period of perhaps two days. With a little zigzagging of course and an anti-radar device previously fitted, their chances of reaching their chosen destination were very high.

"We owe it to Lara to succeed." They said to each other in unison, but then was not the time for kissing. They both felt so wretched, and held each other in warm mutual comfort, as they looked out across the darkened sea.

Erash and Rula could not have imagined what was happening to their faithful friend. Had they known they would surely have returned? As Lara was helped into the guards' boat, the crew did not initially realize the incorrect identity of their new passenger. It was dark, and they took a long time to perceive the real situation by which time Erash's boat had become a mere dot on the horizon. Their fury was crazy. They would nearly have killed Lara there on the spot, but they knew that a dead body would only cause them problems. They had to bring their 'proof' back to port.

Two days later, a very large crowd gathered in the main square of Politir. A poor young woman with her hands tied above, apart and behind her head, as her naked body was laid on a straw mattress in the market square. Two Eunuchs were forcing her legs apart in full view of the gathering crowd. A line of lusty men of all shapes, ages and sizes were paying their money to have their turn. They each walked naked from the waist down, through strong disinfectant once they had partaken of the pleasures of carnal delight. Lara screamed and screamed. Her face contorted as she watched the faces of frustrated men pawing and using her body for their own pleasure. One man was so old and infirm, she was sure that he passed out while he was inside her. In fact the poor man actually died in full view of the crowd. It must have been his last supreme effort.

Blood was beginning to seep from between Lara's legs. Her wrists were torn; the skin was ripped from pulling at the binding. She prayed to die. There must have been forty or more men who had tried their chance with her. Certainly very few were successful but she could no longer stand the shame, and excruciating pain. She felt like she had a large hedgehog in the depths of her groin. The women were standing there ogling at the occasion, and whenever a man succeeded they cheered. Whenever one failed, they spat and screamed obscenities at Lara as if it was her fault.

Lara was left for the day, and then the night alone unattended, naked and bound, guarded only by the two Eunuchs with drawn ceremonial swords. They gave her a sip of water every hour. Passers-by could do whatever they wished with her as long as they didn't tarnish her body.

The following morning they cut her down. A poor brave soul. The two Eunuchs lay her gently on the ground. Her hands found her groin. She stroked herself between her legs. The pained look on her tearful face, the redness around her eyes from continual crying, she whimpered. Her whole body went into spasm. She wretched and exhaled a large volume of air, never to take another.

Her dead body lay there for more than an hour gathering flies. A beautiful young nurse whose voluntary work in a strange country had led her to the depths of human depravity. Her body gave no exhibition of the life that once so proudly lived inside it. There would be no medals, no memorial, no flags, no recognition of her bravery and no mention in a roll of honor. Her sacrifice would just be one more unknown endeavor in the face of human cruelty.

END OF BOOK ONE

***

'An alternative story of Noah and his Ark'

—BOOK TWO—

'Your body is where you live'

CHAPTER 1

Shem and Ham were playing happily on the front porch, a childish game of "Three stones". Noah, the expectant father for a third time, was sitting just behind them in his basket work rocking chair enjoying the warm hazy summer's day. It was a rare occasion these days. The sun was almost perceptible and it was quite late in the afternoon. The mid-wife was in with Naamah; the baby was due at any moment. Naamah had insisted on becoming old fashioned for this birth. She didn't want any modern technology to bring forward and aid the birth. She didn't want to know the sex of her child in advance. She didn't want to plan the movement of her baby's arrival with a convenient moment in the working day. She wanted her new child, when her new child wanted to come. They had both been responsible parents and had prepared for all eventualities, even down to the choice of name. In the event of a girl they would call her Esther, and if a boy he would be Japheth.

Shem was old enough to know what was happening, but Ham was still only a mere infant himself. Naamah had conceived the imminent birth only three periods after she had given birth to Ham. Ham was now no more than a small infant who was just finding his legs. Shem was keeping him very well amused with the three stones on the doorstep.

A noise ventilated from within the house, Noah was not sure if it was he or Shem who heard it first, the music of a natural birth. It was the screaming cry of a newborn child. Noah would love to have been there at that moment but he had another of his bad chests, and couldn't risk infecting his newborn child. He could have taken treatment, but it was no certain guarantee at such an early stage of infection.

The midwife appeared at the open front door, with a small package, wrapped in an old fashioned shawl. The hybrid nurse announced for the world to hear with a clean white toothy smile.

"Japheth is a beautiful bouncing boy-child. Congratulations Mr Noah. I wish that you and your family should have a long healthy life in peace.

Noah stood at the feet of his young baby. He pulled back the shawl just a little. The midwife held him firmly. Noah smiled. He was so proud. He lifted Shem up to see his new brother who immediately tried to poke his finger in his eyes. Noah moved him away.

"Why does he not look at me?" Shem whispered to his father's ear.

"One day." Noah answered in wisdom, "One day Japheth will cast his eyes upon many things, but today, and, yet for a little while longer he has more important things to do."

Noah did not think it a very good idea to stay in close proximity of his newborn infant; he decided to pay a quick visit to Naamah. He did not want to spread his germs around, and anyway it had become tradition for he and Tubal Cain to go out and empty a few bottles of alcoholic wine together to 'wet' the baby's head.

Noah was completely absorbed in his pride as he entered the lift to Tubal Cain's new office. He was proud to be a father of a third son. He so much wanted to tell his brother in law in person.

Tubal Cain's face showed a feint hint of jealousy when he heard the news, Noah could perceive that Tubal Cain's innermost desires were not too far from his own. Noah was sure that he had guessed correctly that Tubal's marriage with Tsionne was as yet proving infertile. They had been married for three years, and although ecstatically happy, Noah was sure that there might be problems with their attempts to have a child.

Tubal interrupted Noah's thoughts.

"Come on old boy. This calls for a drink, but let's not drink alone this time. There is a very friendly bar not too far away from here. Come on I'll take you there." Tubal beckoned to Noah.

Tubal and Noah sat facing each other across a small table.

They were each perched cheerfully on top of a high stool. Outwardly an observing stranger would have perceived two very happy friends enjoying an early evening drinks session together. They were two people in a friendly atmosphere becoming more and more involved in making the other one less sober. No stranger could have known the truth that really existed within their minds. Tubal Cain decided in his office that he wanted to celebrate Noah's third fatherhood amongst people, but he could well have been with his friend in the middle of a large desert for all the effect that the crowded surroundings were having on him. Tubal knew why he could not bear to celebrate Noah's joy with him in private. Tubal was very upset that the celebration was not his own, and very uncharacteristically he had sought the protection of the crowd to give him solace while he gave fuel to aid Noah in his proud moment. Whatever Tubal Cain felt selfishly, he could not bring himself to spoil Noah's day. Very much in passive support, Tubal Cain tried to act out the friendship that Noah was seeking.

Noah could sense a change in Tubal Cain since giving him the joyous news. Noah realized that Tubal Cain was inwardly tormented, but he was not certain of the reason why, although he would have guessed correctly his problem. The only course of action Noah thought would help, he pursued. Inebriation. That would loosen his tongue.

The two men, Tubal Cain, and Noah, once again walked unsteadily off into the sunset, had there been one. They each carried what was left of their almost empty bottles. They were both talking 'cheerfully' at each other. Perhaps Noah was listening to Tubal Cain. He certainly was not listening to Noah.... Tubal was developing verbal diarrhea.

Noah's recent fatherhood had been the laxative of his thoughts. He started to pour out his heart to Noah.

"I love Tsionne. She was my earliest dream come true. We belong to each other. We are one. Yet we are deprived of the one thing to complete our relationship." Tubal began to sober himself for a moment. He knew he was talking too much, but Noah was his friend as well as his brother-in-law. Who else could he confide in? He had to talk; he wanted so much to get his problem out of his system.

"When we were married, Tsionne was innocent, and a virgin. We made love for the first time on our wedding night, and it was perfection in success itself. No book could have written our story with more meaning. We were made for each other. Never have two people created and kept a relationship so perfect." Tubal Cain looked slightly dizzy, and Noah had to offer him physical support for a moment. In fact Noah didn't feel much better himself.

Tubal continued, with a slight slur in his manner.

"Not many brides these days shed blood for their groom especially on their very wedding night. We have been lovers and friends ever since. We are each other. I could not live without her, and am so sad because I feel so much for her. She desperately wants to give me the child she knows I want and that in turn makes her frustrations even worse. She is sad for me, and I am so sad for her. Oh Noah! What can we do?" For the very first time since he had met Tubal Cain, Noah could see a tear of sadness forming in Tubal's eye.

"Have either of you seen anyone who could help you sort this out?" Noah asked carefully.

"Yes. We have been for tests and it proves to be Tsionne's problem. It's anatomical. Her tubes! They don't run wide enough, and don't properly reach their station!" Tubal stopped abruptly….. "I must be mad. I should not be talking about this. It's private between Tsionne and me."

"Don't talk nonsensical rubbish." shouted Noah. I am your brother-in-law. I love you as a friend, and I certainly have always loved Tsionne as your wife. If you understand what I mean. I will respect your privacy, but please let me introduce you to someone who may help the both of you."

"Could you?" Tubal smiled. Noah nodded, and put his arm across Tubal's shoulders. Once again, they walked off under the now very darkening evening sky.

***

The impatience was beginning to show on Svi's tired face. He had had a very busy 'day' acting as a stand-in guide for a pal of his. He had never liked the idea of showing tourists around his own patch in the extra-terrestrial environmental experimentation center, but standing in as a museum guide in the Orbital space center was for Svi, a very friendly sacrifice. Svi could not stand gross ignorance. He just could not tolerate ignorance in anyone, and some of the weird, and uninformed questions that he was asked would have exploded his brain. He just kept telling himself, 'it's only for a day'!

He stood back from the next exhibit as his small group approached one of the early examples of the first orbital space stations, constructed in his grand father's time. He just stood back and listened. He almost curdled up with laughter. There would always be some bright spark that would say it….. It was not very long before Svi heard the remark. This time it was a spotty adolescent lad who raised the question, as the visitors crawled through three at a time.

"Mum?" He started in his half broken voice. "Mum. Where is the main building? This is a very small entrance hall and there is hardly any room to move."

Svi would have excused the ignorance of the young lad who was quite audible from inside the early orbital space station. It was the mother's reply that upset Svi.

'How could anyone be so ignorant' he thought inwardly.

"It must have become detached" she replied with positive authority. Svi had to interrupt and put her straight. He could take it no more.

"No madam" he called out to her as he entered the capsule from the other end. This is the complete example of an early space station. Men lived in this vessel for over one orbital year before returning back to the mother planet. These 'cramped' conditions were accepted as perfectly normal in years gone by. They had to plan their movements up and down the tube, so that their colleagues would not become caught in any embarrassing positions. Do you remember in your history books the terrible accident that took place in station eight when two lab technicians carrying two vials of poisonous gases, collided in their non-gravitational atmosphere and broke the two files underfoot. The four men and one-woman crew died instantly. That was entirely due to lack of maneuverable space within the astro-capsule. Early sub-mariners, had the same problems in their small submarines, but at least they had gravity to help them. No one in their wildest dreams would have expected an orbital space station of these proportions that we have achieved today. When the first space pioneers made their way out of the atmosphere and gravitational environment, they could never have imagined the vast sizes and complicated environments that were going to be achieved in the years to come. It's with thanks to those courageous early pioneers that we are here today. It could be said, that we achieved this level of success on their backs. Who would have guessed even a decade ago, that our orbital space stations would be so large that we would need internal transport to travel around inside them. Three years ago there were only six of these under construction, today there are sixty, and in ten years from now perhaps, six thousand! Perhaps a million or more of these within two more decades will surround the entire globe of the mother planet if we expand the industry at the same cumulative rate of growth. We will achieve that, you can be sure if Noah of Lublia gets his way. Already the flat packed construction parts are coming out into orbit in such massive quantities that these aspirations are ahead of Schedule."

Svi could see the deep interest in the young boy's face. He smiled to himself; perhaps there was some point in showing these relics to tourists after all. Svi had also achieved the inward satisfaction of knowing that at least once he had created an interest in a subject for a youngster, where there had never been one before. Svi was satisfied and was beginning to believe if for that reason alone his day had been worth the effort.

Svi was whistling as he reached his living quarters. He had bought a small floral gift for Lika, and some ice-gel for their 'daughter'. Trin had been with them now since she arrived in their quarters years previously. They assessed that she must be more a youth than a child by now but they had no way of checking her exact birth-date as the records were all anonymous and even though both Svi and Lika have permanent access to these records there was no way to trace Trin's heritage just as with all children of the experimental environment.

Lika was unusually very strained in her manner as Svi entered their apartment. She nevertheless still managed to drop everything she was doing in order that she could give her husband his usual intimate greeting. They were still very much the happy couple but

Svi knew that something was on Lika's mind. She was very anxious and it was very obvious. It was written all over her face, even in her warm friendly voice, and showed in the hesitant manner of the kisses that were always his coming home present.

"Trin is not well! She has a fever. It has come on so suddenly, I don't understand and I feel so helpless." Lika was almost crying to Svi. "We have to get help. She needs medical treatment!" Lika was almost panicking.

"We can't do that" Svi was adamant. "If we declare her for treatment they will need to know her identity….. and after all these years. We have managed to bring her up without problems. The law is to destroy her whatever the reason. She will die. No question. It's mandatory, and if we call for medical help it all becomes official. Up to now we have got away with it. People have helped and closed their eyes to it. When she was ill that time when this section went onto full proportional gravity we coped. Can't we cope now?" Svi was also near to a panic, but he controlled. "Take her down!" He suggested to Lika with a commanding definition in his voice.

"No!" Lika returned her answer without the slightest hesitation in her voice. "No" she repeated "if I take her back to the mother planet we will not be permitted to return until she has completed her early school. No I will not leave you." She ran back into Svi's open arms. "But she *is* very ill." Lika started to cry. "My baby. I love her, but she will die if she stays here." Lika's tears started to empty profusely down her cheeks.

Svi leaned over and kissed Lika all over her face. He loved Trin so very much, but he loved Lika many times more, his heart melted away to jelly when she cried. He would do absolutely anything for that red-eyed, make-up run, tear—stained, messy face.

Lika took Svi into the other room to show him the sad little sleeping child. Sleeping she was, but her young innocent face was in unconscious turmoil as the perspiration dripped off her. The bedclothes were soaking. The room smelled of disinfectant spray. Svi took a sudden intake of breath when he saw their child and after sponging her forehead down for at least an hour he confided to Lika…..

"We have to face it, somehow we have to take her down and get her immediate treatment. We must get her back to health, she is very seriously ill."

Svi trying to stay calm and resolute turned again to Lika and suggested that when Trin's condition was on the mend, they could ask one of Svi's relations to look after her for a few years until she was old enough to return to orbit.

"Then she could come back voluntarily, and legally!" Lika interrupted with a smile breaking into her face.

"We must act immediately" Svi started to get some clothes together and pack some bags. "There is no time to lose. We will all go together. Now!"

***

Jabal was finding life increasingly more difficult during recent years. The morale of his loyal hybrid staff was becoming lower by the day. The attacks by the rogue gangs of rough necks were becoming more frequent. Their raids were often very damaging, several of Jabal's employees had been killed or very seriously wounded. As quickly as Jabal lost hybrid staff he could easily replace them, because his farm was recognized by those who knew it as 'safe'. It was often raided, but as Jabal seemed to 'know' people in high places and was well 'connected' he was left alone as a general rule. The hybrid population seemed to be on the run. They were constantly under attack and many just seemed to 'disappear'. Jabal found no difficulty enrolling new members of staff. There were always hybrids willing to step into a dead man's shoes, or take a position of work vacated by a fleeing brother. Jabal was nevertheless finding maintenance of continuity on his farm very difficult. His staff were constantly changing, he had very few of his original families left. The last three years had certainly taken their toll on Jabal's health, he was looking at least ten years older, his face was drawn and perhaps an early gray hair was beginning to appear in his sideburns. Jabal was a sad reflection of the changing political climate.

Farming was becoming very much more technological, and very much more complicated. The farmer needed to have high qualifications in engineering, mathematics, chemistry and economics before he could even think of turning on his computer terminals to work out his projected four-year growth program. Jabal had developed his ability and knowledge through the experience of years but even he, was finding the new techniques becoming impossible to get to grip with. If he made even the smallest mistake, he could poison an area of land for decades. Jabal was worried, he had ever changing staff with very few who were permanent enough to be useful. He was also worried that they would not have the experience to cope with an emergency. The technological advances of human 'progress' were making life on the farm so much more complicated. The slightest error could yield a traumatic accident. Could they cope? Jabal had this problem constantly on his mind.

Jabal had made a decision; he was going to do something that he had been trying to avoid doing for many years. He called his colleague Lex, and also Rastus his new promoted foreman, into his office. Jabal was sitting behind his desk with a forlorn but determined look on his face. The two men stood with nervous interest as he spoke.

"We are going to make this estate secure. Never again are any of my hybrids going to be the victim of any vicious attack on my land. During the next two or three weeks I want a very deep and wide trench dug around the farm village. If you use a hover-digger you may be able to finish that part of the job in half the time. We will also build a wall around the residential parts of the establishment with gates that will open onto the farmland. This way the staff would be protected, and will probably have no wish to runaway."

Jabal turned to Rastus. "I have every sympathy for your circumstances, but we have to fight these people the only way that they understand." He continued. "By the way, I want you to put hundreds of vertical posts pressed well into the ditch bottom. They must be sharpened to a point at both ends and firmly placed into the soil, so that anyone attempting an entrance by stealth or open attack will fall forward to be impaled on the stakes in the trench. The only way into this village area will be via the specially constructed gate. I am sure it will cost me dearly for this physical defense system, but it will be worth it. Every cent!" Jabal hesitated for a moment, then taking a short breath continued with sincere enthusiasm.

"Yes, when this work is completed, I will give a party. Everyone on this farm will participate on equal terms. We will have a fiesta such has not been seen since Grandpa Methuselah's time. We will invite everyone and anyone. We will tell the world. "No one walks over Jabal or his herd!"

Rastus and Lex looked at each other and smiled. They did not need to say anything; their reaction was blatant and obvious. They were very pleased. It was the catalyst that was needed to get the work done in half the time.

***

Erash and Tubal Cain were engaged in a bitter argument at the central security office of Science and Welfare. Tubal had informed Erash of a secret pact that had been made between the government in Lublia and Fadfagi's 'government' in Bylia. There was to be a cessation of undercover unidentifiable terrorist activities in return for open trade and full recognition of the recent annexation of their neighboring state Orcamo. Bylia had claimed for decades that their western neighbor had no right to independent status as it was so much smaller in size to Bylia and their people spoke the same language and were of exactly the same ethnic origins. The two countries were always at each other's throats. Fadfagi always argued that as one country it would grow from strength to strength. A senior government minister from Lublia had visited Bylia and traded a permanent peace agreement with Fadfagi. The Prime Minister of the Lublian government was about to return with a signed document, and Tubal Cain wanted Erash to meet him with full media publicity at the International Transportation Center. Erash was furious.

"This is a sham. We both know that this man is a chronic pathological liar. He fronts for the most perverse organization in international immorality. He is dangerous. Very dangerous. If one day he were to acquire nuclear weapons he would try to take on the civilized world. That is if he hasn't stolen enough Radiact to have made some already!" Erash was seething. "If I have to, I insist on not being involved visibly. I don't want my face in the same camera frame as that son of dubious parentage. He has many a score to answer for."

"Calm yourself" Tubal tried to slow down Erash's pulse-rate with little success. "We must be seen to be making an attempt at peace. We must just always remember to watch our backs. I agree with you, a paper of peace is not necessarily anything more than a piece of paper, but we must be seen to be making the attempt." Tubal Cain repeated himself. "In fact I will tell you more." Tubal turned to Erash and sat down again behind his desk. "I do believe that if we were to accept this treaty in the spirit of goodwill that was intended, then Fadfagi himself will be coming to visit us soon on a similar mission of goodwill and peace."

Erash stood up and with his stomach churning over inside him he turned his back on Tubal Cain. He knew that if he didn't walk away for a moment, he would have hit his friend clean across the face. Erash could usually contain his temper but on this occasion he really didn't trust himself. He walked across the diagonal of the room to the farthest point from Tubal Cain. He turned with a very reddened face shouted in full volume.....

"Who do you think you are kidding? You are being taken in completely by a raving maniacal genius. He would offer you gifts with one hand and stab you in the back with the other. No! I will have no part of this pantomime." The adrenalin was running in Erash's blood.

Tubal Cain attempted to interrupt Erash's flow of expletives. "Perhaps if you would listen for a few more moments I could explain our plans, and hopes for the future. I really didn't expect this news to affect you this way."

"No?" Erash tried to calm down only to shout more reasoned argument at Tubal Cain. "Who do you think organized the undercover terrorism that takes place using my security office as cover? Who do you think pours money and arms into the group who are trying to destroy the entire hybrid race? Who do you think was the secret author of the 'Final Solution and Destruction of Filth and Vermin'? How would you feel as a hybrid if we entertained all that represented those evils? He should never be allowed to set foot on these shores! You forget the massacres and killings of innocent people. Look what happened to my very own Rula. Have you seen the permanent physical scars that have been left on her posterior? He not only tried to defile her body but he almost succeeded in defiling her mind as well. I have no idea who fathered the child she bore, from his house of sin. She vowed that she would never tell me, and I have never pressed her."

"He's a lovely young lad!" Tubal again tried to interrupt, trying to lower the tone and pace of the argument.

"He should grow up to be a handsome lad. He has Rula's looks and yet a little darker haired that I would have….. " He realized that he was putting his foot right in it. Tubal tried to apologize. "I am really sorry….!"

"Don't try and apologize, that will only make it worse. I am fully aware of that situation and have to live with it. I love the little lad because he is Rula's but I also can't help hating him at the same time because he is also somebody else's. Perhaps we will have one of our own one day soon." Erash was beginning to let his thoughts go off at a tangent.

His mind was beginning to wander away from his aggression. "Listen" Erash continued. Come over to Rula and me for a meal next week. Bring Tsionne, I am sure Rula and Marla will be delighted to see you, and they are both such good cooks. Perhaps in a more congenial atmosphere we could finish this conversation. In the meanwhile I will come with you to meet our government friend, but no way will I meet Fadfagi.

***

Lika could feel the vibrant thump of her heartbeat, and feel the pulse in her neck as it rubbed against her tightened collar. She approached the duty office trying very hard to look nonchalant and normal. She was desperately anxious that she should be able to pick up two tickets for a transfer back to ground base and home. As residents on Orbital space station they were always entitled to return transfer tickets for a visit to home base. There should be no problem for Lika. This was a normal legitimate request. She approached the kiosk window. The problem was that she knew she was cheating and that she and Svi were about to commit a most serious crime, which if uncovered was considered to be almost as serious as murder. Lika knew that, and Svi knew that, but certainly the guard on duty roster would not know that. Nevertheless Lika felt that perhaps he could read her thoughts, perhaps he knew. She reached the window and tapped lightly on the glass. He could not possibly know. Somehow Lika felt much worse when she saw a woman's face behind the counter. Lika imagined that perhaps a woman would have more depth of insight. Perhaps she would see the anxiety in Lika's face.

"Are you alright?" The woman in black and silver uniform asked through the mouthpiece to Lika. "You have gone green. Do you feel alright?"

"Yes! Certainly I'm alright!" Lika replied with annoyance in her voice. She was becoming more conscious of her nervous concern.

"Can I have two transfer return tickets to 'Home Base Ground Control'? We would like to take the next flight."

"You will have to hurry then. It leaves in five minutes. Late arrivals are boarding now. There isn't another one today, so you haven't much time my dear."

Lika grabbed her tickets, and raced as quickly as she could back to Svi who was sitting in the departure lounge with all of their luggage. They had timed it just right. Not even the most heartless guard would deprive a couple from rapid return to ground base when the last shuttle was about to leave any moment. Especially when the woman was obviously very pregnant that she might give birth any moment. The two uniformed guards helped Lika into the gondola with her cases, as Svi struggled with his. There was a very large life like full size doll that he carried so carefully that it attracted the attention of one of the guards.

"She looks almost real. Who made it?" The guard inquired as he stroked the forehead. "Warm. Very realistic, a masterpiece."

"It was an exhibit in the museum. One of the wax models. They had discarded it, so I'm taking it down for the new baby."

"If it's a girl she'll love it when she's older!" The guard called to Svi as the gondola started to move off into the parked Astro-sphere.

"She *is* a she!" Svi mouthed back, pointing at Lika's artificially extended stomach.

Lika could not believe how easy it had been to leave. She only hoped that the sleeping 'Trin' was oblivious to the wax covering that they had so carefully molded all around her naked skin.

She certainly looks like a dummy. Lika just prayed that she would not wake up. They had given her as much sedation as they dared with her being so seriously ill.

Their departure from the space station's parking bay was completely uneventful; in fact it passed almost unnoticed. The only reason Lika noticed it was that it marked a release from the captivity that had held her Trin for so many years since her birth. The final pleasure and relief for Svi and Lika was their slow re-entry into the mother planet's atmosphere only moments later to hover above their home base in wonderful 'real' daylight over the ground control. The hazy daylight was such a welcome for them after such a long period in extra-orbital space. The hazy distant panorama was so different to the clean exact perfectly focused images seen in non-atmospheric orbit. The other feature of arrival back in home environment was the immediate effect of increased gravity upon them both.

Svi for the very first time showed visual concern on his face as he looked across to Lika. He had felt Trin stir very slightly as she had obviously also been affected by the doubling of the effect of full gravity as they reached their stable hover position above ground base.

They would not technically be free until they stepped off the landing vehicle onto dry solid ground and walked away from the terminal building. They still had a long way to go. Would Trin stay the course in her disguise? She was beginning to soak through her clothes. Her fever was worsening. If she became delirious, she would certainly break her cover in the true sense of the meaning. Svi was becoming desperate. They were the last passengers onto the Astro-sphere that was an advantage then. Now it was an acute disadvantage. Their schedule to leave would be with the tail end of the queue. The ground shuttles were traveling backwards and forwards on many return journeys, taking massive numbers of people down to ground-base. Surely their turn would come soon? The restaurant area was at last nearly empty, the loudspeaker called out Svi and Lika's departure code. They rose and moved to the departure gates. Svi was nervous now. He was becoming soaking wet from Trin and it must be showing he thought. How would they get through ground control checkpoint? Svi did not want to worry Lika so he didn't tell her. She would probably have shown her trouble quite openly Svi thought. They moved along in the walking crowd. They had to get their tickets punched at the departure gate. Then only a few moments in flight on the ground shuttle and they would be nearly there.

Svi almost could not believe his luck as they walked through the gate, tickets punched and onto the shuttle. It seemed so easy. The difficulty was surely only in anticipation of danger in his vivid imagination. Suddenly he felt a hand on his shoulder. He turned around; his heart seemed to miss a beat.

"Hallo See! I not forget you. Long time since. You change, and look older. Shoelly you remember me?"

Svi's face changed from anxiety, fright, and then shock to relief, and finally showed pleasure and surprise. He threw his only free arm around the neck of his friend.

"Zarby! I am so pleased. What are you doing here? How did you get a trip into orbit? Gorilla's are not usually allowed out there." Svi was elated to find his friend. Lika had worked out who she was. Svi had certainly told her the story although it was some time previously.

"I have spezial beezniz with people in extra-orbital.

Perhips one day I tell you. I so pleased to see you 'See'."

Zarby gave Svi a loving kiss on his forehead, nodded to Lika and got back into line some way back in the rear end of the queue.

Eventually Svi and Lika had their feet firmly back on the ground. Somehow it seemed so hard, and Svi felt so much shorter. He knew it was just imagination, but it seemed so real. He also felt so heavy, like a Scuba Diver on the surface wearing his weight belt. He knew it would not last very long but how strange to be back on the ground. Passing through ground control checkpoint was another non-event. There were so many people that they only stopped the odd person and fortunately neither Svi nor Lika was one of them.

The couple walked hand in hand pushing their trolley loaded with luggage, and Svi was still bearing the full weight of sleeping Trin. They reached the Taxi rank, and hailed a hover-cab.

"Lublia central please." Svi addressed the driver. They flopped down on the back seat and Lika burst into tears on Svi's broad shoulder. Trin slept through it all. They were home!

***

Rula and Marla had never found it difficult to settle in together as wives to Erash. Their marriage was quite an event in Semir. There was the long walking wedding parade around the inside streets next to the perimeter walls. Eventually with much music and a great deal of fuss the ceremony took place in the main square just around the corner to their "House of Four Eyes". The fact that Rula was pregnant had become very obvious. It was such a shame that she had to parade at the head of the column of guests, looking so much like a 'shot-gun' bride. The fact that the groom had no relationship with the prospective child was of no consequence. She was one of a pair of identical twins, and at the time of their wedding they were looking far from identical. The fact that the groom did not mind was not really relevant. The crowd would not understand. They all thought quite naturally that the child was his, and that was the way Erash wanted it. He took full claim to the bastard child. He loved his Rula, and this was part of his love for her. He knew that his acceptance of that child would keep Rula sane and carry her through all the traumas of their future pains in childbirth, and thereafter. Erash was a very happy man at his wedding. He married both his twins, and the baby was to follow. He was so happy, there were many times when he never permitted himself the luxury of believing that this wedding day would ever materialize. He thanked god quite verbally in his acceptance speech during the marriage service. He made his feelings sound so poetic, so beautiful; he brought tears to the eyes of both his brides.

The happy trio, Rula, Marla and Erash were now living quietly in Lublia in a flat supplied by Science and Welfare. Rula's child completed their family unit at that moment in time, and it was sleeping peacefully in another room as Rula and Marla prepared energetically for the dinner party that was planned for that evening. They were quite looking forward to seeing Tsionne and Tubal Cain once again. For a bonus they had invited Noah and Naamah, but Noah had an important diplomatic meeting so they were going to come along later. Perhaps for the desserts.

Marla's smiling face greeted Tubal and Tsionne as they arrived that evening for what promised to be a wonderful meal. The two sisters had been working industriously all day. The slight subtle aroma of scented herbs greeted Tsionne's keen sense of smell as Marla asked them in.

"You must have been busy." Tsionne whispered into Marla's ear as she handed her coat to her.

"Herbs. They are very difficult to come by these days. So many of the old faithful have become poisonous now with so much soil pollution."

Marla took Tubal Cain and Tsionne into the sitting room where Erash had just arrived to offer drinks. Marla continued.….

"No. I'm very careful with herbs. I use vintage soil from my grandfather's vineyards. They are sheltered, untreated, and protected by law from pollutants. I grow my own herbs in that from seed. I can guarantee the purity of my brand." Marla smiled to Tsionne. "Come on Erash offer everyone a drink."

At that moment, Rula walked into the room cuddling a very tired looking young boy. He was half asleep and seemed not to be very happy about being held under the bright lights of the sitting room. Rula wanted to show her son to Tsionne.

"Do you want to hold him before I put him back to bed?" Rula offered her son to Tsionne who took him readily.

"Oh you know how much I love children, especially this one" She replied to Rula as she cuddled him to her voluptuous chest.

Erash could almost hear himself thinking aloud that he envied the little boy, but Erash managed to keep his thoughts to himself. He always had a soft spot for Tsionne.

Tsionne noticed the look on Erash's face and chose to ignore it. For just a short moment she was scared. Surely Erash was happy, he loves both his wives. Tsionne decided that she must have been mistaken and continued to rock the sleepy child close to her chest. She felt like a broody hen, she looked over to Tubal Cain, and she smiled with such pleasure not realizing what this was doing to her husband's innermost feelings.

Tubal Cain walked over to Tsionne and put his arm around her neck, he looked down on the child, and then kissed Tsionne on the side of her neck. Very quietly into her ear he whispered.

"One day we will have our own, I promise you" he hugged her very tight. Tsionne pulled away in embarrassment and offered the child back to Rula.

"Don't you think you ought to start a family?" Erash called over to Tubal Cain." Then Tsionne won't keep pinching my child."

Erash did not know why he said such at thing in jest, but as the words came out he tried very hard to stop them,.…. without success. The atmosphere could have been cut with a knife. Erash felt terrible. He did not realize until then that there might be problems. Oh dear he thought. What had he done to a very good friend?

Marla broke the silence and called for them all to sit down, as the meal was nearly ready. Rula replaced her son to his bed. It was not long before the hubbub of casual conversation replaced the cold hard silence of embarrassment, which was soon to be forgotten.

The clatter of dishes going into the dish washing machine, and a steamy warm atmosphere of quiet contentment was the greeting for Noah and Naamah on their late arrival. Tsionne was the first to reach the new arrivals as she moved quickly across the room to give a great big congratulatory kiss on Naamah's right cheek.

"I am so pleased for you being a mother of three sons. Japheth is a lovely name, and your eldest Shem, he is growing up to be a fine young lad."

"What about Ham?" Naamah did not want to miss one out.

"I don't really know him, but I understand he is a beautiful child."

"Perhaps one day you will be blessed with a child, Naamah replied quite innocently. The entire room went quiet as they watched Tsionne's face try so very hard to break into a smile.

"Perhaps!" Her answer came without rehearsal. Noah wanted the ground beneath him to swallow him up. How could Naamah say something like that, he thought, but then he had not told her about Tubal's confidence.

***

Rastus was feeling very pleased with himself as he washed the mud and grit from underneath his fingernails. The sink was filling with water that was turning bright orange in color, as the small drops of grime and dirt dissolved into the flowing stream of purified tap water. The job of creating a moat around Jabal's farm had been completed in eight days, well ahead of schedule. Rastus had even been able to place all protective stakes into position. They looked so fierce and foreboding in the half-light of early dusk. Rastus looked out through the half open window of the workhouse, he could see Lex coming across the quadrangle. It was already dark by the time they met each other just outside the door of the washrooms.

"They are delivering the gate from the foundry tomorrow." Lex had come to tell Rastus. "That should complete the fortification well inside the time allowed. The perimeter wall will be finished during this night. With any luck we will be secure by tomorrow afternoon. Perhaps we could ask Jabal if he would like to make the arrangements for his party! Lex said to Rastus as an intentional afterthought, with a smile of personal satisfaction in his voice.

A sudden crack of broken twigs seems to echo loudly across the quadrangle Rastus grabbed Lex's right arm. "Did you hear that noise?" Rastus mouthed quietly to Lex as his grip tightened. He was not scared, but it was the suddenness of the interruption to the tranquility of the misty evening. The character of the noise seems to indicate a running movement away from the compound. Somebody in bare feet. Instinct for the two men begged for them to follow, but Lex pulled at Rastus's arm.

"No. Stay here! If we give chase we may walk or run straight into a trap. Come, let's go and turn on the floodlights. It is about time to test them we haven't turned them on in the dark as yet!"

The duo found their way around the compound to the newly erected guardroom not yet in use. The door seemed to make a terrible loud noise as it opened, even the lock seemed stiff to the key. As they entered, everything smelled so new, there was a very strong aroma of fresh paint. Lex walked over to the large modern control panel, and pressed three yellow buttons. Suddenly there was brilliant light everywhere. The entire farm village was ablaze with illumination. "Shut that light!" Rastus screamed at Lex. "We don't want to light up the entire farm, just the perimeter and beyond. We are making ourselves sitting ducks to any attack with the illumination this way around."

Lex turned to Rastus smiling, as he pressed the four blue buttons and turned out the yellow ones.

"That was a little bit foolish wasn't it?" Grinned Lex, embarrassed at his mistake. The illuminated area changed immediately like a theatrical play, or an example of Son-et-Lumiere. The perimeter fields and beyond became suddenly as if in broad daylight, while the camp enclosure plunged immediately into semi-darkness.

"Look!" Lex was pointing outward across the major field. "Look. See those people running. Three of them, a man and two women. They look familiar, I am sure that I have seen them before, especially the man." Lex watched them with keen interest as the three interlopers ran barefooted, carefully through the dead bracken. "It must be very painful running across rough ground like that."

"They are probably wearing protective socks" Rastus pondered "That's a trick they have picked up from the hybrids who they detest so much."

The two men did not remove their gaze from the distant figures as they ran off almost in a straight line away from the village into an unbroken darkness beyond.

"They took a very great risk coming here like that. They must have had good reason to come." Lex mused.

Two days following the completion of the fortifications, Jabal was sitting next to his sister Naamah, as the full orchestra of their brother Jubal entertained them. Jabal was throwing his party. He was keeping his promise.

***

CHAPTER 2

Noah's face was full of enthusiasm as he spoke so fluently on the subject nearest to his heart. *'Scientific research into the expansion of orbital space'*. It was not often that he was entertained by a non-human in such an extravagant manner, but then this gorilla almost seemed human to him. For a female gorilla, Zarby could appeal quite easily. She was strangely very attractive in a gorilla sort of way. Yes, thought Noah, she has a very kind and loveable beauty about her. He knew that he could be persuaded by her peculiar feminine charm. Noah was sure she was going to get her own way.

"Meester Noah" she interjected as Noah seemed to hesitate for a moment to take a breath. "Please Meester, I leesten with great eenterest to what you describe about future space program. I admire you successes, and envy you wonderful program. I ask you as one of my people, pleese meester Noah, can we joint in. We wood like very much to make a contributeen to the effort! We weel take dangerous risks that hoomans wood not. We can react queeker in an emergency than most humans. Please can we have our experiment in space. Wood the Lublian government spoonser my tribe for a house in space?"

"Do you mean an extra-orbital space station?" Noah questioned Zarby.

"Yees!" Screeched Zarby into Noah's left ear. Noah thought carefully for a moment or two, and turned to Zarby. "We need some groups of people, reasonably well organized who would be willing to test run several pieces of new self-supporting extra-terrestrial equipment. We could set you and your gorilla people to work from an orbital station almost of your very own, but I must warn you…. the work will be extremely risky and dangerous. That will be the only way I could break through basic prejudices and plead a case to let you go. Under any other circumstances there would be public furor about letting gorilla people into space." Noah was firm in his approach, but he still managed to offer friendliness in his manner.

Zarby was ecstatic with Noah; she danced in a circle all round the room before flinging herself at Noah and wrapping her arms around his neck in a tight and gratifying embrace.

"I just hope and pray for your safety." Noah murmured as he pulled away from Zarby's fierce grip. "We ground test everything before it is admitted into orbit. We are very particular about safety on any of these flights, but please tell your people to take extra care. We cannot afford any mistakes; it could set our project back for years, if not cause us to be made to abort it completely. There are many people on this planet, who do not believe it is right what we are doing. They say it is against god's will for us to leave this planet, our place of birth. They will do everything in their power to discredit us, and destroy what we do!"

"Meester Noah. Persecution and prejudice is nothing new to us. Do not worry we will be watching our back all the time. For us that is second nature." Zarby was trying very hard to speak like a human. The contortions on her face were almost causing Noah to smile. "When can start pleese? Meester Noah!" Zarby's face was full of confidence; she walked up to Noah's desk, and leaned over kissing him gently on the forehead.

***

The beeper was vibrating loudly in Tubal Cain's breast pocket; he would have to make his way back to the vehicle to use his videophone.

"Why do I always get called on occasions like this?" Tubal muttered to this blind father whom he was carefully walking, around the local park. Tubal loved his father who many years previously had lost the sight in both eyes due to an atrophy of his sensitive retinal tissues. His blindness, even in these days of transplants and re-creative surgery was completely incurable. Tubal often took his father by the hand and talked him around his enclosed world of blindness. A man like Lamech was really very appreciative of these movements with his son. He was so proud of him, a successful businessman, scientist, and leader. The only thing Lamech wanted now from Tubal was a grandson. Tsionne was a lovely girl, and Lamech enjoyed her company, but he knew that there must be something wrong….. He could sense it…he never mentioned children to either of them.

"There is somebody watching us" Lamech's grip tightened on Tubal's arm. "I sense someone's eyes gazing down upon us." Lamech was most emphatic as he whispered quietly to Tubal. "Don't ask me how I know, but please be careful and don't use your own vehicle's video phone. I feel danger. It's a trap!" Lamech was beginning to panic, he felt Tubal would not believe him, and pulled on his arm even more urgently. "Wait here!" Tubal placed his father neatly on a bench seat some distance from his hoversphere, then walking the rest of the way very purposefully he arrived at the craft still with his bleeper on full volume. Tubal opened the door falling flat on the ground. Nothing happened. He uprighted himself and proceeded across the threshold. His videophone was whirring strongly for attention. Tubal carefully and with as little vibration as possible, lifted the phone, unit and extension lead. Without removing the headset from its rest, he carried the complete unit, still whirring, to the full length of the extension cable. Tubal was now at least twenty or thirty paces from the craft. He lay down on the ground and placed the unit in front of his face, he lifted the receiver. The screen became alive. A familiar face appeared in front of Tubal Cain.

"Perhaps you are surprised to see me, but I am very pleased to see you Mr. Cain. Here is a present for you…..

Tubal Cain was not far enough away from the explosion to be unaffected. The blast moved him at least double the distance from its source. The videophone became immediately disconnected and he still had it in his hands as he landed on the soft drying grass. The hoversphere just disappeared in the blast with a loud noise and a bright yellow and blue flash. There was debris everywhere. Tubal got up and ran to his father. "I told you so!" Lamech smiled "Are you alright. No wounds? No Blood?"

"Come on, we are getting out of here quick!" Tubal Cain took his father by the hand and made with as much speed as possible to the nearby Taxi rank. "Those fanatics will cause a world war if they go on like that!" Tubal said as he helped his father easily into the back seat. "I know the man who did it!"

Lamech took hold of Tubal's hand tightly, and very carefully just about audibly he mouthed into his son's right ear. "I still feel that we are being watched." Tubal looked around to see if they were being followed, as they moved off into the misty afternoon before the crowds arrived.

***

Jabal's party was in full swing. The dancing, the music and the warmth of the campfire seemed to fill the dusty night air with an atmosphere of benevolence and calm that one would always associate with more peaceful times. The happy moving feet were beating the ground in time with the rhythm of Jubal's music. Many pairs of bare feet, hybrid, human and gorilla, were dancing in a moving circle. Happiness and joyous fulfillment was in all their voices. The glow of the campfire was flickering across their faces, as their singing of local folk tunes added to the atmosphere of cosmopolitan merriment. The movement of the closed dancing circle occasionally and without prepared warning would immediately change into reversal motion into the opposite direction. Naamah had often participated in this type of tribal dancing, and even then did not understand how all these independent minds, without clue, or signal, could together change direction in such a manner without breaking the circle. Possibly, she thought, it was related to a change in the rhythm. Naamah was still sitting with Jabal, but could not stop tapping her feet in rhythm with the music. She was becoming entranced by the feeling of involvement. She wanted so much to join in. She stood up, and taking off her shoes, joined in making a place for herself in the moving circle. She could remember this wonderful pleasure as a child when she used to dance in the very center with her father. They would do all kinds of acrobatics to the chanting and singing, as more amateurish music was played on brass metal drums. The parties in those days, Naamah recounted to herself, were less sophisticated, but so much more fun. They made their own pleasures in those days. Today it is all prefabricated and comes in packets.

As if by magic, two figures appeared in the center of the dancing ring. The music went much more slowly, and the rhythm with more definition. Two hybrids a male and a female started to perform a slow love-dance in the living arena. The couple started slowly at first, and then as the best of the music became clearly definite, their movements became increasingly suggestive. The music became more emphatic and the speed began to increase. The male lifted the female off the ground and pushed her feet from under her as she began to spin holding her tightly by the hands in clenched fist form. In rapid time with the music he began to spin, with his partner now well suspended in an outward horizontal position. The male dropped on bent knees to a revolving crouching position and then returned to a rapidly turning vertical situation always spinning fast. If he had let go, the female would surely have shot out into the surrounding crowd.

The crowd went wild, they started to clap hands together loudly in rhythm with the music. The two dancers continued in their circular movement at rapid speed, but by this time they both had their feet firmly on the ground as they skipped through the circular dancing movements.

The shining metal arrow silently and suddenly appeared as it tore through the dancing body of the hybrid woman. She seemed to fling herself backwards with blood spurting in a jet from her chest and her mouth as she twisted and squirmed like a writhing snake along the ground. Her eyes began to bulge, the full light of the fire reflecting in her face as she gave a final pull with both hands on the shaft of the offending weapon. Her death was as sudden as the arrival of the arrow. Her dancing partner knelt down to hold her head in his arms. He was covered from head to toe in her blood. He looked in a worse state than the deceased; there was not a small area of his clothing that was not soaking with her blood. He looked as if he had been injured as well. People began to overcome their shock, and raced into the circle to help. Others ran for cover of the surrounding buildings, suspecting that they were under attack. The happy cheerful gathering was abruptly turned to chaos, and shocked anger.

Jabal and Naamah raced to the guardhouse and switched out the remaining village lights. Naamah showed her surprise as she saw Jabal also switch out all the perimeter lights at the same time. The entire area was in complete darkness except for the relentless glow of the camp bonfire.

"What have you done for that?" Naamah enquired of her half brother. "We won't be able to find our silent foe as he runs off into the dark."

I hope we won't need to!" Jabal replied cautiously. "We have several man-traps buried out there and with any luck....!!" The flow of Jabal's speech was interrupted as a horrific vile scream of pain broke the semi-silence of the darkness.

"That came from the edge of the major field" Naamah grabbed hold of Jabal as they made back towards the door of the guardhouse.

It was not until early daylight that the horror of the previous night's attack became visually evident, as the large pool of hybrid blood left its evidence in the center of the square not far from the dying embers of the lifeless remains of the previous night's bonfire. The unfortunate body of the deceased had since been removed to a more suitable place of rest.

The search party eventually found the unconscious prisoner in the mantrap. She still had her human hands wrapped tightly around the offending bow. There were matching arrows neatly contained in the quiver strapped to her side. There was virtually nothing left of one of the poor woman's legs. The trap had eaten deeply into her upper thigh ripping out her cloths and reaching almost into her genitals. The way she had fallen she had also apparently lost most of her other leg from just above the knee. She had lost a lot of blood but was miraculously still breathing and showing a pulse. The trap itself had save her life, by acting as a tourniquet preventing further loss of blood.

***

Noah was becoming impatient. This was the first time for over a year since he had last allowed himself a trip into orbit. This time was to be something special he was to join Tubal Cain on the large Orbital space unit forty-three. They were shortly to welcome back the largest observatory craft ever built in modern times. It had been on a wide orbit of the sun on a course, perpendicular to the main orbit of the mother planet around the sun. The craft had only completed half its orbit of the sun at exactly the same average speed as the mother planet's related movement.

The two traveling bodies were about to meet up exactly on time on the other side of the sun from where they had started. It was therefore exactly half a year since the original departure of the vehicle. There had been many related observations between the observatory craft and the orbital space unit forty-three which was always in the same position in the mother planet's sky. Noah was very excited about some of the astounding discoveries that were yet to be unwrapped. He was to meet Tubal on unit forty-three.

Noah could not understand why with all the modern technology available it was still only possible to dock one extra terrestrial shuttle at one time. He knew that it was due to opposing compensation forces at the moment of contact. This was still a problem not yet mastered even with related computer technology.

The receiving craft, known as the female, would move with the direction of the arriving craft known as the male, unless precautionary compensatory forces were employed to counteract the movement. Noah had to come to terms with the logic. His craft was in a 'stacked' or parked position until it was their turn to be absorbed into the main structure. The wait seemed to be interminable. He sat at the window looking out at the stars. One day, he thought, they would travel, they would seek, and they would find treasures of the universe undreamed of by humankind. Noah sank into very deep thought as he stared into infinity. Where did it all begin, and why? He thought. Whatever is the purpose for the existence of man? Whatever is the purpose for existence for anything, for that matter? Noah was dreaming and beginning to feel very religious. Was he becoming closer to the reality of his maker, 'The Lord' himself? Perhaps that would be man's destiny in the path of righteousness. Noah's nose was pressed with his forehead against the clear window as he tried very hard to see the bright stars upwards and to the left. He knew it was from that direction that the observation craft would be coming.

For the very first time on this trip Noah felt nervous as he saw the orbital space unit with its large number forty three printed on its side move into view. He knew that at last they were about to dock. Eventually the side of the orbital unit completely obliterated any view Noah had of the heavens. Noah was faintly disappointed, but it was only a temporary experience. At last they had arrived.

After alighting from his transport shuttle into the new destination he went up to the reception desk. He was slightly surprised that his feeling of half gravity did not seem to have much effect on his movement, except that he seemed to run, rather than walk. He had forgotten; it had been such a long time. He decided to take the receptionist's advice, and use the internal monorail to the observation deck where he was to meet with Tubal Cain.

Noah took Tubal's hand in greeting. He saw Tubal's face was somewhat bruised.

"I'm pleased to see you are looking so well." Noah remarked. "I understand you were the victim of a near injury in central park yesterday! Your father told me." He saw the quizzical look on Tubal's face and pre-empted the question with his early answer.

"We have so much information pouring into our data-files that we will be working for ever to unravel it." Tubal said, completely changing the subject. He had real enthusiasm in his voice. "I think we may have discovered something very very exciting."

***

Rula and Marla both greeted their husband with shocked disgust in their manner, as Erash entered into his home on return from a rough day at the office. The expression on their faces was identical, and in no way attempted the concealment of any feelings of the sourness they seemed to contain. Marla spoke first.

"He intends to pay us a visit. That bastard is going to be a guest in this country. Your country!" Marla almost spat at the floor in front of Erash as if it was his fault.

"What are you talking about?" He was taken aback by this unusual and certainly unprovoked aggression from his wives. "Who is coming? What are you going on about?"

"Fadfagi! That's who." Rula pushed in front of her sister as if to attack Erash. "The bastard who had pictures drawn all over me. That's who. Or don't you remember?"

"How? What? When?...!" Erash was completely taken by surprise. He knew it was a possible plan, but so soon, so immediate?

Rula and Marla looked at each other, then at Erash. They realized that he probably did not know, and therefore was unlikely to have been a party to the arrangements. "It was on the holographic news this evening. You have just missed it. Fadfagi is coming on an official state visit in ten days time to discuss improving relations between the two countries. He is coming with his latest and longest serving wife. She must be a real 'goer' who is a good 'stayer'."

Rula was determined to be rude. She hated Fadfagi more than anyone else; she blamed him for everything bad in her life. She continued, "I can't imagine anyone wanting to live with that horrible bearded piece of meat! He is so ignorant, but then you don't have to be intelligent to be clever. He is leading his country down the drain, and perhaps one day if we are not careful, that madman will take us all with him."

Rula was getting all emotional in her rantings. It was very out of character. "Please Erash, keep him away from us, I would kill him if I were to be given the chance."

"I have already told Tubal Cain that I won't have anything to do with Fadfagi, but you know how persistent Tubal is, and he is one for keeping up appearances. Don't worry if I have to give in, I certainly won't let you become involved." Erash tried to calm down his angry wife. He took her two hands and standing in front of her pushed them behind her back, pulling her towards himself, he kissed her warmly on her open lips. A silent, soft and tender, lightweight passion of a kiss, that seemed to draw all the anger out of Rula's mouth. She completely caved in, into his arms. Marla came over and put her arms around both of them. Erash opened his left arm and pulled her in to join them. They made a very happy trio.

Erash was a very lucky and very happy man. He had found the contentment in mutual love so seldom ever experienced by the majority of people in their lives. He had a double helping and he was fully aware of his fortune. He thanked and prayed to his maker regularly, that he could remain capable of living up to his situation. In his good times as well as in his bad ones, he was beginning to find himself often in communication with god as his kindred spirit. He was beginning to become a truly god loving and god-fearing man. He didn't realize that he was becoming quite religious.

"When Tubal returns from Orbital station 43, I will speak firmly to him. I promise." He kissed Rula and Marla very re-assuredly, hoping that they would believe him.

***

The outpatient's department of Lublia's General Hospital was very crowded that morning. Lika could not believe that so many people would want attention at one time. There were persons of all ages, shapes and species. The reception area gave the appearance of a transportation center lounge when a whole day's departures had been delayed a further day. Lika was sure that some people looked as if they had been camped there from the previous night. So many of them seemed so bleary and red eyed, as if they had not seen their beds for at least two days. She was beginning to wish that she didn't have to come to this place any more, but Trin was on the mend now, and she was very grateful for the treatment a week or so before, when they had first arrived back in Lublia. Trin was young and strong; it was not long before her problems were put right. She had suffered so much since her first symptoms in the Orbital Station. 'Extra-terrestrial sickness' the name that is given to such maladies can be very serious in young children, and unless treated early can result in mental retardation, and possible growth deformities. An increase in Iodine in part and short doses of Anti-Radiact soon bring up the blood corpuscles, but until the child is cured, a worrying mother always fears the worst. When recovery is achieved, one very quickly and very conveniently, completely forgets how ill one has been. Lika began to reproach herself for being so selfish. So many of these people in the waiting area were probably very ill. She felt very callous that she possessed such inconsiderate thoughts.

The light came on over Lika's call number. She knew it was now their turn; she walked with Trin over to the examination cubicle. That was quite quick she thought, with all these other people waiting.

"My word. Doesn't Trin look a great deal better now?" Said the medical assistant in a white overall. "Do you remember how ill she was, the day she arrived? She certainly had received a real dose of radiation sickness. How did she get it? Where had you been? It was almost as if you had taken her unprotected into orbit for a few years." The attendant's words hit Lika very strongly. She and Svi had forgotten about the need for body radiation protection in their young one, in spite of the fact that they were partly responsible for it on the environment project.

"What are all these people here for?" Lika tried to change the subject. "They must have been here all night. They look so tired. Look at their eyes, so bleary, sore and red."

"That is why they are here." The medic replied as if surprised. He thought it must be obvious but he was more than polite in his reply.

"The eyes are the problem." He continued. "It is a very early sign of radiation sickness which has for some reason come to this area during the last few days."

"WHAT!!" Lika showed sustained shock and annoyance in her voice. "Here in Lublia. Why? How?"

"We don't know yet for certain, but we believe that it is something to do with the reduction of the ozone layer causing solar radiation to be more freely available. The fairer the skin the worse the effect, but everybody is suffering from 'Blepharitis' inflammation of the inside linings of the eyelids. Chronic itching and sandy soreness. They have all got it. It is not yet very serious, but the implications are that it will be." The medical assistant began to examine Trin, just as the senior registrar appears on the scene. Lika turned to ask him for a more authoritative answer.

"What is this about a local radiation epidemic?" She was certainly blunt and straight to the point.

"Just a rumor with no substance. There seems to be a form of contagious virile infection going around. Don't worry yourself about it. Please just be sure only to use disposable wipes for visual hygiene. Whatever made you think it was radiation sickness?" The doctor enquired.

Lika did not know why she sneaked, but she knew that she would, and did. "Your assistant told me."

The doctor looked startled, and seemed very much taken aback by Lika's remarks. He was pensive for as long as hesitation time would allow and then answered.

"He had no right to give out that information, it is classified and if freely available would lead to untold panic. Please madam, for the sake of calm, don't repeat this information, we shall only deny it anyway. Take simple iodine and Anti-Radiact tablets, and you will be adequately protected in the short term. It will not last very long. Perhaps a few days, or even maybe a full week. Until the ozone hole moves away from these parts. Don't worry."

***

Tsionne was very anxious, she did not want to upset her husband on his return from Orbital station 43, but she was gasping to discuss the interview and gynecological examination results that she had undergone with Noah's friend Bertwin. She knew that she would have to tell him soon, but this was not going to be the best time. She knew that Tubal had not yet been told about his old friend Methuselah, Noah's grandfather. Methuselah had suddenly taken very ill and had been rushed to hospital. Tubal Cain had always looked up to Methuselah with great respect, in fact he had often told Tsionne how he had been influenced by that man to inspire his creation of Science and Welfare. If Methuselah sharp mind and creative influence were to be removed from the scene by unfortunate health, Tubal would be very distraught. He almost looked upon the old man as a son would his father.

Methuselah's body was riddled with growths and malformations, but his mind was still young and agile. Tsionne had also developed a soft spot for 'gramps' as they called him. She desperately wanted to help him. She had visited many doctors during the last few days. Some for her own problems but also she wanted to help 'gramps'. She was now sure of what could be done and had two accounts to consult Tubal about on his return. Although Noah was Methuselah's grandson, Tsionne knew that Tubal Cain would be more affected by the illness of the aged 'uncle' than Noah ever would. Noah's relationship with his grandfather was not always smooth, as being a blood grandson. Noah felt that too much was expected of him.

Tsionne had been to see a specialist consultant who had examined Methuselah and found that his situation would be excellent, and prognosis would be good in the event of transplant surgery. A suitable donor would be found as soon as possible but two people's permission would have to be sought. Strangely enough, one would be Tubal Cain, as executor of Methuselah's "living will", and Lamech as Tubal's father. In the event of Lamech being unavailable, then Noah would suffice. Tsionne had to confront both of them for permission when they arrived back home. Time was becoming short, if Methuselah was to survive the week.

Tsionne was becoming overwrought with anxiety as she waited for Tubal Cain and Noah to arrive at the ground base control, inter flight transportation center in Lublia. She had rehearsed her little speech over and over again. She was word perfect, but she could still feel the pounding in her chest as she saw the large orange Hoversphere shuttle materialize through the thick gray cloud immediately above her head. Tsionne always marveled at the proportions of such a large craft, coming slowly and gently to rest on a small painted spot no larger than a pair of average human-size footprints. A hoversphere was large; it could contain a standard size athletics stadium. It was on occasions like these that Tsionne often wondered at the marvels of modern science.

Tsionne saw Tubal first and almost took off in her speedy attempt to reach him. She ran across the reception lounge, straight into Tubal's arms. He hugged her very tightly to his chest. She laid the side of her face against him, and could hear his heart being...fast!! She was plucking up courage to make her speech.

"I have some good news and some sad news for you my darling Tubal Cain." Tsionne tightened her grip around her husband's waist. She wanted to re-assure him that things might not be too bad. She stepped backwards and away from both men, facing them, that she might address them both equally.

"I would like to give you the good news together and the sad news is just for Tubal and me." She hesitated. Somehow she didn't want it to have come out like that, but now that the damage had been done she decided to continue.

"I have been talking to the doctors who are looking after 'Gramps'. He is very poorly, his body won't last another week, and yet he is still alert and as astute as he usually would be. They recommended a transplant, and as you both are the executors of his 'living will' as Lamech is away at the moment, you must decide, and give permission for the operation."

"How bad is he?" Tubal interrupted

"Why us? Can't he decide for himself?" Noah enquired.

"No, he can't." Tsionne replied indignantly. "His life is in danger, and his will states, that he is at the level for loss of his own power of attorney. It's up to you I'm afraid." Tsionne was being very careful and finding this situation a great strain on her emotion, but she continued. "His body is riddled with malignant growths and malformations. He is having many local electro-radio treatments but his main organs are under maximum strain. His body will not last another week. Somewhere, something will completely collapse. He is taking pain-numbing agents and these will only work to a certain level. He is technically 'terminally ill!'" Noah looked shocked and took hold of Tsionne's hand.

"Tell me. What do they want to transplant?"

"A body." Tsionne whispered in embarrassment." They want to give him a brand new, young fully developed male body!'"

"Brand new?" Tubal interjected.

"Not exactly, brand new, just brand new to him. It will be a body on a life support machine, where the owner became 'brain dead' yet the body is still fully functional."

The two men looked at each other in complete astonishment.

"It can't be possible it's never been done before." Tubal was perplexed.

"I am told that they have successfully performed this operation on several gorillas, and two hybrids have also been done." Tsionne was showing confidence in her replies. She was feeling quite proud of herself.

"I understand that the first hybrid had a nervous breakdown after the post operative recovery, but the second one is still going strong with a new younger life in front of him. It seems that the gorillas offered few problems in re-habilitation, as their intelligence is somewhat lower. The joke is going around the hospital that the gorillas did not even notice that they had a new body, as they all look the same anyway." Tsionne smiled apologetically.

The two men turned and spoke to each other, and then turning to Tsionne, Tubal spoke.

"We will consider it urgently. If we speak to the doctors, and obtain sufficient re-assurance, we will agree. We all love old 'gramps' and we would want him to survive in good health. Wouldn't we?"

***

Jubal and Jabal had decided that as brothers they owed it to each other to sit down with their sister Naamah as a family. They had to thrash these problems out. It seemed that protection was no defense in these times. Even with traps, moats and walls, the farm was always in danger of attack. They could not maintain permanent vigilance on every member of the herd at every moment of the day and at any place in the very large acreage of land belonging to Jabal. After all, the farm was once their family home where they were brought up by their then 'seeing' father Lamech and their mother Adah. Zillah, who was Tubal Cain and Naamah's mother, was the other wife of Lamech, but they were all very happy together. Except that Tubal's exploits into weaponry were not popular with his father. The three siblings sat around the fireside hearth, which was well alive with naked flames. A whole day had passed since the terrible shock of the sudden nighttime attack. What was left of the captured criminal was taken to hospital. It would be days before they could question her.

Together three of the children of Lamech sat around the fireside reminiscing their early childhood. Times then seemed so happy. Life was 'real' in those days. Today, they decided, everything was so artificial. The evening flames of fireside chatter seemed to guide their arguments into constructive ideas about the future.

"Why are you constantly under attack?" Jubal asked a rhetorical question of Jabal.

"I know." Naamah interrupted. Jabal is too kind to his hybrid herd, and he even employs the occasional gorilla." Naamah was being uncharacteristically sarcastic.

"It's the three K's who organize the attacks" Jubal seemed well informed. "They get substantial support from Fadfagi's Bylia. Did you know that? It is said that Bylia funds, creep into the three K's finances through clandestine activities via drug and arms trading on the illegal market. Fadfagi is determined to make the developed world destroy itself, that he might take over control. He sees himself as the all seeing eye. He supports all subversive organizations."

"K.K.K. are a heinous organization. Naamah showed her feelings.

"They hate everyone and anyone who gives help of any description to a hybrid or a gorilla. They wear those white cloaks and remain entirely anonymous. They hide like cowards behind their bed sheets. True fighters who believe their cause to be right and just will always stand up to be counted." Naamah was at her best.

"What can be done about it?" Jabal enquired, in a passive manner. "They seem to thrive on creating apparent chaos and anarchy."

"The roots of the organization! That's what you go for." shouted Jubal the musician. Although a playboy at heart, he was no fool, and when it came to grasping a problem he would always assess the situation and decide on the action within moments. He was seldom wrong. "United they stand, but divided they fall. If you will pardon an old schoolboy cliché, we must make them fight amongst themselves. If we could penetrate their ranks, it would be possible to create a groundswell of mistrust amongst them. If they could be stopped from wanting to compete with each other, and be motivated to compete against each other, then the early seeds of disunity will be seen."

Naamah continued. "They can be vicious and evil people. They have been known to kill and maim just to keep their secrets. They have even killed their own kind who have fallen out of favor for one reason or another."

Jabal had to comment.....

"Penetration of their organization will be very difficult"

Jubal answered with considerable thought and meaning in his manner.....

"I will find a way. Yes," he said pensively. "I will find a way!"

***

Marla was very nervous. She had finally agreed, against her better judgment, to accompany unwilling Erash to the meeting with Tubal Cain and Fadfagi.

Rula had been very firm in her position. She would not attend such a vulgar and hypocritical public function. She realized that Erash had no choice but to support his superior and that one of his wives had to go along, but she was still very upset. She would not even watch the media broadcasts of the event, and they were giving it the full treatment.

The historic performance was due to take place that afternoon in the very large sports arena in the center of Lublia. The sponsors for the occasion were Science and Welfare. Tubal Cain would soon be accompanying Fadfagi and his favorite wife into the stadium where the Bylian leader will make a speech of conciliation and peace. The arena was full to its brim with people. Even the central area used for ball games or large displays, was full of people. They all had their eyes fixed on the podium, which was placed at the far end of the open-air stadium. All the dignitaries and visiting diplomats were seated behind in full view of the watching crowd. Music was playing through the public address system, and a team of warm up girls were dancing in rhythm on the small stage in front of the podium. The uninitiated would congratulate those girls in their performance in that heat, but most people knew better. It was a mere hologram set to music. It appeared to be so real.

From behind, the hologram would be invisible. Marla sat stiffly to nervous attention at Erash's side on the third row up, back behind the podium where all the speeches were to be made. Her hands were clenched, and her elbows pulled into her side as she could feel her anger and anxiety rising up inside her. She would dearly have loved to stand up and shout out to all the televideo and media cameras gathered there, what she really thought. She was sure that many of the gathered dignitaries with artificial smiles on their stiff fixed faces were also feeling the same way.

Marla was looking down on a multi-colored mass of moving heads, a sea of human faces, all waiting for something to happen. The anticipation was probably worse than the event itself. Neither Tubal Cain, nor Fadfagi had yet arrived.

The heat and the haze of the afternoon open-air meeting were in an atmosphere of deep humidity. Marla could feel her posterior beginning to stick to the plastic seat. She felt uncomfortable and dirty. She could almost taste the black dust that always collected in quantity when the heat and humidity became this bad. What a terrible day for such an important event. If only she could use a fan, but she had to remain still and obediently at attention in her seat.

She was sure that she would have dropped off to sleep if she had to sit there much longer without anything to stimulate her interest. She was feeling clammy and damp. How she would have loved to have a shower. At last there seemed to be some action. Marla would even be pleased to see Fadfagi at this stage of the arrangements.

The sudden change in the rhythm of the music on the public address system, then a reduction of volume, which was greeted by a fanfare of trumpets, this was as welcome to the assembled crowd as would have been a gentle breath of fresh air.

Marla stole a glance at Erash and smiled nervously. Erash saw out of the corner of his eye and managed a slight smile back in return. Marla, for that short moment felt warm inside. The re-assurance from her husband said it all for her.

Cheering started in the distant right hand corner of Marla's gaze. The cheering began to move across the entire crowd as if in a wave of motion, as the crowd became able to see the arrival of the guests on the video pictures appearing on the high screens behind Marla's seated position. As V.I.P.'s Marla and the other people seated where they were, in truth had the least advantageous view of the entire program.

Fifteen more people arrived on the stage and took their seats in the front row behind the podium. Tubal Cain took his seat next to Fadfagi, with his wife on Tubal Cain's other side. Tsionne was next, she was to act as hostess and counsel for Fadfagi's wife Rebecca.

Marla thought how strange, she was so very close to these people and not even for a moment could she see their faces. Tubal Cain walked over to the lectern and switched on the microphones. His introductory speech was up to his usual standards, retaining the audience's full interest throughout.

When Fadfagi stepped up and walked over to the rostrum to speak he was cheered and clapped by everybody with full emotion and support. This was evidently due to Tubal Cain's brilliantly constructed introduction, but Fadfagi was no match for Tubal Cain.

The speech delivered by the Bylian leader was full of platitudes, and meaningless ambiguities, which were wholly visible to the sophisticated Lublian audience. As Fadfagi finished and sat down, the applause was more 'polite' than rapturous. Fadfagi didn't even notice, but his wife did, and she was not amused.

The speeches and ceremonies over, the visiting entourage in the front row stood up, and turned to leave. Fadfagi took Tsionne's offered hand to help her down from the stage, and Tubal reached out for Rebecca's. The eyes of Rebecca for a moment looked up and met Marla's unknowing gaze. Rebecca's face showed abject shock, then fury. She reached over the person between her and the third row and spat some fiery words across at Marla, who in her innocence did not understand.

"You left my friend Lara to die, on the beach in Politir. You BITCH! I hate you for all you have done to us and my friends. You piece of perverted filth." She tried to raise her hand to Marla, but Fadfagi stepped forward to interfere. He managed to avoid a very embarrassing incident, especially as all the microphones were broadcasting her every word. By some miracle Erash had been momentarily detained with his back to the incident, so in that short moment their eyes did not meet, as they surely may have recognized each other.

"I apologize to you" Fadfagi whispered to Marla. "Perhaps you and your husband will be our guests on our boat tomorrow evening? Would you come? Perhaps you will bring some friends we will have a party. Please let me know how many? Yes?"

Marla tried very hard to contain herself. She didn't understand. She had heard Erash and Rula talk of Lara but what was the new situation. She was stunned. She could not easily answer, and didn't….. Tubal Cain came to the rescue and accepted on behalf of all of them.

***

Tsionne was very nervously lighting the pair of candles in the center of her dining table as she heard Tubal Cain enter the lobby. These were to be their first private movements together since he had returned from Unit 43 in extra-orbital space, and the visit of Fadfagi had taken up all their time afterwards. At last, in the privacy of their own home, Tsionne could talk of private things with her husband in the romantic atmosphere of a candle-lit dinner. Tsionne was surprised at her own inner nervousness of her very own husband. She was not at all sure how Tubal Cain would react when he heard her personal news, but she was going to do her best to break it to him gently. She could feel her heart thumping between her breasts as the front reception door of their apartment began to glide open. Tubal Cain would be standing there, she looked up, but it was he who spoke first, as he placed an amorous kiss firmly on her left cheek, and wrapped both his arms around her waist. He smiled. "Have I got news for you" he announced. "We can go and visit old 'gramps' later this evening. He's had his operation, and they say that he is doing fine. The funeral of his old body is tomorrow afternoon. Old uncle Methuselah did not want to be cremated, so Noah and I have organized a respectable burial. We hope that gramps will be able to leave hospital tomorrow morning, so that he can attend."

"Attend?" Tsionne queried, "Attend? Do you mean he is going to attend his own funeral?"

"I never thought of it like that" Tubal Cain replied with an embarrassed, surprised expression on his face. After a poignant silence, Tsionne grasped the nettle.

"There is something very important that I want to discuss with you." Tubal Cain sat down like a good little boy eagerly awaiting his wife's every word. She served up the soup. He poured out the wine.

Tsionne coughed politely and began.

"I have been to see Noah's friend Bertwin, the well known gynecologist and I have the results of the tests that he did on me several days ago."

"Well?" Tubal enquired, awaiting every word as his wife took a nervous mouthful of soup. "Well, what happened? What did he say?" He was becoming impatient. It seemed to take an age until he heard her silently swallow.

"We are going to have a baby!" Tsionne pushed out the words determined to continue her sentence, but her involuntary hesitation at that moment caused Tubal to jump from his seat and run around the table to grab his wife around the shoulders.

"What! Say that again!" He hugged her; there were tears in his eyes. Tsionne could see his happiness was all over him. He was like a different man. She had to finish her sentence. It could mean all the difference. Tubal was beginning to 'dance' with joy.

"Sit down!" Tsionne shouted at him. "I have to tell you more. It is not as simple as that. Please sit down. I must tell you more." Tsionne did not often raise her voice, but this once she was in full volume. She had to calm Tubal down. He would not take the remainder of her words in, unless he settled down a little. He sat back down in his chair, and picked up his spoon again as a gesture of sobriety.

"We are able to have a baby with your permission, but it won't be in my body. I am incapable. Parts of me are missing, but I have excellent ovaries and have produced first class eggs. Bertwin has some of your live sperm that he had in for testing. He has the facility in his laboratory to fertilize one of my eggs with your sperm, which he has already done and it's worked!"

Tsionne's voice nearly lifted in pitch due to her verbal enthusiasm. She continued.

"We can watch it grow into a full embryo and become a baby to be born. Our child.…. but you have to agree or he will destroy it tomorrow. He cannot legally grow a human for longer without both parents' signed consent.

"We'll go tomorrow before the funeral" Tubal again jumped from his chair and ran around to Tsionne who was now crying voluminous tears in relief and joy. She had worked herself up into a nervous frenzy not knowing how Tubal would react. It obviously did not mean the same to a man, she thought to herself as she felt Tubal caressing the back of her neck.

She changed the subject a little.

"How could they operate on Gramps so quickly?"

"They had to" Tubal replied. "His body was beginning to expire. He had lost both kidneys and was on dialysis, his liver was on the blink, another few hours and his brain would have been affected. Then what would have been the point? No, they had to act fast. They cut open his skull and spine to the third vertebrae. They took a mould of the bone of the cranium and reformed a new inner skull, which they placed inside the outer skull of the younger cranium. The two will eventually fuse together. Gramps's brain together with his optic nerves and both eyes where then removed in one whole unit and placed into the new molded skull. The rest of his old skull was again copied in the same manner and fused into the inside of his new skull.

The brain of old Gramps could then be placed back into a perfect copy of his original inner cranium. The muscles for the eyes, and the neuro-ganglion and synapses in his neck having been correctly enjoined he would then be in perfect working order. Outwardly except for hairline scarring under his new hair there is nothing to show what has been done. Except that old gramps is now 'young gramps' in a very different body. You won't know him when you see him. The eyes are the same, looking at you out of a very different head."

"Oh! Oooh!" Tsionne found the whole thing sick. She didn't want to hear anymore. "Leave it please. We shall go and see him tomorrow."

***

CHAPTER 3

The entrance lobby was very small, but a hooded member of the three K's was seated there closely tucked in behind his desk. There was little room to pass through this tiny cubicle without getting so close to this man that you could smell the perfume on his breath, even through his white linen visor.

Jubal's heart was beating firmly in his chest, his breathing was forced and he was sure that he would be recognized as a stranger. He carefully walked up to the entrance door of the cubicle, the hooded figure reached out his hand to greet Jubal. Even through his own hood, Jubal was certain he would be noticed as an uninvited stranger to this 'secret' meeting of the three K's. He took a grip of the offered open hand, and together they closed on greeting.

"What are your credentials?" Came the question from under the hood. "You don't come from around here!" The guard seemed to know that Jubal was a stranger, but how, he wondered, as he started to become acutely nervous. He had to give a satisfactory answer, and fast.

"Marwac" Jubal did not know why he said that, "Marwac sent me as a delegate. This is a return visit. It was your delegate who came to visit us last time." Jubal was hoping that he had given a vague enough answer. Marwac was the farthest away village that Jubal knew which had an active group of the three K's. He just prayed that he would be well away from this meeting before they got the chance to check-up on him.

"Enter colleague and brother." The guard was certainly satisfied thought Jubal as he continued along the narrow badly lit corridor, feeling more confident now that he seemed to have passed through that first hurdle.

The corridor came to an abrupt end and Jubal found himself in a large field surrounded by a circle of high stones. It was still dark, as dawn was not due for at least another hour. There were many hooded groups of people sitting around near the various up turned stones. They seemed to be enjoying the informal early morning meeting as a general get-together for a pleasant social chat. They were all wearing the same white linen outfits and were completely anonymous. The only visible part of the anatomy were the eyes, and that was only through the small slits in the uniform, and even then, they were only visible when observed from close proximity in excellent lighting. Jubal also noticed that in one or two of the groups there were some yellow uniforms and an occasional red one. There was never more than one strange color in a group at any one time. Jubal was very curious who these people were and why the strange colors?

Jubal thought it best to approach a nearby sitting group, when another guard took him by the right arm and offered him a greeting holding out his right hand. They shook hands in casual friendship. Jubal was sure that the man must have been smiling behind the facade. He seemed a lot nicer and much more pleasant than the guard on the outside.

"You are not from around here!" The guard interjected. "You are a stranger in these parts?" The guard continued.

"Yes, that's correct," mouthed Jubal. "I came from Marwac as a delegate and representative. I bring greetings and felicitations from our small lodge."

"What is your identity?" The inner guard requested.

"You know that question is in breach of our ethics and one of our prime qualifications for membership in our anonymity. Jubal had been doing his homework.

"Perfectly true, but what is your adopted three K name?"

This remark and question completely threw Jubal off balance.

He was surely now exposed as the fraud he truly was.

"I am not very proud of my name, and I prefer to forget it." While he was speaking he was searching madly for a name that would fit his situation. At last an inspiration and he replied with apparent embarrassment.

"Please don't laugh….. 'Little wet pants'! The day I was to be initiated, I was so very nervous, I slipped on a wet marble pavement and sat down in an oily puddle. Everybody there burst into raucous laughter as they looked at my posterior, which was soaked with green and yellow oily liquid. Of course as you see I am quite tall, and thus the reason for the descriptive annotation of the word 'little'. I think the whole situation to be quite childish if you ask me!"

"That is precisely what I am doing, asking you!" Replied the guard, as he smiled. "That story is too preposterous to be false!" He stated as he burst into sympathetic laughter.

Jubal continued in the direction of a small group of members gathered together under the tallest upturned stone. He started listening in to their conversation as if perhaps to join in and be sociable. He could clearly hear the discussion.

"….. the chance of that happening would be very remote." One of the less well-built members of the group was speaking, he continued….. "If the yellow can prove his strength and bravery today then surely he would reach his full status?"

"Not necessarily" another hooded member of the group interrupted in full voice "You all know what today's test is. We are to prove whether a yellow can become a white, but one of us has to die for him to prove it. If he turns away, he still remains yellow and still survives. I believe that to be very unfair and one sided."

"Don't you remember how terrible and denigrating it was to be called 'yellow'? The term means failure, cowardice, lack of determination…." The conversation continued with another interruption.

"No! The Trial for a yellow to become white should be made at outside expense. Not one of us! There are so many problems in the world outside; perhaps, solving or helping to solve one of these problems would be more suitable than using ourselves as common fodder for each other.

Another man who as yet had not spoken found room to enter into the conversation.

"We may have our chance sooner than you think. I understand that there is something in the wind. Something big. Today's ceremony may be the last one like this for a long time. The Grand Wizard is going to be here today, and I am sure that he will inform us all, about recent events. The last time he came here was twelve years ago when he started the 'final solution' program on hybrids. That has not gone very well. The only success we've had with that, is keeping it low profile. Anyway it sounds so inhuman to do what we are doing, that few people believe it, and those who do, don't want to. We must have halved the potential hybrid population in that last twelve years since we started. Can you imagine how we would be overrun with them by now?" The man was becoming very worked up and his aggression was beginning to show in his hand movements.

The loudspeakers began to crackle, Jubal now very much inside the confinement of his newfound group of members felt more secure. He reacted in the same way that they did as he heard the noises. It was a very antiquated public address system.

Three loud single and separate identical notes came forth from the speakers mounted high above the stones, and then there was complete silence, as the entire system seemed to be turned off.

Jubal had done right to get into a group. He was now completely anonymous amongst them. His linen sheeting was white and exactly the same in every way as all the others. All he had to do was follow what they did. He got up the same way that they did from the left knee then to the right. Finally they were all standing in semi circular lines facing the center of the circle, symmetrical with the surrounding stones.

Music came through the re-vitalized loud speakers, and lasers appeared from nowhere. They danced in rhythm across the sky immediately above them. The personal experience for Jubal was very dramatic and certainly exhilarating. Suddenly people were standing beneath in the center of the erected podium. There were four hooded white clothed members and one similarly dressed but also covered in silver and gold strips. He lifted his hands above his head, and the music and the lasers stopped.

"Are we all present, members of the three?" He called for all to hear. "Demonstrate your loyalty by sign!" Jubal was worried. He could only see the backs of the three men in front of him and certainly could not see their sign. He tried to turn his head very minimally to see if the men at his side could become visible. If he tried to turn too much his movement would become very obvious to all present. Out of the corner of his eye he could see his near neighbor, three down the line, and was able to copy him, quite precisely and in equal timing.

A normal business meeting followed as they all stood in formation listening and occasionally participating. Jubal could sense a change in the atmosphere as early dawn began to appear. The hooded man in silver and gold, who had been taking most of the direction of the business meeting, mounted a further step to stand higher than before. He lifted his arms.

"The grand master wizard demands entry my friends, and is hereby welcomed amongst us." There was a roll on the drums and a fanfare of the trumpets as the form of a man dressed in an all gold-hooded outfit started to mount the stairs to the Podium. Not many moments later after much ritual exchange of greetings the newcomer spoke to the gathered assembly.

"Colleagues, Brothers, take care as I have wonderful news for you today. All being well, this will be the last trial of a yellow, which would result in the death of a white if successful. I bring with me fresh instructions for a new strategy which will increase the rate of the final solution in return for our help in other quarters."

Cheers and applause broke out all over the open field. The Grand Master Wizard lifted his arms above his head, and there was complete silence. He continued speaking.... "Now we see that dawn soon approaches we must continue with the trial."

Jubal soon realized that any member present who was dressed in white linen would qualify for the random choosing of the combatant for the yellow's attempt to improve his lot.

The music had started again and the bucket of white balls was being passed around. Each person was dipping in their white-gloved hand and then holding the white ball in the air for all to see. The music had been playing for some very long time, and the bucket was coming up the line. Very soon it would reach Jubal! There was only one black ball in that bucket, and now it was Jubal's turn. With nervous trepidation he placed his hand blindly and deeply down through the hole into the bucket. All the balls felt the same, and with white gloves it would have been impossible to tell the difference anyway. He made his decision and began to withdraw his hand.

***

Tsionne was holding Tubal Cain's hand very tightly as they entered the amenity area adjoining the surgical section in the West wing of the Central Hospital of Lublia. It was very early morning, and dawn was still only a promise yet to be fulfilled. There were five people sitting watching an early morning hologram on the holographic receiver, while on the other side of the room was a nubile young woman who was practicing gymnastic movements on some wall-bars carefully provided. There were two people sitting at a small table in the middle of the room playing game of checkers. Tsionne looked up to Tubal-Cain and taking close hold of his elbow spoke quietly into his ear.

"So many people about at this time of the early morning. Do think that they are all patients?"

Tubal Cain could feel the anxiety in Tsionne's grip as she spoke. She was certainly worried about their first meeting with "Gramps" following his surgery. He answered in a quiet manner.

"This department of the hospital caters for brain related problems, and this room is one of the therapy lounges. When someone has struggled to perform to a certain physical or mental ability for many years, reduced by neurological damage or function blockage, he or she becomes superhuman when his or her full brainpower is released after treatment. They become super charged and have been known to drive themselves beyond acceptable limits. That is why they constantly monitor post cerebral surgical cases."

"How will Gramps react now? Tsionne interrupted "He will have a new body and his brain is very old!"

"That is a major question." Tubal Cain replied "You may remember Tsionne, when you first told me about this surgery for Gramps that there had been psychological problems with at least one previous operation. Do you remember that Hybrid who had a nervous breakdown? We just hope that Gramps will cope with it."

"I am sure he will. With our help!"

The door opened across the room and a young lad walked in carrying a tray of drinks. He beckoned to Tubal and Tsionne that they should sit down and wait, and placed the drinks for them on a small table from which they had a very good view of the game of checkers. They continued in their private conversation.

"Do you think he will be fit enough to leave this morning.

How could he possibly be well enough to go to the funeral?"

Tsionne queried of Tubal Cain.

"The trauma of the occasion may not be healthy for him either."

Tubal replied, "Don't forget, he will have a young fit and healthy body. He will be able to cope with most physical stresses that would normally be acceptable to a young human body at the 'prime' of its life."

Tsionne was not sure whether she guessed or suspected the identity of the young gentleman before or after she heard him call her by name. The young man who had been concentrating on the game of checkers looked straight into Tsionne's eyes and called her by name. There was deep affection in his voice, unnatural in a complete stranger.

"Gramps!" Tsionne jumped from her chair and threw her arms around this attractive young man's neck. Tubal Cain looked on in complete astonishment. He had not yet grasped the situation. It was all happening so quickly.

"Mind my hairpiece! The real thing will take a few weeks to grow back." Methuselah replied, as he hugged Tsionne even more tightly, and very physically. "Whoops!" Gramps exhorted, "I haven't had physical feelings of that ferocity since my youth. I had better be careful. Sorry Tubal, no offence meant."

"No offence taken" said Tubal Cain with tongue in cheek. Tubal and Tsionne sat staring at this very handsome young man. He was blonde with ginger side curls tall and well built. The only visible reminder of the previous identity were the strong smiling blue eyes of Methuselah staring at them out of that young expressive face.

The burial ceremony for Methuselah's old body was the strangest affair in the humid afternoon heat. The mourners did not know how to react. No one had ever been to such a ceremony before. No ritual, no ode, no religious prayer had ever been written to cater for such an occasion. There, as would be expected lay Methuselah in his mortified state, face upwards in his open coffin. His arms at his side and legs uncrossed but together. He looked perfectly groomed and completely at peace. Someone was heard to remark that there was possibly even a smile on his face.

The visiting friends and relatives walked passed the coffin in single file, occasionally throwing in a small piece of Acacia twig as a symbol of his old life, and the old life in the burned out Acacia bush.

All those people present were finding the situation very hard to understand and seemed to feel uneasy that the young man standing at the head of the coffin was in fact the new body for the 'soul' of the one who's body was lying there in front of him. There was definitely a tear in Methuselah's eye as he stood there rigid and bewildered. He had often heard people joke about how they would love to be able to stand and watch at their own funeral but in fact the truth was stranger than the fiction. New Methuselah felt so sick and uncomfortable seeing his body lying there helpless and lifeless. He had known that friend and been part of it for a whole lifetime. In fact it was the very body that he had been born in. He thought of his parents and what they would think. He thought of his past life and found himself going off into a dream. What of his future, and his family, how will they react in the long term? For the first time ever in his life Methuselah felt very lonely in spite of the fact that he was surrounded by all his friends and his relatives. He took Tsionne's hand in a tight grip. She responded to the warmth of this young man with the same affection. They didn't realize what they were doing, but Tubal Cain was looking on. He was suddenly becoming a very worried man.

***

Fadfagi's large yacht was moored against the harbor wall. There was only a short, narrow and rickety walkway, which connected it to the mainland. The atmosphere between Tubal Cain and Tsionne was very strained as they arrived with Marla and Erash in a small group with several others from the office of 'Science and Welfare'. Rula would still not go, but had said that she may arrive late, although it would be against her best principles to go at all.

The weather was unusually warm for the time of year and seemed to be getting warmer. In fact Marla thought that the sun was so strong, it was almost breaking through the bright late afternoon haze. Black dust was everywhere, and the whole deck area was being hosed down to clear away as much as possible. No sooner was it clear than fresh took its place. "Black Snow" as it was called, was finding itself into the most inaccessible places. Marla hated it and was continually trying to get rid of it. It was some form of carbon deposit, which was being crystallized out of the atmosphere. It has been known in the south to settle like snow quite deep. It clogged up many a street vacuum cleaner. Unlike snow, it did not melt.

The party was just beginning to get into full swing as the newcomers arrived. Fadfagi walked across the deck to greet them. He took Marla's hand and led her accompanied by Erash and the others to a small sun terrace just above the sports deck where the music and dancing was taking place. "I am so pleased that you could come." He was still talking only to Marla. "I am very sorry about my wife's outburst yesterday. She is indisposed at the moment, perhaps she will appear a little later."

"She seemed very upset." Marla remarked. "What is it that troubled her, and what is it that I am meant to have done?" Fadfagi's facial expression seemed to change as Marla spoke. He was not very happy and seemed lost for an answer, he turned to Erash and apologized that he had to attend to some other guests. Marla and Tsionne decided that it was so warm, and as everyone was so happy and friendly, they would go for a swim in the open-air pool. They stripped down to their underwear, which they then removed completely at the poolside. It was very infra-dig these days to wear any clothing in the water. A great cheer rang out as the two girls both dropped their bras and knickers exposing their most private attributes. It had become complimentary for such a reaction from a viewing public. There was no such thing as private modesty any more. They both took a small step to the edge of the pool and then neatly entered the water with identical dives hardly even breaking the surface as they entered the water.

They must have been swimming around in the pool for a little while when Marla looked up and saw Fadfagi's wife enter the pool area. She was also in her undies and certainly was going to take a swim. She turned to face her audience with her back to the pool as she removed her bra and her panties.

Marla swallowed hard. She understood part of the problem when she saw the exposed rear end of Rebecca, Fadfagi's wife. She had the most exquisite shaped behind, which should have been blemish free. Rebecca's complexion was perfection itself, but her rear-end exhibited a very large and somewhat beautiful tattoo. On one buttock there was a six-figure number, which Marla remembered was very similar to Rula's, if not the preceding number. On her other buttock a beautiful picture of an ear of corn by a river. Marla's mind was working overtime. She realized that once again she was being confused with her sister.

Rebecca did not dive into the pool but climbed in down the steps. She still had her back to the water and so did not yet see Marla in the water.

Marla decided that it would be a very good idea if she removed herself from the pool to avoid Rebecca's vengeful orations. She climbed the steps in the wall, at the other side of the pool.

As she raised her wet, dripping naked body from the swimming pool, Marla heard a scream from behind her in the pool.

"You are clean!" The voice came from the water behind her. "Your backside is as clean as the day you were born! I knew that you were a spying BITCH!" Rebecca was screaming at Marla from the water. Marla turned around only to see her adversary climbing naked out of the pool with a most vicious expression on her face. She looked like she would kill Marla and she was moving so fast, head pushed forward, showing her teeth, and pointing her long fingernails at her. She was seething in anger.

Marla was standing naked at the poolside terrified at the approach of this rabid monster. Her only chance was to stand firm and defend herself.

"I've wanted to get even with you, I owe it to Lara!" Rebecca screamed as she threw herself at Marla's neck as if to strangle her. Marla moved quickly sideways to avoid the attack. She was not quick enough and Rebecca placed a long deep scratch wound into her left cheek and down her neck. Marla was now bleeding from her wet face and neck.

Marla felt the wound and saw the blood on her hand. She became angry, very angry. Raising her left foot she kicked her opponent firmly in her stomach, and as Rebecca reeled from the sudden blow Marla punched her hard across the face. Marla had been well trained in her early days with Rula, but the motivation driving Rebecca's madness was far greater than anything that Marla had ever come against before.

Tsionne had left the pool and was on her way for help.

Within seconds Rebecca had returned to the fight, she had jumped so hard at Marla that they both landed firmly on the ground. The crowd was now enjoying this fight between two naked women, and nobody had the courage or the sense to interfere. The two wet woman were rolling on the ground, each trying very hard to get the advantage of being on top. Rebecca was beginning to overcome Marla's valiant attempts to defend herself. She had Marla on her back and had placed her right knee firmly between Marla's legs forcing it into her crutch. Marla had a grip on Rebecca's neck with her left hand and was pushing hard to throw her off but to no avail. Rebecca was now firmly astride her victim's stomach. Her full weight holding her down on the ground. She desperately wanted to finish the job. She was determined to kill Marla and as painfully as possible. Marla was completely pinned down and was wholly at Rebecca's mercy. Rebecca leaned over Marla's head, all hot, salty, wet and very sticky. She spat all over Marla's bleeding face. Marla pulled one hand free, and grabbed Rebecca's neck. Rebecca bent down close and bit deeply into Marla's neck. They were both rolling nearer and nearer to the pool edge. Marla let out a scream as she felt Rebecca slam her knee once again very violently up against her pelvic mound. She felt as if she would be split apart as her whole body vibrated under the shock. Rebecca was now certainly getting the advantage over Marla who made one more valiant attempt at Rebecca's neck.

Rebecca was becoming very desperate and very angry; she noticed Marla's discarded underwear within her arms reach. She fumbled and managed to take hold of the bra! That was all she needed. Within less than a moment she had it wrapped around Marla's neck, and was starting to strangle her. Marla's face was going blue. She was beginning to choke. She would pass out at any moment, as Rebecca was stopping the blood flow to her head. Marla's body movement was weakening and becoming limp.

"Rebecca! What are you doing? Leave my sister alone!" A firm hand was now pulling at the underside of Rebecca's chin. Another was pulling fiercely at her hair. Rula was screaming unrepeatable expletives as she tried to prize Rebecca away from her troubled sister. Rula was livid and all her pent up anger was about to be released. She pulled with such venomous force at Rebecca's head that she nearly bent it back double, until the life-threatening grip on her sister Marla had been released. Rebecca was more worried about her own safety. Rula was holding Rebecca's head so far back that she was looking up into Rula's eyes.

Rula twisted Rebecca's head in such a way that she rolled away from Marla and ended up kneeling face to face with Rula. The expression on Rebecca's face was that of shock, as she saw Rula, twin sister of Marla. It took at least several moments for the reality of the situation to sink into Rebecca's understanding of things.

Rula saw that Marla was regaining her consciousness. Instinct and emotion were motivating her to give full punishment to Rebecca for what she had done, but she leaned over to Marla.

Rebecca was absorbed in a state of confusion. She was finding it extremely difficult to come to terms with the new situation. She just stayed fixed in her kneeling position staring at Rula, and then looking at Marla.

"Twins!" she shrieked, as if in self-recrimination. "You are both the same!" came the inane remark, as Rebecca tried to regain her composure.

Rula was still full of rage; she had spent the last few moments checking to see if Marla was safe and recovering. Satisfied she turned around and raised her arm above her head as if to thrust her finger nails into Rebecca's eyes. As she lunged forward she felt a familiar hand take hold of her arm. She was pulling on a man's grip. She screamed and turned around. Rula could have killed Erash for interfering.

"Now stop this, both of you. Stop behaving like spoilt children. Let us sit down and talk this out. Go and put your clothes on!"

He called to Rebecca and Marla, throwing them each a towel, although they were almost dry anyway and Marla had seemed to be fully recovered, if not moderately bruised.

"I need a shower!" Rebecca retorted, still a slight tilt of suspicion in her voice. "I'm not ready to talk to people like you." She turned to Rula, and then gesturing with her hips she walked off as if in a huff. Erash had to restrain Rula from chasing after her. Tsionne had returned fully dressed and helped Marla to the women's room.

***

Jubal did not dare to look at the content of his gloved hand; he just lifted it above his head and demonstrated his drawn ball for all to see. The music continued, and the next person in the line took his chance. Jubal could not believe it as he looked up at that beautiful glistening white ball that was now his.

The music stopped, and a single drumbeat came over the loudspeaker system. Jubal looked at the raised hand of his immediate neighbor next up the line. There in his hand was the black ball, shining for all to see. A feeling of shocked sickness was deep in Jubal's stomach. That could so easily have been his!

The hooded figure stood his ground, with hand raised above his head, holding the ball, while the rest of the membership stepped carefully backwards, leaving him all alone, the sole lay contributor to the next part of the ceremony. He walked to the very center spot of the circle of stones.

In his mind, Jubal was thanking god, in deep silent prayer. There but for the grace of the almighty could he be standing instead of his unfortunate neighbor in the ranks.

The drumbeat changed tempo and two stringed instruments joined in, making pleasing sounds from a very sensuous trio. The shadows of the surrounding circle of stones were beginning to materialize as the gentle early morning sunlight began to lift itself above the horizon across the distant hills. Just as he could see changing colors across the hilly fields, he could see the central spot in the middle of the circle was also changing its colors. Strangely as the shadows of morning began to consolidate, he could see that curiously the center spot became the pivot of their design. It was a brilliant piece of mathematical engineering. The hooded man was still standing stationary in the middle; his clothing was changing through many vivid tones of hue as the daylight was beginning to take its hold over the dying nighttime shades of darkness.

Two other hooded members, each carrying a golden staff in their left hands, appeared from nowhere. They positioned themselves each side of the new candidate for the ceremony, who immediately stood to attention. Then on the command of the Master Wizard they marched him off for preparation and dressing.

The Grand Master Wizard stepped forward to the podium and announced for the entire gathering to hear . . . "Today's ordeal will be by fire and water. Our brother in yellow will have to kill the brother in white if he is to pass into our brotherhood. Failure cannot result in the yellow member's death, and he will also be permitted to fight another day."

The music started again, and the Klansmen were allowed to relax among themselves. Jubal listened very carefully to the various conversations going on around him. He was intrigued by the matter of fact way in which the hooded brethren referred to the forthcoming ordeal, as if it were only a sport. He was just a spectator amongst them, but felt disgust and sorrow that one of their membership would be killed for the sake of a ritual ceremony. It was so heathen he thought.

After certainly what seemed a very long time, the *'Daylight Bell'* was sounded and the musical background from the tannoy system went quiet . . .

"Await an announcement from the Grand Master Wizard." came the sudden voice of authority.

Although it was bright hazy daylight, Jubal felt that there was an eerie aura about the place, and strangely there was a cool icy wind blowing gently across his face. It was almost with relief that Jubal paid interested attention to the loudspeakers, as a fresh message came to the ears of those congregated. It was one of the Grand Master's officers who was now speaking. "We have wonderful news!" There was enthusiastic exhilaration in his happy voice. "Our white brother has been reprieved. There has been a sudden surprise opportunity, and an immediate change of plan. The duel will continue but under different rules. We have a new candidate as if by a chance miracle. We have acquired an unregistered Hybrid. The fight will be to the death . . . " There was uproar. Everyone was cheering as if they had won a major battle. Some linked arms and danced around in circles.

Jubal's blood went cold. It was one thing when they fought their ritual amongst themselves by mutual choice, but when involving an external stranger unwittingly and certainly against his will, that was seriously wrong. There was such vicious hatred between these hooded people and members of the Hybrid race. The forthcoming fight would certainly be very biased against the Hybrid.

***

Lika had spent most of the last few days in pensive worry about the radiation threat to her child once more. The Ozone layer was sick and had holes occurring in it without warning. As a protective coating to the atmosphere, it was becoming chronically less reliable. Soon it would be so thin that its radiation protection would become purely academic. She was determined to speak to Svi about it when he came home that evening. Her immediate ambition was to take her child away from the imminent danger. Sometimes she had wished that she had replaced the young one back in the environmental research unit from where she had originally come. At least there was built-in protection and as her own child would be, Trin would also be, protected against all severe effects of radiation and its sicknesses. Lika knew that it would be madness. The whole experiment would be ruined if that were attempted.

Most of Lika's day had been taken up with cleaning and tidying their home. She didn't know why, but she was sure that they would be leaving it almost immediately, and she did not want to leave it in a mess. The perspiration was soaking her, the humidity was so oppressive, and that very day the air-conditioning had decided to break down. Every small task demanded a superior effort, but she was determined to complete the job. She wanted their home to be a shining example of cleanliness when Svi arrived home with Trin. He had taken her to the Exhibition of Endangered Species. Trin always came home in raptures over her experiences. The wonderful seldom seen cuddly furry creatures had become so familiar to her on her frequent visits to the local Zoo.

The enthusiastic smiling face of tired Trin, being carried in Svi's arms brought a warm glow of satisfied happiness into Lika's heart, as she let them in the door. Lika grabbed her husband and gave him a tight hug as she kissed the cheeky giggling face of her youngster.

"I would like us to return to the project!" Lika suddenly whispered into Svi's ear. She had been chewing these thoughts over for many days and had programmed herself to tell Svi the moment that he walked in the door. He barely had time to say hello to his wife. A glimpse of a relieved smile was hinting at the corner of his mouth. He leaned over and kissed her firmly on the lips while still holding on to Trin.

"I am so glad darling. I have wanted to return for weeks, now that Trin is so fit and well. I haven't had the courage to broach the subject. The sooner we leave the happier that I will be."

He put Trin down on the floor and went over to make himself a drink. Trin ran off to her room to play.

"What do we do with the young one?" enquired Svi, nodding his head in the direction of the door. "Surely they would not let us take her back into orbit, she is under age. Perhaps she could stay with one of your step-cousins?"

"No! Conditions down here are becoming more risky as every week goes by. Even now radiation levels are growing dangerously high on occasions. At least in orbit the protection is fully controlled." Lika was adamant.

"How could we get back through security? They are now very much stricter on departures than on arrivals." Svi was cautious in his tones. "I am happy to try if you can think of a way. You do realize that if we are caught trying to smuggle a child into orbit we could face the stiffest penalty . . . . . . Full vaporization. All of us!! "

"I think that I know a way," Lika said with some considered authority in her voice. "Your friend Zarby will help us. We have a plan, but it has to be early tomorrow morning or we miss the chance."

Svi was astonished until Lika had explained that Zarby had been in contact with her earlier that day wanting to speak to Svi. They had a long 'chat' on the televideo-phone. Lika then played back the recorded conversation.

Svi could not believe their luck. Zarby and a whole troupe of gorillas were being given assembly work in orbit in exchange for a place of their own. He could not believe it; the gorillas were being given a massive satellite station of their very own. 'That must be the work of that Noah gentleman.' Svi was thinking to himself, and his thoughts continued. 'Perhaps I shall meet him one day.'

"Don't you see?" Lika was pulling at his arm trying to awaken him from his deep absorption in the tele-recording. "Don't you see? Zarby could take Trin with them on the 'Early Riser' tomorrow morning."

"That's true." Svi was enthusiastic. "The Early Riser flights are never over zealously checked, and with a troupe of gorillas we should easily be missed by security."

"No not that way! We go as normal travelers on our usual ticket and Zarby takes Trin with her. They are going to the same place as us, to collect their work. The gorillas are allowed to take their families with them, so Trin will go as one of them. She loves dressing up, you know that Svi. Don't you?"

A nervous smile broke out across Svi's face.

"Come on Lika!" He gave her a very friendly kiss "We have much to do. Let's get moving."

***

It was certainly a new experience for Tsionne and Naamah, as they walked together down the busy city-shopping street. They were arm in arm, either side of their 'new found' friend, 'Gramps Methuselah'. It was very strange taking a brisk walk alongside this well built hunk of a blonde young man.

Tsionne was unashamedly becoming quite attracted to him. She was finding it very difficult to come to terms with the reality of events. This man is her husband's great uncle; he is from a previous much older generation. Tsionne was finding the relationship very difficult to handle. She still adored her husband Tubal Cain, but this new situation was pulling very hard on her sense of reasoning.

"Come on girls." Gramps pulled so hard on their waists, that they found themselves hugged very close to him. "Let's stop for a cable-juice and some nuts perhaps. Here!" He pointed to a curbside restaurant, and sat the two women down either side of him at the nearest convenient empty table.

Tsionne was very aware of Methuselah's glances at her thighs as he sat her down in her chair. She knew that he was having the same problems, and wondered how they would solve them. She felt his hand hold hers for just that little extra time before he let go. She felt his arm help the 'small' of her back and shoulders settle into the chair. She knew that those subtle contacts were more than just an acknowledgement between friends. She was worried, but she liked it, and that worried her more.

Naamah could sense unease, but could not put her finger on it. The conversation had become slightly stilted, as if it were being forced. She had experienced this before, but never with two people who were so close to her. They always had so much to talk about. What was happening, she wondered? There seemed to be an element of shyness, bordering on embarrassment about them. Naamah was not given the opportunity to pursue her thoughts. The strangest experience was about to happen. . . .

"Hya!" A tall beautiful leggy blonde bombshell of a young woman put her arms around Gramps's neck. She ran her longing caressing fingers through his shirt, pulling it slightly open exposing his thickly matted fair-haired chest. She played the hair into ringlets with her left hand, while pulling gently at his head turning his face to hers. The jealous passion in her mouth met his as she closed in on a deep loving embrace. Methuselah was completely involved in this stranger's advances. He was experiencing incredible sexual arousement. What had he done to deserve this, he could not believe his 'luck'. Within moments the passion subsided as the young woman pulled back and spoke directly to Gramps. "Who are these girls? I suppose you'll tell me that they are distant relatives who have just rolled into town! Hi girls!" She said sarcastically, giving them a condescending grin and a patronizing look as she continued to run her fingers, caressing and searching through Methuselah's hairy chest.

The three seated people just could not collect their wits quickly enough. Who was this? Even Gramps did not appear to know. The mixed expression of astonishment and pleasure on his face said it all. He started to reply as the stranger tightened her grip across Methuselah's shoulders. She would have sat on his lap if it had not been tucked so well under the table. His sex hormones were working overtime.

"Yes" he answered instinctively. "They are relatives. Meet Tsionne, my great niece-in-law, and Naamah, my grand-daughter—in-law." He did not understand why he had answered so freely. The words logically appeared from nowhere.

"You're what?" The stranger could not believe his answer. "You must be joking. You told me that your family is small, and these girls must be slightly older than both of us." She started back in a raised voice, and quite uncharitably. "Come on! Who are they?" she yelled.

"More to the point, who are you? " Gramps retorted.

"What do you mean? You know me, I'm Mya, what's wrong with you, and where have you been for the last two weeks? The girl was beginning to show outward signs of panic and a tirade of questions began to follow as simultaneously she started to cry. "...and what are you doing in this part of the world. Are you leading a double life, are you a two-timer? Are you, or have you...dropped me? Are we fini.......?" She just completely broke down into tears.

"I'm very sorry but I don't know you" Gramps tried to re-assure her, "I must have a double."

"No!" she interjected "I know your hair is cut differently, but you have that scar over your left ear where you burnt yourself as a child. Let me see your right hand! There is a small circular scar at the base of your palm."

Naamah took Methuselah's hand and verified Mya's remarks. Mya started to become very hysterical, beginning to panic. It was blatantly apparent that she had had a deep relationship with the former owner of "Gramps's" body.

"What have these women done to you? You don't seem to know me! *Oh Mikash* What has happened to you?"

"Mikash? That must have been your previous identity." Tsionne said quietly into Methuselah's left ear. She tried very hard not to be seen or heard by Mya who was around the other side of Gramps, looking at his right hand.

Gramps stood up, and pulled an empty chair from another table gesturing with as kindly a manner as was within his capabilities for Mya to sit down and listen to him. She did. She was sobbing very nervously as she sat down, deep reddening eyes, and salty wet tears flowing freely onto her face, she could hardly talk and was totally bewildered. She sat with one hand on her lap and another with a paper handkerchief wiping at her eyes as best she could. She was beginning to calm down between intermittent sobs and sudden intakes of breath.

"It seems to me" Gramps began, "that I *am* that person you think I am. But! You may not believe the circumstances and events that led up to this new situation. Perhaps this is not the place to explain it to you."

Mya interrupted amid the tears . . .

"Please tell me why you are so strange. Why you don't know me and why you seem to have become so much more intelligent! You speak so differently. It *is your voice* but you seem to use it in another way."

"That is precisely the answer "Gramps started again "I must explain. Please listen," he continued "Mikash, as you call me, suffered a serious brain hemorrhage last week, and his brain cells died. His body was still in excellent healthy order and was kept fully functional until my brain was safely implanted as a substitute for Mikash's."

"No, No, No!" Mya screamed as she stood up. She leaned over Methuselah's grim face, "Tell me these are lies! You wouldn't do that to me . . ." she feinted.

***

CHAPTER 4

Noah was very nervous. He was about to make one of the most important speeches of his life. Very few government cabinet meetings went smoothly these days; they had been in power for a very long time, having won four elections in succession. They were taking power for granted. So easily had they forgotten who had put them there? It was this argument that Noah was going to use in his opening remarks, as he was about to plead for more investment in 'extra orbital research '. He had some wonderful news to give them, but he was determined to use it to his own department's ends. The blood seeming to leave his fingers, and the apprehensive thumping of his heartbeat were a clear indication of the severe height of conscious nervousness that was trying to overcome Noah as he slowly stood up to speak. Determined to start with and maintain an unadulterated impact throughout that hot humid afternoon, he placed his notes tidily on the lectern and took a breath. With eyes firmly fixed on the Prime Minister, Noah started to speak as if this was meant for his ears only . . .

"Not long ago I returned from a visit with Tubal-Cain in Unit 43 extra-orbital!" Noah's ideas were beginning to gel and he could feel the flow building up within him. "We are making discoveries about our world, our lives, and our relationships with the universe even as I speak to you now. As each moment of the clock ticks by yet an infinite number more of interesting discoveries are made. We live on the edge of the precipice of knowledge. Our destiny is yet to unfold, and our past is sealed in the eons of time gone by. "Noah could feel that he was becoming very flowery, but he continued.

"It is written in our holy scriptures that if we do not heed the warnings of our forefathers, we will destroy ourselves, our home and our destiny. When Adam partook of the fruit of the 'tree of knowledge' the destiny of the human race became *'finite'*, dependent on the limits of its own self-destruction. Had he eaten from the 'tree of life' humanity would have gone on forever in its ignorance." Noah took a deep breath, he had his audience, and he intended to keep it. "We have a duty to humanity to put to right, the wrongs that we have done to others, and to our environment. We are destroying the very home that has supported our nations, a mother and grandmother to us all! "

Noah could feel a strong undercurrent of disbelief coming forth from the gathered ensemble.

"If all else fails, our only chance is to utilize the very technology that has been 'destroying' us, to 'save' us from a forthcoming apocalypse! "

He could feel a growing antagonism to his religious meandering and decided to bring his argument down to their level. The expressions on their faces illustrated an attitude that would be no more than mockery. He began to change his method of approach, hoping that they would not notice.

"There is good reason to believe that this planet is not the only one in the existence of the 'ether' that sustains intelligent life. We have been monitoring coded messages on the Radio Magnetic Spectrum. There are some very interesting results coming from our deciphering laboratories. We even have pictures that were transmitted from a source so long ago it could well be before the crust on this planet supported even an aqueous life form. During our recent scientific stereo-orbital maneuver with our sister satellite on a half orbit around the sun we have been able to locate the exact source of these signals. I have several copies of the sets of transmitted pictures now so far decoded. These are two-dimensional and strictly secret! There are many more versions to be decoded and transcribed, we have not yet mastered their Holographic techniques, but it won't be much longer, and we will have three dimensional pictures, possibly with coupled sound, of their living world!! "

As Noah continued talking, he handed out copies of the sensational pictures received on the de-coders in 'Unit 43 Extra-orbital'. There were gasps of interest and surprise as each person in turn examined the images on the sheets of paper being passed around. He heard a woman state the obvious to one of her colleagues . . . . . "They are just like us! "she was bewildered "but they have more hair." she thought for a moment and then rose to interrupt. Noah yielded to her question. "How do we know that they are not a great hoax or a forgery?" "You don't! But with the correct equipment, which anyone can buy on the open market, and with two receiving sets at least four hundred miles apart, you could pick up enough signals to generate these simple pictures. Wait until we have processed what appears to be holographic material. I am sure that we await those transcriptions with keen interest.

The meeting eventually finished. There had been much open discussion, and Noah came under very strong criticism. They did not appear to like his schemes for increasing the use of astro-technology. They voiced opinion that his extravagances with public money on extra-orbital development were of no real value other than to quench man's thirst for knowledge. Had it not been for these new sensational discoveries of life elsewhere the committee would never have sanctioned further allowances to the budget.

The allowances were agreed but conditional on further satisfactory proof of life outside their solar system. Everyone knew that there was no other planet in their planetary system that could support life, so the challenge was beyond comprehension.

Noah smiled to himself as he left the committee room; he knew he had won. He had incredible proof yet to come . . .

***

Tubal-Cain had not seen Erash so angry since the melt down of the power station at Lyboncher. The two men were seated facing each other across a much cluttered desk in Erash's office. The acute worry was self evident on his face as he spoke nervously to Tubal-Cain.

"Important information has come into my hands about Fadfagi's dealings with Radiact!" Erash could feel the reaction from Tubal-Cain on the mention of the dreaded word. "They are secretly building up vast underground supplies of Radiact material, much more than they would ever need in hundreds of years of peacetime use, and they don't even use it for peaceful purposes anyway. I am told that they have 'acquired' the technology and know how to assemble a destructive explosive nuclear device!"

"How? Where? When?" Tubal Cain was astonished that Erash could be so certain about something that they had suspected for such a long time.

Erash continued . . .

"All the time, while we were entertaining him on his mission of 'Peace and Understanding', and signing pieces of paper, his engineers were busy at work creating weapons of such destruction! . . Why? He must *not* be trusted!"

Tubal-Cain was full of questions to Erash . . .

"How did you find this out, have you undisputable proof?" Erash was almost pleased with his ability to give Tubal-Cain the answer he needed to hear.

"Solid proof." Erash replied "I have a new confidant in the enemy camp. Fadfagi's chief wife . . . Rebecca!"

"What?"

"Yes. After the fight on board Fadfagi's boat the other day, Rebecca realized that she had been mistaken about Marla in the pool, and went to her in the ladies' room and apologized. Marla took the time to discuss her sister's role in the hospital in Larden, and how she had been 'branded' with the other girls. She also told Rebecca the story about how Rula had tried to escape together with Lara and me, with Pollo as prisoner, and how we were spotted by a Bylean patrol boat and stopped. Lara surrendered as a substitute for Pollo so that we could get away. Within hours of Rebecca listening to this story and seeing Rula's tattoo, she had the patrol boat checked out. I have to compliment Rebecca on her thoroughness, she even found out how Lara really died from a Eunuch who was regularly on guard in the market place, where Lara was raped to death."

Tubal-Cain was speechless.

Erash continued . . .

"Rebecca was furious. She knew that her husband could be a cruel dictator, but her excuse for him was that it was the only way he could keep his nation together; otherwise it would break up into factions. Rebecca did not mind the suppression of people for the sake of a country, which was growing stronger, but she was enraged that he should have concealed the blame for Lara's death in such a way."

"I can understand that." nodded Tubal-Cain. Erash reached into the back section of one of his lower desk drawers . . .

"Last night, Rebecca came to my house when neither Marla nor Rula were at home, and she gave this file copy of the Bylean Nuclear Industry."

. . . he pulled out a dusty file, covered by the anonymous title 'Electronic statistics on Semirean Wines'. I always put valuable files inside unimportant ones. They are less likely to be purloined."

He handed the valuable document over to Tubal-Cain who gave it a casual read.

"Very impressive material indeed." Tubal grinned "It is not at all pleasant, but at least we now know how to treat that 'Bastard' and his henchmen, it's a completely different ball game now! Will this Rebecca woman be of future help to us or is this her one and only act?"

"I don't know that yet. At the present she sees herself as a woman spurned or cheated on. Perhaps she could revert back, who knows?"

Tubal Cain called to Erash as he left his Office.

"We must now have a complete review of our defensive security!"

***

The revulsion in Jubal's stomach became even stronger when the Grand Wizard's officer announced play about to commence in a fight to the death. There was a sudden change of tempo in the melodious rhythm of the background music. There followed a strong roll on the drums . . . . . Jubal looked at the small stage out in front of them. The cheers came from the audience to the right first of all, as then simultaneously Jubal could see two very uncertain Hybrids coming on stage from the left.

One was a well built and a very heavy man whose strongest asset was his solid muscular structure and thick wholesome buttocks. He had dark brown skin and an abundance of curly black hair. The other was a half naked female with her hands bound tightly to a loose stake behind her back. She was very beautiful and naked except for a crimson red loincloth, tightly attached to her sumptuous well-formed Negroid brown skin. Two officers placed her in the middle of the open area where the action was going to take place. The stake was driven hard into the ground just behind her back and down between her feet. The poor woman just could not move!

An announcement came from the loudspeaker system. " We have an extra bonus with us. You see in front of you a 'girl friend' of the Hybrid we captured today. The male's ability to maintain her safety will add spice and an extra dimension to the fight."

The two Hybrids stood looking at each other, and then they both looked around the circle of stones, and at the audience, as if to try and remember each individual party in the gathered crowd. When the male looked straight at Jubal's face, their eyes seemed to meet for less than a few seconds, but Jubal was certain that through his linen disguise he had been recognized. This of course would have been almost impossible but Jubal still felt uneasy.

The short silence that followed was completely un-broken until, from the right hand wings of the stage, a young lad appeared and bowed to the audience, then to his opponents. His head was hooded, his identity still concealed, but his body looked good in the tightly fitted yellow linen stretch suit.

"The combat will have few rules" the loudspeaker again broke the silence as it bellowed out to the awaiting crowd, "Our brother in yellow must remain hooded at all times. If the hood is removed, he is shamed out of our organization, and his opponent and female companion will be beheaded. The victor will either be our brother on killing the Hybrid and his mate, or the Hybrid if he can hold our brother's shoulders flat on the ground to the count of five."

A shocked gasp of silence greeted the next remark by the loudspeaker system...

"It is the Grand Wizard's command that the Hybrid and his mate go free with a safe passage away from this place if he is victorious in combat!"

Two officers came forward from the darkness behind. One was carrying a large burning torch on a large stem; the other was towing a large green marble bath on wheels, which was full to the brim with water. He also carried a small bucket on a long handle, which he presented to the Hybrid man. The large oval bath was left in the middle of the floor area. The young Klansman was delighted to receive his torch into his hand. Even through his faceless anonymity his emotion could not be hidden, as his pleasing gasps came from under his yellow hood.

The announcement continued . . .

"The fight will commence with the sounding of two different notes on a ram's horn. Each combatant will be left to his own devices. They will now take their places back to back in the center of the circle. When the game commences they will walk away from each other to the edge of the marked pavement, turn around, and then it is up to them to go for it".

The two men positioned themselves as directed. The Hybrid was already pouring with nervous perspiration, his chocolate colored skin shining under the early morning sunlight. He took a caring casual glance at his mate giving her a wink of reassurance with his left eye.

The impatience to begin was very evident in the manner of the man in yellow as he gently transferred his weight from one foot to the other. They were both at the starting block perilously waiting for the 'off'. Being under starting orders was never an easy time, but this anticipation seemed endless.

The two men hardly moved initially as the horn sounded. They had seemed to forget why they were there. They both moved off with a delayed nervous reaction. The hybrid almost went into a run as he reached the edge of the area. The other man turned around possibly a moment earlier than he should have done. There was a frustrated growl coming from under his mask as he rushed forward with his torch at the hybrid-man. The brown man ran to the bath, filled his bucket and poured water all over his mate. He was now being hotly pursued as he only had the bath between himself and the threat of severe burns. He threw himself violently into the bath, rolling out again almost as quickly as he had entered it. He felt the warmth of the hot torch down his naked wet back. The fresh liquid protection seemed to be working, but for how long? Again the torch lunged in his direction, but he jumped neatly to the side trying to throw a full bucket of water into the torch. He was too slow. Again the torch was lunged at him. This time he was caught full frontal in his stomach. The heat was excruciating, but the hybrid held onto the stem as the Klansman tried to follow through with his push. The hybrid found reserve energy to jump to the side pulling the torch into the bath. The steam went wild. There was almost a complete mist around the event, and the torch was still smoldering. Within moments it was alight again. It seemed to re-ignite from within.

The Hybrid had jumped onto the edge of the bath and was standing high overlooking the area of the event. He could neither believe his eyes or his ears...

...all Hell was being let loose!! Screams and shrieks were everywhere, as perhaps thirty hooded people came running into the gathered crowd. "Run! Run! Run!" He heard a Hybrid voice from under one of the stranger's hoods.

Jubal acted quickly, this was his ideal chance, and he grabbed the flaming torch from the startled man in yellow, and ran to the girl tied to the stake. The other Klansman did not realize that he was a traitor and while cheering him on with full enthusiasm were astonished as he burned out her bonds allowing her immediate release. He grabbed her, and with the wet sweaty hybridman, they ran with the moving crowd of strangers. Jubal's foot caught an elevated edge of a pavement stone, causing him to fall full length to the ground. The moving crowd of interlopers continued on their way leaving Jubal behind to lick his wounds.

An anonymous cloaked arm reached out to help Jubal back onto his feet. It was only a moment later that he was back standing among his hooded 3K companions, looking out across the barren fields at the disappearing backs of the running group of intruders who only moments previously had caused such welcome mayhem. Jubal privately took great pleasure in knowing that he had been an accessory to their escape, but had he been noticed?

"Please re-group. Your attention comrades. The game has been destroyed, and the committee will have to decide on our next course of action." The Tannoy system was in full volume. "We now come to the business part of the session."

Jubal just could not believe how such an extraordinary interruption to their proceedings could be waived aside and without comment.

The brotherhood re-assembled into a semi-circle, an audience around the central podium as the loudspeaker continued to give out instructions . . .

" . . . and that bring us to the next mission. We are going to attack and assassinate a well-known benefactor of the Hybrid and gorilla race. He runs a farm not too far away from here, and is very well known for his kindness to the minority groups that he employs there. We have to eradicate him and teach all those like him, a lesson that they will not forget. These scum who sympathize and support this vermin on our land will understand that we are not to be unaccounted for!! Jabal, the brother of Tubal Cain has to be destroyed, and this will happen very soon. We need some volunteers from among the ranks. It will indeed be very dangerous."

Jubal, although shocked, thought for a moment and his was the second hand to be elevated. He had volunteered!!

***

Lika wanted desperately to look over her shoulder at the small group of gorilla people just about to board the shuttle behind them. She held tightly onto Svi's hand as they sat at a table by the window in the restaurant. They always liked to sit by a window. It was still very dark outside, and Lika could see most of the interior of their shuttle reflected in the windowpane. Zarby! Yes, she could make out Zarby's image in the glass. Sitting next to her, holding Zarby's hand was her small niece, who was carrying a large life-size gorilla-doll. Lika was almost misting up the window with her anxious breathing while she fervently looked for her own youngster. "I can't see Trin anywhere!" She was beginning to panic. She almost raised her voice above a whisper into Svi's ear.

"Don't worry!" Svi re-assured her, "Zarby is quite a bright gorilla, she has to fool those guards, so she will probably likewise fool us. Have faith in your friends!" He gave Lika a confident smile and Lika felt a little calmer inside. The bells and buzzers sounded, it was their third warning that the outside atmosphere was excluded and that they were ready for departure into orbit. An exciting time, just before the early morning dawn.

Imperceptibly they had moved from their stationary position above ground control. Lika saw the lights of G.C.Eton disappear beneath them, out of view. They began to feel the gradual change in gravity as the hoversphere began to move slowly away from their mother planet. They lifted slowly out of the atmosphere, the sunrise began to appear in the North Northeast and they passed across the last remnants of outside air, they could see the beautiful colors of prismatic light reflecting back to them as they left all memory behind, of their mother planet. Soon they would achieve an artificially created half gravity, and then not much later would arrive at their destination, Orbital Environmental Unit Six, as it had been re-numbered.

Neither Lika nor Svi could believe their eyes, as the outside black void suddenly became a maze of bright colored lights, which seemed to be growing rapidly in size and separating into small groups. Their craft and the orbital station that would be their final destination were still in the night shadow of their mother planet. "What are those lights? Are they not beautiful? Why are they growing? They seem to be moving, as if towards us" Lika again moved into Svi's arm for reassurance.

"No!" Svi interrupted, "We are moving towards them! Those bright lights are from the many newly constructed 'orbital units' placed into position since we were previously out here."

"That's not possible, to build so many, and so fast!"

"Multi Functional Integration." Svi continued to answer, "Flat packs of prefabricated parts with pre-programmed radio-magnetic permanent locking joints. Three-dimensional construction takes place as these are locked together in the void of space with no gravity. These units can be put together in an incredible short period of time. The magnetic joints almost put themselves together, with a little help by radio remote control. Parts of Zarby's team are engaged in this type of work.

"We've been away only for a few weeks, how could they build so much so quickly? There must be hundreds of thousands of them!" Lika could not conceal her astonishment. "Most of the basic parts are made back home down below. All that they are doing here is assembling them. Even the internal fittings are prefabricated, complete with internal solid-state wiring. Very little work has to be done out here. The construction of between ten to seventeen orbital units by one gang of workers in a conventional day is not unusual. Look we are nearly there. We will dock into number six, and probably won't recognize it. So much has been done in such a short time."

The window had become full of moving well-lit 'hotels' floating past. Each one seemed brighter and larger than the previous one. They were all asymmetrical and very bright in color. The effect of Noah's pleas to improve the 'fleet' of orbital space stations had obviously not fallen on deaf ears. New *'Hyper Kinetic Gyro Motors'* with accumulative thrust (*'HKG plus'*) had been installed on orbital unit six. It had become possible for the entire unit to travel at almost any speed. *It would certainly one day be able to travel at many times that of the speed of light!*

They seemed to be moving soundlessly towards the large black center of the number 'six' marking of the orbital craft that was their destination. Melodious soft music was being broadcast over the multipoint speaker system in the restaurant. The atmosphere was electric as they entered the big black hole in the oncoming orbital craft. Suddenly it seemed to be daylight outside! Lika pulled again at Svi's arm.

"That light cannot be artificial it is so bright, we nearly need sunshields for our eyes. The glare, it has the quality of full daylight. It just cannot be real!"

"Sorry, but I'm afraid it certainly is! " Svi replied, "A new system of lighting has just been installed, that uses a fluorescent gas in a sealed glass tube. The light it gives out is so brilliant and for the amount of work input required it is very economical to use."

Disembarkation would have been routine if it were not for the anxiety in Lika's heart, as she desperately wanted to make an enquiring glance in Zarby's direction. Trin had been continually on her mind during the passage into orbit, and she was thinking how successfully she had covered up her fear by throwing all her interest into the new environment that was now surrounding her. She followed Svi out of the entrance capsule into the very busy main reception and administration hall, where after a short period of questions they were finally admitted into 'Orbital Unit Six'. At this point she thought that she could afford the luxury of turning around and looking for Zarby.

In the nearby corridor there was a highly polished wall, which shone brightly almost like a mirror. Lika looked very carefully . . . she could see an urgent expression on Zarby's face as a black and silver uniformed guard reached out for the large children's gorilla doll, and went as if to pull hard at its arm. Lika screamed inside herself trying to keep control, surely that could not be Trin . . . No! She thought the doll was far too big to be their youngster. Lika was terrified for her child as the guardsman pulled even harder at the arm of the toy. He could not believe her feelings of anger and deep hurt as the arm of the toy suddenly broke away at the shoulder blade so demonstrating freely to the eyes of the guard the yellow canvas internal padding. Zarby caught the toy gorilla with urgent feeling as the guard threw it back to her.

"Here, you can sew back the arm! " The security officer shouted as he also threw back the broken limb to the nervous female gorilla.

Lika could feel the relief on Zarby's face. She was now sure that she understood how Zarby had done the deed for Trin, and was at last positive about her little girl's safety. Lika smiled to herself in a very private manner.

***

He could feel the warm wet soft sand around his naked feet. The soles of his shoes had worn away weeks before. The hybrid man now had to work in the hot humid daylight without any protective foot cover. Digging this ditch had taken three days and he had lost three friends already due to horrific cave-ins from the loose sandy walls. He knew he must not look up. His downward gaze was compulsory as his digging arms pulled away with the spade at the sand underneath him. Neyl was a hybrid man of mature years. His brown balding head still exhibited a protective margin of thickened but graying curly dark brown hair. His crown was shining, as the perspiration breaking through the sandy scalp seemed to add a gloss to his well-weathered skin. He knew what the punishment was for looking upward into the blue-grey hazy day. The desert heat was horrendous but his unending task of digging was his only salvation from the whipping and flogging that would ensue if he were to show any outward sign of flagging in his efforts to complete the trench by nightfall. Fadfagi's army of enslaved hybrids was engaged in completing a major defensive unit before the winter rains. The underground bunker had to be sealed off from the outside elements before the heavy monsoon that would come in only a few more weeks' time. The Bylean desert was renowned for its severity of changes in weather and the sudden deluge of water that will come with the pouring rains would certainly flood the deep underground bunker that would house Fadfagi's army defense headquarters.

Neyl was well aware of the reason for the urgent haste of his taskmasters to get completion of these trenches in good time for the oncoming flood. These deep dry canals were being cut out of the desert to serve many purposes, but the true value was in the collection of down pouring rainwater into underground reservoirs, and prevention of flooding. When dry, they would act as a defensive retreat and an anti-tank ditch in the case of any enemy offensive.

Thwack! Neyl felt the sudden movement of air against the side of his face. He looked carefully and slowly to his right. The body of one of his enslaved colleagues was now lying face down in the brown wet sand. Deep red blood was spurting from the side of his neck, pumping out of the carotid artery in short but violent squirts! Neyl wanted to help his friend, but knew that he could only act under orders. He let out his frustrations by digging even harder into the sand. He could see his friends dying lifeblood oozing into the bottom of the ditch around his feet. Neyl was now standing in the blood of his dying friend. He was beginning to feel sick, and knew that he would throw up. Self-control was of prime importance as he stood there in the deepening puddle of dark red blood. He never realized that so much blood could come out of someone's neck.

It seemed like ages before he heard the command from the guard. The whole area in which he was working seemed to be covered with blood.

"Put down your spade and help your stinking hybrid bastard friend to load that body thing into the trolley. We don't want any disease here, now do we? " The guard shouted into the trench at Neyl and the other hybrid who was along the line on the other side of the dead or dying body of their once upon a time working colleague.

Neyl was sure that his friend was still alive as they threw his body into the cart that would take it directly down the narrow gauge railway to be tipped into the incinerator for permanent disposal. The two hybridmen treated themselves to a luxurious moment of peaceful meditation as they watched their friend's body on its way down the gentle gradient to its hot fiery end. No sooner had it disappeared, than a shout of command came hard and fiercely from behind.

"If you don't want to feel the cold shaft of my blade, you would be well advised to get back to your digging. That's all you hybrid pigs are good for. Go on clear up the blood! Dig it into the ground and hose it down with antiseptic. We don't want you all ill do we? " The guard was almost pleasant in his manner.

Neyl made up his mind. He had been a slave for half of his life, and things were getting worse. He knew all the problems and had fought through many dangers, but *never* before had he done that which he had now decided to do. He was going to escape!

***

In the half-light of darkness the heavy iron gate of the deep underground prison cell began to move very slowly. The movement was only just perceptible, as the thick vertical bars seemed to slide in a gentle sideways direction. If it wouldn't have been for the feint grinding noise of the ball bearings running very smoothly over the well oiled runners, Girk would not have been sure whether he would have noticed that the only exit from his solitary confinement was becoming open for him. A dark stinking cell that had been his home for such a time, so long, that his life had become paralyzed in a capsule of time so far removed from reality. A human voice whispered to him from the darkness beyond. He had not heard any voice other than his own since his initial incarceration. The whisper seemed like a shout. He had self-satisfaction that even in his sudden surprise he could feel pleased that he was still quite capable of understanding the meaning of the instruction he was receiving. "Just come gently forward three steps, and stand up. You are to come with me!"

Girk lifted himself up to his full height. That was something that he had not done in these recent times. The confined space had made it very difficult for him to move around much. He cautiously stepped forward into the semi-darkness. The authority in the voice that had addressed him just then, had given him the confidence to do as he had been told.

He was certainly disappointed in himself as he walked passed the open iron gate. He thought that he would feel elated, as he would leave the cell that had been his enforced home for what seemed an eternity. He felt nothing! He could not believe it of himself. He had promised himself that he would savor that very moment when he was allowed to exit the cell into the world outside. He had just walked through the gate…and felt nothing!! He almost rebuked himself for taking freedom for granted as he meekly followed his leader without saying a single word, up a steep circular spiral staircase. Girk could feel the cold naked stone under foot as he climbed out of the dark dungeon-hole, his bare feet following its leader to the world outside.

The bright light of day was far too much for Girk. He had to turn away and cover his face with cupped hands as he felt the searing pain of daylight entering his half closed eyes.

He entered the room walking backwards, turning around instinctively when he heard a very familiar voice call his name. "Girk! Is that really you? So we have both survived! What's happened to Ludo? Velmitz called out to his friend in one very excited breath. A man dressed in dark brown uniform wearing a brown peaked cap with pale gold ribbon, called out to Velmitz . . . "Ludo? So that's what his name was. Oh he was executed a few months ago for trying to poach fur in the Mountain Woods of Varg. So he was the third one of you. What a shame we didn't know. We would have saved him for this mission to work with both of you." Velmitz and Girk looked briefly at each other with obvious surprise. This was so much to take in so suddenly, and Velmitz was certainly in the same mental state as Girk. The official continued speaking . . . "In a few moments you will both be introduced to somebody who very much needs your skills. He is going to change both of your lives in a much more useful way. Do not ever forget this opportunity that you are about to be given. To put right all the wrongdoings you have committed through most of your lives. If it were not for the intervention of this gentleman you would have served out the rest of your lives in solitary confinement in those hellholes deep underground. Of this you are both fully aware! "

The guard saw the red light above the main door of his office, and bid the stranger enter. Turning to the two prisoners, he introduced the visitor and benefactor. "Girk, Velmitz, I would like you both to meet Mr. Noah!"

***

The sudden humming noise of the facsimile machine in Jabal's inner office attracted Lex away from his daily routine. He had been placed in the responsible position of general administrator of the farm while Jabal was away visiting his half-sister Naamah. The bleeper was going which meant that the message was urgent. Urgent it certainly was!

He leaned over Jabal's desk and pulled at the extruding paper message. He nearly froze as he read its chilling words. For a brief moment Lex was very unsure how to react. Should he destroy the message or hide it? Its' nature was serious and was certainly very dangerous. After a moment or two of deep consideration, he took the message, screwed it up into a squashed ball in his hand, and then neatly squeezed it between the floor and the skirting board in the corner of the room just behind Jabal's personal filing cabinet. Anyone searching through Jabal's office even violently, should not notice it only thinking it to be waste paper. He knew he had to keep the message in tact at least until his boss had seen it, and that would not be until the next day.

Lex was very unsure how Jabal would react on hearing from Jubal with such news. He would certainly be very happy knowing that his brother was safe, but under these dangerous circumstances as a guest of the three K's! Lex was certain that Jabal would become very angry and worried.

Instinctively he instigated a major security alert. All dugout ditches, the moat, and the surrounding newly built stockade were to be looked at unobtrusively. He could not afford to wait for instruction on Jabal's return. He had to be sure of his master's security, which was under threat of an attack by the three K's, which could happen at any time.

Jabal's arrival home was uneventful, but when Lex gave him the news, Jabal kept very calm and congratulated his friend for his foresight. The fax message said it all. Jubal was well involved with the three K's and had wheedled himself into their plan for his brother's assassination. "I cannot let this threat interfere with my usual commitment to this farm, and I certainly will not interrupt my routine. I must just hope that Jubal can give me fair warning. At least he knows of my daily comings and goings. We will await his next communication!" Jabal instructed Lex with strength of manner that was full of confidence. It was three days later and early evening when the first hint of trouble reached Jabal's ears. Rastus, who was now chief Hybrid Security Officer walked into the office looking very angry. "Perimeter fence has been taken down in three places and is missing. There doesn't seem to be any damage but it needs skill and a heavy vehicle to remove something of that size. There is no trace of anything and no tracks or markings of any description. It is just as if that part of the perimeter had never been fenced. Come and look, it is quite incredible."

"No!" Lex interjected "That's possibly just what they want."

"I am going and you can both come with me." Jabal replied as if ignoring Lex's remark. "Security has to be properly maintained. We have work to do."

Working their way through the heavy undergrowth to the perimeter fence was difficult and the sweat was pouring down their bodies. The humidity was almost unbearable; the days seemed to be becoming fiercer and warmer by the hour. They had to take the old path across the overgrown area of the perimeter field, avoiding the mantraps, and mines. They could not afford to expose themselves to the open areas where they could easily be seen. They could have been walking directly into a carefully prepared ambush.

Rastus could not believe his eyes when they arrived at the first site where the fence had been removed. Everything was completely normal save for a very small carbon deposit at the base of the fence which looked well established and certainly did not appear that it had ever been tampered with at all. Very vocal protestations followed by Rastus. He was certain that this was the spot where the fence had been removed, insisting fervently that they move on to the next one. He was bewildered but determined to prove his case. The next visit proved negative likewise, as they arrived at the scene the fence again seemed never to have been tampered with. Everything was normal except for a small carbon deposit like before, close to the base of the fence. The visit to the final site yielded no more information than the first, with the exception that there were two small piles of black burnt carbon deposits neatly placed at the base of the fence post. They searched the area with keen eyes and suspicious interest but not a single footprint, tire track or any mark of any evidence that that spot had been recently visited. The ground was virgin neither a broken twig, nor any mark of outside intervention. The three pairs of feet turned about and made carefully back home. Very unbelieving and disappointed, the trio made their way back to Jabal's office. They had to reconsider their situation. If they accepted Rastus's story at face value, why was everything replaced, and with such clever careful accuracy?

***

Zarby was having great difficulty in maintaining her balance as she walked weightlessly along the edge of a very large sheet of double-thickness prefabricated cavity wall. The material was of a plastic and metal compounded mixture. Zarby's magnetic boots kept her in contact with the metallic surface, but she was having great trouble keeping her body fully erect as she walked through empty space along this extended expanse of metallic plastic wall! She was very worried that she would completely disconnect herself from the surface and could not get used to the idea of working in three dimensions, weightlessly, and with neither 'up' nor 'down'. There was no fixation point with which to establish her mind. She and her colleagues were working on the assembly of this massive structure but not a single member of the gorilla team was working in parallel with Zarby. These multi-unit cellular buildings, which came out into space in flat packs, were very easy and extremely quick to assemble. With their pre-programmed sealed magnetic permanently lockable joints, a simple assembly unit the size of a small village could be put together in hours once the pieces had all been placed into the approximate correct position in relation to each other. Zarby knew that her teams of gorillas were considered by humans to be only one step better than that of robots. She also knew that there were some people who would consider robots as more efficient than the gorilla. She had pleaded with Noah for a chance for her creed and she knew that success meant that the gorilla would have their reward of an orbital base of their own. She did not want to let Noah down any more than she would have wanted her gorillas to fail themselves in achieving their goal.

For Zarby working in the confines of orbital space was becoming very tedious for her. She knew that being outside the gravitational pull and atmospheric influences of her home planet she was technically open to move away in almost any direction. She felt like a prisoner inside that suit, which sealed in her natural environment. In her land based imaginations was always the idea that there would be a feeling of indefinite freedom when out in orbital space. The teams were working very well, this was their sixteenth session and their production rate was already ahead of schedule. So far only one major incident, when one of her male gorilla colleagues turned the wrong way and took his piece of equipment into what would be have been a permanent orbit of their sun. Fortunately they are all fitted with automatic homing beacons. It was not long before a self-functioning rescue vehicle reached him and brought him with his equipment back to the workplace sector. Zarby knew that this could not be permitted again as slapdash and careless work could cost them their part in the orbital program. The huge form of their new construction was just beginning to take its full shape. This was the dangerous time, when the shadows within the structure became very dark and it was necessary to take serious personal care until artificial illumination became available. Zarby hated the dark at the best of times but when inside one of these newly erected structures, there was not even the tiniest suggestion of half-light. One could smash into a rough edge just as easily as a polished flat wall. Robots were fitted with radar sensors, which under these circumstances did not need the light for maneuverability. Zarby's teams had been fitted with transparent radar units, which were fitted across the front of their helmet's visor. These allowed them to see in a visually enhanced manner even when no light was available. Zarby still found it a most difficult function to get used to even with weeks of training.

All the structure parts that they handled carried with them their own integral circuit structures, which meant that when the structure was finally completed, the last piece when connected would complete the circuit causing all the lights to come on, and air doors to close. Within perhaps only a few more moments, the internal functioning systems, like atmosphere, heating and plumbing would suddenly burst into action.

On this occasion the sixteenth session, Zarby was feeling quite pleased with herself as she went to the main central gallery of the new construction to meet her group for roll call.

"Gozo is missing!" came a scream from the back of the gathered group. This was the first time that one of their numbers had not checked in at the final call. The beacon was not registering, so there was no way of knowing what had befallen their friend and colleague.

***

CHAPTER 5

It's great to see you back!"

Erash called across the room to Rebecca, who was playing a form of 'Abacus', a framed ball game on the floor with Rula's son. Marla was out on a domestic errand, and Rula was enjoying the game with both of them.

Rebecca was becoming a frequent visitor to their home and she had quite attached herself to Rula's son 'Alram'. Erash always welcomed her, as she was so good to Rula and Alram. It was not uncommon for Rula and Rebecca to take Alram out on short trips together. She had become an adopted 'Godmother' to Rula's little boy and seemed to enjoy every moment that they could spend together. Erash believed that as long as this relationship was kindled, then Rebecca would always be a reliable witness and agent for them in the Fadfagi camp. He had grown to adore his 'son' of Rula and although Alram was not his child he fully accepted him as his own.

Together, Rula and Erash had chosen the name 'Alram' for the memory of Lara. His name would always privately remind them of the wonderful person who had helped them to escape to freedom. Both Rula and Lara had found love in an 'Alram'.

Erash was fascinated by the ability of Alram to play 'Bagatelle-Abacus'. It needed an understanding of counting, and a simple ability to plan ahead, and his 'son' clearly seemed to have this, even at his early pre-school age.

"Alram certainly is good at this game!" Rebecca called to Erash as he sat down on the floor with the three of them. "He must take after his father!' She continued in a seemingly innocent manner.

"Do you realize that this game is akin to one of the earliest computers?" Erash wanted to change the subject; he did not like the direction of the conversation.

"Perhaps when he grows up he will be 'Chief Secretary to the Treasury' in Science & Welfare, or even Lublia!" Rebecca continued, "He definitely has the talent."

"I don't want to push him," Rula interrupted sarcastically, "Erash's job will be good enough for him. When Erash has finished with it of course!"

The door opened, it was Marla with bags full of goodies and provisions. Alram jumped up and ran to her, throwing his arms around Marla's right thigh.

"What's for me?" He called up to the towering figure above him. "Wowee!" he yelled as he ran into the corner to eat his small piece of chocolate.

"Have you heard the news?" Marla queried, "Chaudle has just been assassinated!"

"What!!" They all shouted in reply.

"A paresifier at two paces. He was dead while still standing at the lectern. It seems that as he fell his body got caught and remained attached to the stand. It's on the National Holographic Video News now!"

The center of the room suddenly filled with people in panic, as the hologram took its shape, Erash having activated the video viewer. The commentary was continuing . . .

"*. . . . the assailant died only moments later, after exploding a poisonous tablet under his teeth. The Security Forces say that there is no reason to believe that anyone else at the scene was involved. Government sources issued a statement that this is a great loss to peace and humanity. Investigations are continuing and we will keep you infor. . . .*"

Erash turned off the set, as the scene was beginning to attract Alram's attention and it was quite grim.

"That's terrible news" Erash was almost in tears "He was a great leader." He took a breath, "and was scheduled for the International Peacemaker Prize IPP."

"He helped your firm bring my husband to Lublia on his peace mission didn't he?" Rebecca asked Erash.

"You are not meant to know that, even as Fadfagi's wife!"

Erash retorted. The air was becoming very strained.

"Yes but I go to bed with Fadfagi, you don't!" She smiled.

***

"You never told me that the embryo will develop in a stranger's body." Tubal Cain was devastated. When on the way to Methuselah's funeral he went with Tsionne for the first time to the office of Bertwin the Gynecologist nothing was mentioned about surrogacy. They just signed 'approval and responsibility' forms for 'parenthood and conception'. He had never thought to ask for a full explanation, and Tsionne always thought that Tubal had always understood what was involved.

"Do you really mean that our baby is being carried in a stranger's womb?" He repeated.

"Of course! You signed the papers?" Bertwin was amazed at this new turn of events "You must have understood what you signed. The surrogate mother has already been implanted and it would be highly unethical to destroy a healthy embryo in a willing carrier!"

Tubal Cain was a highly intelligent man, and fully understood the error of not reading before signing, he also knew on that morning with Gramps and Tsionne in tow, he could not have been completely aware of his actions when on his way to a funeral.

"I'll have to accept it," he murmured "but I am going to find it very difficult to come to terms with our baby being carried by another woman." He turned to Tsionne "Do we ever get to meet the woman who is to give birth to our child?"

Tsionne turned to Bertwin with curiosity on her face.

"Do we?" She enquired.

"Only if all three parties agree, and this woman I know, would love to meet you both, so I think it would be fine."

"OK. I go with that. It might help me come to terms with this." Tubal seemed a little more relaxed. "When?" He continued.

"Later today. The sooner that you get over this hurdle, the better for everybody!" Bertwin suggested with some apparent caution, and great deal of relief in his voice.

The atmosphere was very cordial, somewhat like a friendly business meeting. Tubal Cain and Tsionne were formally introduced to Arianne by Bertwin's personal assistant. The pregnant woman could not believe that the baby she was carrying was that of such a well-known personality and important celebrity. She gave the appearance of being slightly embarrassed and certainly somewhat timid, but as she sat down opposite the expectant couple she displayed a very trim figure and a pretty doll like face which was surrounded by beautiful thick but short curly blonde hair. She had dimples when she smiled. Tubal asked the first question.

"Have you ever done this before?"

"No!" She seemed shocked at the directness and began to redden a little in her face.

"Why are you doing this for us?" enquired Tsionne. She did not want to answer that question but thought for a moment. .

"I do not like men, but wanted the experience of giving birth to a new life." She continued as if to correct a possible misunderstanding "I have never been with a man, and am very scared of them that way, but this for me will be a fulfillment of life, a form of therapy."

"Will you be happy giving her up at birth?" Tsionne was worried.

"She is not my baby, and as long as I don't see her or hold her, then I will be happy to have been of service. Especially to such nice people. I don't want the responsibility of a child!"

"Will you be prepared to meet with us regularly during the pre-natal period that we could have a direct report?" Tubal was engrossed in the new situation and was almost beginning to enjoy it.

"Of course" she answered "I will be coming up here regularly for tests and training, and you can see me whenever you want me. After all you are the parents!"

***

Neyl could not believe his luck; the guards had all rushed away in a hurry to the nearest video screen. He was now alone in the kitchen sanitation area. He overheard one of the guards speak of an assassination of a well-known world leader. He could not afford the luxury of trying to find out more. He had to act immediately or he may never get another chance.

It was easy taking the heavy kitchen knife from the worktop. It had been carelessly left there, but it was in an area of the kitchen that normally he would not be allowed to get to, it was across the red line. Usually a guard would kill any prisoner who crossed that line, but at this moment there were no guards! He also took a fully functional breathing apparatus from the 'Fire-bucket' stand, and a large netting sack, which was hanging for meat scraps. He was lucky there too; it was almost empty.

Neyl knew his way around the building; he had been there for such a long a time. He knew every nook and cranny, and he also knew that a new meat waste sack meant that the old one was soon to be collected. Everything was quickly falling into place for his attempt to escape. The garbage truck was due very shortly as the full waste was clearly visible through the window, and was well above the full silage level and the bags had been hung out for collection.

He ran around four corridors, only stopping at each corner, in case someone would greet him. He concealed the knife in the netting bag with the breathing apparatus, which he had rolled under his arm. Still no guards, how much longer would his luck hold? He finally reached the area where the collection truck would stand, and again God must have been with him. He could hear the truck coming. Often he had been on truck duty, so he knew all the procedures. He had to hide now, before anyone else arrived to help loading.

He jumped down into the 'sump well' which was always full of thick muddy sludge. He covered himself all over and lay there motionless. He was very exposed, but only partially visible. He did not have to wait long, although to him, it was like an eternity.

As he lay there on his back in the stinking mess, the underside of the truck backed over the trench in which he was lying. It had become relatively dark in the well, and he had the full clean underneath of the vehicle to choose from. He had about seven to twelve minutes to fully attach himself to the vehicle and remain unseen. Tying the netting bag to the underside of the truck was not difficult, but getting into it was almost impossible. He kept getting his legs caught through the holes and it was beginning to become very messy, and more slippery. The smell was awful!

The engine was just starting, he was almost comfortable. Neyl had to be well secure before the truck would move down the security ramp, which was due shortly after the truck had left the kitchen yard. He would be at least three minutes under the disinfectant solution, which had a double use. First it protected the environment from the free transportation of bacteria and second, it protected the outside world from the free transportation of 'criminals'.

As the vehicle went down the ramp, Neyl managed to get comfortably fixed in the bag and his breathing gear attached to his face. He could last up to fifteen minutes on that equipment, which was only designed to get you out of a burning building in a hurry.

He was lying in the bag, back down, looking up, as the vehicle hit the liquid. He went under very fast. His big mistake was lying on his back. His mask was trying to float away; it was not designed to be worn in that manner. He managed to ram it under the net and push at it. This seemed to work. He could not use his hands easily, and on every third breath he swallowed a mouthful of bilge. He cleverly managed to avoid choking by careful respiratory management, but how long would he last?

It was certainly longer than ten minutes later when the engine of the truck started again. It had seemed like forever to Neyl, but with concentration and pure effort, he had kept his spirit going in almost darkness. He nearly lost out at the very end, as the truck surged forward and the rush of liquid disinfectant almost removed his mask.

With no warning, the air around him was clear of liquid and cool fresh dusty air was blowing up his legs as the truck gathered speed on the bumpy road. He was out of that heinous prison. He should be free, but must still be careful, he thought.

***

"I am worried about the future" Noah was talking to Velmitz and Girk on their on their second meeting, " We are losing species of many kinds as we talk, and I am looking to you for help to set some of these losses to right. It is an opinion I have, that very often the best way to do something like this is . . *'to set a thief to catch a thief'*. This may not be directly what we are doing, but you two rogues should get good results because you know your trade so well!"

The two men were openly surprised that events had turned to them in this way. Until that time, they had always hunted for gain, and certainly on most occasions they had not been within the law. Now they were to hunt for the law, and for the future conservation of endangered species. Noah continued.

"If you are successful, we will genetically clone many samples from the various creatures you bring to our 'laboratories'. We will create many replacements for the presently dying families of species with which we used to be so familiar on this planet. In fact, to help with security, and in order to be sure to keep within the law, we will be working from a gravitationalized orbital space unit with keyed in controlled environments, true for each individual creature. "

"Wow!" exclaimed Velmitz "Will we get out there to see it?"

"That depends on your results." Noah replied.

It was a busy day for Noah, he had no sooner finished with Girk & Velmitz when Tubal needed to see him, but on this occasion he was full of enthusiastic anticipation, as more results had been decoded from the previous astro-mission, and Tubal was bringing some of the latest data to Noah's office. He didn't have long to wait.

"We've done it!" Tubal burst unannounced into Noah's office. He was carrying three computer discs in his hand. He put them down on Noah's desk, taking the orange colored one and placing it into the computer drive. He flicked a few switches and then keyed in a few codes before the entire wall of Noah's office came to life with an almost three dimensional picture.

"Hey!" Noah gasped, "That was worth waiting for, where does it come from?"

He was fascinated by the large life-like image of rocky terrain under a deep blood red sky. There were creamy white clouds which enshrouded a brilliant sun that could have devoured any small planet without affecting its' volume. The ground was covered in various places by a greenish brown moss, which seemed to move very slightly in a gentle wave like manner, as if with a breeze which may well have been passing through it.

"Wait!" interrupted Tubal Cain "You haven't seen anything yet, and it gives much better effect on a three dimensional hologram."

As he spoke, Noah took a deep breath as a primitive human type creature crossed the screen rather quickly only to disappear out of the picture.

"What or who was that?" Noah could not believe what he saw.

"The truth of the fact Noah is that we have in these discs transcribed only a minute amount of the data sent from an unknown source, which could be many thousands of millions of light years away. Whatever we have found access to, is very unlikely to exist any more, and there are volumes and volumes of information for us to study, and so many pictures. It's like one long 'Video Newsreel'. Whoever transmitted these data files, certainly wanted others to see them, of that, there is no question. We have hit 'Gold'; I can't believe it!" Tubal almost had tears in his eyes. "Those primitive humans with the long hair on their head, short curly hair down their back and chest, the only bare patches on their body are under their navel, and on their hind quarters. They could look like a gorilla, but they have all the human features that distinguish them from that race. That is only part of what is on show in this program."

Tubal sat down and continued after a sip of cable juice.

"It is as if some other life form was present to take these pictures. Humans in their primitive state. No way were these humans able to do much more than create fire and make stone or metal tools. You will see them move long logs of wood by rolling them lengthways across round stones. They use a kind of rope, which they had bound or 'spun' for themselves from some type of woolly fleece. They must have only just invented or discovered the 'wheel'. It is so strange, but take these discs home and watch them on your Holographic Video with Naamah tonight. I'll bet that neither of you will sleep afterwards. There is also sound which is very eerie and strange in places, as if we hadn't transcribed it properly, but let me know what you think. I cannot believe what we have!"

Noah held the three discs and looked down at them in his hands. From where, how, and why did it come? He pondered.

***

In the mirror Methuselah could see the eyes that had greeted him every morning as he creamed his face to remove his facial hair for the day. He had known those eyes all his waking life, but now they were the only item he had left of his former identity. Every morning now, when he prepared himself for the day ahead, he found it very difficult to acclimatize himself to this 'old to new' situation.

He missed the 'old' body that he new so well, and sometimes felt quite sick when he looked at his 'new' second hand one. He had strange mixed emotions when he stood under the warm flowing water and looked into the full-length mirror, which formed the wall of his shower cubicle. It was a beautiful muscular, well-formed and obviously virile masculine body. The hair was blonde, with a touch of ginger, until of course it became wet. He could feel quite sexually aroused, and it became easily visible, when he thought about what he could do with his new found sexuality. He was always very fond of the female sex, but now all his old feelings were being revived in his new physic. He knew that he was going through a mental turmoil. A love-hate relationship with his new life. He even often felt guilty that he should be the lucky one to have taken over the previous owner's body at the expense of his life. He kept testing his memory and checking on his private and personal thoughts. It was his way of being sure that in truth he was still Methuselah, Gramps, the man his mother had brought into the world a whole lifetime previously according to all normal human measure.

The videophone interrupted his thoughts as he stood there in his shower that morning. Grabbing his towel robe, he threw it around himself as he quickly left the cubicle and pushed the nearest receive button which was not far from where he was standing. Tsionne appeared standing full length in front of him as a hologram image. She was speaking to him. How beautiful she was in her early morning robe, she had only just finished her own shower. How could she do this to him? He knew that his thoughts were wrongful, but he liked it, but she was his step-grandson's wife!

"Hi." She was smiling to 'Gramps' as she called his name again. "What are you doing today?" She enquired, "I'm all alone today, Tubal has gone to a meeting with his security officers at his southern offices, and won't be back for a few days. He asked me to get you busy with your new life. If you will excuse the expression, I was told to get you 'out of your shell'. He doesn't want you moping and miserable. He says that he understands your problems and asked me to bring you out of yourself. Tubal thinks you should rekindle some of your old interests, like farming and the land. Perhaps you could get involved in the new environmental organic approach. He wants me to take you to his section that is studying this new method in Science and Welfare. He thinks that perhaps with your skill, knowledge and experience, you could pull the department into efficient reality!"

Tsionne was very persuasive in her manner. The way she smiled and moved her body, so innocently as she spoke, she would have been able to convince Methuselah to do anything for her.

"OK" He answered without the slightest hesitation, just hoping that the heavy towel would be thick enough to conceal his innermost thoughts.

Tsionne was always correctly dressed for the occasion, and this one was no exception. Gramps was taking her to this meeting with the Environmental Dept of Chemical Farming within Science and Welfare. She looked very business-like in her creamy beige two-piece suit, of which the skirt stopped just below the knee. He thought how lovely her soft fair calves looked as they appeared from below her hem and went directly down to her matching colored shoes. Did she shave her legs, he pondered, or is she wearing stockings or tights? He nearly slapped his own face. What was he doing with his mind? This was his step-grandson's wife he had to keep telling himself!

He escorted her to his own personal hoversphere taking her arm as a grandfather would his own youthful granddaughter. He helped her to her seat, and then proceeded to take up his own seated position at her side. This he thought was going to be a very wonderful day, with Tsionne all to himself, but how would he cope with his emotions. Gramps was again in turmoil, but this time he was more inebriated, than neurotic about it. He just hoped that it didn't show.

The meeting at Science & Welfare went very well, and Gramps saw a great future in the changes he could establish in the organization. He would be keen to pursue it if Tubal agreed, especially if he could depend on help from Tsionne. The whole day he had been engrossed in the problems of Chemical Farming he had not seen a lot of Tsionne, but now he was taking her home, things again were not as they used to be.

They were two different people on their return journey, neither understood the situation that was developing between them, and neither wanted it. Gramps was hoping that Tsionne would not ask him in for a social drink after such a busy day at the office. He knew that he should refuse if asked, and although painful, he had made a firm decision, he would not allow himself to be alone with his step grandson's wife. A gentle quick family kiss on her cheek and he would leave.

Tsionne sat looking at Methuselah, as he seemed to be in unusual deep thought on the route that he was driving. She could not take her eyes away from the handsome masculine person sitting next to her. The firmness of his grip on the Hoversphere's controls, the strength of Gramps's character mixed well with the new body in which he was seated. She also knew that no way would she ask him in to her home on their return, she was resolute in her decision, she could not allow herself to be alone with him, it would be too tempting, and she loved Tubal, he was her husband. A gentle quick family kiss on his cheek and she would leave.

The craft gently came to a stop, in the early darkness of evening, just outside her home. She leaned over to give Gramps his family goodbye kiss.

"Thank you for the ride, I hope you found today worthwhile" She said, and then could not stop herself continuing as if she was not speaking her own words. They just came out unaided, completely without help. "Would you like to come in for a quick drink, I baked some fresh biscuits last night?" as if to add to the persuasion.

Gramps's mouth opened automatically without help, "Yes I'd love to!" came the reply.

***

Tears had been pouring down Lika's face when she cuddled Trin close to her chest. They had sat with Svi and Zarby in Svi's apartments 'great' room in Orbital Station number six. Lika could not believe how lucky they had been that the gorilla doll had not completely fallen apart, when the guard had pulled off the arm. All of Trin's clothes and small personal belongings were inside that doll and it certainly would have aroused suspicion. Zarby had put Trin inside their dirty Laundry basket; she slept among the towels. Trin always loved playing hide and seek, and this was just another game for her. The gorilla team was segregated when boarding the outward flight, and they had to carry their own luggage on and off. Humans could never have done such a thing as everything was packed in the cargo/baggage hold, where the atmosphere was not fit for human consumption.

It was now Svi and Lika's turn to be of help to Zarby's team, Gozo was missing, and Zarby was distressed, she was telling her friends Svi and Lika how her friend had not yet returned for 'roll call' at the end of the last work session. She seemed to be missing.

There could never be anything too difficult for Svi to offer his help on behalf of his friendship with Zarby and her gorilla people. This was one of those occasions when he felt sure that he should.

It was apparent that Gozo was very much a 'loner'. She very much enjoyed her own company and liked to work on her own. In fact of all Zarby's friends, Gozo was the one who preferred to spend most of her time in solitude. She was the thinker and philosopher, and loved working in orbit, because she could be alone and just get on with the job in hand. It was therefore not unusual for Gozo to be the last one back at the end of a work period.

Svi knew that there was an imminent major review of the Orbital System unit "Six" within the next few work sessions. Gozo had to be found before then. The station had been pre-warned already that an important event could be scheduled for the next inspection. No way did Zarby and her team want to become involved in failure. What had happened to Gozo? They were all worried! Svi and Zarby agreed that they should do their own inspection of the work volume that they were involved in during the previous work session. They should check all work sheets and data-files for the relevant period's computer entries to see if they matched. All work done was logged on the Master Computer, direct from the remote control as it was used by the engineer on site as he/she performed the required tasks of construction. If Gozo had stopped in the middle of a job, or an incident had happened, it would show against her work input data. This they decided would be the best place to start.

No suspicion of a problem arose from Gozo's returns, as her input was as usual, perfect, and finished with time to spare at the end of the session. All construction that she had been finishing was complete and firmly attached to the main module, which had become permanently annexed, and a working part of the main body of "Unit Six".

They decided to go to the new section of "Unit Six" where Gozo was last recorded as seen, and was known to have finished working only moments before closedown of that session.

They walked through a maze of new and as yet unmarked corridors following the "map track" which was the construction engineer's markings which at least informed them of where they were in the otherwise unblemished new annex which was later to be a specialist area connected to the environmental research department to which Svi and Lika were still personally involved.

The thick new walls of the newly built volume were well secure, and offered all the protection that would ever be needed from the outside void of intra orbital space. They could walk through these areas without special protective suits or breathing apparatus. There was a small percentage of gravity and temperature control was within human requirements, not too hot and not too cold. All this had been completed from a "flat-pack" in a void space, by one solitary gorilla with a remote magnetic laser control pad in one work session. The decoration would take longer than the construction. Even the plumbing, lighting, and air conditioning were all functional and put together by pre programmed remote control, which automatically registered every move onto the data base of the Master Computer. The feat of human ingenuity always amazed Lika as she marveled at the end product of one session of work in Orbital Space, and probably weeks of work of preparation, fabrication and checking back home on the mother planet.

It was Svi who found it. The remote control, the tool which Zarby had been using to put all this together, the tool which gave her access to the main frame computer, was lying there on the floor as they had turned around a corner of one of those long identical corridors.

It was still warm and still switched to "ON".

***

Weeks had passed since the perimeter fence of Jabal's farm had been damaged and repaired by an unknown source. Life had continued with a very keen sense of increased security, but no apparent incursions and certainly no hostility from outside. Jabal and Rastus were constantly keeping everyone alert to possible trouble, but peace seemed to be giving them all a false sense of security. They had only received one more message from Jubal saying that things will soon happen, and he could not be relied upon to warn them.

Not often did Naamah visit, but Jabal was exuberant that she had brought her children. Shem who was full of playful laughter was into everything and giving it to Ham to play with. Cupboard doors and wardrobes were a challenge to these two kids, whereas Japheth was a baby, much bigger than the day he was born, but still only a babe in Naamah's arms. Jabal thought that he had never seen so much concentration coming from a baby. Naamah was feeding her baby naturally while Jabal sat with her. Noah's wife had always been an environmentalist, and particularly wanted to feed all her babies the natural way. She was not ashamed of exhibiting herself in front of her half brother. For her it was quite normal.

Shem and Ham had moved unseen into the other room where there were many more cupboards with lots of doors with many exciting things inside them. Naamah and Jabal were so immersed in each other's conversation that they had not noticed the disappearance of the two boys. It was the sound of the gunshot followed immediately by Ham's crying that sent Naamah and Jabal virtually flying into the other room.

"My antique gun!" Screamed Jabal "Who loaded it?" He yelled at the two kids crawling on the floor in shock. There was a small hole in the ceiling where the bullet had embedded itself. Shem was on his knees with both hands at his head not knowing whether to laugh or cry. Ham holding his ears like Shem had curled himself up into a ball and was crying hysterically. When they both saw their mother, they ran to her as fast as their little legs would carry them. The revolver lay in the center of the room, still slightly smoking from its' recent use.

"How did they load the gun?" Jabal was mumbling to himself "I keep the cartridges in the other room." He continued in the direction of Naamah.

"There are both safe!" Naamah was almost crying herself but managed to stay composed, although the shock was evident. "I never keep it loaded, and it has not been fired for years." Jabal was bewildered. It was not moments later that Rastus with Lex and several others had burst into the room, all worried about Jabal, they were all talking and nobody was listening as the main siren started to build up gradually and then shrink away, only to re-build again in its volume. The same pattern continued as the house lights all went out and outside people started running everywhere in a somewhat pre-organized manner.

"Man trap!" shouted one of the hybrid guards. "We've caught someone or something in one of the traps identified as D12 Yellow!"

Jabal asked Lex and Rastus to go; as he felt that Naamah and her boys needed him. Lex elected to go with a small group but he insisted that Rastus and Glenshee should stay with Jabal.

It was all happening. The siren dominated the scene and the bright daylight seemed incongruous with the flashing houselights and pulsating searchlights.

Lex and his group moved slowly along the prescribed secret route through the bushy field to yellow section trap D12 out at the perimeter, not too far from the soot scarred fence. Lex looked down at the hooded Klansman, bleeding through his cloak, trapped at the waist in the metal teeth of a deadly tool.

***

Rebecca looked down on Alram as he played with his Abacus. She was very pensive as she considered that perhaps it was her fault that he existed in the first place. The facts would certainly fit. She clearly remembered 'switching' condom powders for an inert similarly colored substance when they were 'residents' in the House of Dolls in Bylia. They would have given Rula no more protection than from a common headache.

Babysitting was something Rebecca truly enjoyed; she was forming a very close relationship with this little boy. She would sit for hours with him on her lap telling him stories. He was a very bright young lad, one of his favorite stories was that of the creation, and how Adam and Eve were the first humans to walk the planet Eden. He loved the part about the apple tree. Since hearing the story for the first time he has always enjoyed eating apples. It was amazing what the driving force could be in a child's mind.

This day was a big day for Alram, he was to start school for the first time, and at midday his parents would be home to collect him, as on this day he was only going for the afternoon for investigative programming. Rula, Marla, Rebecca, and Erash were all going with him. Erash was going to make a holographic home video of the entire event.

Apart from the family interest for Erash and Co. the afternoon turned out to be a non-event. Erash took video of them arriving at the school. He took pictures of the impressive gates, large and very imposing. He lay down on the ground outside as he took pictures for posterity, the big gates opening for the 'little boy'. Erash had in mind to do the same when his 'son' left the school as a late adolescent or young man, showing the gates from a slightly different angle, diminished in size against Alram a then much larger, taller animal.

Rula found the cranial scanning the most perturbing; they entered a white fully tiled room in the basement of the school building, which was also its' medical quarters. In the center of the room was a bed on which Alram was laid down, and invited to look up at the ceiling where there was an animated three dimensional hologram to entertain him and keep his attention. Two matching electronic magnetic blocks lifted up out of the floor and placed themselves at either side of his head at each ear, not quite touching contact. There appeared a strange image on four old-fashioned computer screens, like on an old televideo screen. The lines on two screens were red, and on the other two screens they were blue-green a kind of turquoise.

After taking great care and many readings from the equipment, the nurse-technician touched a green illuminated button on the instrument panel, and all four screens showed the same mixed picture of red lines alternating with the turquoise. A very difficult image upon which to focus one's eyes. The paramedic gently pushed at the top of a pad that looked like a rheostat, and the pictures faded to white, and then black and white as the lines returned. She again pressed, but at the bottom of the pad and the lines disappeared again giving white screens right and left.

"That's done!" The nurse said, as she took her notes and a printout. Then turning off the machine, apologized for its antiquity, and explained that it was all that the school could afford. She told them not to be concerned as she had all the information that she needed, to order a personal headset, for the direct input of educational knowledge into the memory cells of Alram's brain. He had registered a very high reading on the Encephalate Chart, and would very easily be able to take in large volumes of experience and knowledge. He could accept very high-density training systems. He should be completely programmed in early work of reading, writing, and arithmetic by the end of the following week. The teaching staff would be able to assess how long it would take to train him to use his newfound knowledge. Some children take a year, but normally it is a quarter of that, but this nurse thought it would only be a matter of weeks, as he seemed so bright.

***

Tubal Cain and Noah were almost falling asleep from exhaustion. They had been reviewing the entire security program during the years since they had been *'Revenue Inspectors'* in the early days of leakages in 'Subterranean 26'. Everything pointed to a major dangerous conspiracy to create a destructive weapon of such enormous proportions that whosoever was the owner, would be able to hold the entire planet to ransom. The name of 'Pollo' kept re-occurring. It was very strange, she had been positively identified as the person brought from Bylia in the boat with Rula and Erash from the 'House of Dolls'. She had since been reunited with her frozen, but living hand, which she had previously lost in 'Subterranean 43'. Yet she is still quoted in coded messages and still gives orders, and amends instructions to those out in the field of Bylian subterfuge. There must be another "Pollo ". Perhaps 'Pollo' was just a trade name.

The two tired men decided to take a break to discuss the events as they saw them. They agreed that if it were possible to find the new 'Pollo', and catch her then she would only be replaced again. The only way to tackle the problem was to locate her or him, and plant a 'bug' in his or her body so that security would always be up to date with the enemy camp. Erash would be the ideal person to send on such a mission. 'Pollo Two' should not be difficult to find.

Internal security had to be tightened. Leaks and losses had to be sealed. Tubal remarked to Noah that their losses were so regular that they might well have had their own internal mail service to Bylia. Postia was only filtering the thefts. The goods were getting there regardless. Although in very small quantities at any one time, it was so regular it soon added up to a very dangerous picture!

When Noah and Tubal Cain got together and spoke business they always made decisions, as best they could, that way they could prove it was worth the effort.

"We are due to test the new engines! " Noah announced to Tubal as if just to change the subject, "Shall we go together to observe?"

"I was scheduled to go anyway " Tubal Cain replied with enthusiasm in his voice. He acknowledged the pressure and effort that Noah put into achieving this momentous advance in astro-engineering. Noah had worked very hard and Tubal admired him for his character and resolution. Never taking 'No' for an answer from any quarter.

Finally they would try the new super gyroscopic exhaust emitting power source. This would be driven by a mixture of solar and vacuum energy, a form of nuclear fusion. The early engines were small and proved very difficult to trial, because they reached such speeds from which they could never be retrieved, and the return radio signals were still coming but less distinct, and the early engines only reached a speed of twice to three times that of light relative to their source of origin.

The new engines were to be tested with people on board. These engines were mark 4 in the third series, and had been previously tested on a large space observatory slightly smaller than the engines themselves. There were no people on that trip, but everything was pre-programmed to return after the equivalent of three days out from their mother planet. After those three days the vehicle returned to Orbital Space and the deceleration was as spectacular as the initial acceleration six days previously. The internal video viewers that looked backward to the home planet proved to be useless, as the image just shrunk to a spot and disappeared almost immediately after the initial acceleration. With picture enhancement back at base the image was improved, and pointed to some very interesting possibilities for the next generation of 'on board' viewer video camera. These were to be on the next trip, complete with multi magnification picture enhancement.

This would mean linking the speed of travel from the source of origin, the orbit of the mother planet, to the magnification or enhancement of the image produced on the viewing screen. This way, however far they were from the origin of their journey, the image of the mother planet would appear still the same size on the screen. It would just become slightly dimmer as the resolution became less, effectively as the real image was shrinking. An added benefit would be selective enhancement, which would mean that at any moment in time, a section of the image of the mother planet could be seen in the best possible detail. The new technology has increased screen resolution to microscopic proportions. From orbital space it was now possible to read a label on a standard cable juice bottle or recognize somebody's facial features even without much enhancement.

Tubal Cain and Noah both knew the risks of going on this trip. If there was a disaster there would be no person left to that could lead the way. After much consideration and discussion it was decided that the Chief of Science and Welfare, Tubal Cain would go to observe, and Noah should stay behind to guide the mission into the future if any unfortunate event should occur.

"I go tomorrow!" Tubal smiled at Noah "Two days out we turn to come back. OK? We will be away for four days!"

"I am sure that neither of us will sleep!" Noah replied

***

Neyl could smell sea air as the garbage truck pulled to a stop. It was waiting in traffic. They must have reached a busy town, he could see wheels of many vehicles around him, and they were all very dusty and well worn. This was certainly not an area of opulence. Neyl decided that he dared not wait for nightfall to leave his safe enclosure; he had to drop out before the truck reached its compound, or he would likely find himself a prisoner in a new jail, the waste disposal dump which he also knew to be secure from intruders. He vaguely remembered being told once a long time previously that the dump was just outside a town called 'Politir'. They were now in a town, so surely they would soon leave it. He would have to act fast! They were moving again. He just prayed that they would stop a few more times and somewhere useful.

He had loosened the netting and was lying suspended, looking down and backwards, having managed to turn over in his resting place. The truck was stopping again and there was not any vehicle behind, they had just turned a corner. This was a good time to go for it. He pulled the knife quickly through the netting strings that were attached to the truck's underside and did not have far to fall. He still felt the impact of the ground with the lower part of his palms and his wrists. He lay flat on the ground for a brief moment, as if it belonged to him personally. He kissed it and with his heart pounding in his chest, rolled over fast two or three times until he reached the small drainage ditch at the side of the road. Had he been even half a roll later in his movement he would have been crushed under the large rear wheels of the truck.

Standing up was an effort, and he had cramp everywhere especially behind his knees, but he had to move fast. He casually, but as speedily as was possible under the circumstances walked around the corner of the building out of view of the truck, and then he ran.

He knew that he looked a dreadful sight. He could see his reflection in the shop windows as he ran. His prison blue kitchen overalls were almost unrecognizable as they were caked in engine oil and dried-on bilge water. He must have had a very distinct aroma about him. He was amazed that nobody seemed to care as he ran through the streets as if on a jogging exercise. He kept always to the edge of the pavement and sometimes ran in the gutter of the road. Following signs to the seafront was not difficult and fortunately he didn't have far to go before the soft hazy blue horizon appeared to his view. That magic line that separated his planet from the sky, and went from side to side across his vision. He had not seen that since he was a child. Even now it held the same fascination for him as its sharpness and expanse made its own statement to him that even as freedom was now his, God still held him prisoner within the confines of that thin sharp edge of vision itself.

He climbed down the rocks and into the water fully dressed. The sea felt very cooling but also warm. His captivity just seemed to float away in the muck and grime that appeared to come out of his clothing as he swam a little, then submerged and re-surfaced. Although the surrounding water was certainly not pure and hygienic, it held for Neyl the meaning of new life and a freedom that no one *anywhere* could have appreciated as much as he did. He felt salt in his eyes, but he was not sure if it was seawater, or, the fact that for the first time since he was a child, he was crying real tears. He was so happy, so very happy, he knew his mum was with him, and his dad would have been so proud.

He lay back in the water and looked up at the sky. One day, he thought, one day I'll make it up there too!

***

Methuselah was late for his meeting. He had waited for Tsionne for longer than usual, he was concerned that they should leave as soon as was possible. It was becoming almost a regular habit for him to collect Tsionne on his way to work whenever he was going to his office. At last she appeared, her full figure contributed significantly to the shape of the clothes she was wearing. Gramps could not take his eyes off her. He was becoming very emotionally attached to his granddaughter-in-law in a manner that was not healthy. To date they had been very well behaved with each other, although the mental torment was something that they were both beginning to 'share', as they kept themselves apart and yet continued to want each other's company using any excuse.

Tsionne was again wearing a skirt, pale green, and pleated to a hem just below the knee. She knew that Gramps never liked her in trousers, and she also knew that her legs were very much her asset. She did not know why, but she always wanted to arouse her 'Gramps' although she knew that that was very unfair to both of them.

He could smell the soft gentle scent of her perfume as she sat down beside him in the hoversphere. How could she do this to him? He loved it, but how long before he would have to 'explode'? His underwear was beginning to become too tight for him. This was all wrong, he kept thinking, as Tsionne reached for his hand and pulled it towards her thigh. She gripped the hand tightly in her's and she spoke . . .

"Tubal is off today to Orbital Space. They are testing out the new engines and he will be away for the next few days, probably five. He is going with Noah, but Tubal will be on board the test craft and he is so excited, he doesn't stop talking about it. That's why I was late this morning; Tubal was on the videophone. Our holograms were saying goodbye to each other as he takes the next shuttle."

Methuselah was not really listening to Tsionne as she spoke, all he heard was 'Tubal is off for four or five days' and that meant that Tsionne would be alone!

"Let's not go to the office today" Gramps said without even meaning to. The words just came out of his mouth as if self propelled. He had to make a correction and quickly, he continued . . .

"Why don't we call on Arianne and see how the *baby* is progressing?" . . . he thought that may do the trick.

"Tubal went yesterday on his own, yes why not." she replied almost with the same lack of vocal control. What for did she want to see Arianne at the moment, she looked over to Methuselah and gripped his hand tighter to herself and smiled.

Their meeting with Arianne was uneventful and very artificial. Tsionne felt very close to Arianne when she thought about it, when she was with her, and that also reminded her about her husband Tubal whom she still loved as always, but this *feeling* with Gramps was much more physical, and so completely different. She did not feel guilty when with Arianne, that she desperately wanted to get back to the hoversphere with Gramps.

Tsionne could not believe how she was becoming completely disassociated with the memory of old Methuselah as he was and she only now saw Gramps as a 'new person' in that young man. For her now, old Methuselah seemed to have died when his old body was buried not so long ago. This 'new' man whom she was with could be becoming in her mind only a distant cousin of her husband. Tsionne wanted to pinch herself in order to bring her emotional wanderings back to reality, as together they agreed to make the rest of the day a family day afloat, away from the hubbub of their usually crowded day.

She sat down at the back of the boat, and without thinking pulled her skirt well above her knees to allow her thighs some fresh air, as Gramps took the oars and placed them in their rowlocks. He sat facing Tsionne and as he leaned forward, placed the blades in the water and pulled backwards he was given a full view of Tsionne's greatest assets. His underwear was becoming tight once more as they moved well out into the center of the very large lake.

***

CHAPTER 6

Tubal Cain and Noah did not even notice their journey out to Unit 6 Orbital Space; they had so much to talk about. Tubal was again explaining what the new engines would do to their knowledge of speed and he was drinking in the reaction of Noah to the computer video discs, which he had watched the night before. Noah was also absorbed in the *'luggage'* he was taking to environment research and could not contain himself with telling Tubal about it. He was taking the first genetic seeds, which were the result of Girk and Velmitz's exploits in the South Western Continental rain forests. They had found some early forms of a living mammal that were becoming extinct. Noah had frozen sections of recently dead examples of this group in order to recreate the genetic structure of their species in orbital space.

He also had three living Giant Pandas in a large case. Only one was male, but he was going to be busy. This was to be a test case, to prolong another dying breed, about to become extinct by man's inhumanity to his mother planet. Noah was consumed with all the different re-creations he would make in orbital space to regenerate dying species from the planet below.

The video hologram was something else. Noah could not digest all that it contained, but for him, the most striking feature he kept thinking was 'who filmed it, and whose technology transmitted it? Will they ever find out? He wondered. The data was still coming in, although from a distance so far away, its' origin would likely have all disappeared by now. Noah had agreed with Tubal to have another more detailed viewing of the discs, and the updated version would be transmitted to them from ground base as they arrived at Unit Six.

It was a long time since Noah and Tubal had visited Unit Six, and as from the distance they approached the *'building'* they were surprised by its new size in relation to the many surrounding satellites from their mother planet. The new engines had been fitted, and proportionately they were nearly a third of the volume of the whole of Unit Six. The final connections and checks had only been made two days prior to their arrival. Noah could not easily come to terms with the enormity of everything. He knew that the construction of everything from *'flat pack'* form was fast, safe and efficient, but he was secretly worried that perhaps everything was happening *too fast* to be safe.

The new 'Engine Volume' as it was called, was so large that it even contained its own self supporting living and recreational areas for the engineers who had to maintain and care for its ongoing function. A whole new world had been added to Unit Six, another fifty per cent of its original size. Noah and Tubal sat glued to the window of their shuttle as they pulled in towards the entrance port for disembarkation. Unit Six was certainly the largest Orbital Station yet under construction, now that the new engines had been added.

After disembarkation, they left the enormous galleried reception hall and entered the internal monorail, which would take them to the navigational area at the nucleus of the main epicenter of whole station. It sat, a silver dome, perched, like a protruding bubble centrally, from within the structure and with wonderful views of the entire station.

The view from the main control dome was awesome. There was half gravity and therefore they could appreciate *'up' and 'down'* which seemed to add to the quality of the panorama that greeted them as they entered the command center.

Down below was a small city, which could be seen in perfect view in all directions as Noah and Tubal, walked around the perimeter walkway of the circular observation center. As they looked upward, they had a perfect view of their mother planet in all her glory. It appeared as a large blue-white image with attractive swirling cloud patterns and very little exhibition of the land masses that lay underneath, although the icy poles were evident and their appearance at the upper left and lower right could give the impression that the planet was almost nothing else but covered in ice and cloud.

Careful examination of the cloud formation did show the occasional greenish brown land mass underneath, but the blue of the seas was a more common feature. Their planet above them was at midday and gave strong reflected light onto orbital station six below. Noah and Tubal Cain were both seasoned travelers into orbital space, but seldom had they the time to contemplate the stark sharp beauty that so vividly presented itself.

Tubal suggested to Noah that as they had some time to spare before countdown started for the test, perhaps they could review the holographic discs that they had seen separately, and view the up-dated data that was being received as they spoke.

They were completely absorbed in the holographic video presentation of life many millions of light years away when their concentration was broken, as the doors opened behind them and a control center messenger interrupted their thoughts . . .

"The test is delayed for two days as there have been some technical problems. More information will be available soon." He apologized and disappeared back from where he had come.

"I must let Tsionne know or she will worry!" Tubal decided to contact her by televideo, it would be early evening at his home now and she should be back from work.

He dialed the code and the answer came so quickly, even faster than if he had called her from the same street. Tsionne was looking very feminine, sitting in her bathrobe on the reclining couch with a drink in her hand. She was certainly very relaxed.

"Hi" Tubal said, "I am delayed for at least two more days, there is a technical problem. What kind of a day have you had?"

"Oh, a bit different, and I called on Arianne, I didn't get much done today!"

After some affectionate marital pleasantries Tubal had already said goodbye and the hologram was beginning to fade, when he was sure he saw a very casual looking Gramps appear in the background.

***

Svi was worried about Gozo. Since her disappearance, security had been tightened and extra checks were made on all working engineers. Zarby was most concerned that the loss of her pal could reflect on the quality and dependability of employing gorillas, she somehow believed that Gozo was still alive, and that she would still turn up. Gorilla people had very deep extra sensory perception far greater than that of humans, and she knew that Gozo was still among them, in thought, if not in deed. She kept wanting to return to the place where Svi had found her remote control device, and at last she had persuaded him to go with her.

He was a very busy man, Svi had new plant being delivered in to his new genetic investigation Section, and also things were becoming hectic in the human environmental research unit as the monitors had previously to be adjusted for the dangers of high speed travel. They were soon to test the new engines; countdown was only two hours away. Svi still found time for his old friend; he could never let Zarby down. She was so very dear to him and he so desperately wanted to help her find her lost friend.

The gangways and corridors seemed endless, and all very identical, but Zarby knew exactly where she was going and moved with great agility and speed. Svi had his map of the new section, which was still not marked out locally yet, but Zarby was going the correct route without help. Svi was impressed, and when he asked her how come she knew the way so well, Zarby just answered that she knew Gozo was there, and she could feel her in her own thoughts and knew exactly where to go.

Always Svi had been skeptical about 'ESP', extra sensory perception as it was called but if it were possible this was surely a case to prove it. He had some friends who were very well capable of producing the effect, and he knew that Noah and his wife shared a very strong ability between them. He understood that it was common knowledge.

They hurried through the corridors and Zarby jumped down stairwells as in half gravity and with her ape-like talent she could really move. It was pointless really, because she still had to wait for Svi, who although hurrying, could not keep up with Zarby.

She shouted back to Svi that Gozo would be around the next bend as she turned the corner and ran face first into a solid wall. At that point the corridor had a double bend in it and Zarby was not used to that, as it was not the usual pattern of things. She reeled, and then as Svi caught up with her, she ran further down the new corridor at full speed, soon only to turn around and run back to Svi who was not far behind her.

"We've gone pissed her I veel!" Zarby appeared shocked, as if she had seen a ghost. "Plees Meester Svi, plees, I know dat she is very close to here. I feel her mind is talking with mine, in my heed. I know, I know, I know!"

Zarby was almost hysterical, as the lights in the corridor flickered twice, then some gassy steam burst forth from three or four fittings along the corridor, it all went dark, coupled with a distinct smell of burning, and unknown to Svi and Zarby the entire section was now in darkness!

***

There was blood everywhere, Lex had done all he could to bring the dying Klansman back to the house without too much loss of blood, but still it oozed forth, even through the latest new absorptive thick plastic toweling in which they had wrapped him.

Jabal's home was not unused to substituting for a hospital, and there were many available features within, which could help the injured soul. He was in a bad state, and his wounds were almost critical. They desperately wanted to keep him alive and useful. As a source of information he would be invaluable.

There were no more problems, and the alarms were quiet, everywhere was calm. Lex had ordered that a constant security watch be maintained and strict observation and control was to be observed over the patient who was now in their care. As soon as he was coherent he was to be questioned.

Naamah had suggested that they contact Erash through Tubal Cain's office. They should enquire if they could borrow one of the new experimental debriefing modules that downloads the human brain. It was still not proven as safe, but under the circumstances they could use it to copy data out of their captive's mind.

It was daybreak the following morning when the Hoversphere from Science and Welfare arrived. It was carrying the new highly sensitive encephalic scanning device, which would be connected through a headset to the Klansman's brain. Within half an hour he would be ready for output. The system worked very much in the reverse manner of the version commonly used to load information from the educational headsets used in schools and colleges. Input was relatively easy, but download was not yet fully proved, and also there was no certainty that the brain's existing data would not be damaged by stray impulses. The final tuning for taking out information could prove slightly dangerous!

Noah had been on the televideo phone to Naamah from Orbital Unit Six and had told her of the delay in testing of the engines. Although disappointed that Noah would be away for longer, it meant that she could stay with her brother a few more days. She was pleased because it was a difficult time for Jabal and he seldom got to see her children. Also she was very curious to see how the process of downloading would work.

She stood at the back of the room as one of the hybrid nurses placed the headset around the ears of the dozing patient. She watched the screens of the video monitors as the colored diffraction lines were balanced in order to set up the correct wavelength and frequency of the output. Then when all the screens were pure white the technician gave the 'Go' sign and touched the starting mode. There was a feint zig-zag flash across the screens and they again went pure white.

The patient began to slumber and move as if in a deep sleep. The two discs in their drives bleeped rhythmically as they drank the information being fed into them. The task seemed so simple, so normal, and yet Naamah knew that this process was a significant step into 'future—world' technology. She was wondering whether she could come to terms with the morality of such an event. Could it be right? It was certainly necessary, in this instance, to delve into a man's innermost thoughts and nakedly print them out onto a piece of paper. Human privacy was rapidly becoming as historic as nature itself.

Fear and astonishment appeared on the faces of Lex and Naamah as they read into the initial data out-printings from their captive's brain. Some of the information was garbled and most of it was of no significance, but generally there were indications of serious dangers ahead!

It was the sound of the child firing the gun that had apparently brought this Klansman out of hiding into the grounds of Jabal's farm. He was expecting a gunshot as a signal to advance. He had fallen asleep on 'scouting guard watch' and had awoken to what he had been trained to believe was the launch of the major attack. It appeared that the alarms and the lights caught his colleagues unprepared and as there were only three other Klansmen in the vicinity at that time the others must have run for their lives.

It transpired that the three K's were out to destroy Jabal and all he represented. They would be *returning in force* very soon!

***

As Neyl lifted himself, refreshed, out of the water he knew that the first action he had to take was to get fresh clean clothes and perhaps something to eat. He also knew that these were of prime import if he was somehow to reach out and escape across that sea. He would never be safe in Bylia. His face would be everywhere within another day.

Once dried out, food was easy, there was a roadside restaurant just along the road, and he had decided to visit it through the tradesman's entrance around the back. He had to put his clothes on inside out and they looked very non-descript, the green beige lining gave him a different character, that of a delivery man, rather than that of an oily mechanic.

Outside the rear of the restaurant there was a delivery van, which had just left several sacks and packages in the loading bay. There was nobody around, Neyl carefully managed to drop his hand through the very narrow clipped opening of one of the sacks. It was a grainy type of flour. He took some and tasted it. Inedible as it was, he used it as a form of camouflage throwing it carefully all over his clothes and some in his hair.

He walked directly into the main Kitchen. There was only one person in there, a cook or a baker, a plump and heavy man in a white coat. He had thick graying hair and was certainly in no need of a meal himself.

"I've left everything in the loading bay, but I'm a bit of a mess, one sack was slightly open!" Neyl informed the young man whose hands were deep in dough almost up to his elbows. He was kneading it for a kind of bread that he was baking.

"You look a mess!" The baker mouthed across to Neyl, "Your boss has gone up to accounts department to get paid. Sit out in the front shop and I will give you a coffee. Put on this white coat, you'll look better. Let me have it back with next week's deliveries, clean!" He emphasized as he guided the slightly cleaner looking Neyl out into the restaurant.

"Sit down at the back. You've definitely got a short wait. Please help yourself to the salad buffet." The man spoke in short phrased sentences, "Your boss always takes a while. I think he fancies the girl in accounts! He always spends time with her and *I* think they've got something going together!"

Neyl could not believe his luck, and placed himself with a full plate of food and some fresh fruit juice into a very unobtrusive section at the back of the restaurant. He *was* hungry, and the food was excellent. Having no problem emptying his plate in a very short time, he went back to the bar and took some nutrient packs for later, then quickly departed back through the kitchen.

"I'll wait in the truck." He called to the baker who was busy emptying the freshly baked bread from the oven.

Neyl had only just exited into the loading yard as the driver came down to the bakery. If the man had been a moment or two earlier he would have seen Neyl walking away up to the sea front road. He was walking in the direction of the port of Politir where he needed a boat ride.

It was dark when Neyl arrived at the first small harbor, which mainly consisted of fishing boats. He knew that they where of no use to him. They were slow and there would never be a secure place for him to hide. He believed that somehow he needed to 'acquire' something faster and easier to 'drive'.

Neyl felt sure that God was with him, he was positive that his purpose for life was soon to be shown to him. Why did he feel that he would so surely find his way? He was almost singing to himself as he walked along the sea wall looking at the small boats moored beneath him.

He was attracted to a small smart blue Hovercraft with a green skirt and silver trim, which was tucked into a small turn in the harbor wall. Parked on dry land, and powered by engines that he had been trained to build and maintain in his youth. He knew that this was to be his way out of Politir.

There was nobody about and the vehicle was well concealed from any intruding observer, nestled in the dark shadows of the wall. He would have the ability to get the craft moving before anyone suspected trouble.

Getting on board posed no problem, and to his surprise, the interior was immaculate, he could not believe his luck. There were dust covers over everything and the craft was clearly very well maintained. There was an aura of care and attention about the place that was personal to someone who loved it and cared for its' being. The craft was quite old and yet had all the latest equipment. Neyl had worked for many of his luckier early years in servitude as an engineer in engine and body design. He was very familiar with the drives that gave the power to move this heavy bulk out across the water. He was in the cockpit, and the only light that he could afford to use was that of the computer screen. Everything was in working order, even the 'on board' satellite guidance system was in excellent condition. It was so simple that even a baby could fly this thing out to sea.

Getting it started was easy. It only needed a computer password, which was for Neyl easy to find. He had also been well trained in computer techniques, and by throwing out the data directories and turning them around, he soon found the password after a very short process of elimination. The whole system for 'drive' was controlled by the simple keyboard, which was built in to the pilot's desk. He felt like a master in his own world for the first time in his life.

[Enter], backspace, control and shift with F2 and the engine program appeared without problem. The instructions had been written on a panel next to the screen, as if to remind someone how to get to it.

He went to the 'log' and charted out the direction he wanted to go, this course would be steered under autopilot at maximum speed after leaving the harbor. Again he pressed [Enter]. He was now locked into a path, which he hoped would be his *'future'*. He typed the password *'marine'* and the screen offered him three choices "Go" "Wait" or "Cancel". "Wait" was flashing. He looked around to see if all was clear, and gently touched "go" on the screen, which immediately changed to offer "manual" or "auto". He chose "manual", and gently eased forward on the "throttle" lever and the vehicle began to rise on its apron. He loved the feel of power as he eased the steering over to the right and gave a hint of more power to the engine as the craft moved gently down the slow slope on to the water, lapping at its skirt. He did not know the exact moment when he was above the water, or when he had left dry land, but he gently eased the craft out into the thoroughfare of the harbor waters and around the beacon which was perched like a muted quacking duck on the end of the sea wall.

Pointing the nose of the vehicle out to sea, he changed the computer mode to "auto". He could not believe how smoothly everything had happened. Not a murmur from anyone, no flashing blue lights, and no break in his radio silence, which he had left in the 'open to receive' mode. Neyl decided that he had ample capability to travel wherever he wanted, as this old amphibious vehicle would never need to refuel. It survived on stored up solar power, which never needed much replenishment, and as it was partially powered by nuclear fusion, the motor was highly efficient; it was the nearest thing to perpetual energy.

He considered this to be an excellent time to take a well-earned rest, and went for the first time to the door marked "private quarters". As he walked through the door the galley kitchen was on his left and the washing facilities on the right, there were only two cabins for sleeping and only one was usable, the other was laden with sealed boxes neatly stacked and tied, taking up a major volume of the room. It was only the layout of the boxes that gave a hint to the fact that possibly two people would usually sleep in that cabin.

He went to the adjoining room in which there were four bunk beds and climbed into one of the lower ones in the half-light from the corridor. He lay there listening to the soft whirring of the engines, which were almost more difficult to hear than the water rushing past under the canopy skirt on which they were riding. Although there was an almost hypnotic effect, within not many moments he was almost in an unconscious sleep. He was exhausted!

Nobody could have remained asleep, when being bitten so deeply on the shoulder blade. Neyl turned around in the half light of morning, and with explicit shock on his face he quickly remembered where he was, and could not understand how such a beautiful woman could bite so hard, especially with her hands tied together so tightly behind her back.

***

The incoming transmissions of the discs were now in holographic format, and Tubal with Noah were completely absorbed in their content. The panorama was from millions of years previously and yet there in the middle of their viewing room were the images of primitive man as if it would be happening at that moment. Noah felt that he wanted to reach out and touch the grunting human on his slightly hairy shoulder as he sat there eating some form of dead cooked animal. He was crouched at the edge of a small fire around which at least three adults and a child sat in a likewise manner, keeping him company and enjoying the good feast.

"There is no technology here!" Tubal commented, "How and who took these pictures? They are of such high definition and are three-dimensional. No primitive man could produce this effect!"

"That's what struck me most of all!" Replied Noah to Tubal without even a moment's removal of his gaze from the ancient images of a prehistoric human being.

Not long after finishing their eating, two of the group moved backward slightly, away from the fire, and after a few preliminary gestures and plenty of foreplay the two people exhibited in full view of all who would have been present in that viewing room, a procreative sexual act which carried forward to the very climax of its end. Neither Noah nor Tubal could pull their disbelieving gaze away, as the muscular young man and extremely well formed beautiful, also muscular young woman had intercourse in front of them, in the viewing room. They had full view of all working parts and all the necessary sound effects. Both Noah and Tubal could feel their sensuous manhood arise in full strength from within their groins. In fact Tubal felt distinctly uncomfortable, his underclothes had become too tight!

By the end of this explicit session, both Tubal and Noah were exhausted from their experience.

"We can't show this to the committee can we? " Smiled Noah.

The view of the subject on the hologram faded away only to introduce a new panorama of triangular buildings with their apex at the top pointing to the sky. There were humans around the base of these 'temple' like structures, which if these humans were of about the same size as Noah, would make these triangular edifices of gigantic proportions.

"Look those humans are of a more evolved structure and they seem to be more developed. They seem to be more like us, walking more upright but they have more hair on their bodies. I do believe that they are also less sprightly in their actions. This must come from a much later period of their genetic evolution, perhaps many hundreds of thousands of years. How did they do that?" Tubal was completely absorbed in the reality of the past.

"Who took those pictures? Who had the technology, and where was all this taking place?" Noah replied with just as much astonishment in his voice.

The two men were completely involved in the three dimensional visions of what could easily have been the prehistoric and more recent history of the human race in a documentary form. Where and how these wonderful visions were in their possession was also in the back of both of their minds. They were received in transcriptions from radio signals that must have been sent many hundreds of thousands, possibly millions of years previously, from an unidentified source, which no longer seemed to exist. Whoever made these recordings probably also no longer existed, but certainly they were meant for somebody somewhere at sometime in the then distant future of whosoever originated them.

"It appears," Noah whispered "that this could be a documented program of human development, but why . . .?"

"Look!" Tubal interrupted and pointed at the hologram. . "Those men on horseback fighting a battle with long curved knives in that field. Some have ropes with a metal ball on the end. Did you see that? He let it go after spinning it over his head. Ugh! It's vile; his victim just lost his head when it tangled around his neck. The blood is everywhere!"

Noah was shouting "A motorized vehicle, self propelled! At this rate we will be up to date in a very short while!"

"What do you mean *up to date?*" Tubal corrected him, "This happened about a million years ago, *or more!*"

"Yes" Noah agreed, "but not here!"

Suddenly there was a horrific flash of light that lit up the entire room as a mushroom shaped cloud appeared in the center of the viewing area and the hologram disappeared.

Noah and Tubal looked at each other in shocked disbelief.

***

Not very often did Svi and Lika get the opportunity to spend their working day together, but this was one of those rare occasions and they intended to enjoy every moment of it. They were both working on different projects, but it meant them both studying the development of the human environmental research unit. Svi was working on communication and Lika on psychology of the development of the human unaided by exterior modern influences.

"That little girl, she must be quite intelligent." Lika was pointing to a little blonde girl who must have been one of the oldest inhabitants within the unit. The young female was washing herself in the clear waterfall of the gently moving stream that wandered and meandered across the panorama that was visible from the viewing window set within the rocks of a very natural habitat created specifically for these purposes. The little girl showed all signs of developing into a beautiful well-formed young woman. Her breasts were no longer just flat nipples, the volume just an early suggestion but her figure was already enhanced by their appearance. There was no personal modesty as she washed and hummed an unintelligible melody to herself and all to hear. She was very happy as she soaked in the beauty and splashed away in the water of the rock pools around the base of the narrow waterfall.

Her happiness was to be short lived, as around the corner of the rocky glade, another equally aged naked youth appeared, who obviously wanted to 'play' with her in the water. He approached her unseen and unheard from behind and splashed water all over her youthful naked body.

She was caught unawares and turned around. On seeing the expression on his face and the manner in which he was coming at her, the playful atmosphere around her changed to shocked fear as he threw her down into the water and started to pass his hands all over her naked wet body. The young lad was consumed with an unknown desire, which he was desperate to fulfill. The wet fiery struggle continued for a long while and both parties were beginning to bleed in different places as their bodies were often grazed by the rocky surfaces in and around the winding stream.

A third party suddenly arrived at the scene, a youth of similar age also unclothed, and apparently ready to join in and *'play'*. As soon as he was close enough to see what was happening, his manner changed from playfulness to aggression. He ran into the foray and pulled at the hair of the other male from above and behind. The first male had overcome the girl and was pushing her head under the water as if trying to drown her. The new arrival now had him in an arm lock around his neck and was forcing him to release the girl. It was many moments before the partly bleeding youth released her free into the water.

While the fight continued with her savior holding her still struggling aggressor from behind she stood up in the water, and in anger ran hard at him, as he was facing her, and with full force pushed her right knee hard into his genitals. He yelled so loud that maybe it would have been heard at the far end of Unit Six. Even Svi recoiled as in his imagination he felt the implosion between his own legs.

"Wow!" Svi voiced with involuntary movement from his lips. "Did you see that?" Lika whispered to Svi. "That young guy offered protection to the girl. He may have saved her life. Surely that puts them a touch above real animal status?"

They continued to watch as the young rogue hobbled, then turned and ran from the scene holding himself where it hurt most, unaware of the fact that he was grazed elsewhere on his body.

The girl turned also to run, but looked back at her helper who was holing his side with obvious pain. She returned without hesitation and offered a kiss to his right hip to ease the pain. He looked at her, into her eyes, and sat with her on the nearest rock. The young girl began to cry, head on his shoulder. He was her protector.

Today Svi and Lika had seen history, a major step in the early development of human relationships.

***

Neyl had quickly released the woman from her bondage. Her aggressiveness calmed to understanding, when he told her his story. She was a beautiful woman of early middle years, and perhaps well experienced with life. Her soft blonde hair and pale pink skin had certainly helped her to survive until this day. She and Neyl had certainly many experiences, which they shared in common. They had both been captives, Neyl in a labor camp, and she as a prostitute in a house in Politir. She had twice escaped, and this time she was the private possession of somebody very important. Neyl had stolen his craft and gained a potential ally and friend. As an escapee he had not realized how lucky he had been to have tracked his route thus far. He was now aboard a fast moving craft way out of sight of any land with a *'shipmate'* who was an excellent sample of the opposite sex and who was certainly in sympathy with his motives.

The course that Neyl had set would bring them shortly within striking distance of land. The speed that they were traveling would ensure landfall before nightfall. The excitement was building up in Neyl's chest, as he felt the strength of his heartbeat reminding him of human frailty as his destination, perhaps his destiny became nearer with every oceanic wave that skimmed beneath them.

Being thrown together at this time with such a clean and beautiful woman had given Neyl a fresh impetus to succeed, but inwardly he was suspicious how everything had seemed to go so well, and all stages of his escape had fallen into place as if pre-arranged. He kept trying to persuade himself that this was just coincidence, and not some strange detailed plot to involve him. Nobody would assassinate a world leader just so Neyl could escape from captivity! The death was real; he had seen it on the televideo and on all the newsstands as he had run through the streets of that town. "No" he kept telling himself this was quite real, and his imagination was not running wild. He was free, afloat and accompanied by a beautiful woman.

"Would you like a drink or something to eat?" he heard from below deck. "How would you like some breakfast? This vessel is well stocked with food; we have enough to last for days!"

"That's great!" Neyl answered and gestured that they should sit down together and enjoy the early daylight.

Each time Neyl reached across the table for another piece of biscuit, his hand inadvertently touched hers. He thought nothing of it at first, but eventually she seemed to react, as if she was encouraging him to her intentionally.

He took a short nervous breath, and with gentle persuasion placed the fingers of his right hand around hers. She responded immediately clasping his right hand tightly with a meaning that all men understood. They wanted each other.

The two people carefully looked at each other and without uttering a word they joined arms as Neyl helped his newfound friend down the few stairs into the sleeping quarters that they may have some "privacy" for their intimacy together.

Their two bodies gradually became entwined in a carnal adoration. They had found in each other a future, which they somehow knew, held a probable permanence of mutual understanding. The strong contrast in color and texture of their two entwined bodies only seemed to contribute to the beauty of their relationship. This was for real and they each wanted to believe what they had found between them was good and long lasting.

***

"Fire! Fire! Fire!"

The alarms were ringing everywhere. It was pandemonium as Jabal's farm had gone awry with flashing lights and sirens.

The stampede of bleeding animals gave the first clue of the enormity of the problem as many varieties of wild and domestic creature forced their way in blind panic through the center of the farm's residential area. Many were severely injured, and some had damaged limbs or parts of limbs missing. Rastus tried to shoot a few to relieve them of their agony.

There were people running, but nowhere seemed safe. The entire farm had a security drill for just such emergencies, but this was different, the fire and flames were real, and the noise was coming from all directions at once.

It had all started just as Naamah was putting her children to bed. The daylight was fading as the evening sunset reduced the surrounding countryside into a deep dark void. A few of the brightest stars were beginning to appear through an unusually thinly clouded sky. There was a sudden bright flash of light that appeared from across the northern horizon. Within moments what first appeared curious and beautiful, became sinister and dangerous. The fiery rocket was headed direct for Jabal's empty office in the center of the village. As it exploded on target Jabal decided to order the evacuation of all women and children, and Naamah's hoversphere was to be the escape vehicle. Most women did not want to leave their men folk, but they all insisted on their children leaving.

Jabal could not concentrate on the situation while Naamah and her children were still in the vicinity, he insisted that they hurry. Eventually as the vehicle lifted to release itself from the ground, Jabal breathed a sigh of relief only to suffer another major shock as a second rocket propelled missile penciled its image across the darkened sky towards the very spot where Naamah's take-off path was leading her. Jabal could see that the changing movements of the missile's flight indicated it to be 'heat seeking'.

The explosion was immediately above Jabal's head, or it seemed to be, and as the shrapnel began to fall, Naamah's undamaged craft was lifting fast and away from the problem.

Lex and Rastus had their arms about each other in congratulatory glee. They were astonished at their success in shooting down the missile while in full flight. No way could another attack materialize on Naamah. Her craft could move faster that any missile and already it would be far away.

Jabal and Lex with Rastus attempted to put their organized defense plans into action, but the chaos seemed to be winning its' way through to panic. Fire pockets were everywhere and people did not know where to run, or where to hide. So far the only visible enemy was the fire and shrapnel coupled with the uncertainty of where the next explosion would occur.

The multipurpose harvester and crop sprayer had been disabled when the water tower collapsed and fell across its housing depriving access to the outside world for the one vehicle that had the power to lift many people to safety. There was water everywhere, as the supply lines were severed, and the ground immediately around the fallen tower was rapidly returning to it's original state, being that of a natural swamp.

Lex Jabal Rastus and Glenshee arrived in that order, in the underground safety shelter, which appeared still to be in full working order apart from a little water, which was seeping through cracks in the floor. They decided to fight a rearguard action whilst trying to evacuate. If only they could know from which direction the rear was supposed to be!

"The farm is land and cannot be removed whatever these people do, but our people make the farm and as long as we survive we can return to re-create our land. Get everyone clear...."

Jabal was interrupted as the door burst open and two hybridmen threw a filthy bedraggled damp and muddy Klansman onto the wet tiled floor. The Klansman looked up at his brother Jabal.

"Get out before dawn, they have your farm completely surrounded and they attack just after sunrise. They are out to destroy you!"

***

It was late into the evening when Svi and Lika heard the announcement in their sleeping quarters. They were to report for immediate duty to their research unit, as the new engines were to be tested and were on schedule for midnight action. The two young people were to assume responsibility for securing their unit against any sudden or emergent problem.

Tubal and Noah were doing the final checks in the control room of Unit six orbital, when Naamah called in on the Holographic Videophone to speak to Noah. The two men were shocked to hear the news about the attack on Jabal's farm but Noah was ecstatic that she had managed to return safely home with their children, and, at least all was well with them.

Tubal was worried about the unrest and became even more subdued than he was previously when he had caught a glimpse of Gramps on the televideo with his wife Tsionne earlier that day. He tried to make himself believe that there was no need to worry but he could not detach himself from either problem. This was certainly not a time for him to lose his concentration as a lot depended on his judgment. Tsionne would be asleep now as her time zone was already approaching morning. Tubal could not wait to contact her; he had to speak with her again soon, urgently. He wanted to know; everything depended on his sanity of thought. He adored his wife, she was his everything. He was not even listening to the 'count down' checks and he would soon have to leave the Unit for the neighboring laboratory / observatory in Unit 4. Why did everything always have to happen at the same time? Who had attacked Jabal's Farm, and what influence and power had the three K's within his organization. Why now? Was there a deep conspiracy? His silent thoughts hardly showed in his facial expression, but his mind was reeling and his lack of local input was quite obvious. Noah was very concerned, and finally he remarked to Tubal that he should not worry about the attack, that Lex and Jabal would have everything under control. Tubal just nodded and grunted in acknowledgement and continued to push numbers into his personal portable computer. Finally the red and green lights flashed alternately on the master panel of orbital 6. It was final countdown for take-off. Soon, all outside connections would be detached; it was time for Tubal to leave.

Noah took up his allocated position in the Central Observation Area and Tubal gave him some last minute instruction on how everything would work for him. It was probably the best position in which to be placed for the purposes of observation and logging of the flight. Tubal took Noah's hands and stood facing him as he helped him into his 'grand' chair.

"I wish you the best, and that any luck that may be needed should come your way. Take care! This journey will almost effectively take you through time as well as distance. I won't always be able to contact you, neither you, me, but remember how close friends we are, and I'll see you for a double handshake when you return! Just over four days! I love you Noah!" Tubal gave Noah a wide solid hug as they threw their arms around each other with deep strong feeling.

"Don't worry if anything happens for the worst, I'll look after Naamah and the children!" Oh how Tubal had wished that he had not said that. Everything was going to be all right, he did not want to precipitate doom. He chastised himself for being superstitious.

Noah returned the hug, then watched Tubal's exit from Unit 6. He continued to follow Tubal on his video monitors as his every move was logged through the corridors from central control out to Unit No. 4.

Again they spoke to each other, but this time across the airwaves of radio as they each sat in their respective positions checking with each other, their schedule and final data as action time became more imminent.

"Four minutes and still counting" came across the monitor. The air was electric with excitement; the steam was almost visible in the exterior void around the outside of the orbital craft. The hearts of Noah and Tubal were pumping Adrenalin and their concentration was intense. Together they went through their final observations and checked the co-ordinates of the future flight.

Noah saw Tubal's facial expression suddenly change as his holographic video started to form a cloudy image in front of him. Noah could only see Tubal's face, but Tubal could see Tsionne in perfect focus. He felt that he could almost smell her perfume. She was so real, and with him, in her early morning mist of dawn!

"I just wanted to wish you both the best of luck and everything for the flight. Give Noah my love!" She said, and threw an open handed kiss with a depth of meaning, which Tubal truly understood as genuine. The doubt lifted from his thoughts and a satisfied smile broke out onto his face as Noah called over to Tubal . . .

"I heard that! It was Tsionne. That was a nice gesture; she must have got up especially early to do that for us. I could not see her but I heard her, and you look so very much more relaxed now!" Noah was also happier that Tubal seemed more alert once more.

"Three minutes and counting" again a verbal message came out of their active monitors. "Fasten yourselves in, and attach life support systems in case of emergency!" Noah obeyed. It was a long time since such precautions had needed to be taken and it added to the tension. All 'survival personnel' had to be attached to the life support system throughout the 'ship' in order that if anything goes wrong at 'engine burst', they would still be able to be in control of any situation. Noah's heart was at full ahead; he could feel it thumping in his chest. *'Not long now!* He thought.

***

CHAPTER 7

Neyl and his new found friend were standing at the railing in the clammy heat of midday and were looking out across the calming steamy sea at the distant but hazy horizon. The two happy and contented people were only scantily dressed in an excuse for undergarments and the woman's naked breasts were firm and covered in small droplets of sea spray. Neyl thought of it first . . .

"Hey!" He said, "I don't know your name! "

"Rianne" came out of her mouth with a gentleness of flavor that Neyl just had to taste. He turned and grabbed her mouth in his as if to take her spoken name and keep it in his mouth forever. He swallowed it prolonging the enjoyment. He had completely captured her name, and it was now a part of his being. Their tongues touched and played for a while. Neyl could feel Rianne's hands pulling at his back as if to attract his attention. He pulled gently away.

"Look!" she whispered in his ear as she pointed out behind him, across to the horizon, which was now appearing no longer to be a flat and even line. "It's lumpy!" She exclaimed.

"Land!" Neyl remarked, "Come let's look at the charts and see where we are. They climbed the few steps to the bridge and opened the navigation monitors to seek their position.

They could see that their course was bringing them in closer to 'landfall' at a point between two islands in a bay, which Neyl had previously chosen. He had hoped it would have strong implications for his, or perhaps now, *their* future. It was the Central reception area for Ground Control ETON. Neyl was elated, that was exactly where they were headed, and that was where they were going. He could not wait.

As they approached the 'lumpy' area on the horizon it became much thicker and more lumpy, to the point that they could pick up small differences of identity on the widening landmasses growing in front of them. Neyl had decided to aim his craft for the tentative gap between the two shallow lumps as they grew in front of him.

The lumps became much larger as the craft developed speed under Neyl's eager control. He had not noticed that his friend had disappeared inside to put on a few clothes. He was completely absorbed in his next big step to *freedom*

The gap between the two islands had opened wide enough to yield view to the further water behind them. Through that gap there was a new landmass growing out of the sea to the right, behind the maturing shape of the right hand island. That was where Neyl was headed. He took out the electric binocular magnifiers from the 'Captain's drawer' and took a more detailed look. He could see spray on the surface not far off the coast of the right hand island around which they were now to pass. Neyl had forgotten about security, and this was another fast moving craft apparently coming directly out to meet them.

Neyl did not know whether to be anxious or exhilarated, as this strangely shaped craft rapidly approached them. Their hovercraft was traveling at high speed across a relatively flat sea, and yet the other vehicle was moving at least twice that speed towards them. The joint approaching speed would mean that although many miles apart at that moment they would meet within minutes. Neyl tried to fixate his view on the markings of the oncoming vehicle. He was sure he knew from where it was coming, he was certain that he knew that he was where he thought he was. He had driven a pre-set course to arrive exactly that position, but re-assurance would always be greatly appreciated.

He felt Rianne pulling at his elbow,

"Who are they?" she asked, as the spray in the distance became clearly visible to the naked eye.

"Difficult!" came the reply "I cannot yet see through their frontal spray. Wow! It's beautiful! It pushes water out of its' way as if it were a knife cutting into the ocean. It appears so serene, so powerful and so fast. It seems to use the water through which it is traveling as a power source for its' energy. 'GC ETON *Sea Patrol*' is written on the front! We've arrived, we are here!" There were tears in Neyl's eyes. He was almost crying with gratitude, as he threw his arms around Rianne.

***

Rebecca could not believe her luck, she had been asked to organize an international service for the memory of Chaudle. It was thought in the highest diplomatic echelons, that she would have the most neutral of connections and be tarnished with the least amount of stain in the eyes of the international family. She was determined to succeed, and make the death of a world leader for peace, that of a catalyst to a permanent understanding between conflicting nations.

She felt humble, completely inferior and insufficient to the task and yet was so proud when the official letter came by hand to her door in its pretty red, gold embossed, wax seal which she hated breaking in order to open and read the handwritten script content. This was still the way of doing things in the true diplomatic circles. It was this 'old fashioned' way that gave the seed of the idea to Rebecca for a memorial service that nobody would ever forget the man who tried to pacify a world gone mad.

She had firm ideas about where the event should take place in the International area of the League of Nations, but that would have been indirectly sponsored by 'Science and Welfare'. It would not have had the 'real' meaning for collective peace that would otherwise come from a non-political center. Rebecca knew from her connections through her husband, Fadfagi that the 'League' would not be able to exist without the financial support of certain politically motivated organizations. The only friendly and rightful place would be in the homeland of the late Chaudle himself. There was not much time to lose. His funeral was only a day previously, everything was happening so quickly.

Ancana was only a small island state not far off the coast of Bylia, and there was a deep feeling of loss throughout the land. Chaudle as a leader had been somewhat like a father to all who had lived within the republic's shores. The rumor of the news that the possibility of a top-level international gathering would be coming to pay tribute to the memory of their great leader had sent a warming proud feeling throughout the island.

Rebecca arrived in the afternoon of the same day in which she had received her official brief. There was quite a large crowd to meet her at the hoverport, they were subdued but they clapped gently as she walked down the ramp onto their soil. How the people came to know that Rebecca was due nobody could say, she had only decided herself a few hours previously.

Officials met her at the entrance gate and whisked her away in an official government Gyrocopter. As the machine came down to rest on the roof of the Government House, she again began to feel the enormity of the responsibility placed on her shoulders.

Raleph, the assistant governor, met her in his office and after long discussion it was decided that the ceremony could take the form of a re-dedication of an old unused Palace Temple which had strong historical value as a center in earlier days when people met 'together' to worship God. It seemed that Chaudle had only recently had plans passed through parliament for a restoration to its ancient state and a conversion use to a museum to be dedicated to God's peace. The Ancana government had already considered the area should be re-scheduled as a new capital city when it was finished and that rebuilding of the area would take many years. Raleph suggested that they should visit the area and see the old temple.

The area of God's peace could only be reached by ground driven vehicles, as the local people still had their respect for the ancient tradition that no human being could ever go higher than just below the globe on the high pointed spire of the roof of the old temple.

The little village stood on the side of one steep hill, which belonged within the quiet solitude of the seven hills in the very center of their nation. The area was somewhat rugged and overgrown. Its' structures dated back through several lifetimes and had gone into decay and disrepair.

As they drove through the flat aggressively farmed lowland areas with the busy heavy industry factories with their smoking chimneys behind them nearer to the sea, Rebecca could again sense a change in environment as they headed for the hills, which were clearly lifting themselves out of the plain directly in front of them. Around their base there was a distinct color of Mahogany, which became stronger and deeper as the hills became closer. Rebecca had not seen such nature in the raw for many years and was completely inspired by the sight to which they were rapidly drawing nearer. The lower levels of the hills were overgrown with trees, a rare sight these days. They were making straight for them, and a small dark gap was opening in front of them into which their road was to enter.

Rebecca took Raleph's hand for a short moment as their vehicle became engulfed in the semi darkness of the shadows from the surrounding trees. They had started to climb the narrow winding road, which was to lead them up from the plains below, to the mystic city of 'God's peace'. The road was stony tortuous and narrow, it was as bumpy as it was beautiful. Almost untouched by the centuries of previous human intervention the rugged road seemed to climb for what seemed an age to Rebecca but the occasional gap in the trees or the infrequent glimpse of some wild life in the raw, kept her mentally attentive to a scenery she had never before experienced. Real leaves, pretty flowers, she knew that there was still much around but never so much growing naturally in one place.

They could see strong light up and ahead and within moments the soft smell of lavender and pine disappeared to yield the open spectacle of the seven hills of God's peace, with its little village nestled between two of the upper slopes. Diagonally opposite, imposing itself on all that surrounded it was the 'ancient palace and temple' with its high twisted spire and with its large golden 'Orb' which was impaled almost at its top. The original design was that of a genius as if a turning pointed spire had screwed itself through the Orb to show its point atop. The Orb was known to be extremely heavy and it was locally believed that it was only with God's help that it remained in place on such a narrow mast. So long as humankind had faith with its maker and its maker had faith with humankind, then that Orb would remain so perilously balanced.

Rebecca found it very difficult to remove her gaze from the beautiful globe as it shone in the semi sunlight. Raleph disturbed her deep thoughts . . .

"Is this not a beautiful place?"

Rebecca was stirred into reply and suggested that they pull up for a moment in order to stop the heavy engine noise and the sound of the wheels on the stony gravel road.

Not very far along the gentle elevation of the winding mountainous road there was a grassy area, very fresh and green with an uninterrupted view of all the hills and the dark, deep, green valley below into which dropped from high, a waterfall with such a strength of force onto its small lake below. It sent a noisy spray as a mention in the wind for a very wide distance.

The unlikely couple sat down on the grassy bank and viewed the panorama, which surrounded them. Rebecca felt completely involved in her surroundings as she lay prone on the ground and nestled her chin in her hands supported by her elbows. Finally after much meditation, Rebecca lifted her chin and spoke . . .

"I cannot express my thoughts at this moment. The unspoiled nature, the tranquility, the only noise is that of the birds against the background of the waterfall. The color and the smell of this place. I can understand why the people who first settled here called it the place of 'G-d's Peace'."

"Yeh!" Came the sharp reply "We hope to settle more than one and a half million families here when everything is completed!"

"How long replied a stunned Rebecca?

"Seven years" came the answer.

***

Lex and Rastus had been given the privilege of volunteering for the rear guard action to defend the backs of the fleeing families and co-workers on Jabal's farm. Jubal, the 'Klansman' brother of Jabal insisted on staying behind to help.

In the darkness of the night the three got to work with traps and explosives. They were determined to make life very difficult for any invader. Delay was important, that the entire farm could be safely evacuated. Early dawn was less than a few hours away.

The first target to be dealt with was the collapsed water tower. In order to release the Gyrosphere and trailer from their housing explosives were strategically placed around the fallen tower. After some very tense and frustrating moments the full body of the tower imploded to a small pile of trash due to some very clever work performed by Lex. Jubal as Rastus climbed through the mess into the 'barn' where the Gyrosphere was suspended for storage.

Releasing the vehicle posed no problem, and with emergency generators the two men managed to retrieve the machine into the open space outside the barn. The large trailer used for harvest collection was also to prove essential.

While Jabal worked with Glenshee and others to get all the men and their families together, Lex, Rastus and Jubal assembled the elevating trailer globe in which they would all be able to ride, under the Gyrosphere in order to make their escape. The passengers would be considerably cramped, but certainly they could all fit inside the large transparent plastic globe. If all of their body weight was added together there would still be room for almost two thirds of a harvest-weighted load. The idea of escape was brilliant but highly dangerous, and dramatically exposed to the surrounding enemy.

The escape vehicle having been prepared and secured Lex and his team could leave the evacuation to the charge of his boss Jabal whom they had all insisted should go with them in order that he may return at some later date to re-secure his farm with his team of workers.

Lex and Rastus each took pre-arranged routes out to the perimeter defenses. So much had been damaged with the stampede that most of the mantraps and electric fences had been put out of action. There were many dying animals impaled or broken in the traps meant for the human enemy outside. It had been decided that the only power that seemed left within their control was that of trying to delay the imminent attack. That had to be done! The two men each carried a backpack perilously balanced across their shoulders. In these packs was a volatile powdered explosive which when released from its sack and allowed to drop to the ground and come into contact with any organic material would immediately turn into a tar-like substance which would stick to the feet when walked upon. After being squashed to the ground a couple of times underfoot, it would explode violently to nearly one hundred times its own volume, certainly killing the owner of the feet and distributing his pieces over a large area. The two men had set off in opposite directions to form a full perimeter circle before even a hint of daybreak. They planned to meet at the far side of the farm where they would make their joint escape to a pick-up point by Glenshee.

Lex made his pathway to the rendezvous point without an incident and with only a small amount of powder left in his bag. The wait for Rastus was fraught with worry. Lex considered every eventuality; his mind was racing through many vivid horrific imaginations about the fete of his dear friend. He was now late and daybreak was hinting at its early color in the lower eastern sky. Lex listened and looked for even the slightest movement. Hiding in a copse of dead bushes he could just begin to make out the scenery, as the sky seemed to develop a tint of very dark blue gray. He knew that once the light was enough to create a suggestion of daylight shadow then the attack would ensue forthwith. He was worried.

"Hello Lex!" A female voice from behind, he recognized as Glenshee. "Where is Rastus?" Lex indicated by mime that he had no idea, but he was expecting him, and showed his relief at seeing Glenshee.

"We have very little time and I hope to God that he will be here soon. He must hurry!"

Lex saw the trail of fresh wet blood as it reflected in the cool half-light across the path not far in front of him. It was Rastus, crawling and then half walking in a desperate attempt to reach his chum. He had nearly made it when he collapsed in a heap only a few paces away. Lex and Glenshee ran to pick him up taking great care not to get caught by their own explosives. The bleeding Rastus was carefully carried to a small gyrosphere, which had brought Glenshee to the scene.

Lex emptied the rest of the powder around the sphere as they lifted off the ground into the early sunrise. As they moved upward at great speed, the first explosion, then another very close to where the two men had started laying their powder. The attack had begun.

***

All thoughts of Tsionne disappeared from Tubal's mind as the last seconds were counted out to the final ignition of the new engine in 'Unit 6'.

". . . eight, seven, six," he held his breath as he heard Noah's last radio call to him, the words "Good luck".

". . . three, two, one, Go!"

Tubal could not believe it, nothing had happened. Noah sat at his viewer, he could not believe it, nothing had happened! There wasn't even the feeling of initial motion.

"What's going on?" Noah called to Tubal, "We don't seem to be moving but the counting is now going positive at zero plus twenty. What does that mean?"

"Look out of the observatory window" Tubal called back to Noah, you are at least ten or twelve lengths away from us now and accelerating."

Noah thought how strange space flight could be, and how difficult it was to relate to movement and distance. The entire man-made satellite village was effectively moving away and contracting in size at an ever-increasing pace. Soon there was to be nothing left as the entire image reduced to microscopic proportions and disappeared off to the right, also suddenly the shadow of their home planet began to move off in the same direction allowing the dazzling brilliance of sunrise to thrust itself at full strength into the observatory center of 'Unit 6'. This was the first abnormality. Usually this took more than a few moments, as the sensitive photochromic protective transparent cover would change in its density to protect them from the brilliance of the naked sunlight, but with the increasing velocity of their movement, the 'sun' just appeared from nowhere.

Tubal was on the radio again acknowledging the fact that this had not been catered for in the initial trial. It could prove dangerous in the future. Unit six was traveling at almost half of the speed of light at an oblique angle to the solar orbit of their mother planet and away from the sun. They would soon change course to a distant orbit of the sun at several times the speed of light to arrive back within touching distance of 'Unit 4' within four full rotations of their home planet.

The test run was beginning to prove very exciting as the control turned 'Unit 6' around to face backwards to the home planet. They were about to increase their speed into a trajectory course for a distant solar elliptical orbit. Through the roof of the observatory tower Noah and all the controllers could see the wonderful clear image of their home planet, which was now a crescent globe with crystal clear edges, a small dark segment off to the right. The image was huge and took up almost the entire panorama from the roof of the observation tower. The impression of size was much more imposing than when earlier it was so large that the image only represented the ground beneath them.

"Begin countdown to second ignition" came across the loudspeakers, "Secure all hatches and any moveable object, we on board will be entering a new era of velocity never yet experienced by humankind. We will reach a speed many times faster than that of light itself. Two minutes to go and counting!"

Already it was taking a small time delay in the radio contact between Tubal and Noah, but only enough to be perceptible. The distance between them was increasing all the time, but they were still 'technically' visible to each other as 'Unit 4' was still in the seeable dark section of their home planet although getting slowly nearer to its own early sunrise.

The countdown to the second ignition was nearly finished, and both Noah and Tubal held their breath as man was for the first time about to accelerate out beyond the speed of light. ". . . . Three, two, one ignition."

"Wow," Noah looked upward at the home planet, suddenly it was rapidly shrinking in size, and perceptibly turning slowly in the opposite direction as if it had reversed its' rotation. The movement of rotation had hardly been visible before, but now it was visibly revolving in the opposite manner. Noah could see from the clear points on the equator. Also the image, as it was reducing in size, was changing color very gently. Noah had to relate all this to Tubal Cain but contact was now impossible. He checked the videos, as he wanted it all recorded. They were now traveling away from their home faster than the light that was leaving it! In fact, they were now seeing light that had left their planet even earlier and thus was 'older'. That is why their home seemed to be turning the wrong way and was developing a different hue as they were rapidly accelerating away from it!

***

Erash always felt better after having his haircut, he felt relaxed and cleaner as he sat looking into the mirrored wall of the hairdressing establishment. He watched his long red curls being thinned to a more respectable looking neatness. The fresh scent of perfume was in the air in the comfort of the barber's chair he felt that he was for a short time at peace with the world. It was a moment in his busy life much to savored, as these rare moments were for him very scarce. He looked around at the busy salon within the mirror.

There was a fat well-endowed old lady three seats away from him having a hairpiece fitted. A young mother with beautiful long blonde hair was waiting with her two children of different genders each jealously competing for the first place in a non-existent queue for the next spare empty seat.

His eyes were beginning to feel a little heavy and he was becoming somewhat soporific. He allowed his attention to wander and his lids to close for a brief moment.

With his eyes closed he became more conscious of the noises around him, the clatter of scissors, and the hum of the driers. He could hear the scraping of the blades on slightly hairy skin, the general chit-chat of clients as they sat waiting for their next treatment, and the gaggle of oration that was continually flowing from the mouths of the craftspeople at their work. He began to concentrate his hearing on the different action and allowed his eyes to remain closed. A whole new world was around him and he wanted to enjoy it. He was trying to put picture images in his mind to the various voices in the busy hubbub of the salon, when certain words came into his ears that brought him back to reality.

". . . frogs without legs, some with six, one eye or two heads, all deformed in some way!"

Erash lifted himself out of his chair and still with lathered towel about his neck, walked over to the lady who was in deep discussion with her hairdresser.

"Pardon me" Erash interrupted "but who saw this, and where?"

"My young son," she replied "just north, but not far from here. Why?"

"How many people have seen these mutants?" Erash continued ignoring her question but showing her his security identification disc from 'Science and Welfare'.

The woman started to show her concern, "Just my son Dork and his girlfriend. I am sure that they would take you there.

"No!" Erash replied quickly "but we must check the kids out first for radiation or poisoning. If they can just direct us I will go out there with an environmental inspection team, but we must see your son first!"

"They have brought a few home with them already!" The woman was beginning to show signs of panic. She also got up from her seat. The two lathered people stood facing each other, it was almost humorous, but they were not laughing as the soapy bubbles dripped down their toweled bodies.

Erash turned to the assistants . . .

"Clean us both up, we will be back later, send both bills to Science and Welfare, here is my card."

Within moments the anxious couple were mobile, on their way to Erash's office at Science and Welfare to get kitted out in order to meet with the lady's young son.

Dork went to answer the call at the front entrance door. He was expecting his girlfriend Evila and was unsure how to react when he opened the door. Standing in front of him were six thickly green suited beings of which one was certainly his mum. He could clearly make out her blurred outline through the thick translucent material.

"Mum? What's going on? Why are you wearing that garb? Why the helmet and breathing apparatus?"

*****

The black and silver logo on the prow of the fast approaching sea vessel was clearly that of G.C.Eton. Neyl and Rianne slowed down their craft to a stationary drift and threw out a sea anchor with the obvious exaggeration that would show the oncoming security patrol that they were willing to acquiesce to their demands. Neyl had the bright idea of raising white and yellow flags to suggest willingness to be boarded. He remembered as a young cadet in his childhood days when he learned historic signs and seafaring emblems. He hoped his message would be recognized.

They did not have to wait long to find out, as the fast approaching craft slowed down and pulled alongside. A strong loud voice came across from the speakers of the security boat only to echo through their own on board speaker system. Neyl had left their monitor navigation system switched on and they were receiving a double volume of communication. Neyl went to his microphone to reply.

"We have escaped from capture in Bylia in this purloined boat and seek sanctuary within your borders. Please we have so much to tell, we know that we have come from what for you must be like another world!"

The police vessel took them in tow and at a relatively slow speed they approached the coastline then through a narrow strait to a large lake, which they began to cross in a somewhat erratic path in order to avoid the tops of buildings, which seemed to be growing up through the surface of the inland sea.

Neyl remembered that as a child he had learned how the world seas had been rising due to thermal changes in the planet's atmosphere. Now he was seeing the obvious effects for the first time. He knew that from where they had come the coastline had been rebuilt many years previously, but now in this new place for him he could see clearly what was happening. How could humankind be so stupid? These buildings represent an old city that had drowned beneath the gradual rising tides of the melting snows at the ice caps. He could see how some strong tall edifices that once stood so erect and proud were now tilting at different angles, some perilously, as if below they were trying to find their own new levels and gentle resting places in the ever-changing soft slippery silted ground beneath them.

In contrast in the distance Neyl pointed out to Rianne the tall out dated towers of the rocket propelled vertical take off vehicles that a few generations previously had been the only way known to get into orbital space. They were going to drive passed the historic museum of ancient space flight. Neyl took Rianne's hand and held it tight; he had tears in his eyes. He had never been here before, but he felt that he was coming home. He would have kissed the ground if he had landed at that moment. He was completely overcome with emotion. He knew that this was what he had been born for. This was his reason for his existence. He grabbed Rianne tight around her waist, as they were moving by the old relic gantries of space flight of a time gone by. He was almost openly crying into the wind, as they stood at the rail of their hovercraft in a helpless tow behind G.C.Eton patrol boat No.649.

***

The sudden change of speed from 'Sublumic' to 'Superlumic' faster than the speed of light didn't go passed unnoticed to Svi and Lika. They were taking a well-earned rest in their cabin and had turned off their partial gravity in order that they could enjoy the comfort of each other within the deep padded walls of their sleeping cell. They were in a mad passionate self taught embrace with emotions building up to an orgasmic climax. Svi was well inside his wife as suddenly they were thrown backwards against the padded wall behind Lika. Svi was effectively hard and heavy on top of Lika as the ship continued at great increasing speed creating a new source of gravity probably two or three times that of the ship's normal.

"Wow!" murmured Lika into Svi's well-chewed ear, she sighed and let out a long increasing wailing gasp of satisfaction. Svi could not control himself as his sensitive point reached the ultimate intimate depths of its greatest achievement within the damp wet walls of Lika's femininity. He could feel her internal vibrations around his weapon as finally the strength of his masculinity discharged itself into the awaiting chamber of Lika's abdomen.

"Wow! Wow!" Lika was holding Svi so tight he could hardly breathe. "How did you do that?" she whispered to Svi "We came together at the same moment. Give me a kiss!" She grabbed a hold of Svi's waist and pulled hard at him with her open legs wrapped around his buttocks. "More" she gasped "More she repeated with a jocular smile wide across her satisfied face.

"Later" replied Svi "I seem to have temporarily run out of ammunition."

"I'll help you to reload" Lika was already creating a cuddle between them that Svi knew would send them both to a well-earned blissful sleep

Noah was finding the inability to contact Tubal Cain very frustrating. When he tuned into the frequency he was using previously all he could get was interference and audible blurb, which although synchronized, made no logical sense to his ear or equipment. When played at a slightly different speed he could make out voices not unlike his own and that of Tubal Cain speaking in a language strangely unfamiliar to his ear. Soon that disappeared to become someone else's which was completely unrecognizable to him. He could not figure it out and it worried him, he decided to go for a walk into the observatory area on the outside edge.

Noah knew his astronomy; he had been brought up on 'star charts' and 'astro-maps'. As a child he had had an insatiable desire to follow the stars and planets of the extra orbital dimension. He had a collection of old books, tapes and discs, which were all devoted to the subject. He knew where every common star or illuminated object should appear in the sky. Even when out in orbit he could self adjust to compensate and relocate his positions from the common star formations, like the triangle, the square and many well-known rhombuses and parallelograms. His 'space geometry' was so good that he used to lecture in it in his early days of Astro research.

He could not believe the appearance of the panorama, which greeted him as he reached the viewing deck not far from his office desk. His view of space was astounding to him as he looked out through the panoramic astrological reflecting video telescope, Noah was very proud of this new accessory, it was his original idea and had a computer grating support program which automatically logged all that was recorded as it scanned the heavens. There was a hint of parallax movement among some of the formations, some were appearing to move together and others were moving apart. The most familiar stellar constellation known to Noah seemed to be getting perceptibly larger as the other points within it were increasing their separation. On the opposite side of the panorama the stars were a slightly different hue and were growing closer together. Occasionally a really bright light would pass across the 'sky' and disappear like a comet of short duration.

Noah was fascinated. Their speed was now about six or seven times that of the speed of the light that started to travel with them at the moment of their first 'superlumic' acceleration. The objects around them and the stars of different distances would now all have a different visual relationship with their craft. Effectively outer space was traveling at all different speeds related to their own trajectory. A new experience he had to record. It was then that Noah realized what could be happening to his radio receiver. He went back to play with it again.

***

Gramps could not wait another moment; he had to see Tsionne once more, and had offered to take her once again to visit Arianne. New emotions were developing inside his young body and he so very much did not want to betray his grandson Tubal Cain. Tubal was away and Gramps Methuselah did not want to take advantage of the situation, but he knew that he had a strong enough sense of responsibility to control himself for he did love and enjoy Tsionne's company.

While waiting in the entrance lobby of Tubal and Tsionne's home, Gramps was becoming very nervous. From nothing his stomach was entertaining a whole family of butterflies. They were becoming very busy as Gramps stood there looking at the crack of the door for a small clue as to when it may slide open to reveal the wife of his grandson.

Within moments and what to Methuselah seemed an age, the door parted open to yield to an extraordinary well-presented Tsionne who was classically dressed in a beautiful dark navy blue suit. She was smiling and twice placed a fond and friendly kiss to both of Gramps cheeks alternating from one side to another, while she firmly held both of his shoulders. Gramps nervously started to pull away as if embarrassed.

"What's wrong? Tsionne asked,

"I have a cold and don't want to be generous with it" he lied.

The trip to Arianne would have been very uneventful except that Gramps could not take his eyes off the gap in Tsionne's clean cut skirt where he could see the fold of her knees and the best part of her fleshy right upper thigh.

"Keep your eyes on the road" she called out to Gramps as he took a corner somewhat faster than he should have done. In reply he accelerated out of it just as a young adolescent would as if showing off to a girlfriend.

"What are you doing? What are you trying to prove?" Tsionne was bewildered by Gramps youthful attitude, as regardless of safety he continued at speed down the narrow road. Tsionne pulled at Gramps arm . . .

"Slow down! What are you doing? You'll get us both killed!"

Just as quickly as he had pulled away at speed, he slowed down and pulling over and off the side of the road, he gently brought the vehicle to a stop. He leaned, head forward over onto his folded arms, which were across the driving controls and in a voice that sounded almost in tears softly mouthed an apology to Tsionne.

"I cannot come to terms with this! This young body is giving me all the strong emotional and physical stimuli that I had almost forgotten from nearly two whole generations ago. I am a young man again with all the biological wonders of that time forcing themselves back into my brain. I am finding it very difficult to cope. It's odd the old expression in reverse. 'Mind over matter' has very much become 'matter over mind'! You are my grand daughter in law so to speak, and I am so strongly physically attracted to you . . . Oh! I should not have said that!"

Without forethought Tsionne leaned over to Gramps and pulled him closer to him in order to offer him comfort and solace in his despair. A friendly gesture to help calm his thoughts. He completely misunderstood her and pulled her even closer to him giving the most erotic and passionate kiss full frontal onto her soft young fleshy lips. He found her tongue in a state of shocked surprise, as his free hand reached for that inviting gap in her skirt. He could feel her silky-smooth frilly underwear. In an instant his youthful hand was working overtime to find the warm wet treasures within Tsionne's groin. Sensibility came quickly to Tsionne and with very firm resolve; her right hand came hard across Gramps' face. He pulled back and looked at her like an embarrassed young man who knew that he had gone too far.

***

The frogs varied in their deformities and posed a great problem to the research investigation lab. There was no measurable radioactivity and no indication that the abnormalities were anything other than that of normal growth. One frog had one leg shorter than the other, there was a little black mottled frog, which looked almost normal in the body apart from its color, but it had only one eye in the middle of its head, the other one was only visible when it opened its mouth.

Erash had ordered a complete evaluation of this mutant species and wanted quick results. When he had found that these specimens were not irradiated and in no way radioactive he ordered a team of investigators to go to the area in which they had been found. The group had returned with more frogs, a few reasonably normal looking, but many with an extreme variety of abnormalities. Still no radioactivity. The investigative group leader gave Erash a very comprehensive report all done in the greatest of detail, and in the speediest of time. There was no apparent abnormality present in anything else living in the area, and certainly no local radioactivity.

There was one exception to the list of completed tests, the local water although not appearing radioactive had not yet been tested for anything else. Erash had become quite angry at this discovery and demanded more extreme tests on the local water.

Solvents and industrial waste had been found in the streams where the frogs had made their homes. Spawn had been laid in the reeds of the almost stagnant ponds at the edge of the slow flowing streams. Under close examination this spawn showed the containing gel to be contaminated with the smallest amount of radioactivity so small that it almost made no impact on the counter as it was placed in the correct position of most sensitivity.

"Things are going from bad to worse! " Erash wrote in his memoir report of the day "It won't be long before we contaminate the entire water supply of this continent." he murmured to himself as he read his detailed report. He had seen reports like this before. Water, which had always been man's friend and support, could very well become his most dangerous enemy. It was bad enough when the entire nation's water supply had been intentionally contaminated with anti-biotics to protect the human body from disease, contraceptive chemicals to protect from unwanted births, and fluoride to protect the nation's teeth from decay, but now thought Erash we are contaminating our water with destructive and dangerous pollutants. The lifeblood of nature could very soon be its own destroyer! The concentrate in this particular mountainous area had not been very strong, but Erash knew that elsewhere it was worse. Water had to be treated everywhere, and treatment plants were becoming quite an industry with Science and Welfare at the forefront of suppliers. After all it had been proved that of all pollutant industries, Science and Welfare were among the highest offenders.

Erash found working in the Micro-biological Water Research Department very frustrating. The people there employed where far from communicative and even with his high understanding of scientific jargon he still found it very difficult to understand very much when they did explain it to him.

He was called over to one of the specialist benches across the very busy working research lab. He was finding it very uncomfortable walking in his sealed pale blue laboratory suit. The guy who was working there was acutely anxious and full of emotion. There was a mixture of shock, surprise and horror visible on the technician's face as it appeared through his sealed facemask.

"This is beyond the understanding of G-d!" he murmured with a trace of anguish in his voice, "Look, I mixed these two drops of untreated pool water from different areas together by mistake and it developed all the properties of simple saline except one even more major problem . . . it's become dangerously radio active!!!"

***

Rebecca was elated it was only a few days and already nearly everything was arranged as planned for Chaudle's memorial service in the small mountain village of 'God's Peace'. The personal invitations had been sent out to all nations of the world and most had favorably replied. As yet, there had been no refusals but there were still just a few more replies outstanding, she had never expected such a success. It was as if this man's violent death was to be a major factor in bringing peace to the world. Peace, strength and stability could only result from the meeting of all nations on an occasion such as this. Perhaps, she thought, even her husband could change in his attitude to these people around him. She was soon to see him for the first time in nearly a week; she had so much to tell him.

She did not usually enter her husband's office unannounced but on this occasion with nobody at reception she walked straight through. He was behind his desk, busy in conversation with three other guys. She had not seen that stern anxious expression on his face for a long time, but as he lifted his eyes to greet hers his appearance deliberately softened to a gentle smile. He purposefully wrapped up the discussion with the three men whom she was sure were from doubtful background and gestured for them to leave. Rebecca did not feel comfortable in their presence, she felt one of them looking right through her, and he was wearing a monocle in front of his right eye and had short graying dark curly hair. He stood hard to attention clicking his heels loudly together in greeting. She accepted his warm clammy right hand as he acknowledged her presence and bade her good bye. He and his two 'colleagues' walked out of her husband's office. "Who were they? She asked "and why do they each wear the black and silver snake ring of Science and Welfare?"

"They work for me!" Her husband tried to brush off the event as trivial and with his arm placed gently around her shoulder moved her to take a seat opposite his across his large desk.

"What's up?" he questioned "You are early, have you got a problem?" He was as abrupt as ever. Rebecca had grown to like that quality in him. He was a man of direction and always gave the impression that he was in full control and having complete knowledge of all that was going on around him.

"No! Precisely the opposite "she replied, "The memorial service is working out well. I am astonished how strongly this guy was admired, almost worshipped."

"A great loss to us all!" her husband agreed, "Give him all you've got for a memorial. It is important that the whole world sees and appreciates his loss. I'll be there with you, but please Rebecca put me in an obvious position, I very much want to be seen. I want it to be known by all that I was there!"

Fadfagi and his wife sat discussing the service at length and her husband offered some helpful hints before they decided to go to a local restaurant for dinner.

Despite being sat facing a wall in a secluded corner of a very fashionable eating-place, Rebecca could see in the mirror on the wall the three men seated a short distance away across the room. The same men she had seen earlier in her husband's office were now sitting three or four tables away with a woman who appeared to have only one useful hand.

Rebecca became concerned; she just hoped it did not show in her voice as she settled into a fond friendly evening with her husband. 'An occurrence that did not happen very often these days' she thought to herself.

***

CHAPTER 8

The end of the fourth day was bringing great excitement and almost a festive mood on Orbital station Unit No.6 on its return journey to their mother planet's orbit.

Since slowing down a little on the other side of their Sun two days earlier when they would have been perhaps less than a twelfth of a light year away from 'home', they had again accelerated back at the same superlumic speed in a slightly different homeward direction passing around their sun from the other side.

Noah was watching the radio and video receivers with keen interest as the colors of distant stars assumed a new hue as the craft again moved back in their direction towards them. Their mother planet was becoming the largest and brightest object in the astro-panorama in front of them. It was almost possible to see its sunlit crescent shape with the naked eye. As Unit No.6 was approaching from an oblique angle far out in space their sun was no longer behind them therefore its shadow on the far side of the mother planet was becoming more evident as it grew larger in the 'sky'. The orbital ship was beginning to change course to align to a returning orbit of its' mother planet and a final rendezvous with unit 4 and a repositioning in its own original astronomical area of orbit. They were moving rapidly nearer and the orders were broadcast on the internal communications system that after a ten-minute countdown the powerful engines would be turned effectively forwards causing the ship to sharply reduce speed for its 'glide' into final orbit. Noah could see the rotation of the home planet clearly on the electronic binocular micro-telescope. With infra-red enhancement it was possible to make out the continents, which gave the appearance that, the globe was rotating in the normal direction but faster than usual. Perhaps a day at a time, as if it were trying to catch up with their approach!

Svi and Lika jointly checked out their environmental area, that all gravitational functions were working normally. They viewed all area monitors to inspect the residents that they were all in a safe and satisfactory state. The forthcoming rapid reduction of speed would be compensated for within the environmental area by the sincere strategic use of gyroscopic gravitational compensatory motions, but with this new situation of super velocity reduction it would just be possible that accidents could happen.

As with the original acceleration all the 'children on the environment center were put to sleep by generating a mild anesthetic gas into their atmosphere and the when asleep they were physically placed in secure safety straps within a secret shelter adjoining their area. Here they were to sleep until the danger was clear, being the released and laid back in the same position from which they had been taken, knowing nothing of what had been happening around them.

The engines had been placed into correct mode and the countdown was proceeding, they had already learned not to reduce speed too quickly, so the deceleration program had been adjusted to stretch over a longer time period. . . four . . . three . . . two . . . one . . . go ! ! !

This time Svi and Lika could perceive an increase in their attachment to the floor on which they were standing and also could feel that they were becoming slightly heavier, not too seriously, but noticeably. Usually normal changes in speed would not be apparent as they were compensated with artificial gravity gyros, which all units carried. Obviously not capable of handling speeds and speed reductions beyond the speed of light, but on full power and with astro-velocity reducing at an increasing and even rate they were slowing down to the natural speed of light.

Noah watched their home planet now quite easily visible, but no longer was its rotation clear in fact it was hardly moving. 'No', he thought, *it was stationary.*

Svi and Lika could not feel their body weight any more and the floor was no longer an attraction as the gravitational machines had once again taken 'full' command.

Tubal Cain was watching for them through his observation port with an electronic digital binocular telescope program. He could line log-on to the exact point that Unit no.6 would appear. He watched his video-scanner, there was nothing, and then out of the corner of his screen he could see an image appearing but it was not very clear as if changing in size and color. Then came the flash as if an explosion . . . .

A clear image appeared just as it had disappeared four days previously in a flash of light and apparent implosion, as the craft was to disappear into distant oblivion. Tubal Cain knew all was well as the radio and video signals kept coming, but slowly and elongated as they were stretched through the distance of time. Tubal Cain was excited they were absolutely on time, and within less than an hour would be back in their correct position in orbit.

***

Sad it was that such a day should be the first public outing for Noah's son Shem. Chaudle's Memorial Day had been arranged almost entirely by Fadfagi's wife Rebecca, and it was her genius idea to involve children at the memorial service. Chaudle loved children and, as he often said, it was for them and their future that he had fought so stolidly for peace. Rebecca had decided that all adults attending should bring at least one of their children with them. If they had not any children then they were to bring their nearest child relative. She wanted the world to appreciate that it was for their children's sake that Chaudle's cause should be continued. It had been universally accepted and praised that this was what Chaudle would have wanted as his memory. The beautiful valley of "God's Peace" had never seen so many people at one time, the remote and serene village that stood on the side of one of those quiet peaceful hills was awash with lines of people all trying to 'push' to the front to be nearer to the 'Old Temple' site where the gathering of political celebrities were taking their seats for the formal service of honor and thanks for the work and gift to humankind of such a man as Chaudle.

The spirit of the message was genuine, as even the crowds who were gathering had brought their children in their masses. Everywhere there where parents with young children either holding hands or on their shoulders, and all had brightly colored re-cycled paper garlands around their neck. The brightness and contrasts of the multi-colored adornments, coupled with the magnificent splendor of the multi-colored clothes that all the people were wearing out of an almost 'holy' reverence for this wonderful man now deceased. The strength of the color generated a happy warm glow across the hazy sunny countryside.

The atmosphere was at peace, and the people were in unison with their appreciation of the solemnity of the event. Through their quiet and peaceful meditation even the children hardly made a sound as the three-dimensional sound of gentle mystic and magical music flowed melodically across their crowded ether.

An embarrassed latecomer carrying a small child pushed his way politely along a row of seated mourners and sat himself down next to Tubal Cain.

"I have to speak with you, and not here" Erash whispered into Tubal's left ear, "It's too dangerous but we must speak!" Tubal nodded slightly in recognition and lifted his flattened palm from his lap in answer. They would meet later out of earshot and then indicated politely that the first speaker was about to introduce the leader for the ceremony. Rebecca approached the podium and spoke gently to all present and almost the entire listening world. To those close by and also the closest of television cameras there could be seen the dampness of the suppressed tear on both eyes.

"I would like to introduce to you the deputy leader of the 'Council of G-d's Peace' who as a youngster knew Chaudle as his playmate and having similar peaceful aspirations it was felt correct that he should lead this service of homage to this benefactor of humankind, a man loved by us all!"

Shem was not listening to the ceremony but was intent in looking around at the gathered crowd; there were so many children, virtually every other seat contained a young person and the atmosphere was very somber. He was amazed that from so many children not a noise was out of place, not a murmur of disrespect, not a fidget of boredom. He knew that like himself they were probably not listening to the oration but their behavior was subdued each out of respect for the strength of the occasion.

The ceremony seemed to go on forever for Shem as he had a small part to play in the proceedings and he was becoming nervous as the time slowly passed. He knew his lines; he had learned the words overnight and his uncle Jubal had listened to him that very morning. He was perfect. Shem had faith in God, just like his father, and he knew that God would not let him down but just to make sure, he gave a quiet prayer.

The people around him began to turn their heads towards him in a good luck gesture, for there next on the ceremonial list was Shem's name and the task he was about to do.

"I now call from among us gathered here, 'Shem' the son of Noah, a senior minister of the government of his country. Shem is going to repeat those famous words uttered by Chaudle at the last world peace conference at which he was talking about 'worry and faith' in the context of humankind."

Shem had now reached the podium, he was still only a little boy, and this would give full effective strength to the words he was about to utter. He shuffled his feet a little to make sure that he was standing firmly on the ground and looked out and across to smile and wink to his daddy. A soprano-like unbroken voice then uttered out of his mouth . . .

"There is no point in worrying about the past,
it is gone, you can only feel guilty.
There is no point about worrying about the present,
for it is gone in an instant, you can only suffer it.
*Nevertheless, you '**should**' worry about the future,*
so that perhaps you can change it for the better!"

Shem nodded a small bow of his head, turned and descended back to rejoin his proud dad. The words coming from such a small child on such an occasion said everything!!!

***

Tubal and Tsionne sat patiently in the waiting area of their local hospital. The warmth of Tsionne's head gently leaning against his gave Tubal the emotional strength to cope with this new situation. He continued to think of the danger that his father may be in, but with Tsionne's gentle hand stroking at his thigh he could contain his worries. This was just a routine procedure that Lamech was undergoing but his many internal hemorrhages of the past few days had already caused great concern. It was not known how long he had been passing blood in his stools because he himself could not have looked, as he was blind. He was undergoing video examination using mini-cameras, which had been injected into his blood stream and also taken by mouth in the form of small tablets. They were eventually to dissolve and disappear forever but at the moment his whole body was under close computer based examination, all parts of his body and particularly all vital organs were completely internally accessible to the scrutiny of the computer. Once upon a time the eye was the only direct window into the world of the general health of a patient. One could see naked blood vessels and nerve endings, but now this computer visual examination of the human body was becoming the window to everything. The latest advances could even download the human mind possibly the soul itself.

Tubal's thoughts were wandering through the technological advances of recent years; he had almost drifted away from the problems of his father who was erratically losing blood. He began to think back to the early days of his childhood when his seeing father used to take him everywhere. How he loved to go to the Nature Park and walk in the long grass, which often would come over his young head and barely up to his father's waist. His memories were rambling on as his thoughts began to dwell on the soft sweet smell of flowers with the thorny spiky stems, the sunshine that occasionally illuminated a deep blue sky, which upward seemed to be everywhere that he looked. He remembered the days that his mother and father had taken the family to the seaside, and how when playing among the rock pools at the water's edge, he would be astonished by the many mini creatures living therein. He recalled how each time he arrived for the first time at the coast, how amazed he was and the deep impression he experienced when he saw that 'line' of the horizon that went cleanly across his vision. Did anyone who went out there ever fall off? He used to think. They stopped coming to the seaside, he remembered, as his father started to find the light too bright and could no longer tolerate the headaches that would follow any such visit. It was not much later when his father started to trip over things and become a lot more irritable to his family. His father was slowly going blind. Tubal controlled his thoughts and he pushed his memories back further into the past, he wanted his father seeing again in the happier playful times of Tubal's childhood days. He remembered the times when they would visit the mountains and sit by the flowing stream as it moved gently downwards winding its way through the rocks and gullies downward and downward to the valley beneath. They used to follow as best they could by walking down and keeping in close contact through the small tree groves and across the occasional mountain field of greenish grass until they reached the wide moving river in the valley they loved. Tubal thought to himself, how strange that his childhood memories always brought him back to water and green fields. Nature had changed so much since his early years and he knew from old films and videotapes that life was even cleaner and more beautiful in his father and grandfather's time. He was completely absorbed in re-thinking his childish thoughts and childhood memories when he felt Tsionne's hand tighten suddenly against the inside of his thigh.

A nursing attendant dressed in a surgical gown was walking towards them at a brisk pace, Tubal could not believe what he was thinking, and he just prayed that he was wrong!

He was not wrong . . .

. . . the intruder spoke directly to Tubal. "Tubal Cain?" He nodded recognition, "Your father is no more!"

***

Rula and Marla were sitting on their deck trying to enjoy the warmth of the early afternoon in the hazy sunshine. They were both anxious about the state of their husband's health. Since Erash had been frog hunting in the northern marshlands he had become more irritable and his skin had developed a nervous type of rash. Even his eyelids were red and sore, he just was not right. He had taken to wearing sunglasses most of the time just to protect himself from the strong hazy light of the day. He would not stop working and even as they spoke he was out on another task related to his work with Tubal Cain.

The twins were certainly unsettled in support for Erash, they both loved him very much, as much as they loved each other but they could see changes in him and in his character. He was becoming impatient and sometimes a hint of aggression in his manner, which for Erash was foreign to his nature.

Their worry was that the nature of Erash's problems was having a corrosive effect on their family life to the point of making them all miserable. Since their marriage to Erash they had only produced the one child and of that Erash was not the father, although he had always treated him as his own, spending all his time with him.

Rula was talking at length about the last time Erash had been home for more than one day, when Marla interrupted her . . . "I have to tell you this" she bent over to speak closer to her sister, as if to keep a private conversation even more secret in the privacy and seclusion of their own home. There was nobody about and Alram was out with Rebecca, she continued in a whisper . . .

"I've missed my period and I'm very late with the next."

Rula was not ruffled in her reply,

"Have you done a test?"

"Yes."

"Well?" Rula was a little pushy in her tone.

"Positive, and very strong!"

"Phew!" Rula got up from her chair and crossed over to Marla, throwing her arms around her sister with tears beginning in her eyes "I hope it's twins" she said and continued to whisper into her sister's ear . . .

"I think that I'm pregnant too!" she smiled.

"What!" Marla almost shouted in disbelief "How wonderful, how long?"

"Same as you, very late for my second period, tested positive but average strength, doubtful whether twins."

"Twins are very common in our family", Marla was thinking aloud.

"We must not neglect Alram" Rula remarked "he looks upon Erash as his dad, and worships the ground he walks on. Perhaps when Erash has his own children he may not take such an interest in his stepson. It worries me!"

It was the glassware that caught Rula's eye as it started to quiver and crawl along their shelf in the display cabinet above and behind Marla's head. It began to tinkle as it rubbed together with its brothers and sisters as they seemed to shudder in spasms, the cabinet door sprung open and a thin metal tray fell over clattering out of the unit taking some glass cups with it, with glass shattering into many small pieces around Marla's feet on the floor below. "Can you feel that?" Rula called to Marla in astonishment "It is as if a train is rolling along underneath us, but it is solid ground and there is no railway or sewage tunnel anywhere in this area."

"It was enough to cause *this* damage!" Marla breathed in . . .

"A groundquake!" she shouted.

***

Noah and Tubal were enjoined in conversation around a large conference table in the Scientific Assessment Offices of Science and Welfare. They were both feeling very satisfied and full of feelings of well being, as once again they were back on the luxury of the solid ground of their mother planet.

Noah had called this informal meeting of the 'Astro—Board' prior to his arrival back at ground level. He had wanted to assimilate all the relevant data into a generally discussed future policy document.

"We have discovered many new items of interest during the last few months and can now put together some important statements of fact . . ."

He handed out twelve copies of his original document, one to each of the other people present.

"Please read it and remember that this information although scientific fact, is classified secret within our department, and must at present remain as such."

The introduction of the document read . . .

'1 . *The speed of light is purely a relative measurement, and it is not a prohibitive limit to man's future speeds of travel.*

2. *Examination of the universe reveals past developments of beings not dissimilar to humankind itself, although from where those 'people' come is still as yet a mystery.*

3. *There is documented and taped evidence of the creation of one similar system of planets to this one already being in existence approximately only four or five hundred light years away from here, merely half one generation's lifetime.*

 Within that system there could well by now have developed a planet that would support life, possibly similar to that of humankind. Some of those planets have their own natural moons and could form a very interesting basis for further examination.

4 . *Pollution on this planet is becoming a major problem as the energies of humankind become more parasitic and destructive. It could be said that on a colored topographical map of this planet 78% of it is now affected directly by human pollution and as can be seen from the affixed statistics, nearly 50% of the whole is almost irretrievable in the short term.*

5. *There now exists sufficient living space in orbit to accept 10% of the population of humankind from this mother planet and as such could be a useful source of industrial growth for the future.*

6. *We have new unsolved problems in the general water supply, the weather, the ozone protective layer and even the air we breathe.*

7. *Humankind's insatiable thirst for possession and jealousy for power over his fellow human, is causing great concern as the build up of horrendous nuclear weaponry is still ongoing although in secret and under the possible potential power of some very unscrupulous self-opinionated political leaders.'*

Noah asked them just to read through the introduction to themselves and then each section that followed was to be discussed in detail. Tubal Cain was full of emotion, at last a direction was beginning to formulate in front of them, and with a little more effort and some concrete decision under his belt he may be able to influence government itself.

After a short while the papers began to shuffle and a murmur of whispers began to emit from the eleven other gathered members of the committee, as Tubal Cain looked up at Noah as if to say, what a wonderful mammoth task, already partially complete. How did they manage to come so far? Although Tubal had not uttered a word, Noah could read every word that he had thought just by looking at his face, it said it all. Noah smiled back in full acknowledgement to Tubal Cain; he knew what this so far achievement had meant to him, to both of them.

***

'The Third Rising'
The beginning of the end,
or, towards the end of the beginning . . .

Many periods had passed since Neyl's admission to ground control at ETON and now this was his first time in sole charge of the engineering section of an intra orbital shuttlecraft from its base on the ground below. They were scheduled to dock very shortly with an orbital space station. He was in charge of the engines and all technical work had to be channeled through him. He was directly responsible to the captain, his immediate superior officer. As chief engineer Neyl had progressed fast and far since his arrival on the mainland with Rianne.

Neyl looked out of his office window as the ship began to turn very slightly on its axis in order to achieve its exact locater with the entrance port of Orbital 6 of section 43. They were approaching under autopilot and Neyl could just sit back and admire the view. He was in charge, but he only had to monitor the equipment unless there was a problem. This gave his mind time to wander to that time when he was a prisoner within the narrow confines of human captivity, followed by the freedom as he lay at the edge of the sea shore and looked skyward at the dark night of stars. He remembered the vow he made with himself that he will never again be robbed of his freedom. He would always go wherever he wanted and as far as he desired, never ever again to be trapped by the confines of white man's limited space. He never dreamed then, that he would one day escape from the very limits of his captivity on mother planet herself. He was there, in the outer environment of orbital space. Free and completely at will, away from captivity down there in that little blemish of territory on that planet below. He allowed himself the luxury of thinking of Rianne, his beautiful woman with whom he had built up such a strong friendship and personal relationship, that they were almost man and wife. This of course was illegal. Marriage was not allowed between hybrid and human but so long as one was sterilized it was allowed for them to be partners. With Neyl's sudden promotion they had been forced to make a decision and Neyl insisted it should be him. Any way it was always easier for the Hybrid to 'get done' than the white person. He knew that children were out of the question, a family would likely never be theirs, but they could still have each other . . .

Docking procedures were nearly complete, and Neyl had to come back to reality. Routine had to be followed and procedures completed, with preparations to be made for their return journey. This would be his very first complete tour of duty solo, since his recent promotion. Perhaps soon, he thought, he could bring Rianne along for the ride so that she could see what he does. After all, it was an exciting experience. It was almost as exciting as going up in an elevator, or lift, except that sometimes in this craft one had a good view.

The first passengers were now disembarking, as Neyl went over to the control panel and, on the captain's orders, started the automatic countdown to final departure for their return journey. This involved recharging the magnetic solenoids and rewinding the gyroscopes. He had to bring the engines back up to full capacity in order that the power was there that they would be able to make a soft stable landing back on the ground at ETON. This was a relatively long procedure as it was one of the older varieties of craft that had been modified. It could now land directly back on the mother planet and also elevate from there without a small supply shuttle, as had always been the case in the past, this vessel did not recharge in flight. One day perhaps thought Neyl. He sat there at his desk guiding the procedures with his computer mouse as if it was all a children's' game.

***

Rebecca appeared at the twins' door, the expression on her face said it all. Worried shock affected people in many different ways but Rebecca's pale worried brow and quietness of speech barely above a whisper demonstrated a depth of anxiety to the root of her emotions.

Rula gently took her hand and carefully guided her to a comfortable seat in their family room. Marla prepared a warm leafy drink that she had kept in her stores just for such occasions.

"We heard about Fadfagi's illness, is it that serious?" asked Rula while leaning over to her friend's ear in a whisper.

"Terminal . . . but . . .!

Rebecca hesitated as if she should not have said that, even to Rula. She nevertheless continued ". . . please don't repeat this, the media must not be told, it will cause panic in our country and people will climb over each other for their piece of power. It will be bad enough when it happens, but let my man sort this out himself. He is very much the egotist, but I am sure he won't let his country down! He's told me so."

"What's wrong with him?" asked Marla as she handed Rebecca her warm brew.

"Terminal cancer, it's gone too far, he was always too busy to seek medical advice, now it's too late. Even a body transplant won't work, because mild traces have been found in his brain fluid and although not well established, it rules out his chances of even mediocre survival into a new body. Otherwise, you can be sure he would have commandeered one from one of his subjects even if he had to 'kill' for it. Several medical opinions have told him that he would guarantee a shorter life if he had a new body. The shock would be too much for his brain to sustain without adverse reaction. There is no hope. Perhaps only a short while longer before pain will take him over. I am worried about what he will do then, with all that power. He could certainly be very dangerous!"

"We will have to tell Erash!" said the twins in unison. "That's why I am here." Rebecca continued "Please keep this quiet from the public gaze, but with that in mind, you must tell Erash, and then Tubal Cain and Noah will know. It is very important I believe, just for the sake of survival. Fadfagi is capable of anything, he could be vindictive."

"What for instance?" asked Rula.

"He has weapons of mass destruction hidden away. He has been testing them for years. Remember those ground quakes? Those were of his making, and his ego is supreme."

"Why does he subscribe to being a peacemaker? He made himself so obvious in his presence at Chaudle's memorial service. He has been well-represented at all environmental conferences; he has even signed the "Radiact Non Proliferation Treaty!" Marla queried.

"He wears the halo of an angel to all those who don't really know him!" Rebecca was becoming red with frustration, and certainly very disturbed.

"Thank you for telling us!" We will contact Erash at once on his 'red' line. He must be told immediately. We have to prepare for the worst case scenario!" Marla voiced to Rebecca and her sister.

Rebecca had not yet left when Erash arrived home to his two pregnant wives. They were due at anytime soon. "I want my children to have lives to live, and a future to look forward to enjoy. This guy of yours could bring pandemonium to this world of ours. You were right to come to us. I will not let this become public knowledge. He is the devil himself. We can only *pray* for his salvation," Erash hesitated . . . "tell me, do you love him?"

Rebecca was shocked by the directness of the question . . . "I used to, but now I am just sorry for him and I only wish him well in the hope that even at this late hour he might change.

***

"Clone! Clone! Duplication? No, it isn't ethical, it's immoral!" shouted Lika, at Velmitz, whose face immediately changed from that of an achiever to one of surprise and temporary embarrassment.

"That's what we are here for. We have been given the task of renewing species that have been almost eradicated on our planet below. For those of which we have found structured cell tissue we have been able to genetically restructure species that are extinct. Recently using special computer assistance we have recreated an ancient bird, which could not fly. It used to live in the frozen Polar Regions. We believe it to be the very first recreation of its' type. It has wings, which are not developed, but it uses them as fins with which to swim in the cold waters of that area. It has furry skin, which resembles feather, but isn't. These creatures are we believe just how G-d originally created them, or as they were meant to have evolved G-d's way. Surely this cannot be wrong, to bring back one of G-d's creations and remove it forever from the list of extinct species?"

Lika did not know how to react; she was completely shocked. Sure she thought, this was wonderful to bring back an extinct species, but what right had they to take on G-d's work, on the other hand, were they just putting right an error of destiny of a creature that was brought about by humankind itself. In defense she threw a ludicrous remark into the argument . . .

"I suppose that you will be doing that with human beings next!" she said with mild conviction in her voice. "We are! Didn't you know? This is illegal down below, but up here in orbit we have been working on it with people who have studied this for years. This is being done in another station, similar to this one only a few blocks away from here!"

"We discussed this a long while ago." Svi interrupted, he could feel the confusion in Lika's thoughts as he moved up to her and warmly placed his arm around her waist. "Up here," he continued, "we have a job to do, attempting to continue life as it was once meant to be. It is the continuance of the battle for survival, which is in-built as a motive for all living creatures. The innate desire to procreate and continue to exist is to us God given, and what we are doing up here in orbital space is just one more way for us to follow in G-d's direction!"

"What right have we to touch life with our finger, to bring about engineered pre-designed life, lives that are only to exist by the efforts of human ingenuity?" Lika reacted as if thinking aloud.

"What right have we to kill?" asked Svi.

"For survival, yes!" answered Lika in a quick response "Not for any other reason. We should not play games with creation and certainly not just for the fun of it. You can't tell me that much of what we are doing is for the benefit of survival."

"It could be!" Velmitz interjected. "Who knows what may happen in time to come, in future centuries. Who would have guessed at a time only three and a half human generations ago that mankind's subsequent generations would have done so much to destroy the very planet upon which they had fervently depended for survival?" He thought to himself, how much he had changed since his earlier days as a poacher and bounty hunter.

Lika was thinking of Trin, who was she, and from where did she come? What about her own child? Would she with Svi ever find out what happened to their offspring? Oh what were humans doing with life and G-d's creation? What had she become? Was she nurse or soldier?

***

"'AEF'. What is that?"

"Accelerated Electro-magnetic Frequency'", Replied Tubal Cain, he was absorbed in discussion with Noah about the recent findings from a pioneering probe that had been sent nearly half a generation previously out into the depths of the unknown void of space. He continued . . .

"When this early probe was sent on its unmanned mission, it was fitted out with a laboratory of robots which although primitive by modern standards, could produce some very near human movement. They worked under command from our home base here at ground control. The only problem was that it was soon to go out of useful electronic communication range that the time delay between one order and the next would become very impractical. Work of any purpose over such a far distance was to become laborious and somewhat impossible. Rather like a computer with a slow drive due to over-filled memory. Our early pioneers nevertheless had foresight and at that time were working on a way of accelerating the impulse generation of the electromagnetic spectrum, using magnets and metal coated strips on a rapidly rotating drum. Today it can all be done using computer programming and a 'super speed' has now been produced where the velocity of radio waves, even various light waves can be increased with very little difficulty well beyond their natural speeds. In fact they have reached speeds thirty or forty million times their natural speeds. Can you imagine something out there in space at least one thousand light years away; it would effectively be on our doorstep! We could communicate on the *'waves'* without much time delay, if any!" Tubal sat down and took a long satisfying sip of his warm steamy drink. "We now have the ability and capacity to directly communicate with this craft and have adapted it using new programs within old technology and have been able to establish a return transmission module using 'AEF'. We have been able to communicate on an immediate basis with this pioneer craft for several weeks now and have come up with some shattering results, almost unbelievable. The views of 'ancient' heavens are so similar and yet so different. There are symmetrical movements of stars and some asymmetrical, we would never have known the degree of this before. It gives us a whole new meaning to the origin of matter itself." He had Noah completely involved in his oration and continued . . .

"The several electronic telescopes that we have on board are feeding us with vast amounts of information, too much to assimilate in such a short time. There is also the *'time warp factor'* as the origin of the astronomic data that we receive from the craft is older by more than a half of a human generation, even as it looks back to this planet it shows us in immense detail our home as it was then, that long ago. Just think our planet can be seen exactly as it was when our fathers were our age. We have attempted to push pioneer faster farther outward into space but it won't travel fast enough to make any immediate difference to our results of today."

"This will make extraordinary changes in our abilities for space exploration." Noah mused with a pensive smile almost exuding with his enthusiasm. "Can I have a detailed report on a specific area out there? Is it possible?"

"Of course you can, it would prove most interesting, and especially when you see by example the intricately detailed manner in which we look at this, our home planet."

Tubal took out a large poster size folder and opened it out onto the desk. It was full of brilliant color pictures of the surface of their home planet in various degrees of magnification.

"What strikes you most about this?" Noah says to Tubal and continues, "The weather patterns, they are variable, all over the planet. There are swirls of cloud and clear skies. Look whole large areas, which are basking in open clear warm sunshine. The greenhouse effect had not yet materialized and pollution had not yet reared its' ugly head. Look at those rivers, the detail no scummy foam just clear water and you can often see through to the bottom.

Noah scribbled instructions on a piece of artificial paper and handed it to Tubal Cain.

***

CHAPTER 9

Gramps answered his videophone; a tearful three-dimensional picture of Tsionne stepped into his room. The new holographic technology made everything so realistic. He could almost be tempted to put his arms around her.

"Arianne has disappeared with the baby. I should never have employed her as nurse. She was becoming too close . . . I should never . . . She took my baby . . . Oh! Oh! . . . Oh Gramps what shall I do? Tubal will be furious, he never wanted Arianne around after the birth but I felt sorry for her. He'll kill me!"

"Don't be absurd, Tubal couldn't kill a fly! How long has she been gone? What makes you think she has taken off with the child?"

"I don't know, but I just know that she has gone!"

Tsionne sat down partially out of camera sight, so that only her head and shoulders appeared in front of Methuselah, the lower part of her body disappeared into thin air. Her head and shoulders were suspended in the middle of the room with nothing underneath, almost ghost-like. She began to cry almost uncontrollably.

"I'll come around to you right away, where is Tubal Cain?"

"No please don't come, everyone will talk! Tubal is with Noah, a special meeting. I'm worried about security. Arianne could be quite evil. I'm beginning to see what Tubal meant. She could be very dangerous. Oh Gramps, what shall I do?"

"Call Tubal on his mobile, tell him what has happened. I am sure that he would prefer to be in control. Do not keep it from him, or then he never will forgive you!"

"You are right!" The image of Tsionne faded away without even as much as a goodbye. She faded into nothing as she turned off her terminal. Gramps still could not get used to the reality of the technology, only paled by the reality of this sudden situation.

Tubal Cain was still absorbed in deep conversation with his 'chum' Noah, when his mobile phone buzzed in his ear . . . it was his wife.

"What makes you think that she's not coming back?"

"I don't know, but I just know that she isn't coming back. She has taken some of her personal things, not all of them, and none of baby's things just the carry cradle and wheels. That's it! That is what it is; she has taken her toothbrush and make-up tray. She would not want to be without it . . . and her hairbrush, but nothing of baby's. Oh what shall I do?"

"How long has she been gone?"

"Since mid morning at least, she was here for breakfast."

"It's only mid afternoon now. That is not long!"

"I know, but believe me, woman's instinct. I know that she has gone, with our child. Oh . . . Oh!"

"Was there any sign of a struggle, a mess or anything of that sort?"

"Not really, but it does look as if she was in the middle of cleaning up and left in a hurry."

Tsionne was beginning to cry again and one thing that always got to Tubal was his wife when she cried. He always loved her more for it. His stomach and heart were competing with each other for emotional attention.

"I will alert security, and will return home immediately now! Love you darling. I will see you soon. Don't touch anything. We will find our baby, there is probably a good explanation for everything . . . Don't worry!" On those not so remarkable words he turned off his mobile and looked at Noah . . .

"Our child has possibly been kidnapped by its' surrogate mother, *its' Nurse*!"

***

Erash arrived home in the middle of the day, without warning, and he had Alram with him. He had collected him early from school.

"Where is Marla?" he asked Rula while holding his son's hand tightly as if he didn't want to let go. The fear was plainly obvious on Erash's face; he was almost white as if he had seen a ghost. He became very authoritative in his speech "Where is your sister?" he asked again almost aggressively.

Rula had never seen her husband like this before, and they had been through a lot together.

"Marla is out with Rebecca, but should be back very shortly."

"Get packed! Everything for both of you, and Alram, we are leaving and may not be back perhaps ever. I want to leave here as soon as it gets dark. This is an emergency, take Alram and let him choose a few of his favorite things. Two travel bags each, that's six in total, you can take two more for me," he said as if an afterthought, "but I am not sure if I can make it immediately, but take my baggage anyway. I will catch up with you later!"

Rula shouted at Erash . . .

"What's got into you?" She yelled, "Why have you brought Alram home so early in the middle of the day?" She pushed her son out of the living room door. "Go upstairs and do what your daddy says." She called after him as he obediently went about his chores, almost as if he knew the importance of the situation.

"Now what is this all about?" Rula queried again, trying to calm down the urgency in Erash's voice.

"How is Rebecca?" Erash asked, as if it was in answer to Rula's question.

"What has that got to do with it?" Rula was becoming impatient.

"Everything" he answered, "Her old man is up to no good. He's dying and there is every reason to believe that he is concocting the worst epitaph of human history. I want my family safe, out of reach. Now please get packed as I ask and I will explain when Marla and Rebecca get home, but for now please get packed. This may be our last chance. We could be going on a very long journey. Please believe me I have it on very good authority. Oh and by the way, don't tell anybody, or panic will break loose and then we will all be trapped. Now please go, I have papers to prepare, electronic-mails and faxes to send.

Erash had been at work in his office at home for quite a while when he heard the door go and Marla walked in. She saw Erash, the mess of papers and the beginnings of a collection of packed luggage. They both spoke at the same time . . .

"What's this mess, what is going on, why are you home?"

"Where is Rebecca?" Erash was trying to look back through the door behind Marla.

She has gone! She was too upset, and could not stop; she wanted to go back to her husband. He has taken a turn for the worse!"

"I know!" Erash answered with authority. "He has become very dangerous, and we have to act fast!" at that moment Rula came back into the room.

"What is this all about? Marla called to her sister "Why all the bags, where are you going?"

"Not just Rula, all of us" Erash interrupted by calling across the room "I want my family safe, and out of reach of Fadfagi's horrific sick warlike arms. He is going to leave a dramatic memorial that those who survive will always remember him, and I have that decoded on excellent authority. I wanted to tell Rebecca to be aware and perhaps come with us."

Rebecca appeared at the door as if directly on cue.

"No! I must go to my husband, he needs me, and his country needs me, if I am to save this world from a holocaust. I love you all, but I must do what I have to do!"

Rebecca disappeared back through the door as quickly as she had appeared.

***

Noah could not believe what had happened; he was pacing up and down his office. Tubal had promised to contact him with news, the moment that he arrived home. Poor Tsionne must be demented with the pain of not knowing. Even he, Noah was unable to relax. The young infant had been constantly on his mind from the moment that Tubal Cain answered the call from Tsionne. If Noah was feeling like that, how must Tubal and Tsionne feel? He kept pacing back and forth. There was no way could he concentrate on work. Every time the fax, phone, or holographic video machine clicked into action, Noah's heart missed a beat! How could anyone do that to Tubal?

After what seemed an indeterminate length of time, there was a buzz on his greeting board telling him of a visitor at his private entrance. Not many people knew where that was and few had access to it. He flashed on his video security and took a deep breath. It was Naamah with her brother Jabal.

Noah was feeling unusually insecure as his wife and brother in law appeared at the private back door to his office. What was the purpose of their sudden visit? Naamah was appearing very formal in her manner and why did she bring Jabal as her escort. Every logical point was rushing through Noah's brain as he opened the door and began to question them. "What's going on? Why are you here? What is happening?" Jabal answered very quickly, as he placed a rolled scroll into Noah's right hand.

"This was received by Naamah earlier this afternoon on your private emergency domestic fax line. It was from Erash, and he has encoded it. Look it's marked *'Extremely URGENT and for Noah's eyes only!'* It arrived at your home and Naamah did not want to bring it to you alone. She says that there is something about it that scares her, although we cannot decode it. Perhaps it is the fact that Erash chose to encode it in the first place, especially as it was on your private line. "Let me have a look at it," replied Noah as he began unrolling it out of its' tube. Noah took a thin plastic sheet out of a concealed drawer at the back of his desk; date coded it, and then held it over the script.

"Sit down both of you. This is extraordinary! Erash can't be right. I'll read it to you . . . "

As the words came out of Noah's mouth Naamah took Jabal's hand and gripped it tightly with tears almost lacrimating into her eyes. Slowly the truth of what was about to befall their lands became more apparent to them as Noah went farther and deeper into Erash's decoding script.

At an opportune moment Noah took a long breath and the three shocked people took an aghast look at one another as the truth of a possible Armageddon began to dawn on them. The artificial silence went unbroken as the depth of meaning began to sink in. The momentary pause in Noah's narration seemed like an eternity as again Noah continued into Erash's long message, almost oblivious to his listeners and nervously realizing more and more with every word, the responsibility that was being thrown upon him.

" . . . and with that, I am anxious to bring this to your notice Noah as at this time it would be unfair and unwise to lay more burdens on my immediate superior Tubal Cain. Please keep this message only for your own protection, and do not place it in the archives. I have no objection in your showing it to Tubal Cain, but at this time with their baby being stolen, that must be your choice and not mine. We all love you Noah. Sorry, from Erash!"

Naamah usually could somewhat control her emotions, but fighting back the tears she threw herself into Noah's arms saying . . .

"The horror of this situation I can cope with, we have had good lives although unfinished, but our children, and all those other children who have hardly had a blink at life. Those poor souls. What has humanity done to G-d, that he should seek such revenge?"

Although somewhat stunned by reaction and remark relating to the shock report from Erash, Noah spoke with strong resolution in his voice . . .

"I believe that G-d gave us all life for a purpose and a meaning only known to him. This life that I have been given has now been shown by G-d, the purpose for which it was meant and I must follow G-d's way. *Come . . .*" He held out his hands to Jabal and Naamah saying . . .

"We have work to do!"

***

There was suddenly a lot of activity on Orbital craft 43. Svi in section 6 was trying very hard to concentrate on his job at hand, but with all the maintenance staff chasing their tails, checking and listing, it was becoming very difficult even just to collect and put together his daily statistics.

"What's going on? Why such a hive of activity? Why are you guys all so near to panic?" Svi asked one of the engineers. "Orders! Orders from above. It seems that big guns, top brass are coming to visit, with their families. That has never happened before. Children in Orbit! Big names! We have to have everything perfect. Even 'Velmitz the Spiv' has been given special orders. Why him?"

The small engineer continued on his task. A somewhat tiny man as was often chosen for such jobs being as he could creep so easily into sections and volumes that most normally sized people would find an effort, or a difficulty. 'Mind your head' signs for this guy had never had any meaning other than 'I wish'.

Not far away from Svi, Neyl was standing with one of the 'check-in' guys who examines, notes down and checks off the cargoes that were being unloaded from one of the recently more frequent visiting astro-trucks. The trucks catered for all the needs and demand of the orbital industries and residencies. Goods were brought on a regular basis, as was the waste re-cycled and often taken back to home planet for disposal. Neyl was now well entrenched in this kind of work, as a chief engineer. He enjoyed it very much. Some days it would be passenger shuttle, or on another it could be goods. One or two transports could do both. All the very latest machines did both and were more profitable.

"What are you carrying here in these sealed boxes?" The security guy was being more inquisitive than usual.

"It says medical supplies, rare specimens!" Replied Neyl as if to say isn't that obvious, it's written on the label. "I want you to open it please!"

"That is dangerous! I cannot open it, I'm not authorized!"

"Then take it back on board your truck, or we will have the legal right to destroy it."

"No!" shouted Neyl at the guy "Perhaps we should call the person who is officially responsible for this material. He can make the choice!"

"OK! But you only have a few minutes of unloading time left."

"Velmitz Sharon" said Neyl as he pointed to the recipient label on the large case.

"No idea!" replied the officer guy shrugging his shoulders. "Although there is a special department on this craft where they do medical experiments. I believe a Dr Sharon could be there!"

"Don't touch that!" screamed Velmitz. He had managed to run at furious pace to get to the loading bay with only a few moments to spare. He opened his jacket and pulled out his pass showing a much superior rank to the security officer. "I have a much higher rank than you, and when in uniform I have much more silver braid on my black uniform than you. In fact my rank is so high that the silver on my trousers makes it very difficult to sit down!" Velmitz's humor was lost on the security officer who stood his ground and went to his belt. Holding his paresifier and making it obvious that he was setting it in a ready to use mode he answered Velmitz . . . "Unless you open one of these cartons, I will have to destroy them. If you make one false move, I will shoot you. This is my job whatever your rank. Sir!"

"This may be your job, but if you open these outside laboratory conditions, you will be stopping me doing my job, and possibly depriving the world of some very rare specimens of organic material!"

"What for mother's sake, specimens?" asked the guard, while beginning to show that he was losing his patience "Perhaps this will help!" Velmitz pulled out of his wallet a government seal of office authorizing his use of listed organic material, signed by Noah himself.

"Why didn't you show me that before? Sir?" shouted the guard saluting and standing to attention.

"I didn't think." Came the reply.

***

"Don't worry. Our baby will be safer than you are! I will keep in touch with you. Love, Arianne."

"Don't worry. Our baby will be safer than you are! I will keep in touch with you. Love, Arianne."

"How many times are you going to play that godforsaken message on our voice-mail? You will wear out our answerphone machine." Tsionne was never rude and always kept her temper, especially as far as Tubal Cain was concerned, but things were going from bad to worse, and she was beginning to blame Tubal for the loss of their baby. It was his fault that he was so famous. It was his fault that he was so wealthy, and so involved in politics. Good gracious it was his police force that was virtually in entire worldwide control. His black and silver uniforms were everywhere. Why had he made himself such a target for kidnap and blackmail? Tsionne knew that the truth was a different reality, but the picture could easily be painted in the manner that she was thinking, and it was causing her strong emotional discomfort. How could life be so cruel?

Tubal turned off the machine, feeling the fractious manner in Tsionne's voice.

"There is a clue there somewhere" he replied "Why does she say 'safer than we are' and why does she sign off 'love' Arianne. There must be a reason for that, and she doesn't ask for anything. Does she?"

"Have you traced the call?"

"I tried, but it was a public call box out in the countryside near Gluma Hills. There is nothing out there, at least nothing of interest. Nobody lives there, it's partially barren, a few old dried up orchards, and of course up in the hills there is some preserved forestation. That's why there are still public telephones there. Oh there is an entrance there to a subterranean unit, I've forgotten the number, but unless she's gone mental, for what would she have gone to that area?"

"I feel sick" Tsionne's face was turning green. She could well have been telling the truth. She did not look well. Her beautiful pink face with pouting lips and dimples had changed to one of sick worry, and Tubal did not seem to be of any help at all.

"What are your police doing?" she asked.

"They are running a trace on all Arianne's movements during the last few months. They can compile a full dossier, possibly even when she went to the toilet. We can find out where she's been, how she most likely traveled, what she bought, almost everything of importance. We can possibly also find out whom she is associating with."

"How do you do that?" Tsionne's face became minutely more relaxed. Something was being done. "How can they find out so much?"

"Her credit and debit banking cards! They leave a wonderful trail behind her. Every transaction tells a story. The date, the time, what she bought, exchanged or cashed, and the place she was at that moment. Sometimes now, we can even also have video or still pictures of her at those places. We will have a full dossier on her by sunset. We have one of her card numbers from the receipt she gave us from when we paid her. We can get everything else from that."

"How?"

"She has credit card insurance, and under these circumstances we can obtain all her other information from that."

"Wow!"

Tubal Cain sat down next to Tsionne and put his arm tightly around her pulling her towards him. She came willingly and put her head across his chest turning to look up at his face. He held her like a baby.

"I love you," Tubal said "I will never let you down. This terrible thing will sort itself out, I promise you." Tubal looked past Tsionne's face at the floor as if in a bewildered dream and he continued talking to the floor, as if thinking aloud.

"I do not understand that message she left. It is not threatening, it's somewhat passive. The keywords are '*Safer*', '*love*' and '*our*'. Why? Why did she put it that way, and she seemed sad not happy."

Tsionne jumped up and ran to answer the telephone.

"It's Noah, for you!"

***

Rebecca's return home went completely unnoticed and uneventful, as she had covered herself in very concealing religious clothing. She was dressed in a manner not too unusual for a woman in her country and she could pass most security points without question. It was already dark when she entered her room and the dust had already accumulated on most polished surfaces. This was a major problem in that part of the world, and she had only been away for a couple of days.

She had decided to try and curb Fadfagi's endeavors whilst secretly trying to engineer a new stronger branch of government. She was placing herself at great risk. If her husband found out she would suffer the direst of consequences. She had many true friends in government, and also people she could trust, but there were many opportunists and hangers-on She would have to be sure of whom she would trust, and could not give any wind to the others, or she would surely die before her husband, and he only had perhaps less than a score of days left to live. She had decided on her plan of action and was already working within it.

She was to see her husband within the hour, and was completely ready for it. Her inner self wished that he would pull through and his sure health would return, but of that it would take a miracle from the Almighty himself, and she knew that no way could he qualify for that kind of help. He could be so gentle, so kind, and so understanding. His warmth to others could be highly contagious but he could switch it on and off at will. Even she, Rebecca, could not be totally sure if he was ever genuine.

A small growing drip appeared underneath her husband's nostrils. She sat there next to his bed holding his left hand. He had certainly deteriorated in the last few days since she had last seen him. He was a mere shadow of the man she had known and who had known her in their headier days in their early relationship. She thought back to those happy days when she worshipped him and walked around in the happy ignorance of his ruthlessness and evil abilities. His love for animals, the way he almost risked his life to rescue a small marooned cat caught in the eaves of an old bridge over a fast flowing river. She thought of those times that they used to spend away from the madding crowd locked in each other's arms buried in the dusty muck, up in the private hills of their own private countryside. A naked swim in their local 'fresh water' pond, almost clean of pollutant, the only one in Bylia, and her husband had it all for himself. She was blind to his evils; She saw only the good things he did. How could she have been so naive?

Now she had a duty to herself and the world. She had to stop the forthcoming evil Fadfagi had prepared as a horrific memorial to his life, and leadership. She had to help to re-create a truly democratic 'leadership' government in her adopted country that someone like her husband could never again take the reins of power and ultimately control the destiny of an entire world.

The hand she was holding began to move very weakly and her husband was about to speak. Although outwardly he appeared quite healthy, the inside of his body was going through torment as his cells of life were having a re-creative orgy in reorganization. He was finding speech an increasing effort but if he 'took a run at it' once he got started it became easier for him. He started very slowly . . .

"I am so happy that you are home, I ask that you don't leave me again at least until I have been buried. Stay by my side; at least don't go far away. You are the only wife that I have ever had whom I love, . . . so much! I don't insist, like the leaders in our ancient times, that my favorite wife or wives should be in attendance on me after my death, in my personal tomb, to be buried with me. I could, you know. No I want you to bare witness to my epitaph and try to help re-build this world in my image. I have left a secret "will": which is to be opened by the chief secretary of defense in the presence of two out of three other Government ministers. You will find their names inside the personal flap of your private diary, the one you have with you now, in your handbag. You will have to be there too. Just to observe that my wishes are carried out to the letter. Even as I now speak these decisions are irreversible, except by me in front of the same people. So please don't go far away.

He held her hand even more tightly, very firmly as if he could break her hand. He still had brutal strength when he wanted it. He leaned over to kiss her. With tears in her eyes she kissed him warmly on his mouth.

***

It had been a long time since Svi and Lika had been able to snatch some private time together and eating out was something that they rarely did. They lived on a diet of tablets, pastes, and crunchy bars, something to which most orbital dwellers had become quite accustomed. A perfect balanced diet of bio-chemically constructed products, which could feed all human needs in a perfectly balanced way, and caused the least amount of waste product. It was not accepted by the older generation, but even the waste product of excreta and urine could now be re-cycled into food products and had been for years, but because of prejudice among some people especially the older generation, these products had to be clearly labeled. There was one version of this food that Svi had become particularly fond of, it had a very pleasant and distinctive flavor. He could not understand the distaste among these people for such things.

Lika was keying her way through the computer pages of the *'Cooked food menu'* on the keyboard built into the top of the restaurant dining table at which they were sitting, with a wonderful windowed view of their planet alongside them. It seemed so near that one could imagine reaching out to touch it.

"Natural duck in wine sauce, with capers, onion and potatoes. That sounds interesting. Do you think they kill a duck, and are they real onions?" Lika asked to Svi curiously. "It has to be what it says, that's the law, but of course we don't know how old these products are. It's not like buying them in a shop; they could have been stored for years. We don't eat this food very often so spoil yourself, order whatever you want.

Svi selected his menu choice from the data screen in front of him, using his keyboard from the table, pushed 'enter' and the banner appeared across the screen, 'do you want to be served and billed with the other person at your table? . . 'Yes' or 'No'? He pressed 'Yes'. The answer came up with a further question. Credit / debit card number please. He punched it onto the keyboard and then there was a flash of light across his face as his facial picture was taken and a final message came onto the screen saying . . . 'Your order is being processed along with that of your companion. Your waitress is Salzi and the meals will be along in six minutes. If it takes longer you will qualify for free desserts'.

They would not qualify for the free desserts. At the end of the fifth minute the meals were placed on the table immediately in front of them. Svi felt somewhat nostalgic when he saw his waitress. It was a long time since he had been served food by a gorilla.

"You know, it's a long time since we have been able to enjoy quality time together. Seeing that gorilla just now, reminded me of those student days of ours, and the time I was in the forest in the care of her species. How would you like a holiday trip back home, could visit one of those sea resort spas on the coast, or we could climb a mountain, go skiing, or shopping in a busy city mall, or even just take a deep-sea trip and enjoy natural life. Let's go back to our home planet for a long break. We need it, and we have earned it."

"Things are beginning to change out here in orbit" Lika replied "Our environment is becoming very busy with visitors and we have just had this accommodation count. It seems that they want every conceivable domicile or residence that it is possible to occupy. I understand that we are to have an influx of new people, including 'children' for the first time. They are said to be staying for a long time, but we have no schools up here. If we didn't teach Trin she would have no education at all. *We* knew that but do these people? Maybe they will start a school. Wouldn't that be wonderful for Trin? She will also have friends of her own who aren't adult." Lika took a breath and a thought for a moment. "Our jobs are secure and our new accommodation is beautiful, so many rooms, a palace. Why not!" she mused, "Why not, let's take a long break and enjoy a paid holiday back on our home planet. Perhaps we could even meet your gorilla friends if they have returned from orbit. Lika smiled to Svi.

***

Tsionne and Tubal had decided to go to the area where Arianne was last known to have been when she made her telephone call. It was now early morning and the sun was brightening up the hazy sky. The warmth of the day was already making itself known to them even at this early hour.

"Today will be a real scorcher!" Tubal Cain remarked to Tsionne as they rounded the final bend before arriving at the park entrance. Forestry parks had become a well-established tourist center and were very popular with nature lovers in these times of natural austerity. There were an unusual number of vehicles in the line for entry into the park and so early in the morning. The worried couple pulled over to the telephone bay and Tubal got out to look at the numbers on the boxes. He found the one he wanted and it was the first one he looked at. That made sense, the phones were not very busy and that was the first in line. Arianne was probably the only one there when she made her call. Now what should they do? Tubal and Tsionne had almost memorized the long report from the tracing agency of the police force. Tubal had managed to get their final version very late into the evening of the previous day. They now had a reasonably clear outline of the person they were tracking. She had been preparing for a siege and buying produce and baby products as if there was to be nothing left in the shops tomorrow. She had rented a large covered hoverwagon, which she had no doubt loaded with all this produce etc, and last filled up with fuel inside the forest. She did not take much, so she either did not have far to go or she was just topping up the system to full.

Tubal and Tsionne were both highly concerned when they saw some of the items that she had only recently purchased. The phone call from Noah had highlighted their anxiety even more. What did she know? How and why?

The line of traffic into the forest was not normal. Usually it was just the odd car, or hoversphere, enjoying the day in the park, looking for the odd bear or gorilla to play with, but today it was like a slow moving line, a queue of people, all in their various sorts of vehicles slowly moving in one direction along the narrow winding forest road. Tubal looked hard in front of them as they joined the slow moving flow of traffic, he pointed out to Tsionne, it was like joining in a long column of refugees all trying to run away.

They all packed their vehicles to their fullest capacity, some were pulling filled up and overflowing trailers, and some had their roof racks filled to overflowing. On one occasion he noticed an old fashioned television set at the side of the road, dumped as if forgotten and left for posterity. Whoever did that was in serious trouble, as when traced they will pay bitterly for leaving litter especially on forestry land.

"Where they all going?" Tubal asked Tsionne. It was a non rhetorical question, they both knew the answer, but did not want to recognize it.

"Subterranean!" Tsionne and Tubal mouthed at the same time. "How do all these people know? Where are they coming from?" said Tubal Cain.

"Look!" shouted Lika, "Complete families, and all their belongings. It almost looks organized!"

"Noah was right, we must call Erash and tell him, do you know his mobile telephone number?"

Tubal dialed Erash on his scrambled line. After a long wait the two men discussed the situation at length. Tubal terminated the call and turned to Tsionne.

"Everything depends on Rebecca now, but we have to make very quick decisions Erash is taking his family out to Noah and his family in Orbit. We can't make it, and won't without baby. Baby is probably with Arianne in there, and I vote we go straight there. Fortunately we did the same as Arianne, copying her habit and we are well stocked up with supplies. Let's go underground!"

"What about Gramps?" said Tsionne?

***

Velmitz almost felt like screaming, he needed more help. Noah in his wisdom had sent him so many cell specimens of living creatures from their home down below that he was finding it very difficult to sort them and file them against the incoming supply of fresh supplies. He had pleaded with Noah to stop, but it was like banging one's head up against a brick wall. Noah would not budge. This was a problem and Velmitz had to deal with it. He could not understand why Noah was sending up such perfectly ordinary specimens for tube filing. These species were prolific and would never become extinct.

Noah was going to arrive in orbit with his family in a few hours; perhaps he would get a clearer picture when they meet. Velmitz had already been informed they would.

Most of the specimens were cell structures with 'mapability' for re-creation but some of the creatures were living and habitat homes had to be found for them in a hurry. Why? Velmitz was completely bewildered. This was a major change of policy in less than a few days. It did not make any sense at all.

Storage of cell specimens was no problem; there was a special 'freezer' library set by solely for Velmitz's department usage. This allowed him to store everything that would be sent to him with space left over. The problem was that he needed more librarians working with him. Categorization and filing the phials was not an easy job, particularly with such a shortage of staff, but the budget would not stretch to more help, Velmitz had always been told. Now Noah was sending up so much volume, it would take far too long to sort it. He would be working for years and still not yet get straight. Fortunately the way the phials were packed, he could keep them as they are in 'astro vacuum freeze' until required, without even opening the cartons. Nevertheless, it was imperative to record and file all stock, and Noah wanted it this way.

Velmitz looked up from his computer screen to see a grave quiet face of Noah looking down on him. Noah looked terrible, there, appeared to be a man with the whole world's worries on his shoulders. This was definitely not the right time to ask for more help, he would have to make do with the staff he already had.

"This place is a mess!" Noah said without even a 'Hello'. It was most unlike him. Anyone could see that he was a very concerned and worried man.

"I don't take a break, and I only have four trained librarians working for me." Velmitz defended himself. "Here are very special cell phials, I want you personally to put them somewhere very safe and mark them for my attention only. They are very important to me, and I don't want them filed with anything else. Call them 'Noah's assortment' I will hope never to need them, but if so, it will only be me who can ask for them. Each one is labeled but in my own coding. They are to be destroyed when I die unless countermanded beforehand by me personally. Did you hear that?"

"Yes!" came a timid answer from Velmitz.

"Please sign here for them." Noah handed him a standard receipt, which he duly signed and stamped. "Now, what were you saying about this mess?" Noah continued.

Velmitz answered. "Organization is very difficult without help, when suddenly there is this great influx of material. All of a sudden what originally started out as an extinct or dying species program, which would be easy to maintain, you now ask us to perform for everything. You started the change by sending just a few species that were not dying or extinct, but now you are sending so many varieties of specimens, that it would appear, dare I say, that you want to be able to re-stock the entire world!"

"Maybe so!" answered Noah in a quiet worried murmur. "It depends entirely on Rebecca!" he mumbled under his breath.

"What was that?" Velmitz did not hear him properly.

"It does not matter!" Noah seemed to try to pull himself out of his nervous lethargy, stood up straight to his usual full height, a changed man. He had realized that his task was a much easier one than Rebecca's. He continued . . . "You can have another sixteen librarians, that should be enough, and also as long as you like to complete the job, but with one proviso: Not one specimen seal can be lost. As you know there are quite a few cell phials in each seal, but not one can be lost. Keep them properly preserved."

"What about living animals?"

"You will have a group of about thirty five veterinary surgeons to look after their special needs. You only have to create the list of habitats for the animals."

"Why live animals?"

"That's another story." answered Noah with just the weakest trace of a smile.

***

Fadfagi was becoming very short tempered, and this was one of his periods out of bed. He was walking backward and forward like a locked up animal with the frustrations to match. This man was angry although he did not know with what. Probably his illness he thought, but no, he thought again it wasn't his illness that caused this ineptitude around him. Why could not he get things done like he used to? Rebecca, she could help, they generally listened to her.

"Darling" he turned to his wife speaking to her in his sweetest voice, and then he said something to her that he had never said before . . .

"Please," Rebecca looked up "Will you organize a meeting of my second defense council. I can trust *those* people!" He knew that he should not have said that. It meant that there were others that he could not trust. Even Rebecca should not know that, for her own safety. He sat down.

"Don't worry darling" she acted as if she had not heard everything he said and continued "I will arrange a meeting in one hour for you. The second defense council you said?"

"Yes."

Rebecca left her husband dozing off in his chair. She went into the adjoining office and opened her diary. Two of the names on her mysterious list were on that council. Her pre-conceived plan was to be given its first opportunity. She could feel the adrenalin rise in her body and her heart was thumping as she picked up the videophone to speak to the first member of the second council. She was pleased that she could only get through to talk to his secretary. He would be there and that was all that mattered. Only one of the members she spoke to direct and he was the only one who could not make the meeting. He was also not in her diary flap.

The council members bar one all turned up at the same time and took up their places at the round table as if pre-rehearsed. Rebecca's husband sat in his usual seat to chair the meeting, his wife sat down beside him on his left.

"First of all, I would like to thank you for coming at such short notice, but we have a lot to discuss. I would also like to introduce you formally . . . ." He had to take a breath, and after a bewildered sigh continued ". . . to my 'Prime Wife' Rebecca!" She will now be attending all . . ." Again a sigh and a breath ". . . meetings in the future as my nursing attendant in order to keep the necessary degree of secrecy required by such . . . meetings!" He made it to the end of his sentence.

Fadfagi felt that he had to over-react to his hesitations and over-acting would help his cause. He wanted Rebecca present at all times now. He felt safe with her.

Rebecca was delighted with Fadfagi's hesitations, and he was obviously over reacting to a small reality, but he was certainly playing into her own hands. She needed help to do what she had to do, but she didn't expect it to come from her very own husband.

The meeting went into full swing and generally it was about finance, and future developments. Rebecca had already noted a few items on the rushed agenda where she could try to get Fadfagi to bring down the sky on them.

The first of the items was called and voted off the agenda as not enough time had been given to be advised for the meeting.

The second was about the usage of women and legislation for allowing them in the army. Rebecca's presence at the meeting took that item off the agenda.

Rebecca was not doing very well, she had to get at least one hit at this meeting.

Only a moment later it happened when the guy brought around the cable juice. The delegate on Fadfagi's right reached across him to the tray to get his juice, and dripped onto her husband's notes causing the ink to run just a little. Her husband went berserk, and egged on by Rebecca very quietly under her breath in his left ear she took out her 'kerchief and started to mop up the small drip on his note pad intentionally causing the mess to look worse. Her husband went mad and to the astonishment of all around him, started screaming at the guy who did it. He was shocked, and apologized profusely, but the damage had already been done. Fadfagi abruptly called the meeting to a close with no excuse, saying he will re-call them in the morning.

***

CHAPTER 10

Svi was surprised at the number of flights back home. The shuttle service had increased about fifty fold, or more. There were so many flights; he had had no trouble getting tickets for the two of them. A thirty day break back on their mother planet was just what they needed, and so easy. He could not wait to tell Lika. They had the choice of seats.

Lika could sit in the restaurant at her favorite window place. They were to go that evening, arriving in midday only just over two hours later on the other side of the world.

There were so many special new assignees to help with their project work that they had had very little trouble in delegating their work for their whole period of temporary absence. It had never been so easy to go back home, Svi was elated and wanted so much to tell Lika. He would not telephone her. He wanted to see her face when he told her . . .

"Just the two of us?" asked Lika full of enthusiastic hugs, as she threw her arms around Svi's neck, and kissed him hard almost swallowing his tongue. He pulled back a little, just in order to answer.

"Trin stays here this time." said Svi. "Where shall we go? We have the world at our feet!"

"Literally!" Lika responded giving a smile and an extra hug and then continued

"What about starting at 'Foggy Springs' with the mud pools and the steam heat. It's one of the last safe and natural wonders of the world. We can float in the sea there; it is so thick with salt. The area is now a health spa; it could be good for us. Let's start there for a few days, and then go to a real seaside where the water is almost normally clean. We could go underwater sea-life swimming with tanks and mask."

"That's more than we have ever done in orbit!" replied Svi. I have never been in a space suite properly for the use of; although we have both worn them for training and traveling we have never had to use one properly! 'Tank and mask' swimming sounds great to me." He hugged her tight as if he was in competition for who was the strongest.

Packed and ready, the happy duo made their way to the ticketing and departure center. The noise was astounding; there were people everywhere.

"Where has everybody come from?" Lika asked, as if Svi knew the answer. "Look over there!" she pointed "Arrivals! It's like an immigration center. There must be thousands lining up for entry into our vessel. What goes on? Why does everyone come here? There must be an extremely major convention or something. So many people, but there are so many children. Every adult seems to have children with them. This is incredible. There is no experiment except ours with children, we would know about this. All these people and they look as if they are in a state of shock!"

"I don't like this!" Svi whispered under his breath to Lika as they moved further forward towards *'check-in'*.

"Look there are very few people here, there is no line, no queue. What's going on? Those people over there have gone through to departure!" He noticed, pointing it out to Lika, "and some of them look like they don't want to go.

"Let's speak to that woman over there, she's crying, I wonder why." said Lika pulling at Svi's arm.

They walked through the gates to the departure lounge without any trouble carrying what small amount of baggage they had brought with them. They intended to stock with new things when they touched down on the ground back home.

The woman was no older than Lika in appearance, and had been crying for a long time. Her tears were almost exhausted and eyes very sore and red. She had a box of highly absorptive tissue plastics on her lap, and was holding onto her small overnight travel bag, with such ferocity, as if it was all she had left in the world. Lika leaned over, down on one knee and spoke gently to her asking her what was wrong, and if she could be of any help.

"Everything was normal yesterday. I had my family and home back down there in Semir." she began to cry again, trying very hard not to. "Then the telephone rang for my husband. It was a strange voice almost sounded like a recording. I called him to the phone. He was obviously prepared for the call, he went white, as if with shock and his mouth dropped open. He turned around putting his back to me. I'll never forget those moments as long as I live. That was when our life changed and I believe forever. The voice on the phone asked him one question; I seemed to know that by the way he answered." She took a breath and gave a sigh.

"What was his reply?" asked Lika.

"Up!"

"What happened next?" asked Svi.

"It was as if he had rehearsed this program for years. He went to a cupboard that I did not know existed and pulled out this bag, he gave it to me." She began to cry again and started stroking the bag. "He sent me with the bag to the local transportation center in Semir telling me that he would get our Susi from school, and I haven't seen him or her since." She calmed down a little, as she obviously felt that she would be getting help from Svi and Lika.

Lika spoke again "How did you end up here?"

"I don't really know, but at the transport center, they asked for my ticket and I didn't know anything, so they pointed to my . . . this bag. I opened it, it was yellow they said. I handed them my yellow plastic 'ticket'. They slid it through a ticketing machine, and told me to take a seat in their lounge. They gave me a cable juice, and I vaguely remember traveling in a slumber on several machines. I finally ended up in arrivals across the way. I have only recently woken up properly, but I feel so sad. Where's my husband and daughter? Why am I here? They tell me that I must stay and await my husband and daughter here. I can freely go back, but this is my one and only chance to stay here. If I leave, I can't come back. No one it seems is allowed two goes, and you can only come here now if you have a child or children with you. Children on their own are allowed if they can get here. Is it something to do with those rumors?"

"What rumors?"

"That there's going to be a nuclear war!"

***

Perspiration was pouring down Tubal Cain's face, they had pulled to a stop in the occasionally moving column of what had become stationary traffic. The air conditioning had ceased working, and the heat of the day was still rising. The hovervehicle in which they were trying to travel could normally move best and at high speed when clear of the ground. It could even reach the flying height of a two story building, for short periods, but in this area nothing other than government vehicles were allowed off the ground. The air conditioning could not take the strain of being permanently on the ground.

"This is a real scorcher of a day, and its only mid-morning!"

Tsionne murmured to Tubal Cain.

"I'm soaking wet." Tubal replied, trying very hard to unstick his trousers.

"So am I!" Tsionne began to undo her top. "I hope you don't mind!"

"There *are* other people about! No I don't care!" Tubal was usually the prude, but this situation was different. "Just make yourself comfortable my darling. I love you!" He turned and gave her a warm salty kiss on her shining oily lips. For just one short moment they forgot everything as they went into a tight, wet loving embrace obliterating the hot sticky world around them.

"Eh'mm! The traffic is moving!" Tsionne broke away and made herself as straight and tidy as she could. They were beginning to move for another short few moments.

It was well into the middle of the afternoon when they turned the last bend in the forest road, and the two hot sticky bodies of Tsionne and Tubal Cain arrived second in line from the entrance to the subterranean local section.

"Subterranean 3374. I was wrong. I thought that we were farther north than this. We are only in the 'three thousands' here!"

"Further north, with *this* heat? Darling you *must* be mad!"

Tsionne replied to Tubal with a lot more life in her voice, now that they had arrived. She did up her blouse, and tidied herself up, while her husband did the same.

"Entry cards and ID please!" said the Policeman in black and silver uniform as he placed his open hand through the driver's window into their heat stifled home.

"I beg your pardon!" replied Tubal Cain.

"Your entry papers and ID. Please! There is an infinitely long line behind you. We cannot delay. You should have been prepared, you've had long enough!" The policeman was irritable, and the heat did not help."

"I have our ID's, but we have lost our entry papers!"

"Oh!" The policeman stood back and gestured to pull over to the right into another line of vehicles. "You wait there! You will be seen eventually perhaps. If you find your papers, come back to this office on foot and we will process you immediately, if not, well . . . you will certainly have a very long wait and I cannot guarantee that you will finally get in." He again gestured for them to move, and stopped, walking back to their window. He looked in with his face hard against the vehicle in order to see inside better. "Where are the children?"

"What?" They both replied in unison.

"Already inside. Down below!" Tsionne replied in an instant, as if so pleased to be asked.

"OK!" said the policeman, "What is her name?" Tsionne again answered with enthusiasm.

"Baby Cain." she smiled. Perhaps this will prove a match, perhaps this meant that they have found their baby. "We had not given the baby a name yet, but here is the identity number and the bracelet from our baby's arm on the day of the birth." It was not legally necessary to register a name, as long as there was a number, and this they had.

"It's here, on the screen, who brought the child in?"

"Our help. Arianne!"

"Take that line over there on the left. The number will be checked and found. Your entry nevertheless is still waitlisted until you find your papers! You may or may not get in or your child-carer can change her place with one of you. That would be quicker!" I can't waste any more time on you now."

The impatient policeman had become rude, and directed them to move into their new position in line.

***

It had been a long night for Rebecca, she had tried to sleep in the same bed as her husband, because he had wanted it that way, but he was heaving and pulling so badly, at times he would shout as if delirious. He had kept her awake to the point that she had to get into the other bed. She had hardly slept at all, but now early sunrise, she had work to do. Her husband, he was now fast asleep, out to the world, sleeping softly and sweetly like a baby. She was sure that he possibly had a feint grin on his face.

She was still feeling somewhat tired when she went about her first chore of the day. She had to prepare the first committee room for the re-arranged meeting of the second defense council. She had a plan and it did not take as long as she thought it would. She was just closing the door when she heard something from an office down the corridor. Who would be working this early? She thought. Curiosity took her in that direction and looking over the low-screened wall into the office her surprise turned to shock, then to horror. A man she knew, but not by name, had just withdrawn a blooded blade from the neck of one of the second defense council. There was blood everywhere. It was oozing all over the man's desk, dripping into drawers, the carpet, everywhere. The assailant turned completely and met Rebecca face ways on. As their eyes met the man became scared, his calculating look changed to that of fear. Fear of being found out, perhaps?

"Why?" Rebecca found her lips mouthing words out loud to this assailant. She was speaking without forethought or due care.

It must have been the shock, she determined to herself as her voice carried on, almost without her. "Why did you do that? What had he done to deserve it?"

"You are Rebecca, aren't you?" The man replied, as he wiped the blade with desk tissues and dropped them down the waste.

"Why did you do this?" She continued, "Possibly I can help you!" She did not know why she said that but her female instinct told her that this was a good man who needed her.

She continued again, but she was now beginning to regain control of herself. "Please tell me, it is important to both of us. We may be working on the same side!"

"How could you be?" The man said foolishly as he continued to give away his position. "You are Fadfagi's wife!" He completed his position, and Rebecca was right.

"Quick!" she said, "I'll help to clean this up. With your strength we can drag him to the basement corridor from where we can drop him into the drainage sewer. He will be flushed out to sea.

Nobody will know that the body originated from here. We can take him in a laundry bag. I'll get one!" She disappeared into a nearby cupboard. They managed to pack his body very quickly and within moments he was in the laundry shaft to the basement, only to disappear below to the sewer through the trap door in the basement floor.

"You will have to help me clear up this mess in the office while there is still no-one around. You can tell me what you are doing. I know that we are on the same side! "Rebecca continued while they returned to the office.

"How do I know that *I* can trust you Rebecca?"

"You don't!"

"You could have me arrested!"

"I can do that anyway." She answered

"How can I betray my cause and my colleagues?"

"How can I betray my husband?" She did not know why she said that but continued, "What is more important? My husband or humanity? I vote for humanity and my husband is sick."

"We know."

"Who is *'we'*?"

The man hesitated, his hands began to tremble, what had he said he wondered. He went for broke, and answered. "The Democratic Freedom Army. We are small but we are in places that count.

Rebecca had hit the Jackpot; she held her breath and then took the chance of her lifetime . . .

"Will you help me?" She asked.

***

"You have to leave, you have already checked out!" said the official in the arrivals window.

"We have decided not to go! Svi was getting annoyed. "You can't make us leave."

"You are quite correct, we cannot make you leave. You can both stay in the departure lounge for as long as you wish, you can live there if you so desire, but your only way out of there is to board a shuttle."

"What about our new friend here, Naomi?" asked Lika, "She can get back in can't she?"

"As she has also gone through to departures she cannot come back either, unless her husband turns up with her daughter. Unescorted adults are no longer allowed up here."

"Since when?" questioned Svi.

"Since a few hours ago! A major policy change."

"It must be. We work here, surely that's important?"

"Certainly is." replied the guard who was beginning to become impatient with Svi. "Even more reason why you should have stayed where you were."

"We want to!" shouted Lika

"You don't understand madam. Once you have checked out, which you did when you walked through those gates over there, then you become the same as any other outsider, and can't come back!"

"We have a child here, in fact we have *two* children here!" Lika put the truth in for good measure.

"I see that on the data bank," said the guard, but that doesn't change anything, as they are already here and technically you are not. It does nevertheless allow you to change places with two other people, one for each child. Hey no! I'm wrong. Only one of you can change, as one of your children is the property of this section as such cannot be used for a trade off."

"This is damn stupid!" Svi interrupted "We live here, and have just moved into beautiful new quarters. We are the senior administrators in the . . ."

"In the H.E.P, Human Environmental Project" the guard interrupted "It's all here on the screen. I am powerless; there is nothing I can do. I'm sorry! They will not allow anyone up here anymore unless pre-approved, or they have a child with them, and I have heard rumor that even that arrangement is soon to be cancelled, we are running short of accommodation."

"We have our own." Lika was becoming tearful, but managed to hold her cool.

The guard answered her.

"You may have a home here, but as I understand, it can be confiscated if you have left. There have been a few cases already."

Svi turned to Lika and suggested that they sat down some distance away still in the departure lounge, but out of earshot of the officers at the gate.

They moved over to a small seating area near the telephones and television, and sat down after helping themselves to a hot drink out of one of the machines. As they sat down a scream of joy came from across the lounge, as they saw Naomi jump the gate, put her arms around her daughter and then give her husband the strongest and longest hug.

"Well that is someone who is happy!" Svi whispered to Lika across the small drinks table.

"We have to do something!" Lika whispered back to Svi.

"We could do nothing!" came the answer from Svi. "We could just sit this out. Even the guard said that we do not have to leave; we could stay in this lounge for a few days or more. There is food, and toilet facilities."

Lika pondered for a moment, and turned to Svi.

"I believe that this area is going to start becoming very crowded very soon when more people get turned away, or are made to go home. We ought to mark out our place. Somewhere a little more private perhaps."

They looked around and decided that they were best where they were. Svi went to a public phone, rang a number and left a message.

"Whom did you call?" Lika enquired, as they sat down very close to each other to watch the Television screen immediately above them.

"I called Noah and left a message. If we make a run for it, they could legally send us back! So now all we can do is pray!"

***

Determination was a quality that had helped Neyl to survive so far. He was always aware of what was going on in his life, and he knew that the only way forward had to be initiated by him. No one else would likely do it for him. Nobody did anything in life for other than selfish reasons, whatever they did. Even martyrs gave their lives for a self satisfaction and for a cause or a love that they believed was selfishly their own. He knew that his world was under threat, and that he was now a mere bus driver carrying escapees to their new emergency home. He knew that soon it will be his last journey, and he wanted to be sure that their last journey ended in the safest situation, in orbit. He was also concerned about Rianne; she must come with him. He would not leave her behind; they meant so much to each other. He would find it very difficult to get an Orbital Travel License, 'OTL', but Rianne would have no problem he had thought. This had proved wrong since they changed the rules, she had no children, and Neyl was not allowed to give her one. His only hope for Rianne was for her to make an illegal trip on the last available shuttle, which had to be his. Otherwise she would be sent back to imprisonment and possible death on ground base ETON.

In his position as chief engineer on his shuttle, he had access to all incoming intelligence, and military movements. With a little skill and good judgment he could obtain a clear picture in his mind of the dangers that were happening almost as they occurred. It had become his unofficial duty to keep his captain informed of events. They had decided to work together. The captain also wanted to save his family and having no children he had arranged for Rianne to join up with his sister, wife and mother in law. He had no other living family. They had to judge their moment with the greatest care.

Intelligence was showing strange things coming up from below. The worldwide defense modules were on full sensitive alert at the highest level, yet there seemed to be no aggressor. How come? If there was no aggressor, what were they all worried about, and why all the preparations? These precautions were real, the refugees were real, and the disorganization was real!

Everything pointed to genuine fear of mortal attack, but from where? This uncertainty meant that Neyl and his captain had to rethink their plans. They may never recognize an attack until it actually happens, and then of course it would be too late!

Neyl thought back to his time in the desert in Bylia, the underground bunkers he had 'helped' to dig and the secret defense systems that had been built. Why did they seem so important at that time he wondered? Now it was beginning to dawn on him the reason why.

It was of prime importance to act sooner rather later. Neyl was thinking about this next trip. That was when they had to take their passengers on board. They could come on board through the crew's quarters perhaps. Neyl decided to talk with his captain.

This meeting proved to be far more traumatic than Neyl had envisaged it would be. When it came to the crunch his superior officer seemed to be proving himself somewhat fearful of the consequences of anything going wrong. Neyl had to hold himself back from calling the captain a coward to his face! He managed to control his anger when his captain refused to accommodate, and deferred the decision to a later date. His superior officer had far too much to do at this time, he said, his wife, sister, and mother-in-law would have to wait another few more days. Neyl went angry within himself. How could this guy be so blind? The world as they knew it could be gone, before they had docked back into orbit on their next trip.

Neyl had fought his way through life for freedom, and this he had achieved without any help from another mortal. He only had had G-d at his side, and with that strength he knew that his next mission would be successful. Neyl made up his mind and prayed that with divine help he would succeed. He radioed to Rianne's private ground receiver that he would pick them all up when they land this next time. He also added that Captain Dandar was not to know.

***

Rula, Marla & Alram's arrival at the orbital departure shuttle so late into the night was very carefully unannounced. Publicity had to be avoided in order not to create panic. The twin expectant mothers, with Alram looked very much like tourists, and they certainly had never before traveled out of their planet's gravitational caress. This was to be a new experience for all of them.

The twins were very concerned about Erash and wanted to stay with their luggage and wait for him to arrive at the departure station. They waited for two shuttles, but still Erash had not arrived, Rula & Marla knew that they could not wait any longer, and Erash knew where they were going. If they had waited any longer it would be dawn, and they would be at greater risk of being recognized, and once the media got hold of the story of the family of Science and Welfare's Chief Security Officer running away in the middle of school term-time into orbit, then real panic would break out.

If it had been under any other circumstances, Rula would have enjoyed the new experience of lifting gently and slowly out of the night sky into the black vacuum of darkened orbital space. The spectacle of the horizon changing color from invisible black through deep red to the silver of sunrise, then blue white and its disappearance completely as the shuttle rotated about itself as it turned into it own temporary orbit of their home planet.

'Rendezvous' with the orbital station was almost an anti-climax except for the outstanding gigantic size of the building. She had never imagined anything could be built that large, almost automatically and in such a short time. It was now a city as large as any respectable city back on home planet below. She also noticed on arrival that other smaller neighboring units where being attached with small couplings. The idea seemed to be, to bring all the nearby vessels into a unit of one. Why would they want to do that she wondered. Rula must remember to ask her husband. It would surely be safer to have them separated and distances apart.

There was a surprise for them at the arrivals gate. It was not Erash but Noah who had come to meet them. He had a warm smile on his face as he reached out to Alram to take his hand as he steadily mounted the ramp up off the shuttle's exit way into the slightly higher artificial gravity of the orbital craft. From the one-third gravity on the shuttle it had gone up to just over one half of that of their home planet. It was a remarkable feat of engineering by humankind. Marla remarked about how her pregnant body felt a little heavier again. She had to lose weight. Rula agreed with her but replied that of course that although both pregnant they still weighed almost half that of what they weighed down below in their planetary home.

"Erash is working very hard. He has to, with Tubal Cain being inactive at this time." Noah was speaking to the twins and had picked up Alram and put him on his shoulders, one leg either side of Noah's neck. He knew that all kids liked that, and Alram, he found, was no different. Noah continued speaking . . .

"We believe that Tubal Cain has been purposefully distracted to take him out of our system at this critical time for our defense system. It was essential to get you all safe, so that Erash can do the work for both men unhampered. Things are very serious, and we are having to change the rules on a regular basis. Erash is now elsewhere in orbit and will be joining you soon, but for now he should know that you are all safe." Noah dialed on a 'holographone', and Erash appeared in three dimensions in front of them. The girls could not believe the reality and Noah remarked to them that with low gravity the machine is more efficient and produces a cleaner and clearer image. As Erash's image faded away Noah suggested he would like to show them personally to their quarters.

***

The Democratic Freedom Army was very interested in the names written in Rebecca's diary. She had fought hard within herself to make the decision of disclosure but she knew that she had so little time to spare, and the world was in mortal danger. The 'Dem Group' or *'Dg's* as they called themselves for short, agreed that they should meet with Rebecca before the Second Defense Council meeting which was to be later that morning, such was the anxiety that time was of the essence.

Her new friend worked very quickly.

She only just had enough time to shower and clean herself up, when her personal mobile telephone rang as she was getting dressed.

"Waterfront Café, have a hot juice and wait. Take necessary security precautions. Come now." Rebecca knew that 'necessary security precautions' meant do not be followed, and check yourself for wires and hidden microphones. She always did that, it had become a routine, and it was second nature for to her. She decided to return to her adopted religion and dress accordingly. It was a wonderful cover for her. She would look just like most other cloth covered women walking across the local streets. Even her husband had not recognized her in her dark brown half mask or veil as it was sometimes called.

She walked an irregular route to get to the waterfront going into a building and up in the lift to one of the high floors, walked down a flight of stairs and took a fresh lift back down to the lobby area again, leaving by a back exit. She waited outside and nobody followed. Wandering in and of shops and hotels she eventually arrived at the 'Waterfront Cafe'.

She took a seat in a visible position, asked for a hot juice and waited. She took out of her bag her personal sweetener dispenser and popped a single tablet into her drink. It fizzed and disappeared. She thought for a moment how these small tablets can make so much difference to the taste of an otherwise sharp bitter drink, and how her supply never seemed to empty. She hoped that perhaps *she* could have the same sweetening effect on her husband. He needed sweetening up.

A pretty young lady sat down opposite Rebecca, with a bright smile across her light brown face. Her long wavy brown hair was showing favor to the gentle wind that was blowing at Rebecca's thin gossamer covering.

"Would you come inside?" she asked Rebecca, who noticed a light accent in her voice that indicated perhaps that she was not from this area but from much farther north. The two women walked together in through the restaurant, and up some very narrow steep stairs, which were only a body width as they ascended to a small concealed room above the dining area.

There were five more people in the room. One she knew from a very long time ago, and the other was her newfound murderous friend. She tried to remember from where she knew the person. It was a long time ago. There was something about him that made her uneasy. Why did she know that he looked older now and why was the memory connected with something horrible? She began to worry, and was barely aware that she was being spoken to.

"We need to know how much we can depend on you." A small man who was bald and shiny headed, but was supporting a fine thick ear-to-ear gray beard. He leaned over the table and at full stretch tried to monopolize Rebecca's left ear. He continued in full voice. "We will be acting very quickly. Probably this evening. We know that the world is in mortal danger and that it is imminent. We are going to . . .!"

He was stopped in mid sentence as his neighboring co-conspirator kicked him under the table and then pulled him back to his seat. He was then successfully interrupted.

"We do not anticipate any problems, but do we have your continued support in a change of government after, ehm, when your husband has gone?"

Rebecca felt that she was surrounded by amateurs, transparent and oh, so foolish. She knew what they were up to and had to stop them. She tried to make the best use of her answer.

"Of course I will support any democratic attempt at government after my poor husband is dead, but for now we have more urgent a problem. We are safe as long as he is alive. He has made sure of that, but as soon as he is pronounced dead, there will be a funeral, and as his epitaph he has already given fatal instruction to launch murderous attacks which can only be rescinded before he dies. Only in a certain manner and with certain witnesses present."

"Oh God maybe we are too late!" said the little gray man.

"Perhaps I can help?" said Rebecca.

The little gray man reached forward again . . .

"Our wheels are already oiled and in place, our plan is so secret that even we do not know what is to be done except that it is tonight!"

"You must have an abort contingency?" asked Rebecca

"No!" They said almost in unison.

"We could not trust ourselves and joint decision was taken last night. The only person who knew anything outside this room was killed by us this morning." said a young fair-haired man from the other end of the table.

"Why was he killed?" asked Rebecca.

"He was a security risk!" said her murderous friend. "That's the guy we threw away this morning!" He continued.

"Well did you or he have any contacts for this contract on my husband?"

"As we tried to tell you, the guy who did, the guy who arranged everything is now dead!"

***

Tubal and Tsionne were again becoming irritable in the heat, which even in late afternoon was becoming even more oppressive. The humidity was so high that it was possible to see damp patches on everybody. Even outsider heat hardened types were showing their discomfort. The birds had all gone, and apart from people noise the area was deathly quiet. There was a strange eeriness about the atmosphere as if a storm was brewing and was about to explode. Tubal took a full bottle of drinking water out of the vehicle's ice box and opened it, offering some to Tsionne who took only a sip. She was seasoned in working through the heat of Postea but would loved to have taken a few drops more, but she knew that only a sip at a time was the best way. She offered it back to Tubal who took a large gulp and poured a large amount over his head soaking everything around him.

"What did you do that for?" Tsionne was furious after she had been so careful.

"I'm going outside and that should help me for a short while!" he replied, "The mobile phone doesn't work in the vehicle and there is so much electrical activity here. I must ring my office. I'm going up there." He pointed to the ridge on the crest of the valley way above the entrance to 'subterranean 3374' All the electrics are on this side of the valley behind us, so I *should* have a clear line."

"Are you sure?" asked Tsionne.

"I should know! I helped design this subterranean system. Here, use your facial make-up mirror and use the plain side to shine that rare image of the hazy sun, up to me if we are to move. I will get back very quickly because I can almost jump down into the sand below. Do you see?" Tubal pointed to the mountainous piles of loose sand that were conveniently placed all round the entrance to '3374'.

Tsionne watched Tubal Cain climb the walkway that went up and over the entrance to the subterranean. Normally people used to do that as a pleasant climbing walk, but in this heat it was a formidable task. There was almost no shade and the sun was almost naked in the sky. In her lifetime she had never seen it so clearly. It was certainly too bright to look it directly and it was immediately above and behind Tubal Cain who was now nearly at the top. She watched his silhouette against the bright blue white sky as he mounted the crest of the ridge immediately above that marked the boundary of their valley with that of the next. She was sure that he was holding something to his ear. Yes she saw it glint in the sun for a very short moment. He was using his phone.

"Tubal Cain here! Please convey a scrambled message to Erash. Subterranean 3374 . . . Oh! Hello. . who are you? I was going to leave a coded voice-mail!"

"Crap!" came back the password, which continued in the correct manner "It's coming in from everywhere! Hold and I will put you on a scramble line direct with Erash."

Tubal Cain could not believe his luck, he was deep in the stinking hot Gluma Hills, hours from anywhere, and now he was about to speak direct with his chief of security whom he believed to be out in orbit somewhere, and when he heard Erash's voice it was as if he was standing next to him, so clear and uninterrupted. Tubal felt safe, a scrambled line could only be received by another phone with the identical code settings. Tubal answered Erash . . .

"Very difficult to gain entry, but Arianne is in there with our baby. Could you arrange for us to get in?"

"What?" said Erash in shock "Didn't you have a permit from Science and Welfare?"

"No! We never registered. Never thought it mattered, kept putting it off. Don't say it. I know it was stupid of me but please we need to get in there. Urgent!"

"Should be no problem, but here in the meanwhile use my numbers with Alram. We are not using them, that will get you in temporarily."

"Thanks!" Tubal said as he noted down the numbers and then turned off his phone just in time to see a flash from Tsionne's mirror. He was down in a tenth of the time that he took to get up there, and was busy brushing off the sand as he approached Tsionne at the vehicle's open window.

"We have to move the hoversphere." She announced to Tubal.

"They have again changed the rules, and we have to go back into the old line over there!"

"No we don't!" said Tubal as he walked back to the gate and spoke to the officer. A few moments later he indicated to Tsionne to drive over to him. They were going in.

***

Lika was quite right. It was not long before the departure lounge began to fill up with rejected applicants for temporary residence in orbital space. Why they could not reject them on ground base was a mystery to Lika. They surely had to be approved for orbital residence before they left. Svi had said that they were constantly changing the rules as the situation was changing down below, and that the powers that be were trying to avoid a mass panic.

They were finding it very difficult to defend the small area that they had foolishly made for themselves so close to the telephones and television. It was very much the place that most people wanted to be. Lika was most put back when she saw her first child in their reject area. It was a syndrome child, one with slow developmental problems. It affected Lika deep in her stomach. She knew that they were thrown out of the environment system whenever the odd one appeared, and there were not that many but this was the first time she had seen one, so much older and really so full of life. An adoring young mite, she thought, but rejected and being sent back as unwanted. Lika knew it was for the best, but it hurt her deep down.

There were many people waiting for the next return shuttle, which was due very soon, and Svi found himself in conversation with a young man, who was now well established in a teaching career. He had no children and was rejected for entry. It seemed that teaching was a profession that had actually been listed as a forbidden profession on the 'ARK', which was now the adopted name for the orbital volume immediately under Noah's command. Svi could not believe his ears. How things were changing. What had happened to the G-d loving, G-d fearing man in the character of Noah? All these new rules and the regular altering of them. How come and why? Why all these children and why no teachers. If they have to stay out in orbit for possibly years, why no education? What is going to happen to the children, and upon them the whole human race? Where are Tubal Cain and the organization of Science and Welfare? How come everything has been taken over by a government minister? Svi's mind was running wild with his thoughts as Lika came and squeezed into the space on the seat beside him.

"This is horrible!" she said, "So many people, good people! What is happening to our world? Why does G-d do this to us? They, whoever 'they' happens to be, are selecting who can stay and who cannot. I don't know why, but I expected this to happen. It all matches up with the rules we have to follow with our humankind environmental studies. Selection, segregation, and basics. Why?"

"Did you know that with all these children in orbit, they are not having any teachers? It's a forbidden profession!" said Svi.

"What?" Lika's mouth stayed open with disbelief. "Why hadn't we been briefed? None of this makes sense. We should have been warned, and we should never have 'left' our poor children of 'HES'. They will need us, Trin what about her? Oh dear!" Lika put her head on Svi's shoulder for some consolation as a tear came into her eye. "How can man do this unto man?" she whispered into Svi's chest.

Svi gently stroked the back of his wife's head and pushed his fingers through her curly light brown. He loved her so much. He would rather die than ever leave her. He quietly thanked G-d for their love for each other and prayed that he would stay with them and get them through this horrific situation.

As if in answer to his prayer an echoing call came over the loudspeaker system.

"Would Svi or Lika of the Environment Studies Program please report to arrivals gate six." The message was repeated three times before they had managed to wade through the crowds to gate number six to be met by the somber but half smiling face of Noah! He nodded to the officer in charge and turned to Svi and Lika . . .

"Welcome back." he said.

***

It was going to be much easier for Neyl to conceal Rianne and Captain Dandar's family on board their craft. He was making a return journey to the home planet laden with people. It was a long time since there had been so many people on board a trip back to home soil, and Neyl had never experienced this. Only recently the outbound journeys were full to capacity, but on this trip he was taking back at least two thirds as many as he had brought out. He was pleased that he had had the foresight to contact Rianne and she was arranging everything.

Each time they gently entered the atmosphere of their home planet; there was a slow gas like flow, which passed along the window of his office. A window, which gave him privileged views of the world or worlds outside. He was a senior officer and had the status of an 'outside' office with an adjoining residential suite. The crew was allowed family visitors or personal guests to stay, but not for longer than two return trips at any one time. Officers' wives were allowed to stay, but only recently that rule had been rescinded as unfair to the crew.

Neyl had arranged for tickets of visitation to be issued to Rianne and the Captain's family. They could stay in their respective residential quarters. The problem was that this could only happen for two return trips, and perhaps one more, as they still allowed one extension. Neyl was determined to overcome that problem and thought that he may have found a way, but he only had one chance to crack at the nut, as afterwards they will close the hole.

The outside gradually turned from a black starry night followed by the cloudy gas passing by, until the stars were obliterated in a pale gray white fog.

Within moments there was a deep dark sky outside his window which was becoming the deepest of blue black colors then through the many blues until the beautiful brilliant blue of what once used to be a bright summer's day. It was usually then that Neyl knew he would see his world appear as the clouded horizon would come up into the view of his window, as the ship turned slowly about its axis with ground contact only to be moments away. Down through the hazy clouded atmosphere to lower altitudes the window became a bright white.

Ground contact was felt by Neyl to be a little rough on this occasion. Something was not right. He had to check it out, so he made his way to engineer control.

"What's wrong?" he asked his first officer "Why did I feel the landing?"

"We had the wrong settings, we should have had it on 'auto' but we can disembark faster if we bring her in manually. We are under instruction, as you know, to make speed in our turn-arounds, which is why we are working this way.

"What went wrong with manual? That should be perfectly safe and OK with Capt. Dandar at control." asked Neyl.

"It was my fault!" said the second officer. "I had forgotten to adjust our weight with so many people on board."

"Check for damage" Neyl gave the order, I will have to notify the captain."

"We already have checked." Came the first officer's reply,

"We have buckled our landing gear, and will need urgent replacement. This has not happened previously to one of these crafts, so we do not know how long it will be. We have been told it could take anything from an immediate turn around, to three days, if they have to get one from the suppliers."

Or perhaps never! Neyl thought to himself, knowing, that possible Armageddon could not be far away!

"Can we take off without one?" Neyl asked, already knowing the answer.

"Not in a straight line, and its illegal!" came the answer.

***

CHAPTER 11

The 'Second defense council' meeting was very quick. Fadfagi went through the agenda in rapid time, as if there was a train to catch, and he was already late. He took almost no discussion, and vetoed and voted on all items. If such records were kept, Rebecca was sure that the meeting she had just witnessed must have taken the least time, and there was quite a medium sized agenda.

The meeting terminated with a well wish to Fadfagi and a promise of allegiance, which made Rebecca's husband very happy and proud. As the council were leaving he called back after them.

"All I want to be remembered for is what I did for my country, and how I gave it power over the rest of the world!"

Rebecca found that remark somewhat out of place. It was not like her husband to say something like that unless he was never going to see them again. She became a little cautious. She began to worry. He knew that there was a new danger. It was in his voice. He had never been able to read her mind, they had never been that close, but she knew that something was wrong. There was something new. What could she do? Her plan was almost in ruins. She had to get his will changed quickly, and she was almost back to square one. She could try and call a meeting in his absence of the people on his list, but that could go wrong and backfire. Her husband could go mad and give murderous orders himself. No, she thought, she had to discredit her husband to the point that his advisers would countermand his will for the sake of peace.

"Rebecca!" Fadfagi called, "Come into my office while I sit down for a few moments. I'm tired, that was a tough meeting, and I had to finish it quickly."

"You can say that again," said Rebecca "You must have broken a record for efficient use of time. Why did you have to finish so quickly?"

"We have to get away from here for a few days" Fadfagi leaned back in his reclining chair as if trying to hold back a smirk from appearing on his face. "And we are leaving immediately. Darling you go and get your things. I am already packed."

Only a short while later Rebecca was helping her husband out of the lift on the roof of their building and into a special hoversphere of Fadfagi's special service fleet. They didn't travel very far; within moments they were on the roof of a nearby building, where they very quickly disembarked into the lift of that building. Rebecca knew exactly where they were the moment the doors opened for them to get into the lift. The memories and horror forced their way back into her body. For the first time in a long time she remembered.

"Why are we here?" she was half crying as she asked her husband. She desperately wanted to know what was going on. "I have to speak with you privately" her husband replied as they went down in the lift to the third floor. "We are going to my private suite. Only I have access there and we will not be disturbed."

The lift stopped on the third floor, but instead of the doors opening Fadfagi had touched the floor buttons three, two, and one simultaneously, and the mirrored rear of the lift opened out as another door that was concealed in the mirror behind them. Her husband asked her to help him as he mounted the small step into a darkened hallway. As his foot touched the floor of the hall the entire area became illuminated in its extravagant beauty of yesteryear. The lift door closed behind them and Rebecca heard it disappear into the bowels of the building below. With difficulty Fadfagi guided her that she should help him to another door. It was numbered '39'. He took out an electric keycard and put it in the lock. The door opened to reveal another lift. Her husband invited her to step in with him. For a brief moment an element of pain flashed across his face but he winced and carried on regardless. They stepped into a very strange place. The floor, ceiling, and all walls were mirrored in brilliant amber yellow, and subtle diffused lighting around all the edges. Everywhere you looked there were hundreds of diminishing sized Rebeccas and Fadfagis. Up, down, left right, front, back everywhere, and they all moved together, and kept blocking the view of distant infinity. What a powerful image. It could be very sexy at the right time, with the right person, in the right mood. This 'room' had been so skillfully made, every image was in a perfect line, and the gentle curve of images disappeared into a distant infinity, wherever she looked.

They were going down and had been for a short while. The mirror room slowed and came smoothly to a halt. The door opened and Fadfagi asked Rebecca to get out and help him.

"This is my private apartment within this the 'House of Dolls'. We are deep under ground and well below sea level. Only I have access to this place, with the exception of a small group of special service people whom I have vetted in depth. They all have family, and I know them all well. These people cannot afford to let me down. They love their families too much."

Rebecca now knew that she had a major problem. Never before had her husband ever admitted his evil ways to her. He must have reason to doubt her or he would have kept up the charade. He moved her gently to the most lavishly decorated fully mirrored symmetrical eight-walled bedroom with a very large circular bed in the geometric center. There were multitudes of reflections in every direction.

Wow!" came out of Rebecca's mouth, involuntarily and with meaning. She wanted to cuddle her husband; she needed to, no matter how sick he was, she had to caress him. It may be her last chance. She mounted the bed and indicated he should join her. She undid her clothes a little showing her legs, and gently opening them that her husband should see that she wasn't wearing anything underneath. He moved towards her, keeping his eye in line with her treasure, showing pink and moist.

"Where did you learn that?" he asked.

"Here at the 'House of Dolls'." she said, as she remembered where she had seen that man from the DG's earlier in the day.

＊＊

Many times had Tubal Cain been inside Subterranean, but never before with people in it. He had attended trials and rehearsals but this was the first time that real people were involved. In the past tourists and group bookings were not uncommon for the beautiful recreation areas, but now all the emergency stations were open and the color coding had been changed through green, brown, blue, and was now at amber. He prayed that it would not go to red. Erash quite rightly had ordered all entries and admittances to be on a 'red' basis because if 'double red' was declared everything closes and no one would be allowed in or out.

Madness of one dying man half a world away was causing such mayhem. There was nothing that Tubal Cain could do to stop it. The only possibility that could save this fiasco would be Rebecca. Even a first protective strike at the originating bases in and around Bylia could not prevent a catastrophe. They knew where many of them were but this guy had put so much below ground in silos under lakes, sewage farms, hospitals, schools and many other similar sensitive places. If these sites were to be attacked and they were wrong, what would the rest of the world say if these areas were destroyed? What would happen if as would probably be the case they did not put them all out of action? Anyway first strike strategies had been voted out by government as not morally prudent, and with the modern defense systems of interception it would be almost impossible for anything to get through.

That did not help much, the feeling of being a sitting target was supremely self evident by the manner in which a low panic had been initiated among those of the population who for one reason or another had been privileged to have been informed from the very center of government. It was like living under an unexploded bomb, which probably had no detonator.

A recent search through computer files within the immediate 'Subterranean 3374', showed that a young women with an infant child had been recorded using the baby changing facilities in the 'lakehouse' out at valley 616, which was nearly one hour's journey from the reception's transportation center by 'Super Fast Underground Monorail'. Tubal and Tsionne were elated at the news, but wanted to await fingerprint identity confirmation before proceeding to follow. If it was she, then she would show up again very soon. She must be sleeping somewhere, and she only had to insert her security identity card to use one of the facilities and her bar coded fingerprint will be read and identified. It would not take a long time to locate Arianne, as she will have developed a relatively narrow pattern of movement. Every time she used her keycard it would register her personal details. Tubal sat with Tsionne in the first class V.I.P lounge waiting for the fax phone to ring indicating a possible locater for their lost baby. "There is a match, and she has visited the same changing facility again. In fact she is there now!" The cheerful security officer called to Tsionne who was sitting in a comfortable reclining chair very close to his office. "Go now and if I were to give an accurate guess, you would be with your child before she is ready to feed the infant again, and you may catch the feed."

Almost as if it had been pre-arranged, but that would have been impossible, a monorail train was sitting waiting for them at the platform, doors wide open, and a first class carriage directly in front of them. Tubal could now use his rank and position to get these services now that they were inside the subterranean and he used his Science and Welfare ID as his key card.

They made themselves comfortable in reclining soft seats next to a small low table, sat back and waited. Tsionne was too excited to think of anything other than her baby. She was now worrying about whether she would be all right and how safe she was with Arianne. These were things that she had not concentrated upon so much until this time a reality of meeting again was becoming so close.

The train moved out of the station and accelerated with strength into the tunnel, into which the train fitted so well like a hand into a glove. Tubal was often bemused that such a vehicle should be almost entirely window, in fact almost transparent, and yet spent most of its life in a tunnel. Of course it was permanently in the secure precincts of the Subterranean Network, but it would sometimes come out into the artificial open volumes of the subterranean parks or artificial landscapes. The train sped along its track, passing through many stations, at great speed, too fast to read the names, just mere flashes of light and the occasional image of a busy platform. Express trains moved at such severe speed through a station that it traveled on a separate single rail and was cocooned within a transparent plastic tunnel, which saved the visitors to the station from the discomfort of suffering the fierce slipstream that moved with the train.

It was not long, but seemed like an age to Tubal and Tsionne when suddenly their carriage was illuminated by the artificial 'natural' daylight of the open world around them. They were in a mountainous area with a bright blue sky. The sun was shining and casting bold sharp shadows on the ground. Tubal could not take his eyes off Tsionne's face as she looked about her. This was a world like that which her great great grandparents may have known. Pure, clean, clear and it all was so 'real'. A bright sky, green fields that stretched as far as the eye can see and beautiful mountains some with summer snow on their caps. The blue, the green and the beauty. It was astounding. She knew that it existed, but the reality was bewildering. The sky was so high, with the occasional fluffy white cloud. She noticed in the distance reaching forward from the edge of the horizon, there was a deep dark gray, almost black, clouded area, which seemed to be approaching in their direction. It had a magnificent bright strong silver edge to it as it was concealing the sun from view as the train moved into its darkened shadow. The mountains were disappearing behind them as they passed at speed another station and then entered again into a tunnel, still traveling at speed, but not for long. Tsionne was just becoming used to the change in illumination as the carriage again broke into broad daylight. They had arrived at a lake surrounded by mountains that looked so beautiful even through the torrential rain that was falling upon the train causing visibility to be difficult.

"We are here." Tubal called across to Tsionne who was now occupying a completely different position on the kneeling shelf in order to achieve a better view, with her nose pressed hard against the window. She jumped up with double enthusiasm, knowing that the reality of the moment would soon have to be faced when they meet Arianne. Again, her heart was beating fast and firmly in her chest, and she worried about their child.

"Is this place amazing?" asked Tubal Cain to Tsionne as they stepped out of the train "The sky and the tops of the mountains are just holograms, everything else is real. Even the sun is partially genuine, it is prismatically redirected from the surface through transparent lead protectors, which prohibit dangerous radiation, but allow the sun to come through. The system is so sensitive that the sun can even be received through thick hazy cloud. It makes living underground almost better than living on the surface."

They reached the recreation center where Arianne was meant to be and checked with the registrar. Yes, she had been there but they had not seen her for a while and her room had not been used to sleep in.

"She must be due to give another feed very soon, let's wait there," said Tsionne.

They sat in reception behind the entrance doors so that they could not immediately be seen and waited, but not for long.

The doors opened and in came a woman with a young baby. Tubal looked at the woman who was dressed in a long headscarf and a thin shawl. He looked at the child. It could have been anybody within those baby clothes. Tubal held Tsionne back from jumping up. He was a little unsure what to do. He indicated to Tsionne that as they had not yet been seen they should wait until she was changing the child. She could not run away at this point.

The woman placed her keycard into the door slot. Tubal read his computer. Yes! It was she. Her key could be read direct into Tubal's personal security system.

Moments later, they walked up to Arianne, who was changing the baby's dirty nappy. The woman turned round and Tsionne screamed. "You're not Arianne, and where is my baby?"

***

Opening the door to a home full of dark haired strangers was the last thing that Svi and Lika suspected would happen to them. They had been away for just over one working day and already it appeared that their new home had been purloined by the powers that be. Lika went straight to the bedroom while Svi entered into argument with one of the men. They were both very rattled and jointly decided to call security. Lika entered the bedroom and her shock changed to distress as she saw the young children playing with her things that she had so carefully packed away. A little girl had painted her face in various different colors with stripes going in all directions. The two boys had found that with low gravity, it was fun to lift a normally heavy 'medicine ball' and throw it with one hand across the large circular double bed to the other side where the other young lad would usually catch it, but he obviously didn't on several occasions as there were two broken lamps and a shattered mirror, fortunately on the opposite wall there were only dirty marks as there was nothing else that would have interfered with the movement of the ball when the other boy failed to catch it.

It was all Lika could do to refrain from screaming at the Kids. She could not believe her own sense of responsibility and attitude of manner as she walked over to the small girl and then took her by her deep violet painted little hand, and carefully walked with her to the door, asking the two boys to accompany her with the ball. Svi was fighting back his laughter when he saw the cute curly black haired, hazel eyed, pale skinned little girl with the multi-colored striped face, blue-yellow and violet hands and limbs. Every visible part of her body had been touched by color. Svi felt very sorry for Lika. How much damage had the little girl done to Lika's private make-up collection? Within less than the blink of an eye, Svi's medicine ball came careering through the door and luckily just missed an old clay ornament that once belonged to his maternal Great Grandmother. Then the two young boys appeared, each with a soft persuasive sweet smile on their face as would melt anybody's heart.

Svi did not know whether he would laugh or cry but the better man within him made him hold his cool, and decide to wait for the arrival of security. He nevertheless turned and faced the same man again asking . . .

"Where is the children's mother and are you their father?"

"Yes I am their father and this is my brother and brother in law. My wife has taken the two older daughters with her to order in provisions. We generally like to see what we are getting rather than ordering on the TV channel or the 'Net'." Svi thought for a moment that this guy was obviously very wet behind the ears. The food one can acquire in orbit is nothing like that which one can get at home. He'll soon find that out.

The man was still talking . . .

"Anyway, who are you, and what rights have you to walk in here? We live here now as of today. You will have to find somewhere else. We got here first; we need the space with five adults and five children. We are informed that the people who live here will never be coming back. By the way how did you get through the door?"

"We have the keys! Why not? This is our home!"

The father of the children turned to look at his brother and brother in law, as if in disbelief. "We were directed here from 'residential allocations'. This home was vacant, and we have been drawn to recover it for our use.

The front door buzzed and a warning light over the front door flashed on and off alternately red and amber. Svi pushed the video screen next to the door. It was the security men.

Two large security police officers entered after showing their ID's. They always looked impressive in their black and silver uniforms.

Svi started talking "We have just come home and find these people trespassing on our property!"

"Yes and they have caused so much damage." Lika found herself interrupting.

"We have been allocated this apartment by the residential agency, and we believe it to be ours." The newcomer said in his defense. The Policeman took a small hand held computer out of his belt and tuned it to the correct channel. He pushed several keys then the address where he was standing and waited for a moment.

"I am afraid that there seems to be a problem. The occupants have left the ark and no longer have right to this and no longer have the right to their property in orbit. He turned to Svi and Lika and asked, "Who are you?"

***

Rebecca woke up, and remembered clearly where she was. There was extravagance and opulence of the decor, the comfort of the warm cushions, and the luxury of the perfumed bed beneath her. She looked to her right and there clearly looking right at her, were her husband's naked knees. She felt good inside as she tried not to move and looked downwards at her sleeping husband's face which had a clearly happy smile across it's' mouth from end to end. He would have been looking directly into her personal parts. She remembered; that was how he had insisted on falling asleep. She could not believe that her husband was so ill and could only have a few days to live. He had been like a man possessed; his lovemaking was superb, just as it always was. He could easily have been a professional. There would be few women who would have experienced such a beastly love maker with such a high understanding of women. He was good. Wow! She thought for a moment, how it could be said how lucky she was.

She quietly got out of bed, and pulled the covers over her exhausted sleeping husband. The 'shower pool' was wonderful with very warm water coming down, powerfully up, and sideways also with somewhat force of spray. She stood in a frame that would move on request, placing her at any angle to the water sprays that she desired. Fadfagi had bought a few of these machines from a guy who made them for orbital usage where gravity was very much reduced or non-existent.

She was toweling her dripping body when she heard her husband's call, and throwing on a lightweight loose fitting robe she went to him. He was sitting upright on the bed, with his head in his hands and elbows on his knees, staring at the floor.

"Rebecca, I don't feel well, it is difficult for me to talk, my throat is rough and very dry, but I have to talk with you. You have some explaining to do. I thought that you loved me."

"I do love you, you know I do! Wait a moment and I will get you a drink." She went to the clear water dispenser and filled a drinking cup for him. She sat down next to him on the bed, again showing him very subtly all that a man would like to see without showing everything at one time. She wanted to keep him in a friendly mood.

"Of course I love you. I always have, since we first made love together here in the 'House of Dolls'."

"You knew it was here?" Her husband seemed somewhat surprised.

"Of course it was here. I worked here didn't I?"

"Yes." Fadfagi turned his face in shame, and then changed his mind. He turned to her, held her under her chin with his hand and was just about to make a loving remark from his warming face, as suddenly without warning a twitch appeared to the right of his face pulling at the right of his mouth as if he was doing it voluntarily. Although Rebecca knew that this was not the case. He tried to talk but it was no more than vague rubbish that was coming out of his mouth. He made to get up out of bed, and fortunately fell sideways onto the edge of the large circular bed.

He was wide-awake as Rebecca managed to move his feet to a more normally comfortable position. He lay there awake, trying to talk, and Rebecca did not know who or what to call. She was in fact a prisoner in charge of her sick captor. She had nursing experience, but all she was able to do without any facilities was keep her husband comfortable. This she did, and he was desperate to talk.

"Lay still." she said as she stroked the back of his head with gentle massage. "Don't try to talk. Not yet. Just calm down a bit and wait!" She kept him lying on his side by using the very large pillows and punching them up behind him. Again he tried to speak.

"Tape 'cording . . . discick . . . please . . . lis . . . ten . . . love . . . you . . . too . . . much . . . Ehhh . . .!!" He stopped, as if in mid sentence and went into what seemed like a deep level of subconsciousness. His breathing was normal and heartbeat seemed OK, but he was out to the world. She made him comfortable, and pushed the red button marked 'service'. She noticed next to it a small box with her name on it. She took it to the bed and sat next to her husband and opened it. There was a letter and a recorded disc.

'Dear Rebecca,' it said,

'I wish that I didn't have to write this letter but my thoughts are important to me, and you should know what I think.

I have always known everything about 'everything' about you. You may wonder how, but I never missed anything of your life since we first met at the 'House of Dolls'. I have monitored every step of those lovely legs of yours, and every movement of those luscious lips of yours, and I have listened to every word uttered by that powerful tongue of yours, and heard every sound absorbed by those wary ears of yours, but I still love my loyal wife, and treasure her as mine. Please don't desert me at this time to the DG's, and please understand my motives and feelings.

If I have died when you read this, then possibly everything has already happened. If I am still with this world then please do not interfere with my last wishes.

Love Fad.

Rebecca was almost struck dumb with shock. How could he know about the DG's? What did he have on her? She could not understand and thought best to play the recorded disc. Samples of conversations she had had with Rula and Marla, their child and so many more inane items of her life were recorded for all to hear. How could he do that? He had not wired her up and she always checked herself, her clothes and her food. She regularly checked her belongings, and there was nothing that she always carried everywhere. She thought, except her sweetener!

***

Tubal Cain was trying very hard to placate his wife she was crying uncontrollably. The poor woman who was changing her child could not understand what had suddenly befallen her. They had managed to remove themselves from the baby changing room with a clean baby and sat themselves down in a nearby comfort lounge where the woman fed her baby from a bottle.

It appeared that unknown to the woman her ID card had been switched with that of Arianne's. Also the PIN number had been transferred from this young lady's own card to Arianne's so they must have met or been very close at some time. Probably at these changing rooms where one is so easily distracted and there are plenty of the wall machines around. Everywhere the young lady had been since was indicating incorrectly as that of Arianne. Arianne must have searched hard to find this woman, because like her, she was using one of the older ID cards without a photograph, and also she fitted in closely with the child's age group. There would be no problems for either of them, at least not for a long while.

Now all they had to do was chase the identity of this new lady to get back her card and isolate Arianne and their child. Tubal Cain was desperately trying to explain this to Tsionne, when at last the security police arrived with more information.

"We have found Arianne, at least we have found where Eryl's card is being used. Believe it or not there is another person looking as well."

"Who for?" said Eryl.

"You'. Said the officer.

"Do you know who he is?" she asked, whilst looking quite startled.

"His name is 'Ardo' and his ID is confirmed."

Eryl took a deep breath and tried to control herself. She hugged her baby and kissed it. "Your father! I thought he was dead! Please, please find him for us!" The young woman looked up at Tubal Cain and held the baby up, very close to Tubal's face. "Find my baby's daddy. We thought he was dead!"

Running upstairs was something Tubal Cain did not do very often, and this was the second time in one day that he had done so. He was so pleased that he had been a keep fit addict.

They only had to take one short stop on the monorail in order to reach the apartment block where Arianne was staying. She had recently moved in using Eryl's card. Tubal had to get to the seventeenth floor by running up the stairs from four flights below because they did not want to rouse her suspicions of unwelcome visitors. Tsionne and Eryl were waiting with a security policeman in the lobby below. Tubal had promised Tsionne that he would call down for her when he had found their child. Emerging from the emergency exit Tubal found himself in the corridor, only an arm's length from Arianne's front door. He pushed the 'welcome' buzzer and hid around the corner of the staircase. He felt like a small boy playing 'Tag', but he was out of view of the security camera. He could not believe his luck as the door partly opened only wide enough to speak through.

"Who is there?" came the obvious question. "Why are you hiding? Show yourself or go away! Came the order. Tubal Cain recognized her voice immediately; it was Arianne.

He called back in a friendly manner.

"Arianne, it's me, Tubal Cain. Please let me in." The door flew open as if on an impulse it was so fast a response. Arianne ran out and threw herself at Tubal. She was crying as if full of relief of the world's pressures on her shoulders. She just pulled Tubal Cain into her apartment and took him to the baby, and holding the baby and leaning against Tubal Cain's chest she just wept without shame. Shortly afterwards, when Arianne had pulled herself a little bit back to normality Tubal called for the two women and the security officer to come, which they did.

Arianne threw her arms around Tsionne and kept apologizing and promised to explain but first wanted to apologize to Eryl. The two women sat down, while Tsionne sat across the room holding and cuddling her baby. The world could have exploded around her, but Tsionne would not have noticed. She was happy she was reunited with her child.

It appeared that Arianne had taken several calls from a gentleman with a very unusual accent who kept asking for Eryl, and she could not palm him off with excuses. He said he would call again, and kept asking how the baby was.

"What?" Tubal heard Eryl shout. "How did he know about our baby?"

***

"The law is the law, and if we did not observe it the rule of anarchy would prevail and cause havoc amongst us. Legally those people in your home are entitled to be there." Noah was doing his best sorting through the legal pages on the computer screen in the Orbital Six Security Office with Svi and Lika. "This is all recent law, but emergency law which we are under at the present, can be made by dictate, and is law immediately. Tubal Cain, Erash, and now I, are capable of making law for immediate consumption. As yet I haven't needed to, but Erash is virtually running the show from another orbital station and he did right by this law or we would be in a shambles here with unplaced refugees. We of course all hope this to be a temporary situation, but we have to think the worst. Don't we?"

"What do we do?" Lika interrupted, almost in tears.

"Nothing!" Said Noah "We will re-accommodate you immediately and I personally will bargain with these new residents to change to another property in the meanwhile.

"They smell, and the children are doing so much damage to our home and to our personal belongings." Lika was becoming very impatient with Noah.

Svi picked up on the suggestion made by Noah only a moment earlier.

"What is the 'worst'? How long could we be here?"

Noah answered grimly with another question.

"Worst case scenario. Do you really want me to tell you or can you guess?"

"I can guess, but I want to hear it from you!" Svi said nervously with a drying mouth.

"Never in our lifetimes to return to our mother planet. That is the worst case scenario!"

Lika screamed and ran to Svi's arms. Together they stood gripped in each other's tight embrace both looking at Noah, and waiting on his next word. "The best we can hope is that we should only see partial destruction on the ground, followed by a short safety period, and then a massive return to whatever there, has survived for us to reconstruct lives and communities."

"What's the best possible situation, under the circumstances as you know them?" Asked Lika.

"It would certainly have been done by now!" Noah replied "The problem is, he is officially a peace-maker, and we cannot locate all his weaponry. Some of it he moves around and it crops up in many different places only to disappear again. If we obliterated 70% of his force, the final thirty per cent would be capable of major destruction and that launch would be guaranteed. As I understand it we could probably expunge ninety-five per-cent of his weaponry before it hits its target just by tracing their launch and killing them at high altitude. We can do that from here in orbit."

"Could we be attacked here in orbit?" Svi asked. "No. Fadfagi has not got that type of weapon, and we have such accurate response ability that anything that is launched in that form of weaponry can be destroyed before it can do any damage."

"So why the panic? What's the problem?" Lika wanted to know.

Noah looked directly into her eyes saying . . . "When somebody holds a fully armed loaded gun pointed at you, how sure are you that your bullet proof vest is going to work?"

***

Fadfagi's breathing seemed to alter very slightly and a tension in his body seemed to ease a little, but he was still not reacting to any stimulation, and all local tests that Rebecca knew, and was able to perform were proving negative. He was in a deep coma. Rebecca's instinct was to look after her husband and care for him as best she could until help arrived, but she could use this period to try to alter things for a more secure future. She only had a very short time. She could be very callous and leave her husband just as he was lying there, and remove all evidence of her being there. There was no point in that. She knew her husband, he would have built in video cameras and everything that had taken place would be clearly recorded on disc. She loved her husband and did not want to cruelly leave him to fade away unattended, but the entire world was at risk while he 'slept'. She knew what she had to do, and fast. Her loyalty and love for her husband was superseded by her responsibility to mankind.

She had almost an entire daylight day in which to alter the forthcoming pattern of events that would have permanent effect on the future of life on their planet. She had very little time and she had to be back with her husband before the cleaning staff come around on their evening shift. She pushed the 'Please do not disturb' button on the inside wall as she had opened the door to leave via her husband's private elevator. That would keep out the early morning cleaners, and any callers until the button cleared after midday. The cleaners would again be due that evening. She had to be back there before then.

Making her way back to the palace in the early morning mists of sunrise, dressed in her religious garb and alone was not a situation to which she had given much prior consideration. The narrow bending streets were deserted, and she felt that as a single woman dressed anonymously the way she was, made her feel very uneasy. She felt that she was being watched or followed, that someone would 'jump' out on her without warning. She listened hard for the following footsteps, there were none. She looked carefully in all the doorways and for her reflection in all the glazed frontages. She was definitely not being followed. The odd single streetwalker was always male going about his early morning business, and as he walked, would respectfully gently bow his head to her on passing. He did not know who she was; he was just respecting her dress.

She was listening very hard when suddenly she could hear the sound of alarms and police sirens in the distance, in the direction of where she was walking. As she proceeded nearer they were becoming much louder, almost deafening. She turned the corner and almost walked directly into the back of a uniformed policeman. She pulled back without being seen, walking quickly up a back street staircase onto a narrow terrace which she knew would take her to just above the rear alleyway giving her access to the tunnel entrance into her private dwelling area in the palace.

Cautiously she moved as fast as her silent tip toeing footsteps would allow her, along the upper outside corridors of terraced street while trying not to be too obvious of speed. There were now many more people all curious to what was causing the alarmed attention now not so far away.

It was the smell in the air that first changed her mood. There had been an explosion of some sort, and not long previously. She had her suspicions, and when she turned the next corner her suspicions were justified. The private living quarters of the palace had been completely destroyed by a horrific explosion. Dust and damaged bits were everywhere. The corner of the building where she was standing had protected the area behind her from the blast, but everything in front of her, the whole residential wing of her husband's palace had been destroyed and lay as a dusty ruin at the bottom of the steps directly in front of her. Through the shock, she started thinking . . .

'What was worse? People thinking her husband to be dead, or knowing him to be close to it?

***

"They have blown up Fadfagi's Palace!" Neyl called to Capt. Dandar who was preoccupied with the maintenance team who were trying desperately to refurbish the landing gear with parts that were from another older craft. The new whole piece of equipment that was needed was not yet available. A serious mistake had been made, the manufacturers had only made *'left'* ones, and it was the right one that was broken and no way would the left one fit into a right sealed unit even if squeezed the other way round.

It was a wonderful opportunity for Neyl to put his rescue plan into action, while his captain was so involved with other things. He would not even notice if his first officer was gone for a short while.

The new type of craft that Neyl had been working with was one of the few that could make a direct ground landing and also make a snug neat fit into one of the orbital craft's new loading bays. His craft could take passengers direct from ground into orbit, something that had not been available for many years of space adventure except in cargo, construction and maintenance vessels. This was going to make Neyl's task all the more easy.

No one could ever hide such a large craft. It was one of the largest 're-entry and touchdown' crafts ever built. As Neyl rode in his hovercab through the main street of downtown Eton he could look back across the rooftops of the tallest of buildings and still see the upper two thirds of his beautiful vessel sitting perched on its landing pad. It was quite spherical, but to his trained eye he could see even at the distance that he was, that it was slightly tilted off its axis. A vehicle of that size would never have previously got off the ground if it were not for the new high-tech "Radical Spin Mechanism" known as RSM. The invention of which made this new vehicle possible.

He arrived at the central departure arena for passenger check-in, which was crowded almost to breaking point with people, all with the most horrible sense of urgency in their faces. There were women yelling above the heads of others with pleading hands pointing aimlessly in all directions. The line of applicants reached forever in distance outside the building. The local roads had been closed to traffic. In the large entrance hall the throng was unbelievable, the crowd noise could be heard from outside of downtown. There were men becoming most aggressive, pushing and pulling at their neighbor in line, an epidemic of family arguments had broken out, there were people busy filling in forms at the writing bureaus, or talking into video questionnaires. It was pandemonium! Neyl was pleased that he had given Rianne strict orders where to meet him and what to wear. He spotted her in the bright yellow outfit, which held so tightly onto her body just as if it had grown there. He could see every contour of her body. He had forgotten how much he loved her, as her face turned to his from across the large hall and a cool clear smile crept slowly across her face. The fact that the smile was slow, Neyl knew meant a sign of cautious nervousness. He was very soon to find out the reason why.

"I would like you to meet Lemka, Capt Dandar's Wife."

Neyl noticed that this quiet unassuming dark haired lady who although somewhat buxom, had a gentle appearance, and a soft skin complexion which belied her age making her look a much younger woman than he knew her to be. Her full figure gave her a very female appearance that could make any man very happy. She introduced Neyl to her sister and her mother, each who in turn could have been his captain's wife. All three women had retained an appearance of health and fitness akin to much younger years. The trio all sported long curly black hair and very soft skin. They were obviously very closely related as a family. Rianne stepped forward nervously announcing "I have two more passengers".

She reached behind the three women and pulled out two cheeky little smiling children.

At once Neyl knew why Rianne was worried. One was a bouncing young boy with golden curly hair and a smile from ear to ear, which made dimples in both of his cheeks. This young lad would be an asset and would make at least one of the women legal. It was the other young fellow that Neyl was worried about. He was completely illegal for orbital travel. This child was a possible first generation mixed species, between hybrid and traditional human. His black curly hair and dark complexion with his large wide smiling thick lips gave way to a nearly standard human nose.

"The fairer one will be your child," he said to Rianne "does he have any papers?"

"No" said Lemka "His family took them when they went below, he got lost and knocked at our door. They have already closed out the Subterranean sites, this afternoon, so even if we knew where they were, we could not take him there."

"Who is his friend?"

"Laski" Lemka answered with pride in her voice. "He is one of Luki's best friends. Luki went to find Laski and when he returned his parents had left with the rest of their family. Luki's mother is or was a friend of mine, she left screaming for her son, but she had three other children and had to get them to safety. Her husband works for Science & Welfare, and had a license for more than two children. That's why they had 'early day' passes for a Subterranean Unit."

Neyl knew that Laski would never have made it through any subterranean entrance. His color was wrong. Likewise he would not even get aboard his vessel, even with a 'platform ticket'."

"The three of you are all dark haired and obviously a family. If we could disguise this young lad just to get him on board, at least that would be a start. Come with me." he beckoned to Laski, "We must go to the toilet."

The two males proceeded to walk through the crowd to the gentlemen's room. Neyl took Laski by the hand and they went into the adjoining baby changing room. Nobody was in there, which was lucky. Neyl closed the door behind them and pulled back his fist. Without any warning he punched the young boy squarely across his mouth, and as he took his hand away, Laski started to scream and bleed at the same time. "One day you will thank me for that!"

Moments later he reappeared with Laski in tow, crying and whimpering a little, but covered in bandages, around his now swollen mouth and hands.

"This poor lad had an accident! He fell out of a hovercab, grazing his mouth and hands!"

***

"All entrances and exits have been put on 'double red'!" Tubal Cain called out to Tsionne. "The interior has been upgraded to single red. We are now locked in, and the world outside is now locked out. I believe that even I cannot get out with my most superior rank."

"Why double red? What's happening?" Tsionne asked calmly. "Fadfagi's home, his palace quarters have been blown up. Now the rest of the world could be in mortal danger. They haven't found his body yet, but they believe him dead. If that is the case then it will be a long time before anyone will see natural daylight again, if ever." As Tubal Cain finished speaking the obvious out loud, the truth suddenly hit him and he began to develop a nervous shiver, and seriously needed to relieve himself. He made for the toilet in a serious hurry, leaving Tsionne and Arianne to care for the baby.

Tsionne took the opportunity of Tubal's temporary absence to try and find out more from Arianne about her sudden departure with their baby a few days previously. It appeared that Arianne had received a message on her voice mail to collect her child and run to Subterranean while the only admission qualification was to have a child as a companion. Soon it was going to become much tougher, and Tubal with Tsionne would always qualify. The message continued that no attempt must be made to inform anyone of her intentions or whereabouts as this would prevent her from reaching safety. Within days, she was told the world, as we know it would be in turmoil and she must go there with the baby, and go prepared for a siege.

"Why did you go? Why did you believe that?" Tsionne asked.

Arianne answered, "It was my father who gave me the message! He loves me, and he never lies to me. I could not tell you anything, I felt awful, but it was all I could do. My father knew about something and he wanted to save my life."

"How did your father know?" Tubal's voice asked, coming from behind them.

"I don't know, but he is a sea Captain on an ocean going liner and his contacts are very secret. He also said that he will be in touch with me soon."

"How will he find you?" Tsionne interrupted.

"He gave me a message box number to call to let him know where I entered subterranean, from that he could contact me. He also told me how to switch cards and with whom, although that person must not, and was not to know that I had done it. In the end my father said that she would be very happy.

"So you spoke with your father?"

"Yes I called him back and luck had it that he was at home, but in a hurry to leave. We spoke for only a very short while. He said that he would see me soon, if he makes it, and then he said . . . 'Go, Go, GO!' I could hear the panic in his voice, so I ran. The message I left for you was out of love, and hope that you would follow, I could not say anything that would give the game away, as my dad said that I would be watched."

Tubal changed the subject . . .

"Well now that we are to be here for an indeterminable length of time, I believe that we should seek out our living quarters that have been allotted to us."

They arrived at the offices of central administration along with thousands of others. Of course those with a pre-booked reserved 'ticket' would have been able to go direct to their accommodation, but Tubal Cain had never taken his own warnings seriously and had no booked space. A strong case of *'the cobbler being the worst shod'* if ever there was one.

Tubal left Arianne, Tsionne and the baby in one of the snake winding lines and continued, passing everyone, to the front of the line, he had a theory and hoped he was correct. There where sixteen administrators in their booths, three other booths were vacant, and one more had an older man inside, above his head a badge with the title of "Gold & Silver Only". There was nobody waiting in this special line. Tubal smiled a little and walked directly up to that booth. "My name is Tubal Cain, Executive and most senior officer of 'Science and Welfare'. I have changed places with my colleague Erash Raan, he is with his family in Orbit, this is his security number and I have his Personal Identification Number in my head. You can call him if you wish; I can't, as my phone will not work down here. Please scramble any call that you make."

"Mr. Cain, I know who you are, and Erash has already called. Everything is arranged. I'm pleased that you had the foresight to come straight to this desk. You will have the suite by the 'Grand Lake'; it will accommodate between seven and ten people, and certainly has good facilities for children. I understand that Erash was planning a large family." Tubal thanked him, and asked the officer to communicate with Erash. The administrator replied . . .

"You can do that! There is a private office in that apartment with direct ability to communicate with Orbital Fleet HQ. You can speak with Erash yourself."

"I should have remembered that!" Tubal smiled even more, and looking up at the artificial sky mouthed a sweet 'thank you' to G-d and Erash, in that order.

***

Lika was used to being in orbit, she seldom went home to the mother planet, but she was inconsolable. Svi held her close to him, her head against his chest. They had sat in the next office from Noah for an agonizing length of time. He had been looking down at the back of Lika's head for ages. The wait and the uncontrollable grief were almost too much to bear. Not since they had waited for their blood test results had their plight been so tense.

Noah appeared at the half open door behind them. "I'm still working on it" he said "but perhaps you will be better off if you would go back to your lab, which is somewhere that you feel at home. Don't worry! We will get you back to your apartment, something similar or perhaps better."

"It's not just our apartment, our home, it's everything! Svi answered without turning his head, but looking at the reflection of Noah in the brightly polished plastic paneled wall. "To be in space is every young lad's dream, but not to live there forever. Never to go back to our home planet environment, never to walk free under a real sky, never again to enjoy the real time of day. I feel quite sick inside."

"It's not just me then?" came from the direction of his lap. Lika had stopped crying. She sat up and faced both Svi, and Noah who had now entered the room. Lika's face was very red-eyed and tearful, but she managed to regain her composure and continued speaking. "Will we really never be able to set foot back down there at our planet home-base? Will we never again be able to breath natural air rather than this recycled stuff? Will we never be able to visit an animal sanctuary and see wild animals as they used to be, before man destroyed their habitats?"

"I have all the answers to those questions" Noah interrupted, "but I may first say that I believe in G-d, I believe in the Supreme Being, the creator of all. I would imagine the unhappiness and tears in our creator's feelings when he looks upon the ruin that man has brought to one of his beautiful creations. How could he allow it to continue? I believe that we may have been chosen to save what we can in his name, that we will be able to help in the recreation of the world as our ancestors would have known it, that G-d's work could be continued without torment of man's destructive knowledge and ability. To self indulge in the thoughts of returning to our original home is motivated by purely selfish reasoning, and should be quashed from our minds. It is to those uneducated and untarnished human youth, where our future as a species may lie and that is where you must put your constant concerted endeavors. *Never* and I repeat *never* should they gain any outside knowledge. They should continue through their lives based solely on their instincts, cocooned in their natural ways, without hindrance or help.

"Do you really believe what you are saying?" Queried Svi, with obvious support from Lika. "You think that we were put out here by G-d, and that these circumstances are not of man's making?"

"They are of man's making in their origination" Noah replied "It clearly states in our ancient writings that the first man partook from the 'tree of knowledge without permission. This is why we are where we are today! Otherwise humankind would have continued forever in its ignorance, but happy in its primitive existence."

"We have a serious job to do!" Lika called over to Noah "We have to preserve the security of our environmental domains, and ensure the health and safety of our inhabitants. They are to be our future! Is that right?" Lika pursed her lip for Noah's answer.

"Yes that's right!" he replied.

"Then what is to become of us?" Lika enquired.

***

Rebecca was quite out of breath when she reached the 'Waterfront Cafe' and rushed directly inside, trying her hardest not to be noticed. She felt that she just wanted to disappear into obscurity. Sitting herself down at a table in a dark corner, just beneath the entrance to the narrow staircase at the top of which she met the DG's, she looked toward a fair-haired young waitress who was walking towards her.

"Rebecca?" she said, quite surprising the recipient of the question.

"Yes that is me! Who is asking?" Rebecca replied nervously.

"You are known to us, please come upstairs to my room. I need to talk weeth you. It is very important and could be life saving." She pointed to another small staircase entrance lobby immediately across the hallway. "Those through there" She indicated quietly.

Rebecca noticed a slight accent in the woman's voice, but obeyed, being quite confident that she was doing the right thing. After all, that was why she was there; she had to find the DG's again. They could help her with Fadfagi and it was probably those people who had tried to kill them earlier that previous night.

The waitress almost pushed Rebecca up the narrow dark steep staircase to a small ill lit landing of ancient timber framework, which creaked, to every movement of their feet. The girl politely nudged Rebecca through a half opened door into a much friendlier and moderately well lit room. This young lady was obviously very proud of her home, it was a model of neatness and tidiness and her walls said everything about her. She was an obvious lover of good music, and apart from many other well-known artists there was a very sexy picture of the young 'Jubal' when he was a well-known musician with his band many years previously. There where many pictures of life being lived to its full. Rebecca felt guilty. This young lady was probably about to die, with millions of other young men and women like her all because of her late husband's need for immortality. Suddenly the young woman spoke . . .

"You are safe here, but not for long, you must go somewhere else, I will write it down, no better still here is a card with a local map on the back. Go there immediately and I will arrange for you to be met, but first you will need to change. You look too familiar in that clothing and you can easily be recognized by anybody that knows you. Here put this on." The pretty young woman removed her mop of beautiful long curly blonde hair to reveal natural short reddish brown hair underneath. "Please take one of my trousers' suits, possibly a scarf and one or two of my accessories, just to look the part, Soften up your make-up and tone down your coloring. No one will recognize you."

The 'new' Rebecca arrived at 'The Castle Wall Inn' in excellent time. It was still not yet midday. Although her time was running down, there was still hope that she could still sort things out before her husband was discovered by the cleaners.

At the gatehouse of the magnificent old castle there was an attached inn, which had served meals to the weary traveler for many centuries past. The inn was one of her country's most famous tourist's spots, and it was still preserved almost much as it was meant to be, when it was built out of natural wood and heavy gray stone.

An extremely smart looking heavily overdressed 'flunky' type man with high black sided boots, long shiny dark leather britches and a bright red lightweight overcoat with tails walked up to the door of her hovercab to open her door. He wore a dark leather triangular hat, which exactly matched his tight fitting britches. This hat he immediately removed when he opened her door for her to alight. He made a polite bowing gesture greeting her by name as she stepped down onto the hard cobble stoned ground. He bade her to follow him into the inn.

They were there already. All of them. She recognized them all. The DG's had assembled, this was to be their last chance. Rebecca sat down and watched their stunned and somewhat grateful faces when she told them that they had not killed her husband, and as far as she knew was still alive. They reacted in almost one voice when they decided that they had to act fast. They had to collect him from the 'House of Dolls' and somehow prove him to be still alive and well. At least until they could change his 'death wish' on the world.

Rebecca decided to take them to Fadfagi through the roof, the way he had taken her. She knew that there was also an underground route via 'Subterranean' but she did not know its detail and could not take the risk.

The afternoon had hardly moved on when the large hovercab landed gently on the roof of 'The house of Dolls'. They all jumped out like paratroopers following their leader, as Rebecca took them via Fadfagi's private elevator system to his private quarters where they had spent the previous night.

"He's still breathing!" Rebecca announced, as she cradled his head in her arms.

"Come on, let's get him out of here!" called out the leading DG. "Look at the security monitor," he said, "There is someone coming up in the elevator!"

***

CHAPTER 12

Acool dry smile very much wanted to creep across Neyl's face as he showed his newly found passengers around his personal private quarters on board his disabled vessel. He had all the facilities that a person could need in a semi permanent home. It was a large apartment, within a craft that resembled a very large mobile hotel. Neyl's rooms were large, spacious and could certainly for a day or more accommodate the additional souls he had brought on board. It was only the sleeping facilities that would be in short supply. There were three old-fashioned design cupboard beds that could be pulled out of the wall, these did not offer any privacy for the women, but would certainly please the two boys. They were fun to be climbed into and one could almost hide inside. Neyl was not worried about Arianne or about the boys, but how could he keep his captain's family under wraps. He did not know whether to tell his family or not at this stage. His captain did not believe that an early rescue of his family would be more risky for their protection through the days that would follow, if their stay were to become prolonged.

The two boys were already occupied. They had discovered the tilt of the ship's floor had given them a new game that they could play. They had found a bottle full of glass and plastic small colored balls. They found that by rolling them in a certain manner up the sloping floor, they would eventually roll back down again. They had made some sort of competitive game out of it, and were mimicking some TV performers with their voices. They were already having fun.

Neyl turned on the holographic video (HV) and put it onto one of the news channels. It burst noisily into the center of the sitting room. He had the volume too loud. The women jumped at the shock of the sudden intrusion into what had been a relatively peaceful tranquility. Their shock became more apparent when they started to see and hear the latest news that was being placed so realistically in front of them.

". . . and all stations and gateways to Subterranean are now closed to all comers until further notice!"

Neyl decided to go and break his own news to his captain and proceeded to his office on the bridge. Captain Dandar was nearly always there. Neyl had checked the engineers at the site of the repair and the captain had not been there for a while. The repair they said, still remained unfinished and could yet take a few more days. They desperately needed the correct parts. It was almost impossible to make do and mend. Neyl entered his captain's office only to see a very clearly anxious and worried captain at his desk whose face turned abruptly to anger when he saw Neyl.

"Where do you think you have been?" he started a fully oathed outburst at Neyl. Captain Dandar would have hit his first officer if he hadn't been a gentleman and respectful of the uniform. He continued to shout at Neyl with clearly defined panic as an undertone . . .

"Rioting has broken out in several cities and people are starting to panic. They have closed down every access to Subterranean. Ground control center and departure terminals have just been closed down due to bomb threats. This is terrible and we are even in serious danger here. I have sent second officer Perwee to fetch my family. You were nowhere to be found, I was told that you were gambling at the casino!"

"That was my cover story Sir!" Neyl replied, trying to remain calm. The captain continued . . .

"What have you been doing?" Neyl had never seen his captain so angry. He was almost screaming at him with rage. Neyl tried to get a word in before his captain completely lost his cool.

"I've been into town to collect your family; they are safely here on board."

"Whaaaat?" Captain Dandar screamed and ran to Neyl from around his desk, and throwing his arms around Neyl he spoke warmly to him. Where are they? Why didn't you tell me before? How are they and how long have they been here? Oh! Oh, and *thank you*."

"They are well and are in my quarters at the moment." Neyl did not want to complicate matters by mentioning the boys; his captain was nervous and may throw them off his ship. The captain then surprised Neyl with an abrupt change of manner and re-assuming his more familiar captain-like aura of responsibility, he picked up his personal telephone unit. "Perwee? . . . Good . . . Come right back . . . . At once!

Yes, they are here on board. Be quick we cannot wait for you. I am going to give the order now of *twenty* to take-off. I wish you the best of luck. From where you are you barely need *'ten'*. Be careful and come in via the engineering depot. The crowds don't know that way yet. You should get through, I'll pray for you. Do not bring anyone else with you . . . Yes that's OK! How did you pick up your daughter so fast? Never mind! Tell me when you get here." He put his handset back on his desk and turned to Neyl. "Start take-off procedure from 25 as per regulations."

"What about the undercarriage sir?" Neyl remarked enquiringly. "We are not safe at the moment, we have a serious tilt and maintenance have no firm support in situe. We at least need that!"

"Tell them to put the digger track vehicle under our broken shaft, and adjust its lift to bring us up to 5.5 degrees passed the correct vertical angle. We will lift off with maximum spin and minimum thrust, once we lose ground contact we can increase our thrust to give severe and serious lift and with the 5.5 degree error in our favor we should drop back to just vertical for just those few moments that matter. Oh by the way, tell the engineers doing that task that if they wish they could come along with us. I don't think there is anyone left checking anyone on board. They have all boarded themselves and have brought some family with them. Strange, how did they all know so quickly?"

Neyl turned to leave, but the captain continued . . . "You can give your order here, from the bridge." he said, and directed him over to the control panel. Neyl contacted the administration and gave all the necessary orders for take off on 25.

"I hope we can wait that long, Captain Dandar said to Neyl, as he pointed to the perimeter security screens which showed a massive crowd amassing near the main gates and the 'Cargo approach' entrance. Things are getting dangerous. 'Serenity' and we are the only two crafts here ready to leave for orbit. Everyone in this game is so busy these days. Orbital construction, as you know has taken the major part of the workload. We are by far the larger ship and will attract the most would-be refugees."

"They've broken down the gate, and there no defense forces around, they have all run away. Perhaps most are here on board. What the devil is going on?" Neyl called out mouthing a serious oath at the same time. "We surely have to bring take-off forward?" He called to his captain, "and if so, what about Perwee?"

"We cannot take off until we have 95.5 degrees over true horizontal in order that we take off vertically. As you know if the error is too great we could roll over and continue rolling like the ball we are, possibly all the way into town. Many thousands would be killed".

"If we take off early and the men below are not out of the way they will all be killed"! Neyl remarked.

It seemed like only moments later when the chief outside engineer called up. "We have 95.5 degrees from the horizontal in favor of lift. Do we come on board?"

"Yes and quick, we are to launch immediately, at 4, not 14 as at present scheduled!"

The captain called for all units to advance 10 calling for a take-off of under 4.

"I just hope Perwee has made it! Close all outer doors, and hatches, we are on our own." The captain retained his cool authority as he looked at the monitors. There were people everywhere. The departure assembly points had become unrecognizable. Amassed with screaming, crying and angry people. They were throwing things, anything of which they could grab a hold. The craft was built to withstand meteorites, but it was still becoming very distressful. Several camera fixtures had become bent, and a few went out of action giving strange views of peoples elbows and feet or the sky or just plain blank screens.

The captain then announced . . .

"Countdown advanced to 'one' we cannot wait around anymore."

"The ship is half of one degree off set axis and still moving finitely to a minimum, it reads 95 degrees exactly now." Called Neyl, who then looked at a working monitor just above his head and screamed across the office to his captain . . . "They've found the digger and are trying to move it. The crowd is everywhere like ants!"

"Go, Go, Go! Now!" Called his Captain into the intercom.

***

Tubal Cain could not believe the images appearing on his HV. Why had riots broken out? People had gone mad up there, and yet no public announcement had been made of any damage. What had driven these people to this? He wondered. Tubal had been on the original design committee for Subterranean and he privately knew that there were 'places' that were secure and safe 'exits' and 'entrances' for specialized protected craft that could withstand any radioactive attack and, as long as protective magnetic belts were worn by the people on board it was possible to have the freedom of the skies during these times. Even on double red status there could be exceptions. "I'm going out to have a look!" Tubal announced to Tsionne, who was nursing her baby.

"Don't be long." She replied, with a nappy pin in her mouth and without looking up "You know that we will be eating soon."

"No!" Tubal corrected, "I'm going up top, outside Subterranean to assess the difficulties." He said to his wife who screamed back at him . . .

"We have just got here, we are just settled as a family and you want to go play policeman. How can you?" she screamed at Tubal, making her baby cry and eventually throw up.

Darling if we do not straighten this out up above, it is possible that it will take years to sort out."

"They are all going to be killed anyway," Tsionne moaned "and the radiation that will persist afterwards will probably go on for years and years, and will certainly finish the job. What is the *point* of going outside?"

"We can probably contain any attack and survive." Tubal replied seemingly quite convinced. "This subterranean is just an insurance."

"You are beginning to believe your own propaganda!" His wife shouted in full volume, Tsionne was now becoming extremely irate. Tubal Cain walked out in a huff, almost breaking the automatic door release button as he kicked it hard on leaving. Tsionne started singing to her feeding baby as if trying to prove that nothing previously said mattered, and she didn't care anyway.

Tubal felt heavy hearted and a little sick, leaving his Tsionne like that, but his emotions were soon changed to nostalgia when he arrived in the deserted Grand Entrance Hall of Subterranean 26. It was here that he first came with Noah. They were disguised as Revenue men and had come to search for stock shrinkage of strategic materials. It was a strange phenomenon, but he could remember the explosion now, more clearly than he could then, at that time. He recalled his stay in hospital and then thought about how much had happened since those more carefree days. Oh how he missed Noah, and they hadn't been apart very long. Noah was his friend, confident and brother-in-law, he was safe in Orbit with his sister Naamah.

The Gyrosphere was a gleaming orange in its floodlit launching bay. It was late afternoon and the outside sun would be lower in the sky, so its' prismatic illuminating effect was very much less, which brought an eerie contrasted aura of starkness and singularity to the machine standing above him, there on it's magnificent grandiose tripod frame.

There was nobody about, he was completely on his own. This was as it should have been. He was one of very few people who had known of the existence of these machines, and certainly less than twenty people had access to this particular subterranean area of the Grand Entrance or Exit Hall. Tubal's personal security tag would get him through anywhere in the entire system.

He would have to drive the vehicle himself, and this he quite looked forward to. Even a baby could work these controls.

The first thing he did was electronically to switch the rescue craft's skin color from orange to a mélange of green and brown patches as if for ground camouflage. He was not going to use it as a rescue vehicle. The outer double skin of the gyrosphere had chromatic polarization facility. A technology that can change its appearance to suite the electro-magnetic command placed upon it.

Tubal gently pulled back the throttle and simultaneously released the harness holding the sphere in place on the tripod. The machine began to rise vertically upward into the artificial sky. His view of the ground below made a strong impression on him. He had never seen so many people in such a small space. He had looked down into Subterranean many times before, but this time it was busy with people. It was akin to looking down on an ants' nest. Only the arrival and departure areas were deserted. The holographic effect of the sky meant that as he rose the artificial horizon began to break up and eventually disappear and the true appearance of the dugout cavern took its natural physical shape. This of course could not be seen from down below where everywhere had a natural horizon which would change color with the weather, just as it did in the earlier days before the greenhouse haze took over.

Suddenly it all disappeared completely as Tubal's craft entered the vertical shaft and took up speed as it rose through the darkness. Tubal checked his magnetic radiation protection belt, that it was switched on, or the vessel would not have been able to pass through the final exit six into the seventh area jokingly nicknamed by the people below as 'heaven'. If he made through to 'seventh heaven' he would be above the true surface of his planet and in the natural environment created for them by G-d himself.

Tubal saw the water surround his vehicle as he entered the bottom of a sludgy, muddy lake. It was still traveling upward when it broke into fresh air. The waters were falling back leaving behind a memory of small droplets on the gyrosphere's panoramic transparent windows. He had made it back to the planet's surface, the glare was horrific, and he had not brought protection for his eyes. He turned up the density of the photo chromaticity, in order to darken down the cab. It worked! Now he had a job to do. Solo. He was on his own.

***

The human species under Lika's care and observation now assumed a different roll in her mind. They were more important than the concentrated long term experiment that she had understood it to be, when so long ago she and Svi together had opened their sealed orders.

She sat with Svi at one of the centrally located 'in sky' observation bays. This bay was located in the artificial sky and was completely invisible to the people below within their enclosed environment. As Lika looked down on their children below, she began to realize that the youngsters were now of a new importance and were one day in the multi-distant future, to become the ancestors of the then new human race. It was her duty to make sure, that in their profound ignorance of the evils surrounding them that they will survive to perform that task.

Some of the older children were now becoming mature enough to understand their basic instincts, but as yet she had not seen anything procreative. She often wondered whether she had innocently seen her own child, and whether indeed it had survived so far. All the children of the environment were anonymous. They would never have any family history other than the pre-checked pre-birth DNA construction checks that prevented abnormality being born into their orbital environment.

Svi nudged Lika gently with his elbow; he didn't want to say anything out loud. He knew that these humans had almost supreme hearing ability and he did not want to speak even through holographically concealed and highly insulated double-glazing. There were three young boys standing on a small hillock, watching some sort of strong movement coming up from what looked like dirty and deep hole in the ground. Svi had pushed his nose close against the bay window and hinted for Lika to do the same. A young human was digging with bare hands and kicking the dirt out backwards. The hole was already deep and quite wide. What was the purpose of this action, and was it a male or female doing it?

Eventually after what seemed like an age, a dirty young man emerged from the hole, and brushing himself down he ran over to a nearby stream and washed off the dirt. He then proceeded to break off some nearby relatively strong evergreen branches with some thickness to them, and dragged them to his hole. The shorter ones he placed across the top of the width of the hole, and the longer ones he weaved through the shorter ones, placing them across the length of the hole. He then squeezed between the leafy branches and disappeared into his newly made 'home'.

"Wow!" said Lika "That man has become a property developer. He has built a home for himself in the ground. He doesn't need our caves anymore. He has the knowledge enough to make his own independent way." Svi touched Lika's hand that she should wait a moment, as two of the watching boys moved over to the hole and stood on the branches, jumping and kicking at the stick roof. Within moments one of the lads fell right through, followed by the rest of the roof. Only a breath later the offending destroyer emerged somewhat sore and bruised. The 'home owner' stayed behind to clear up the mess as the other three boys ran away across the fields.

"Now what is going to happen?" Svi quietly whispered to Lika as they both continued to watch the hard working young man. They did not have long to wait, when no sooner had the young man disappeared back into his hole than a young canine animal appeared over the hillock and started sniffing at the ground around the hole. On finding several convenient places where ends of branches were striking skyward, the young dog stood and lifted one of his hind legs, and with his nose pointing proudly to the heavens; he proceeded to water the wood beneath him. After about three or four procedures, as if the dog was mapping out territory, the young man pushed his head through his roof in order to see what was happening. Then with a face full of trepidation he reached out his hand to the dog, which pulled back for a moment, then moved forward as if to bite the boys outstretched hand. The boy had the courage and kept his hand, palm facing downward, still like a statue. The dog moved more slowly, sniffing as he moved quietly forward. His nose touched the longest fingers, which still did not move. The boy had been working very hard and had physically worked up quite a 'sweat'. It may have been the salty taste or just the friendship, but the dog just licked the hand until it gently moved and began to stroke the dog under his chin. In response the dog licked the boy's now smiling affectionate face. Two new friends had established a relationship!

***

Fadfagi seemed to groan a little as they lifted him gently, but smartly into their hovercab. Rebecca held his hand as they lowered the stretcher into the swing grips, which were meant for that purpose. Although he looked very pale in the face Rebecca thought he looked very sweet in his comatose ignorance lying there immobile and peaceful as the vehicle with everyone on board lifted off from the white paved flat roof.

"Wow, that was close!" the curly brown haired young man spoke for very first time and as he closed his mouth a splintered hole appeared at the side of the craft immediately followed by an explosion of blood from within the young man's forehead and neck as he slumped forward, completely ignorant of what had happened to him. He rolled onto the floor, oblivious to any pain or discomfort, no movement of hands or legs to protect himself, but serious blood everywhere. Rebecca felt his pulse, and in a controlled manner as if this kind of thing happened every day announced . . .

"He's dead! Where did it come from anyway? Let's get moving down nearer to the ground. We must be closer to the streets. Get some buildings in the way, fly at a low level" she shouted to the pilot.

"They must have seen us and they are sure to follow." Said the short bald man with a curly gray beard from ear to ear. "We have to hide my husband as if he has been kidnapped. That will give us time, or at least a little bit more time." Rebecca held her husband's head cradled in her arms like a baby.

"If they could get such an accurate shot into this craft, surely they must have seen your husband on the stretcher?" The younger blonde guy interrupted momentarily.

Rebecca put her hand up to her mouth indicate silent discretion. Perhaps they were being heard, perhaps the place was bugged. Then she proceeded to announce out loud . . . .

"They don't know that you drugged him," she said "Perhaps they think he is ill, on a stretcher. Perhaps we could keep up the pretence." she winked carefully to her comrades. "Where are we going now?" she asked as the cab slowed to turn a street corner at the height of about the fourth floor of the nearest building. She looked again at the cab driver. "He's not the driver that we had coming?" she whispered to the guy with the gray beard. "Did you change him?"

"It should be Marco, he is our usual driver. Let me have a look. All that I can see from this angle is the back of his head. He is in a very small compartment. He stretched over Fadfagi and could get the same view as Rebecca. "I've never seen him before. Where is Marco?" The elderly guy looked as if he was about to panic, and Rebecca managed to restrain him, and calm him down, indicating that they may be 'bugged'. She whispered to her bearded colleague, "Is there any one of us that can drive one of these machines?"

"Only him!" He answered, pointing to the dead blooded body on the floor. "I wonder if that was the reason that he was killed. How could they know? This is terrible! Where are they taking us? Do you know where we are going? This is definitely not a familiar area of town to me."

"We are going in the direction of the State Prison." Rebecca replied in disbelief. They have a superb hospital wing, but surely that's not the reason."

"No!" said her bald friend "It's secure, and there is the secret major military headquarters underneath. I do know that!" he said with perspiration pouring down his face. "It will be from there that the first steps will be taken to execute the Armageddon!"

"Then let them take us there." Rebecca was firm in her manner "The likelihood of killing off the lion, should be easier in its den!" she tried to smile and gave her husband a visible cuddle. "Oh you stupid fool!" She whispered in his ear.

***

No sooner had Dandar shouted . . . "Go! Now!" into his intercom, than they saw the outer rim of the outside skin start to move. It developed its' spin very quickly, causing many objects and people on the outside to fall away, or within moments be forcibly thrown from the vehicle's outside framework. One external camera that had not been damaged picked up a horrific picture, which appeared above Neyl on one of his working monitors. Two young men were holding on to the edge of the frame work of the outer rim as if they would be saved, both of them were suffering from the centrifugal effect and their legs were horizontally displaced outward. As the spin progressed one of the men disappeared outward like a bullet, he just went, and he disappeared in an instant from the screen. On closer examination it could be seen that the other man had strapped his hands to a grid on the exterior skin of the vessel so that he would remain in that position. He surely did not believe that he would survive the upthrust when it came or the loss of air as they moved up out of the atmosphere.

The enhanced spin became very strong and the body of the craft suddenly began to feel as if it was standing alone with a tremendous force pushing into it. The people inside could feel the pressure, it was very strange! Almost the opposite of a centrifugal force. Even Neyl, who had experienced this before, felt the force more than ever before. He kept looking at the monitor above him, suddenly all that was left was the bleeding red hand and wrist of the man who had strapped himself to the outside grid, and the rest of his body had gone, disappeared. Why had he attempted that, he wondered?

Neyl watched the 'angle of elevation' dials that had been set for vertical take-off. The spin was fast enough now for disassociating with the ground. They could almost release themselves with a mini-upthrust. Did they dare? Captain Dandar gave the order to release the land grip and issued instruction for elevation of less than one hand width from the ground. Neyl watched the 'angle of inclination'; it was at corrected vertical, ninety degrees. Then the vibration started as if from nowhere. The needle on the vertical moved backward and forward between 87.5 degrees and 92.5 degrees. At least it was even.

Vibration meant danger. That was the last thing that they wanted, but so long as the craft did not deviate from an even projectory it could lift freely into the heavens.

Neyl noticed that an effective tilt was beginning to be indicated as the needle moved one degree off vertical axis, to average an angle 91 degrees, which was one degree off vertical and the variation was showing signs of widening. If his captain did not give the order to lift, he felt almost obliged to give the order himself. What was he waiting for? His captain seemed to take an age to give the order, but in truth it was only a moment later that he pushed the control and the vibration stopped immediately as the far horizon appeared in the screen. They had moved upward very freely but slowly. The gyros were holding the exterior spin as they began to rise. Neyl could see a feint angular movement of the horizon, they were elevating not quite vertically, which was fine as long as they didn't go into a roll, this would shoot them downward without warning.

The horizon was holding a more or less horizontal image on all monitors that were working normally, and the craft began to rise well above the height of the city. It began to accelerate its upthrust by increasing engine velocity. Neyl was pleased; perhaps they had made it with only a makeshift track vehicle as an effective temporary undercarriage. Unless they could re-construct a new working landing gear while in orbit, they would never be able to land this machine again on natural ground.

The sky outside was going through all the blues. It was becoming darker as they were losing their surrounding atmospheric blanket of daylight that represented a normal day on their home planet. They were almost in orbital space.

A bright flash of light lit up the entire craft as the area beneath them seemed to explode as if to engulf them in fiery gasses. This was no normal explosion. It was as if the city below had taken a direct hit by the most horrific weapon known to man. A large mushrooming head of cloud was approaching them fast and could well be about to engulf them deep into its center. Everybody had moved to a downward looking viewing bay. It was a beautiful sight, but horrific and very much lacking the meaning of the terrible destruction that had taken place in that instant below. Anyone who could have seen that sight would never forget the awe of the occasion. The area below was becoming larger, almost reaching out to the horizon, but it still had no chance of reaching their altitude. The size of the mushroom head began to reduce as they moved away. Its apparent color changed through most of the seven colors of the visible spectrum until it began to look like it was bleached out and a large gray colorless mess as it resettled back on the ground from which it had risen.

"Fadfagi must be dead." called Neyl to anyone who may have been around to hear. "We just made it to safety!"

Neyl got down on his knees to thank G-d for his delivery. In that brief moment he remembered his days of captivity digging those trenches in Fadfagi's desert, his promise to himself to escape, and the distance he had come, just to get his freedom. He kissed the floor and tears found their way into his eyes. He felt guilty, oh so guilty at being saved, when so many of his old comrades and friends down below deserved better than him.

***

Her clean long dark straight hair was shining under the bright hazy sky as Rosie Cag stood on her platform at the end of the swimming pool. She was about to take her final race to qualify for the great international event in which she would represent her country very soon. She was a favorite to go streaking ahead of all others in her class. She was almost certain to win. All eight female competitors stood there on their individual podiums with adrenalin at full supply waiting for final sound of the traditional starting gun.

The gun went, a perfect start for all, but only the tips of Rosie's fingers ever reached the water. *Gone*, gone in a fierce flash of such extreme heat. No witnesses, no memory, nothing, they were all gone, nothing!

Little Edin Scod with his cheeky smile and short-cropped blonde hair was always very slow when he followed his mum along the walkway across the busy main street. His mother turned around to call him to hurry, they had shopping to do and she couldn't push baby and wait all day for her baby's older brother. She stopped and placed the pushchair in the doorway to stop the door from closing while three paces she walked back to take her son's outstretched hand, they never touched. *Gone*, gone in a flash of such extreme heat. No witnesses, no memory, nothing, just radioactive dust, they were all gone. Nothing!

Mowing the lawn in the late afternoon was a privilege that gray haired and weather worn Polgo always enjoyed. The local nature museum was one of the few areas in that region of the world that had a carpet of grass, which had survived man's attitude over many decades of ruinous environmental destruction. Polgo was proud as he sat with bared legs atop his vehicle specially designed to create the lines that followed it of freshly cut grass. He always attracted a crowd. There was no substitute for the smell of freshly cut grass, and the beauty of the polished appearance of a neatly finished lawn. Many people came just to enjoy a good sneeze, or even a slight reddening of the eyes. It was worth it, just for the memory. He came to the end of a clean-cut band and lifted his gear to turn around to start the next lane. It was two thirds finished. Even he stopped for a moment to view the difference between fresh cut and uncut. He smiled to himself as he dropped the cutting bladed rollers back down to continue again. They never touched the ground. *Gone*. Gone in a flash of such extreme heat. No witnesses, no memory, nothing, just radioactive dust, they were all gone, nothing!

Family gatherings were unusual for the Wach family, but the new baby of only a day. Celebration was called for in these 'troubled' times. When many influential friends had gone away for a short while or just disappeared, it was natural for a family to be full of joy and happiness when they had all managed to re-unite for even just a short while to welcome the newest member of their family. Of all those invited, not one was absent. They had all made it to the party. They had already washed the baby's head and asked for G-d's blessing. The feed up was about to begin. A large cake on a trolley was wheeled into the dining room, which seated the thirty-eight people present with room to spare. The grandfather of the baby was called to make a speech and light the very first light for baby 'Flo'. He mumbled a few words about being asked to keep his speech short, and then there was nothing. *Gone*. Gone in a flash of such extreme heat. No witnesses, no memory, nothing, just radioactive dust, they were all gone. Nothing!

Corpan had a full compliment of passengers in his hoverbus, as he passed over the last tall building to make his landing in the town's main square. He was able to carry 26 people and with himself that was twenty-seven. He was returning a school trip with two teachers and two dozen children to the parents standing below at the landing stage in the public square. No one will ever know if they saw it coming because the epicenter of the flash of light contacted at the very same spot where in the Town Square, as the hoverbus at that identical moment would have touched the ground. No smiling faces, no chitter chatter of homecoming, no "Look mum what I have got!" no kisses and hugs of reassurance. *Nothing* except the fierce flash of explosive heat, no witnesses, no memory, nothing, just radioactive dust, they were all gone. Nothing!

"Serenity" was still preparing to take on passengers when all hell let loose. Captain Dandar's ship had already left and people had been scattered everywhere. No semblance of order existed and it appeared to be everyone for him or herself. All the long passenger gangways were not yet fully in place against the last possible orbital passenger ship "Serenity". Nevertheless, human ingenuity was working fast as the force of the crowd pushed gangways into full position where they were not already connected. People were climbing across each other, and pulling at loved ones just to get them on board. The crew had obviously been instructed to start 'Cut and run' procedures. The exit doors at ground level, possibly through charitable kindness, had been left open for as long as possible. Everywhere else was secured for take-off. The whine of the engines had started, and external skin spin was due to start at any moment. The external doors were very strong and their closing force caused living struggling bodies to be crushed and squeezed with their blooded innards splitting out through their bodies. These poor people did not have enough time to enjoy their pain as the sudden flash of extreme heat came down upon them, no witnesses, no memory, nothing just radioactive dust, everything was gone. *Nothing!* Just a ginormous blot on the landscape where once so much had been before. A returning tidal wave of water drowned out the remaining piece of land as it fell deep into the sea. G.C.Eton was no more.

Tubal Cain was airborne, among the hills near the entrance to Subterranean 26. There was an eerie peace and calm, or was it in Tubal's imagination. He saw an odd bird fly from one spot to another, there was a small child playing with a hoop outside her home. The mother ran outside and grabbed her as if she thought that Tubal's craft was a danger. The day was bright and hazy, but Tubal felt ill at ease, and moved his craft towards the shadow of the line of nearby hills, which were towering above him. There was a sudden gush of 'down-draught' as if everything from the other side of the line of distant hills had been violently thrown or pushed, causing dramatic fall-out on his side of the valley.

"The bastards!" Tubal shouted but there was no one to hear his hopeless call, as he fought to control his craft in a torrent of hot dusty air as it forced his craft into a sudden spin.

Using the craft's own spin, he managed to gain some control, and of course the ship's magnetic active field protector would have double the effect because of the additional protective field belt that Tubal was wearing. He had to get back to the muddy lake if he could still make it, and if his entry signals would work. He could see the darkened valley there in front of him, dipping his angle of approach very slightly he managed to submerge his craft in to the dark deep murky mire. He opened the safety box under his seat and stepped into the protective rubber suit, which immediately did itself up, around his body, even accommodating the vital protective anti-radiation belt. He had to go it alone. There was no chance that he could take the craft back down below, it was contaminated, but he could decontaminate himself, if he could only find the entry drain. He left the craft and with full downward illumination from his head covering, he thrust downward with his strong swimming movement. He could see the welcoming beacon, flashing deep violet, just down and ahead.

***

The last thing that Rebecca wanted at this time was to be kept waiting. Time was of the essence and her husband was very sick. She had given her bald friend in the DG's the nickname of 'Doc' as he had being paying so much attention to her comatose husband since they had rescued him from the 'House of Dolls'. The hovercab had landed within the prison walls and they had been sitting there in the hot humid afternoon, still in the cabin and with no engine running. The air-cooling system was not functioning. The perspiration was so bad that all the unwilling passengers were soaking through their clothes. Her husband just seemed to be peacefully asleep. Mid afternoon humidity was the worst and the cabin was almost completely transparent. It was a horrendous ordeal for them and the captors knew it. The driver had left them on landing and he had gone a long time previously. The prisoners could not leave, they were locked in and there was no one able to drive the complicated machine even if they could have climbed into the driving compartment.

They were fighting to stay awake by talking rubbish to each other, taking it in turns to initiate a conversation. Any body listening in would have wondered what their language was, it was quite nonsense and meaningless, but to an outsider it could have sounded like code. It was very quick of Rebecca the way she caught on and joined in. If anything would create an outsider's attention, this form of talking most certainly would.

"Glate pergal wontwick?" came the question from Doc to Rebecca. They all knew that there was no meaning, but as they were being monitored it may attract attention, Rebecca almost felt like laughing as she replied, the heat was becoming horrific.

"Wellcofos marfle pume sec!" Came her answer in a non-descript language.

"Gregle, gregle, gregle . . ." Fadfagi began to try to speak. Nobody had noticed a sudden change in his condition. He was apparently coming round to a more conscious state. Rebecca couldn't believe it, and shouted across to Doc that he should try to cool him down.

"What with?" came the reply as Doc looked around him for a miracle.

Fadfagi was certainly improving, he was trying to move and his arms were wandering aimlessly around as if he was trying to get a hold of something. He found and grabbed Doc's shoulder-pad and using a very strong force; he tried to pull himself up into a sitting position.

Rebecca jumped with surprise and moved rapidly across to help Doc. They both supported Fadfagi into a seated position. He was dazed wet and tired but was certainly gaining conscious awareness.

"Bec!" He called to his wife. He had not called her that since their very early days together, when Rebecca was in his service at 'The House Of Dolls'.

"Bec!" he repeated. "What are we doing? Why are we here? Who are these people?" He was speaking so lucidly, his mind had certainly cleared. It was almost as if he had not been ill at all.

No sooner had Rebecca wiped a small tear away from her eye than all of a sudden there were people everywhere. The hovercab already surrounded by guards was attracting a new brand of uniform. That of the dreaded security police in their black and silver with their hideous logo. A badge of evil. Three of them were coming on board in a hurry. Rebecca detested these people and now, after all these years they were once again her captors.

Rebecca's vivid memories of those evil times came flooding back to her as the security police with their black and shiny silver striped uniforms pushed and pulled at her body and that of others including that of her husband. They threw a black trash bag over Fadfagi's head as they brutally bundled him like a captured wild animal into a caged trolley on the ground beneath. Rebecca was screaming as she saw this happen only to find herself encased in a similar manner, and with male hands pushing and pulling at even her intimate parts, she felt enquiring fingers underneath her private clothing, suddenly she was falling blindly through the air until she landed on what seemed like thick straw, and a lot of struggling moaning bodies.

She was certain that she must have injured the person upon whom she had landed. She heard further screaming from above and a falling body caught her on the side of her head. She yelled as the wind was forced out of her body and her neck was jarred with pain, both arms were temporarily numbed but the pain was short lived as her adrenalin rushed back into her body and the tingling stopped. She could hear her husband. He was talking coherently.

"Get me out of here! I am Fadfagi, your leader. Cut me free or I'll have your arses. I know who you all are! Do you know who I am?" He yelled. Suddenly there was a thud as a boot was kicked into his mouth. The force was so strong it must have broken his jaw.

"If *that* don't kill yer, *this* will!"

Rebecca could hear the movement so clearly as the security policeman again lifted his leg as if to kick him once more. "Stop that at once!" Came from below them. A senior officer appeared to be giving an order. "No blemishes, nothing that can prove we did it! Stop! Keep him and her clean. It don't matter about the others, they are not for show."

Rebecca did not hear much after that, as she felt the sharp sting of a needle. She tried to struggle but went out like a sleeping kitten only to wake moments later to the sound of someone calling her name.

"You have been asleep for ages, so much has happened!" said the stranger's warm friendly deep male voice. She was still in a blindfold.

"My husband?" she asked "What . . . How is he?" She realized that her hands had been tied quite professionally and she was no longer wearing any clothes. She was tied to a bed, naked on her back. She was beginning to feel bruised all over. "Who did this to me? Where is my husband? What have you done with him?"

"Oh he's dead!" came the nonchalant reply. "He died with you last night in his Palace when it was so brutally bombed by the DG's. We have been given your living body beautiful to play with. You will also be gone soon. Unfortunately, because you are nice, and there is no way I can help you!"

"What about Fadfagi's memorial attack? Is that to go ahead, or have things changed?"

"The bombs? No that started at lunchtime today. They said that you both had been killed in the palace bombing. My governor just had your husband blown to bits. They will find them tomorrow morning alongside your remains in the palace ruins. Rebecca's attempt to do the impossible had failed. She began to cry as she thought how stupid her husband had been. She thought of Rula and Marla and the children due. She thought of Alram and Erash.

"Oh!" She quietly prayed within herself for the first time in many years.

"Please . . ." she continued, "please save the souls of the righteous that they may go onto better things. If it were to be possible for them to know how she felt . . ." she prayed, ". . . please let . . ."

Her prayer never finished. *Nothing*, just extreme heat, no witnesses, no memory, just radioactive dust. Nothing. No longer would there be any relevance in the Palace bomb, for this one was multi-proportions larger. The city was completely destroyed, not even rubble was left. The blast had flattened the entire area. Nothing, no one, not a soul was left to tell the tale.

***

"We were so worried about you!" Marla had tears in her eyes as she spoke to Erash on the Holographic Video "Where are you and when will we see you back here with us? Here with your orbital family at this awful time!"

Erash could see Rula and Alram in the background crying.

"I am coming home immediately as we are transferring our command lines. I will tell you when I see you." Rula could see apparent organized chaos going on in the background behind and around her husband. People were shredding paper, destroying computer file discs, and generally trying to pack essential items into large voluminous crates. There was an element of fear on their faces and it was of the type that could become contagious. Rula kept quiet, hoping that in her cool perhaps Marla had not noticed. They would hear it all from Erash when he returned.

Erash continued . . .

" . . . In the event of my not making it back to you, contact Noah for direction. Tubal Cain is safely in Subterranean, but his command is now only planetary. It had previously been decided that under these circumstances that the most senior government minister in orbit would be expected to assume Orbital Command. That would be Noah. We are responsible to him, and until such a time that proper government can be re-established, Noah is in total command. I cannot say any more from here, but you can find the regulations on the 'World wide Information Network' under 'Contingency Plans'. You know the code. It's privileged information. I'll be back soon." He disappeared, as the three dimensional hologram dissolved into the air in front of them.

Marla turned to speak with Rula and decided not to say anything when she saw her sister's fraught face. She moved nearer and threw a wide arm cuddle around her sister and her son Alram. They fully understood the meaning of the situation and if it were not for Alram's presence they would both have cried volumes of tears. Instead they forced a tense smile and sat Alram down with one of his toys.

After many anxious moments, it was not long before they heard that Erash's office had arrived for attachment to their orbital craft.

They wanted to run and meet with him but that was not what Erash would have wanted. He would have called for them both if he had wanted that. The girls had decided to prepare a meal while they had waited and it could well have been ready before he arrived, but it had kept them occupied.

Both of Erash's wives threw their arms around him as he limped into their apartment. They had not realized how much tension that the three of them had been under as they broke down onto their large couch with Alram closely in tow. The family of four 'plus' were choking back tears of joy and happiness. They were all together again in spite of everything. They had only been apart for a couple of planetary days but it had felt so long and so many terrible things had happened.

It was Marla who first noticed that Erash was bleeding from his upper thigh, badly enough to show through his clothes. "An old wound!" he replied as Marla pointed at the stains. "We were hit by a missile. One of Fadfagi's! We don't want people to know. It is bad enough already. We have lost so many people. If it hadn't been for Zarby and her band of gorillas we would have lost even more! I could not tell you that on the 'HV'. We could have started a wild panic. This is being played down and all undamaged material and sealed workable units are being attached to this station or orbital city!"

"What did Zarby and her team do? Are they all right? Are they safe?" Marla queried, while hugging Erash as Rula pulled away at his clothes to expose the wound, which was still bleeding and appeared to need some form of treatment.

"They were incredible, and such imagination. I saw it all happen. We were hit by one missile, which exploded on impact; they have a trigger mechanism in their nose. We could see more coming towards us on the Radar but they were well behind. Zarby and her gang were out collecting debris from their construction work with their electro-magnetic nets. They always listen in to traffic control, as they have to keep the orbital routes clear of dangerous construction objects. All of a sudden and without warning they took their net in a different direction and started trawls with magnetism at full power. It was unbelievable. The missiles just kept coming but the gorillas' net was causing phenomenal attraction. Zarby's people had moved their nets effectively out into open space relative to orbital city. They were placing themselves in great danger, with only their space bicycles to keep them mobile. The missiles came, there were six more of them, but luckily the net activated none of their trigger mechanisms. The gorilla people audibly laughing as they tied together the spent missiles still with fully loaded warheads, into their cargo area for further consideration. We now have six unexploded missiles with no power to fire them. They are being placed safely in the supply vessel attached to 'Fortune One', which is part of Noah's own fleet which is accompanying this orbital craft!"

***

Docking into Orbital 26 was proving very difficult for Dandar and his crew. Their sudden take off from home planet had left a few bent and partly damaged sections of the lower body of their machine. Also the radio-magnetic sensors which were needed to align their craft with the entry dock of the orbital vessel were out of line and could not locate the 'entrance sensor' in order to gain automatic entry into their port. In other words they only had one choice for docking, and that was manually. The other alternative was to leave their vessel 'outside' and ferry in the passengers, which would take the equivalent of a couple of days on their home planet. Neyl suggested that he went outside and with a 'Space Bike' using it as a 'tug' he could tow them into port. This could be highly dangerous as the 'Hoverglobe' or 'Gyrosphere' was so enormous he could crush himself on entry if he put himself in the way, between the vessel and the interior of wall of the orbital craft's entrance lobby.

He sat on his bike with towrope behind and attached to that was the important leading edge of the 'under carriage point' specially made for this purpose. He did not want to move very fast.

Capt Dandar had placed their vessel in a perfect stationary position relative to the Orbiting Unit 26, and was such a short distance away from the entrance port.

The mass of the machine that Neyl was about to pull did not matter; it was the speed that was important. He had to be able to stop it as well as move it, and that was when he could be out of danger. A solo job would be far easier and more accurate, but would take longer to perform.

Neyl looked about himself. For the first time in outer space he was able to appreciate the true meaning of size and distance. With such a large mass towing behind him and an even larger mass coming up towards him with the clouded blue-white surface of the planet that had always been his home in the distant background. In this scenic panorama he could appreciate his orientation in relationship to the enormous size of the home from where he had come. Already there were significant smoky gray scars appearing in the cloudy surface cover of the silent distant scene that was once his home. There were serious large areas developing from beneath yielding to a deep blue, and on one area toward the distant horizon he could see a patch of deep clear blue and the greeny brown of a land mass, as seen only in historic photographs from times long ago. Something terrible was happening down there below, but there were areas where there would now be clear blue skies allowing the naked sun to warm the land and water as had not happened for previous generations of humankind. Would there be any human alive down there to appreciate nature's unfortunate dividend. Would there be anyone there with eyes to see it. Neyl pondered.

As Neyl made steady progress with his tedious mission, slowly but with due care and caution, he was continually distracted by the changing shape of the surface weather formation of the planet below. Usually the changes of cloud pattern were continuous although imperceptible, but now there were several areas of rapid and violent change.

He was an orphan and his younger sister and older brother had died at the hands of derelict and devious white humanity. He had no living family, he had nothing to regret, nothing and no one left behind except the memories of happier times in his early childhood. The only person who meant anything to him, he had brought with him. Now looking back at his once upon a time home, on which he had spent more than two thirds of his life entrapped as a prisoner of humanity itself. He could not pull out of his imagination the smallest thread of sympathy or pity for those poor suffering souls down there. They were getting perhaps what they deserved. He was now free, he could make his own decisions, and he could be treated as an equal. He could fulfill his life in a manner of his own choosing.

Neyl's mind was suddenly brought back to reality. His efforts to load his captain's craft into the entrance bay was almost complete. He carefully pulled himself over to the wall-mount for his bike and dismounted whilst beginning to secure the main vessel for downloading the passengers. They had made it!

***

In that earlier moment when Neyl was gazing across the void of dark open space onto the planet from where he had come he could not have known the tragedies and problems facing the surviving beings below.

Tubal Cain had managed to reach the drain cover of the emergency shaft, but his key was buried beneath his protective suit. A small detail which had been overlooked and no practice run had ever shown up this contingency. This was the first time that all entrances had been sealed secure at one hundred percent. In order to release his security disc he had to force open the neck of his protective clothing. He just hoped that his radioactive protection belt would keep him healthy and secure. After a squeeze and some gentle but difficult maneuvering he succeeded in exposing his security disc which to Tubal's delight and relief resulted in his being able to slide back the drain cover in order that he could enter the shaft below. He carefully slid through the narrow gap and resealed the grill behind him.

Swimming down through muddy water he came to the next entrance, which was full of stagnant thick leaded metallic water. Through this he found it almost impossible to swim, but having had many previous sessions of learning how to swim through this thick and dense medium in a downward direction, he managed to reach one of the portals for entry below. Again his security disc allowed him through but this time he was accompanied by an inrush of thick heavy wet compound. He was now able to stand up in an empty resealed chamber out of which the thick metallic sludge was being quickly pumped out in exchange for pure atmospheric type air. Within moments Tubal's suit was pristine clean from serious jet washing. The treated water was also being washed away and the chamber had become warmer and absolutely dry. A door slid open in the wall exposing an elevator room into which he stepped. As the door closed behind him there was a strong motion downwards followed by severe and rapid deceleration. The door again opened, he was at subterranean base reception level in administration headquarters. Organized mayhem had appeared to become the rule of the day. Red and green lights were flashing everywhere.

"Groundquake warning! Groundquake warning! Proceed to your local designated shelter . . . Groundquake warning . . . follow the flashing blue lighted trail . . . proceed to your local shelter . . . Groundquake warning . . ."

The repeated pre-recorded message continued to come out of every speaking output. No one was to miss it. Tubal Cain had to find his family. He checked in his suit and pushing his way through the moving crowd he ran to his family's local shelter.

"Tubal!" Tsionne threw her arms around her husband almost pushing him to the ground. "Where have you been and what happened? Why these warnings? Has Fadfagi died? Are we under attack?"

Her husband did not have time to answer the question as his emergency bleeper buzzed at his waist for the first time ever. He ran for his mobile communicator, picked it up, turned it on and held it to his ear.

Tsionne saw his face go white with fear. She had never seen her husband in such a mood. He held himself steady and spoke very quietly but with firmness of voice, and strength of command. She could not hold back a scream of terror when she heard what he said into his phone.

" . . . but that's Gramps area of safety if he made it" she was screaming and burst into tears. Arianne rushed over with the baby in her arms and tried to consol her. Tsionne continued shouting at Tubal. "That is very near here! What happened?"

"We sustained severe damage!" Tubal answered as he threw his arms out to Tsionne and the baby, he was holding both women and the baby in his arms. They were all in shock and the baby was crying in response.

"What happened?" Arianne repeated.

"There is water everywhere in the lower Eton area. We have sustained severe underground damage. It seems that these Bylians had a weapon we had not known about, 'Groundquake bombs'! They hit the ground and burrow for some distance before they explode with maximal nuclear devastation. We have to seal off a large area of destruction in subterranean 462, and there is serious danger of the radioactivity spreading!"

***

CHAPTER 13

Svi was scratching his head in bewilderment! He was reading Noah's new orders. Since the recent failed missile attack upon their orbital city, and reports of small successes elsewhere, Noah had sent Svi and Lika a copy of an extremely sensitive and very secret encoded package which had already been sent to Erash. It was specifically marked for their eyes-only.

They had only just settled into their new apartment, which was twice the size of their old one and were happily getting themselves sorted out when the private sealed message was delivered to their door.

Noah was informing them that they would be moving out of orbit very shortly and that their entire orbital city and all its attachments in their entirety would be seeking out a new home in orbital reach of a planet not unlike their own in an entirely new different planetary system. He would explain later, but it was about 64,124.7 home planet light years away and would take about 444 home planet years of traveling time to get there, which was just over half of a human's expected lifetime. It would be equal to forty years of the new planet's bi-annual year. They would be traveling at about an average of about 144.43 times the speed of natural light allowing for slippage.

Noah's reason for being so informative to Svi was the need to enforce the importance of the meeting of their minds and the needed dedication to the continuing environmental space program.

A minimum of four hundred and forty seven of their home planet years cooped up in an interstellar space traveling city was almost too much for Svi to come to terms with or comprehend. He could not imagine how Lika would receive the news. She had popped out for a moment and would be home very soon. They would be spending half of their lifetime on board this city and having already lived what is usually one quarter of it already down on their home planet, it would leave them only about one final quarter of their lives to lead under the umbrella of the new planet's skies, that is assuming that they survived and would be permitted to land on the surface below. Svi had enough sense to realize that if the powers that be had been to so much trouble to keep the new generation of human race so isolated and separate, then surely they must be the people to receive full landing rights of the new as yet lightly inhabited new planet.

Svi set himself a target; he was going to work on a mind-bending project, which could ensure that he and Lika would be able to qualify to land in the same manner as all his laboratory family. Perhaps, if his idea gels and succeeds, even Noah and his family would be able to stay to enjoy their newfound lands. He had more than sufficient tools for the job, and would certainly have time to do it. This was to be his new personal project. He had convinced himself. The only person whom he would trust with it could be Lika.

It was only moments later that his wife appeared through the entrance port. She had been out to get some domestic supplies, but when she saw the orange colored envelope, she knew it to be an important message from the powers that be. She put down her packages and hurried over to Svi. They sat down together on a large beige sofa as Svi gave Lika the largest of hugs, as she tucked into his right arm; she read the decoded note quietly to herself.

Svi waited for a reaction from Lika, and was amazed at her lack of it. Holding her so tight he could feel her every movement. Not an iota of surprise went into her body. No reaction, no sudden shudder, no movement. She finally took it out of their private decoder machine refolded it and replaced it into the orange envelope for Svi to keep safely or destroy.

"Why could they not put that through our interline network rather than send it to us by hand?" Was the first thing that Lika said.

"Computers cannot keep secrets" came Svi's reply, but he was still waiting for more as he could feel Lika's deep profound thinking.

"What is going to happen to us?" she said as if without pre-meditated thought. "We can cope with nearly four hundred and fifty years up here. Those people at home get nothing, but are we, us the non-participants in orbital research unit going to survive? We will have about twenty new planet years left. That is about a quarter of our lives remaining. Are we then to *die* in space, *travel on*, or *re-settle* on the new planet with the others? What do *you* think darling?" She cuddled in to her husband's chest resigned to an unknown and narrow future. "But at least we have each other and we have survived so far." she whispered into his chest.

"Listen to my idea!" Svi answered. We have to be able to join our friends from in there "he said pointing in the direction of the environmental laboratory. "Then we will be able to land, just like them." He said with the authority of seeming to know the answer already. "If I can do it, then nobody in the city needs to stay behind. We will all be able to make landfall."

***

Tsionne threw up; her face had turned white, her dried lips pointed down at the ground as she leaned over a sidewalk guide rail waiting to repeat the function. Arianne grabbed the baby and Tubal held his wife, as she was about to throw up again. They had gone down two levels to visit their local shopping mall just to collect some supplies for their new home, when a hospital train pulled into a nearby station. The paramedics were helping to unload injured people, and were checking each one with radioactivity sensors. A few of the injured and walking wounded were separated as apparently contaminated and put back onto the other end of the monorail underground train. The others were being loaded into heavy-duty buses to be taken elsewhere. Some contaminated people were screaming that they wanted to go with the other people on the buses with members of their families or very close friends. This was not being allowed, but uncontaminated healthy or injured were being allowed to go back on the train to join the contaminated if they wished.

It was when Tubal explained to Tsionne what was to happen to the contaminated that she threw up. They were being taken to a safe sealed destruction site, where their remains would be neutralized into de-activated dust and then blown down through strong narrow vents with horrific force deep into the depths below. They did not let it be common knowledge or the unfortunate ones would rebel and not go willingly to their end. The loved ones, friends or carers who wanted to stay with the sick contaminated were allowed also to go to join them in their end. Tubal explained that this had been made a policy many years before. It was known that with destruction they would lose many of their supplies and also the means to create them. For this reason it would also be necessary to 'lose' a certain percentage of population.

It was just too much for Tsionne she finally vomited again making a large horrible yellow mess on the ground beneath her. This time it really was too much for her as she collapsed unconsciously into Tubal's arms.

Two security officers standing close by saw what happened and indicated with urgency to two nearby paramedics who were dressed in orange and silver protective full bodied suits with full head covering. An alarm sounded and a verbal warning broke out on the speaker system that everyone should avoid contact or proximity to unapproved wounded or sick. Approved sick or wounded carried large blue tags around their right wrists.

Tubal grabbed Tsionne. He knew that she was clean and would pass a contamination test without any problem, but he was wearing a wristwatch measure of radiation absorption and he knew that he would fail, only just, but he would fail, he had only recently been outside and although cleansed and de-activated there was likely to be still some dust on him. He did not dare to stay and take the chance and find out.

The three of them ran for an escalator going up, as it was a much quicker way to the next two levels. He made it with Tsionne unconscious across his shoulders. She was quite lightweight for her size he thought, or maybe he was just very fit. He looked back, Arianne was much slower, she was smaller and had baby and a cradle.

Tubal indicated that she should go the longer way and take the lift; they would meet at home. Tubal made it with Tsionne to the top of the first escalator; he ran most of the way up the moving stairs.

"Please step over there!" the paramedic called to Tubal Cain as they met face to face when Tubal stepped off the stairway. Tubal was trapped, he had no means of escape, and he had no choice but to obey. They took him and his now semi-conscious wife into the nearby examination room.

They threw a testing scan across Tsionne's body and then asked her to go into another room. They did not even suggest checking Tubal Cain.

"We need to know a little bit more about this lady. Can we see your papers, and what is she to you?"

"Here is my ID card and that lady is my wife. What's wrong? She only feinted when she saw those unfortunate people coming off the train below."

"No!" The paramedic said quietly. "Did you know that your wife is pregnant?"

"What!" Tubal Cain broke out into his first smile for many a day. "She can't be. That's not possible!" Tubal was happy and shocked.

"Why are you surprised?" The stranger said, "Are you not the father?"

"Don't be disgusting! She was not able to have children."

"You got that wrong!" came the reply.

A widely smiling Tsionne appeared in the open doorway in a wheelchair. She looked great, alert and refreshed. Her smile went from ear to ear, with teeth glistening white under the bright surrounding illumination. Her expression said it all! "You know!" she said, "You've been told. We are going to have a baby! We will be complete."

Tsionne climbed out of the chair and slightly unsurely walked over to Tubal's outstretched arms. They kissed and cuddled, oblivious to there being anyone nearby.

***

Svi and Lika had become consumed with their new private project and were turning over part of one of their bedrooms to the function. They had found three new computers that they had managed to purloin from another department as no longer needed. Svi was refitting some of the circuitry and inventing and adapting some of the parts to his specialized needs. He was becoming very excited.

Lika was assessing the stages of improvement, and planning the forward needs of their project, that they should always be up to date. She could foresee a breach of many moral codes. There would be problems, but the outcome merited the experimentation, and until some serious results could be determined they agreed that the project they had set themselves should be maintained as low profile, and completely secret. They would refer to their program as their 'House Guest' and no one, not even Noah or Erash should be informed of it. At least not for the present. Svi and Lika agreed that when presented as job already completed, then everybody would be happy, but not before!

Elsewhere in the city Noah and Erash were meeting face to face in the same office for the first time in a long while. "We are in mortal danger if we stay here any longer in orbit than is absolutely necessary!" Erash said gravely to Noah. He continued . . . "We have to change position and move a long way out of range of these missiles."

"That's not possible." Noah replied "As you are aware even if we change position our wireless waves will soon attract the missiles from wherever they are coming. The only way to be rid of them for sure will be to travel outward away from our planet at a speed somewhat seriously faster than them, but if we slow down, they will always eventually catch us up. They have been pre-programmed to do so."

"I know!" said Erash "We could continue collecting them in the same manner as we have done using Zarby, but for how long will they be lucky?"

Noah closed all security valves in his private office and turned on the noisy extractor fan.

"What's the problem?" Erash asked Noah. "Do you think this place is bugged?"

"I know that it is! I ordered it, or at least Tubal Cain ordered it, but it was my idea."

"Bugging your own office. That's a novel idea."

"No it's not, many people do it. It's called security and adds to job security, and I am in control. Anyway, permit me to draw us back to the orbital problem. A few hours ago I gave the order to commence 'long countdown' to move out of orbit."

"Out of orbit? 'Long Countdown'! What does all that mean?"

"As I sent you in my memo, we cannot survive in this position, and shortly we will hear from Tubal Cain that our old home will have become irretrievable, that is if it has not already!"

"Do you mean that you are still in touch with Tubal Cain?"

"Yes," said Noah " . . . and so are you. He is living in your apartment in Subterranean."

"How did you know that?" Erash smiled.

"Let us just call it security!" Noah smiled then once again became more serious. The Subterranean Territories are becoming partially damaged by groundquake bombing and cannot remain for very much longer a certain sanctuary for these scared refugees down below. The geological balance is becoming unstable and within this, or the next generation it will probably implode or explode. It will certainly fall apart and probably self-destruct. These groundquake bombs are new, and we certainly never considered them as possible enemy tools. In fact we didn't even have them on our drawing board."

"What are you saying? Is this the end of our planet home? Are those poor souls down there unlikely to survive?" There were tears in Erash's eyes, and a paradoxical nervous smile was attempting to show itself in the curves of Erash's mouth. There was surprise on Noah's face as he saw a feint glimpse of this.

"I'm sorry," Erash continued, "I often smile when I'm anxious. I always have, it is a form of nervous reaction. Like shock!"

Noah brushed aside his remarks and continued . . .

"We await Tubal Cain's contact, and if we have his permission we will leave orbit on an outward bound course forever. *Never to return*."

***

"How can it be raining?" Tubal was standing at the door of his waterside home looking across the lake. A clear blue sky and a bright sunny day, yet large drips of rain were falling on the lake. Just not real, thought Tubal Cain. Perhaps something was wrong with the weather programming and this was the result. Large globules of water were dropping vertically from a clear blue sky and were bouncing into the lake quite visibly and frequently. He decided that he should investigate.

It was later in the day, mid afternoon, when Tubal decided to re-contact his pal and brother-in law, Noah out in the Orbital Rim. He had established a private office within his home with direct audio-visual contact with Noah on a *Va*riable *S*peed *A*ccelerated *L*ight basis, known as 'VaSAL' the latest adaptation of the most recent technology. This innovative technology would make it possible for Tubal and Noah to communicate with each other even when the distance between them is increasing at speeds many times faster than that of the speed of light itself.

There was perspiration pouring down Tubal's face and the heat was becoming severely unpleasant. It showed as Tubal's clothes were sticking to his sweat sodden body when he appeared clearly on Noah's three-dimensional holographic video. Tubal was standing in the middle of Noah's office and apparently dripping onto the floor.

"This is the only way to keep cool!" Tubal spoke first, and continued . . . "I have soaked my clothes in a cold shower. It was Tsionne's idea, and it works. This started mid-morning not long after the rain had begun to stop. Something is seriously wrong with the air-cooling and freshening system. These ground quakes are doing something very serious to our structure. Alarm signals are going off everywhere and when we check them out, there is seldom any problem. It is becoming quite chaotic."

"Thank goodness this call is coded secure and scrambled" Noah interrupted.

"What difference if it wasn't?" asked Tubal completely out of character "All the damage has been done. I don't rate much future down here in Subterranean or on the surface for that matter!"

"Do you want us to try to come and fetch you? We could send a scout ferry to attempt to get you and your family out of there."

For only a brief moment Tubal's expression changed and then realizing the futility of any effort of rescue he gave the anticipated answer with a great firmness of meaning. "No! My place is here with the people. I must help to save what I can and perhaps there is some room for continuance in the eyes of G-d. This planet can survive and I will make sure that some of our species survive along with it. Go Noah! You have your job to do, but all I ask is please keep in touch. This new 'VaSAL' technology will keep up with any speeds your 'ship' can achieve. Go! Take our human race to new frontiers, but as previously agreed, let us reproduce in ignorance, that we do not desecrate our new horizons just like we did the 'old'." Tubal Cain was either crying a little or his sweat droplets were worrying him, as he was struggling to keep his eyes open with the tears.

"I hear what you say Tubal, and you know that neither you nor I would be able to stay on any planet that was to be humankind's new home. Our knowledge would one day destroy it as we and our ancestors have destroyed this one. Perhaps you will make a better job of keeping the old, than I will of obtaining the new sanctuary for the human child. Sincerely Tubal, I love you and wish you the best and for all your family. We shall depart before your nightfall, and leave the Orbit of Eden traveling in the direction of that position in interstellar space known to both you and I. That new solar system we both discovered not long ago. I will keep you in touch; let's hope that that stays possible. The technology as such is as yet untried."

Tubal seemed choked when he replied to Noah.

"Please take care and make it worth while, let there be a future for the human race that all that went before is not wasted. I know that we both have faith in G-d and all cannot be lost. He has indicated his vengeance to reign down upon us but he could not mean complete annihilation for us, Noah, you are going to be an uncle. Tsionne is pregnant. It was surely a miracle; it was G-d's will. Why?" Tubal stepped back one pace to indicate departure, or an end to the call; he had a broad wet smile across his worried face.

Noah threw Tubal a long parting kiss of congratulations as he faded out from the center of his office. The small wet patch on the floor immediately dried into nothing.

***

Making love in low gravity was difficult and wonderful, but Svi and Lika had acquired a small private gymnasium in their new home, which had some exquisite pieces of equipment. They could also turn off the effect of gravity completely, an innovation only recently installed into sections of orbital city, and only then into very expensive residences and select dwellings. Making love without gravity at all and using one of the exercise benches as a fixed base made love making an art that they were loath to interrupt, but interrupt they had to do. Their *'alert buzzers'* started without warning and their red and amber attention warning lights started to flash at that very moment when lovers always are at their most vulnerable.

They rapidly moved to answer their call, and turning on the reduced gravity fields they put their warm naked and smelly bodies under a warm shower.

Together they had to prepare their 'Children of the Environmental Study' into a protective form of dormant stability in order that they will be safe and unaffected by the changes as the city is moved out and away from its fixed Eden orbit. They will be saying their goodbyes to Eden forever.

Again the routine of atmospheric applied sedation was to be used to make the environmental people drowsy and finally fall asleep where they lay in order that their sleeping bodies could be secured in their ignorance from the rapid changes of movement that could cause them to be injured.

It was Lika who suggested that they should contact Zarby. They had been informed that the gorilla people had chosen not to leave with Noah but had their own ideas for their future. Their orbital crafts had formed a small version of their own Orbital City and they had decided to stay a while longer, with plans to move off in a completely different direction. Their life span was shorter than that of the human and they were more skeptical about leaving on such a long trip. They had hoped to return to Eden if things calmed, but if not they would *'self freeze'* into a hibernated state of *'suspended animation'* and at a much slower, almost normal speed planned a completely different destination for their future. It could be thousands of years before they would awake to view their new home wherever that may be!

Saying goodbye to Svi and Lika on holographic video (HV) brought tears to the eyes of all concerned. Zarby broke down when she saw Trin and almost changed her mind about not going with Noah. It was strange. No gorilla from the orbital community had been refused the ability to travel with Noah's Ark of vessels that made up the Orbital City, but every single gorilla person had voted to travel with their own kind and under their own momentum. Lika was crying overtly as the last images of Zarby and company disappeared from the center of their living room and the last parting words had been said. Lika snuggled up with Svi, and even Trin was crying as they cuddled tightly in their now empty living room.

Noah had a sudden surprise, while during the countdown there was an unexpected interference on the message screen and Naamah came running into Noah's office screaming with delight. She threw herself at her husband and was ecstatic with open enthusiasm. Noah could not understand what Naamah was saying; she was speaking so fast with tears pouring down her face, and nervous hiccups in her voice.

"Glenshee!" she screamed "Rastus and Lex" she continued. "They are out there!" she was laughing and crying at the same time. "I thought that they would be dead. They are on their way here!" She was out of breath from running, "They stole a satellite cargo ship and escaped before all went mad down there. They have news of Jabal and Jubal. They also survived, but are still on Eden, but made it to Subterranean along with Gramps and a few others. Can you believe it? Oh Noah? Can we wait until they get here before we leave orbit? Their craft is very slow and no one aboard can navigate. They have almost got here on their own and it's taken ages. They are out of any food supplies!"

"No darling, if they can make it, they must do it themselves. We cannot alter this marathon count. We have to secure and leave at a prefixed time or we could be in serious danger from our own engines which are still new and are also somewhat untried technology!"

Naamah screamed and banged both fists several times on Noah's shoulders. "Don't be so stubborn. Is there nothing that you can do?"

Noah pushed his wife out of the way and went over to the nearest internal communicator.

"Whose the guy that brought that broken 'tub' of a Gyrosphere into dock?" he said to some distant controller. "Neyl? He repeated into the phone. "Yes! Get him to call me immediately, I have very urgent work for him, and alert the safety station from his area that an astro-craft be made available for him. The best you've got! Yes!" he repeated, "The best you've got! *It's urgent!*"

***

As the ground quaked and shook once more under foot, a large piece of powdered rock came falling from above, broken into the tiniest of pieces and covering the ground around them like freshly fallen white snow! The quakes were different now. They appeared to be self initiated, happening in their own right and not driven by the force of the exploding creation of a man made bomb.

"This could prove dangerous! I believe that we should join the others and move to a different section of subterranean. We may be able to find people whom we know. Mya if it wasn't for you, we would not have found our way this far. There is no way we would still be alive and almost safe!"

"Definitely!" called out Jabal as he brushed off the concrete dust and wiped the grit out of his eyes.

Jubal, who was still finishing his meal, pushed his plate to the side, as it was no longer appetizing covered in white powdered dust.

"Methy!" called Mya "I love you more, now that I have got to know *'you'* better, but it was 'Mikash' whom I thought about as I brought you and what I could of your family here to safety, and I do agree, that we should move on, but we should all try and keep together. *'In unity we have strength'* that is what Mikash would always say to me. I cannot believe that he is no longer with me. I know that his body is with me and that helps, but he was buried inside your old one and I never said 'goodbye'! She was becoming tearful but managed to retain self-control.

"We are a group of sixteen with your family and mine. We must stay together, and it's my pleasure that Mikash's mother has come along with us." Methuselah leaned over and put his arm around Mya, just to re-assure her in a most gentle of manner. She turned and pulled hard at Methuselah's neck drawing his face close to hers. Immediately she drew back as fast as she had created the close encounter. Looking directly into Methuselah's eyes, she had started once again to become emotional, although somewhat controlled from within herself.

Methuselah or *'Gramps'* as he was still known by his family had realized for a little while that it was not an easy task for either of them to come to terms with each other, but he hated feeling mercenary, had it not been for Mya and her interest in his new body, then Jabal, Jubal and a few other members of their family would by now be ashes and radio-active dust on the planet surface not too far above them, and he did fancy her body very much indeed. He felt like a fraud. Especially when vivid images of Tsionne, sounds of her voice and her extra special smell kept creeping back into his memory.

"We could take the first train that is going south, which has room." Jubal interrupted, being the adventurer at heart. He was astonished at the enthusiastic response. Everyone to the last person, even the two children agreed. It was very pretty where they were, not far from one of the great underground lakes, and a center for one of the main underground service industries. There was a local leisure resort and the whole area was not over populated, but these ground quakes were becoming more frequent and more forceful in their effect. A decision had been made and the two brothers Jubal and Jabal took it into their hands to organize the exodus. It was only a very short time later that sixteen people with all of their luggage were on their way to a better safety and another Great Underground lake.

It would not be long before they were to find out just how lucky they had been that they had so quickly made their decision to move on. Their train was gliding gently without friction along its' monorail when suddenly they could feel shuddering apparently coming from below, and the gentle smooth forward motion became a sandy grinding feeling as the train, while seeming to drop no more than a finger's width, started to slow and grind almost to a stop. Then as if held in the space of a moment's limbo continued again without finally stopping. It suddenly lifted again as if under a resurgence of power and speedily moved gently and friction free onward to their final destination. They were later to find out that the entire area from where they had come had imploded under a severe 'natural' groundquake that had now become the plague of Eden, and centered in the lower regions of the Northern Subterranean. They were very lucky that their train had had enough momentum to escape the failed power supply and travel into the healthy one of the next subterranean county.

***

"We have you in our scanner!" Neyl screamed with great joy. He had thought that he was on an impossible mission. If he was to be able to return to the 'Ark' of Orbital City" he would have to find his quarry in double quick time. His ship had been attached by a long 'real' umbilical cord to the Ark City, but his distance had long been too far and now his craft was only attached by an 'electro-magnetic umbilical' which was virtual and well proven. There had never been a failure except due to main power loss and that was very unlikely. It would cause the 'Ark' as much trouble as it would cause Neyl. Countdown on the Ark was continuing and he knew the score. He could return to the Ark whenever he thought it was dangerous to stay out, but he trusted his umbilical and thought if he can get the others to physical contact then all of them would be safe even if the Ark all of a sudden disappeared from the skies above Eden into the far distant interstellar space. The umbilical magnet would surely pull them all with them. Neyl was almost sure. He was a serious distance away, but at least he would be able to get back to his physical tow, which was bleeping away back down their long trail.

Within moments Neyl had maneuvered his astro-craft alongside the large ancient cargo vessel. Neyl smiled to himself at how these people had managed to get such an old tub off the ground.

"We are going to have to play 'tag'." Neyl announced to them as his very small mini-vessel pulled up against their machine and was completely obliterated into its shadow. "We are tagging you with cable-ties and we will tow you to our bleeping guide . . . "

Neyl's expression changed and his voice became much warmer in manner as the image of one of his to be rescued people appeared on his video screen, he continued with a gentle smile on his face.

". . . which we will re-attach to us and then together we will rejoin 'Noah's Ark of Orbital City'. We must hurry as they are about ready for *Interstellar Acceleration*. *'IA'* as we call it for short. When that happens we are certainly safer if we are physically tagged, as it will pull us with it. I am not sure if our magnetic hold will be strong enough. It has never been done before. I'm pleased that I found you, so quickly, we have every chance of making it." he said with re-assurance. "If we can, we shall take that battered old cargo vessel with us, but in the meanwhile you are safe staying there, because as I talk, we are already accelerating back to our bleeping beacon. It would be too dangerous to transfer you until stable speed is maintained and that may not happen until we reach the 'Ark'.

For Neyl this rescue had become much more personal as he looked at the friendly smile of Rastus framed in the video. One of his kin, a man like himself, and Noah had apparently risked all this to try and save him. He knew that Noah was kind to the Hybrid people, but he thought that might only be a lip service. Now Neyl was beginning to believe more in the man who was becoming his savior.

Rastus smiled in surprise that he was face to face with one of his own kind and tears of affection and appreciation began to show around his eyes.

"I would like you to meet my wife." he turned and called for Glenshee to get into the area of the camera. They hugged each other close as they both peered into the screen at the smiling and almost tearful face of Neyl.

"How many of you are there on board?" Neyl enquired, "Six" came the reply "We have one young child, and then there is Lex with his mother and sister. We don't think that there is anyone else on board. Lex has been searching the ship since we left. It doesn't make sense. The control room was empty when we walked onto this ship through an *open* door. The elevator worked without problem and all systems were 'go' for take off. There was nobody around; it was very eerie, almost as if it were meant to be especially for us. Lex pushed a few buttons, released the elevator shaft from this old vessel, it fell away without any problem, and it was all so easy! We sealed her, and having confirmed all air locks, we just very gently left the ground. It was extremely slow; we thought that we would never make it. We fully expected to fall backward to the ground at any time. We seemed to get slower and slower as we felt our feet becoming less attached to the floor, then suddenly it was dark outside and we were floating a little as gravity left us. We knew then, that we had made it into orbit. There is no one else on board. We are sure, but where did they all go? How was it possible for us to 'steal' this ready made half loaded and apparently unguarded ship?"

"What is the cargo?"

"Don't Know. We couldn't open it. Special tools are needed and we don't have any, although I am sure we will find them eventually."

Neyl was called by his colleague. "We have the bleeper, and I have attached the beacon, we are back in touch!"

Neyl relayed the message to his new friend on the video screen and then continued . . . "You had better secure everything that moves, and warn your friend Lex and his family to strap down like us. The Ark is due to start 'IA' very soon. We may have just made it. We will be pulled with it at a relatively faster speed as the tow coil is rolled in at both ends until we meet the Ark."

The noise of the winding metal cable could be heard very clearly as their gentle journey to the Ark continued. They were still very far and outside discernable range.

"Radar approach says that we will have contact with the Ark in fifteen marks, that's not long." Neyl called out for all to hear.

"Look at the stars" Rastus replied " they are moving slowly backwards and off to the left. I've never seen constellations move before. That's not possible. Are we spinning or tumbling? What's happening? Have we lost our tow?"

Rastus was anxious and Neyl spoke calmly and full of reassurance.

"No!" he said, "We have started 'IA', we are on our way to a new home. Let us pray together that we make it. Fare ye well Eden, we pray for you too!" Neyl had tears in his eyes.

***

Erash had been with his family at the very moment of commencement of IA. He could not believe it had started, and that the countdown had finished. Nothing had happened, apart from the feeling of gravity building up slowly from behind them instead of from below. They were attracted to what was effectively the rear wall of their apartment, but only very slightly. Even the loose dishes on the coffee table hardly moved, although Rula had to move fast to stop one falling off and spilling.

Marla was looking out of a window from her strapped position, when she saw her sister's reflection was still moving around. "Get belted!" she shouted at her, "soon we will be under the effects of 'IA'!"

"We are already," she answered whilst seating herself on a convenient window seat and belting into place. "Did you not see the cup move?"

"Look out at the star's constellations" Erash interrupted "they're perceptibly moving backwards towards the same direction as the rear wall. 'IA' has definitely started."

Erash turned on the large pilot monitor screen in the ceiling of their apartment. "Wow, look at that, we are already at the speed of light and increasing very slowly. Our rate of acceleration is slow but we are moving very fast. Artificial gravity compensates automatically, but it surely won't cope with this if we accelerate more quickly or erratically?" Erash was talking aloud but to himself. He was fascinated by the event. Soon they would be at 1.5 times the speed of light. He switched to looking back at Eden on his viewer; it didn't appear any different, just slightly perceptibly smaller and shrinking more. It was apparently revolving backwards just a little. "How strange to see that!" he thought out loud.

"What's strange?" Marla called out, and Erash proceeded to tell her.

"As we go faster, the light reaching us from Eden will be older, and the planet will start appearing to revolve in the reverse as long as we are accelerating. If we go fast enough and stay able to enlarge and enhance the microscopic pictures, we will see our Eden get younger. If we could magnify the images by billions we may be able to see Noah's 'Gramps' as a baby. You would be able to go back to Adam & Eve, even perhaps the beginning of our planetary time. Who knows?" Erash was starting to ramble, when suddenly a message was broadcast over the public emergency intercom system. It was clearly the artificial voice of a computer.

"We have now reached a speed, twice that of the speed of light. We are now going into phase two, and in 15 marks we will be increasing IA by 5 fold, and will be reaching the speed of 11.1 times that of the speed of light at which point we will reduce IA for a short while when damage control teams will inspect. Please prepare yourselves for major movement, and secure everything that moves. You now have 14.75 marks before IA increase. 'Security before comfort'. Remember!"

Erash had rehearsed his family many times that day and they all knew what to do and where to be. They just lay watching the stars, waiting for them to move faster. They were looking at the monitor, which had reference figures rapidly digitally changing in display panels at its periphery. There was a clear but shrinking view of their old home Eden. The planet would normally have disappeared at this stage but the camera was viewing Eden through an Astronomical Microscopic Telescope, which also had built in visual enhancers. This kept the image of their old home large enough to see in relative detail. It was beginning to notice that it was in backward rotation, and strange clouds were forming around its equator. The northern hemispheres were beginning to clear just a little, and then the image returned to its usual cloudy state.

"What happened there?" called out Marla

"Oh we have possibly seen the reverse movement of those horrific explosions that were created only two days ago by our old 'friend' Fadfagi, that maniac leader in his last death throws. We are now seeing the light that came from our planet over fourteen days ago. If it were possible to look carefully and in deep detail we may be able to see you sitting with Rula outside on our patio. Do you realize that we will very soon in the next short while be able to look upon Eden and see what it looked like in the time of many generations back of our great great grand parents over 2,000 years ago?

***

As Jubal dismounted off the train he was sure that he recognized a voice in the crowd only paces away. There were people everywhere. Railway train stations were always busy but this time it was different, everyone was hot and sticky and finding it very difficult to move in any direction. People were lying down on the 'cold' or 'cooler' stone floor, and were covered in different degrees of a gray white dust that was sticking to their clothes and more so to their wet sweaty skins, The longer they had been there the more thick and greasy. One short fat man was fighting for his breath and had to be administered rapid oxygen assistance by a friendly young and pretty blonde haired nurse.

Jabal was, as always, keeping up the rear and an eye that all their party was complete, and that all their luggage and personal property was all together to be loaded onto the absent trolley. The platform was cluttered with people and their belongings. The smell was foul; the air was thick, hot and humid. There was this gray ash-like dust everywhere. One needed a handkerchief over one's mouth to avoid taking it orally. Jabal called out to Jubal from just within the door of the train that they were all complete and that everything was squeezed onto the crowded platform. As he alighted from the carriage a bell sounded and the *'scrummage'* started for all the waiting people to enter the train. Suddenly the pushing and shoving started for the passengers wanting to enter the train and Jabal was sure that caught in it were many people who did not want to be. When the doors pulled closed, Jubal and Jabal would have been quite surprised if every person on the departing train were there out of choice.

"Jubal! It can't be Jabal! It is! How did you both get here? From where have you both come?" Tubal Cain threw his dusty arms around the two brothers pulling them both towards him. His surprise was only too evident, as his enthusiasm erupted at meeting some of his family, safe, in such a G-d forsaken place. "You must come home, Tsionne will be here in a moment and she will be delighted to see you. How many of you are there?"

"Sixteen" came the answer from Methuselah, as he ran up to Tubal Cain and threw his arms around his shoulders wishing to pull him closer to him. Gramps then continued to narrate their travels and troubles to Tubal, and the scene of family reunion was becoming somewhat emotional. Especially when Tubal announced Tsionne's great news in her absence. He had been on the adjoining platform waiting to meet her. She had been one stop up the line to see her 'Gynie' friend 'Bertwin' and Tubal had just arrived to meet her when he saw Jubal getting off the other train just across the platform. With so many people about and the state of near chaos, Tubal found it difficult merely to cross over the platform through the crowd.

"I can't believe you got here safely!" Tubal continued, "There was a severe groundquake just at the previous station down the line. There are many people dead and injured. The damage control unit has reported that it will be able to cope, but it will be days before we can get those trains running again. This station will be the terminal at present for the 'up' lines."

"How is Subterranean going to stand up to the bombing?" Jabal asked Tubal Cain.

"We did not expect 'Groundquake bombs'" Tubal replied, "The unexploded ones that we have in our possession indicate a high degree of technological 'know-how'. We underestimated the enemy's ability. We had never pursued that course. Our version is very primitive and certainly cannot go down so deep underground. It does not burrow like these do! Ours only scratch the surface".

Tubal broke off; as they had finally located a large baggage trolley and having loaded it thanked Tubal for his welcome invitation. No sooner than his invitation had been graciously accepted than the other train pulled in on the other side of a relatively empty platform. Tsionne had arrived and the 'reunion thing' was repeated while Tsionne became very emotional. Then came the sudden silence between two people as they looked upon one another from beyond an arm's length distance. It was the first time in quite a while that Tsionne had seen Gramps.

***

Svi and Lika were well aware of the commencement of "IA" but were much too busy over viewing their flock to take in the external consequences. There had been one tragedy already; Svi and Lika did not want another. Small accidents could be coped with, but the loss of a human child was unforgivable. They had already lost one and they did not want to lose anymore. A young blonde haired child of about twenty two Eden years old, had perhaps reacted very badly to the inhaled environmental anesthetic, she must have been very sensitive and had fallen face down under its influence into a shallow rocky pool of water. There was not enough water to cover her naked body, but enough that it prevented her from breathing and she proceeded to drown in no more than a small puddle. Her poor limp body was taken and stored in the security of a deep freeze that it could be used in later years for transplant and spare part surgeries if and whenever needed. Children's parts were always most difficult to come by.

Lika was very distressed at the loss of the little girl. She had taken it very personally, believing that all the children were her responsibility and that she had failed this little one by not being there to save her. The child could not have known anything about it as she went into what was to be her permanent peaceful death, but that did not console Lika.

Everything was quiet and as the ship was yet still continuing under IA for a very short period longer, Lika and Svi were strapped in their bunk seats and were viewing their domain on various three dimensional holographic monitors. The dead child had been discovered earlier not much after the initial input of anesthesia into the Environmental Atmospheric Control (EAC). Androids, robotic type machines that had been preprogrammed to act normally under unusual gravitational conditions, were used to remove the poor young body to the freezer in a hold quite far away.

Only a very short distance away from where Svi & Lika were seated, Neyl and his rescued were undergoing the final stages of their docking with the Ark of Noah.

Neyl was thrilled when he realized that they would possibly make it just before the end of initial IA, because if the Ark was to reduce its acceleration even a tiny amount it would in effect be slowing down related to the movement of Neyl on the tow. The net result could mean Neyl's ships just crumbling into the back of the Ark, effectively being crushed by the differences of momentum and the physical contact on the Ark which could be devastating. Neyl took the necessary precautions of pre-programming his tow and the tow to the Ark, that in the event of an acceleration reduction and or a slow down of any nature their crafts would push out sideways with a small movement so that they would in effect continue passed the Orbital City and then slow down to be at their speed in the front. Neyl would then release the tow from the Ark and be able to drive his two attached crafts gently into a convenient docking bay. 'Eureka' they will have made it. The event of reaching the Ark at the moment of IA reduction was the only problem that could cause alarm and that seemed to be more and more inevitable. Neyl had to re-think and fast! IA reduction and the point of contact with the Ark were rapidly approaching the identical time. He had spoken with Noah's control room and asked for the IA reduction to be delayed by even 2 seconds. This was not possible; it would spoil their overall trajectory. It was up to Neyl and Neyl alone. He asked if they could increase the speed of the tow absorption, but this was at a maximum.

Neyl decided that he had to arrive late and attempt to pass as the Ark was reducing its relative acceleration. He gave control instruction to reduce tow absorption and he did the same so that they were at least reducing their relative acceleration with the Ark. They would now arrive at the Ark later than reduction of IA giving them time to move sideways as he previously had programmed, but he now had to re-program his sideways movement to the new tow program. There was not much time left, but with moments to spare, he completed his task. He did not have to wait to find out if it was correct, they were on a moving course sideways to their Ark approach, as Ark IA had been reduced and was continuing to reduce. Soon the Orbital City would be no longer increasing its speed related to Eden, but would be at constant speed moving away from it. All Neyl had to hope for was that the 'tow-rope' did not snap or become disengaged when they reached full forward extent having passed the Ark. Within moments he found out as a jolt within his cabin told him that they had reached full distance and were all now at the same reducing acceleration as the orbital City.

There were cheers in Noah's Control room and tears in Naamah's eyes as the rescued evacuees were admitted through the entrance lobby followed by Neyl. They had made it without any kind of loss!

***

END OF BOOK TWO

***

—BOOK THREE—

'The Third Rising'

CHAPTER 1

'The Journey'

There had been a passage of many years on Eden since the Ark's departure from its orbit. Tubal Cain and Noah had kept in constant touch as far as the physics of communication would allow. More than four or five weeks could go by without any good reception. Sometimes due to faulty equipment, or due to its newness and early technology, the 'time slip' did not always work and Tubal or Noah would receive the same messages as if they were new. It was very difficult, but overall the two men had managed to keep up with events, and together plan the Ark's future.

Tsionne now had had her first natural child, a brother for their surrogate baby. They could not believe how much alike the two children were, although the younger one was born with thick red hair like his great grandpa Methuselah. Tubal was very pleased as he was very much a member of the family and he was spoiling it profusely.

Gramps and Tubal Cain had virtually taken over the running of Subterranean, and Jubal and Jabal had found their own niches for contributing to their new environment. Jabal was again back in agriculture where he was best and Jubal always the playboy and adventurer was very much involved in the attempt to recapture human usage of the planet's surface. As yet it was still proving almost impossible due to 'radio-activity'.

A council had been created to legislate and control the way of life in Subterranean and Tsionne had found herself in the chairperson's seat of the Family Division. There was a small community of Gorilla people who had made it to Subterranean; they had a small-forested zone near one of the underground lakes, which was truly beautiful. Their representative on the council was Bozo, the twin sister of Gozo who had disappeared in orbit during construction of Orbital City many years previously.

With the help of Tubal Cain and Noah, the Ark was now halfway into its journey at a speed of double digits faster than that of the speed of light. A feat that to neither of them seemed like a reality. Even the miracle of being able to communicate at standard wavelengths but at enhanced speed equal to that of the craft was an unbelievable experience. Although unreliable, it more than often worked!! Without that Eden would have disappeared into the radio space of the future unknown.

Noah, with Tubal's distant help, had set a course in the direction of an interesting and potentially friendly planetary system, in which there were three planets out of nine that looked like they could be possible re-settlement locations. With the inaccuracy of understanding the time slip in their signal communications the final destination would have to be decided when the Ark would be in a closer vicinity.

This was one of those luxurious moments when Tubal and Noah were having perfect three-dimensional communication and they were dissecting old data received from an early exploring probe sent in that direction many years previously.

They were able to see the volcanic surface of what appeared to be a partly water covered planet which had become partly elongated at one end, like that of a bird's egg. It was rotating on an uneasy axis at a variable 90 degrees to its' longest dimension, but it was still making it, with apparent turmoil from within. When Tubal accelerated the recorded replay on fast forward, they could see images of a planet throwing out a small proportion of it's innards in a round 'lava-like' volume with an umbilical sinking back into the depths of the original planet. The waters of the large forming ocean absorbed the umbilical almost to the center with a trail of small islands disappearing into the central depths of a warm peaceful ocean. The sudden loss of planetary volume resulted in the immediate break-up of its largest single continent in the East. A third of it broke away and moved toward the newly creating circular ocean from where the first dry dusty moon of that now wet and many continented planet had been created. The new rounded shape of the mother planet now appeared much more at ease with itself as it continued on its way with a new slightly tilted axis around the sun at the center of its orbital system. The new moon stayed facing that mother planet destined ever to orbit around it approximately twelve and quarter times in one of its years. After even more fast forwarding they could see that apparently seven continents had developed with seas and oceans filling in the gaps. This was forming into a beautiful deep blue paradise planet, which could be full of all the vital elements needed for the survival of humankind.

Perhaps . . . ?

***

Dissatisfaction was becoming rife among the people of the Ark and Noah knew it, and understood why. His speech to the nation of the Ark was his first significant communication with everybody in their years on board. It was not what he had said to them that concerned Svi and Lika, but that which had not been said.

There was so much 'who-ha' in the build up to the speech, which was to be made in the large three dimensional games arena. There was a simultaneous TV broadcast on all channels, and holographic video communication was blocked also to receive it on all channels. There was no choice, the speech was being made, and all were meant to see it and hear it. All sound channels, even in the love making cells, shower rooms, or toilets, there was no choice but to listen. It would be very difficult to find anyone who didn't at least *hear* it. Even external engineers working on the outside had to have it plugged into their working background, and as if a miracle there were no emergencies throughout the entire broadcast which continued without interruption. Noah took questions at the end, but answered them like a true politician, either with another question, or if he did not like the question, he would answer the question he would have liked it to be.

Noah was indeed surprised to greet Svi and Lika at his office he had previously asked for an appointment with them to be put in his diary, but why were they looking so nervous? He thought it best to come straight to the point; he needed to break the ice . . .

"How did you like my speech?"

"Is that for real Mr. Noah?" Svi answered, almost involuntarily.

"What do you mean?" Noah retorted.

"We are concerned about our children!" Lika interjected, trying to aim at a tangible argument. "What is to become of them?" She knew the answer, but thought it best to start from the obvious, as she and Svi had previously agreed. "You do not have to worry about them," came the reply from Noah, "that is why they are on board. It was originally thought to be a *'best way forward'* idea and as such was always a secret project of government and Science and Welfare. It is best still to play it down. Keep it in low key. I will explain."

"Please do." nodded Svi, with hurt feelings.

"Do you believe in G-d?" Noah asked Svi directly. "Yes, without question!" came the immediate reply, with Lika nodding in clear agreement. She did not want to be missed out.

Noah continued . . .

"Do you accept the story of Adam and Eve?"

We accept its' meaning." answered Lika with Svi's nod of approval.

"What do you understand by its' meaning?" asked Noah.

Svi answered . . .

"Humankind as represented by Adam under the influence of Eve his wife and persuasion of a snake disobeyed the ruling of G-d by eating from the tree of knowledge. Having eaten the fruit of knowledge he destined the human species to a future of fixed length, G-d having thus barred him from reaching the tree of life. The knowledge and understanding of things were to be its final destruction. In other words, with man's ability to understand and use his knowledge, it would finally result in his permanent destruction, that being the end of the human race. His ability to destroy himself!"

"No doubt taking a large piece of environment with him." Noah agreed, "If we are to save the human race, we have to eradicate that knowledge, we have to go back to before Adam ate from that tree. We have that opportunity now. We have to preserve all that is good in humankind."

Svi and Lika could see directly where Noah was leading them, and they both understood that this would not be the correct time to interrupt. They let him continue.

"We are almost certain that in the not so distant future we will be within the vicinity of a small planetary system of ten planets including its' sun. There are three possible planets in that system that could be habitable by natural man. As we approach the system, all will become clearer to us, but we do believe we could be safe with either number six seven or eight as we go in towards its' sun. At present our investigations into the three planets show that each one at a time in its' development could support or perhaps could have supported human life, but we are not certain about the time in which we are viewing them. The most likely candidate is planet number 'seven'. It was still forming, but we are observing tapes of light that we believe was created many million years ago, collected from the far reaches of outer space from ancient light reflected and re-transmitted back to us from one of our earlier probes. On our second-generation early probes we had the ability to transmit signals at extreme speeds never known before to man. We could do that with accelerated wave radio, but up until now we had not been able to move solid matter that quickly.

"Planet Seven? If it is friendly to man, are we going to disembark everyone?" Lika asked, knowing the answer already.

"It will not be possible!" came Noah's stern reply. "As I just explained, only those of us, who have never eaten from the tree of knowledge so to speak, can permanently land on the new planet. We will destroy it if we take our knowledge with us! There must be no trace of previous human endeavor, no reason for man once again to set about his own destruction! The only people safe to go would be your children of the orbital environment project, and similar from other areas on this Ark of Orbital City."

"What do you intend to do with the others?" Svi queried. "There is unrest. The people on board are not fools. Why are they here and where are they going? What is to happen to us, and to you for that matter?"

Noah hesitated. "We have the idea that we may have found another system many light years away from this first destination, we believe it could be habitable to man, but we need to do some more work on it, and we have the years to do it in! This situation must at present be kept secret and you are bound by law to do so".

"You have no fear of that, there would be a riot, and no-one would get off this vehicle alive."

Svi replied. "Mr. Noah, we may be able to help you. Give us a few more days."

***

Neyl was busy spraying his wounded shoulder with some fresh artificial skin from an aerosol can when the nurse walked in. Rianne had called for emergency help when Neyl had come home from work that day. He was often getting himself into minor incidents and this was just one more. He had been opening up a disused corridor in order to create a new area for a viewing tower, which would house an external *'super'* telescope that was almost finished in the laboratory workshop. He cut into a wall and a loose live cable thrust itself out at him and lashed itself across his shoulder causing a moderate burn.

"What are you doing?" The nurse yelled at Neyl, while pulling the can out of his hand.

"I need new skin urgently." He replied aggressively. "What about disinfectant and sealer?" The nurse admonished him.

"I don't need sealer if I didn't use disinfectant!" He smiled cheekily.

"What!!" Rianne and the nurse in unison.

"No, I never used disinfectant when I was a prisoner, working in absolute filth. No way do I have to do that now! Anyway I was working in sterile conditions and they had been sealed off since this place was built. The live cable was wedged behind a loose panel; it had not been capped for some reason. It was as if the work had not been completed and was just left in the middle of the job. As you are here nurse, please you might as well check me out, as I have to go back to work and finish this job that I left so suddenly."

Rianne threw her arms around Neyl's neck. "You are wounded my darling, you can't go back to work like that. Please rest! Nurse please will *you* tell him?"

"I must go back, there was something not right there. I must find out! There was unfinished work, why?"

Neyl felt quite physically confident as he went back down the corridor in his new clean work suit. He was worried that others may have tampered with his work in his absence. He had put roped beacons around the working area before he left for dressing his wound. *'Beware live electricity'* notices were always a good deterrent. He looked carefully, nothing had been touched, and his assistant was still there dozing on his sitting stick. Neyl took great pleasure in waking him up.

On the end of a telescopic two way telephone lead Neyl entered the small space that ran along the double wall of the disused corridor. Eventually it opened out into another wide corridor as if from nowhere. He had to locate the origin of the uncapped cable. Why had it been left incomplete and the entire unit sealed off? It was a whole unused corridor between two large halls constantly in use. It did not make any sense. The corridor led nowhere, but looked as if it was meant to be a major feature of the building. He managed to move along in the darkened area using the light from his helmet in order to see. The place was immaculately clean; the tiled floor was shining brightly. He had entered the corridor at its' end and by the escape arrows patterned on the floor he was going in the opposite direction, so he was proceeding to the beginning. Everything smelled new, it was just as pristine clean and polished as when it was built. The corridor was not on any map, and finished from where he had just come, in a dead end with a live dangerous cable hanging unattached. A mystery. Neyl was almost running along the long corridor, he was determined to find out where it started. Moving around a wide bend his headlight reflected back from a glass panel at the other end. There was something on the floor lying half inside what appeared to be a half opened door. As Neyl approached he could see that it was a body of a work person dressed in woman's overalls. It had apparently been trying to attract attention through the door wedged half opened by her body. The only problem was that the door opened onto a thick outside wall that had possibly been built incorrectly across the doorway.

He gently moved the body, which looked stressed, but asleep, her eyes were closed. She was dead, but complete and as if death had only recently visited her. She was relatively still warm! Her helmet still offered her an airtight environment and there was no breathable air left in her suit. She had died of lack of good oxygen mixture. The suit was still working and was powered although weak; it was that which had kept her warm. There had been no gorillas on board since before 'IA'. Who was *this*?

***

Tubal Cain was on the accelerated communication link with Noah when Tsionne broke the latest news. She was again with child. Tubal had tears in his eyes as he turned away from Noah for a brief moment to throw his arms around his Tsionne. They could see that she was effervescent with pride and overflowing with affection as she hugged her husband covering his face with kisses. Tubal pulled gently away and turned to tell Noah.

"I heard!" The holographic image of Noah said before Tubal could open his mouth "Wonderful news! How long? When is it due? May I tell Naamah? She'll be delighted. Just think how difficult you found things, and now you are blessed!" Tsionne turned to Noah "Are we blessed? Why does G-d want people born down here? It will be centuries before any return can be made to the surface."

"What about us?" Noah said, "We on the Ark of Orbital City, as was, are destined to a possible journey into the unknown for generations to come."

"I do not believe that!" Tsionne interjected "You already have a possible destination, a beautiful planet with all you would need on it for survival."

"Not for me, nor my family, we will have to wait, and if G-d is willing, we will find somewhere else for us to destroy in future generations. As I see it, only humans who are ignorant of past life experiences, living on basic instinct would it be correct to place on a virgin planet! That way they will survive, as will their natural environment. Only the uneducated, ignorant children from our environmental unit would qualify to land in humankind's new home."

"That is terrible, but I see what you mean! How sad that we cannot trust ourselves to keep the place tidy. A group of human beings are just like 'pigs' to the trough!" An alarm sounded in the background.

"Is that yours or mine?" asked Noah.

"Ours!" called Tubal, "they've found an old unexploded groundquake bomb at the bottom of our lake. The news is flashing on our internal monitors. This could be serious. I'll get back to you shortly, when I know more! I'm signing off for now, see you!" With that Noah gave a brief hand wave and faded away leaving Tubal to sort out a new problem.

Groundquake bombs had ceased their work not long after Gramps, Jubal, Jabal and company had arrived in the sector where Tubal and Tsionne lived. Occasionally there was a rogue bomb discovered and they were very difficult to diffuse. There had been a few accidents, but now one in their local lake that *was serious*. If it was to explode it could take the whole lake with it. The possibilities were horrific!

The submersible vehicle carried a working team of four. One was the captain of the vehicle, and as the driver he had permanent responsibility to ensure its' safety. The other three were bomb disposable experts. They rotated their responsibilities on each job. These 'jobs' as they were called were becoming fewer by the week, as the belligerence from the outside had finished a long while back, not long after Tsionne gave birth to her first natural child. The discovery of unexploded bombs was more uncommon now but when one was found it was usually in a very difficult and not normally visited place. This was once again the situation in this instance.

The three men donned their submersible sealed suits with air tanks and masks, shook each other's hands in ceremony, and then departed through the air/water valve out into the warm lake. They snaked their way around the rocky bottom of the well-established lakebed until a bright blue flashing marker beacon came into view.

The plumpest of the three men swam forward to the front with a small box clipped to his elbow. He moved slowly up to the silver gray nose cone of a rocket shaped object which had a drill-screw appearance on the apex of its' nose. The screw was slowly and gently turning freely in the water and the attitude of the rocket was nose upward with the rest of its' body sticking up out of the ground. The bomb they knew was as long as the three men would be if their heights were added together, and its' diameter at least that of their three waists in a in a tight belt. One third of the bomb, the rear end was still buried beneath it, in the ground from where it had come. It had not gone off, but that did not mean it would not. It was even now extremely dangerous.

The plump guy placed a suction microphone on the nose just behind the fin of the rotating nasal screw. He then moved downward to the base that was barely protruding out of the ground and placed a similar suction mike in position. After securing two more mikes elsewhere he reported back to his colleagues showing four fingers then the circled thumb and forefinger indicating four fitted and AOK.

It was many hours later, almost a whole working day when Tubal received the message. "Bomb disarmed and sending for disposal". It said nothing about the trials and tribulations of the men in their efforts, and near death of one of them with his foot caught under the fin when loosening the machine from below. It said nothing of the two seconds at the end of the countdown that could have gone the wrong way if they had tweaked an incorrect wire. They had complete faith, and with divine help, they conquered.

***

"I've looked through the records of *'missing persons'* and that is why I have come to see you" Neyl announced nervously across the threshold of Svi's front door. He handed Svi his ID, "Can I come in? It could be very personal, and certainly private!"

Svi waved him to enter and took him into the enlarged sitting room. A very fatigued looking Lika appeared at the door of the adjoining *'casual room'*.

"This is Neyl, a chief engineer in the 'Astro-Fleet'. He has something important and possibly sensitive to say to us. Come on darling, leave our houseguest for a moment, I am sure he won't mind."

"I'm sorry," said Neyl, "I did not think that you would have company at this time of day. Shall I come back?"

"No, please stay, Lika was only going through an analytical problem with him that can wait until later. What is your difficulty? How can we help?"

"I found your name on the official 'Found' list for a remote control lost years ago in section 26 orbital."

Svi thought for a brief moment . . . "Wow! That's right, I remember!" Svi was astonished, he had forgotten about it, and almost felt guilty about doing so. He felt that he had let Zarby down badly. "How and why were you looking?" He did not want to give any information away freely.

"I do some private sub-contract engineering work in my spare time, and I have a lot of that at the moment. I was breaking open an old area to restore it to use. As you know, the powers that be are about to install a new powerful multifunctional external telescope between the two great halls in section 26 and apart from getting near electrocuted on a live cable I found a kind of 'dead' gorilla. She is still sealed in her pressure suit. I have heard that you could know who she is. Only one Gorilla ever went missing that has never been accounted for, and you found her remote control. Is that right?"

"Gozo!" Lika called to Svi without thinking of the consequences.

"I still have her! Or her body!" Neyl interrupted. "She looks just like new and is still warm according to her suit monitors. We still have her in our working area, although we have moved her into an empty side cupboard. If we report this I'll be grounded until they solve the problem of her demise, and that could be forever. I could not believe my luck when I saw your name annexed under the 'missing persons' for the discovery of this remote control. I thought that someone like you may be able to help, certainly to identify her and then with a possible pre-solution to this problem. Can you help me?"

It was only a short while later that both Svi and Lika were bending over the *'dead'* body of Gozo. Svi could see her face asleep in the darkened helmet. He had only met her once or twice that he could remember but she had a distinct deep voice for a gorilla, and he could hear her mispronounced language so clearly as he looked at the face. It almost brought a tear to his eye. He turned his face to Lika; she was trying to suppress a few tears.

Svi acknowledged who she was and pointed out that her suit had technically kept her alive in the *'Prime State of Being'* a form of *'life support hibernation'* but her body was too far gone to be regenerated. Yes she was warm. Her organs would still have been weakly fed and the suit would have sustained her enough in order to bring her back to life after two or three Eden years, but this length of time would be impossible.

Neyl showed signs of surprise, he had never heard of such a suit. Svi explained that they were only on trial and only gorillas were issued with them. It had saved at least two lives to his knowledge.

"So there is no hope for her?" Neyl asked.

"There may be something." Lika interrupted, but we will have to insist on strict secrecy at this moment. Will *you* and *your colleague* co-operate?"

"He usually does, but I cannot guarantee that."

"How about for a few days?" asked Svi.

"What are you going to do?" Neyl was curious.

"We cannot tell you, but let us say that it could make a difference to everyone on this craft. We will all have a much more secure future" Svi was full of enthusiasm, although whispering his reply.

"It is definitely what Gozo would have wanted." Lika interrupted again.

"We may be able to prove that to you" announced Svi

"Do you mean that? Can you show me proof now?"

"No! Perhaps in a couple of days. Anyway we will have finished with 'her' then and I will speak to Noah and Erash myself. For that you have our personal guarantee. Will your colleague keep quiet that long?"

"I'm not sure."

"All right, just tell him that we are taking her, and we will attend to all the paper work. We'll send security down in two or three days for your reports on the discovery. You have no need to worry."

Neyl smiled and reached out his hand with a thank you, and Svi put Gozo, still in her suit, into a large body bag for transport back to their quarters.

Lika could not believe their luck and Svi knew that this would have been Gozo's last wish. Dare he think it; perhaps there was divine intervention. Surely of that they would both soon know the truth.

***

Their black uniforms with the silver strip stood out strongly against the surrounding beige and cream office furnishings. The air was foul smelling and sour with the acrid fumes of illegal smoking of a nicotine product mixed with that of a hastily overcooked meal. The two security officers were sitting facing each other, each with a cigarette in his hand. Having previously disengaged the smoke alarms, they were in close discussion over the remains of their seriously badly prepared meal.

Almost nose-to-nose, they were arguing their problem in the privacy of their small smoke filled office in the security block of Noah's fast moving 'Orbital City'.

"……….. there is no way you are going to go home! Home does not exist anymore." Koel was almost spitting his words into his colleague's face. His temper was beginning to rise in frustration.

"We are not going anywhere. We are trapped in this old bucket of ships forever if Noah gets his way!" Kraut burst out in angry reply. "We are not to land on this new planet! You heard his speech! If you read between the lines, the only people to be allowed to disembark onto this new planet will be within the environmental experiment. You heard him!" Kraut banged his clenched fist on the table his adrenaline beginning to rise.

"Where did you get that from?" Koel enquired knowingly. "His reference to 'knowledge'. He suggests that only the ignorant of the previous achievements of man in the face of G-d should be safe to land, in order that we do not destroy the planet, like he says that *we destroyed* the old one!" Kraut's speech was starting to slur as he was becoming angrier. Perhaps trying to calm himself down, he drew a mouthful of smoke, inhaled, waited a brief moment and then exhaled directly into Koel's face. "Even Noah, by those rules will not be able to stay. Where will *we* go? There is no place else, except home. Anyway I don't want to be a castaway on a planet without the comforts to live a normal life. Do you?"

"As I already said," came the reply "home does not exist anymore, or at least it won't very soon. Even if we get back home in time, do you want to return to its' inevitable destruction? There is a chance we might find that other planet which the high-speed 'air and water' sensitive probe found its' way to. It sent signals back from that nearby galaxy cluster. Both Noah and Erash have mentioned it as an alternative."

"They are not sure about it, but it could be another seventh of our lifetime away even at serious speed!"

"Noah will also want somewhere for his family. He is human just like us. He must believe in the other planet being reachable!" Koel was trying to rationalize the situation and attempting to calm them down a little.

"No! I believe that Noah will take his family down to the first planet and will stay there. He will feign an accident or something. He will find a way. Anyway I want my comforts and I want to go back home. I would rather die early there, than live out my life in poverty!"

Koel walked over to the entertainment system and substantially turned up the volume of the music sound system, he needed the noise.

"We will have to prepare a plan, and will have to be very careful that we should not involve others unless we have no alternative." Koel walked slowly around the small room, as if deep in thought, occasionally breathing out nicotine fumes as if with somewhat relief pushing them vertically upward into the already thick smoky layer above his head. He then sat back down in his chair and placed his calculator notebook on the table. Touching the keys with energetic enthusiasm he turned to his colleague and cautiously smiled. "I have a seed for a plan, but let me make some enquiries." he said putting his forefinger to his mouth, and then pointing to his ear as if to indicate that someone may be listening and it may be dangerous. He stood up suddenly as if prompted by memory and reached for the nearest deodorant aerosol and sprayed to the highest regions of the room. It was a while before he thought it safe to turn the smoke alarms back on. "We can't take these risks anymore he murmured to his friend as he ran the sink flusher which always generated an acceptable noise. They decided to put the dead meal plates in their garbage as they were so badly burned it would give them a good cover story should they so need one. They only just made it to re-activation of the smoke alarms, for if they had taken even a moment more of free time, the main fire detection system would have taken control and all hell would have been let loose. They would have also become very wet, and have a great deal of explaining to do!

***

Lika could barely hold back her emotions as she listened to Gozo's deep 'hoarsey' voice coming out of the computer's audio system. It was so real, as if Gozo was sitting in the room with them. The only reason that they could use Gozo's real voice was because the computer that Svi had purloined a while back had the early maintenance crew's voice recognition system in it and Lika had located it by accident.

Gozo's helmet had been removed from her head and she, or her body still in its' protective uniform was lying prone on her back on a workbench in Svi and Lika's casual room. Svi was carefully recording everything that Gozo was saying. The diligent duo had effectively been up for two days and two nights working and watching the unfolding of an apparently completely successful experiment. They could not leave Gozo's side for even a moment or it would not prove their experiment. There always had to be somebody present to ensure a safe result. She was now ready to have her helmet replaced and re-connected. They could then check to see if they had been complete in their success. If her body functions were still responding to the uniform, and all reported back as normal, then Gozo had unknowingly saved the Ark's people from a possible demise in interstellar space!

They checked the suit readings, there was a minimal reduction in body vivacity, but that was to be expected, as the helmet had been removed and Gozo had been exposed to normal atmosphere such as it was. The work that Svi and Lika had just finished on Gozo had in no way affected the brain's ability to work and control the body of its' host. Technically Gozo was still brain alive, if they had had a new body available which matched, then she could have lived again in her new body, except that the brain was not powerful enough to manage it. Had Gozo's body been discovered a few years earlier, then possibly they could have rejuvenated her, but now she was technically dead. When they turn off her suit's life support system she would just stop functioning completely.

The big breakthrough that this experiment had proved was that they could download a brain and erase all its' memory and ignore that part of the brain which deals with the basic body functions needed to keep it going, and also retaining its programming for its' basic instinct.

There were tears pouring down Lika's face as Svi hugged her and suggested that she . . . "Go and get Mr. Noah!"

Noah's initial reaction after chastising Svi for misusing a 'dead' body was that of shock and disbelief, coupled with an obvious optimism that this would remove an enormous weight off his shoulders.

"Before I will let you loose even on a convicted criminal, I have to know that it works and is safe."

"You can try it on me!" Lika shouted at Noah. She was determined to get her way. They had discovered the moon and she was convinced it would work. She uncharacteristically leaned over to Noah in a most suggestive way, almost offering to kiss him directly should he say yes.

"You are sure of yourself, aren't you." he said and looked over to Svi.

"I wish it could be me, but at this stage only Lika and I can work the program and a female's brain is mildly different from a man. It is more complicated. When we prove we can restore a woman to her basic animal state capable of performing all functions at the same time. We must prove that a woman can perform, 'The Brooding State', and then we know that we are fully successful. Gozo proved it works; now we have to prove it to you. Lika is our only choice!"

"No!" said Noah. "I want real proof. It cannot be Lika. We need you both. Hand Gozo's body over to security for cell storage and I will cover you for what you have done. Give me a day. Go and get some rest, I will arrange a suitable subject for you" He turned to leave and then as if an afterthought, "By the way, you will be able to return this person back to her normal knowledgeable state afterwards, won't you? We still have quite a few more traveling years out here in deep space."

"Of course!" They said smiling in Unisom.

***

Neyl was becoming very restless. Boredom was something that throughout his life as an enslavened prisoner he had always been able to cope with, but now his main obsession had been removed, that of needing to escape. He was constantly able to find a way to keep himself occupied with an endeavor to break the shackles of captivity. It was now several years since he had achieved freedom and met up with his beloved Rianne. Their relationship was not generally approved of within the Ark, but they had both accepted sterilization and their mutual involvement was therefore quite legal. They neither of them wanted children, they just wanted each other, but now Neyl was desperate to get back to work. He needed to occupy his mind. He was looking for any opportunity to get some work in what he knew best, and he also needed very much to involve Rianne. The opportunity was very soon to happen, there was going to be an emergency and Neyl's help would be indispensable.

The temperature within the Ark was seriously regulated and continually kept at 'comfort' zone temperatures. Slightly cooler in sleeping quarters than within the workplace, but always within natural comfort limits. At first no one noticed, but on four consecutive days the general temperature had been dropping slowly. It was Erash of security who spotted the danger on one of his routine visits to security control.

"There must be a heat leak!" Erash called across the office to a controller sitting alone at a similar monitor. "Look at program H16!" Erash called into his headset "If we keep losing heat throughout the Ark at this rate, in fifteen days from now our water will freeze! All atmosphere valves are normal, our fuel and energy reserves are at constant regeneration and replenishment, and all filtration systems prove normal. Why are we losing heat from our atmosphere? There is no logic, but it will need someone to go outside! Go look for an engineer in 'Maintenance'. It could prove to be a very dangerous assignment but we must know what is going on, and he must know what he is doing."

A request for a volunteer was sent to Neyl. Outside work was his forte and they could trust him. He was a professional, the best. He could handle all eventualities.

Neyl had a contented smile on his face as he showed his Rianne the small private control room aboard his tiny independent astro-vehicle. He appreciated a warm proud feeling coming

412

from within as he guided Rianne through the controls. He had at last found himself a much-wanted assistant. She had recently finished her training and now it was just the two of them out in the astrosphere with a serious job to do!

"Steam!" Rianne pointed to a small section on the eastern side of the moving city. "We are leaving a small vapor trail behind us!"

"But it's not *behind* us, It is not like one would expect to see on Eden in its' atmosphere. We are in a vacuum with negligible gravity. It is moving along with us and going outwards from the side of our body mass, not backwards! This is serious!" Neyl continued with both eyes glued to his binocular telescope. That indicates a major gas leak under pressure, we have to locate it!"

Rianne followed closely the navigation instructions as issued by her other half, and systematically brought their astro-vehicle around to the volume of leaking gas.

"Not too close." called Neyl. "You could spoil the highly polished surface of our vehicle if you drive through it. Its heat may be contagious under these circumstances."

They both took a very close look; it was very clear to them what was wrong, but where were they to begin in correcting the problem before it got worse. As they watched, the steamy waste exuding from a fracture at the base of a damaged antenna, began to dislodge some of the bolts, which held it in place and they could see the small hole gently grow in diameter. The gas was being pushed out through the gap and as they looked on in awe one more of the many bolts came out and went off obliquely to that of the spray of the yellow gushing steam.

Together, Rianne and Neyl worked hand in hand outside their vehicle, re-affixing the bolts that were lose and sealing the surface with an elastic solvent which set hard, moments after being released into the astro-vacuum. Neyl knew that the physics of what they had successfully done was only temporary until the inner atmosphere effectively eroded away the chemical elastic seal causing an even larger hole than that previously.

"We have to go back inside the city and locate the area from where that gas is bleeding, and then remove it, forcing an internal vacuum. Then we can seal and repair everything. It could be difficult but not impossible".

***

Tubal Cain was concerned that there may be a problem aboard the Ark. He was delighted to speak with Noah.

"We *are* drifting a little off course, but that is due to pressurized atmospheric seepage on the east side of the Ark." Noah was replying to Tubal's question. "We will return to our original course when we have rectified the problem. With this guy Neyl on the job that should be very soon I would think. We won't need very much energy to correct our course settings to make good the error. We may arrive a few weeks later at our destination, but we should cope with that."

"What difference?" Tubal commented, "The only people who would know that would be the 'temporary landing escorting party', and they would not be staying. What difference to them whether it is sooner or later? They are not going anywhere."

"They believe that they are!" Noah contested, ". . . and they are becoming increasingly agitated up here. There is an undercurrent of antagonism to the fact that they think that our children of the 'environmental investigation' are getting preferential treatment. The residents of the City of the Ark believe that they are going on to 'AC', *which* will take some many extra years travel out of their lives. I am beginning to sense great difficulties ahead." Noah believed that it was too early to mention 'the experiment' and chose not to mention it to his best friend and brother-in-law Tubal Cain.

"What is wrong with 'AC'?" Tubal appeared to be surprised that it had been mentioned.

Noah continued with an answer to Tubal's interruption . . . "We do not know enough about its' environment, it would be a gamble. At present, as you know, we are aware of the fact that there is a planet at about the correct distance from its' sun at its star's center which gives it about the correct surface temperatures, and there is an abundance of nitrogen, oxygen and water, but we cannot guarantee the ability to sustain human life. We have sent out preliminary probes and only some results have been retrieved. We are traveling too fast and these earlier probes do not contain the newest technology."

"Perhaps I can help from here. Give me the tracking frequencies, and we could collect the data and forward it to you using this new accelerated technology." said Tubal Cain with a kindly smile on his face.

"Why didn't I think of that? Great! OK, but let's see if there is something I can do for you in return." Noah enquired, "Yes, you could come back for us all!" replied Tubal in good humor.

Noah turned around to see that Erash had just entered the office and the three men exchanged some small pleasantries with Erash keeping tight lipped about the experiment, it was classified and although he was sure that Noah had told his brother-in-law, Erash had no right to mention it.

After final arrangements had been made for data transfer of information from the probe to 'AC', Tubal Cain took his leave saying that he would report within a few Eden Days.

Erash looked at Noah in Tubal's absence and indicated that they were ready for Svi and Lika, whenever the experiment was to begin.

"What have you done with the children?" Noah asked. "Alram is old enough to help to look after them, but Rula wanted Marla with her to view the proceedings. One of Lika's senior staff nurses is supervising all the children while Rula undergoes this task. Rula has made a living will in case things don't go exactly as they should.

They walked through to a small technical laboratory, which was attached to Svi and Lika's home. Svi and his wife had created quite a remarkable workbench in order to conduct the experiment. They wanted it to be impressive, they had to prove their right to success and the people of the Ark, unbeknown to them were depending on its successful outcome.

Lika was cradling Rula's head into a soft felted headrest.

***

"We have to do something about this" Shem, a tall lean young man in his early married years of youth, with fine long blonde hair around his shoulders which swayed in movement every time he forcefully turned his head, was interrupting his brother Ham who always liked to encourage his own point of view. Officially Shem was the oldest son, but it was quite debatable which one of the three sons would be head of the family in the event of Noah's demise, they were each very well qualified with their own strong personalities.

This was an impromptu family gathering of the three brothers to discuss in their father's absence, their future and how they would plan for it.

Shem continued . . .

"We are all lucky enough to be married to wonderful wives and we would very much like to settle down and have our own families. We are certainly not going to do that here out in space. It could be said that we are lucky to be here, many others didn't make it, but we did, and we owe it to ourselves, our species, and our kind, that we should go forward and procreate a new human generation. According to dad we will not be able to leave the Ark at our first stopping place; we will have to wait. We must have an alternative in as much as where do we go from here?"

"Whatever we think, we can't go against our father, or at least we cannot be *seen* to be!"

Japheth put in his contribution. "We have to be careful or we could be the instrument of a revolution."

Ham sat in deep thought, scratching his early balding head with gentle persuasion. He was younger than Shem, but he was a little shorter and more stoutly built. His hair was also blonde and fine not unlike that of his two brothers but his was already thinning and the crown at the back of his head was already proudly shining through. He coughed and quietly interrupted . . .

"This insecurity is very unsettling, and all the surviving people of this world have their eyes on us, the next generation of Noah. They watch our every move, and if we were to put a foot wrong there could be a riot. We have to keep cool!"

"I just said that!" Japheth called out, apparently quite hurt. He was somewhat younger than his older brothers, and was married very young to his school time sweetheart on his parents' advice. They could see this exile situation approaching and wanted to secure all their children's futures. Shem and Ham always treated Japheth like the 'younger' brother; he was always being made to feel that he had to prove himself to them. His being married, he thought would enhance his position in his brothers' eyes, but it did very little to help. They would not belittle him intentionally in front of his wife, but they could be very patronizing. Japheth would often think that thank goodness the three wives got on so well together, even with his wife being so much younger than the other two, she was the 'baby', and all three women were very beautiful.

Japheth was determined to make his point. For once he wanted to be listened to.

"If we follow the rules, keep within the law of the 'Ark', we cannot go wrong. There is nothing to stop us from creating a landing army of helpers to organize the landings when we finally arrive at our destination whenever that is to be. It will give everybody a goal to work for and could contribute to relieving the 'unrest' in the 'Ark'."

"The Science & Welfare security guards are well trained in that exercise." Shem pointed out.

"I don't trust them!" replied Japheth.

"We'll work on your idea, but I believe that we could cause trouble with the force of Science & Welfare, perhaps Ham could speak with Erash about it" Shem stated condescendingly to his youngest brother.

"I'm not sure that Erash has all the control of his security forces that he is meant to." Japheth answered, but Ham nodded apparent agreement and then said that he would report back to them after his discussion with Erash.

***

CHAPTER 2

The perspiration was pouring down Lika's forehead and the salty sweat was getting in her eyes. She was acutely nervous about the whole affair, and sincerely hoped that she was not dripping onto the equipment. Wearing fine protective gloves should have been sufficient she thought, but even through those she was sure that she had felt a few drips. Lika had even resorted to wearing an absorptive headband, but in her tension that would not stay straight and was slipping over her eyes, she could sometimes not see clearly, having to push it upward with the inside of her forearm.

Svi was busy at the first monitor screen and the keyboard, while his wife was maintaining the connections to Rula's skull. Working on somebody they knew did not help their attitude, both operators were acutely aware of what they were doing and although the functions were very easy to perform, they understood the permanent tragedy of doing something wrong.

At this moment they had only just begun copying Rula's memory onto a small condensed disc, they were not even near any danger to Rula's mind, but Lika was still acutely nervous. 'What will happen when I start full download?' she thought secretly to herself and began to feel even more anxious.

As the copying process continued Rula made a sign with her hand that she wished to speak. They had not sedated her for this process, it was not necessary, and they had asked her to give her comments at will. They just wanted her to give a sign in advance that she was about to, in order that their equipment would not be affected.

"This is a very strange experience" she remarked "I am passing through my life's history as uncontrolled thoughts just seem to flash through my mind, it's involuntary and very strange because I can still think parallel thoughts at the same time about something else! Like now when I am talking to you!"

"That is good," said Svi "Men do not have that same facility. The man is the hunter and concentrates on only one thing at a time. He cannot well put all his conscious energies into more than one thing at a time. It is as if he can only run one computer port at a time, whereas a woman's brain can run a bank of ports without any loss of quality, although it is arguable that her quality is not as excellent as the man's singular quality. The woman has the 'brooding instinct' built in and can watch over more than six different things at the same time whereas a man can only concentrate well on one. Man was the born hunter, woman the born carer of her brood. She knows at all times what each one of her children are doing and can watch over them well."

The copying procedure was finished without incident, with the small exception of when Rula experienced the brief sight of the memory of her painful incident when she was imprisoned in Larden. For that single moment her mind was concentrated on that brief moment of her life. She suffered it all over once again, the pain, the embarrassment, the humiliation and the hatred. She had forgotten how it had affected her and how she had fought against its' emotional effects at that time. Just suddenly it all came back with a vengeance, and again she had to fight.

"How do you feel?" Svi asked Rula. "How do you feel about going to the next stage? We have everything on record now, a full copy, and download will be perfectly safe, we can put you through full erasure apart from 'life essential' and 'body motor zones', including 'basic instinct'. That is, we will leave you with all vital body and brain functions that you were in possession of when you entered the world as a new born baby."

"I now have fully developed breasts, a working menstrual cycle, all my teeth and body hair. I can chew; I can walk, swim, understand and speak a mutual language. What will happen to those things? How will my brain cope with that?" Rula showed a little anxiety in her voice.

Lika replied before Svi . . .

"Those are very sensible questions, and you have virtually nothing to fear. The only thing that will change for us is language communication. We won't have anything more than that of a baby, all other conditions that you have mentioned will come back as normal except perhaps swimming, for that you will have to re-learn, but it is in your basic instinct, you will quickly learn to paddle like a dog. The children of the environment experiment quickly learned to do that without being taught. Your brain will also update itself on all body changes and will immediately convert and compensate its functions in alert to those changes, such as teeth, hair and sexual awareness. I do believe that you will walk within moments of re-awakening because crawling is not what we are built for. We are built to stand up and walk. Again, look at the children of the environment. They eventually walk and run, and they were never taught. The early ones found out to do it themselves in their ignorance."

"There is one thing that Lika missed out." Svi interrupted, "Artificial aids will have to be removed and discarded unless they are implanted already in the anatomy, such as false teeth or glasses or contact lenses. People who have had refractive or other surgery will not be expected to have that undone. You have to come to terms with bad vision if you have it but don't forget we will not be able to read as no written word or letter will exist any more. I can see that you have had a lot to understand and digest in the last few moments, how about a break for some cable-juice and cake. Perhaps we can then proceed with the download and erasure. Do you feel ready for it Rula? We promise you that you are perfectly safe and we do have everything about you completely saved in here, and an extra two copies on these two separate tapes." Svi pointed to the condensed disc, and held up two sealed boxes of electro-magnetic tape.

***

Neyl and Rianne found their way to the corridor in which Gozo's body had been found. He had not realized in his mind that the place where they had found Gozo was that same place under which there was a hole in the roof.

"We will have to return in air sealed work suits! Then we will be able to evacuate all the air from this compartment and seal it off for repair."

It took Neyl and Rianne longer than they would have expected to find their own personal electronic astro-work suites. They had been moved from where they had put them on board their craft and probably innocently hung in the staff quarters' changing rooms.

When they returned to the 'corridor' with the problem Neyl noticed that something was different. He could not quite put his finger on it, but he was worried. The wires that he now knew so well were bound in a different manner to the way that he had done it, and the door to the emergency access unit had not been firmly closed. He was most precise in these matters and his years of imprisonment had made him very aware of even the tiniest things.

"We had better get down to work." he called down the corridor to Rianne who was bending down tightening up the clip on her boot.

"I will check the atmospheric pressure for you," She replied, "while you prepare the air evacuation equipment."

Neyl and his partner worked energetically for quite a while in preparation by sealing off the affected compartment down to the last detail. No way was it going to be possible for air to escape into their working volume. When they had retrieved what atmosphere they could into storage by suction, in order not to waste anything, Neyl was determined not to allow anything more than a vacuum to exist in his working space.

After some time Neyl heard Rianne call out on her suit's intercom . . .

"It all checks out. We have a vacuum."

"Let's have a break for a short while and then re-check the vacuum and see if it still exists, then we will be sealed in and safe to continue." Neyl suggested.

They spent some glorious moments on the observatory roof looking at the stars. The roof was a building site. The new telescope had not yet arrived but the housing for it was already completed. They sat together against its' wall looking out across the Ark to the stellar beyond. In the context of the large city beneath them, the scenery of interstellar space was truly a magnificent sight taken in the perspective of the size of the Ark, which was all around and below them.

"Look" Neyl said softly to Rianne through his helmet intercom "Look" he said again "There is no steam, no gush of gas or vapor leaving the tower like there was a short while ago."

"Nothing," Rianne answered, "We have managed to block out the leak, now we have to find it and seal it."

"That won't be easy. We will have to re-fill just the outside section of the observatory with air, as that is where the leak is. The pressure will be low, so then we can repair it without any danger to ourselves."

"Look!" Rianne said softly to Neyl, her voice also coming clearly and fondly through his helmet intercom. "Look! What I found on the floor at the end of the corridor when I was re-securing my boot-lock." Rianne put her gloved hand into her unzipped external suit pouch and pulled out a gleaming silver lightening flash broken button. I thought as much!" replied Neyl. "Something strange is afoot, and I do not trust security!"

Rianne nestled up tighter to Neyl as close as their astro-suits would allow, smiled and began to mumble . . . "When you look out there at the stars in order to see from where we have come, you would not believe the misery and evil that is out there within all that peaceful scenery!"

Slightly changing the subject again Neyl asked Rianne, "Have you noticed that there are no *natural* shadows?"

"Yes that's true. Apart from our own generated light there is only starlight and more so from the brightest stars in the sky. There is no definite shadow except where our own lights create it."

"Look, just to the right of the direction of where we are going." Neyl motioned for his wife to turn, as he pointed behind them to the front tip of the Ark, which was clearly visible from where they were sitting.

"Another bright star, I see it."

"That was not there until a few days ago. I noticed it and now it has become at least twice as bright since then."

"It could be the brightest star in the sky. What do you think that is, and why are you so interested?"

Neyl smiled and held Rianne closely.

"I believe that is our future. If you use logic, we know from where we have come, so that . . ." Neyl pointed back to where they were first looking. ". . . is where we came from." He then stood and turned around again. ". . . and that is exactly the opposite direction giving a degree or so error. We are moving in that direction, and fast. Look at the slight movement of the heavens. It is just perceptible to the naked eye." Neyl again pointed, pulling up Rianne to stand next to him. "That is to be our new home. Please G-d."

"Not according to Noah." Rianne replied curiously.

"We'll see about that." Neyl murmured with a degree of uncertainty in his voice.

***

Svi sent Lika to tell Rula that they were ready for her. As Lika approached the door she was sure that she could hear sobbing from within the room. Marla answered the door, she was red eyed and embarrassed and tried to whisper into Lika's ear, so as not to be heard from within the room. "We are very emotional. My sister has just remade her will and also a living will. The reality of the situation has just hit us, but we are still volunteers."

"We?" said Lika almost out loud.

"Yes, I thought you knew that I will substitute for my sister if there is any problem."

"There won't be! All the difficult work is done." Lied Lika ". . . But thank you anyway." She gave Marla a gentle kiss on the cheek. "We are ready now!"

The controlled erasure of the relevant parts of Rula's mind *was* quite easy. Svi maintained complete control using his two monitor screens with his keyboard, while Lika continued her vigil on Rula's headset. The same type of headset used in education and installation of knowledge was this time being used to erase it. There were a few differences this time. Rula was generally anaesthetized and lying prone on her back on a specifically constructed hospital type bed. Svi had obtained the services of a registered anesthetist and his nurse for the occasion. As the procedure continued they noticed substantial changes in Rula's demeanor. On one occasion her sister had to apply a diaper-like towel to her groin, where she had appeared to have inadvertently lightly urinated. Fortunately she had not eaten that day or the previous night so that was the worst that happened, but Marla felt quite embarrassed.

"She is nearly gone!" Svi announced with a serious sense of relief in his voice. "Start to reduce the anesthesia."

It was not long before Rula's naked head re-appeared from the headset and Svi turned off the monitors. They carefully pushed the bed out of the theatre of operations into a large comfortable side room where they removed Rula onto a settee-bed and lay her down on her side. She lay there like a piece of meat.

"When this actually takes place in future, things won't be quite like this. The sedation will last a lot longer, there will be distant supervision and of course the subject will be naked or almost naked when he or she awakes. That is yet to be decided." Svi narrated as they made Rula comfortable. "We shall see some action very shortly. We have the patient's pre-permission to videotape proceedings from hereon and she will see it first before permission will be granted not to destroy it.

Marla was watching Rula's lips and holding her hand, she felt some life coming back into her consciousness. The Anesthetist's nurse was checking her vitality signs and nodded approval as all the correct numbers appeared on the anesthetist's mobile monitor screen.

"Don't expect anything," Svi called out to Marla, "she will act just like a baby and you won't understand her, neither she you!"

Rula started to breath easily and suddenly opened her eyes then she broke into a broad smile and looking up at her sister pulled her down as if she wanted a kiss. Marla kissed her warmly as a sister on her mouth for a brief moment and withdrew. Rula started to cry uncontrollably and Marla threw her arms around her as if to help her.

"Don't do that!" Lika called out "She is nervous and doesn't understand. Consolation at this time could be counter productive in the world outside. Leave her, watch her and listen to her for a short while."

Rula cried continually until she fell asleep again, but this time it was much more fitful and appeared to be very satisfying to the patient who curled up into the fetal position and placed her thumb in her mouth and sucked herself gently into a deep sleep

***

"My goodness, what a fine young man you have turned out to be, but you are too young to lose your hair, perhaps that's why you grow the rest so long."

Ham was always accustomed to being ragged by his uncle Jubal, and on this occasion he had turned up at Erash's office only to be greeted by the electronic holographic video-mail, which was taking in a long message from Jubal on Eden. Ham switched it over to live at his end in Erash's office and directly picked up the communication with his uncle. They had not met for many years.

"What are you doing in Erash's office? I wanted to leave him a message." Jubal enquired.

"I called in to speak with him, but I saw your hologram standing in the center of the room, I knew it was active, so I wanted to speak with you. After all, you are my uncle and you are on Eden, or should I say under it? Aren't you?"

"You could say that I am *in* it, but at present I am in Tubal Cain's office as this is still the only way to communicate with the Ark."

"How are everyone, Tsionne, uncle Tubal, great Gramps, and all?"

"Tsionne is expecting her fourth child and we are all growing older every 'day'. Uncle Tubal is having trouble with his cough from the inherent dust that we get down here, and Uncle Jabal is as usual, always busy. I understand that life on the Ark is somewhat boring, is that true?"

"Yes! We go to the occasional three-dimensional ball game. The low gravity gym is quite good fun, but the *best* is sex in almost full Eden gravity, but that is a rare and expensive commodity out here, we have to order the gravity in advance, so it doesn't have the same effect when its pre-planned so far in ahead. One thing is great, we don't have to use contraceptives because it is in the drinking water, which goes into almost all that we eat and drink, so no one can get pregnant on this trip. Not even me!" Joked Ham.

"I would never have guessed!" replied Jubal, quite the known expert on such a subject. "But *you* have put on some weight since I last saw you. Turn around, let me have a proper look at you."

Ham obliged and Jubal continued. "They say that the Holographic makes one look fatter, so let's just blame that."

"It's two dimensional video that does that." said Ham, "but I'll accept what you say graciously."

"What did you want to speak to Erash about?" Jubal asked Ham again.

"Security! A question of security! Ham answered with the first thing that came into his head. He did not want to be pre-empted. "Why are *you* wanting to speak with Erash?" Ham asked in quick reply.

"I didn't want to speak with Erash" Jubal continued, "I wanted to leave him a message on behalf of Tubal Cain. I knew that Erash was out with his wives at the moment, and Tubal asked me to call him with a message. That's all, but it was great speaking with you, I will call him back later and leave the message then. I'll say goodbye to you for now and please give all your family my best regards."

"Can I take the message and give it to Erash?" asked Ham.

"Sure." said Jubal without even considering any consequences. "Tubal wants Erash to keep him posted when he intends to make the course alteration in order that he can keep our planning up to date. Also it will affect our directional communications at superlumic speed. He says that we have almost achieved consistency now and it would be sad to lose it at such a late stage."

"I have recorded your message for Erash and I will also instruct him myself directly when he returns to his office. Have you any idea how long he will be, as you know so much about his movements?"

"All of today he will be out and possibly also tomorrow." stated Jubal from so many light years away.

After terminating their conversation almost moments later, Ham rushed out of Erash's office with what he thought to be sensational news for his brothers. He would still get to speak with Erash but at present 'time' was obviously not of the essence.

"They are going to change course, soon! Where are they going now?" he wondered to himself as he walked off to consult with his brothers.

***

Kraut was desperate to freshen up. He removed himself from his warm shower and rubbed his body all over with his heavily powdered towel. He had to remove all traces of engine oil and get himself pristine clean. His image in the bathroom mirror looked good in his black and silver security uniform. He always felt impressive when 'dressed'. He had a moderately high rank and was always willing to use it. He truly enjoyed the authority over people that his position carried with it. He took pride in his uniform and took out his clothes-tape-brush and used it to clean it from top to bottom.

'Wow I look good' He smiled to himself,

Koel was already seated at his office desk when Kraut walked in unannounced.

"Well? How did it go?" He asked Kraut.

"I did it, and know that I was not seen, but I've just cleaned myself up."

They had to be very careful with what they said to each other, but they already had a private code of conversation that seemed to work. They could certainly understand each other. It was important that no one else would. They knew that their office was wired, and so even might they be. *What do you mean you weren't seen?* Asked Koel with some consternation in his face.

"It's meant to be a surprise for my girl 'Airit'" He got himself out of that mistake quite easily. "I don't want her to know do I?"

"I suppose not," replied Koel with a smile. "Have you hidden it out of sight?"

"Yes. Until I'm ready to give it to her."

"Great! Sit down we can play checkers."

"3D or flat?"

"'3D'. It is more concentration Koel answered." While Kraut set the pieces in the cube, Koel stood up and put on the locally piped music channel. He had the volume very loud which made it very difficult to hear because of the electrical interference drowned out the good stuff. He turned, complained and sat down. Kraut then switched on the Kettle to boil some water. The whistle, which would sound when the water boiled, was also very loud and would seriously affect the reception from any wire that had been placed in their office. The two men knew that they themselves used the identical monitoring system elsewhere on the Ark.

Without necessarily moving their pieces, the two men spoke to each other as if they were playing a completely different game.

"That piece you just placed is well tucked away. It will cause havoc later in the game, but it is hardly noticeable hidden away in that corner at present."

"It will carry such a force of strength for such a small piece. It is where I have placed it that matters. You will see!"

The two men continued their game of Checkers, with the casual comment that bore no relationship to the game in front of them, but to a 'fictitious' game in their dreams.

There was a short 'rap' on the office door, Koel went to answer it.

"Would you sign here please?" said the laundry deliveryman. "Why? We don't usually have to." Answered Koel. "This is a regulation working uniform suit. It is standard delivery."

"Yes that is right, but it's damaged, and we didn't do it, so *before* we clean it, we have to have you acknowledge the damage. We can repair it, but at your cost."

"That's OK." came Koel's reply "We can claim back uniform repair costs. It is just bureaucracy gone mad. By the way whose suit is it and what is damaged?"

"It's Kraut's and an official button is broken in half. Only part of it remains and as it is silver it will be expensive to replace. You know that it is an offence to wear the uniform with a broken button."

"We are aware of the regulations." Koel signed the form. "There, take the uniform, repair and clean it. Be off with you! We are security officers you know!"

***

Rula was sleeping peacefully when Marla and Erash entered the room. Marla bent down and kissed Rula very lightly on the center of her forehead. Rula began to stir.

"You were wonderful," Marla whispered quietly to herself "a true and honest example of courage and honor. Words that have disappeared from many people's vocabulary." Rula stirred again as if she was hearing Marla's soft voice in her sleep and was beginning to awaken. "Noah was very impressed." The excitement in Marla's voice was bordering on ecstasy or devout relief that the ordeal had proved itself. Rula began to wake and on seeing her sister attempted to sit up, but fell back as if it was too much effort. She lay there with her beautiful but sleepy sticky eyes looking up wide open at her sister, then at her husband, then back to Marla.

Rula lay relatively still for a few moments as if surprised at her surroundings and appeared to be carefully taking it all in. Erash nudged Marla to look at Rula's mouth, he was sure that she was attempting to make a sound, as if she wanted to speak. Rula, like her twin sister, had a determined nature and would win even if it were only mildly feasible to do so. She wanted to talk, and talk she would. She made a noise from deep in her throat, as if she would wish to hum baritone. She moved her lips to open and close and found that it worked. She could hear her own noise. Continuing along the same lines she practiced for a few moments then went quite quiet and relaxed.

"Wha..amy? Ah,my..bak?" Came suddenly out of Rula's mouth, with such effort, she became exhausted immediately and closed her eyes for a few moments, before a nervous smile crept across her alert face as she re-opened her eyes and looked lovingly at her husband and clearly spoke. "Erash" she said.

"Darling. We have been here all the time. Noah is delighted.

Can you remember?" Was his reply.

"Where am I? Am I back?"

"Yes," said Marla almost in tears of relief. "You are 'back', you had us worried, but you did so well and you have had your mind re-instated as was, but Svi and Lika explained to Noah that your initial recovery was only artificial and you won't remember it. It was like deep hypnosis, but you are back with us now aren't you?"

"I feel exhausted!" said Rula, "but otherwise no problem.

Tell me all about it and I will just listen." "When you are ready you can see the video of yourself and how you acted and re-acted when your brain was newly born out of erasure."

"You were wonderful" Marla interrupted Erash "You were great, but certainly you have made us all aware of a few problems for which they will need to be prepared. Noah has asked Svi and Lika to make some suggestions for alterations and report back to him. You will see the video, but no way do any of us wish to be reduced to that level as adults."

"But we may have no choice!" Erash commented, "If we want to survive onto the new world."

"Tell me, what was the main problem?" Rula needed to know.

"It may be easier for you if I prepare you for the video." Erash continued, "The main problem was your frustration. Your body was fit and well and ready to go, but your mind was so primitive, you kept becoming aggressive, and even at one point violent. You started to masturbate and tried to attack me sexually. We could not communicate with you, and you would not slow down enough to understand."

"Does this mean that I was a failure? I have a feint recollection of recognition of what you are saying. Why is that?"

"Svi is better suited to answer that, but I believe that he could not erase *all* the fresh memory of today and yesterday. He said it would be too dangerous for your vital support system. He did say though that it would be well buried in the lower reaches of your subconscious and should not disturb you. No you are not a failure, when you first came back with us with restored brain memory and life experience you were traumatized. It was too much for any human to digest back into the central nervous system, but you coped and fought, within a miraculously short space of time and with your sister's help you regained your cool old self. You are a lady of honor and distinct courage. We all admire you. You could have collapsed, but you knew that the people of this Ark depended on your success."

"What is going to happen now?" Rula asked.

"Noah is depending on Svi and Lika to come up with an alternative program which will correct all those glitches. Svi is relatively confident."

Erash gave Rula a long affectionate kiss and he cuddled his two wives in a blissful temporary peace.

***

On arriving back in his office Noah found Velmitz Shawn anxiously awaiting him. They exchanged pleasantries and each thought to himself how much older the other had become. Videos seemed to lie about appearance and they had not met for years even though it only seemed akin to yesterday when Noah had entrusted Velmitz with his four 'cell phials'.

"Are there any difficulties?" Noah came directly to the point "I know that you finished your initial agenda of listing and cataloguing years ago. How are you getting on with your latest assignment?"

"Oh that is no problem. We had a few setbacks with cell division, but we solved that. It was the general water supply. There is contraceptive in it, so we have to make and bottle our own water. It is very secure and labeled 'poisonous substance'. No that is not why I have come to see you." Velmitz hesitated for a moment and then continued by asking Noah directly. . . "Why? For what reason are we doing this? It is hard work and all my colleagues and associates are becoming restless to the point that they took a vote which was almost unanimous that I should come and ask you person to person across your desk."

"You have been given the awesome task of carrying G-d's creation one step further into the future. Is that not enough for you?" asked Noah.

"Yes, but where is our future and what will happen to us and all these creatures?"

"The original idea was that the rare species were to be cloned, re-created and laid back onto Eden in order to multiply and procreate that they could once again be citizen creatures of our planet home. History was to change that and it was seen that this established form of science was to be used for even higher reasoning. Eden was under threat, its possible survival was in balance, so as if directed by the almighty himself, we had the ability there already to enhance and clone even mundane everyday creatures living or dead in order to preserve life forms as we knew them before."

"But we are not going to return to Eden!" Velmitz interrupted.

"That is true, but our motives are still the same. We owe these creatures little, but we owe it to G-d, our maker, to re-establish his work rather than allow it to disappear into oblivion. We must do all we can to re-establish these organisms with us the human species. Another thing or another way of looking at it is environment. We destroyed the environment of Eden to a great extent due to lack of consideration and selfish greed. We need the chain of nature to survive in our natural state, and as you know the new children of the Ark will need a familiar ecological balance if any of them are to survive. By importing with them familiar nature we stand a better chance of helping human survival on a new planet."

"What is this *us* and *them* business you keep referring to, and what about disease? Will we not be importing our diseases onto the new planet? Is that all right?"

"Us and them! That is a problem, as I mentioned in my 'Arkle Speech' to the nation of the Ark. We cannot take over a new planet in order to destroy it, as we did on Eden. We should not take with us our knowledge or technology onto this new home. Until very recently, privately we have accepted that only special circumstances should permit, other than our environment children, to settle on the new planet. You would be allowed to supervise your deposits as Svi and Lika would theirs, but just as with other privileged visitors, they would have had to return to the Ark."

"Would have?" queried Velmitz.

Noah hesitated; he knew he had said too much, he had gone too far.

"Would have. As I speak to you now, in confidence, and if it gets out, I will know whom to arrest, because this is a privileged discussion. Have I your word of honor? Honor amongst thieves or should I say poachers?" Noah asked as if with tongue in cheek.

"I would like to say yes but I am not in the position to be honorable!"

"Then I cannot tell you any more, except . . .," Noah thought for a moment "There is a strong chance that I will announce a serious change of policy in the next few days."

***

Shem and Japheth were agog when they heard Ham's news. They just could not believe it. Why would Noah decide to change course at such a late stage. They could be well into the final third of their journey to the seventh planet as it had now become called. They knew that all recent checks had proved it to be the best bet as a landing site from the lips of their own father. What was up now? What dramatic change had taken place, and why hadn't their dad told them? The three boys had become very uneasy with the uncertainty. "I think that I should still go and see Erash about our original plan, it can't hurt, and if in conversation I can get the chance I will casually ask about the change of course." Ham decided out loud for his brothers' approval.

Elsewhere on the Ark two security officers, Kraut and Koel were glued to their security audio monitors. They were aghast with surprise as they listened in on the 'live' fruitful conversations of Shem, Ham and Japheth.

On arrival at Erash's office Ham nodded a brief hello to Neyl who was just leaving. Erash will not keep you very long" The secretary at reception desk announced to Ham who impatiently waited at the water fountain. It felt like an eternal period of time before Ham was able to face Erash across his desk.

"Sorry about the delay, but I had to attend to a few urgent matters." Erash greeted Ham warmly with a handshake.

"Did you get the message from my Uncle Jubal?" Ham found himself coming straight to the point. He was a little bit upset with his own pre-emptivity. He had prepared a completely different approach but the delay in his seeing Erash had resulted in completely unsettling him. "Yes!" Erash smiled as he sat down, while motioning Ham to do the same. "I received both messages, the first *and* the second. Thank you." Erash answered with a small degree of innuendo in his voice.

Ham decided to attempt to stick to his original plan of discussion with Erash and continue in that vein. "My brothers and I want to be of help. We know what is going on, our dad keeps us informed" Ham stated in his ignorance. "We would like to help with the landing of passengers on any strange soil when the occasion arises. We would like to create a 'landing army' or policing force that will monitor and direct landings in order to help it go smoothly. We are willing to submit to training."

"Why?" Erash was surprised at the request.

"We are frustrated and feel that we would like a goal in our travels. We wish to contribute to the community."

"We already have a security force. How would you be any different?"

"We would be 'independent'!"

"Well, what difference, what does that mean?" Erash was suspicious.

"May I speak freely? Without fear of incriminating myself?"

"On this occasion, yes, as a favor to your father."

"Cult!" Ham took a breath and with courage, continued "Your 'S & W' security has over the many years become a form of cult! It does a good job, but many people are scared of their authority, and may I say it? They are not trusted! It has been said that they are politically on the far right wing!"

"Wow! You could be arrested for that!" Erash hesitated, stood up and walked around his desk, then placing his rear end on the desk in front of Ham he continued after deep thought, and looking down at Ham . . .

"I agree!"

Ham could not believe his luck; the first hurdle was now behind him, he could continue.

"Come back to me with proposals and I will speak to your father." Erash smiled.

"One more thing" asked Ham "Why are you changing course, and where are we going?"

"Planet seven of the Solar system! Why? Oh the message!" Erash suddenly realized. "I have just seen Neyl, and I kept you waiting while we changed course. I also notified Tubal Cain that I have done so. The gas leak over the last few days caused a minor course deviation. We have now corrected our alignment as the leak is repaired!"

***

Noah felt that his office was like a railway station. All day there had been an interchange of people involved with the administration of the Ark. He was doing his best to cover all aspects of a necessary policy change in the event of a successful conclusion of the experimental project of Svi and Lika. They had even perfected a second experiment on their young recently married daughter 'Trin', all within a very short period of time. Noah was astounded by the energy emitted by these two guys. He wanted so much to give them a break, but he knew that there was only one way to change things, and he needed them and their success in order to do it.

Two tired people entered his office, and Noah threw his arm around Lika's shoulder and directed her to sit down in a comfortable chair. Svi sat himself down next to her as Noah sat behind his desk.

"You both look exhausted!" Noah informed them, "Do you feel hungry?" They acknowledged 'yes', and Noah ordered some food and drink on his intercom. He turned to Lika and asked . . . "How is it going? Are we on board yet, or is there more to do?"

Lika half smiled, understanding the full gravity of what they were about to announce, but also the pleasure of their work being finished and that it was successful.

"We are up and running and ready to go!" Lika's voice was choking with fatigue. They had not slept for more than an odd moment during the previous days and it showed. "There are certain provisos and some careful decisions to be made, but on the whole we have several spare programmed discs and subject to some rules we are able to proceed." Lika almost started to cry and Svi carried on with her announcement. "We can perform this task on each subject in less time than it takes to administer the anesthetic, so long as we are not saving what we erase. That would take ages as you know!" The more machines and the more attendant staff, the quicker we can work, but it would require an enormous amount of organization, because those who have not been downloaded must never see or never be seen by those who have, with the exception of those people who have been specially trained. If this were not so, there would be a catastrophe, which could result in an uncontrollable riot. People who have been reduced to their basic program of vital life function, all of a sudden, can achieve inordinate strength. As you saw when Rula attempted to rape her 'husband'."

"We will have to re-build a volume of the Ark to cater for this, with one way movement of passenger traffic, like at the airport terminals".

"That should not be difficult" Noah said while making some notes. "What happens after download, how long will they be under general anesthetic?"

"Well," said Svi, slightly embarrassed "they will have to be naked and their openings and orifices will have to be searched before the anesthetic wears off. In case they are trying to cheat and bring items with them. Scanners won't detect everything. We also understand that you do not want any prosthesis or artificial aids with them so they will have to be removed. In cases like that we feel that they should be given the choice not to go. We don't know how you will handle that."

"There should be no problem with that, they can have the choice. In fact I have no problem with anything that you have said. It seems well thought out, but you *are* Svi and Lika. I believe that you are a wonderful team. One of the best we have on the Ark." Lika began to show tears in her eyes but kept quiet. Noah continued . . . "We will have to make these 'rules of possession' known well in advance in order that people can cater for all eventualities. For example nothing will be allowed that will *not* die and disappear naturally with the body when the person dies. That also applies to our vets' department. I will give you some human examples." Noah took a sip of cable juice and continued trying not to be too boring. "I will tell you what will be allowed, that is easier at present. We will permit as I said just now, anything that will rot and disappear with the dead body. We would allow natural transplants such as human or clone grown organs, implanted teeth buds for third sets of natural teeth, refractive surgery where everything is natural, or auractic surgery of the ear or hearing canals where natural perishable products have been used. These are just a few of the principal forms of allowed items. Anything that will give a historical legacy or is so obviously manufactured cannot be allowed. It would incite interest and suspicion from the 'new' population. I would suggest that all people be given the opportunity to become wholly perishable in order that they may leave with the landings on planet seven. Most people could have that choice and I believe that we have just about enough time to do everybody who will want it."

"One more thing!" Lika needed to finish, "When the newly mind-erased people have been released from their anesthesia they must not ever again come in contact with uniformed security. These people have in built anathema to the black and silver.

They will react very badly to say the least!"

***

As if with urgent feeling Kraut was passing each of the fingers of his right hand through the long straight auburn hair of Airit who was lying across his lap while they sat partially watching an old holographic 3D video movie. Airit was enjoying one of their few moments when they actually had some real time together. The old video movie was just an excuse for them to be able to sit together and 'talk' for a while.

"Where are you putting your hand now?" Airit smiled up to her lover. "You know that's forbidden territory!" as he moved his hand down to a fresh region around her groin. "I am a security officer. I have to check you out don't I?"

"Do you do that with everybody?" she smiled as she encouraged him to do more.

"I do not discuss my clients. Professional ethics you know." Kraut answered as he smiled with a large deep prolonged kiss into Airit's wide-open mouth. He felt the warmth of her emotions coming through to him as he caressed her and experienced her tongue with even more force and deep feeling. At that moment in time he truly believed that he loved her and he knew that she loved him. They were so close only full sexual intercourse would have been closer, but Airit was very old fashioned. She was still a 'virgin' in as much as she had never done anything more with a man than they were doing now, but they wanted each other very badly. Airit was strong; as was her man and she would not give in. Kraut accepted it with respect, but not for lack of trying.

Their lovemaking was beginning to affect Airit's ability to maintain control; she carefully pushed her man away and stood up, straightening herself out.

"I am sorry darling but you are an excellent lover and I have to slow down. Airit stepped back slightly. "Would you like a drink?" She walked towards the kitchen as she spoke. "A hot roasted bean drink would be a fine brew, black with some sweetener." He threw her a kiss as if to say 'thank you'. Taking the remote control in his hand, he re-wound the video for a few short moments for them to resume watching when Airit came in with the drinks. He wanted her happy, he had a very important question to ask her and he wanted her in a good mood.

She was gone for some while, but when she returned with drinks on a tray, also some light biscuits to nibble, he noticed how beautiful she looked; she had re-done her face make-up to perfection. 'How does she keep her hair so neat, and so smooth' he thought to himself. He brushed away at the table for her to put the drinks upon.

Sitting down almost next to him she lifted her drink to her mouth. "What do you want?" she asked completely out of thin air. "I know you only too well. You are so attentive, much more than usual. You obviously need something from me. What?" Kraut was taken aback. "What do you mean 'What'? I am always attentive, I give you most of my time and I think about you *all* the time."

"Do you *love* me?" Airit asked.

"Well of course I do."

"You don't sound convincing." Airit said with a soft kindly smile. "Enough to get married?" she asked.

Kraut now had a problem with what he would say next. He felt trapped. Of course he loved her, when he was with her and sometimes he looked forward to seeing her, but not always. He thought that he could love her, but he was not yet ready for it.

"Is that a marriage proposal?" Kraut asked.

"Not exactly, that is not for me to ask." Airit spoke softly with deep care in her voice.

"I want the security of marriage, just as you do!" Kraut continued "But at present for neither of us, is our future secure."

"What do you mean by that?" Airit enquired in surprise.

"They are going to change course and I do not know where we are going now." Kraut had made his point in an opportune manner. "You work in 'Admin' can you find out? It will make an enormous difference to our future." he reached across and gave her an affectionate warm friendly cuddle followed by a comforting kiss as if to alleviate any of her 'worries'.

***

CHAPTER 3
'SELEKTION'

Ham could not believe his luck. On going through a required *'clearout'* of Erash's apartment he found a small closet that would have been Tubal Cain's had he made it to the Ark as he was originally supposed to. Erash and his family had now taken up temporary residence in an apartment next to Svi and Lika, as they were so much involved in the forthcoming download.

Had it not been for the kidnap of Tsionne's surrogate child they should all have been 'safe' on the Ark at this time. Instead Tubal Cain was back there on Eden, and Erash who should have been in charge on Eden, was on the Ark acting out the commands of Tubal Cain and Noah. Now the time was approaching for general download and erasure of most of mankind's minds in order that those landing would be cleared to do so.

They had reached the outer edges of the "Solar System' and its' sun was now large enough to be visible with the naked eye. Very soon they would be slowing the Ark down to more normal levels in order that they could navigate through the orbits of the various planets and following their own solar orbit and using the Sun's gravity they would slow down even more in order to land there cargo on Planet Seven. Planet Six and Planet eight had already proved as uninhabitable for human life. Planet eight appeared that perhaps once upon a time it could have been, but planet six was an enigma, and would cost too much human endeavor even just for a landing. No everything was right with planet seven, so why go anywhere else? Nature had smiled upon this planet, and G-d had been kind to it. Man could walk naked there if he so chose and nature could provide most of his needs.

Looking in the full-length mirror, Ham could see his own image fully dressed in one of Tsionne's beautiful laced silk creamy beige nighttime outfits. He was quite physically aroused as he pranced around pretending to be Tsionne. Although Ham was getting on for early middle age, these outfits dated back to her early days with Tubal Cain and were very sexy for bedtime wear. On Ham they looked stupid, but he could not see that. He could only feel the previously worn sexy clothes against his body and imagine Tsionne's young image in the mirror. Ham heard someone coming and in less than a moment had returned fully dressed in his own clothes.

It was his brothers Japheth and Shem who appeared behind him. Had they seen him he wondered? He didn't think so or they would have said, or looked surprised, but they were very matter of fact when Shem spoke to him.

"We have come to help you finish the job. Erash's apartment has to be cleared out for the security guys to take over. As you know they have elected to continue their journey after we have all left for Planet Seven. They are to use Erash's apartment for their headquarters residence." Ham was unhappy at being interrupted and he hated being hurried.

"Tell me something that I don't know already!" he replied. "The download program is about to start and we will be required very soon on the 'Airside'. We have to help. As you know we have the responsibilities for security tasks on the 'Airside' as they do not want any black and silver uniforms through the gate."

"I thought that they were not going to start brain downloads until we had decelerated from superlumic speeds." Ham *was* surprised.

"That starts tomorrow Planet Seven Time." Japheth added and continued, "It has just been announced that from now on we are to cease using **EST**, **Eden Standard Time**, and all times from now on are to be as that would be on planet seven, '**PST**'. The Eden year is 1/11th that of Planet Seven and our new days will be very slightly shorter"

"Wow!" said Ham with a sarcastic smile "You *have* told me something new!"

"I will tell you something else that's new." Japheth interjected . . . "The Planet Seven has a large airless moon which orbits around it just about twenty eight **PS** days at a time. It completes one day more than thirteen times as Planet Seven completes its year of orbit around its' Sun."

"You *have* been studying your subject." Ham paid a patronizing compliment to Japheth.

"We have one complete moon orbit of Planet Seven which is to be known as one 'Moonth', to prepare for download and we must have everything ready for go!" Japheth said quietly.

***

"We need at least two moonth's supplies." Neyl whispered into Rianne's ear as she prepared her list.

"That is about eight weeks on Planet Seven."

"Yes!" replied Neyl.

"I find all the new times and terms very difficult to get used to!" Rianne complained.

"If we were going to be downloaded, we would not have to learn these new things. So be grateful that we have this other choice." Neyl was becoming impatient. He knew that the *Intersteller Deceleration {ID}* was scheduled to start the following day, when their extreme speed would be reduced to sub-lumic within six days. They had a very narrow time window in which they could proceed into their next adventure. Neyl was always determined, and this time he knew exactly what he had to do. He was an expert on escape. He always tried to keep it so simple.

He continued . . .

"I have prepared our astro-vehicle, it is fully serviced, cleaned and super loaded with full fuel resources. We even have our modified gorilla safety suits on board. We must be the only humans ever to use them, but as you know, they work well. I have fully tested both. We will be ready for any eventuality, but let's just hope that we don't need them. I have even found and hidden on board, four neatly folded parachutes. We go later this evening, when the Ark is busy preparing for *Intersteller Deceleration* and are busy with safety precautions we will be going outside to do the necessary 'checks' that are required for *'ID'*."

"You have brought enough provision for an army!" Neyl reacted when safely on board their Astro-vehicle. "You are lucky that we have so much space as we have no cargo."

"I got my maths wrong," Rianne replied "There are just over eleven Eden years to one Planet Seven year and that is not important in this case, but in error I brought just over eleven times too much."

"Never mind, I just hope that nobody spots it before we leave." Neyl was always aware of the obvious. Why should they need so many provisions for such a short trip?" Rianne went through all the safety checks of their craft with Neyl, and then checked with control to request 'disengage' and the opening of the loading bay doors for their exit from the Ark.

They had to proceed with their work around its 'perimeter skin'.

"How long are you going to be disengaged?" The control tower requested.

"Now that the Ark is completely about turned and facing backwards we will do four orbits of the Ark at regular speed, and we will keep in touch." came Neyl's nervous reply. "Good. Beware; 'ID' starts on what would be your sixth lap at normal speed. You must be back and attached before that or you will lose us forever, as you will continue at superlumic speed until you meet an object in your path. You do not have the power in your vehicle to avoid anything or even slow down!" The answer came from the control tower in a soft female and very persuasive voice.

"That is only a computer!" Rianne assured Neyl.

"I know!" smiled Neyl. "What a pity!"

The 'all clear to proceed' came back after a long nervous wait for approval and the loading bay doors opened just enough for Neyl's small craft. Rianne carefully and slowly moved their astro-vehicle out of their housing through the air lock to the outside.

"Look." Neyl pointed out to Rianne, "Still no shadows, only our own artificial light and a small degree of starlight, but that is evenly spread around us. When slowed down and nearer to the new Sun we will have proper daylight and true sharp shadows.

"There is a very slight hint of a shadow if you look at the telescope housing. The edge has a sharp edge to the shadow but it is very feint. Look!" Rianne pulled on Neyl's shoulder and continued speaking. "The new solar sun can be seen with the naked eye back there it is as if we have come from its direction."

On their third lap Neyl indicated to Rianne to roughen up their radio with some pre-recorded static and then temporarily shut it off, change wave bands and then re-transmit on another channel. This she did and then following their pre-rehearsed schedule . . .

"Hallo control. Hallo control. We appear to have lost contact! We appear to have lost contact! Over!"

Neyl and Rianne smiled at each other while they waited during at least one more trip around the Ark. Then came a reply . . .

"We have you. Wow! Good thinking to use another channel. Where are you? We need you back to attach immediately. Any problems?"

"No, none!" called Neyl "Except this radio is on the blink. We are returning to port now. Over and out."

With that announcement Neyl turned off the radio and turned the Astro-vehicle around, taking it very slowly to just underneath the new telescope housing under which he had previously created three firm capstan type fittings on which he could firmly attach his craft. Technically they were between the Ark and a firm fixture that was part of the Ark, so when it slows down they would sink gently onto it rather than pull away at speed. In this position, Neyl had found out that because it was new, the control tower was completely blind to that part of their perimeter.

Control tower was panicking and called Erash for approval. "There is an Astro-vehicle which has not returned after radio interference cut off its' radio. We are only moments away from 'ID', shall we delay?"

"No we cannot," replied Erash "We have only a small window or we will miss the Solar system altogether. At this stage we cannot afford a delay of even one full second. Go with or without. By the way who is on board the craft?"

"Neyl with Rianne!"

"That is a shame!" said Erash "One of our best, but we cannot wait. It is now just about time. Continue with the countdown and depart exact on the nail!

***

The initial countdown to 'ID' although announced, went completely unnoticed by all passengers on the Ark. There was no sudden surge and no change in position of fragile or badly placed objects. The reduction of speed was so gentle and so slowly put into action that anything loose in the craft barely moved. There were a few minor incidents of non-secured objects falling over as deceleration increased, but it was all so subtle that almost nothing went wrong. Eventually the deceleration was increased multifold and people felt the new gravitational force coming from the back of the Ark which was now apparently coming from the direction in which they were meant to be traveling.

Most people had strapped themselves in at this stage and many went to bed early, as that was the best way to handle the increasing gravity from the back of the Ark. All residential apartments had the ability to change bed arrangements from floor to wall as most rooms had soft quilted wall areas, in order to cater for all eventualities. It would have been far worse if it weren't for the gravity compensators built into the engine, which were gyro-driven. they were helping by providing negative artificial gravity to reduce the overall effect.

Lika and Svi had one of the most difficult tasks, with the children of the environment research unit. They once again had to find all of their people sedated somewhere in the volume, collect them, mark and photograph the spots where they were discovered that they could be returned there afterward. They would then secure them in a large dormitory that had been created for them since the initial 'IA', which seemed like history now.

These people were no longer children, but young adults. Many of them had found out what their bodies were for. Many of them had tried to enjoy each other's anatomy, but as yet the contraceptive system was working one hundred percent. Lika had brought it to Svi's attention that as yet only a few couples had found an apparent kinship and they were all old enough. She thought that perhaps it was the absence of childbirth that was generating this affect. This item had helped Svi and Lika sort out one of the major problems with which they had been faced . . . 'Kinship'. There were families on board who were scared that they would not know, or want to know each other on download. Svi and Lika had finally found the section of the brain, which was associated with Kinship using some environmental children to do so. They used some couples who had become very close and also some people who had not. Also they used some normal family volunteers and some unattached who were from within the Ark passenger list.

Svi and Lika managed to confirm many things that they already knew but were quite astonished by some of their findings. Three couples among the whole group had one partner who had some deviant sexual interest; they were bisexual. They each knew it, but would never admit to it. There were two young men and a woman. They were not related and did not know each other. Neither Svi nor Lika was going to tell them their secret.

Noah and Erash had been wonderful to Svi and Lika; they had accumulated educational headphones in such large quantities. These items were previously forbidden on the Ark. Svi was doubtful of their origins, but they worked. The computer workshop had been working non-stop to provide systems and units that would fulfill the demand for download. Noah had allocated the Great Hall and Stadium for the two functions of collecting people, 'Arkside' and 'Airside' as they were becoming known. The Ark was already being divided physically into the two different sections and it was beginning to look quite impressive. The general feeling among the population was that in spite of "Download' the majority wanted to go. Noah and Erash thought that perhaps the people had not yet realized what was going to happen to them. There were so many takers.

There was a mammoth job in front of all the people of the Ark and Noah did something that had not been done on Eden for many generations. He had made some studies from some old books and videos. With Naamah and Glenshee's help, they were both great believers, he organized a full prayer meeting to give thanks to G-d for deliverance so far and to ask for his help in their next stages of survival. Not for many generations had people prayed together in a single place. They were to use the great hall and it was to be televised on all channels for those who could not make it.

Noah was astounded that out of all the people on the Ark nearly everyone applied for tickets. Many of those who did not apply were security guards. Erash was not surprised.

***

"Nobody has been out here since we tied up!" Neyl whispered to Rianne. "If we hold on and secure our suit with our tether to the lead rail, we should be able to mount the external steps to the 'new telescope'. I know the security codes, so there should be no problem on entering the airlock from the outside undetected. We have to be careful not to be 'blown away' by the deceleration, which is still on going. If we let go of anything it will disappear in a flash. One moment it will be there in our hand, the next moment gone forever, as it disappears at the speed we were when we let it go. If there is any part of the Ark in its' way it will just go crashing hard into it! If there is no Ark in its' way it will just go on at superlumic speed passed the Solar System and on forever or until it hits or is pulled to something of a larger mass."

Eventually the intrepid duo left their astro-vehicle securely tied and fixed as previously to the Ark. They climb the outside emergency steps to the 'New Telescope'. With any luck and with due certainty they would make an unannounced entry into the airlock. Neyl was not one to take unnecessary risks, and he knew the security system so well that he was not taking a risk. Rianne was carrying a food parcel and two drinking pouches.

It was a difficult climb up the circular steps, which went around the base of the telescope and seemed to go on and up forever. On one side nearest to their destination and facing to the back of the Ark, the pull of the rail on their tether and the inability to walk properly was fearful as they rounded the corner and disappeared toward the front of the Ark facing Eden from where they had come, the deceleration was pushing at them and although walking was less fearful they were being pulled 'down' toward the wall of the telescope housing. Neyl looked back at Rianne when they were around on what was a relatively 'safe' side. One of the attached drinking pouches had disappeared. That is a warning he thought. They were only half way there and at this stage there was less protection as technically they were well above the Ark and with this strange invisible force going across them, they could be blown off sideways and the Ark would disappear forever in an instant. They would not even see it, as they would still be traveling at their super lumic speed of that moment.

Neyl indicated to Rianne that they could climb up another way from there. Why had he not thought of it before? There was a problem that there was no guide rail to tie or hold onto. They would have to use their magnetic climbing spikes. He indicated. He showed Rianne that he had released the spikes from the soles of his boots and the palms of his gloves. They were magnetic and would grip onto almost anything but they left marks on the surface. Neyl did not think that at that distance away and outside there is any way that anyone would see them.

He asked Rianne to follow him as he climbed the side of the tower to the telescope entrance on the outside nearest to the front of the Ark, which was the side farthest from where they were going. This way they could almost walk up the side without any fear of being 'blown off'. Physiologically crawling although slower was more reassuring as they could also hold on with their hands. The physical exercise was good for them.

Entering the telescope office was easy and no alarms were set off. Neyl checked for electronic bugs, he had a security detector as part of his regular engineer's kit. He also temporarily by-passed the sensitivity detectors to the Control Room so that for the short while that they were there; they could have their lunch, use the equipment and return to their astro-vehicle completely unannounced to anyone.

The large objective lens of the telescope cast a shadow on the room

below. Rianne pointed out to Neyl that in the true darkness of the stellar light, the shadow proved how strong it was.

"The large objective lens is what gives the superb detail of inter-stellar objects that we observe. Let's just have a quick look at where we are going." Neyl said, like a little boy with his new toy. He set the computer for the nearest planet.

"Nothing! It won't register, says it's too blurred." He followed correction instructions given by the computer. "That must be due to deceleration from superlumic speed affecting the light reception that we get from relatively close objects!" Rianne knew her stuff; she had studied Physics in her spare time.

"I have it. Them!" said Neyl in surprise as he looked at the digital reference screen. "Solar Planet Two is very close to Solar planet One and they are both about the same distance from us.

"Let me have a look." Rianne pulled the viewer around so that they could both see. "Look the illuminated crescent of Solar Planet Two is enormous related to the sunlit crescent of Solar Planet One, and Solar Planet One has a clearly visible Moon, whereas Solar Planet Two has one visible and a larger one hidden with many other 'bits' floating around it. The picture has gone!"

"We will have to go in again to view but as we are decelerating it won't hold the live picture for very long. We will have to save it as we do it each time and that will leave a trace that we have been here. Let's go and come back shortly at the end of deceleration."

***

Communication with Eden had been impossible during deceleration. On one occasion Noah had received an old message from Tubal Cain about a groundquake bomb in the lake, he received another of his own messages returned as unsendable, when he knew that Tubal Cain had seen and replied to it on his video mail. The situation was not serious, but upsetting that they should have lost contact with 'home' even for a few days. In earlier times they had been out of contact for many weeks and that was quite common, but they were more frequent in their communication now as technology had been improved. They had become accustomed to it.

Noah was at his monitor trying to get in touch with Tubal Cain. He tried 'variable speed technology' and 'accelerated bounce' signals that went fiercely faster than any speed that they had traveled in the Ark. Tubal knew the wavelength and should have been able to catch them on the 'bounce' and slow it down to transpose it and watch. There would be 'live' communication when that had been completed, but still no sign of success. Suddenly the screen lit up with a picture. Two planets and several moons, 'Where did that come from?' He wondered. Instinctively he turned up the sound and there was a commentary. It was a woman's voice.

" . . . *the illuminated crescent of Solar Planet Two is enormous related to the sunlit crescent of Solar Planet One, and Solar Planet One has a clearly visible Moon, whereas Solar Planet Two has one visible and a larger one hidden with many other 'bits' floating around it . . .*"

The screen and sound disappeared. Noah tried hard to retrieve the picture or the sound, but he could not. Strangely enough he thought that he had heard that distinct female voice before, and unfortunately he had not had the presence of mind to copy it. Where did those pictures come from? They were the first two planets in their path to the center of the Solar System. How? Why? He thought to himself. It began to worry him.

The door behind him opened, it was Erash unannounced. "I have been speaking with your sons Japheth and Shem. What nice young men!" Erash walked over to the musical player and turned it up loud; he also indicated that they should speak in the bathroom where he turned the tap on to full. "Their wives have asked them to tell me and indirectly you. They couldn't face you themselves!"

"What!" Noah was awaiting each word out of Erash's mouth. "Ham! Your sons came upon their brother Ham, acting out his fantasies in woman's clothing. The boys think he is a transsexual. Poor guy!"

Noah was startled and sat down, he poured out a cable juice for both of them and thought for a few moments. He was trying to control his thoughts between disappointment and anger. "How sure are they?" He asked Erash.

"Positive. They stood almost behind him and watched dumbfounded as he played out his fetishes in a mirror. They felt sick that it was their brother, and quite sorry for him. They did not want to be seen and by some miracle a door closed in the outer corridor behind them causing Ham to think that someone was coming. He jumped behind a screen and quickly changed. It seems that he still doesn't know that they saw him."

"We should not take this on board as yet." Noah was thinking loud. "It is his and his wife's problem. His wife will be desolate if she were to know, unless she does already. What do Japheth, Shem and their wives think about Ham's wife. Do they think she knows?"

"This is third hand but it was mentioned and they believe that she is truly oblivious to his sexual deviation. Otherwise she is putting on a wonderful prolonged act of adoration." Erash said quietly.

"Then leave it, and wait." Noah said.

Erash was concerned. "We will have to be careful! The boys will be starting a new job in Two days time, in control of security on 'Airside'. They will be in charge of the examinations of naked downloads for concealment!" Put Ham in the male side, he should be kept safe away from the women. Organize it somehow. Use women for women, and men for men, and keep someone on a discreet watch on my son all the time!"

***

"According to my watch and readings on the astro-vehicle's control panel we should, at any moment, be at the end of the sixth day **Planet Seven Time**." Rianne called across to Neyl who was clamping down the cargo and securing all the loose fittings.

"We have to be very careful." called back Neyl. "Even the smallest loose object could be like a bullet through the hull or the windscreen of this machine when we finish deceleration, if they get it even slightly wrong and it is not a smooth transition from constant reduction of speed to constant reduced speed. This vehicle was not built for the kind of speed changes that we are experiencing. Although we will still be traveling fast, we will be sub-lumic, and at constant speed until we reach the orbit we will make around the Sun. Each time we pass a planet our path will alter very slightly but that is all catered for in our overall pre-flight plan. When we pass a large planet we have to be careful not to drift away from the Ark if we are not attached, so in future, as we are unsure we must keep tethered at all times. We do not want to use up too much of our suit fuel reserves for playing, do we?"

"We are very close to termination of deceleration. We are already 'sub-lumic'." Rianne was watching the monitor very closely and she knew that they were almost at the speed they wanted. We were at the speed of light 'three hundred thousand' just twenty-six 'PST' seconds ago. We are still slowing down and the sixth day is due to finish in fifteen PST seconds, 13, 12, 11, counting down, 8, 7, 6. Hold on, 3,2,1. Nothing happened, but the dials are no longer moving, we are now at constant speed. Look at my pencil, it's floating." smiled Rianne.

"You fool!" Neyl shouted at Rianne "If we had been only slightly out, that could have killed us by being loose."

"Anyway it didn't!" Rianne realized her error and started to cry! "This is all too much, I can't go on!" Neyl moved over to comfort her and gave her a very masculine hug, which seemed to do the trick. Especially when he said "Sorry darling!" into her ear.

"Do you feel that?" Neyl suddenly said.

Yes! You mean a hint of gravity?" replied Rianne, no longer emotional. "Where is my pencil?" She took it from the monitor panel 'grip' and holding it out in front of her let it go. It fell like a dead leaf in the autumn backward onto her face. "I'm right" she said "We have a little gravity and it is now coming from behind us from underneath the Ark. We have artificial gravity again."

"They must have re-started the Gyros, but as you know the effect is felt much more inside the Ark than outside, and if we lose our contact with the surface the gravity reduces down to a minimum very quickly as we move away from the Ark. So we must still tether ourselves when outside this astro-vehicle. Hey, what is that?" Neyl pointed at the New Telescope, a light just went on inside its' office, but it did not stay on for very long. Neyl thought it to be very strange that somebody would want to use the telescope so soon after the end of deceleration, which had only just occurred. They must be in a hurry for something perhaps.

Neyl discussed the situation with Rianne and they decided to go and investigate. They knew it to be a risk, but they were convinced that they could handle it.

Having proceeded to climb back up to the new telescope under slightly easier conditions Neyl let them in through the same door as previously.

"Careful!" Neyl whispered to Rianne ". . . and do not turn a light on, we will get enough light from the corri . . ." Neyl stopped abruptly as his boot caught some kind of package on the floor. "Look, a body!" he stopped and went down on his knees. "A woman and she is alive!"

"Look at her clothes." Rianne tried to make her look decent She has been attacked and she may have been raped. She has certainly been beaten up, look at the bruises, and the tears on her clothes. She has been in a fight. She has damaged finger nails and some residue in between." He pulled a cushion from one of the bench seats nearby and placed it under her head. He then took a small body scanner out of his suit kit and ran it over her entire body. "No breakages, no structural damage and her circulation is sound. She is a good-looking woman poor thing. What beautiful long auburn hair!"

***

"I didn't know that there were so many young children on the Ark! Can we give him something to stop his crying?" Svi asked Lika as he surveyed the line of people for 'Selektion' and processing for download.

"There are a few children who were born on the Ark, but that was allowed to balance families and compensate parents in very special circumstances. They had a special license and were allowed to bypass contraception."

"How did they do that?" Svi asked.

"They each took a pill. It was an antidote."

"Wow, so simple, taking a pill in order to *have* a baby." Svi smiled to himself.

"We have so many black and silver uniforms on show. Do we have to have so many security guards?" Lika was showing visible concern.

"We cannot afford any panic, and they are generally disliked. Erash and Noah thought that they would have a sobering and stabilizing effect on the people. The public does have a respect for them or at least their uniform." Svi whispered.

Lika nudged Svi "That one over there has a black eye and his face is badly scratched. I wonder what he has been up to!" She said while looking directly at Kraut who was busy removing a suitcase from somebody in line. "I thought that they were allowed to keep their belongings until they were 'Airside'." said Lika.

"They are, but the guards make occasional checks on peoples' bags in order to stop forbidden items getting into the 'Selektion' area. With scanning and heavy security we seem to have prevented any problems as yet, but we *have* only just started."

Svi and Lika proceeded to enter through the security gates the first secure area called 'Selektion'. This was where all the people were given a full medical exam and scanning. Those who failed were given two options and neither of the choices was to proceed to 'Download'. For these people this was not available as they were not going to 'Planet Seven' For the occasional failure, they were allowed to go back to try again, having availed themselves of the Ark's specialist services, such as having false teeth removed, mechanical non perishable hip joints replaced with new perishable, or the removal of any unnatural non-perishable item on or within their body. The notice that people had taken previously of this warning had pleased Noah. So many surgeries had been performed in preparation for this; he was surprised how successful the results had been. The most popular was Lasik and dental tooth bud implantation because they were quick and somewhat natural and certainly perishable. Most people wanted to be able to see clearly and to eat. A one legged man was happy if he could eat and see, he would always *manage* he thought with one leg.

"This place is very sad!" Lika spoke quietly to Svi. She almost had tears in her eyes. "We are splitting up families and putting fear into their hearts. It's all wrong!"

"No!" Svi was very firm with Lika "Just think about the alternative. Just think about what we have done for them. We have given them the possibility of a new life. Look what we have achieved with our download system. We can now select a few important areas to leave unerased, such as 'kinship'. We are able to fully anticipate the reactions of nearly all subjects of download and as yet we have not made any mistakes!"

"We haven't done many yet, it's too early to say such things. We still have a month of traveling. Where will we put them? The 'children of the environment' area is as full as we can afford and are able to healthily administer. The unused areas, which are separate, are now almost full of the younger people we have downloaded, but soon we will not be able to take any more and we haven't even fully started yet. What does Noah expect of us?" Lika's frustration was outpouring. "We are to meet with Ham and Shem shortly. It seems that they are going to 'deep freeze' the patients before releasing them onto 'Planet Seven' and we have the facilities for that but we will be told more about that very soon. Surprises will never cease!"

***

Neyl and Rianne decided that they could not leave their discovery where she was, there lying on the floor of the Observatory Office. She was comatose and would not recover without help immediately. All her body functions registered as normal. Rianne suggested that she took off her suit and that they dressed the body in it, with Neyl taking her to the astro-vehicle. It would be easy enough and then he could leave her there safely and return to the Observatory with Rianne's suite. Neyl pointed out that there were several problems with that scheme. If she recovered consciousness at anytime with only Neyl around to help her she could kill them both from traumatic aggression. If she were to recover while Neyl was returning to get Rianne the problems she could create in the astro-vehicle were unthinkable. They could restrain her, Neyl thought, but it was then that he had the most brilliant of ideas. Neyl was on his knees looking up at Rianne who was standing right over him.

"Look behind you!" he said. She moved as if defensively and swung around instinctively as in training, with both hands ready, down with bent arms and knees. "No!" said Neyl "Don't panic! Look on the wall, the cupboard with the transparent door, over which there is a sign . . .

'For Emergency Use Only, Break plastic to open!'

Something we always see but never notice, why didn't we think of it before. We can use one of those; they are multi-sized, for man or woman. The emergency exterior working suit."

Rianne was just about to break the transparent plastic cover when Neyl again shouted at her...

"No don't do that, you could set off the alarm! I have a key in my kit. I *am* an engineer. We don't want any more people down here yet."

They managed to dress the body in the suit, but finding it very difficult getting her head into the helmet without aggravating her bruises. Her beautiful long hair only added to the problem, but eventually they made it and with the slightly richer atmosphere within the suit the girl showed signs of possible revival.

"Is it a bright idea, taking her back to our astro-vehicle?"

Rianne was having second thoughts, but Neyl had an answer. "What else are we going to do? Her attacker could be due to return to do far worse to her. She needs help and we could be the only people around here for a long time. Do you suggest that we just leave her here?"

"No we can't! I suppose not, but we are blowing our cover and exposing ourselves to capture."

"Perhaps, but if we keep her with us, at the moment we are safe."

They checked that her suit was airtight and completed their own attire, then using the airlock they managed to get the three of them quickly and hopefully unobserved back to their astro-vehicle. Of course Neyl before leaving the observatory office smashed the transparent cover to the emergency suit cupboard hoping to throw any pursuer off the scent. No alarms went off to his knowledge.

A bed was made for the injured soul on the spare trapeze hammock that they hung for her in a sympathetic gravity situation above their cargo. Removing the suit was slightly easier although Neyl had great difficulty in not removing any other item of her clothing at the same time. Working together Rianne and Neyl managed to lift her into the hammock, where she slept peacefully for quite a while before any sign of life began to come from her.

Neyl took a look at her; she was still asleep, but no longer out 'cold'. She had been sleeping fitfully since they had put her in the suit. Neyl took a second look, he thought so. She was still asleep, but there were tears pouring down her cheeks. She was crying. Crying in her sleep! They did not have to wait much longer. Neyl and Rianne had been watching the distant observatory office for any sign of life when suddenly the light went on, and shortly afterward went off again, to be followed by a feint moaning and sobbing from behind them.

Rianne moved back very quickly to the hammock. The girl was awake, bewildered and very distraught. For a little while, Rianne, without introduction or in fact many words being exchanged at all, kept plying the young woman with small sips of cable juice. The two girls were silently building up a 'rapport'. Rianne appeared to know exactly what to do. Not a word was being said, but the two girls understood. Finally after a comparatively long while, Rianne, with a warm smile spoke. "My name is Rianne, what is yours?"

"Airit." was the short answer as she once again broke into tears.

***

Kraut needed an alibi; he knew that many people had seen him at the line for 'Selektion'. He made an obvious point of needlessly searching some poor soul's bag, and made sure that he could be identified perhaps even by Svi and Lika themselves. He thought how lucky he was that they had made their appearance just after his. He had to return to finish what he had started. He was furious with Airit for not preventing him from making a fool of himself. She never told him what the change of course was all about and for days he had worked under an illusion. Now it was his turn. He knew that in truth he did not love her, he had just been using her, but it seems that perhaps she had just been using him. That was definitely *not* allowed. He was determined that he would get his way with her and then he would kill her. That is why he needed an alibi.

Intersteller Deceleration had been over for many hours and he had to get back to the observatory. He went to the men's toilet and changed out of his uniform, and then checking that he was unseen, he took the bag with his uniform and dropped it in a security locker, taking the key.

The observatory office was just as he had left it, but where was Airit? He knew that he had left her out cold, and she would be in no condition to move. He had even administered a mild amount of anesthetic that he had on his handkerchief, to keep her out for longer. Where could she have gone, he wondered. He had secured her from escape by locking the only exit door at the end of the corridor. Her clothes were torn, especially where modesty was important, there was no way that she could, or would want to go back to her quarters, assuming that she could have escaped through a locked door. Kraut walked around the desks, he thought that perhaps she was hiding. Turning to look if she had tried to leave from behind him, he saw the broken plastic cover. Suit number one and its' helmet was missing. Kraut was astounded. He went to the airlock to check its' status. Was she in there and had it been used? Yes it had, as it was closed on both doors and it was still a vacuum. The last door used was the outside door. She had gone! Where? He had to finish the job! She could tell, but no one would believe her. He could not risk it. Why didn't he plant a transmitter on her? He had thought to do that, but what if she had found it? Anyway that was all too late now. He had to find her; he had to finish the Job. He must have his way with her, he had been honorable up until the last, but she had insulted his uniform, she had deceived him, he would take her virginity and kill her. Her body would be easy to dispose of, just like the others were, but he had one problem, where was she? She could not go far if she was still outside and the emergency work suit only had regenerative atmosphere for about a day (PST). She would have a radio in her helmet; if he could get her to transmit he could locate her from security headquarters. He had high rank. He would try.

One of Kraut's colleagues . . .

"Calling suit number 01, calling suit number 01, calling suit number zero one! Please come in, we know that you are out there."

Neyl and Rianne had been hearing the message coming out of Airit's helmet for the last few hours. This was no surprise to them, it was a logical step for the security forces to follow, as when it was answered they would immediately be able to track down from where the transmission was originating, but Neyl and Rianne had other plans.

Leaving Rianne and Airit behind to do the necessary female things, to dress Airit's wounds in private and freshen her up, Neyl went to deposit a copy of the helmet's transmitter in a suitable place. Being an engineer of severe sophistication, he had rigged up a remote control, with a pre-recorded taped message so that he could transmit from an unlikely distant situation. He knew that this would throw them wildly off the scent. He even managed to acquire an extra suit from the security section of the Ark. He reset the new helmet for the original waveband in order to receive. He had keys to everywhere. He was a master in his trade and the rank he held was subject to very few who were senior.

When Neyl had returned with the new black suit with the dark blue helmet Airit was already very much better and becoming more settled. Rianne had established for her that she was still untouched, a virgin, although brutally bruised thus all the aches and pain between her legs. She had been kicked with a heavy walking boot in her groin to the point that left a blooded print. She had bled quite profusely causing staining to her clothes. Kraut must have known how much damage he had done. Airit had fought a brave battle. She had successfully defended her honor, but he was very aggressive and he had a horrific temper.

She knew that she would inevitably see him again, he would see to that, but when she did, she had to see him first and finalize him before he finalized her.

***

Noah and Erash were getting concerned at the interest of the passengers in seeing the passing planets. The Ark was approaching its' orbit with the sun at an oblique angle to the general planetary orbits of the 'Solar System'. Everybody now knew that they were making for

Planet Seven and they needed one trip around the sun to slow them down enough to create their own temporary orbit of their Planet Seven. By virtue of their obliqueness and different positioning of the Solar Planets in their own individual orbits Noah knew that they would only get close enough to six of them in order to see sufficient detail of consequence with the natural human eye. There were many requests to use the 'New Telescope' in the observatory, but only experienced astronomers were allowed to apply. Their work and commentaries were played on one of the popular holographic video channels for all those interested to see. The problem for Noah and Erash was when one of the planets was near enough, everybody ran to their nearest volume of the Ark in order to get a glimpse. Although sub-lumic, they were still traveling very fast and these 'new' planets went by very quickly. By virtue of the fact that they were traveling towards the sun the planets appeared as small thin crescents and as they passed they grew in width to almost full size as the Ark reached the sun ward side and its passengers could look back to the planets that they had passed. There was very little time, they grew and shrunk within a day (PST), but it was truly a wonderful experience for those few short hours and if it were to be possible, would leave an indelible memory within the viewer's mind. They saw vast and sometimes colorful planetary rings, gassy surfaces, many unusual moons, and many craters and for one or two viewers they spotted a few odd comets floating in a similar direction to the Ark. The sun was ahead of them and Rianne was enjoying measuring the increase of the angle and increasing brightness and contrast of the surface shadows upon the Ark.

Their astro-vehicle was well hidden in the valley between the observatory tower and the deepest side of the great hall. It was a brilliant piece of camouflage work by Neyl. The deep black shadows created by the tower upon the roof and wall of the Ark disguised the visible edges of their concealed machine. The surface of the Ark was extra highly polished, so was the astro-vehicle.

Lika could feel Svi's arm tightly around her waist as they stood in their privileged position looking out of the fully glazed domed roof of the observatory tower. "It is as if this were another world!" Lika said wistfully to Svi.

"It is!" Svi pulled Lika tighter to him. "That was a dumb thing to say, but it does explain how I feel. I cannot get used to the fact that we are no longer on and around Eden and will never return home. I have to consciously think to myself that we are not there and will never be able to go back!" She snuggled up to Svi and looked up, at the large rings surrounding the planet almost above them. They watched it quietly pass them by with its' strange reflected light creating deep, sharp-edged, slowly moving shadows on the observatory floor. Eventually it shrank to a small almost imperceptible bright star amongst the many millions of others in the 'empty space' behind them. "I feel very privileged that I have been able to see that with my own eyes. Was that not a beautiful sight? There was a strange silence, an eeriness of color and motion. It was almost as if whatever was 'in there' was welcoming us to their planetary system. As if they were the guardians of whoever came and went. I felt strange as it passed us by. That gaseous container of chemistries and physics that most likely mankind will never know. Strange to say that, isn't it?" Svi put his head on Lika's as if to acknowledge and answer her words of apparent meaning.

For the first time in his career on the Ark Velmitz was aware of restlessness amongst the animals in his care. Solar Planet number Five, the largest of all the planets in the Solar System, had just passed them. Although its rings were not as impressive as those of Planet Four the strange eerie feeling seemed to permeate itself through to the animals. They seriously calmed down to almost normal once the offending planet had passed them by.

Neyl looked at his astro-vehicle's gyroscopic-compass which was used for interstellar navigation, based on standard physical principals of magnetism and useable for direction finding anywhere in the universe. It always points in the direction preset at the origin of one's journey. It had been spinning at an alarming rate during the passing of Planet Five. The spinning dial had finally come back to rest motionless and only a few minutes off its original setting. That Neyl worked out was the precalculated change of course due to Planet Five's gravitational pull, but why had his gyro-compass been spinning, and at such a phenomenal speed? It had never happened before!

***

CHAPTER 4

Noah was talking to Svi and Lika in the 'Suspended Animation Unit'

"I agree that we are running out of space on 'airside'. Perhaps we should have kept to our original plan and not started downloads so early. We have the facilities to 'freeze' everyone on the Ark, but neither Erash, Tubal Cain nor I, like that idea. It was originally a government decision to put this facility on board for 'suspended animation' for very long journeys through generations, but it was finally to be used for a completely different purpose. It was to freeze criminals for parts. It was thought to be more useful than the death penalty. That is why it became nicknamed 'Death Row', a great misnomer. I don't mind the 'tissue bank' and 'cell storage' features that we have next door, but that is from the already dead. That place is for 'living people'! Nevertheless I will try to help you all that I can and we will open this place up for you, but I do not like it!" Noah almost had tears in his eyes as he spoke to Svi and Lika with deep emotion.

"Has this facility ever been used?" Svi asked Noah very carefully.

"Only for tests, without any problem. When we tested out the new engine for this vehicle, we took on a large number of volunteer convicts. They got a reduction of their sentences. Only one was sick, and he was probably sick beforehand. He still survived and I understand earned his release, but the main reason for this establishment was far more sinister. 'Body parts'! Thank G-d it never came to that. The only criminals that we had on board were new and were sent back to Eden on one of the last shuttles." Noah walked over to the nurses' station and sat down in the chief nurse's seat. "OK! I will set this place up by tomorrow. You will have a full settlement nursing staff and transport to collect and deposit 'downloads' here. We can accommodate the entire Ark in this facility; there will be no problem. We pack them in drawers, in alternating patterns, head, feet, head, feet and so on. We can get thirty people in one drawer and each download will be drip fed and completely anaesthetized. It is a little old fashioned, but the correct way to use these facilities would be very long term, two or three generations of lifespan, but when we acquired the new engine technology and it was fitted, this facility to freeze a people became redundant. The gorilla people have gone in a different direction to us and they are using this method to survive the enormous distances that they have chosen to travel. We will be probably sixteen generations further on before they reach their destination. They did not have the high tech engine that we do."

"Will this form of hibernation affect the people, will they be aware of it?" Lika asked innocently.

"Once they have been through brain erasure, they will be personally searched while still under anesthesia. They will be stripped naked and placed in a re-useable trolley where they will be sent by rail to reception at this nurses' station, still in the trolley. The nurses will have complete control of the railway trolleys and can arrange for people to be put carefully in their correct drawer. They will all be clearly labeled around their left wrist and opposing right ankle and we have color coded them according to their origin. Each one also has a different identity number and families are easily recognized: so are predeclared friendships. Mono-sexual relationships are not approved and if they maintain this tendency through download they will have to find their own way and their own companion. The committee refuses to allow you to intentionally maintain that problem, but as a gesture of fairness we are not going to prevent its manifestation as it must have been the will of G-d, but we must not encourage it. In answer to you Lika, from the moment that they are under download anesthesia, until they are released onto their destination on Planet Seven, whether onto the edge of a rock pool, under a tree, or onto a grassy field, they will know nothing until they wake-up. Their memories will start from that moment. Just as you first instructed us when you showed us how it will be done."

"That will work," said Lika, "but it is essential that they have no conscious contact from that pre-downloaded moment until they re-awaken at 'point of arrival'. What about children of the environment and the conscious downloads who are living in the artificial environmental status as of now?"

Noah gave his reply . . .

"They will be sleep induced as we do before acceleration and deceleration, for security, but this time they won't wake up until they are there at the point of arrival on Planet Seven. This is humane and completely sensible. These people will have a head start of the others because they will not need downloading and the others who have been but are in the 'new area' will not be very different."

"What about the marshals, porters, nurses and administrators like you and Svi? What happens to us?" asked Lika.

"No problem! Security wants the Ark after we have finished with it, they want to go on and discover another world not affected by my constraints with landing upon it. We are offering any of them who want it download and permission to 'arrive' on Planet Seven otherwise they can stay with the Ark and continue. These people will down load us and we will be in the last group. I made a deal, a long time ago with two of them separately. They each both know that there is another one of them but they do not know whom. Neither do they know that in fact in reality there are three. I have to protect the principals for which we are doing this. They all three know that they have to account for all the people previously and still present on the Ark into the Master Control Room Database when we have completed arrival on Planet Seven. If they disobey and not all are legitimately accounted for, the Ark will self-destruct on its' departure Orbit from Planet Seven. They will have to balance the books, in order to leave."

"What if they decide to land on Planet Seven?" Svi enquired.

"Once I have entered download I will have consciously signed off on hand magnetic—print identity that only those with pre-recognized identities will be able to accompany me. My party will then be landed on Planet Seven. We have a few mechanical robotic people with good large brain capacity on this Ark, and we will be landed in their charge on the same automatically returnable landing craft that the majority of people will be using to land on Planet Seven. Until that final craft has returned empty of life-form to its' loading bay the Ark will be in constant danger. It would also self-destruct if they try to land any 'manned' vehicles after my 'sign off'. The last download which will be you, Svi, and you with your family will be in my group."

***

"You are going to have to make up your mind very soon Airit, which way you want to go. You can come with us, but you can also go with them. Nobody else will ever have that choice, but you will have to decide that very soon or we may lose the opportunity to get you back on the Ark. We trust you implicitly, we know that you won't give us away, but we know that by allowing you to return we are putting ourselves at risk!"

"How safe is it for me to come with you and will I put you at risk?" Airit asked Neyl.

"We are at risk either way, but perhaps much less if you were to come with us." Neyl replied with Rianne nodding mutual agreement.

"Will I be able to go back to the Ark first, before I come with you?"

"No!" both Neyl and Rianne replied in unison.

"Why?" asked Neyl.

"I have something that I must do!"

"A matter of honor?" asked Rianne

"Yes!"

"Then we will bring him to you, will that suffice?" Neyl announced with serious insight and Airit nodded agreement. He took out a remote control and pushed a button. "There . . . he is on his way."

"What have you done?" Airit became suddenly full of fear. Her face went white and she became nervous.

"I have pre-recorded a computer voice reply in a high pitch tone which could be that of any women, asking for help to get back on board. Your 'friend' is calling out for you, he wants to locate and trap you. This way we trap him. How do you like that? Neyl said with a smile on his face.

"Won't it blow our cover?"

"I like the 'our' bit. That proves loyalty to us. No of course not, any more than it could have been blown already. He will try to trace your old helmet transmitter and will certainly locate it now that it is transmitting."

"Where is it?" Airit asked.

"Nowhere near here, and I have already booby trapped it. He only has to touch it and it will explode. It is filled with shrapnel and bits of metal. He will not survive; his suit will be punctured. He will get what he deserves!"

"No!" Airit replied "There is a well used expression, that 'a person is known perhaps to have a nasty streak in them', in this particular man I would alter that description. I would say that in that evil and perplexed man, it could be seen that perhaps somewhere, he has a nice streak in him, if only he could find it. I want to give that guy one final chance and then I will not feel in the remotest part guilty when I kill him!"

Neyl and Rianne both pleaded with Airit that it was not necessary and were still pleading when a voice from the Control Tower came out loud from Neyl's radio link-up.

"We read you and note your position. We will be sending a party out to rescue you! Do not move from where you are as we can protect you. Code 'R' and out."

"I have to go! Tell me where? Please!" Airit was pleading. Neyl reached for the black suit and dark blue helmet. "I anticipated this. He won't expect someone in a security uniform. This suit will give you an element of surprise and so will this, use it!" He handed her a loaded paresifier.

"These suits already have paresifiers in their pouches as regular issue, everybody knows that. Why do I need this one?" Airit enquired.

"The issue ones are always kept in the same pouch and Kraut will know if you are using it or if you are going for it. Put this one in this behind your neck!" and Neyl presented her with a sling-like holster that hung invisibly behind her neck, completely unseen but easily accessible when wearing her helmet.

"You will have to be careful." Neyl told Airit "Do not un-tether yourself from the Ark. We are again about to reduce speed shortly after passing very close to Planet Six which is due to arrive very soon. You will go flying onwards much faster than us. Out of control if you lose hold. Please be careful. We will have no way of collecting you, you will be irretrievable."

***

To a complete stranger it would look as if Tubal Cain, Noah and Erash were all in conversation in the same room, but they were not. Tubal Cain was light years away, but with the marvels of modern communication it was now made possible for them to sit in comfortable chairs and talk together as if in the same sitting room. On two occasions, Marla and Rula had come in, and on two other occasions they were visited for a short while by Tsionne and Jubal. Their image communications over the years had improved to such a high degree of technology that it was unbelievable the distances that were being covered with almost no perceptible delay. There was an occasional fading image or crackle in the voice, but that was only minimal and reminded them that this was not real.

Tubal Cain was speaking . . .

"You are very shortly about to pass very closely to Planet Six of the Solar System. You will then commence your severe deceleration to a much lower speed. Communication is going to be even more difficult for us and may even disappear altogether, perhaps forever. Your signals will become very much interfered with by the Solar Energy, once you are in the vicinity of Planet Seven and higher. From where we are, so far away, the resolution with current technology would have to be higher than we can detect using accelerated light and radio technology. It is very doubtful after passing the orbit of Planet Six whether we will ever be able to contact one another anymore. So very likely as we all know this is our time for sad goodbyes." Tubal had visible tears in his eyes.

"Certainly not in our lifetime" Noah replied "but I personally believe that if we keep our covenant with G-d, at some very distant time in the future there may well be a new continuing generation of humankind who will be able to look at itself in its ignorance to suffer and enjoy life, due to the efforts of you Tubal, you Erash and all of us who have worked to this end with the help of the Almighty."

"It was Erash to whom we must direct our gratitude. Without his efforts we would never have been able to reach this stage of placing our brothers and sisters on Planet Seven." Tubal was becoming very emotional and continued trying not to show it . . . "Noah, I know that for you to give your name to the new planet would be a forbidden suggestion. It would also be of no value to anyone who lands there because they would be ignorant. No to us here on Eden it is important that your new home has a name. May I suggest that we give it the name of the person who has devoted himself to our cause and without whom none of this would ever have taken place?"

"Erash?" Noah answered with a question.

"Of course!" said Tubal.

"Erash it is! Do you have any problems with that?" Noah spoke to Erash who was very surprised and had become somewhat pensive.

Lifting his head he said a few words in reply. "I accepth with humilithy, buth ith isth thoo much for me tho understhand why you thould choothe me." He was having slight difficulty with speaking; he could not pronounce his 'sh's and 't's very easily. He had had to discard his false teeth a few days earlier and had been implanted with real tooth buds in their place. At present he had a few gaps in very strategic places, so when he spoke, it came out distorted.

"'Erath'" he said "I am very honored 'Planet Erath'. Thank you, buth I do noth deserf ith, buth thank you." He smiled and grabbed both his wives who appeared for the occasion and hugging them both he gave them both very affectionate kisses. All three had tears in their eyes.

"There you go!" said Tubal Cain "'Planet Erash' we love it!"

"'Planet Erath'" said Noah in partial jest, "Erash is having problems with his speech. Perhaps we should recognize that and call it just as he did . . . 'Planet Erth'!" Noah did not get it quite right.

***

The light was very eerie and strange as Airit glided securely on her tethered guide rail across the whole length of Orbit village, which now constituted Noah's Ark. It was a real 'Castle in the Sky'. She knew that it was large, she had spent many years on the inside of it, but now she was outside securely tethered but moving freely across its' surface. There were narrow volumes where certain parts of the 'old' orbital city had been joined with new or other previously existing sections and it was through here, one of these 'holes' that Airit was able to pass safely to the underside of the massive craft.

She had been told where to go and she was determined to complete the task that she had set herself. She wanted to give him a chance. Perhaps he would be decent, a rare hope indeed, but it would ease her conscience.

Moving around the lower quarters of the city, she was in and out of shaded and well-lit areas of the lower underside of the Ark. As she approached the leading edge of the city she saw the image of planet six, way out in front of them, and the small red arc was growing in size quite markedly. If she used her imagination she could think that she could see the red glow was moving directly towards them. She could already see the crescent shape and the sharpness of its' edges. It was no larger than a quarter size of her small fingernail, but already there seemed to be a soft reddening of the colors that had imaged themselves on the surface of the Ark. Strangely the Sun was large enough to create a daylight effect from the distance and just under the front elevation of the Ark, which when mixed with the much paler effect from the 'red planet' in a slightly higher elevation the shadows began to become more diffuse as the two different light sources began to separate even more.

She turned around the underside of a protruding dome and again had perfect image of the forthcoming glow, then she saw her target, up against the forward edge of Orbital City, being the old disused power station cafeteria. The suit was screwed up on the floor of the airlock, open to the outside void of any atmosphere. It was a vacuum space. There were some lights switched on inside the cafeteria, but no one was visible through the very large windows. Airit realized that this place was atmosphere tight and still contained emergency food supplies. This would have been an ideal place for her to hide had she needed to. It seemed very logical. Neyl had thought this through very clearly. With the airlock open and her suit on the floor Kraut would go in to examine it. If he touched it the blast would kill him instantly. Airlocks are built so thick that it would take an asteroid collision to damage it or its' seals. If Kraut did not seal the airlock when inside the damage liability would be even less. If the airlock was sealed and re-filled with atmosphere, the damage would all go to the external door.

Airit decided to sit in a concealed spot and wait. Kraut should arrive quite soon. She looked up and forward, the crescent of the red planet was getting nearer and had moved its position to slightly higher in the sky. Airit realized that it was getting quite close and she knew from Neyl that the crescent shape would eventually appear as large as the fifth planet because they were to pass much closer to it. Eventually it would take up almost the entire upper part of the sky in relation to the Ark, as the crescent opened out to almost a complete round, in the same manner as with planet five. She prayed that Kraut would come very soon as she wanted to be able to return safely to the Astro-vehicle.

'Very soon' came very quickly. Airit was just thinking to herself that she could see a major part of the larger ice cap quite visibly and knowing the shape of it in advance, she correctly perceived it as being the 'north'. The rest of the planet appeared to be slightly tilted away from the sun but she imagined its' other pole which was smaller was out of sight at the top and yet it was the 'Southern' pole. Everything appeared upside down to the way her training manual had stated, and then she realized, they were approaching it from above at an oblique angle, so of course the South Pole would appear to her to be above the North.

Her attention was diverted from the increasing size of the small Arc of planet six when she was attracted by a reflected flash, which suddenly came to her notice. She was sure that she could see the silhouette of a dark security suit with its' bright silver flashes which went down both sides of the suit. Its' helmet was dark blue and in it she could see through her binoculars was a bright red reflection of the planet that was growing above them. She looked up at the red planet, the arc of which was now much larger and wider in the sky. The whole specter was about to grow past the front of the Ark and across the upper side. She of course was underneath.

The solitary dark suit was making for the open airlock and it was moving freely and un-tethered. Airit decided to act and fast. Keeping herself tethered to the Ark's guide rail system she moved carefully so as not to create a shadow or a reflection of the Sun in Kraut's direction. The overhead planet was now creating a bright redness of colored glow coming off the highly polished surfaces of the buildings of Orbital City. In Eden terms she could say it was 'almost daylight'. Even though she was on the underside the bright red light coupled with some oblique direct and reflected sunlight was illuminating anywhere that had even the faintest view of the passing Sixth Planet. The planet crescent was almost completely round now and occupying the entire sky on the upper side of the Ark. Already Airit was worried about being seen in the shadowed light reflected off the highly polished underside. She could now see the sun clearly and directly in front of her. She had to turn on the suit helmet protective light feature. If Kraut turned around she was sure that she would be seen, but she had to stop him touching the suit lying in disarray on the airlock floor. She spoke gently into her helmet microphone . . .

"Can you hear me? It is me, I see you! You are alone, who are you?" She hoped that it was Kraut and that he was tuned in to her wavelength, which was standard in all emergencies.

"I see you lying there, wait I will help you!" It was Kraut but he had disguised his voice by changing his microphone pattern as if it was in error or faulty. She new it was he.

***

To enjoy the view of the craters, canyons and deserts of the Red Planet at such close quarters was something that neither Rianne nor Neyl were able to do. They were both thinking of Airit who was now completely out of sight on the underside of the Ark. They could hear her every word, but that only made them more anxious.

The Red Planet was at its' nearest to them in its largest state when Airit's voice came on sound. They also heard Kraut's reply and Neyl recognized the distorted voice. It was the same one that they had heard earlier. They also heard Airit's reply, and then there was silence, just the feint sound of static indicating that the lines were still open and the occasional heavy breathing as one of them moved more physically than normal.

Eventually after what felt like a lifetime, Airit spoke . . . "Don't touch that suit! I'm some distance behind you, what do you want?"

"You! I've come to rescue you, to take you home." The voice in the suit replied. "If you are not in that suit, where are you?"

"Identify yourself, clearly." Airit shouted. She was becoming nervous.

"I am your rescuer, or do you want to die out here?"

"No, enough, tell me who you are and verify it, then I will present myself to you. I will come out of hiding." There was no point in lying, Kraut decided, as time was of the essence, he had to be back inside before deceleration started once again. For each moment of time lost, he felt that he was being cheated of satisfaction at Airit's expense. "Kraut!" he said smugly "You know me very well, need I say more?"

"Yes! What did *I* used to call you, privately?"

"Poopsie!"

"You tried to kill me, why?" Airit responded.

"I didn't try to kill you, but you deserved what you got. You deceived me!" Kraut answered with some sincerity in his voice. "You allowed me to make a fool of myself. You disgraced my uniform, and that is a crime!"

"I am over here, wearing my uniform!"

"Whaaat!" Kraut saw the security guard astro-suit and was completely taken aback. "What are you doing in that? You have no right. That is the uniform of the *'SS'* the Security Services. I have every right to kill you for it."

"No you haven't. I am your superior officer; I hold senior rank to you and as such can identify myself. My number ends as 707, and you know that yours is 722. Only a fellow officer would know that. We all know our 'PI' numbers, as we cannot always carry our 'ID' cards around with us. Especially when working under cover. Which I was."

Rianne took close hold of Neyl's arm and they looked at each other in shock. They could not speak because they would not risk being heard.

The planet above them was beautiful, but rapidly moving away down the Ark, presenting almost its' full sunlit surface to them as it began to shrink into the distance. They would be starting the engine very shortly. It would be in reverse thrust as they were sublumic now and did not need to turn the Ark around. How much longer did they have? Rianne looked at her watch and showed it to Neyl. Inwardly they had grown very close to Airit, and did not want to lose her, but this revelation threw a new light on their very own situation. If both Kraut and Airit died, their own personal survival was guaranteed, but that was unthinkable, although those thoughts momentarily crossed their minds. "I must help my senior officer." Kraut said clearly into his helmet as he ran forward fast towards Airit with a knife openly in his hand. "Come with me into the cafeteria until the end of deceleration it will be safe in there!"

"No!" she said "You only want my body, and I aim to keep it for myself." Airit knew that she could be heard in the control tower and by Neyl and Rianne. Kraut also knew so he had to be careful with what he said, but not what he did. He threw himself at Airit grabbing her arm and with the knife he cut the connection of her radio antenna. Her signal would now become very weak. He also took the knife to his own antenna. Now they could only hear each other. Both Control tower and Neyl could thus only hear static and the occasional uttered word of Kraut or Airit, but nothing made sense. Deceleration was about to commence so there was no time for anyone to go out and interfere.

***

Before proceeding to finish wrapping up their children in the same old sleepy way, Svi and Lika, the only two people not to suffer from the passing spectacle of the 'Red Planet' sat in a privileged position in the Control Room Observatory Tower. These two had the sole responsibility of the environmental children, and the Red Planet never appeared in their children's sky.

Lika could not believe that something so small and so far away had become so large and so near, so quickly. The ease with which one could see into the canyons, the way their shadows made them look so deep. The snow or ice crested mountains that first met them as the planet began to drift passed. They could see the razor sharp outline of the mountaintops on the far edge of the planet where the sun's light disappeared over into the distance and oblivion. They could see the appearance of the North Pole, which had a screw-like circular appearance as if created by a movement of cyclonic wind. For Svi and Lika, for just a short moment, this was a simple time for thoughtful meditation.

For Erash and Noah, this time it was like a nightmare. Every person who could walk had attempted to reach a good viewing position on the Ark. Fortunately nobody had the mind to try and exit to the outside, but what Noah and Erash had to contend with was bad enough. Every body wanted to see the 'Red Planet' at close quarters. They were so close that they felt that they could touch it!

The viewing of it was no worry for the Ark administration, which was easy. The real problem was immediately afterwards. Deceleration was imminent and everyone had to be in his or her bunk for the initial stages, just in case of any serious interruption to the gentle build up of full deceleration. This was not foreseen as a problem the many years previously when the route-map and flight plan was established. The rapid deceleration within the solar system so immediately after passing Planet Six was too soon. Originally Planet Six, Seven and Eight were thought to be possible destinations, but when it was discovered that Planet Seven was the best location, no thought was taken of public reaction when passing the other planets.

The view of the Red Planet was a truly awe inspiring experience. As they were approaching it obliquely from above, the North Pole was the first recognizable mark. Its' circular screw like appearance was most interesting to the human eye. The South Pole was not visible as it was above and out of sight beyond the global horizon of the planet's tilt. The colors, the textures and roughness of the surface, the occasional misty cloud, very much unlike that of Eden caused anxiety and fear in some of the people. This was once considered a possible home for humankind in the earlier stages of their journey, so what will happen when they reach 'Erth', Planet Seven?

The alarm sirens started sounding warnings as the surface of Planet Six shrank away into the distance well beyond the back of the Ark. The assembled crowds began to break up, but there was a new tension in their minds as they moved away to return to their quarters. One or two people were arguing about right of way and pushing. A small fight broke out in one of the narrow corridors. With the sirens going and the strong tension in most people's minds, organized evacuation of an observation volume began to turn into organized chaos and possible tragedy. Many 'black shirts' Security Service guards appeared on the scene almost immediately as if from nowhere. It was not long before many injured on stretchers and several bodies were released from the crushing mess of people.

Noah almost wept when he heard the news and Erash wanted desperately to take the blame on himself for his lack of foresight. Noah would have none of it. They had very little time left before deceleration and if aborted the dangers would be worse.

Erash ordered his 'black shirts' into action and it was not long before the 'SS' had cleared the deluge, leaving a few small signs of rough handling.

***

Rianne grabbed Neyl's hand; she looked as if she was seeing a ghost as she pointed to the rear airlock hatch of their Astro-Vehicle. Neyl was sitting in his pilot's seat and Rianne was facing him in her reversed chair-seat. She could see all the way to the back of the craft. Airit's space suit was entering the airlock from the outside. They had given her the combination code; it could not possibly be anyone else.

The airlock 'buzzed' closed on the outside and there was the normal release of compressed atmospheric gasses. Airit was obviously well versed in the use of such devices, she waited the necessary time before attempting to release the internal hatch and it opened on her command.

"You made it back!" Rianne flew forward across the cargo and down onto Airit with such force that she knocked her over, but pleasure and relief was all over her face. She threw her arms around Airit's chest as she helped her into an upright position. The new gravity situation was coming from the front of the Ark so the floor of their Astro-Vehicle had a real gravity effect at that time. It was almost correct to stand upright. The new deceleration had started some while before and its' gravitational effect was quite reasonable. "What happened?" Rianne enquired.

"I got him!" There were tears of relief flowing down Airit's face "He's gone, but it was a very near thing! He would have killed me if I had given him the chance. He wanted my body. He saw it as revenge because he thought that I had offended his uniform. I had to defend myself didn't I?" She sniffed and looked up to Rianne as if *she* would know the truth. "Of course you did!" Rianne tried to sound comforting but was aching to hear her story and ask a few questions. "How did it go?" came from the front of the Astro-Vehicle.

Neyl wanted to be part of the 'homecoming'.

"Let me get out of this kit and I will tell you. Oh by the way, thank you Neyl, this is yours." She reached over the cargo and handed the paresifier back to Neyl. He examined it. "It hasn't been used, the safety catch is still switched in." he said somewhat in surprise.

It was not much later, cable juices in hand, the three of them sat together in the front cabin of the astro-vehicle. Airit was certainly very alert and sober in the manner which she told her detailed story . . .

"I have both of you to thank for saving my life and I won't and can't forget it. Without you I would have met the same end that was waiting for Kraut."

There was a deep intake of breath by Rianne. She could not believe that she was listening to the same Airit she helped only a few days previously. She and Neyl had virtually scraped her off the floor of the observatory towers and brought her in 'ruins' to their astro-vehicle. Now she was firm, resolute, upright and full of life. Airit was talking . . . "I know how much you heard because we were transmitting our sound until Kraut cut through the antennae connections. After that you may only have heard the irregular disjointed word."

"That's right." said Neyl who was listening attentively. "Kraut started by trying to play it softly although he had become quite violent," Airit continued . . . "he said that he loved me and would take me back to the calm and safety of his lodgings, but I knew that he was overwhelmed by the uniform that I was wearing. He believed my statement about my rank and he had to respect my uniform. That is the law!"

"Your statement about being an SS officer, was that true?"

"It *is* true! I still *am* an SS officer, and that is my true rank, but I have been working under cover. This Kraut guy was a serial killer and a pathological power pervert. He was using his uniform to his own ends, he killed nine women to our knowledge and he disposed of their bodies!"

"What! You must be joking. How did he dispose of their bodies?" Rianne asked in shock.

"The same way that I disposed of him, or should I say that he disposed of himself."

"Tell us please." Neyl pleaded somewhat timidly. "He was trying to hassle me and once he cut our radio connections, he tried to force me over to the airlock of the cafeteria. To start with, as my training had taught me, I went to his command, appearing to be willing but always secretly on my guard. Once he got me inside I achieved the ability to escape his grasp when he felt more secure, while closing the airlock from the inside. I slipped out just as they were closing to their final segment. If he had tried to follow me he would have been crushed. With the doors being closed and with me on the outside, I stayed on and tethered to the Ark just above the level of the monitor cameras immediately above the airlock exit. Moments later he was out of the re-opened doors and looking for me. I pounced from above and put both my legs astride his neck and squeezed his helmet tightly between my legs. He grabbed my suit at the right knee and tried to dislodge me. Fortunately I had taken his knife and thrown it away. The force of my surprise pushed him forward onto the polished surface of the Ark deck and he started to slip downwards to the front of the Ark. Slowly at first, he was holding onto my trousers and I went with him. The deceleration must have just started, because he was only drifting gently towards the front and his only attachment was to me manually. Then I felt the pressure increase and I was also moving to the front of the Ark. We were together moving faster and faster toward the very apex of the Ark. I tried desperately to loosen his fingers but could not. We both went over the edge, missing the final rail by a hair's breadth. He was on his own out in space except that he had got a hold of me. I had one last chance and kicked his helmet as hard as I could. It did no damage, but it must have jarred his head and he let go. I found my way back to the Ark after pulling hard on my tether and scrambling back on board. I turned around and saw his pleading face as if he was waving to me as an unwelcome goodbye, as he continued on his way on the Ark's original course at the original speed to go into orbit around the sun in perhaps a few weeks from now. He will surely die beforehand, but he deserves the death he had awarded others on several occasions. I don't feel guilty!"

***

'*Selektion*' was the way that applicants for download were sorted out as qualifiable for eventually going to 'Erth'. A law existed on the Ark that only those people who were completely perishable were to be allowed a download, and download gave one the ticket to land on 'Erth'. Lika was becoming upset by the number of people who were separated from their families and having to make their sad goodbyes as they were not classified as completely perishable owing to the need for dialysis or ongoing diabetic treatments, hip joint replacements or other prosthetics etc., etc. She did not realize just how many people had heart movement monitors or pacemakers. So many people were refused permission for download that when it was granted to a person it was accepted with great excitement, as an achievement and when a whole family got through first time round there was a celebration. When she thought about it, Lika found the reactions quite strange. It was a paradox. The people were happy that they were going to have their brain disrupted and best part of their knowledge destroyed forever. 'How could they be so happy?' she thought.

Things had recently changed and there were more people returning, re-applying at 'Selektion' for download. There were people who previously had had implanted artificial seeing eyes, artificial prosthetic kidneys, diabetics who had had synthetic liver tissue, and similar types of cases listed on the records as having artificially manufactured implants who were returning having had new natural implants from human donation. How could there be so many and so suddenly? Lika wondered where these donors came from and decided that she would investigate. She was happy to see families re-united with their kith and kin. She loved to see the joy on their faces but from where did these spare parts come and why now? She had to know.

Svi was upset to see the anger on Lika's face when she appeared late at the door of their apartment that evening.

"What's wrong?" Svi asked as he saw beads of perspiration or were they tears pouring down Lika's face? She was very angry.

"The SS bastards!" She threw herself into Svi's arms and started to cry profusely. "That uniform ought to be destroyed and burnt just like everything it stands for!" She started once again to sniff and could not catch her words to mouth them.

"Calm down, come and sit down and I will give you a warm cup of cable juice which will help, and then tell me all in slow tempo. Come take a few breaths and sit down." Svi put his arm around her shoulders and led her to the most comfortable chair. She sat down with him holding her head against his hip. He stroked the base of her skull through her thick curly hair. She was still crying. After a short while, when she had calmed a little he brought her a pleasant drink of warmed juice.

She sipped it, sat backward and began to tell Svi her story.

"I could not understand why all of a sudden there was a large supply of natural organs and tissue parts that so many people were able to appear and successfully re-apply for download. I went to investigate. I started at the tissue library in which there were plenty of raw materials. That took me to a small sealed-off area of the 'hibernation unit' which had drawers crammed full with bodies of all shapes, sizes, and . . ." Lika sobbed and again took a breath ". . . ages. There were even young children. There were lists of all the bodies, their blood types etc., and how and where they 'died'. Very efficient, even the tissue parts were labeled with the blood groups and cell types, blood types and from where they had come. I cannot believe how truthful they are in their evil deeds." She once again began to become emotional.

"What evil deeds? Who?" Svi begged the questions.

"The SS, they have printed price lists of all the parts, tissues, and whole organs that are available from each body quite openly and these prices are extortionate. I simply asked where all these bodies had suddenly come from!" She again became emotional.

"Where?" asked Svi.

"From those that they killed and maimed in the riots on corridor four after the passing of the 'Red Planet'. *It's immoral!*"

***

Instructions were given out from the Ark Administration that walls of the Ark on daylight side as it had become called were to be avoided at all cost. There was severe risk of anything coming in contact with an area of inner wall, which was not properly insulated with the outer wall on the side of the Sun. This was a temporary problem, the engineers were trying to sort out all hot spots, and in the meanwhile everyone was to beware. This was early days, they were to make their three quarter orbit around the Sun and already the Ark wall that was nearest to the Sun was becoming very hot indeed. The electronics were mildly affected and their internal radio was full of static. It was decided to take moderate evasive action. They were going to continually rotate the Ark on its' traveling axis, so as to avoid too much exposure at any one time of one part of its surface to the brilliance of the Sun. Also there were built in irrigation units which on demand automatically would pour cold water across the inside surface of that wall that was exposed to the Sun so that the external heat would not too much affect the interior. The material of the wall was made of such composite materials and so finely polished that a large proportion of the heat was not absorbed and there was very little expansion or contraction. As long as they kept to their pre-planned orbit of the Sun they would not get near enough to have any surface buckle but continual monitoring was done although difficult because of all the static. Noah was very seriously considering moving their solar orbit outward but it could add up to a **PST** year to their journey. If only he could talk it over with Tubal Cain, but that was out of the question at present. Perhaps they would speak for a last time when they get nearer to 'Erth' and farther away from the Sun.

Neyl was getting very hot under the collar; in fact they were beginning to roast in their Astro-Vehicle until the decision was made to rotate the Ark. That at least alleviated the situation for a little while at a time. It was Rianne who came up with the idea of internal irrigation of their vehicle, and at last it had proven useful that she had calculated the supplies by over eleven times the necessary amount even for the three of them.

Their cooler or refrigerator worked in conjunction with the vehicle's air conditioning unit. Neyl, the engineer stripped down one of the emergency air hoses that would usually be used for extra-vehicular activities such as long term repair work on the Ark which could mean a long period of being in space without replenished air tanks. He unwound the air-line and connected it to the water exhaust of the cooler in the air conditioning unit. Then having attached with adhesive tape the long tubing around the apex of the curved roof of the vehicle he used a small hand drill and laboriously drilled holes in the tubing so that when switched on it would flow through the holes and a fine spray would run down the inside of the windows and walls to be collected at the bottom in medical trays adhesively sealed against the skirting at the base of the window and walls at floor level. He found the trays in the medical chest under the pilot's seat. This was improvisation at its' best. They would have to turn the air-conditioning unit up as high as it would safely go and that would need a lot of water or it would become dangerous in the great heat. Neyl smiled, they had plenty of bottled water, over eleven times more than they would need to drink even for the three of them.

After a few moments of checking the connections, the taps and faucets, Neyl turned on the system and pushed the working output level of the cooling unit up as high as would be safe. Two things happened. The water started slowly at first, then quite smoothly a simple flow of water rippled down the windows and walls to be collected and drained away in order to re-cycle what they could back into the system. The other thing that happened was that the sunlight very noticeably seemed to be becoming less bright. Rianne and Airit lay on the floor of their craft and looked up out of the right forward window, at that time it was only way that they could see the sun which was just coming around the observatory tower and shining through two thickly tinted walls of dense window glass which made it almost safe to look.

"There is a lump missing from the Sun!" Airit remarked in her innocence. "Look at the top left hand corner because it looks like somebody has taken a bite out of it."

"An eclipse!" Rianne commented knowingly. Of course Airit would have no idea what an eclipse was.

"What is an eclipse?" Airit queried, as Neyl laughed quietly to himself. Rianne responded in a kindly voice. Even security officers did not know everything.

"There is a planet between us and the Sun, so its dark side is facing us and the body of it is silhouetted in the globe of the Sun. It should move across the upper region of the Sun until its complete circle blocks out a considerable amount of sunlight. I would imagine that as this would be Planet Nine, the nearest to the Sun, and we are very close to Planet Nine's orbit of the Sun, we would therefore be moderately close to that planet. It follows that it will take out approximately one third of the light of the Sun when Planet Nine is directly between us and the Sun. You will see, but don't stare for too long as it could be permanently dangerous to your eyes!"

It was not long before the black circular disc moved across and away once again exposing the full glare of the Sun and its' brilliance which appeared regularly into their cabin as the Ark rotated almost on its' axis. 'Planet Nine' began to appear in the sky towards the right of the sun as a brightly lit thin narrow cratered crescent. As time went by it moved slowly away becoming smaller but wider in size, much more slowly than Planet Six. Their deceleration and partial orbit of the Sun had begun to take effect. The sun had hardly moved from its' position in their rotation but Planet Nine was definitely growing more round but slowly, very slowly smaller. It moved out and away from the Sun then began once again to get nearer and finally disappeared from the sky completely, behind the Sun perhaps!

***

There were relatively few people left who had not been downloaded when Planet Eight was close enough to see as a bright light in the sky a long way away. It was almost a non-event except for those people still privileged to use the electronic telescope. The position of Planet Eight in its' orbit was beyond the Sun on the same side as Erth but still too far away to see with the naked eye, other than as a bright 'star' in the sky. When the Ark was previously around the other side of the Sun they were on the dark side of Planet Eight, but now a substantial amount of it was visible as a wide crescent, but only to those with eyes through the electronic telescope. It appeared as a somewhat gaseous cloud covered planet, very bright in the sky and completely lacking of any features.

After passing through the Solar orbit of Planet Eight, for those who knew, the anticipation began to rise and the days were beginning to be counted before the Ark's first full orbit of the Erth, Planet Seven.

Noah was trying his utmost to raise Tubal Cain on his high-speed communication link. Neyl was preparing with Rianne their next delicate step in their adventure. Airit agreed to close her eyes. Svi and Lika were very heavily occupied checking out their children. Trin had become somewhat independent but agreed to wait for them to be downloaded all together as a family. Lika felt very broody. Where was her real child, what was it, and is it still alive? Erash was enjoying sometime at home with his family. Later he spent some time checking through the hand over of the Ark to the SS who in the main were going to run it when the majority of the residents had left. He was again talking reasonably normally as his mouth had settled down and his teeth were beginning to grow.

Velmitz had big problems. He did not have enough staff. They had genetically generated many young of many species and his professional veternarians had nurtured and classified each and every puppy, kitten, cub, chrysalis, tadpole and lava etc., etc., etc., into their correct environmental area. Noah had supplied him with an Erth ecological territorial map accorded with the natural elements of each area, but Velmitz and his gang were way behind in sorting out where each individual being was to go. They were due into Erth orbit in less than one half of one moonth. He was beginning to feel panicky.

Rula and Marla had become somewhat emotional, they knew that they were not going to download until nearly the end along with their Husband, but they had become worried about their tenure on their children who were still quite young. They had great faith in the 'kinship factor' that was to be retained, but what if something went wrong? They were both very worried and imagining the worst things. Alram had agreed to keep himself, his family and his wife's family close together and Erash had given permission for them all to be done together and to be placed in the in the same batch destination to be in the same place on Erth. Somewhere called *'The Sea of the Middle Erth'*. Thought to be a truly beautiful place and very environmentally sound for humankind.

Shem Ham and Japheth were working very hard, they had performed their duties like champions, but fatigue was an unwelcome guest at their table and they needed to slow down just a little.

Rastus and Glenshee had organized the group of hybrids into a strong negotiating position. They had been allowed to choose to be downloaded all together and travel to Erth together as a unit. They were to have their own area for landing as small groups.

Lex had found himself a close friend on the Ark, and she was also a close friend of Rula and Marla, so Erash had pulled Lex in to do a lot of work for him. Lex and his 'wife' were to join Erash when it came to their turn for download.

***

A major discussion developed aboard the Astro-Vehicle, Neyl started it, but they were all pleased that it had been brought into the open.

"Of course you can trust me!" said Airit "I owe my life to the both of you. I would not betray either of you. You are both more important to me than my uniform. I believe that I have completed my task of loyalty to the SS. I am certainly not staying with the Ark on its' departure from Erth's orbit. It has become an unwritten rule for all SS officers to stay with the Ark. I believe that Kraut with guys called Koel and Klaus had a lot to do with the setting of that rule. They were sometimes nicknamed the three 'K's for obvious reasons. They were the epitome of selfishness and I owed them no allegiance. If it is possible I would very much like to come with you. I do not know where you are going, but I do know that we think the same way and I completely trust you. Is it possible to come with you?"

"Oh yes!" screamed Rianne in deep relief as if a profound tension had been removed from her. "I would share anything with you, including my life." She threw her arms around Airit almost strangling her with emotion.

Neyl looked dumbfounded and helpless. He was a practical man and 'how were they going to do it?' he was thinking.

***

CHAPTER 5

'Arrival'

The Sun was directly behind them, which meant that Erth was in full phase, a complete circle of blue with apparently stationary white cloud patterns across its' surface. It was only just visible to the naked eye as the brightest star in the heavens and it was certainly very bright, growing in size by the moment.

Noah and Naamah were together in their bedroom when Tubal Cain appeared. He was standing there right in the middle of the room at the foot of their bed. He was a picture of health and a face full of smiles.

"Tubal!" Noah shouted across the room "I can't believe it. Wow! We were just going to bed. I would have switched this off in a few more moments. How wonderful. We have missed you very much, please talk as much as you want"

"We have been working on an upgrade to the *'com.system'* as you know and we have finally got it right." Tubal was full of smiles and spoke with much verve. "You cannot imagine how easy it was. Even I understood the first time, when it was explained to me. This new *'Quasar'* technology is very interesting. We have uploaded it for your use at your end, but of course you won't have much use for it very soon. What is happening with the Ark when you are all gone?" Tubal asked.

"Security Services are taking it over." Noah replied. "They want to search for that other planet that we knew about. They want to settle without losing their acquired knowledge. I cannot be their judge that is for G-d to decide. Anyone who does not qualify for Erth landing will be going with the Ark under SS rule. They should be quite safe. I have taken all pre-agreed precautions for our departure and they know that it would be fatal for them to depart without placing the last downloads safely on Erth. That of course will be Svi and me, with our nearest and dearest. After the last shuttle of downloads, it would be equally impossible for them to try and make a separate landing on Erth."

"I don't trust my own security guards," Tubal interrupted. "They became an autonomous organization which worshipped its own uniform and its members thought that they replaced G-d. It's best for you, that we withdraw the uploaded upgrade before you download it. It would be dangerous for us back here in Eden if this system fell into the wrong hands. They could send us viruses and spy into our systems if we were to allow it to continue. I am really sorry Noah but this will most likely be the last time that we will communicate together." Tubal Cain had a well-defined sadness in his voice.

"I can agree with you in every way," Noah remarked "but as this could be our very last communication, tell me, how is it on Eden, how is your family, and what's the latest news?"

"I will answer you as best as I can. We have completed a massive geological survey and the results are horrific." Tubal took a deep breath and continued.

"There is an early developing problem within our crust as the pressure is building up, slowly but certainly. The report says that it could be fifty to seventy five generations before critical point is reached, or a lot less. One thing it says with certainty that Eden is a planet, which does not have a long time future. It will blow one day! There are already some small cracks underground and on the surface. We still suffer the occasional groundquake."

Tubal adjusted his seat and continued "The family? Well, as you know, Tsionne is almost permanently pregnant and she can get quite big, but when she isn't she has almost no increase in her normal body weight. When without child, she always has quite a remarkable figure. Gramps has had a new girlfriend now for almost a year, our time, and I find her very nice, but Tsionne doesn't like her at all and she is generally a very good judge of character. She thinks that 'Thia' as she is called is only after what she can get and Gramps is very well established and has a lot of influence down here. He is highly respected. Tsionne thinks that Thia spoils his image. Jubal is very much involved with reclamation of the surface now. There is a possibility that there are small surface communities scattered across the globe that did not suffer from the radioactivity. Jubal has made contact with one, which alleges that they have contact with others, but he is still cautious. He suspects a hoax, but he is further investigating. His brother Jabal is still the farmer and without him active, we would not be able to guarantee a full crop every year. He is a genius at synthetic weather effects. His results are astounding and sometimes very frightening but they work. I look at my children and two of the boys remind me very much of my father Lamech. I miss him very much now, and I am sure that he is with me. I am sure he 'sees' my children and Tsionne. I am sure that he approves. I am sure that he is proud. He never did see his daughter-in-law but he always used to tell me that she sounded very beautiful. Now that he is no longer with us I feel that he is with us even more than before and I know that he thinks that Tsionne is beautiful. In fact I don't think that he can keep his eyes off her. I know that I can't. Hey! What about Naamah? How is my sister? Hi Sister!"

Tubal could see that Naamah was very well and that she had a great friend in her husband, Noah.

"If you enjoy Noah as much as I do Tsionne, then we are very lucky siblings."

"This is the strangest feeling," Naamah replied "I feel as if I am on death row, and they are about to call my number, but I am actually looking forward to it. It is uncanny and I cannot explain it. The only thing that worries me very much is that I am going to lose my image memories of you and my brothers. I will probably even lose any knowledge that I ever had of my family that I no longer will see. Please forgive me and I hope that when I eventually die one day, we will be re-united under G-d's hand."

Noah pulled his arm very tightly around Naamah giving her a firm hug as if to say 'that *will* happen, but in a very long time, way forward from now'.

***

Lika's heart was beating and the vibrations were loud enough to waken all her sleepy people. At least that was what she felt as she held tightly on to Svi's hand like a little girl would hold that of her father. The bewildered duo were standing at the viewing rail on the gallery airside, looking over 'section one' of their sleeping children, They were the first group in the Atrium below awaiting orders for loading into the deep crimson padded cushioned drawers of the crates that were due to be used to cargo them down to Erth below.

Svi and Lika were using this moment to take a breath from their chores and overview the procedure. They were also awaiting instructions from Shem who had not yet arrived. Across the Atrium was the grandest sight that had ever yet met mankind. Through the enormous full field windows that formed the roof of the Atrium chamber was the reason for Lika's deep emotional feeling. There, presenting itself in full glorious color was the blue, brown and green partially clouded surface of what was to be their new mother planet, 'Erth'. It occupied the entire sky and was barely discernibly moving. Being so close, closer than any man had ever been before with the entire panorama above them. It was an awe inspiring experience now that they could pick out features in the minutest detail, never yet before seen with the naked human eye. They were still on the sunny side and must have been in the midday position slightly north of the planet's equator where they were due to stay for the next few days whilst intricate data was taken and sorted for the arrangement and deposit of humankind and other species onto its' soil.

"We will be staying in this orbital longitude of midday for the next seven days." Shem interrupted their thoughts. "We are going to examine in fine detail the surface as the Erth spins on its axis and we are to move up and down the midday longitude from pole to pole thus in effect completing seven or eight orbits of the Erth's own rotation. At present we are in the same orbit of the sun as is Erth, we are just a 'tad' nearer to the sun."

"Hallo Shem, look at those snow covered mountains, an enormous range, coming so crisp, and sharp from the ground. There is almost no cloud cover over to the left, and the shadows are very deep. They must be high," remarked Lika who could not take her eyes away from the specter of Erth above them.

"Those are fold mountains, created when the ice came down from the north during an ice-age cycle at the time of early creative stabilization of this planet's rotating axis. We have seen it happening on Dad's video. The ice pushed the rocky ground beneath it up high to form a high mountainous plateau and then withdrew when it melted back slowly to form the polar cap almost as it is now. Some of the mountains are very high and the one over there, just visible at the edge of the cloud cover is the highest mountain on Erth. That area would not be the most hospitable to human kind except perhaps in the lower valleys where there is fresh water." Shem was pointing with his hand. "Due to the high water content on Erth's surface there is continual convection of warmth into the atmosphere which results in ever changing condensation of water which returns to the ground as rain. The condensation patterns appear in different stages as cloud formation, more or less like it used to be on Eden. They can look quite solid in appearance, but you can drop right through them."

"I can see that since we started looking at the Erth we have already moved northward further, we can just about see the other side of the North Pole if you look at our superimposed latitude and longitude markings on the large computer monitor screen on the other wall." Lika pointed. "It must be spring in the northern hemisphere."

"How did you work that out?" Shem was impressed with Lika and showed it in his voice.

"Well, we can see the darkening sky of night on the horizon far away to the other side of the North Pole, but it is still daylight for quite a distance beforehand. It must be early spring."

"How do you know that it is not the autumn?" Asked Svi, a little skeptically.

"The general ground temperature in the northern hemisphere is somewhat cooler than the equivalent in the southern, so it has not been able to warm up yet, therefore in the south it is Autumn, in the north it is spring, which is the best time to land humankind. Either we are very lucky because that is where the land mass is in most supply, or it has been well thought through and pre-planned." Lika smiled quite pleased with herself. "How are we to judge where to put humankind?" She asked Shem.

"Yes, it was planned. We wanted to give our species and most of the others, the best chance to prepare for their future using their basic instincts. We needed to be sure that food and water was plentiful, and in the spring it will give them the smartest chance to learn."

Lika smiled and preened herself like a cat. She had got it right and she was pleased. As Shem continued to answer her question, Svi listened intently with deep interest.

"The most important substance for survival of humankind is water, fresh water. We could not survive on seawater. There is too much salt in it. We would soon die, unless we boiled it and collected the vapor. That is going to be too technical. No it has to be near rivers or lakes to start with, where fresh water is, or flows in abundance. Have you noticed that the second or satellite planet of Erth, its' moon, has a serious gravitational effect on its' partner. It causes all the water on Erth to follow it, just like the water on Eden followed its' Sun, but here there is the Sun and the Moon, so the water faithfully follows them both in their cycles. They cause tides of the seas and oceans, also changes in the weather patterns. The constant erosion has created sandy beaches along many of the coastlines. Whereas these look attractive to the eye they would be generally completely lacking in fresh water. The best place for man is some distance up the river, certainly a distance from the sea, unless mountains or hills drained down towards that area supplying fresh water. At this stage the human will not know to dig a well for water and if he did and was too close to the sea, it would not be fresh. We will avoid areas like too high or too low, too near to the sea. Eventually the human will find his own way, but to start with we must give him the chance, should we not?"

Svi and Lika nodded approval.

"Thank Tubal Cain and my father!" said Shem.

***

"This is it, the moment that I have been waiting for, all my life! Freedom! Let's go." Neyl had already released the blocks holding the astro-vehicle on the capstans and sitting proudly in his pilot's seat with his craft pointing skyward he pressed all the release buttons and with the engines gently running, he moved the vehicle upward just perceptibly away from the Ark. "Disengaged!" he announced with unadulterated pleasure as if he had been waiting to say that for all the years of his life. He moved his machine vertically upward from the Ark at rapidly increasing speed. They could feel an increase of the gravity coming from behind them.

"This is strange!" said Airit to Rianne; they were sitting sideways facing each other. They had to re-arrange the seating to include Airit. "If we look back, is it up or down? And if we look forward is that also up or down?"

"Soon after one orbit on the dark side it will be very obvious that 'up' is in fact 'down'." Neyl replied with a touch of sarcasm. As we get nearer to Erth, the gravity will begin to be more noticeable. The astro-vehicle was moving on a course at a gentle tangent to the Erth, they were about to go into their own orbit of Planet Seven.

As they approached the dark horizon a new spectacle came into view, it was the Erth's satellite the Moon rising above the horizon. They were going to pass between the two planets, both in half darkness, what a sight? What an experience? The changes in the illumination as they moved between the two planets with craters on the one side and Erth's inviting freshness on the other created shadows and ghosts of shadows. The umbrae and the penumbrae gave a morbid eerie feeling of foreboding and bewilderment, but no sooner had they passed through into the oblivion of complete darkness than a new horizon appeared on their left of Erth's morning as the sun began to rise on its' surface yielding itself to the fresh day for those below.

"Yes!" said Rianne, I can feel it, I can see it, and I know it!

That is down!" She pointed to the Erth.

"We are now in Superior Orbit." Neyl replied, "We have to now select where we want to land. We can only afford one orbit for this luxury. If we take any more we will have no more fuel for emergencies and we are more likely to have one if the Ark admin become aware of our presence. We have to avoid that if possible. We left in their one blind radar area of the Electro-Telescope. I disabled their radar at that point when I was out working a while back. We followed that blind area outward into orbit of the Erth when we became too small to be noticed. Now that we are in morning we are back in view of the Ark, but we are tiny and would not be noticed except by accident because we are not moving towards them. Only then would it flash up on the screen as a warning. Where do you think looks best to make landfall?" Neyl asked.

"There!" both the girls pointed to the same place and looked at each other smiling.

"That's amazing, outvoted in only one word," Rianne said as she put her arms around Neyl's neck and gave him a large sucking kiss on his cheek.

"That *is* amazing!" Neyl agreed, "It does look beautiful and it's right in the center of the upper hemisphere. They call that area 'The Middle Erth Sea' and if we make for that northern area in the hills we could lose the astro-vehicle in that large volcano on the seashore. There would never be any trace of it if we were clever. We must lose it or the SS may come after us, and they will have every good reason. I am going to place us in stationary orbit above that area while we prepare for our jump."

Neyl had given Airit one of the extra parachutes that he had brought which were originally meant for use on the cargo, but he had also said earlier that there was a chance was that the cargo did not need two parachutes anyway. They bound up all their cargo in the crate in which it was bought and attached the closed parachute. Neyl affixed a small device to the grasp handle and moved the entire unit to the opened airlock inner door. "We can place this in the airlock and re-close the door temporarily. We can eject it when we leave, which will be very shortly. Take anything that is important to you, your luggage must not be affixed to your body. Do not forget that you may fall on whatever you have attached to you, so make sure that you are well equipped with padding. Put whatever you can in your pack. We don't want any accidents do we?"

"How are we going to jump?" Airit asked.

"Together all four of us at the same moment out of the open airlock. I've been through the routine with you many times. We will put the astro-vehicle into a governed decent, using its' engines to keep it falling slowly and always above target. It will fall gently in the sky, like a feather, so as not to get burned by the atmosphere. We will jump out when we reach the safe height to do so, but the vehicle will turn its engines as we jump and will push just a small tad to give it a little more speed to fall to the ground. It will then automatically use its' engines and fall below us suicidally into that large volcano. I have preset the ground-seeking device to those co-ordinates. It will dive directly into the center of that orifice."

"How are we going to release the cargo parachute, it won't open without help. Are we going to hold it until the time?" asked Rianne.

"No! It is too dangerous. We keep away from it. I have a remote control to release the chute when ready. It will also do a copycat maneuver to follow my path as long as I remain in front of it. I will have no problem with that. We are making for those hills above and north west of the volcano. It is some distance. When we are ready let's go!"

***

"You can't do that!" Lika yelled at Ham, who was lifting up the crimson silk cover of one of the naked sleeping children.

Ham turned to face Lika dropping the cover back into place, with his face almost as red the sheet. "I was just checking that everything was alright and that they all are properly labeled!" said Ham very embarrassed.

"Well? Said Lika also embarrassed, for something better to say, "Are they all correct?"

"Yes, although this is a real mixed bunch of kids."

"That is the way that they are meant to be. It makes them genetically stronger." Lika was getting out of her embarrassment. "Are you coming to Erth as an escort with Svi and Shem?"

"Yes. We are all going and we have to help unload at the other end. There will be six of us this time with Shem, Japheth, Svi, Lex, You, and me. Lex is working with Erash and has been assigned liaison duties for all landings. Erash couldn't handle it all by himself."

"That is great. How long do we have to wait?" Lika enquired.

"We are all ready and are in fact all waiting in the 'air-lock office' for you. Svi is also there. I was waiting out here to *tell* you." Ham smiled.

They walked down the corridor to the 'air-lock office of the Atrium where Lika was introduced to Lex. He was assuming charge of the proceedings.

"We are ready to go, the crates of section one children can be loaded direct, and they don't have to go through Hibernation Unit as we are already airside."

The six people stood back in a small group as they oversaw the trays of children being gently loaded into the cargo hold of a small hoversphere that would take them to Erth. Lika and Svi asked to sit at the front of the cabin in order to get a good view. They were scheduled to be only taking the trip once in their current condition; they wanted to see the landing on the Erth at first hand.

They embarked onto the hoversphere on the Erth's side of the Ark, which meant that they were in the dull luminance of 'Erthlight', a secondhand sunlight that had been reflected off the Erth's surface.

As they moved slowly away, the reflection of their hoversphere could be seen clearly in the highly polished surface of the Ark. The newer volumes of the Ark had been finished in highly polished material. Lika's expression changed dramatically from that of profound pensivity to obvious awareness of all around her, as suddenly they came out of the Ark's shadow and were greeted by full sunlight directly onto their hoversphere. Round them apart from the Ark, the Sun and the warmth of Erth, was a deep blackness of the vacuum of extra-terrestrial space that surrounded them.

"It is like putting your elbow in warm water to test its' temperature or getting slowly into a hot bath!" The pilot, Captain Dandar, said as they moved very slowly Erthwards. "The atmosphere is very thick, like on Eden. Birds can wrap it in their wingspan. It can blow fast enough to pull out trees; it can burn up and melt heavy metal if we try to enter it too quickly. Atmosphere is very powerful and yet when we walk in it we can hardly notice that it is there. That is almost how slowly we have to make our initial entry. We are going in very carefully at first, just like we did on Eden. I have the co-ordinates from mapping. We will be down very shortly."

Lika had never had that explained to her so simply before. She knew the reasoning but it was interesting to hear it from the pilot himself.

The 'blue' just seemed to develop around them as they dropped slowly into the sky. It was a warm hazy blue mixed with a pale silver-gray steamy haze. Lika nudged Svi to look down below them, there appeared to be a large lake. No she realized that it was 'Middle Sea'. Her sense of size was wrong; they were still quite far away. They moved nearer and the 'blue' got bluer and brighter, the sunlight became more diffused in the atmosphere causing a painful glare to her eyes. How will the children cope with this, she thought? She could see the greenish brown of the sea below where there were slight ripples on the surface. Perhaps they weren't so slight she thought. "Surely we aren't going to land in the sea?" she said to the Captain.

"No." Dandar answered, "We are going inland. I have been told to follow a certain river from its' mouth to a point further north where we are to place 'section one' in a safe position."

"It will be just before midday as we land." Lex started speaking "The Ark will be almost immediately above us. If we place the children in the shade under the trees we can initiate their awakening then. They will not wake up until we have left and gone out of their view forever. I am told by you Lika," he looked at her directly, "that as it is almost midday, they will work out for themselves well before dark that they will have to make or find hiding places or homes for safety from the sun and other hostile beings."

"Yes, that is correct! You know your stuff, thank you." Lika smiled to him.

Their landing among the trees almost at the river's edge was almost unnoticed; it was smooth. Unloading the cargo did not take very long, certainly much quicker than it had taken to load it. The three sons of Noah supervised by Lex placed the sleeping naked bodies in small groups under the shadows of the trees in the long grass. Ham took a ripe cherry from one of the branches; it was delicious. They re-packed the empty crates into the sphere and prepared to leave but Lika asked Lex permission for Svi to sit with her under a similar cherry tree just for a few moments alone in order that they could give private thanks to G-d for such a wonderful gift as 'Erth'. They sat there in prayer for what seemed an eternity when they heard shouting from the sphere. They ran to find out.

"Where is Ham?" Shem called out "He has disappeared! Have you seen him? We have to leave very shortly."

"No I haven't seen him." Said Svi, "But we will look around!" Lika had a very good idea what Ham was up to. She looked at the naked sleeping bodies in the long grass under the trees. Where were the most attractive and most exposed body parts? She looked, and then saw the long grass was waving in the wind, but there was no wind! She left Svi for a moment and walked very carefully through the long grass around the back of the waving grass stems. There on his knees, she found Ham masturbating in full view of the sleeping naked young couple with all their genitalia exposed for him to see.

***

Noah had decided that he must go to Erth with Naamah, his boys and their family, just for a visit before download and this is what he did.

In order not to be seen by any of those people whom had already been disembarked, Captain Dandar, under instruction, took the family of six for a short visit to a beautiful but mountainous region just north east of the 'Middle Sea'.

When the door of the sphere opened Noah stepped forward and took a deep breath. He opened his mouth for more.

"Wow!" he said, "this stuff is addictive. There is a smell to it, a smell of . . . !!? I don't know, I have never smelled that before, but it is a wonderful smell"

"It is the atmosphere," said Capt. Dandar "It's the first breath or two that has a definite smell wherever you are. It has been known to make people cry. The first breaths of Erth's atmosphere have a pungent, but sweet fresh smell. It has a taste doesn't it? I had to fight back the tears, but it makes you want to breath some more. It is a whole new experience, and yes, it is addictive as you put it! Yes that's right, it's addictive!"

Noah stepped forward asking his family to follow, and Naamah did cry when she took her first deep breath of Erth's atmosphere. Both daughters-in-law joined her when for a short moment she cried almost uncontrollably as she got down on her knees and kissed the ground with her husband Noah beside her. They were almost prone on their knees kissing the soft grassy ground in prayers of thanks to G-d. Their children joined them; even Dandar and his crew of five men joined him in prayer. The ten men and four women were all on their knees kissing the grassy ground beneath them in deep meditation, when suddenly as if in answer to their prayer, there started some heavy rain. It came down so strong as if to wash away any sin that had befallen them. They were all standing under a large overhanging rock when Noah pointed to the sky as the cloud of rain continued, but the sun was also trying to make its' presence felt.

"Look!" Noah cried "The colors. Look at that 'bow' in the sky, it is surely beautiful. G-d is making a covenant with humankind that as long as humankind respects the world that G-d has given them it will endure. This rainbow is a symbol for man to see, to remind him that without G-d he would not be. As long as there will appear a rainbow in the sky it will remind humankind of the truth." Noah took a breath with some tears under his eyes. "We now have to return to the Ark and sustain our final preparations. My children, it is G-d's wish that you should return to Erth as with your cousins of the Ark that you should go forth and multiply."

Naamah pulled quietly on Noah's hand indicating that they should walk for a few moments out of earshot of their children as the rain was beginning to stop and the sky was a sunny blue with some white fluffy silver edged clouds over to the west. Naamah spoke to Noah as they walked through the luscious green countryside.

"The hand of beauty has painted itself across this land. We are fortunate to be able to see this and understand its' splendor, its' nature. This is nature in its' natural state. Take a breath of the air try a drop of this water from the stream. It is all so clear and healthy. 'Pollution' is a word that does not exist here at all! Do you remember from where we have come? Can you remember? Everything here is in abundance; there are leaves on the trees, dew on the grass, and plants in full flower *without* help. You can use your *nose* and smell the herbs that grow free, the blossoms and the flowers, even the muddy stream has its' own identity. We are in a garden in a grand scale. Can you remember when we sat on the bank of our polluted river and all we could smell was sulfur and smoke rising from the valley? We had black dust raining from the sky every day and never saw the sun. Please do not let humankind do that again to Erth. Please G-d let it be that humankind has learned its' lesson. Please let us be happy in our ignorance and *always* remain so!"

"Amen!" said Noah as they walked back to their group.

Not far away from the spot where Noah and his family had been kissing the grassy soil were some human-like eyes that were watching over them in shock, horror, and awe. Who were these people? Strangers, so different, and from where did they come?

The rain finally stopped and within moments the ground was dry.

"We had better return to the Ark. I have another run to do almost immediately, we cannot afford any more time." Capt. Dandar announced to his companions. Come on I want to count fourteen on board."

Only moments later they were above Planet Seven making their way back to the Ark. The occupants of the hoversphere felt clean, well washed and at peace and it was not due to the rain.

***

The cargo was the first to go, followed by Rianne who had jumped only once before, then Airit who had not, followed by Neyl who's experience was well established through training. They all 'flew' together as they watched their astro-vehicle still under power drop slowly but slightly faster than them. They had a short while before they would open their chutes; they were still in free fall. They watched as their once upon a time temporary place of residence began to turn in order to make for its new home, the center of the large slightly steaming volcano. It was at that moment that Neyl was made to remember his old friend in the trenches of servitude when the missile went passed his right shoulder missing it by a hair's width it seemed. Fortunately, Rianne, Airit and the cargo were to his left as they fell. He had the sharpness of mind and sense to give the spontaneous order . . .

"On the count of four, open your chutes—4,3,2,1. Now!"

Both girls heard his signal through their personal intercoms and Neyl using the remote opened the cargo chute at the same time as his. He then negotiated to the front with the cargo following behind. The girls obediently followed as Neyl indicated speed of fall to the northwest was essential if they were to miss the heat of the blast as the radar-seeking missile destroyed the astro-vehicle. He just hoped that their parachutes would not be seen from above, tempting a further attack.

It was almost enjoyable watching the two objects falling almost together towards the large volcano on the coastline on the north eastern coast of what had become called 'Middle Erth Sea' It formed a volcanic island peninsular, and was a truly pretty sight just attached to the mainland by one narrow causeway of rocks.

"Whoops!" Neyl made an involuntary noise as suddenly the astro-vehicle made its appointment with the volcano, at the exact same moment that the missile hit the astro-vehicle. For a brief milli-moment nothing seemed to happen, and then all hell was let loose. Thick yellow and brown vapor just seemed to rise as if it was coming up to meet them. Neyl found out how suddenly one can learn to pray. He felt the up-rush of air as it caught the inside of their chutes and the three of them with the cargo seemed to be carried upward into the higher altitudes once more, but it was not cold and smelled of hot cinders and burning dust. He looked up at the chutes. As if by a miracle they were still fully filled with atmosphere and apparently undamaged as he could feel that once again they were beginning to fall, but so was the dust.

Neyl indicated that they must keep their chutes full, and drift north-by-north west if possible. Eventually they made it to the ground, all within sight of each other and although filthy from the powdered cinder, no other ill effects.

"These chutes can substitute for tent covers until we build a home. They are made that way." Neyl said as he suggested immediate retrieval of their tatty dusty material. "Look at the volcano! It is still erupting and the gaseous waste has become very steamy. Leave the cargo, it's quite safe" said Neyl, "Let us climb to the top of that hill. From over there we should get a good view of the volcano, although it seems to be quietening down a bit and the exude is turning into a steamy cloud."

They reached as far up the hillside as they could easily climb and looked down onto the coastline below. The volcano that had stood so proudly against the coast had almost completely disappeared taking missile and astro-vehicle with it. There were still large bubbles and plenty of submerged activity, but it was all coming up from the seabed.

The volcanic island was no more, it had appeared to have slid almost sideways collapsing into the sea leaving a small crescent like coastal area completely surrounded by water. They carefully retraced their steps back down to where they had left their things. The cargo box had been opened, but whoever or whatever had probably been disturbed, as nothing except one box of tissues had been taken.

"Hey!" called Airit. "Look at this!" she said pointing the soft muddy ground. Beneath her finger was a human-like fresh bare footprint, but slightly longer and narrower, there in the mud.

***

Svi and Lika were becoming experts at dispatching downloads to Erth and Lex had become a very good friend. They had placed almost the entire population who qualified onto the ground in a multitude of different places. All continents had some human representation although only in safe areas. In general near fresh water and natural shelter. They knew that the human would find his own way and adapt very much as they did under experimental conditions on the Ark. As long as they were safe for the coming night and future day, then the team felt that they had correctly done their job. Lika had been aching in her heart that she wanted to go back to Erth with Svi, just the two of them. Svi did not want to set a precedent by asking, but he could see how remote Lika was becoming within herself and finally agreed to ask Lex.

"Of course!" came the surprise reply without even a moment of thoughtful consideration. "Do you want to go with the next batch? You will have to go with a delivery, and we have to be certain of the area, you cannot go completely on your own or you may unavoidably be seen by earlier new arrivals that are unaware of our existence. As you know that must never come to notice."

"Now?" said Svi in complete surprise "Great, I can't wait to tell Lika."

Svi thought that Lika would strangle him with the gratitude she had in her heart and they both ran like children to the dispatch room on 'Airside'.

Velmitz was there waiting for them. They were using the large cargo craft for this trip, it had been converted from the 'old tub' that Lex and Rastus had arrived in when the Ark was still only an orbital city of Eden. It was time to deliver the Pandas of Varg to their new home in the hills towards the eastern end of Erth's largest continent. There was an ideal spot for them and plenty of natural bamboo.

"This will be a bumpy ride," said Velmitz "but this old vehicle is very tough and extremely dependable. They don't build them like this any more."

"No." said Svi with a smile "They don't build them at all any more."

Velmitz was friendly but seemed a little agitated. "We have to leave immediately he said as he ushered them into the large craft. "There has been bad weather in the region and we only have a short window to deliver and set up these wonderful creatures whilst the weather remains good which it is now. There has been so much rain."

Only moments later they were on their way and the big hoversphere was very fast for its age.

"Were you waiting just for us? Lika enquired.

"That's right!" said Velmitz with his head down looking at charts and columns of figures.

"Thank you." both Svi and Lika responded in union. "Can we be of any help?"

"No thanks, except to leave me to check out these figures if you don't mind?" Velmitz was apologetically abrupt with them. They could see nothing below except the soft curly vaporous top of white clouds. They were covering all that they could see from horizon to horizon.

"We certainly have to trust our navigation equipment in order to land." Lika whispered to Svi,

"I understand that we are due to land in a very hilly area and all we can see are the clouds below and we are getting nearer to them."

Suddenly they were surrounded by misty cloud and rain on the windows. Eventually they were through and to Lika's surprise they were underneath the clouds, which were now quite dull and gray, but they were still quite high up. They could see the ground and it *was* very hilly, but covered with trees and foliage.

"A most beautiful terrain but it would look much nicer in sunshine," said Lika.

"I'm worried about the Pandas," said Velmitz as he looked up from the charts. "We have very slightly less gravity here than on Eden, but we have just over twice that of the Ark. These Pandas are very sensitive animals and most of them have never known Eden weight. I am concerned that they will cope with the new gravity. In effect they will weigh twice what they are used to. We have been strengthening them up during our approach through the Solar System, but will their hearts stand up to it. They are naturally heavy animals."

"We have had the same with our environmental children." said Lika "We even tried putting an area unknown to them in artificially higher gravity just a fraction more than Erth and all of them adapted very quickly. Long term, who knows, but as long as they can reproduce a new natural generation then we have in effect done our job. Think about it, when you land on Erth or Eden for that matter you notice that you feel heavier, but eventually you don't notice it anymore. As long as they are physically healthy, twice their gravitational weight won't kill them. Anyway their original specifications were to cater for gravity, which was similar, and those haven't changed. It would take many generations for evolution to take care of that."

They hovered above a sloping hillside in a stationary mode. "You cannot do this in the newer craft. Only the older vehicles can hover. Watch!"

Eight long metal folding legs moved outward and down from the lower segment of the craft. They each contacted the ground independently of each other. Then the craft settled into an upright, 'bubble in the hole' level position.

Lika was grateful to Velmitz for the deep-legged boots that he had loaned her from the craft, but she still needed help from Svi walking through the mud as they went in quite deep and sometimes stuck as if by suction. It was easier to walk under the trees in spite of the continual dripping of water which always somehow found its way to the back of her neck. There was often a sudden deluge when a tree animal jumped from one branch to another. On looking up on two occasions Lika got a faceful of tree water and she never did see what caused it.

Svi saw them first, and then Lika almost immediately afterwards, she screamed out of shocked surprise causing them both to run away. On the ground ahead of them in a small clearing among the very tall trees, had appeared two very slim human-like 'apes', unlike the gorilla people on Eden, there was a naked male and a naked female. They had looked shocked themselves, gave a second glance in Svi and Lika's direction and then ran away into the bushes.

***

"Describe them to me." Said Noah sitting in his comfortable office chair listening to the astounding narrations of Svi and Lika.

"At first glance they appeared to us as no more than naked apes, an unusual version, not one to which we are accustomed. Initially we were both quite shocked and turned to go back to the sphere when they bolted through the bushes. They were very fast, and their reactions were very sharp, and yet they were almost human. A human could not have jumped that high bush as if it was not there."

"Definitely almost human!" Lika interrupted. "They walked or ran with a very slight stoop in their back giving them almost round shoulders." continued Svi. "They jumped medium sized bushes with impunity, at least twice their height or possibly more. When they landed they gave the impression of being very sharp witted."

"They were *like* humans, but ape," said Lika again "They are like a human would be if he was an ape, or like an ape would be if it was a human." Lika said with devout conviction. "The guy was quite attractive for an ape!"

Noah laughed . . .

Svi was prompted to say something. "The female was considerably sexy and also not unattractive." He said as if trying to compete. Noah and Lika laughed together.

"That's it!" shouted Lika "Their faces were human, well almost!"

"They would pass for humans in a crowd." Svi stated and hesitated as if he wanted to add something more. Noah lifted his hands to stop him and then he spoke with a voice of considered authority.

"We have known about these people for years, but we do not think that there are many of them. They are at man's latest stage of evolution on this planet. They are an underdeveloped form of humankind, and if left alone, much like the gorilla people on Eden, they won't interfere with us, if we don't with them. Tubal Cain and I discussed this possibility across the vacuum of stellar space, when we finally examined this planet in minute detail. It is just a shame that you discovered their existence before your download. We are going to let everyone find them for themselves and leave nature to take its' course. They will not harm you, they do not usually eat their own kind, and to apes *or* humans we are their own kind. Just leave them alone, let nature take its' course." He repeated.

Little did Noah, or anyone else in that room know that Noah and Tubal Cain in their ignorance together, had in making that decision so long ago, effectively signed the death warrant of the evolutionary species of 'Neanderthal Man' the so called missing link in the chain of human development according to Darwin.

The human species brought with it from Eden disease and viruses with which Neanderthal man could not compete. Most people on the Ark, even the Environmental Children had been inoculated against most strains of effective disease when they were young. It was almost unheard of for a human to be ill from that kind of thing, but the Neanderthal had no chance.

Svi and Lika found that they could be attracted to these 'apes', they were not, they had each other, but as time was to go by there would be some inter-relationships with this superior kind of animal and the Eden human would find his ranks contained some hybrid forms of Neanderthal, but many generations later there would be no more trace of Neanderthal anywhere. It would be a complete wipeout. Tragedy? Or nature taking its course?

Svi and Lika felt somewhat deflated after the meeting with Noah and decided to return to their tasks at hand. They had already decided where they wanted to be, along with Trin and their family, at the western end of the mountain range that stretches east across the north of the 'Middle Erth Sea'. West of the so-called 'pan-handle' of the 'old boot' as it had become nicknamed. There was a place just below and to the west of the mountains with a fountain of water, which came from somewhere underground. The water was fresh and there was shelter and food. That is where they would go. They held hands and waited as they waved goodbye to the very last transport down to Erth. All that was now left were the marshals, messengers, admin, Noah, his family and associated workers, their families, and of course Svi and Lika with Trin. Wait, there was one person left in a crimson cushioned crate.

"What is she doing here? Asked Lika to Svi as she gently lifted the cloth off the sleeping youthful face.

"That is my present to you as the highest token possible of my love on this momentous occasion now that our work is complete." He hesitated and smiled. "Our daughter!"

Lika screamed a stifled scream and Svi putting his arm around her continued,

"She showed up a while back. I had secretly programmed our 'DNA' into the 'Children of the Environment' database, and her 'Kinship' tests proved it. She is ours, and she has no other ties."

Lika was crying with happines as if she had inherited the world. "We can now go to Erth with our whole family." Lika was full of tears and threw herself into Svi's arm. She knew she could not awaken their daughter lying there so peacefully in the red cushioned crate.

"She very much looks like you, when you were a protesting naked student, carrying that pole in your hands, and all you were wearing was an old pair of sandals." said Svi giving Lika that extra big cuddle.

. . . and they all lived happily ever after?

***

"Ba'reshit"

I truly am amazed that as I lie here naked on my back, I am not afraid. That which is to come is of my own design with the loving help from Lika, my wife, without whose energies I would never have achieved this great event. I am the last to undergo this experience and I am contented that all downloads before mine, with one exception, have been perfect. Loukash, a few days previously was a problem, I believe that in truth he really did not want to go and eventually we managed to upload his entire memory back to its place of origin. He then tested positive and was scanned containing no errors. He has elected to stay on board and will travel with the others.

At last it is my turn and I am ready, I am awaiting the experience without trepidation.

I am so looking forward to rejoining Lika. I use the word 'experience' so lightly, but in no more than a few long moments I will have no experience on which I can any longer dwell my thoughts. I am about to be downloaded onto a disc for posterity. No longer will my thoughts be available to me for I will have just basic instinct and life essential brain memory. The only luxury that will be retained is the love recognition emotion of family and close relatives. I will know Lika and she will know me.

"Svi? You OK?" The soft voice of a young male nursing attendant enquires as he brings the headset to my side. "I am ready to complete my task, you are positively the last one to be done. You have done enough yourself to know how easy it will be. The last transport is waiting and your place is secure next to Lika and company. The shuttle is pre-programmed to return here empty and as planned there will be no crew. Your disembarkation from the shuttle is to be completely automatic and aided only by robotic androids. They cannot stay with you and if one does in error it will self-destruct, dissolving into the atmosphere. That is what was arranged is it not?"

"Yes! Exactly!" I know that I smiled as I ask him once again his name.

"My name is 'Porgelet' but surely that is of no consequence as within moments from now you will no longer have need of it and your memory will be gone?"

"Not quite Porgelet." I answer, wishing that I hadn't for I knew that my brain is to be downloaded and with all the others *secretly* directed to a multiple backup disc elsewhere for data record in the possible event that humanity will catch up with itself in many thousands of years yet to come.

I feel warm all over very suddenly; the headset is now in place and has a very high-pitched whine. I know what that is. The first thing that the headset will do will be to make my brain cool my body down by about ten percent which is why I feel so pleasantly warm and sleepy.

My thoughts are beginning to race, a strange feeling indeed. It is so real as if it is really happening just here at this very moment. My memories are in their most infinite detail; so immediate and yet so short lived.

***

'The Legacy'
Many people will pose the question . . .
"What happened next?"

With the final arrival back at the Ark of the large empty Gyrosphere, the *SS* researched the passenger lists on the computer databases in order to check and verify that all was in order. They kept registering two short, but after checking each person on the Ark individually against their entry on the register they found that they were still short. There were a further eight women missing and unaccounted for, but their entries, which were on, the register had been deleted from the database. Only when they checked the old back-ups could they identify who deleted the originals. It was Kraut and he was now missing with another security officer called Airit. Neither had been present at the pre-download seminars and both held high ranks. Airit had a secret higher rank than was before known and in truth was only answerable to Erash who had now gone and was no longer contactable

They had a problem and neither Klaus nor Koel knew the answer, but Koel seemed to be unduly worried. He had not seen Kraut for weeks. There was a report of him not having returned from a rescue mission and the person he had attempted to rescue was Airit. At that time they were unaware that Airit was working within the 'SS' and certainly were unaware of her superior rank. Who was she reporting to? These were all questions going around in Koel's head. He knew that he had a job to do for Noah and that there was another high-ranking officer with the same job. He also knew about the top secret 'klone bank' of Noah's and his family that had been held by Velmitz in the event of an aborted mission but it was not needed and was destroyed as previously ordered. He desperately needed to find the other officer who knew the charge of Noah, otherwise he would have to take the decision on his own and that may not be the correct decision!

As a result of misdirected thoughts within the 'so-called' leadership among the crew, there is a horrific explosion on the Ark completely destroying it. Henceforth to become a gaseous comet and reverting to an orbit of the sun somewhat resembling that of its original, returning it in the direction of from where it came but only far enough to return to the solar neighborhood approximately *every* 72 Erth years or 800 Eden years. (It was later to become known as Halley's Comet?)

Multitudes of generations later after the extinction of the Neanderthals due to imported alien disease and complete destruction as a result of selfish brutality by humankind, three kings bring gifts of gold, incense and myrrh to a newly born child in a stable in a small crowded town near the sea of middle Erth whilst following a new bright star in the sky.

The new 'Star'? Could *it* be a comet? Could it be the death of a once
upon a time haven of the human race? *'Eden'*? Will we ever know?

Perhaps one day . . . Why is man so pre-possessed with always looking up at G-d's skies? How many times will Adam eat of the fruit of knowledge? If he *was* built that way, was it his *fault*?

***

EPILOGUE

What a pity that Noah had not been able to predict the future, that one cannot reverse the decisions of G-d. I wonder whether he would have done the same and put the people of the Ark through the same had he been able to foresee how mankind would again redevelop his skills, re-perform his wasteful activities, and re-organize his inflictions upon his fellow man. I personally guess that if this story were to be true, Noah would have done the same as he did, as would any decent thinking man. Only G-d would have the right to make permanent change. In the light of recent events all related to culture and religions, at least Noah deferred the inevitable for a while.

Perhaps one-day man will cross that territory known only to the almighty and/or in our death we will know the answer? Why are we here anyway? Why *is* anything? Why is G-d? Why? And why is it anyway, that it only seems to be humans who ask?

***

A PERSONAL THOUGHT BY THE AUTHOR
Howard J Peters OD

The passage of man through his life whether fortunate or unfortunate, whether happy or unhappy, or perhaps both, to the approximate three score years and ten (PST) is guided by G-d and of his personal experiences, none are more important than those of the second half of his earliest decade. His so-called 'formative years' when he has already learned to do the physical things for himself, like walk, talk, eat, drink and go to the toilet. He is then beginning to take in the world around him and learning how to react and survive within the world and among people to whose lives he or she is also causing effect.

With that in view I would like to offer my best wishes and thanks, apart from offering to the souls and spirit of my father and mother and thanks for the birth and love of my brother, but to those people who I am sure unknown to all of us had an everlasting effect on the creation of our lives that were then in front of us . . . *(All then in the UK)*

(Please forgive spelling, but it is as I remember it)

David Edridge (Cedar Rise)
Terry Custance (Friars Walk)
Michael (Hippo) Harrison (Cedar Rise)
Geoffrey Rubinstein (Cedar Rise)
David Smith (Friars Walk)
Tony Gosling (Oak Way)
Lenor Stofer (Cedar Rise)
Susan Clifford (Cedar Rise)
Jean Bigden (Cedar Rise)
Tony Smith (Cedar Rise)
Linda and Ian Duque (Powys Lane)
Leonard and Raymond Gold (Oak Close)
Robert Winston (Arnos Circle)
David Puttnam (Eversley Park Road & Salcombe School)

also my very own Scots cousin—Michael Brown (Rockburn Drive, Glasgow)
and fondly my cousin—Dodo Scriven (Hamilton Avenue, Birmingham)

There were many others who later in life were to affect changes in me, but it is the 'formative years' that are in my opinion the subject for thought with regard to this story.

***

I would like to offer my sincere thanks to Eve Shirley for her encouragement, and to Mae Elliott who helped me to become inspired in this, my story.

Also thanks to Manuela deGroot, my better half, for contributing the photographs for my front and back cover.

***

*I do hope that man will **learn** from his 'bite of the apple'* that if he is to survive that his children and his children's children for generation upon generation may enjoy the fruits of their endeavors; then let ***this*** in truth be their legacy!

—0—

965988